Five hundred ca........
supporters in th........
their struggle fo........
But would the r........ reach their proper
destination? So many people wanted them and
plotted to snatch them for their own devious
purposes.

There was only one man whom Major-General
Houston could trust to collect the rifles and
deliver them safely – a man who was ready to kill
anybody, renegade, Mexican soldier, or anyone
who dared to interfere. That man was Jackson
Baines Hardin who was known throughout the
West as a 'lil ole devil' when it came to a fight.

*Title awaiting publication

J.T. EDSON OMNIBUS
Volume 9

YOUNG OLE DEVIL
OLE DEVIL AND THE CAPLOCKS
OLE DEVIL AND THE MULE TRAIN

CORGI BOOKS

J.T. EDSON OMNIBUS VOLUME 9
A CORGI BOOK 0 552 13863 0

PRINTING HISTORY – YOUNG OLE DEVIL
Corgi edition published 1975
Corgi edition reprinted 1981

PRINTING HISTORY – OLE DEVIL AND THE CAPLOCKS
Corgi edition published 1976

PRINTING HISTORY – OLE DEVIL AND THE MULE TRAIN
Corgi edition published 1976

Corgi Omnibus edition published 1992

Corgi Books are published by Transworld Publishers Ltd.,
61–63 Uxbridge Road, Ealing, London W5 5SA, in
Australia by Transworld Publishers (Australia) Pty. Ltd.,
15–23 Helles Avenue, Moorebank, NSW 2170, and in New
Zealand by Transworld Publishers (N.Z.) Ltd., Cnr. Moselle
and Waipareira Avenues, Henderson, Auckland.

Printed and bound in Great Britain by
Cox & Wyman Ltd., Reading, Berks.

YOUNG OLE DEVIL

For the two beautiful Barbaras (French and Innes, in alphabetical order) of the White Lion Hotel, Melton Mowbray, although this probably won't induce them to serve me an extra pint of lager-and-lime after closing time.

YOUNG OLE DEVIL

author's note: *This to explain briefly how the events recorded in YOUNG OLE DEVIL were caused and came about.*

Early in February 1836 a Mexican army was marching northwards, its numbers increasing as the Militia of various States and other volunteer regiments were called into service by *Presidente* Antonio Lopez de Santa Anna. Having consolidated his position as absolute dictatorial ruler of all Mexico south of the *Rio Bravo*,* *el Presidente* was intending to crush the opposition to his control of Texas.

Neither the Spanish Constitution nor the various régimes which had supplanted it after the formation of the Republic of Mexico in 1822 had ever made a serious effort towards opening up, developing, or even utilizing to any great extent, the vast area of land which they had named 'Texas' after the Tejas Indians who had occupied a portion of it. Instead, it had fallen upon foreigners to do so.

Having received a land grant on the Brazos River in 1821, Stephen F. Austin had been encouraged to form a swiftly-growing Anglo-U.S. community. Other grants – such as that acquired by the Hardin, Fog and Blaze clan on the Rio Hodo – had been made by the Spanish and earlier Mexican régimes and had allowed the Texians† to extend their holdings. By 1830, there were close to 15,000 of them living in the hitherto unoccupied and unproductive territory.

Such immigrants had proved to be beneficial to their adopted country. Hard-working and industrious for the most part, they had been willing to improve and develop the land which they were occupying. Being capable fighting men, skilled in the use of weapons, they had been able to stand up against the hostile bands of Commanche, Wichita, Tonkawa and

*Rio Bravo: the Mexicans' name for the Rio Grande.

† Texian: an Anglo-U.S.-born citizen of Texas, the 'i' being dropped from usage after the Mexican War of 1846–48.

7

Kiowa Indians and, unlike many of the *Chicano** population, did not expect, or require the protection of the Mexican army against such foes. Furthermore, as they had increased the potential value of their properties, they had formed a useful source of revenue of the Mexican economy.

However, despite all of the financial and other benefits which had accrued from the Anglo-U.S. colonists, the authorities in Mexico City had grown less and less enamoured by the prospect of an ever-increasing foreign population, even when it was occupying and making productive land for which they had little use themselves. Diverse languages, customs and, in some cases, religious beliefs had combined with basic differences between the Texians' and the Mexicans' conceptions of democratic government to form constant sources of friction.

The incessant political upheavals, as one unstable régime after another gained power, caused a growing sense of discontent among the Texians. Each successive party to form a government had appeared to be worse than its predecessors. Fully occupied with trying to remain in office, none had given any consideration to the immigrants' request that Texas be established as a separate State – it was regarded as a territory of the State of Coahuila – with representation in the government. They had, nevertheless, continued to levy taxes and duties against the Texians and had attempted to deny entry to further immigrants. As the Texians who had already become established, and not a few of the *Chicanos* had pointed out, such a prohibition would ruin all hope of further expansion and revelopment.

While the majority of the Texians had accepted Mexican citizenship in good faith, the refusal to grant representation, and other treatment to which they had been subjected by the various régimes caused them to revise their atitudes. More and more of them had come to agree with the faction, amongst which Samuel Houston had been prominent, which had insisted that the only secure future for themselves and their descendants lay in the annexation of Texas by the United States of America.

On coming into power, Santa Anna had quickly shown signs of being more ruthless, vindictive and oppressive than any of his predecessors. Adopting the invariable tactics of every dictator or despotic régime who seeks to impose his, or its, will

* Chicano: a Mexican-born citizen of Texas.

upon a population, he had decreed that the ownership of firearms was illegal and had sent an order to his brother-in-law, General Martin Perfecto de Cós, that all the Texians were to be disarmed.

Santa Anna's edict regarding firearms proved to be the final straw which had broken the colonists' patience. The Texians had realized that to surrender their weapons would leave them defenceless against the hostile Indians and criminal elements, none of whom would have given up *their* arms. What was more, it would effectively prevent the immigrants from resisting further impositions by *el Presidente*.

When the garrisons of the Mexican army – showing an energy which had been noticeably absent when called upon to deal with Indians or *bandidos* – attempted to carry out the disarmament, the Texians had refused to obey. There had been rioting and open conflict at Anahuac, Gonzales, Velasco and other places. Such had been the fury of the Texians' resistance that most of the Mexican troops had been compelled to fall back and join General Cós at San Antonio de Bexar. Faced with what amounted to an open rebellion by men who still possessed the means to resist and were generally superior to his own soldiers in the handling of weapons, Cós had not been able to enforce *el Presidente's* wishes. Nor, despite having been aware of the gravity of the situation, had he attempted to have the disarmament edict rescinded or tried to bring about a peaceful settlement.

Realizing that there was no hope of obtaining an amicable and satisfactory relationship with Santa Anna, the Texians had decided to sever all connections with Mexico. They had set up a provisional government, with Henry Smith and James W. Robinson as Governor and Lieutenant Governor respectively and had sent a commission headed by Stephen F. Austin to the United States to try and obtain arms and provisions. Samuel Houston had been appointed major general and made responsible for organizing an army to defend what would – at least until annexation by the United States, which everybody was confident would be a foregone conclusion, be an independent republic under the Lone Star flag. Prominent and wealthy Texians, such as James Bowie, William Barrett Travis, Edward Burleson, Benjamin Milam, the Fog brothers, Edward and Marsden, James W. Fannin and Frank Johnson, had raised regiments – few of which had a strength exceeding

9

two hundred men – so as to be ready to meet the attempts which all knew Santa Anna would make to subdue their bid for independence.

The earlier stages of the rebellion had been successful as far as the Texians were concerned. Several minor skirmishes had gone in their favour, as had the only major confrontation to have taken place. On December the 11th, 1835, after a battle which had lasted for six days, Cós and his force of eleven hundred men had surrendered to Colonels Milam and Burleson at San Antonio de Bexar. Although there had been objections from some of the other senior officers in the Republic of Texa's army, the co-commanders had allowed all of their captives to return unharmed to Mexico on Cós having given his parole that he and his men would not participate in further military action against the Texians. If the reports which had been brought in by the Texians' scouts had been correct, the protest of some officers had been justifiable. Cós was accompanying his brother-in-law and clearly did not intend to honour the conditions of his parole.

While the various successes had boosted the morale of the Republic of Texas's army, they had proved a mixed blessing in that they presented an incorrect impression of the struggle which still lay ahead. The victories, as Houston and most of his senior officers appreciated, had been achieved against poorly-trained, badly-equipped, and indifferently commanded troops.

Due to Texas being so far from the centre of their country's affairs and offering few opportunites for gaining distinction and promotion, career-conscious officers of good quality had avoided serving there. Houston knew that such men would now be coming and would command battle-tried battalions which had fought in the various struggles between the factions who were attempting to take over the reins of government. They would be a much more dangerous proposition than anything so far faced by the Texians. Not only that, the Mexicans would have a tremendous advantage in numbers.

Being aware of the disparity of the size of his own command and the army which Santa Anna would be able to put into the field, Houston had been disinclined to meet the Mexicans in open battle except upon his own terms and on ground of his choosing. With that in mind, he had ordered all the scattered regiments and people in the western sector to assemble at San

Antonio de Bexar. Once they had done so, it was his intention to withdraw into East Texas and make their stand where, if things should go against them, they would have an avenue of escape by crossing the border into the United States.

Although many of the Texians who would be compelled to abandon their homes had seen the wisdom of withdrawing, realizing that *el Presidente* would show them no mercy if he laid hands on them, not all had done so. Four hundred men, under the command of Colonel Fannin, had declared that they would not retreat and intended to hold the town of Goliad.

There was, however, another and more serious threat to the unity of what remained of Houston's army. Eager for fame, acclaim and glory, Colonel Frank Johnson was planning to invade Mexico along the Gulf Coast route and was willing to go to any lengths to make his scheme succeed.

CHAPTER ONE

I'M FIGHTING FOR THE LIKES OF *THEM!*

'I DON'T doubt Sam Houston's courage, or his integrity,' Stanforth Duke stated, after one of the men who had accompanied him to San Antonio and was mingling with the other customers, acting as a stranger, had asked for his views on the current situation. Since entering the Little Sisters *Cantina*, he had spent much money buying drinks and had made himself so popular that he felt sure that the crowd would be willing to listen to him. Knowing that there would be some present who held the Commanding General of the Republic of Texas's army in high esteem, he did not want to antagonize them by too blatant a criticism of their hero. 'But I do question his judgement when he talks of burning homes and crops,* then running away from the Mexicans. Don't get me wrong, though, I've no stake in this personally. I live up north near Shelbyville. But if my home was down in this part of the country, I'd be damned if I'd be willing to put a torch to it, up stakes and run. Especially as we've licked the greasers every time we've locked horns with 'em.'

'It ain't right for you to be talking that ways, stranger,' protested a second member of Duke's party, who was sitting at a table some disance away from the first man. 'You know the General figures that's the right thing to do.'

'With respect sir, I don't agree that I shouldn't be saying

---

* In addition to withdrawing, Houston had wanted to adopt what would one day become known as a 'scorched earth' policy. He had sound reasons for such a measure. By burning their homes, crops and other foodstuffs which they could not carry with them, the Texians would have left their enemies with a difficult supply problem which would increase, rather than diminish, the further Santa Anna advanced beyond the Rio Grande. Despite having this explained to them, there had been such strenuous opposition and refusal that Houston had been compelled to drop the proposal.

Sam Houston's wrong in how he wants to handle things,' Duke answered. The interruption had been made to anticipate any similar protest from genuine supporters of the General. 'The way I figure it, the Republic of Texas's a free country where a man's entitled to speak his mind about anything, or *anybody*, no matter how important they be. That's one of the reasons we've taken up arms against Santa Anna.'

Having delivered the comment, the burly, well-dressed man paused so as to study the response to it. Clearly nobody suspected that he and the lanky, buckskin-clad protestor were working together. There was a brief, yet general rumble of agreement. Satisfied that he had made his point and would be allowed to continue without interruption, he swept his gaze around the crowded bar-room.

The customers who had assembled at the Little Sisters *Cantina* shortly after noon on February the 18th, 1836, were a cross-section of the male Texian population who had gathered at San Antonio in answer to Houston's summons. Some of them had on home-spun garments of the style common among the poorer communities of the United States. There were others clad in buckskins, after the fashion of the mountain men. Several wore clothing derived from the working attire of the Mexican *vaqueros* which was in the process of evolving into the traditional dress of the Texas cowhands. A few, such as Duke, sported broadcloth or cheaper styles of town suits. Scattered among them were a number of soldiers whose fatique uniforms – black leather, *kepi*-like forage caps which could be folded flat for packing; waist-length dark blue tunics that had high, stiff stand-up collars but lacked the pipe-clayed white crossbelts; lighter blue trousers decorated by stripes along the outer seams of the legs; black boots with spurs on the heels – had been copied, with minor variations, from the United States' Regiment of Dragoons by Colonel William Barrett Travis and supplied to the members of his command.

Although only Travis's men wore recognizable uniforms, Duke knew that there were representatives of every regiment in the vicinity present. So he had an audience which was ideally suited for his purposes. He had come to San Antonio with the dual purpose of recruiting men for the force with which Colonel Frank Johnson was planning to invade Mexico, and to persuade those who remained to compel Houston to make a stand instead of withdrawing. If the latter could be achieved,

14

the attention of the whole of the Mexican army would be directed against Houston and it would greatly increase Johnson's chances of success. Neither Johnson nor Duke were over concerned with the adverse effect such a stand might, probably would, have upon the General's outnumbered force.

'What'd you-all reckon we should do, mister?' asked a stocky man in a cheap town suit, from another part of the room.

'Attack the greasers before they can even cross the Rio Grande,' Duke replied, accepting the cue which had been fed by the third of his associates. 'That way, there'll be no call for you to leave the homes you've worked so hard to build. You'll stop the greasers before they can get near to them.'

'By cracky, that's right!' enthused the stocky man and there was another mutter of fairly general approval.

Standing behind the bar, William Cord listened to the conversation with considerable misgivings as he guessed what it was leading up to. It was probably the last opportunity that Cord would have to do business for some time and he had benefited by the amount of money which Duke had spent. For all that, he wished the burly man had stayed away from his *cantina*. Being whole-heartedly in favour of Houston's strategy, even though following it would mean that he must abandon his hitherto lucrative place of business, he did not approve of what he guessed was a carefully organized attempt to change it.

However, after the clever way in which Duke had established his right to freedom of expression, Cord could not see any way of preventing him from airing his views. For the *cantina's* owner – a known supporter of Houston's policies – to attempt any kind of intervention would, he realized, evoke protests which might erupt into open conflict between those who were in favour of the General's strategy and those who opposed it. Cord suspected that the men who had supplied the various comments were in cahoots with Duke. He had a good idea that there were at least two more of the agitator's companions in the room, although as yet they had not spoken. Big, burly, unshaven, dressed in poor quality town suits with grubby, collarless white shirts, they had a strong family resemblance which suggested they might be brothers. Like the other customers who were lining the bar almost elbow to elbow, they were standing with their backs to Cord. However, instead of looking at Duke, they were watching the crowd.

Turning his gaze in the pair's direction, Cord noticed a man coming through the batwing doors. Approaching the counter, the newcomer moved with a Gascon swagger which reminded the owner of the arrogant, over-proud, French-Creole dandies he had seen in New Orleans. Although he was not French, the man exuded a similar cocky self-importance and – assurance. His clothing was clean and he had a well-scrubbed look.

Bare-headed, with his wide-brimmed, low-crowned black hat dangling by its fancy *barbiquejo* chin-strap on to his back, the young man – he would be in his mid-twenties – was six foot in height and had a straight-backed, whipcord lean frame which was set off to its best advantage by his well-tailored garments. He had a thinly-rolled silk bandana which was a glorious riot of brilliant, if clashing, colours knotted about his throat so that its long ends trailed over the breast of his open-necked fringed buckskin shirt. His tight-fitting fawn riding breeches ended in the tops of highly-polished Hessian boots. The belt into which he had hooked his thumbs carried a long-bladed, clip-pointed knife – of the type made by James Black, the Arkansas master-cutler, which had already become known as a 'bowie', in honour of the man who had designed the original – in a decorative Indian sheath at the left side. There was a slanting, two inch broad leather loop attached to the right side of the belt. Into this was thrust the barrel of a good quality pistol so that the butt was pointing forward and would be available to the grasp of either hand.

However, it was the newcomer's face which attracted Cord's main attention. The black hair was taken back in a way which made the sides above his temples protrude and look like short horns. That combined with the brows of his coal black eyes that were shaped like inverted 'V's, an aquiline nose, a neatly trimmed moustache and short chin beard gave his features an almost Satanic expression.

Coming to a halt on spread-apart feet, the newcomer studied the crowded front of the bar. Then his eyes came to rest upon the two men whom Cord suspected of being members of the agitator's party. Becoming aware of the scrutiny, the pair turned their eyes towards the man who was looking at them.

'Would you *gentlemen* mind moving so that *I* can get through to the bar?' the young dandy inquired, his voice that of a well-educated Southron.

Seeing the pair stiffen as if somebody had laid a quirt across their rumps, Cord could tell that they did not care for the

16

manner in which they were being addressed. Politely worded though the appeal had been, the speaker's tone and attitude were more suitable to the deliverance of a demand which he believed he had every right to make. Everything about him suggested that he felt he was dealing with unimportant social inferiors.

A shrewd judge of character, Cord concluded that the newcomer's behaviour was more liable to rouse the two men's wrath than to lead them into compliance with his wishes.

'Come on now!' the young dandy continued impatiently, raising his voice and causing it to sound even more autocratically commanding. 'Step out of the way there and let me through!'

Such was not, Cord could have warned the newcomer, the wisest way in which to speak to two obvious bullies and roughnecks. They were certain to take exception to his assumption of superiority and would be most unlikely to treat him with the servile deference that he clearly considered he should receive.

'Can't rightly see no reason why we should,' the slightly taller and older of the pair stated, conscious of the glances being darted at them by their immediate neighbours along the bar. 'Can you, Brother Basil?'

'I ain't got no better eye-sight 'n you-all, Brother Cyril,' the second man answered, scowling balefully at the dandy. 'Which being so, I'd say you should try it on some other place, fancy pants. We ain't a-fixing to move.'

The brothers had loud, harsh voices which they made no attempt to modulate. So their words were spreading beyond the person at whom they were being directed. Several pairs of eyes swung away from Duke as he was starting to explain how Johnson's proposed invasion of Mexico would benefit the Republic of Texas.

'Now look here, you two!' the dandy said coldly, also raising his voice to a level which was louder than necessary. 'While the likes of you have been propping up a bar, I've been out scouting against the Mexicans. So move aside and let me through.'

Glancing around as he heard the voices and noticed that he was losing the attention of his audience, Duke located the cause of the disturbance. The discovery caused him mingled annoyance and anxiety. He had spent a fair sum of money, buying drinks to ingratiate himself with the crowd and make them

17

more receptive to his agitation, so he did not want anything to distract them. From what he could see and hear, there might be a serious distraction developing. Of all the men in the room, the arrogant young dandy could hardly have selected two more dangerous than the Winglow brothers upon whom to try and impose his imperious wishes.

Being aware of the delicate nature of his assignment, Duke had tried to impress upon all his escort the need to avoid trouble if possible. He had repeated his reminder at Shelby's Livery Barn where they had left their horses before coming separately to the *cantina*. Clearly Cyril Winglow, who was always a bad-tempered bully, had forgotten his instructions.

'He's sure dressed fancy for a feller's done all that there scouting, ain't he Brother Basil?' Cyril asked, looking the young màn over from head to foot.

'Don't let the way I look fool you, *hombre*,' the dandy advised, his Mephistophelian features growing even more sardonic and mocking as he returned the scrutiny. 'I've done plenty of fighting in this war. So I don't need to go around hawg-filthy to try to make folks think I have.'

'Hey there, gentlemen!' Duke called, seeing the anger which came to the brothers' faces as the barb went home. Hearing him, they looked in his direction and he hoped that they would take a hint from his intervention. 'Let's have no unpleasantness.'

'There won't be any,' the young dandy replied, but destroyed the relief which Duke had started to feel by continuing, 'Just so long as these two yahoos stop hogging the bar and let me through.'

'Here, sir,' Duke put in hurriedly, speaking before either of the brothers could do more than stare at the newcomer. Oozing an amiable bonhomie which he was far from feeling, he stepped forward and waved a hand to the gap he had left at the counter. 'You can have my place.'

'Thank you for the offer, sir,' the dandy drawled, without moving or taking his attention from the brothers. 'But I want *them* to make way for me. Damn it, I'm fighting for the likes of them!'

'Fighting for—!' Cyril began, slamming his glass down so that it shattered on the floor.

'Hold it!' Cord bellowed, snatching up and cocking the bell-mouthed blunderbuss which he kept on a shelf under the counter. 'She's loaded with rock-salt and I'll use her should I have to.'

'Are you siding with him?' Cyril demanded, spitting the words over his shoulder. However, having heard the menacing clicking as the weapon's hammer was drawn back, he stood still instead of leaping at the newcomer.

'I'm not siding with anybody,' Cord corrected. 'Just protecting my property is all. If you feller's got things to settle, go outside and do it.'

Although Cord had acted instinctively in the first place, his training as the owner of a *cantina* having taught him the advisability of trying to prevent trouble on his premises, he had seen how he might turn the present situation to good use. If the men went outside to fight, the majority – if not all – of the other customers would follow to watch. That would put a temporary stop to the agitator's speech-making and allow Cord to send his son with a warning of what was happening to General Houston's headquarters.

'Surely there's no need for that, gentlemen,' Duke protested in a placatory manner, duplicating Cord's thoughts on how the crowd would react. He moved closer, looking at the brothers rather than their challenger. 'At a time like this, we can't have fighting amongst ourselves.'

'I shouldn't reckon they'd want to do any fighting with anybody,' the dandy scoffed.

'Easy, Brother Cyril!' Basil said urgently, having taken notice of their leaders's obvious disapproval. While just as much a bully as his sibling, he was somewhat more intelligent. Being aware of how vindictive Duke could behave when crossed, Basil had no wish to antagonize him. There was, he decided, a way out which would avoid any suggestion of them having backed down. 'He's got a knife 'n' pistol and neither of us is armed.'

Realizing what the younger Winglow had in mind, Duke nodded approvingly. Nobody could blame the brothers for refusing to take on an armed man when neither was carrying weapons. Nor was it likely that the arrogant young dandy would be willing to consider fighting with this bare hands against a heavier opponent.

It was a good try, but failed to produce the desired result.

'Shucks, I'd hate the gents here to think I'd need weapons to deal with the likes of you,' the young man remarked, sliding the knife from its sheath with his left hand while the right pulled the pistol clear of the loop. 'If somebody will hold these for me—'

'Here, mister,' offered the burly sergeant of Travis's regiment, who was sitting at a table near to the dandy. He came to his feet and held out his hands, 'I'll take them for you.'

'*Gracias*,' the young man drawled, relinquishing the weapons without hesitation. Then he swung his sardonic gaze to Cyril and went on. 'Now it's entirely up to you, loud mouth. *I'm* ready, but *you* might not have the stomach for it.'

'I'll show you whether I have, or—!' Cyril roared furiously, ignoring Duke's prohibitive head-shake and making as if to lunge at his tormentor.

'Not in here, you won't!' Cord interrupted firmly, tapping the muzzle of his blunderbuss on the counter to give emphasis to his words. 'If you're set on fighting, go outside where my furniture won't get broken.'

'That suits me fine,' the young man announced as, taking heed of the owner's words and action, Cyril restrained his impulse to attack. 'I'll be waiting out there, loud mouth. You do what you want.'

With that, the dandy swung on his heel and swaggered towards the door. He presented his back contemptuously to the brothers and did not so much as glance over his shoulder as he left the building.

'Damn it to hell, Major Duke!' Cyril protested, turning to the agitator and, in his desire to exculpate himself, ignoring the fact that they were not supposed to know each other. 'The son-of-a-bitch ain't giving me no choice.'

An almost uncontrollable rage filled Duke as he watched Cyril removing his hat and coat, but the incautious words had not caused it. Probably nobody else had attached any significance to them. All around the room, men were finishing their drinks and shoving back their chairs. Duke's anger was rising as he saw that what he had feared was happening.

'Hey!' whooped a soldier excitedly, as Cyril passed the garments to Basil and set off across the room. 'Come on. Let's go see what happens.'

Watching the mass movement to go outside, Duke knew that he could neither do nor say anything to prevent the disruption of his work. Stimulated by the drinks which he had bought for them, the crowd clearly considered that watching a fight would be more interesting and entertaining than listening to him. Duke silently cursed the brothers for not having remembered why they were in San Antonio and refusing to make room for the newcomer at the bar. One glance at him ought to have warned them that their response would make such a proud, arrogant young hot-head determined to enforce his demand.

'By cracky, mister,' enthused a leathery, buckskin-clad old timer who was standing at Duke's side, breaking in on his train of thought. 'That feller's going to get taught a lesson. It don't pay to rile up young Cap'n Hardin that ways.'

'Who?' the agitator inquired, realizing that the other did not consider the 'lesson' would be given by Cyril Winglow.

'Cap'n Jackson Baines Hardin of the Texas Light Cavalry,' the leathery man elaborated. 'He's a lil ole devil in a fight.'

CHAPTER TWO

LET'S SEE HOW YOU STACK UP
AGAINST A *MAN*

STANDING in the centre of the street, Jackson Baines Hardin
watched the crowd streaming out of the Little Sisters *Cantina*.
They spread each way along the sidewalk, talking excitedly,
making bets and jostling each other for the best positions from
which to see what happened. If he was perturbed by what he
had done inside, his Mephistophelian features – which, in part,
accounted for his generally, used nickname 'Ole Devil'* –
showed no evidence of it. Rather, if his expression was anything
to go by, he regarded the prospect of fighting with a heavier
man as an enjoyable relaxation from the serious and dangerous
business of scouting against the Mexican army.

There was a hush as the Winglow brothers emerged, with
Basil carrying Cyril's hat and jacket. While the young man's
comments had been directed at both of them, they had realized
that the crowd would not allow them to make a combined
attack upon him. Nor, if it came to a point, did either believe
that it would be necessary to do so. Each of them was heavier
than the slim dandy and they had both acquired considerable
ability at rough-house brawling.

'Sorry you ain't going to get a chance to whip him, Brother
Basil,' Cyril announced as he lumbered from the sidewalk.

'That's all right,' Basil answered, halting at the edge alongside the sergeant who had taken charge of Hardin's property.
'You go do it good, Brother Cyril.'

Even as the younger brother gave his magnanimous blessing,
Hardin showed a reluctance to wait for Cyril to come to him.
Instead, he darted forward. Doubting that the young man in-
tended to meet him toe-to-toe, Cyril lunged forward and

* Another reason for the nickname had arisen out of the fact that
other men before the old timer in the *cantina* had commented upon
him being a 'lil ole devil' in a fight.

spread open his arms. By doing so, he intended to circumvent the other's attempt to swerve by at the last moment. He discovered too late that such had never been Hardin's plan.

Gauging the distance which was separating them, Hardin bounded into the air as he had been taught by a master of *savate* – the French style of foot and fist fighting – in New Orleans. Drawing up his knees towards his chest, he caused his body to tilt backwards. Then, straightening his legs, he propelled the soles of his Hessian boots into the centre of Cyril's chest. All the air was driven from the burly man's lungs and he was flung backwards by the powerful, unexpected attack. To the accompaniment of laughter and startled comments from the onlookers, he collided with the left side hitching rail. That alone prevented him from falling on to the sidewalk.

Rebounding from the leaping high kick, Hardin landed on his feet with an almost cat-like agility. He clearly had every intention of following up his advantage before his opponent could recover. Gliding forward, he smashed his left fist into Cyril's belly. As the man gasped and started to fold at the waist, Hardin's clenched right hand rose to meet the bristle-covered chin. Lifted erect and held that way by the stout bar of the hitching-rail, dazed and winded, Cyril was in serious trouble. He was clearly unable to stop the continuation of the attack.

Seeing his brother's predicament, Basil set about relieving it. Dropping Cyril's coat and hat, he sprang forward without waiting to remove his own. Before Hardin realized that Basil had intervened, he felt a hand grasping the back of his shirt collar and another catching his right wrist to twist it into a hammerlock.

Having obtained his two holds, Basil tried to use them as a means of pushing the young dandy away from his brother. Allowing himself to go until he had regained his equilibrium, Hardin came to a stop when sure of it. Setting his weight on his left leg, he thrust his right diagonally until it was alongside Basil's left foot. Doing so caused his body to swing to the right and he crouched slightly, bending his left arm at the elbow. Although he had not tried to jerk his right wrist from Basil's right hand, the turning motion had brought it from behind his back. Giving the other no chance to return it to the hammerlock, he snapped it upwards with his palm towards his attacker. Doing so caused Basil to loosen his hold a little.

23

Instantly, Hardin's left knuckles ploughed into Basil's *solar plexus*. Letting out a croak, Basil released hardin's shirt and felt the wrist snatched away from his fingers. Coming around, Hardin delivered a right cross to Basil's jaw which turned him in a half circle. Nor did he let it end there. Bringing up his left boot, he rammed it hard against the seat of the younger brother's trousers and pushed hard. Unable to help himself, Basil went staggering to fall on hands and knees half way across the street.

Brief though the respite had been, Cyril had recovered sufficient of his wits to take action. Shoving away from the hitching rail, he swung a wide, looping round-house punch which struck the side of the young man's face. Although the attack came just too late to save Basil and, due to Cyril still being somewhat dazed, arrived with less than his full strength behind it, the blow caught Hardin before his foot had returned to the ground. Pitched sideways, he knew that he could not prevent himself from falling. So he let himself go and concentrated on landing as gently as possible. Alighting on the street, he rolled on to his back.

Lumbering forward, while his brother was rising, Cyril dropped with big hand driving forward to clamp on to Hardin's throat. It was also his intention to ram his right knee into the dandy's body. Although Hardin could not escape the hands, he managed to writhe so that the knees missed. That made his position a little easier, but he knew that he was far from being out of the woods. Kneeling at his side, Cyril raised his head with the intention of banging it on the ground. At the same time, Basil was running forward to help with the attack.

Strolling from an alley along the street, a man of about Hardin's age stopped as he saw what was happening. Six foot tall, heavily built, he conveyed an impression of well-padded, comfortable lethargy. He had curly, auburn hair showing beneath his black hat, and his sun-reddened fetures lost their amiable, sleepy-looking expression as he took in the scene before the *cantina*. As he was dressed – with the exception of his scarlet silk bandana – and armed in the same fashion as Hardin, it seemed likely that he was connected in some way with the dandy. He too appeared to have bathed, shaved and donned clean garments recently, Although his pace changed from a leisurely amble to a run, he knew that he would not be able to reach the fight before the second assailant had returned to participate in it.

Being unaware that help was coming, Hardin set about saving himself. Bracing his neck, without making what he knew would be a futile attempt to free it by sheer strength, he managed to lessen the impact as Cyril shoved downwards and the back of his head met the ground. Then, as he was raised for a second time, he pivoted at the hips to send his left knee with some force into the burly man's ribs. Immediately after making that attack, Hardin thrust his right hand upwards between Cyril's arms. He did not close it into a fist. Instead, he jabbed his first and second fingers into Cyril's nostrils. Pain roared through the recipient of the attack. Leaving Hardin's throat, his hands went up to try and staunch the blood which gushed from his nose.

Rushing up, Basil arrived just after his brother had been compelled to release Hardin. Coming in from the opposite side to Cyril, Basil launched his right foot in a kick. Rolling to the left, Hardin swung his left arm so that the base of his fist met the advancing shin just above the ankle. Working in smooth coordination, his right hand grasped the leg of the trousers over his left fist. Having halted the kick, Hardin returned his shoulders to the ground and hauled the captured limb above him. Then his own right leg snapped around and upwards, aiming the toe of his boot at Basil's groin area. The kick caught Basil on the inside of the upper thigh. While painful, it was not sufficiently so to incapacitate him. It did, however, combine with the pull being exerted upon his leg to throw him off balance.

Giving Basil's leg a twisting heave which toppled him over, Hardin released him and bounded up. Snarling incoherently in his rage, half-blinded by tears, Cyril lunged and with bloody hands tried to grab the slim young man.

'This's for the *Chicano* boy!' Hardin told the burly man savagely, pivoting into another *savate* kick.

Propelled by the powerful gluteus muscles of Hardin's buttocks, his right boot came into contact with the bottom of Cyril's jaw. The burly man's head hinged back until it seemed that his neck might be in danger of snapping. Lifted from his knees he began to crumple like a punctured balloon and collapsed flaccidly on to his face.

25

Having disposed of the elder brother, Hardin turned his attention to the younger. Moving clear of Cyril and standing with his back to the spectators, the young dandy studied Basil who was once more on his hands and knees and staring at his sibling as if unable to believe his eyes.

'Come on, you lousy son-of-a-bitch!' Hardin ordered coldly and his face seemed even more Satanic as he swept the second of the Winglow family with a contempt-filled gaze. 'Let's see how you stack up against a *man* instead of a *Chicano* boy.'

Swinging his head so as to glare at the speaker, Basil became aware of the significance of the comment and did not care for what it suggested. Apparently the dandy had another reason besides arrogant self-importance for picking the fight.

Although the Winglows and their companions had believed that they were the only human occupants of the livery barn, they had been mistaken. Shortly after the rest of the party had taken their departure, the brothers had heard a scuffling noise. On going to investigate, they had discovered that a pair of boys – a Texian and a *Chicano* – were hiding behind some bales of hay. Guessing that the boys had heard Duke giving his instructions, Basil and Cyril had decided to frighten them into keeping quiet and had tried to catch them. Being older than his friend, the *Chicano* had tried to hold the brothers off with a pitchfork while the youngster escaped. Although he had been partly successful, the Texian boy having fled, the *Chicano* had been less fortunate. Disarming him, the brothers had slapped him around and finally left him bloody and unconscious on the floor.

Partly because they had been told to pretend that they did not know the rest of their party, but mainly due to believing that Duke would disapprove of what they had done, the brothers had not mentioned the incident on their arrival at the *cantina*. From what he had said, it seemed that the dandy had found the *Chicano* and, learning who was responsible, had for some reason decided to inflict summary punishment upon the men who had carried out the attack.

Letting out a bellow of rage, Basil thrust himself erect. Recklessly he flung himself forward with big hands reaching to grab hold of the dandy. It proved to be a costly error in tactics. Before his fingers could close, the object of his intentions seemed to disappear.

Crouching under Basil's grasp, Hardin let him have a punch

in the pit of the stomach. It halted him and, as he doubled over, Hardin's knee rocketed upwards. For the second time, Basil was fortunate in avoiding the full force of an attack. He had fallen back just enough for the knee to miss his face. Struck on the forehead, he was lifted upright and staggered rearwards for a few steps. However, he did not go down. As Hardin advanced, Basil caught his balance and swung a backhand blow with his right hand. Although it was almost at the end of its flight when it connected on the side of the dandy's head, it brought him to a halt. Basil followed it with a much more effective punch to the chest, sending Hardin up against the hitching rail. Wanting to make the most of his success, Basil lunged forward.

On seeing that his cousin had escaped and rendered one attacker *hors-de-combat*, Mannen Blaze had slowed to a more leisurely pace. He had complete faith in Hardin's ability to take care of the remaining assailant. Satisfied that his assistance would not be required and thinking that his arrival might bring some of the burly man's friends into the affair, he halted and leaned against the hitching rail of a store on the opposite side of the street to the *cantina*. While it was clear that he did not mean to intervene, he was ready if anybody else should do so. Although he did not know it, such an intervention was at that moment being suggested.

Standing glowering angrily at the crowd, Duke felt a touch on his sleeve. Looking around he found one of his party at his side. Tall, gangling, the man's sombre features and black clothing were indicative of his profession. He had been an undertaker before joining Johnson's regiment.

'Shall we cut in, major?' the man inquired, watching Hardin side-step Basil's rush and move into the centre of the street.

'No, Jolly!' Duke replied. 'Those two stupid bastards deserve all they get, letting themselves be riled into a fight.'

The force with which the punch had landed on his chest had been a warning to Hardin that a toe-to-toe slugging brawl would favour his heavier assailant. So he had had no intention of being trapped in a position which would require that he fought in such a manner. Having evaded Basil and gained room to manoeuvre, he swung around to await the next development.

Instead of having learned the futility of such tactics, the burly man continued with the methods he had employed with

27

some success in previous fights. They proved disastrous against the swiftly-moving dandy, who refused to stand and trade blows or to come to grips where brute strength would have prevailed. It soon became obvious that, barring something unforeseen happening, Hardin was going to win. However, not all of the punishment being meted out went one way, Basil managed to land some punches in return for the many which were being rained upon him. All in all, the appreciative spectators were treated to a pretty good fight.

Despite seeing that his cousin was justifying his confidence, Mannen Blaze was perturbed as he remembered what had brought them to San Antonio. Devil could, Blaze reflected have picked a more suitable time to become involved in a street brawl. That belief was increased, as was his perturbation, by the sight of two men who came from an alley further along the street. Recognizing one and making an accurate guess at the other's identity, Blaze could foresee stormy times ahead for his cousin.

One of the new arrivals was grey-haired, very tall, broad-shouldered and powerfully built. Clad in a buckskin shirt, brown bell-bottomed *vaquero* trousers and high heeled, spur-decorated boots, with a wide-brimmed black hat tilted back on his head, he had a bowie knife – more correctly *the* bowie knife* – in a sheath on the left side of his waist belt.

Seeing Colonel James Bowie approaching was not the cause of Blaze's consternation. In fact, the legendary knife-fighter and adventurer appeared to be amused at finding Hardin in a fight. The same did not apply to his companion.

Lacking two inches of Bowie's height, the second man was also more slenderly built. He wore a uniform similar to those of the soldiers on the sidewalk, except that it was of better material and more decorative. There were bullion shoulder scales on his tunic and his head-dress was a black felt *shako*. Further indications of his rank were supplied by the red sash, knotted at the right, around his waist under a belt with a sabre hanging by its slings, and by a row of five brass buttons on each sleeve's cuff. He marched rather than walked, striding out as if on parade.

Blaze assumed, correctly, that the officer was Colonel William Barrett Travis; already noted for being a tough martinet

* What happened to the knife after the Alamo is told in: *The Quest for Bowie's Blade*.

28

and disciplinarian. Judging from his expression, he did not approve of what was going on.

'Stop this damned brawling immediately!' Travis bellowed, just after Hardin had knocked Basil staggering with a right to the jaw.

Turning his head to discover who had spoken, Hardin duplicated his cousin's identification of the two men. However, carrying out the order was not possible. While Hardin was willing to obey, the same did not apply to his battered and bloody assailant.

Catching his balance and coming to a halt, Basil once again charged wildly at the young man who had inflicted so much pain upon him. Hearing the other approaching, Hardin knew that he would not be responsible to words. Avoiding the bull-like rush, he whipped around a *savate* circular side kick which propelled the toe of his boot into the pit of Basil's stomach with considerable force. The burly man let out a belching gasp, folded over at the waist and blundered onwards a couple of steps. Pivoting, Hardin delivered a second kick. It landed on the seat of Basil's pants and kept him moving. Pure chance guided him to the supporting post of the hitching rail. As he still had not straightened up, the top of his skull rammed into the sturdy timber. Rebounding from it, he fell as if he had been boned and with blood pouring from his scalp.

'Sorry, colonel,' Hardin said, breathing heavily but turning in a respectful manner towards the approaching men. 'I don't think that feller heard what you said.'

'I see you've not forgotten how to fight, young Ole Devil,' Bowie remarked with a grin, glancing at the motionless brothers.

'You know him, Colonel Bowie?' Travis asked, before Hardin could reply and in tones which suggested that he and the great knife fighter might not be on the best of terms.

'Don't you?' Bowie inquired, sounding puzzled. 'This's Captain Hardin of Ed Fog's Texas Light Cavalry. Devil, may I present Colonel William Barrett Travis?'

'My pleasure, sir,' Hardin responded, although he felt certain that the sentiment would not be mutual under the circumstances.

Like his cousin, who was coming slowly towards him, Hardin silently decided that of all the senior officers in the Republic of Texas's army, Barrett Travis was the last whom he would have wanted to arrive at that moment. Even if the colonel had known the reason for the fight, Hardin considered it was unlikely to have met with his approval.

'Sergeant Brill!' Travis called, turning to the spectators on the sidewalk, without offering to acknowledge the introduction. 'Take our men back to the camp and find them some work.'

'Yo!' answered the non-com, giving what was already developing into the accepted cavalry response to an order.

While Duke could see that he would be losing some of his audience, he expected that the rest were going to re-enter the *cantina* and allow him to continue with the work which had been interrupted. Even as the thought came, he heard bugles playing a familiar and – under the circumstances – infuriating call.

'That's assembly, boys,' Bowie announced. 'Means we're all wanted back at the camp. I'd be right obliged if you'd close down for a spell, Bill.'

'She's as good's done, Jim,' Cord answered, and he could hardly restrain his relief as he realized that by doing so he would prevent Duke from resuming the agitation. 'I'll open up after sundown, gents, but there'll be nothing else served until then. Collect your belongings.'

'Whose outfit are those two with?' Bowie asked, indicating the unconscious brothers.

Nobody replied. Glancing at Duke, his men received a prohibitive shake of his head and kept silent.

'Looks like they must have come in to join somebody,' Bowie went on. 'Here, Ed, Tim, see to them.'

The men named by the knife-fighter belonged to his regiment. Swinging from the porch, they went to carry out the order. While Travis's soldiers were forming up, the sergeant returned Hardin's property to him.

'We'd best have 'em toted to a doctor, Colonel Jim,' suggested one of the men who was examining the brothers, and he pointed to Basil. 'This jasper's head's split open pretty bad and, way young Ole Devil there kicked it, the other'll be lucky if his jaw's not broken.'

'That's *very* good!' Travis snorted, in tones which implied exactly the opposite, scowling at Hardin who had donned his hat and was returning the pistol to its loop on his belt. 'Thanks to you, *captain*, we've lost two men who could have fought against the Mexicans.'

'No excuse, sir,' the young dandy answered, stiffening into a ramrod straight brace as rigidly military as the uniformed colonel's posture. His Mephistophelian features displayed a complete lack of emotion, certainly he did not appear to be contrite over having deprived the army of the brothers' services. 'Permission to leave, sir?'

'Granted!' Travis replied. 'And, unless you wish to indulge in further brawls and to cripple a few more members of *our* army, I'd suggest that you get about whatever business has brought you to San Antonio.'

CHAPTER THREE

YOU'VE NO INTENTION OF BELIEVING US

'TOMMY'S not here yet,' Mannen Blaze remarked, looking languidly around as he and his cousin entered Shelby's Livery Barn.

'I was hoping that he wouldn't be,' Ole Devil Hardin admitted, and touched his bruised left cheek with a careful forefinger. 'With any luck, I'll have time to tidy myself up again before he comes to fetch us.'

'I'm going to stick with you this time, cousin,' Blaze declared with a sleepy grin. 'That way you'll maybe keep out of mischief.'

On their arrival at General Samuel Houston's headquarters that morning, Hardin and Blaze had delivered the report of the scouting mission which they had carried out. They had been told that the General would not be able to see them for some time, but wished to do so eventually. Wanting to look their best, and having an aversion to being dirty for longer than was necessary, they had left the third member of their party at the headquarters' building and gone to try and make themselves more presentable.

Visiting the livery barn where they had already left their horses, the cousins had asked advice of its owner. An old friend of their clan, Allen Shelby, had told them to go to his home and make use of his toilet facilities. As the senior officer, Hardin had been the first to use the bath and change from his travel-stained garments. While his cousin was bathing in turn, he had returned to the barn to see if their companion had arrived. Finding the *Chicano* boy and learning what had happened, he had set off to deal with the matter alone instead of waiting for Blaze to join him.

Although Hardin had achieved his purpose, he had accepted Colonel William Barrett Travis's comments and curt dismissal from the front of the *cantina* without making any attempt to offer an explanation which would exculpate him. Accompanied by his cousin, who had prudently remained in the background during the brief discussion with Travis, he had made his way back to the livery barn. They had arranged to meet their companion there when he came to fetch them for the interview with Houston.

During the walk from the *cantina* to the barn, Hardin had satisfied Blaze's curiosity regarding the trouble. He had also explained why he had not told Travis of the real reason for him picking the fight. Far from being the slow-witted dullard which he pretended to be, Blaze had conceded that his cousin had acted for the best and hoped that their superiors would share his sentiments when they heard.

The barn was still unoccupied, which did not surprise Hardin and Blaze. Shelby had been on the point of departing for a conference at Houston's headquarters when they had come to seek his advice, and had said that all of his employees were occupied with preparations for leaving with the army.

'Mrs. Shelby's too busy to want me bothering her again,' Hardin drawled. 'I'll have a wash in the horse-trough.'

'You shouldn't need to change your clothes again,' Blaze commented. 'I reckon we can brush most of the drift off.'

'I hope so,' Hardin replied. 'I don't have another pair of breeches until Mrs. Shelby sends the pair she's having washed. Let me get a towel out of my warbag and, while I'm washing, will you get the rest of our gear out of the office? Then we'll take the horses, go out to headquarters and wait there until the General can see us.'

'I'm for *that*,' Blaze declared. 'There'll be less chance of *you* getting into trouble again if we do.'

Although the cousins' and their companion's saddles were hanging with several more on the inverted V-shaped wooden 'burro', which had been erected along one wall for that purpose, they had removed their bed rolls, rifles and other weapons. Shelby had suggested that with so many strangers in town – and as the barn would be untended – it might be advisable for them to leave their more portable property somewhere less public than on the burro. Putting his private office at their disposal, he had given them a key so that they could retrieve their gear when they needed it.

By the time Hardin had finished his ablutions, Blaze had fetched their belongings from the office and had removed most

33

of the dirt stains from his shirt. Donning it, Hardin replaced the towel in his warbag. He was about to refold his bed roll when footsteps sounded and a group of men came through the open main doors.

Six in number, the newcomers formed a rough half circle and halted just inside the building. In the centre of the line, standing with his hands behind his back, was a tall, gangling, mournful-looking man wearing a black hat and suit. Studying him, Blaze thought he might be an undertaker and wondered what had brought him to the barn. Although the others wore a variety of clothing, it was clear that they were with the black dressed man. What was more, their attitude suggested that they might not have arrived for the harmless purpose of collecting their horses.

'What're you pair doing in here?' Erasmus Jolly demanded, after looking around to make sure that nobody else was present.

Having seen that he would not be able to carry out his assignment as long as the *cantina* was closed and the men returned to their regiments, Stanforth Duke had been furious. He had guessed that when Houston heard what he had been trying to do, he would take steps to ensure Duke was not given a second opportunity. Being of a vindictive nature he had decided that the indirect cause of his misfortune should be made to suffer. So he told Jolly to take their men and revenge themselves upon the young dandy, while he went to see if there was any chance of resuming the task which had brought them to San Antonio. Having discovered that their victim was at the livery barn, Jolly had come with his companions. He wanted to provoke Hardin into starting a fight so that he could claim, if questioned, that he and his companions had acted in self-defence. After what he had seen at the *cantina*, he felt confident that doing so would be easy.

'That depends on why you're asking,' Hardin answered truculently, coming to his feet and darting a quick look to where his pistol – which he had removed while washing – lay on his saddle just beyond his reach.

'There's a fair few fellers' gear in here, including our'n, with nobody to keep an eye on it,' growled the biggest of the party, standing to Jolly's right. Clad in *vanquero*-style clothing, his name was Stone. It had been he who had asked the questions in the *cantina* which had allowed Duke to start commenting upon

34

the military situation in Texas. 'So we're a mite curious when we find two fellers taking things out of somebody's warbag.'

'It's *my* warbag,' Hardin stated coldly, acting as Jolly hoped he would, and flickering a glance past the men towards the main entrance. 'And I'm putting something in, not taking it out.'

'How about them other two bed-rolls?' the former undertaker challenged, as he and his companions moved slowly closer. He still kept his hands behind his back and continued in an officious manner to which he felt sure the dandy would take exception, 'Seems to me that makes one more of 'em than there is of you.'

'We're taking our *amigo's* gear out to headquarters with us,' Blaze explained in a placatory manner, after having darted a look at his cousin which, Jolly believed, was imploring him not to make trouble.

'Your *amigo's*, huh?' Jolly sniffed and brought his party to a halt about fifteen feet away from the cousins.

'He's waiting out there,' Hardin elaborated and swung his gaze past the men as if searching for somebody to confirm his statement. Then he eyed the black dressed figure sardonically. 'Only you've no intention of believing us.'

'You're damned right we haven't,' Jolly confirmed, bringing his hands into view. The right was grasping a cocked pistol, which he lined at the slim young dandy. 'Stand still, both of you.'

'Best do it, Devil,' Blaze advised almost tremulously.

'Shed your weapons,' Jolly went on. 'We're going to take you to the constable and see what he reckons to your story.'

'That suits me,' Blaze declared, starting to draw the bowie knife from his sheath with the tips of his fingers. He looked at his cousin, continuing, 'I'd do it, was I you, Devil. The constable knows us and he'll soon clear things up.'

'That's for sure,' Hardin agreed, giving a confirmatory nod. Then he also took out his knife and let it fall. Oozing arrogance and indignation, he scowled at Jolly. 'And when he has, *hombre,* we'll be expecting an apology.'

'You'll get it,' the former undertaker sneered, watching the bulky red-head's pistol following the two knives. 'Move away from 'em.'

As the cousins obeyed the order, going into the centre of the barn, Jolly congratulated himself upon the way in which he was carrying out his superior's instructions. While desirous of vengeance, Duke had decided that it should be restricted to a severe beating with fists and feet. There must, he had stated, be no shooting as that would attract unwanted attention. So, with such a restriction placed upon him, Jolly had been determined to ensure that their victims were also denied the use of weapons. Satisfied that he had achieved his intentions, he was about to tell his men to do their work when he heard a soft footfall from his rear. While his men looked around, he kept his eyes to the front.

A small figure appeared in the main entrance. Bare-headed, he had short-cropped black hair and sallow, cheerful, Oriental features. He wore a loose fitting black cotton shirt, which was hanging outside trousers of the same material that were tucked into Hessian boots, and he was unarmed. Apart from the lack of a pigtail, he might have been a typical Chinese coolie, one of those who were already to be found in the United States.

'Devil-san!' the new arrival began, hurrying across the room and passing between Stone and Jolly. 'General Houston says for you to co—'

'Hold hard there, you yeller-skinned varmint!' Stone bellowed, shooting out his right hand to grasp the back of the small Oriental's shirt neck and starting to tug at it. 'Get the hell out of—'

As either Hardin or his cousin could have warned the burly man, such an action was ill-advised to say the least. While Tommy Okasi was undoubtedly of Oriental descent, he did not belong to the Chinese race. He was, in fact, Japanese and possessed a sturdy fighting spirit which the Chinese coolies, with whom Stone had been acquainted, only rarely exhibited.

Five years ago, a ship commanded by Hardin's father had come across a derelict vessel drifting in the China Sea. The only survivor had been Tommy Okasi, half dead, and with no possessions other than the clothing on his back, a pair of swords and the bow and quiver of arrows which were now leaning against his saddle. On recovering, he had proved to speak a little English. However, when questioned, he had given no explanation for his presence aboard the other vessel. Nor had he evinced any desire to return to his native land. Instead, he had stayed on in Captain Hardin's ship attaching himself to his rescuer's son. What was more, while he had a very thorough

36

knowledge of his nation's highly effective martial arts, he was content to act as Ole Devil Hardin's valet.

Even before the events which had caused Hardin and Mannen Blaze to leave Louisiana and join other members of the Hardin, Fog and Blaze clan in Texas, Tommy had been of great service to his employer. Since arriving and becoming involved in the struggle for independence, he had taken a full part in their activities and had shared their dangers.

All in all, Tommy Okasi – even without his two swords, which for some reason he was no longer wearing – was not the kind of man to be treated the way Stone was doing.

Feeling the hand take hold of his collar and himself being jerked roughly backwards, Tommy reacted with devastating speed. Instead of allowing himself to be flung by his captor and out of the door, he contrived to go towards Stone. The loose fit of his shirt did nothing to impede his movements. Twisting his torso to the left, he bent his right arm in front of him. Then, at exactly the crucial moment, he reversed his body's direction and propelled the arm to the rear.

'*Kiai!*' Tommy ejaculated, giving the traditional spiritual cry as he struck at his assailant.

To Stone, who had not expected such a display of aggression from a member of what he had always regarded as being a passive and easily bullied race, it seemed as if he had been kicked in the *solar plexus* by a mule. Releasing the collar, as all the breath was rammed from his body by the force of the impact, the burly man clutched at the stricken area and folded over. He retreated hurriedly a few steps, trying to replenish his lungs, before tripping and sitting down.

Having liberated himself, Tommy continued to move with rapidity and deadly purpose. Jolly's head had swivelled around as he heard Stone's agony-filled croak on being struck and the pistol's barrel wavered out of alignment. Before he could return it to its original point of aim, the small Oriental turned his unwanted attention upon him.

Around and up whipped Tommy's left arm. He did not strike with his clenched fist, but the result was just as effective. Keeping the fingers extended and together, with the thumb bent across his palm, he drove the hand so its edge passed under Jolly's chin and chopped into his prominent Adam's apple. Jolly might have thought himself fortunate had he known how effective the *tegatana*, hand sword, blow of *karate* could be, for

37.

he was just too far away to take it at full power. As it was, the result was not to be despised. To Jolly, it seemed that his wind-pipe had been assaulted by a blunt axe. Reeling backwards, making a sound like a chicken being strangled, he involuntarily tightened his right forefinger on the pistol's trigger. The hammer swung around, propelling the flint in its jaws against the steel frizzen which hinged forward allowing the sparks to fall on to the priming charge. A spurt of flame, passing through the touch-hole, ignited the powder in the chamber. With a crash and cloud of white smoke, the weapon fired. As its bullet flew harmlessly into the wall, the recoil snatched it from Jolly's grasp. Not that he gave its loss any thought. Staggering towards the wall, with hands clutching at his neck, his only interest was in trying to breathe.

'Get the bastards!' yelled Bellowes, the stocky townsman who had 'asked' for Duke's advice at the *cantina*.

'Know something, Cousin Devil?' Blaze inquired, sounding almost plaintive, as he watched two of the quartet reaching for the pistols in their belts as they all moved forward. 'I don't reckon they'll listen to reason.'

'I never thought they would' Hardin answered.

To give Lacey – the big, burly, buckskin-clad man who had 'protested' against Duke's criticism of Houston's policies – and Bellowes their due, they intended to use the firearms as clubs in accordance with Jolly's instructions. However, they found that doing so was far easier to plan than to carry out.

Timing his action perfectly, Hardin demonstrated his *savate* training by kicking Bellowes's hand as it was dragging the pistol free. Having done so, while Bellowes yelped with pain and dropped the pistol, Hardin turned on his second attacker, who was called Tate and who was dressed in a similar fashion to Stone. Ducking beneath the man's hands as they reached towards him, Hardin caught him around the knees and, straightening up, tossed him over to crash to the floor. Even as Hardin disposed of Tate, Bellowes retaliated by delivering a right cross to the jaw which sent him across the barn to collide with the burro.

Employing a rapidity of motion that was vastly different from the slothful manner in which he had been behaving up to that moment, Blaze gave his attention to Lacey. Bounding into range, the red head flung forward his knotted right fist. Carrying the full weight of his body behind them, his knuckles made

38

contact with the centre of Lacey's face. Despite having almost reached the end of its flight, the blow was still hard enough to make its recipient release the pistol, which had just come clear of his belt, and he lumbered backwards a few steps with blood flowing freely from his squashed nose.

Although the smallest of Duke's party, the fourth attacker did not hesitate to try to avenge Lacey. Dressed in the fashion of a French Creole dandy, McCann was a cocky young man who considered himself to be very tough. Catching Blaze's right shoulder, McCann tugged and, as he turned, drove a punch into his stomach. While the blow landed fairly hard, it made little or no impression upon the solid wall of muscle with which it had connected. Startled by the lack of distress which he had expected to cause, McCann sent his right fist after the left, and with as little effect.

Looking almost benevolently at his assailant, who seemed diminutive in comparison with his own bulk, Blaze shot out his hands. Alarm came to McCann's face as he felt the lapels of his jacket grasped and he was lifted from the floor as if he weighed no more than a baby. Then, as Lacey – who matched the red head in size – came back with the intention of repaying him for the blow to the nose, Blaze gave a heave and flung McCann aside. Although he alighted on his feet, the young man had no control over his movements. Unable to stop himself, he rushed onwards until he collided with and disappeared over the bales of hay behind which the two boys had hidden while eavesdropping upon Duke's instructions.

After having struck and disarmed Jolly, Tommy watched the attacks being made upon Hardin and Blaze. He was ready to go to either's aid if the need arose. Behind him, Stone lurched erect breathing heavily. Rubbing his torso where Tommy's elbow had impacted, the burly man moved forward. Hearing the other approaching, Tommy turned. He was only just in time, a huge hand was reaching for him. Before Stone's fingers could close on the small Oriental, he felt his wrist gripped with surprising strength and given a peculiar jerking twist. Just how it happened, Stone could never imagine, but the barn suddenly seemed to revolve as his feet left the floor and he sailed over Tommy's shoulder to land heavily on his back.

Still croaking hoarsely and having trouble breathing, Jolly had started to move in when he saw Stone rise. He was amazed to see his burly companion thrown with such ease, but, hoping to take Tommy by surprise, he charged forward. He met with no greater success than Stone, being treated to a similar *kata-seoi* shoulder throw and deposited almost on top of his companion. Having done so, Tommy darted away to help Hardin who was being attacked by Bellowes and Tate.

The fight continued to rage. It was fierce and hectic, but, despite their numerical superiority, far from satisfactory where Jolly's party were concerned. They had come to the barn expecting little difficulty in dealing with Hardin and Blaze. Instead, due to Tommy's intervention, their victims were able to turn the tables on them.

As when dealing with the Winglow brothers, Hardin relied upon his speed, agility and knowledge of *savate* to defend himself. Blaze lacked his cousin's qualities, but was stronger and just as able to take care of himself, using skill instead of relying upon brute strength. By far the smallest of any of the combatants, even McCann being taller, Tommy Okasi was anything but the least effective. His use of *ju jitsu* and *karate*, which were all but unknown in the Western World at that period,* more than off-set all the advantages his opponents had in the matter of size and weight.

Matched against three such talented performers, Jolly and his companions found themselves outclassed. In eight minutes, it was just about over. Having returned to the fray, McCann was put out of it when Hardin kicked him under the jaw. Shortly after, Blaze removed Lacey and Tate by coming up behind them while they were attacking his cousin, catching them by the scruff of their necks and banging their heads together. He had been free to do so because he had knocked Bellowes towards Tommy, who had deftly applied the finishing touch. A *nukite*, piercing hand – thrust into Bellowes' stomach folded him over so that Tommy could follow up with a *tegatana* chop to the base of the skull which dropped him as limp as a back-broke rabbit.

With all their companions sprawling unconscious, Jolly and Stone found themselves faced with the uninterrupted attentions of the two young men who should have been their victims. Both of them were soon being knocked around the barn, driven by Hardin's and Blaze's fists. While his cousin delivered a *coup-*

* Until the visits by Commodore Perry U.S.N.'s flotilla in 1853–54, there was little contact between Japan and the United States of America.

40

de-grace to Stone, Hardin caught Jolly with a left uppercut which flung him backwards through the door. Going out to make sure that the undertaker was finished, Hardin heard shouts and running footsteps. Halting, and ignoring Jolly as he lay supine and motionless, Hardin – who looked anything but tidy or dandified at that moment – turned to see who was coming.

In the lead, striding out angrily, his face registering extreme disapproval, was Colonel William Barrett Travis.

CHAPTER FOUR

A MISSION OF VITAL IMPORTANCE

'WITH respect, sir,' William Barrett Travis said, after having read the contents of the dispatch which had been received that afternoon and heard what the General Samuel Houston intended to do about it. 'I don't think that Captain Hardin is a suitable man to carry out such an important assignment.'

'Why not, Colonel?' Houston inquired.

Seated behind the desk of the big Spanish colonial style mansion which had been donated by its owner as Houston's headquarters whilst in San Antonio de Bexar, the commanding general of the Republic of Texas's army was an imposing and impressive figure. Big, thickset, with almost white hair, he had blue eyes that seemed strangely young in such a seamed, leathery and deeply tanned face. Although he would have preferred less formal garments, he was wearing the kind of uniform which the enlisted men expected of one with his exalted rank. The dark blue, close-buttoned, single-breasted coat had a high, stand-up collar. It was ornamented by gold shoulder scales, bearing the triple star insignia of a major general and by two rows of nine blind buttonholes in a 'herring-bone' pattern. He had a red silk sash around his waist, but his leather belt with a sabre hanging from its slings was on the hat-rack by the door, as was his black, bicorn chapeau. His tight-legged fawn riding breeches ended in black Wellington leg boots with spurs on their heels.

'If his behaviour since arriving in San Antonio is anything to go by,' Travis replied, looking straight to the front and ignoring the man who was sitting at his left, 'he's reckless, irresponsible and can't – or won't – avoid getting involved in fights no matter what duty he's supposed to be carrying out.'

'You know young Hardin, Jim,' Houston remarked, looking at the third occupant of the room. 'What do you say?'

'I can't deny that Devil gets into fights, Sam,' James Bowie admitted. 'He's a fighting man from soda to hock*—'

'That's as maybe, Colonel,' Travis interrupted. 'But an ability to get involved in brawls isn't what I'd regard as a desirable quality for the man the General needs. He has to take on a mission of vital importance.'

'I'm not gainsaying that,' Bowie answered, glancing with asperity at the other colonel. 'Devil might get into fights, but I've never known him to start one without good cause.'

'That depends on how you interpret good cause,' Travis countered coldly. 'From what I've been told, he became involved in the one at the *cantina* because he insisted that two men made room for him at the bar. In addition, not content with disabling them, he got himself into another fight, even though his man had come to tell him that the General wanted to see him.'

'Way I heard it,' Bowie objected, 'those fellers didn't give him any choice but to fight.'

'*He* started the one at the *cantina*,' Travis insisted. 'According to Sergeant Brill, he walked in and deliberately provoked those two men—'

'If he did, he must have had a damned sight better reason than just wanting to get through to the bar,' Bowie declared. 'And, as far as I know, 'nobody's got around to letting him tell his side of it as yet.'

Watching the two officers glowering at each other, Houston felt perturbed. He wondered if it would be wise to leave them together in San Antonio after the rest of the army had withdrawn to the east. Each in his own way was an excellent fighting man and a capable leader, but they had outlooks and natures which might prove to be incompatible. Their differences could easily damage the effectiveness with which they carried out their duty of defending the Alamo and, if possible, delaying Santa Anna for long enough to let Houston reorganize his forces ready to meet the Mexicans in battle.

'Suppose we ask him now, gentlemen?' Houston suggested, acting as peace-maker as he had had to do many times when there had been clashes of will or personalities between the leaders of his various regiments. 'Will you ask him to come in, Jim?'

* In the game of faro, the first card of the deck is called the 'soda' and the last is the 'hock'.

43

'Sure,' Bowie answered, coming to his feet and crossing the room.

Despite knowing that he had successfully completed a difficult and dangerous scouting mission, delivering much useful infirmation about the Mexican army's strength and progress, Ole Devil Hardin felt distinctly uneasy when Bowie opened the door of the study and passed on the General's summons.

Colonel Travis had been anything but pleased by the discovery that Hardin and his cousin, Mannen Blaze, had become involved in a second brawl and had rendered more members of the Republic of Texas' army unfit for duty. Nor had he been in any mood to listen to explanations, particularly when he had learned what had brought Tommy Okasi to the livery barn. Instead, Travis had suggested icily that the cousins would be advised to pay greater attention to their military duties and should reserve any further inclination for fighting for use against the Mexicans. Accepting the comments without argument, and not permitting Blaze – who was seething with indignation over what he regarded as Travis' unjust treatment – to speak up in his defense, Hardin had once again tidied himself up ready to report to Houston.

On Hardin's arrival at headquarters, he had been told that the General could not see him straight away. A messenger had brought in dispatches of considerable importance which required Houston's immediate attention. Before hurrying away, the General's aide – a harassed-looking young captain – requested that Hardin should remain in the hall until he was sent for. Returning with Bowie and Travis, the aide had taken them into the office. Taking note of Travis's cold scowl as he went by, Hardin could guess at the report which would be made regarding his activities. So he had misgivings when he was finally called in by Bowie.

Little of Hardin's perturbation showed as he went by Bowie, into the room and came under the scrutiny of the two senior officers. However, he was not as composed as he forced himself to appear. In fact, by the time he came to a halt in front of the desk he felt downright ill-at-ease, even though he was managing to conceal it. Standing at a stiff military brace which Travis would probably have approved of under other circumstances, he looked straight ahead. For all that he was conscious of Houston studying his bruised left cheek and swollen top lip.

After what seemed to the young man to be a very long time, Houston said in flat tones which told little of his feelings. 'I hear you've been in trouble this afternoon, Captain Hardin.'

'Yes, sir,' Hardin answered, allowing his gaze to drop to the speaker's tanned and expressionless face.

'On *two* occasions,' Houston went on, still giving no indication of how he felt about such conduct.

'Yes, sir,' Hardin agreed.

'Do you make a habit of picking fights?' Houston inquired.

'When it's necessary, sir,' Hardin replied respectfully.

'And you considered that it was necessary this afternoon?'

'Yes, sir.'

'Why?' Houston asked, glancing from Travis to Bowie who had returned and was standing alongside the straight-backed young man. 'You're at ease, captain.'

Relaxing slightly, Hardin explained how he had found the *Chicano* boy at the livery barn. Learning who had administered the beating and why, he had made his way to the *cantina* to investigate. Before going in, he had listened to the agitator answering questions and had taken notice of who was asking them.

Recognizing the threat to Houston's military strategy, Hardin had decided to intervene. However, he had known that to attempt anything in his official capacity would avail him nothing. Enlisted men in the Republic of Texas's army, being volunteers, were generally not so well disciplined that they would obey orders given by an officer who did not belong to their own respective regiments. What was more, his clan were known to be supporters of the General's policies. So the agitator and his assistants would know why he was interfering and would have resisted his attempts, which could have caused fighting to break out between the rest of the customers.

With those thoughts in mind, Hardin had formulated a plan which he had believed might serve his purpose. Identifying the *Chicano* boy's assailants and making an accurate assessment of their natures, he had approached them in a manner that was calculated to make them angry. He had been gambling that the rest of the customers would prefer to watch a fight than to sit listening to the agitator talking.

'I'd heard that Bill Cord always made anybody who was

45

spoiling for a fight take it outside,' Hardin concluded. 'And I figured that when he did, pretty near the whole of the crowd would follow us.'

There was a brief silence as the young man came to the end of his explanation. All the time he was talking, he was also watching the General. Not that the scrutiny had produced any result. Houston's leathery features had remained as impassive as if he had been one of the Cherokee Indians with whom he had lived for several years. However, Hardin had heard Bowie grunt appreciatively on two occasions and figured that there was at least one person in the room on his side. He had not attempted to look at Travis. Nor had he heard anything to indicate how the bow-necked colonel was responding to his story.

'You figured it right,' Bowie declared in a hearty and satisfied voice, turning his gaze to Travis. 'And I reckon we can be thankful that you did.' Then, seeing that the comment was puzzling Hardin, he continued, 'The other boy's daddy came to tell us what they'd heard, Devil, which's why Colonel Travis and I were headed for the *cantina*. Had an idea it might be as well to get the fellers out and away, only I reckoned we could have trouble in getting them to leave; especially the ones who weren't in our regiments and had been drinking. You getting them outside that way helped us do it, wouldn't *you* say, Colonel Travis?'

'It helped us,' Travis conceded almost grudgingly. 'But there was still the second fight.'

'There was no way we could have avoided it, sir,' Hardin stated politely. 'They were the agitator's men, the ones who'd helped him get the conversation going the way he wanted at the *cantina*. I recognized two of them and figured they weren't exactly coming to thank me.'

'What happened, Devil?' Bowie inquired, determined that the young man should be completely exonerated and that Travis should admit he was wrong.

'They pretended to think they'd caught us robbing the barn,' Hardin replied. 'Then the one who looked like an undertaker threw down on us with a pistol and made us shed our weapons—'

'You let them *disarm* you, knowing what they were going to do?' Travis asked.

'I thought that it was for the best, sir,' Hardin answered,

46

without showing any resentment over the interruption. 'Way we'd been acting, particularly cousin Mannen, they didn't have any notion that we knew who they really were and putting off our weapons clinched it. They were sure that we didn't suspect them. We were gambling on them not wanting to do any shooting as it would bring folks to see what was happening when what they wanted was to work us over with their fists.'

'There were still six of them against the two of you,' Travis pointed out, but there was a subtle change in his voice and it had become slightly less critical. 'I'd say they were very stiff odds, even without shooting.'

'Yes, sir,' Hardin conceded. 'But we'd lulled their suspicions and, with Cousin Mannen acting scared, they were likely to be over confident. Besides—'

'Go on,' Houston prompted, having observed the change in Travis' tone.

'I'd seen Tommy Okasi coming, sir,' Hardin obliged, wondering if he was winning the General over. There was nothing in his attitude to supply a clue, although Travis appeared to be softening a little. 'He could tell there was something wrong, so he made sure they didn't hear him until he was ready to let them. When he saw us dropping our weapons, he guessed what was going on and left his swords outside so that they would think he was harmless.' Try as he might, Hardin could not restrain a faint smile over the thought of how Stone, having fallen into the little Oriental's trap, was disillusioned. 'Which they did and that evened the odds up considerably.'

'There's others have made the mistake of thinking that little feller is harmless and come to regret it,' Bowie confirmed with a broad grin. 'You've never seen anything like the way he can fight, Sam. Fact being, those yahoos are lucky they didn't get hurt worse than they did.'

'Is that all, Captain Hardin?' Houston inquired, displaying no emotion at all. His face could have been a figure drawn upon a wooden fence.

'Yes, sir,' the young man replied, stiffening slightly as he realized that judgement would soon be upon him. 'I apologize for the delay in reporting to you—'

'Think nothing of it,' the General boomed, and he smiled broadly. 'I couldn't have seen you straight away if you had come and it sure as Sam Hill wasn't your fault that you got delayed.' His eyes swung to the seated colonel and he went on,

'He could have spent his time in worse ways, don't you think, Bill?'

'Well, sir,' Travis answered, his sense of fair play having caused him to revise his opinion of Hardin so that he eyed the young man with approbation. 'I don't approve officers being involved in brawls with the enlisted men, but I'm satisfied that it was justified on this occasion.'

'Thank you, sir,' Hardin ejaculated, showing his delight at having received what was tantamount to an apology and an accolade.

'You could have explained what started the fight when Colonel Travis questioned you outside the *cantina*, or at the barn,' Houston pointed out. 'It would have avoided any misunderstanding about your motives.'

'Yes, sir,' Hardin admitted, but tactfully decided against saying that he doubted whether Travis would have listened to an explanation in either instance. Instead, he went on, 'Like I said, the agitator had established his "right" to freedom of expression. So I figured that if he heard me explaining things to Colonel Travis after the fight, he might be able to use it against us. He could have said that one of your officers had picked on and hurt bad a couple of fellers rather than let him speak his piece. So I concluded it was better to keep quiet and explain in private.'

'Not every young man would have seen it in that light,' Houston praised.

'I must admit that I misjudged you, captain,' Travis declared, standing up. 'The circumstances of our meeting led me to assume that you were a reckless, hot-headed trouble-maker and finding you'd been in a second fight did nothing to change my opinion. I was wrong and I don't mind admitting it. You may have taken some chances, but they were calculated risks and not made recklessly.'

'Thank you, sir,' Hardin answered and he could not entirely hide his relief as he saw Houston nodding in agreement. 'Anyway, we came through it all right.'

'Which's more than can be said for that damned agitator's men,' Bowie remarked, showing his satisfaction over the way in which his protege had been exonerated. 'I don't reckon he'll be able to use any of them for a spell.'

'He's still around, sir,' Hardin warned. 'I could go—'

'You *could*,' Bowie grinned. 'But you're not going to. Don't

48

be a hawg, young Ole Devil, you've had your share of the fun. Leave us old timers have some.' His eyes turned to the general and he went on, 'If it's all right with you, Sam, I'll go and ask that feller if he'll head back and tell Johnson that we're happy with the way things are being run, but don't take kindly to folks trying to enlist men who're already serving.'

'Do that, Jim,' Houston confirmed, anger clouding his features for a moment. 'Damn Johnson—' Then the imperturbable mask returned and he looked at the other colonel. 'I can't see any objection to letting Captain Hardin take on the assignment, can you, Bill?'

'Not any more, sir,' Travis answered. 'If there's nothing further, I've duties which need my attention.'

'Go to them, Bill,' the General authorized. 'If the rifles arrive in time, I'll send some of them to you.'

'Thank you, sir,' Travis replied, although he, Houston and Bowie all realized that the Alamo Mission would most likely be under heavy siege before the weapons could reach it. He turned to the young man, whom he now regarded in a far more favourable light than when he had first entered the office, extending his right hand. 'Good luck, Captain Hardin. I won't advise you against getting involved in fights. Just keep on thinking before you do it.'

'I will, sir,' Hardin promised, shaking hands.

'I'll go too, Sam,' Bowie drawled. 'If that's all right with you.'

'Sure, Jim,' the General confirmed. 'Try to send that feller back to Johnson in one piece. I'd hate him to start thinking we'd got something against him and his men.'

'I'll do my level best,' Bowie grinned, then offered his right hand to Hardin for a warm and friendly shake. 'Good luck, young Ole Devil, in case I don't see you again before you pull out. Could be you'll need it before you're through with the assignment.'

Watching the two colonels turning from the desk, his fingers still tingling from Bowie's grip, Hardin wondered what kind of assignment he was to be given.

CHAPTER FIVE

A VERY DELICATE SITUATION

WHILE waiting until James Bowie and William Barrett Travis had left his office, Major General Samuel Houston studied the tall young man who was standing at the other side of the desk. Watching Ole Devil Hardin, and thinking of the assignment which he was to be asked to carry out, the General liked what he saw.

That had not been the case when Hardin first entered the room. Seeing him then, the General had been inclined to accept Colonel Travis's assessment of his character. However, as the interview had progressed, Houston had revised his opinion. Despite the way in which he had walked, with a free-striding, straight-backed confidence that came close to being a swagger, he was anything but a strutting, self-important and over-prideful hot-head who relied upon family influence to carry him through any difficulties that he himself had created by his attitude and behaviour. It was, the General had concluded, the beard and moustache more than anything which gave his Mephistophelian features an aspect of almost sinister arrogance.

On the other hand, Houston conceded that Hardin was no Hamlet filled with gloomy foreboding, misgivings or doubts when faced with the making of a decision. Behind the externals, there was a shrewd, capable reliability. As he had proved since his arrival in San Antonio and – if the report of his scouting mission was any criterion – on other occasions, when he found a situation which required immediate attention, he was willing to act upon his own initiative. What was more important, to Houston's way of thinking, he was prepared to stand by the consequences of his actions.

The latter had been apparent as Hardin had been facing the inquiry into his conduct that afternoon. While he had been somewhat perturbed on entering the office, he had hidden it very well. Yet, even though he had known he had acted for the best of reasons and had achieved his purpose under difficult and dangerous conditions, he had not tried to carry off the affair with a high hand. Nor had he counted upon his not unimportant family connections with Houston or Bowie to gain him automatic absolution. Instead, showing no resentment towards Travis's hostile attitude, he had explained his reasons with a polite modesty which had commanded the General's respect.

Summing up his impressions, Houston decided that young Ole Devil Hardin was brave without being foolhardy. He could think not only for the present but also for the future. That had been proven by his reason for not having explained why he had been fighting in front of the *cantina* when by doing so he might have gained exculpation and Travis's approbation. With such qualities, he would be the ideal man for the important mission.

What was more, the General felt sure that Hardin – provided he survived – could become a figure of considerable importance and a guiding hand in the affairs of Texas, whether it became an independent republic or one of the United States of America.

'Sit down, Captain,' Houston drawled, as the door closed. He pushed the humidor across the desk after raising its lid. 'Help yourself to a smoke.'

'Thank you, sir,' Hardin replied, taking the chair which Travis had occupied and helping himself to a cigar. Then he winced a little and gave his right side a gentle rub.

'Are you all right, boy?' Houston inquired solicitously and his concern was only partly motivated by the possibility of the younger man being unable to carry out the mission.

'Just a mite sore, sir,' Hardin replied with a wry grin.

'Would you like a drink to soothe it away?' Houston asked. His face took on an appreciative expression and he stamped on the floor. 'Don Sebastian keeps a good cellar and he's given me the use of it. I'll soon have something brought up if you're so minded.'

Although the General did not know it, his words were the cause of consternation to a man in the wine cellar. Short, plump, middle-aged and wearing the white clothing of a Mexican house servant, he was kneeling on the top of one of the wine racks. He held a glass tumbler with its bottom to his right ear. The upper end was pressed against the ceiling, which was also the floor of the study.

The Latin temperament had always been highly susceptible to intrigue, and the wine-rack being used by the man was sited to allow eavesdropping on private and confidential conversations in the study. Don Sebastian Carillo de Biva had had that in mind when turning over his mansion to be used as Houston's headquarters. A wealthy land owner, de Biva was running with the hare and hunting with the hounds. So, although he was giving his support to the Texians, he had also allowed his *major domo* to organize a spy ring with which to supply information to the Mexicans. By having done so, he hoped to emerge from the present situation no worse off than he had been before the declaration of independence whichever side should be the victors.

De Biva and his family were no longer at the mansion, having moved west to their *hacienda* in what would later become the American State of New Mexico and which was not involved in the Texians' bid for freedom. Staying behind, the *major domo*, Juan Juglares, had put his knowledge of the premises to good use. He spoke English far better than he admitted and, by listening from the top of the wine-rack, had already been successful in his spying task.

Having noticed the excitement caused by the arrival of a dispatch rider, Juglares had sensed that something of more than usual importance was in the air. So he had come to the wine cellar and taken up his position. From various comments that he had overheard between Houston, Bowie and Travis, he realized that the matter under discussion was likely to prove well worth the risks of listening. He had no wish to be driven from his point of vantage while there was still more to be learned.

'Not for me, thank you, sir,' Hardin replied, much to Juglares' relief.

'Have it your own way, boy,' Houston drawled and indicated a sheet of paper which was lying on the desk. 'Let's get down to business. You'll most likely know why Stephen Austin's Commission went to New Orleans, seeing that your Uncle Marsden was one of the Commission.'

'Yes, sir,' Hardin agreed. 'To try and recruit men, obtain weapons and generally raise support for our cause. That's pretty common knowledge, sir.'

'Too common,' Houston grunted, and went on as the younger

man stiffened. 'I'm not blaming Marsden for *that*, boy. We never tried to keep it a secret.'

'Is that a report on how they're getting on, sir?' Hardin inquired, relaxing as he saw that his uncle was not being held responsible for disclosing the purpose of the Commission.

'It is.'

'Are they being successful?'

'To a certain degree, although they're having some difficulties. However, they have obtained five hundred new caplock rifles and ten thousand rounds of ready-made ammunition for them and are arranging for them to be shipped to us.'

'Five hundred *caplock* rifles?' Hardin repeated eagerly. 'That's *bueno*, sir. We can really make use of them.'

'I see that you're one who doesn't have any doubts about the caplock system,' Houston remarked.

There was considerable controversy between the adherents of the flintlock and the newer caplock mechanisms as a means of discharging a firearm.

'I don't, sir,' Hardin confirmed, and indicated the weapon in the loop on his belt. 'This Manton* pistol of mine's percussion-fired.'

'But not your rifle?'

'It is too, sir, in a way. You see I use what Uncle Ben Blaze calls a 'slide repeating' rifle. He bought it from some feller called Jonathan Browning† while he was up in Illinois last fall. Way I see it, though, the caplock's going to replace the flintlock completely. It's more certain, easier to load – I'm sorry, sir, but I feel strongly about it. In my opinion, for what it's worth, five hundred caplocks are worth double their number of flintlocks; particularly in wet weather.'

'You don't have to persuade *me*,' Houston stated with a grin. 'Some of us worn-out old fogies can see the advantages of the caplock as well as you smart young men.'

'I'm sorry, sir,' Hardin apologized.

Down in the cellar, Juglares moved restlessly and wished that the men above him would get down to business. Every

* Joseph 'Old Joe' Manton, gunsmith of London, England, an early maker of percussion-fired weapons.

† Jonathan Browning, gunsmith father of master firearms' designer, John Moses Browning. John Moses appears in: *Calamity Spells Trouble*.

minute he remained in such a compromising position increased his chances of being caught. Retribution would be swift and final if that should happen.

'Anyway, boy,' Houston went on, waving aside the apology. 'They'll be at Santa Cristobal Bay, that's about ten miles north of the Matagorda Peninsula, in seven days. You'll collect them from the ship and deliver them to me at Washington-on-the-Brazos, or wherever I might be at the time.'

'Seven days, sir?' Hardin repeated, thinking about the distances involved and the type of terrain which he would have to traverse. 'How long will the ship wait?'

'No more than two days, and it will only run into the Bay at night. While we're in control pretty well from the Brazos to the coast, there's the Mexican Navy to be taken into consideration. They've a frigate blockading Galveston, with a ten-gun brig patrolling between it and Matamoros. So the captain daren't hang around in the vicinity for too long. It's vitally important that the shipment doesn't fall into Santa Anna's hands.'

'I can see that, sir. Those five hundred caplocks and their ammunition—'

'It goes much deeper than that, boy,' Houston interrupted. 'In fact, it could have an adverse effect upon any future supplies and aid from the United States. We're involved in a very delicate situation. As I said, we didn't try to keep the Commission's purpose a secret. Santa Anna found out what we were hoping to do. So his consul in New Orleans and the Mexican Ambassador up at Washington, D.C., are raising all manner of protests over it.'

'That's only to be expected, sir,' Hardin pointed out philosophically. 'But it won't stop our kin and friends back in the United States from helping us.'

'It might,' Houston corrected. 'There's considerable opposition from the anti-slavery faction to any suggestion that, after we've won our independence, Texas should be considered for annexation by the United States. Their contention is that by allowing that to happen it might result in the formation of further 'slave' States.* Rather than have that happen they'd sooner see Texas remain under Mexican rule. So they're de-

* The Texians had suggested that, after annexation, in view of the vast area of land which would be involved, Texas could be divided into three or four separate States.

manding that the United States refuses to allow even private support or aid for us.'

'But surely we've our own supporters in Congress, sir,' Hardin protested.

'We have,' Houston conceded. 'And they'd be willing to stand by us more openly if it was only the Mexicans and the anti-slavery faction involved. But Santa Anna's made representations to various European countries. He's claiming that our "rebellion", as he calls it, is preventing him from bringing about settled conditions which will allow expansion, development and overseas trade. As the Europeans are interested in the latter, seeing a chance of profit, they are taking the line that the United States has no right to interfere in the domestic problems of another country. So far our supporters in Congress have been able to evade the issue by pointing out that there is no proof that aid has been given since the declaration of independence.'

'And the shipment would furnish that proof, sir,' Hardin said quietly.

'It would,' Houston confirmed. 'It's true that the arms were donated by private individuals and have nothing to do with Congress, or the United States, but it will embarass our supporters and lessen their chances of winning the annexation issue. So you can see why it's very important that the shipment doesn't fall into the Mexicans' hands. If it does, there will be pressure put on Congress to stop *all* aid.'

Crouching on the wine-rack, ignoring the ache in his legs and neck, Juglares was congratulating himself. What he had heard was of the greatest importance. Not even the discovery that Bowie and Travis were going to hold the Alamo Mission had been of such value. While his first inclination was to leave immediately and arrange for the information to be passed on without delay, he refrained. The more he could learn, the greater use it would be.

'Even granting the extra two days, sir,' Hardin said, after a few seconds' thought. 'That doesn't leave me much time to have Company "C" join me from the regiment, then get to Santa Cristobal Bay. Particularly taking along wagons to carry the shipment.'

'It doesn't,' Houston admitted. 'Especially as the longer the ship is delayed, the greater chance of it being captured. There's one thing, though, you won't be using wagons. Like you said, they'd slow you down too much. Mules're faster and better suited to the kind of country you'll be covering.'

'That's true enough, sir. But do we have enough of them available?'

'Ewart Brindley does. Do you know him?'

'I've never met him, sir. But I've heard tell of him—'

'And most of what you've heard is true,' Houston said with a grin, having noticed the inflexion in the younger man's voice. 'Old Ewart's just about as ornery and cross-grained a cuss as ever drew breath or drank corn liquor; but there's no better hand at working a mule train.'

'That's what I've always heard, sir,' Hardin answered.

'And that's one of the reasons I'm sending *you*, boy,' Houston went on. 'Your Uncle Edward has already spoken highly of your ability to get along with people. You'll have to handle Ewart real carefully though, even with the letter I'll be giving you for him. It's no good going along and expecting him to doff his hat, touch his forelock, say "Yes sir, captain," and take your orders. He's too cantankerous for that and, the way he sees it, as they're *his* mules, neither you, I, nor anybody else can tell him how to use them.'

'There's some might say that it's his duty to use them, sir,' Hardin commented.

'If they did say it, he'd tell them to go straight to hell and take their notions of duty with them.'

'Isn't he for the Republic, sir?'

'Old Ewart's never been *for* anything in his whole life,' Houston warned with a grin. 'He's always *against*. Bear that in mind when you get to his place at Gonzales and you'll get along fine.'

'Will he be there, sir?' Hardin inquired.

'Di sent word he would be, getting everything ready to fall back with us.'

' "Di", sir?'

'Ewart's granddaughter. Her name's Charlotte Jane Martha, but I wouldn't advise you to call her any one of them. He's reared her since the Kiowas killed her momma and daddy back in 'Twenty-Two. They do say she can throw a diamond hitch faster, tighter and better than any man. That's where the "Di" comes from. Old Ewart thinks the world of her. So if you can get her on your side, that'll be as good as half the battle.'

'I'll keep it in mind, sir,' Hardin promised.

'You do that, boy,' Houston ordered, but in a friendly manner. 'Now, about an escort. I can get you as many men as you think you'll need from one or other of the outfits who're in town.'

'I'd sooner not do that, sir,' Hardin objected. 'For one thing I'd rather not be using men I don't know and who don't know me. And, anyway, to get them we'd have to explain to their officers why they're wanted. I think the fewer who know about the shipment the better. There's less chance of word getting to the Mexicans that way.'

'I'll go along with you on that, boy,' Houston conceded, nodding his approval. 'So far, at this end only you, Colonels Travis, Bowie and I know about it. And they don't know when or where it's due to arrive.'

'In that case, sir, I'd rather not take an escort from town. It would attract too much attention. From all I've heard, Ewart Brindley and his muleteers are pretty tough *hombres*.'

'They are,' the General confirmed. 'They've taken mule trains through Indian country more than once and come back with their hair.'

'Which means they can hold up their end, comes shooting,' Hardin said with satisfaction. 'If it's all right with you, sir, I'll not take an escort from town.'

At that moment, Juglares heard the handle of the cellar door being turned. With a surge of alarm he realized that whoever was outside would be able to enter. Such was his eagerness to overhear as much as possible of the General's conversation, that, on arriving, he had merely closed the door behind him—

And had left the key in the lock!

Even as the door began to creep slowly open, Juglares acted with commendable speed. He knew that he could not stay where he was and hope to remain undetected. Although it was late afternoon, the window in the outside trapdoor – through which barrels of wine were lowered into the cellar – was still letting in too much light. Nor could he think of any acceptable reason for being on top of the rack and the tumbler might give away his true purpose.

Swiftly, but quietly, Juglares rolled across the rack and lowered himself to the floor with it between him and the door. Having achieved this without making enough noise to betray himself, he peered between two of the shelves to find out who had disturbed him.

The intruder proved to be a thin, sharp-featured infantry soldier. Before entering, he looked back into the basement in a furtive manner. Apparently satisfied that he was not being observed, he advanced, subjecting the cellar to a similar cautious scrutiny. His whole attitude implied that he was not carrying out any official, or even lawful duty.

For a moment Juglares thought of remaining in concealment and allowing the soldier to do whatever he had come for and then depart. However, he saw the objections to such a course. Having stolen some of the liquor, which was almost certainly his reason for visiting the cellar, the soldier might lock the door on leaving. While Juglares could still escape by the trapdoor, the grounds were heavily guarded and he would be in plain view of a sentry. Of course, as *major domo*, he had every right to be in the cellar; although he would have to think up an explanation for making his exit that way instead of through the basement.

The decision was taken out of Juglares's hands.

'Hey!' yelped the soldier, coming to a halt and staring at the rack behind which the *major-domo* was standing. He seemed to be on the verge of turning and dashing out of the cellar. 'Who-all's there?'

'Only me, *senor*,' Juglares answered in soothing tones and, knowing that to do anything else would be futile and would arouse the other's suspicions, he walked from his place of concealment. 'Can I help you?'

'Who're you and what're you doing down here?' the soldier demanded, but his voice lacked the authority of one who had the right to be asking such a question.

'I am Don Sebastian Carillo de Biva's *major domo, senor*,' Juglares said, adopting his most imposing tone and manner. 'It is one of my duties, particularly in Don Sebastian's absence, to take care of the wine cellar.'

'It is, huh?' the soldier grunted, sounding impressed but still dubious and suspicious.

'*Si, senor*,' the *major domo* confirmed and went on craftily, 'If you wish, we can go and see the first sergeant. He will tell you who I am.'

The gamble paid off.

'Shucks, there ain't no call for that, *amigo*,' the soldier said hurriedly, just as Juglares had believed that he would. 'I've been sent down for a couple of bottles of whiskey, if you've got

58

'em. So if you'll give 'em to me, I'll get going and leave you to your work.'

'Certainly, *senor*,' the *major domo* replied. 'Don Sebastian keeps whiskey for his Texian friends. I will get it for you. Will two bottles be enough?'

'Well,' the soldier began, his eyes taking on an avaricious glint. 'The cap'n did say three now I come to think back on it.'

'Three it is, *senor*,' Juglares declared without hesitation.

Walking to the rack in which the bottles of whiskey were stored, the *major domo* felt relieved and cheerful. He was sure that the soldier had lied to him, but he did not care. The information he had already garnered was worth far more than the three bottles he had been asked for. Once he had handed them over, the *gringo* would go. What was more, he would be unlikely to mention that he had found anybody in the cellar as he should not have been there himself. When the soldier had left, Juglares hoped to resume the eavesdropping and find out if there was anything else to be learned.

Before the *major domo* could take out the first bottle, he heard heavy and authoritative footsteps descending the stairs and crossing the basement. So did the soldier and an expression of consternation came to his face. It grew rather than diminished as the burly figure of First Sergeant Gladbeck loomed through the open door.

'What's all this?' boomed the non-com, looking from the soldier to Juglares and back.

'I heard a noise in here and come to see who it was, serge,' the soldier answered. 'Found this feller here. He allows it's all right for him.'

'It is,' Gladbeck stated, having recognized and identified the Mexican. 'But you'd best get going afore I grow all suspicious and ask what you was doing down here in the first place.'

'Sure, serge,' the soldier replied and scuttled hurriedly away.

'What was he after, liquor?' the first sergeant inquired, turning his attention to Juglares.

'*Si senor*,' the *major domo* agreed. 'He said he'd been sent to collect three bottles of whiskey.'

'Three, now that's what I call being greedy,' Gladbeck grinned. 'Have you got everything you need for tonight? The General's entertaining his senior officers to dinner, there'll be eight of them.'

59

Since the non-com's arrival, Juglares had been thinking fast and had revised his line of action. While he had hoped to continue listening to what was said in the General's office, he had now decided against taking the chance. He already knew when and where the shipment of arms would arrive, that the officer charged with receiving it would go first to the town of Gonzales, and that he did not consider it necessary to take a military escort. Such information was far too valuable for him to risk being caught eavesdropping. What was more, he had just been given a perfect excuse for leaving the mansion and passing on his findings.

'Eight extra, *senor*,' the *major domo* said doubtfully. 'In that case, I'll have to go into town and make some purchases.'

As Juglares and the first sergeant left the cellar, Ole Devil Hardin was finishing outlining his plans for the collection of the shipment. Houston agreed that, as only he and the young man were aware of the date and place where it would arrive, the line of action which had been proposed stood every chance of succeeding.

CHAPTER SIX

I'D HATE TO GET KILLED

ALTHOUGH the rain had ceased to fall about half an hour earlier, Ole Devil Hardin and Tommy Okasi were still wearing the waterproof *ponchos* which they had donned to keep their clothing, saddles and other equipment as dry as possible. The moon had broken through the clouds and its pallid light was sufficient for the two young men to make out some details of the small hamlet at which they were intending to spend the night.

Having followed General Samuel Houston's advice and allowed their horses to rest at Shelby's Livery Barn overnight, Ole Devil and Tommy had left San Antonio de Bexar early that morning. Instead of accompanying them, Mannen Blaze had returned to the Texas Light Cavalry so that he could take command of Company 'C' during his cousin's absence.

Ole Devil had had no idea that his conversation with the General had been overheard and reported to the enemy. Nor did he suspect that plans were already in motion to circumvent him on the assignment, but he and Tommy were too experienced as campaigners to ride along the main trail which connected San Antonio and Gonzales.

All of the Mexican army's garrisons might have been driven out of Texas, but that did not mean military activity was at an end. Some of Santa Anna's volunteer cavalry regiments, the Rancheros Lancers for example, were comprised of *Creole* hacienda* owners' sons and their *vaqueros*. Hard-riding, tough and capable fighting men, they were sufficiently enterprising to carry out raids north of the Rio Grande. There were also groups of *Chicanos* who supported *el Presidente* and were always ready to strike at any unwary Texians with whom they came into contact. In addition, marauding bands of *Comancheros* and white renegades roamed in search of loot and plunder.

* Creole: a Mexican of pure Spanish blood.

61

Any such foes could be expected to watch a trail that carried traffic between two fair-sized towns. So, even though they had not been able to make such good time, Ole Devil and Tommy had ridden parallel to, but out of sight of it. That meant they were approaching the hamlet from across country. With the wind blowing from the east, the scent of them and their horses was being carried way from the buildings. Due to the rain, the ground was soft and their mounts' hooves were making little noise.

'There're some horses in the lean-to at the back of the *cantina!*' Ole Devil warned quietly, bringing his linebacked dun gelding to a halt about two hundred yards from the nearest building. 'But the rest of the town looks deserted.'

'Perhaps they belong to some of the men who have stayed behind to guard their homes,' Tommy suggested, stopping his bay gelding. His sibilant tones were no louder than those of his companion. 'Or they could be a patrol who have taken shelter from the rain.'

The two young men were not worried by the deserted aspect of the town. They found that less disturbing than the presence of the horses. On passing through while going to report to General Houston, they had found its population on the point of leaving for the greater security offered by the larger town of Guadalupe.

'It could be either,' Ole Devil agreed. 'But, if it is a patrol, is it from our army or Santa Anna's?'

'A wise man would make sure before letting them know he is close by,' Tommy pointed out.

'You're riding with a wise man, believe it or not,' Ole Devil declared, swinging to the ground and removing his hat. 'I'll drift on over and take a look.'

While Tommy was dismounting, Ole Devil hung his hat by its *barbiquejo* chin strap on the saddlehorn and strugged off his *poncho*. Folding and tucking it between the cantle and his bed roll, he removed the powder horn and bullet pouch which were slung across his shoulders and suspended them from the hilt of his sabre. There was an oblong leather pouch attached to his belt in the centre of his back. Although it held the means to load his rifle, he left it in place. To have removed it would have entailed drawing the belt through the loops of his breeches and the slot of the pistol's carrier. He had not worn the pouch in

San Antonio, but had fixed it into position before leaving that morning.

During the removal of these items which would be an encumbrance to swift and silent movement, the young Texian was examining the hamlet on the off chance that he might discover something to supply a clue to the identities of the horses' owners. He failed to do so, but did not advance immediately. Instead, he waited while his companion prepared to cover him as he was carrying out the scouting mission.

When the rain had started, Tommy had removed the string from his bow to prevent it from getting wet. The six foot long weapon – which had its handle set two-thirds of the way down the stave instead of centrally, as was the case with Occidental bows – was hanging in two loops attached to the left side of his saddle's skirts. To keep the flights of the his arrows dry, he had suspended the quiver from the saddlehorn and covered them with his *poncho*.

Allowing his horse to stand ground-hitched by its dangling, split-ended reins, Tommy duplicated Ole Devil's actions by removing hat and *poncho*. Then he retrieved his quiver and swung it across his back so that the flights of the arrows rose above his right shoulder and would be readily available to his 'draw' hand. With that done, he restrung the bow and nocked an arrow to the shaft.

'Are you taking your rifle?' Tommy inquired, when his companion made no attempt to pull the weapon from its saddle-boot.

'I can move faster and quieter without it,' Ole Devil replied and nodded to the bow. 'If you *have* to use that heathen device, try not to stick the arrow in my butt end will you?'

'I'll try,' Tommy promised, grinning as he heard what had come to be the usual comment under such circumstances.

Despite his remark, the Texian had complete confidence in his companion's ability as an archer. It was, in fact, very comforting to know that Tommy was ready to cover him if it should prove necessary. While the odds were in favour of the horses behind the *cantina* being owned by friends, Ole Devil did not discount the possibility that they might belong to enemies. If so, and if he got into some kind of trouble, he might need all the help he could get.

Tommy might be small, but Ole Devil knew he was

63

completely reliable. He was as deadly effective with the bow as he was with the *daisho*, the matched pair of slightly curved, long hilted swords which he carried; the thirty inch long *tachi* hanging by the slings at the left side of his belt and the eighteen inch blade *wakizashi* dangling on the right.*

Walking forward with his eyes continually raking the buildings for any sign of danger, Ole Devil found himself revising his opinion regarding the wind being from the west. Earlier he had cursed it when it had occasionally contrived to send some of the rain down the back of his neck. Now he had to admit that it was coming from an advantageous quarter. It was not carrying their scent to the horses behind the *cantina* nor had it caused their mounts to become aware of the other animals.

Leaving his big bowie knife sheathed and the Manton pistol in its belt-loop, Ole Devil drew nearer to the lean-to without being challenged. Aware of the danger, he took precautions against startling the horses. Hissing gently through his teeth, he alerted them to his presence and arrived without causing them to take fright and betray him. After giving his surroundings a thorough scrutiny and satisfying himself that he was not being watched by the owners of the animals, he stepped underneath the roof.

'Easy now, boy,' Ole Devil breathed, going up to the nearest horse in a calm and unhurried manner. Laying his left hand gently on its flank, he stoked it and went on, 'You're cool now, but I'd say you were out in the rain for a time.'

Having made this deduction, the Texian turned his attention to the horse's saddle. It was still in place, with the single girth† tight enough for the animal to be ridden. The large horn and bulging fork wooden tree covered by sheep-vellum and lined with wool, to which the girth and stirrup leathers were attached by simple straps, was typically Mexican in origin.

However, on going to the next animal, Ole Devil found that it was carrying a different kind of rig. Even before the conflict of interests had caused hostility towards the Mexicans, Texian saddlers had begun to develop their own type of horse's equipment. They were already producing a saddle with a smaller

* The *wakizashi* was traditionally carried thrust through the girdle, but Tommy Okasi had had his fitted with belt slings since arriving in the United States.

† Due to its Mexican connotations, Texians rarely used the word 'cinch'.

horn, little swelling at the pommel, a very deep seat, wide fenders to the stirrups and double girths. The horse was fitted with such a rig and, like all the others, had a bed roll strapped to the cantle.

Continuing with his investigation, Ole Devil discovered one more Texas 'slick fork'. The other three horses had on double girthed rigs, but with a quilted, hammock-type seat and no horn, of the style made popular around 1812 in the Eastern United States by James Walker, a Philadelphia saddler. Unfortunately, the diversity of types supplied little or no information regarding the identities of the men who had ridden on them.

Standing by the last horse he had examined, Ole Devil was able to see into the alley which separated the *cantina* from its neighbouring building. Although the rear of the *cantina* was as dark and apparently deserted as the rest of the hamlet, there was a glow of light from the side window.

Leaving the lean-to, the Texian crossed to the alley in the hope that he might gain more information silently he crept forward, halting to peer cautiously around the side of the window. The light was supplied by a single lamp which was standing on a table in the centre of the room. Of the four men who were sitting at the table, one was a tall, slim *vaquero* whose *charro* clothing showed signs of hard travelling. The rest were hard-faced, unshaven white men dressed in buckskins. Yet another *gringo* was standing behind the bar cutting up pemmican. There were four flintlock rifles leaning against the counter.

Crouching below the level of the windowsill, Ole Devil went by and reached the front of the building. Instead of turning the corner, he looked around it cautiously. Nursing a rifle, a fifth man was sitting on a chair by the door.

Even as Ole Devil looked, the man lurched to his feet!

Although the young Texian felt sure that he had not been detected, he instinctively drew back his head. There was no outcry, nor anything else to suggest that he had been seen. For all that, without conscious thought, his right hand went to the most suitable weapon for his purpose in case the man should prove to be an enemy and come to investigate whatever he might have seen.

With that in mind, Ole Devil did not reach for his Manton pistol. Instead, his fingers enfolded the concave ivory handle of the bowie knife. Under the circumstances, it would be more

65

effective than the firearm and would not cause a general alarm. Weighing forty-three ounces, the knife's eleven-inch long, two-and-a-quarter-inches wide, three-eighths of an inch thick blade, and the scolloped brass butt cap, made it as good a club as a cutting and thrusting implement.

There was, Ole Devil told himself, no real reason for him to be taking such precautions. While the men were dirty, unshaven and not very prepossessing, they were not especially different from many members of the Republic of Texas's army which, in general, was more concerned with fighting efficiency than in trying to present a smart and military appearance. Nor was finding a *vaquero* with the buckskin-clad white men cause for alarm. Several regiments, Bowie's Texas Volunteers in particular, had *Chicanos* serving in their ranks.

Despite that, the young Texian felt uneasy. Try as he might, he could not think of any reason why he should be; but the feeling persisted.

After about thirty seconds had gone by without the man approaching the corner, Ole Devil once again surreptitiously peeped around. The man was now standing at the edge of the sidewalk and looking to the west along the trail. Then, making a gesture of impatience, he turned and stalked towards the *cantina* without so much as a glance in the young Texian's direction.

'Ain't no sign of him, Sid,' Ole Devil heard the man saying in protesting tones and a Northern accent as he went through the door which had been broken open. 'I bet he's holed up some place out of the rain and'll be staying there until morning.'

'Get the hell back out there and keep watch in case he ain't!' roared a second voice which had a harsh New England timbre. 'I want to be ready for him if he comes.'

Turning before the man reappeared, Ole Devil withdrew along the alley. He went as silently as he had come and just as carefully. Bending as he reached the window, he passed without attempting to look in. Then he straightened up and strode out faster. On coming into sight, he signalled for his companion to wait and hurried to rejoin him.

'There are six of them, Tommy,' Ole Devil reported *sotto voce*, and he described what he had seen, concluding, 'I'm damned if I know what to make of them, except that they're definitely not men from the town acting as guards. All I know is that I don't like the look of them.'

66

Neither Ole Devil nor Tommy attached any significance to the fact that two of the white men spoke with Northern accents. They knew that not all Texians had originated in the Southern States.

'They are waiting for somebody?' Tommy remarked.

'From what was said,' Ole Devil agreed. 'Just one man, the way they were talking.'

'Then, as they haven't unsaddled their horses, they may be expecting to move on when he joins them,' Tommy suggested. 'We could stay here and wait to see if they do.'

'Trouble being, if he has taken shelter from the rain and is staying there for the night, they'll not be leaving,' Ole Devil argued. 'Then again, they're not trying to hide the fact that they're in the *cantina*. If they were, they wouldn't be showing a light.'

'That doesn't mean they are friendly,' Tommy pointed out. 'They would know a light would lure anybody who was passing.'

'I'm not gainsaying it.'

'Then what shall we do?'

'I hate puzzles, Tommy,' Ole Devil replied. 'So I'm just naturally bound to get an answer to this one. Thing is, I'd hate to get killed before we've collected those rifles. General Sam and Uncle Edward'll be riled at me if I do. So as we can't play it safe we'll have to handle it sneaky.'

'Very wise old Nipponese saying, which I've just made up, says, "Always better to be sure than sorry",' Tommy announced soberly. 'What do you intend to do, Devil-san?'

Despite the light-hearted comments, neither Ole Devil nor Tommy was forgetting that they were engaged upon a mission of considerable importance. However, they also realized it was their duty to try and learn who the men might be and what they were doing in the hamlet. It only remained for them to decide how they might most safely satisfy their curiosity.

'I'll take both horses and swing around so that I ride into town along the trail from the east,' the Texian answered. 'You go through the alley on foot and be ready to cut in if there's trouble.'

'I expected that if there was walking, humble Nipponese gentleman would have to do it,' Tommy sighed with mock resignation, watching his companion gathering up the horses' reins.

67

'If you're *that* humble, you shouldn't be riding in the first place,' said Ole Devil and swung astride his tall, line-backed dun gelding. He started it moving and the no-smaller bay followed in response to his gentle tug on the reins. '*Sayonara*.'

'Remember old Nipponese proverb, which I've just made up,' Tommy counselled. ' "In time of war, wise man treats all others as enemies until they have proved differently".'

'I'll bear it in mind,' Ole Devil promised and caused the horses to move faster.

Keeping the arrow nocked to his bow's string, Tommy set off to carry out his part of the plan. Before he had reached the lean-to, he could neither see nor hear Ole Devil and the horses. Which proved to be fortunate.

The sound of footsteps on the planks of the sidewalk in front of the *cantina* reached the little Oriental's ears. Darting to the lean-to, he halted behind its back wall. So quietly had he been moving, even during the last brief dash, that the horses were unaware of his presence and he did not disturb them.

Two of the buckskin-clad white men, each carrying his rifle, came along the alley. However, Tommy had already attained his place of concealment and he listened to what they were saying as they approached.

'You reckon we'll come across him, Al?' asked one of the men, almost petulantly, his voice suggestive of a Northern origin. 'It's out of his way if he's going to—'

'I know it is,' the second interrupted and he too did not sound like a Southron. 'But we were told's he'd be heading for Gonzales first and this's the trail's goes to there. So we'll ride out for a couple of miles and see if there's any sign of him. If there ain't, we'll come back and see what Halford wants us to do.'

'But if he's holed up, he won't be along until after daylight,' the first man protested. 'And I don't cotton to the notion of hanging around here after sun up.'

By that time, the pair had reached the lean-to. Tommy was hoping to find out who they were looking for, but did not. The conversation was terminated as they collected their horses. Leading the animals outside, they mounted and rode away to disappear into the alley at the opposite end of the *cantina*. Tommy clicked his tongue impatiently over his failure to learn anything. Even the fact that the man did not wish to be in the hamlet during the daytime proved nothing. He might be a loyal

Texian who believed, like Ole Devil and Tommy, that the trail and locality could become unhealthy due to enemy raiders.

Waiting until the sounds of the two horses had faded into the distance, Tommy walked from behind the lean-to and into the alley. He adopted similar tactics to those used by Ole Devil as he came to the window. Holding his bow and arrow, low, he looked in. The Mexican and two of the white men were now standing at the customers' side of the bar eating a meal, as was the third, except that he was behind the counter.

Moving on, the little Oriental reached the front end of the *cantina*. However, he halted in the alley and listened for Ole Devil. Once again, the rain proved to be beneficial. The normally hard surface of the street was sufficiently softened for the horses to approach with little or no noise.

Holding the animals to a walk, Ole Devil was scanning the buildings on each side of the street. He had noticed that the lookout was no longer outside the *cantina* and wondered whether that was because the man whom they were expecting had arrived, or if he was now keeping watch from a less exposed position.

'Two have left, Devil-san!' Tommy hissed as his companion rode by.

'*Bueno!*' the Texian answered, in no louder tones, without halting until he had turned the horses to face the hitching rail near the cantina's door.

Shortly after the party had broken into the *cantina* their leader, Sid Halford had ordered Joe Stiple to search the building for liquor to supplement their meagre supply. Although Stiple had failed to do so, he had stayed behind the bar. Having been a bartender, he always felt more at home on the sober side of the counter. Standing there, he was the first to become aware of Ole Devil's arrival.

'Hey!' Stiple ejaculated. 'Somebody's just rid by the window.'

'It could be Soapy and Al coming back,' suggested the lanky man who had acted as lookout, speaking through a mouth filled with pemmican.

'I don't reckon so,' Stiple objected. 'Looked like there was only one man and he's come from the east.'

While the brief conversation had been going on, Halford, the lookout – whose name was Mucker – and the *vaquero* Arnaldo

69

Verde, had turned towards the door. They heard the horses being brought to a halt and leather creaking as the rider dismounted, but as yet they could not see him. Halford and Mucker reached towards their rifles. Behind the bar, Stiple was duplicating Verde's actions by placing his right hand on the butt of the pistol that was thrust through his belt.

'Easy there, gents,' called the newcomer, as he crossed the sidewalk. 'I saw the light and came in to see if I could stay here for the night.'

Studying the tall, whipcord slender young man, and giving first attention to the way he was dressed and armed, Verde then examined his features. He was reminded of pictures he had seen of the Devil.

Juglares had said that the man being sent by Houston to collect the rifles had a face like *el Diablo*, the Devil!

On receiving the *major domo's* information, Verde had known that he would need help to deal with it. The nearest available assistance had been a group of white renegades who were working for the Mexicans. Going to their camp, he had told their leader what he had learned. It had been decided that Halford's party would accompany Verde and kill Houston's officer. Once that had been done, the band would go to the coast and capture the shipment.

Guessing that their victim – who, according to Juglares, would be travelling alone – was almost certain to make use of the trail between San Antonio and Gonzales, the party had sought for him along it. Finding the hamlet deserted shortly after the rain had started to fall, they had forced an entry into the *cantina*. Discussing the matter, Verde and Halford had concluded that the man they were seeking would also use it for shelter when he arrived.

The gamble had only partially paid off!

In some way, the Texian had eluded Al and Soapy who had left in the hope of locating him. However, he was strolling into the *cantina* and clearly had no suspicion of the fate that awaited him.

For all that, Verde realized things could go wrong. Finding himself confronted by four men, all of whom were fingering weapons, the newcomer had halted just inside the door. If any of the party attempted to raise a pistol or rifle, he would leap back out of the building. Before the swiftest of them could reach the sidewalk, he would be mounted and riding away.

70

It was a moment for rapid thought!

Having done so, Verde put his scheme into operation and silently prayed that his companions would guess what he was doing and respond correctly.

'Hey, *amigos,* it's all right,' Verde announced in a hearty tone, taking his hand away from the pistol. 'I know this man. It's *Captain Hardin* of the Texas Light Cavalry. *Saludos* captain. It's good to see you.'

With that, the *vaquero* started to walk forward. His manner was friendly and he held out his right hand. In a sheath strapped to the inside of his left forearm, hidden from sight by his jacket's sleeve yet ready to slip into his grasp when necessary, was a needle-pointed, razor-sharp knife. He was an expert at producing and using it unexpectedly.

71

CHAPTER SEVEN

THEY WERE WAITING FOR *YOU*

OLE DEVIL HARDIN watched the *vaquero* coming towards him, but also devoted some of his attention to the three white men. That they should have reached for their weapons on his arrival neither surprised nor alarmed him. It was a simple precaution that anybody would be expected to take in such troubled times. However, he had noticed how the lanky former lookout had thrown a startled glance at the biggest of the party on hearing his name. What was more, despite the *vaquero's* apparent friendliness and his announcement of Ole Devil's identity, the trio were showing little sign of relaxing.

Watching Verde advancing, Halford suddenly realized what the welcome meant. He turned his head just in time to see Mucker, who was not the most intelligent of the party, starting to lift his flintlock. Taking his own right hand from his rifle, Halford gave the lanky man a swift jab on the arm. On Mucker swinging a puzzled gaze at him, he scowled prohibitively and shook his head. Looking back at Verde and the Texian, Halford replaced his hand on his own rifle. He did not notice that, although refraining from lifting the weapon, Mucker did not move his hand away.

At first, Ole Devil had decided that the white men might have an antipathy towards officers. However, having observed the by-play between Halford and Mucker, he felt decidedly uneasy. His instincts suggested that everything might not be so amiable as the *vaquero* was making out.

Showing nothing of his suspicions, Ole Devil stepped forward. He did not recognize the *vaquero*, but knew that meant little. Without growing boastful about it, he knew that he had already carved something of a name for himself since arriving in Texas. What was more, his appearance was so distinctive — particularly since, as a joke more than anything, he had grown the moustache and beard to augment his Mephistophelian features – that he attracted attention and remembrance. Possibily the *vaquero* had seen him somewhere and was wanting to impress the three white men by a pretence of a much closer acquaintanceship than was the case.

Despite the conclusions which he had drawn, Ole Devil could not throw off his sense of perturbation. Something, he felt sure, was wrong. The burly hard-case had stopped the former lookout from lifting the flintlock, but had returned his own hand to his rifle. The third man's hands were hidden by the counter and might already be grasping a firearm.

However, the *vaquero* continued to draw nearer. He was still smiling, with his right hand extended to be shaken and the left hanging by his side. Neither were anywhere near the heavy pistol which was thrust, butt forward, through the silk sash around his waist and he had no other visible weapon.

Although Ole Devil was not yet within reaching distance of the *vaquero*, he too thrust out his right hand. He realized that he might be doing the occupants of the bar-room an injustice by mistrusting them. They would find such an attitude offensive if they were innocent of evil intent. Being aware of the kind of pride and temper possessed by many Texians, he was alert to the possibility that they might try to avenge what they would regard as an insult to their integrity and he wanted to avoid trouble of that nature. Also, to continue delaying a response to the *vaquero's* friendly greeting was almost sure to arouse their suspicions if his own feelings should be justified.

'*Saludos, senor,*' the young Texian said, but he did not relax his vigilance and was ready to react with all the speed if the *vaquero* should try to draw a weapon. He took the opportunity to study the men at the bar, continuing, 'Howdy, gents.'

Elated by the success of his scheme to lull the newcomer into a sense of false security, Verde gave the special twist to his left arm that liberated the knife from its sheath. Without needing to look, he caught the hilt as it slid into his hand, which was turned with the knuckles forward to prevent his potential victim from seeing what was happening. Easing back the hand so that it was concealed by his thigh, he turned the weapon deftly until its blade was extended ahead of his thumb and forefinger.

All was now ready for an upwards thrust into the unsuspecting Texian's stomach!

The blow would be delivered as soon as they were shaking

73

hands, so that the victim could not step back and avoid it.

At the bar, Mucker started to grin broadly as he watched the knife appear in Verde's left hand. He darted a delighted glance at Halford, but it was not returned. Equally aware of what was going on, the big man began to lift his rifle with the right hand so he would be ready in case something went wrong and Verde failed to do his work.

One more stride would bring Ole Devil and the *vaquero* close enough to shake hands. While the other's features still retained their friendly aspect, the Texian noticed that his left hand had, apparently by accident, swung until it was out of sight. Glancing past the *vaquero*, Ole Devil observed the expression of triumph on Mucker's face, and the movements of Halford. He sensed that the situation might be far less innocuous than appeared on the surface.

Suddenly the young Texian felt as if a cold hand had pressed against his spine.

The *vaquero* was armed with a pistol, but did not appear to be wearing a knife!

Ole Devil realized that not every member of the Spanish or Mexican races had a natural affinity towards knife-fighting, but it was extremely rare to come across a *vaquero* who did not go armed with one. If it was not sheathed on his belt, or thrust through his sash, it might be suspended beneath his collar at the back of the neck, carried in the top of his boot, or hidden in some other way.

There was one place of concealment, Ole Devil remembered having been told, which assassins in many lands made use of.

Reaching to take hold of the young Texian's hand and confident that he suspected nothing, Verde tensed slightly and was ready to bring out the knife. Before he could do so, he felt his intended victim's fingers make contact.

But not with his hand!

Hoping that his motives would be understood and his apologies accepted if he was mistaken, Ole Devil acted with deadly speed. Instead of allowing his hand to be trapped, he changed its direction slightly. Without giving any indication of his intentions, he grasped the *vaquero's* right wrist tightly. As he did so, he took a step to the right and rear and swung so that, for a moment, he was standing at an angle away from Verde. Before the *vaquero* could resist, he jerked on the wrist with all his strength and pivoted himself around on his right foot. Bending

74

his other leg, he swung it in a circular motion which propelled the knee into the advancing man's stomach.

Taken unawares, Verde could not prevent himself from being dragged forward. The knee met his midsection with considerable force. With his wrist released at the moment of impact, he was driven backwards. His knife slipped from his fingers and clattered to the floor as, partially winded and starting to fold over, he twisted away from his assailant. It was an almost instinctive action, designed to shield him from any further attack by the Texian, and he stumbled against the table at which he and his companions had been seated.

'Get the bastard!' Halford roared, snatching up his rifle in the expectation that their potential victim would turn and run.

Seeing Verde's assassination attempt fail, Stiple started to respond without needing the burly man's advice. What was more, he was in a better position to do something than either of his companions. Knowing that he could do so without being seen by the Texian, he had already drawn the pistol from his belt. Jerking back the hammer, he started to raise the weapon above the level of the bar which had previously hidden his movements.

Although startled by the unexpected turn of events, Mucker made a grab for his long rifle.

Instead of justifying the burly man's expectation and running, Ole Devil set his weight on his spread apart feet. Bending his knees slightly and inclining his torso forward a little, he made preparations for fighting back.

While prudence might have dictated that the young Texian should adopt the course Halford was anticipating, he had no intention of running. Hot-tempered arrogance had nothing to do with the decision. The fact that the *vaquero* had identified him in such a manner aroused disturbing possibilities which he considered must be investigated. Nor was his decision to seek a solution made rashly. He had devoted a lot of time, thought and effort to developing the means of defending himself in such a situation.

Even before coming to Texas, Ole Devil had realized that there were several flaws in the training which he had received in handling a pistol. His instructors had regarded a handgun as a duelling implement, with rules and conventions limiting how it could be used, rather than as a readily accessible defensive

75

weapon. With the latter purpose in mind, he had worked out a technique that was very effective.

Turning palm outwards, Ole Devil's right hand flashed to and closed around the butt of the Manton pistol. To slide the weapon free from the belt's retaining loop, he used a system which would eventually be developed into the 'high cavalry-twist' draw.* However, unlike the gun fighters who perfected the method in the mid-1860's and later, his sequence of firing could not be carried out with just one hand. Instead because of the shape and position of the hammer, he had to use the heel of his left palm almost as if he was 'fanning' the hammer of a single action revolver.

The unorthodox method of handling the pistol did not end with the way it had been twisted free from the belt and turned towards its target. Instead of adopting the accepted stance — sideways, with the right hand fully extended at shoulder height, left arm bent and hand on the hip — of the formal duellist, he stood squarely to his point of aim. Crouching slightly, he elevated the weapon to eye-level and, after cocking the hammer, his left hand went around to cup under the support the right. While doing so, he was selecting the man who was posing the most immediate threat to his life.

Not for another thirty or so years would the idea of fast drawing and shooting become widely known, or practised. So Ole Devil's actions came as a surprise and a shock to the three men at the bar, particularly to Stiple. With his pistol lifting to the firing position, he found himself looking into the un-wavering muzzle of the Texian's weapon. The hole of the barrel seemed to be much larger than its usual .54 of an inch calibre.

Having made sure of his aim, Ole Devil squeezed the trigger. On the hammer driving forward, the superiority of the caplock system became apparent. Striking directly on to the brass per-cussion cap, without the need to push clear the frizzen and create sparks, it was much faster in operation. Flame and white smoke gushed out of the muzzle about two seconds after his hand had closed around the butt.

Ole Devil fired the only way he dared under the circum-stances. Flying across the room, the soft lead ball went by Hal-

* A more detailed description of the 'high cavalry twist' draw is given in: *Slip Gun*.

ford as he was swinging his rifle towards his shoulder and struck Stiple in the centre of the forehead. It ranged onwards, to burst out at the rear of the skull accompanied by a spray of blood, brains and shattered fragments of bone. Killed instantly, the stricken man was flung backwards. The pistol dropped from his nerveless hand as he crashed into the wall. Then he crumpled as if he had been boned and fell out of sight behind the counter.

Although somewhat perturbed by the young Texian's spirited and very effective resistance in the face of danger, Halford still continued to raise the rifle. He drew consolation from the realization that, no matter how fast and capable a shot the other might be, the pistol was now empty. Long before Hardin could reload, or try to protect himself in some other fashion, Halford would have drawn a bead on him and sent a bullet into the head.

Even as the thought came to the burly man, he discovered that – in spite of the information which Verde had given on the subject – their intended victim was not travelling alone or unescorted.

Having moved silently down the sidewalk, bending low as he went by the window, Tommy Okasi was standing alongside the door by the time that Ole Devil had passed through. The little Oriental had not shown himself until he had heard the commotion which had warned him that his intervention might be necessary.

Darting across the threshold and into the bar-room, Tommy studied the situation with the eye of a tactician. One glance told him which of the remaining enemies was posing the most immediate threat to his companion. The *vaquero* was sprawled face down across the table. At the bar, showing his bewilderment, Mucker was making a belated grab for his rifle. Neither, Tommy realized, was so dangerous as the burly man. His weapon would soon be lined and able to open fire. At such a short range, he was not likely to miss.

Coming to a halt with his feet spread to an angle of roughly sixty degrees, Tommy turned the upper part of his body to the left and looked at his target. In a smoothly flowing, but very fast move, the long bow rose until perpendicular and was lifted until his hands were higher than his head. Extending his left arm until it was straight and shoulder high, he drew the string back and down with his right hand until the flight of the arrow was almost brushing against his off ear.* By the time his draw was completed, he was sighting so that two imaginary lines – one extended from his right eye and the other out of the arrow – intersected on Halford's left breast. Satisfied, he released his hold on the string.

Liberated from its tension, the bow's limbs returned to their previous positions. In doing so, they propelled the arrow forward. Hissing viciously through the air, the shaft flew towards its mark. On arriving, the needle-pointed, razor sharp, horizontal head cut between the ribs. It sliced open the heart in passing, to emerge through his back and sank into the bar.

Involuntarily throwing aside his unfired rifle as a spasm of agony ripped through him, Halford wrenched the arrow from the counter. Then he spun around with his hands clawing ineffectually at the shaft which was protruding from his chest and crashed dying to the floor.

With his left fingers closing around the barrel of the rifle so that he could elevate it into the firing position, Mucker saw first Stiple and then Halford struck down. He continued to lift the weapon instinctively, turning a worried gaze on the men who were responsible for his companions' deaths. What he discovered was not calculated to reduce his anxiety. The young Texian was starting to move forward, transferring the still smoking pistol to his left hand so that the right could go across to the ivory hilt of the bowie knife. Beyond him, the small 'Chinaman' was already reaching for another arrow.

Lying across the table which had prevented him from falling to the floor, Verde was also studying Ole Devil and Tommy. While a capable knife-fighter and no coward, the *vaquero* had more sense than to tangle with the Texian in his present condition. Not only had he lost his knife, but he also lacked the other's ability to draw and fire a pistol swiftly, and he was still feeling the effects of the knee kick. What was more, contrary to Juglares's information, their would-be victim was not alone. Nor was he likely to have restricted his escort to one small man armed with such primitive, if effective, weapons. In all probability, the rest of the escort were approaching ready to support the advance pair.

While these thoughts were passing through Verde's head, fright was spurring Mucker to move at speed. Already the butt

* A description of Occidental archery techniques is given in: *Bunduki.*

78

of the rifle was cradled against his shoulder and its barrel was pointing at the centre of the Texian's chest. His right hand drew back the hammer, then returned to enfold the wrist of the butt and his forefinger entered the triggerguard.

Deciding that discretion was by far the better part of valour under the circumstances, Verde lurched erect. Moving around, he hooked his hands under the edge of the table and flung it in Ole Devil's direction. Precipitated to the floor, the lamp – which the party had found behind the bar on their arrival – was shattered. It was almost out of fuel, so did not burst into flames. Instead, it went out and, as the moon had disappeared behind some clouds, the room was plunged into darkness.

Holding the pistol in his left hand and with the right engaged in drawing the bowie knife, Ole Devil could do nothing more than leap aside as the table was thrown his way. However, the evasion saved his life. Mucker's rifle roared an instant before the lamp was extinguished and its bullet passed where Ole Devil's torso had been a moment earlier.

Turning as soon as the darkness had descended, Verde ran across the room. He was making for where an oblong, slightly lighter than the surrounding blackness, marked the window in the left wall.

Realizing that he had missed the Texian and hearing his companion's footsteps, Mucker did not hesitate. He had no intention of testing his strength against such an efficient fighter as their victim had proved to be, especially as Verde clearly had no intention of staying. Having reached his decision, the lanky man flung his rifle towards where he had last seen the Texian so that it revolved parallel to the floor.

Luck was on Mucker's side.

Starting to follow the *vaquero* with the intention of intercepting and capturing him, Ole Devil felt the barrel of the rifle passing between his legs. He was tripped, pitching forward through the blackness. Instinctively he let go of the pistol and the knife, so that he would have a better chance of breaking his fall.

There was a shattering crash of breaking glass and timber. Covering his face with his forearms, Verde had hurled himself through the window. Carrying the ruined frame and broken panes with him, he plunged into the alley. Landing on his feet, he darted towards the lean-to.

At the door, Tommy had started to draw the bow and was

79

watching the window as he had guessed that the *vaquero* would attempt to leave through it. When the sound of Ol Devil falling reached his ears, he could not prevent himself from looking in that direction. The commotion caused by Verde's departure brought the little Oriental's attention back to the window. He realized that he was too late to stop the *vaquero*. Nor was he any too sanguine over his chances of being able to do anything about the lanky white man, who he felt sure would follow the *vaquero*. Accurate aiming in the almost pitch blackness of the room was far from easy. In fact, Tommy could not even be sure of exactly where his arrow was pointing.

Listening to Mucker as he sprinted across the room, Tommy waited with the bow fully drawn. When he saw the other's vague silhouette, he loosed the shaft. It flew high, but came very close to scoring a hit. Mucker felt the hat snatched from his head as if by an invisible hand and heard the thud as the arrow which had impaled it drove into the ruined frame of the window. The sensation gave him an added incentive to leave. Letting out a screech, he flung himself recklessly through the hole. Although he came down on his hands and knees, he was up like a flash and racing after his companion.

'Are you all right, Devil-san?' Tommy called anxiously, lowering the bow.

'Sure,' the Texian answered, feeling along the floor for his bowie knife. 'See if you can stop them!'

Satisfied that his companion was not hurt, Tommy turned and went out of the door. He found the linebacked dun and the bay were moving restlessly, but not so badly frightened by the commotion that they were threatening to pull free the reins and bolt. So taking another arrow from the quiver, he nocked it to the bow's string and trotted along the sidewalk.

Even before Tommy reached the alley, he could hear enough to warn him that he might not be able to carry out his companion's order. The moon was still behind the clouds, which had reduced the visibility. While he could not see that far, the sounds suggested the two men were already leading their mounts from the lean-to. Leather creaked as they swung into their saddles, then the animals started moving.

Tommy increased his pace, but by the time he arrived at the rear of the *cantina* the men were galloping to the west. Although he brought the bow into the shooting position, he did not bother to draw back on the string. Having only twenty arrows, he did not want to chance losing one while trying to hit a practically impossible target. Waiting until he was sure that the pair did not intend to return, he replaced the arrow and walked through the alley. On reaching the street, he found Ole Devil was standing on the sidewalk.

'Any luck?' the Texian inquired, sheathing his knife.

'They were gone before I could shoot,' Tommy replied. 'Who were they?'

'I don't know,' Ole Devil admitted. 'It's a pity we couldn't have taken at least one of them alive and questioned him. I've an idea they weren't here by accident, or just to shelter from the rain.'

'You mean that they were waiting for *you*? Tommy asked.

'I started to think so,' Ole Devil answered. 'But this isn't the shortest way from San Antonio to Santa Cristobal Bay. So, even if they'd learned about the shipment in some way, they wouldn't have expected to find me on this trail.'

'Unless they knew how you are going to carry the rifles,' Tommy supplemented.

'How could they?' Ole Devil demanded. 'Only General Sam and I knew that.'

'I heard the first two that left talking as they went,' Tommy explained. 'One was saying something about the town being out of the man they were expecting's way and the other said they'd been told he was going to Gonzales first.'

'Then it could have been *me* they were after,' Ole Devil breathed, remembering the conclusions he had drawn from the men's behaviour when he had arrived.

What was more, the young Texian saw the implications if his assumption was correct. Somebody very close to General Houston must be a traitor and was supplying information to the Mexicans. He also realized that there would not be time to return and warn the General, then reach the rendezvous with the ship. Before he could do so, it would have been forced to depart and the consignment of rifles would be lost to Texas.

CHAPTER EIGHT

IF YOU CAN'T HELP ME,
DON'T HELP THE BEAR!

DESPITE the fact that he arrived at Gonzales without any further difficulties or attempts upon his life, Ole Devil Hardin refused to let himself be lulled into what he suspected might be a sense of false security. Even the fact that he was now riding across the range between the town and Ewart Brindley's property did not cause him to relax his vigilance. Rather the knowledge tended to increase it.

Having taken precautions in case the *vaquero* and Mucker should return with the two men who had departed earlier, Ole Devil and Tommy Okasi had made their preparations to spend the night at the hamlet. After attending to their horses and those of the dead men, they had made a meal from the rations of jerked beef and pemmican which they were carrying. Then they had resumed their investigations into the ramifications of the incident at the *cantina*.

A thorough search of the two bodies had produced one very significant piece of evidence. In a concealed pocket at the back of the larger corpse's belt there had been a document bearing the Mexican coat-of-arms and a message written in Spanish. It was to inform all members of Santa Anna's forces that the bearer, Sidney Halford, was working for the Mexican Government and must be given any assistance that he requested. Although his companion had not been in possession of a similar authorization, it was convincing proof that they were not loyal to the Republic of Texas.

Unfortunately, there had been nothing to suggest why the renegades were at the hamlet.

Being aware of the very serious issues involved, Ole Devil and Tommy had discussed the matter at great length and in detail.

First they had considered the way in which the *vaquero* had acted when Ole Devil had entered the *cantina*. If the gang had merely been awaiting the arrival of a companion, there was no reason for him to have behaved in such a manner. He might, of course, have been alerting the other members of the party to the fact that the newcomer was rather more important than a chance-passing member of the Republic of Texas's army. However, the lanky man's reaction to the introduction had implied that he, for one, wanted to discover who had arrived.

Against that, the gang had apparently expected only one man. If they had known who was being sent to collect the rifles, they must have acquired their knowledge from what had been said in General Samuel Houston's office. Which meant that somebody had been able to listen to the conversation without the General and Ole Devil being aware of it. However, if that had been the case, the eavesdropper would have known that Tommy was accompanying the young Texian. Unless, as the little Oriental had pointed out, for some reason he – or she – had been prevented from hearing all that had passed between them.

There was, Ole Devil had realized, only one course open to him. If there should be a spy with the means of gathering such confidential information, the General must be warned so that he could take precautions. Producing a writing-case from his war bag, the young Texian had composed a report for Houston. In it, he had given a comprehensive description of the incident and of the conclusions which he and Tommy had reached. He had also said that he was retaining the document which identified Halford in case he might find a need for it during the assignment.

The next morning, after having spent an otherwise uneventful night in the *cantina*, Ole Devil had sent Tommy back to San Antonio de Bexar with the report. Using one of the dead men's horses, which the fleeing pair had been in too much of a hurry either to take with them or frighten away, the little Oriental was to ride relay. After delivering the information to Houston, he would follow and rejoin Ole Devil on the way to the rendezvous at Santa Cristobal Bay.

Taking along the second of the horses which had been left in the lean-to – the contents of the bed roll on the cantle of its 'slick fork' saddle, although supplying no information of greater use, suggested that it had been Halford's property – Ole

Devil had resumed his journey at dawn, Tommy was using Stiple's mount, which had a Walker-style rig, having lost the toss of a coin to determine which of them should take it.

Once again the young Texian had not stuck to the trail. While the two men had fled and not returned, he doubted whether they and their companions would give up so easily; especially if they were aware of his assignment and were trying to prevent him from carrying it out. He had reached Guadalupe without having seen any sign of them. Visiting the town, he had found its population were preparing to take part in the withdrawal to the east.

The commanding officer of the town's small garrison had listened to Ole Devil's story and, without having asked too many questions about the nature of his mission, had promised to send a patrol to the hamlet. They were to search along the trail on the very slender chance that the four men might still be lurking in the vicinity. Although Ole Devil had described the quartet as well as possible and the officer had said that he would try to find out if they had been seen around Guadalupe, he doubted if he would be successful as there were so many strangers present. However, he had offered to supply Ole Devil with an escort as far as Gonzales. Wanting to travel faster than would be possible if he was accompanied by a number of men, as well as having no wish to reduce the other's already barely adequate force, the young Texian had declined the offer and had ridden on alone.

As was always his way, Ole Devil had given much thought to the situation. While he had remained alert and watchful, he had not expected to run into any trouble before he had passed through Gonzales on the final five or so miles which separated it from the Brindleys' place. His reasoning was that if the men were hunting him because of the shipment, and had been told of at least part of the arrangements he had made in Houston's office, they would know why he was not taking the most direct route to Santa Cristobal Bay. After the way in which he had arrived at the hamlet, they were likely to assume that he would adopt similar tactics and stay off the trail. While there were a number of ways in which he could travel from Guadalupe to Gonzales, once he had passed the latter town his route would be more restricted.

In view of his conclusions, Ole Devil was willing to bet that they would be spread out and keeping watch for him somewhere between two and four miles beyond Gonzales. Nearer to the town, or closer to the Brindleys' ranch, any shooting would be heard and might – almost certainly would if there was more than one shot – be investigated. Now he had already entered the region where, if his assumptions were correct, he could expect to find them.

Slouching comfortably in the saddle of the borrowed horse, with the linebacked bay walking at its right side, the young Texian kept his eyes constantly on the move. He was passing through rolling, broken and bush-dotted terrain which would offer plenty of scope for ambush. What was more, there were numerous areas of high ground; vantage points from which the quartet could keep watch for him. However, it was also the kind of land that allowed a man to move without making himself too conspicuous if he knew how to utilize it and did not mind winding about instead of trying to go directly to his ultimate destination.

Since his arrival in Texas, Ole Devil had learned how to make the most use of such land when he was traversing it. Despite his upbringing, in fact because of it, he was no snob. Nor had he ever been so self-opinionated that he would not take advice and learn from those who knew what they were talking about. Working with experienced frontier men, he had watched, listened, remembered and put his findings into practice. He was doing so now as he rode along, leading the dun with its reins held in his left hand.

Having called at Gonzales and obtained advice on how to find the Brindleys' ranch, Ole Devil had kept to the bottom of draws, or passed through areas of bushes instead of going across more easily negotiable open ground. When he had been compelled to expose himself by crossing a ridge, he had done so with great care and only after scanning every inch of the land ahead and behind.

The raucous cackle of feeding magpies came to Ole Devil's ears as he was approaching the top of a bush-fringed rim. Suddenly, one of the black and white scavengers gave an alarm call and they rose into the air. The young Texian realized that it was not his presence which had frightened them.

Slowing down his horses, Ole Devil approached the rim with extreme care. Making use of the screen of bushes, he peered over the top. About a hundred yards away, a buckskin-clad figure carrying a rifle was walking towards the partially eaten

85

carcass of a mule that lay in the open some thirty yards from a clump of buffalo-berry bushes.

Although the figure was dressed in a familiar manner, except that he had on Indian moccasins and leggings instead of boots, and despite the brim of the hat hiding his face as he looked down at the carcass, Ole Devil knew he was not one of the white men who had been in the *cantina*. About five foot seven inches tall, while neither puny nor skinny, he lacked the thickset bulk of the one who compared with him in height. In addition, he gave the impression of being younger. His horse, a black and white *tobiano* gelding with a 'slick fork' saddle that had a coiled rope strapped to its horn, but no bed roll on the cantle, was standing ground-hitched some thirty feet away. It was staring in alarmed manner at the dead mule.

The horse, Ole Devil decided, was showing better sense than its owner.

Even as the thought came, there was a rustling among the buffalo-berry bushes. Ole Devil looked that way and a sense of chilly apprehension drove through him. From all appearances, the youngster's desire to examine the dead mule had led him into a potentially dangerous situation. Rearing up on its hind legs, a large bear loomed over the bushes. It had been lying up in the shade after feeding on the carcass, Snorting and snuffling, it stared at the intruder advancing towards its kill.

For a moment, Ole Devil was alarmed on the youngster's behalf. Then, with a feeling of relief, he realized that the bear – despite its size – was of the black species and not, as he had first feared, a grizzly. Despite the many highly-spiced, horrifying stories told about its savage nature, *Euarctos Americanus*, the American black bear, was generally not especially dangerous to human beings. If the creature in the bushes had been a Texas flat-headed grizzly, the youngster's position would have been very precarious. Fortunately for him, that part of Texas was somewhat to the east of *Ursus Texensis Texensis*'s range.

With the realization, Ole Devil felt the apprehension leaving him. He had no wish to advertise his presence and attract unwanted attention by shooting. All the black bears he had come into contact with had never lingered any longer than necessary in the presence of human beings, even when disturbed after having fed on a kill. It was merely curious and puzzled. Being short-sighted like all of its species, it was not sure what kind of creature was standing near its prey. However, as long as the youngster did nothing to antagonize it, there was a better than fair chance that he could withdraw in safety.

'You mule-killing son-of-a-bitch!'

Even as Ole Devil opened his mouth to call and advise the youngster to back away slowly, the boy yelled at the bear and started to raise his rifle. Excitement, or fear, had given his voice a high pitched, almost feminine sounding timbre.

Hearing the youngster, the bear showed that it might be different in habits from most others of its species. Instead of giving a 'whoof!' of alarm on hearing the human voice, spinning around and taking off for a safer location at all speed, it cut loose with a short, rasping and menacing, coughing noise.

Ole Devil had only once before heard a similar sound, but he had never forgotten that occasion. It had happened during a hunt in Louisiana and the bear had given just such a cough before charging through the pack of hounds to try and reach the hunters. Several bullets had been required to put the enraged beast down.

Instead of taking warning from the bear's behaviour, the youngster stood his ground. Lining the rifle, which he must have cocked as he was approaching the carcass, he squeezed the trigger. The hammer fell. There was a puff of smoke from the frizzen pan, but the main charge failed to ignite for some reason.

As if realizing what the hissing splutter from the rifle meant, the bear gave another of its threatening coughs and lurched forward.

To give the youngster credit, he might have acted in an impulsive and reckless manner by yelling and trying to shoot the bear, but he was no fool. Nor, despite how his voice had sounded, did he panic. As the bear dropped on to all fours and burst from the fringe of the buffalo-berry bushes, he let his useless rifle fall and turned. However, having already been disturbed and made nervous by the bloody carcass, or perhaps because it had caught the bear's scent, the *tobiano* gelding did not wait for its master to return and mount. At the sight of the rage-bristling beast erupting into view, the horse gave a squeal of terror and, disregarding the dangling split-ended reins, bolted.

Growling a curse, Ole Devil used his spurs to set the borrowed horse into motion. Feeling the tug at its reins, the dun advanced and kept pace with its companion as they topped the ridge. However, as much as he would liked to have done, the young Texian knew he could not delay or slow down and transfer to his own mount.

Once again, the youngster was displaying courage. Certainly he had sufficient good sense to keep running. He had a lead over the bear which might just about prove adequate providing that he could maintain or increase his pace. Unfortunately, he was going away from Ole Devil. To call on him to change direction would be fatal. So the young Texian kept quiet and urged his mount to a gallop. Then he discarded the dun's reins to leave both his hands free.

A black bear could attain a speed of around twenty-five miles an hour when charging, but it needed time to build up to its top pace. With its eyes fixed on the fleeing youngster, it hurtled after him and ignored the departing horse. Nor was it aware of Ole Devil dashing down the slope in its direction.

Urging the borrowed horse to its fastest gait, the young Texian gave thought to how he might best deal with the situation. He had heard that some Indian braves had so little fear of the black bear that they regarded it as being unworthy of death by arrow, lance, tomahawk, firearm, or even a knife. Instead, the warrior would beat the beast's brains out with a club and apologize to its spirit for having done so. However, having done a fair amount of bear hunting, Ole Devil had never believed the story. He certainly was not inclined to try and duplicate the feat, particularly under the prevailing conditions.

Nor, despite the fact that the Browning rifle when loaded — which it was not at that moment due to the difficulty of carrying it in a condition of readiness — would have offered him the advantage of five consecutive shots without needing recharging, did he regret that it was in the dun's saddleboot. To have drawn it and made it ready for firing would be a very difficult, if not impossible, task when riding at full speed. What was more, from his present position, all he could take aim at was the bear's rump. A hit there with the comparatively small calibre rifle would not stop it quickly enough to save the youngster from a mauling. Ole Devil would have to place a bullet in exactly the right spot to achieve his purpose. Luckily, due to having transferred his weapon carrier to the borrowed horse's saddlehorn, he would have two shots at his disposal instead of only one. For all that, killing the bear would be far from a sinecure.

When in motion at speed, a black bear's rolling, loose-haired hide and the placement of its feet combine to present ever-changing contours which made accurate aiming a difficult proposition. Throughout its stride, its legs 'scissored' rapidly to add to the confusion. One moment the forepaws would be under the rump and the back legs up close to the nose, bunching the vital organs. Next the body appeared to become extended out of all proportion, causing the target to change its position in relation to the now elongated frame. The young Texian knew of only one area where he could rely upon hitting and bringing down the animal immediately.

There was, however, a major objection to Ole Devil firing even a single shot. It might be heard by the *vaquero* and his companions, causing them to come and investigate.

For a moment, Ole Devil contemplated trying to effect a rescue in the manner of a Comanche brave going to a wounded or unhorsed companion's assistance. He had practised the method with other members of Company 'C' and was proficient at it. Doing so under the prevailing conditions would be difficult and dangerous, yet it might be possible if the youngster co-operated. The problem was how to acquaint him with what was being planned. Calling out the information was not the answer. It was sure to distract him and would cause him to slow down, or could even make him stumble if he looked back to see who had spoken.

Then another factor arose to lessen the already slender hope of scooping up the youngster and carrying him to safety. A worried snort burst from the fast-moving horse as its flaring nostrils picked up the bear's scent. Controlling its desire to shy away from a natural enemy, Ole Devil managed to keep it running in a straight line. Clearly the borrowed mount lacked the stability of temperament for him to risk that kind of a rescue. An unexpected swerve, a refusal to respond to his heels' signals – his hands would be fully occupied with the pick up and could not manipulate the reins – or a panic-induced stumble might see them all on the ground and tangled with the enraged bear.

While a black bear could not equal the grizzly's armament, its teeth and claws were sufficiently well-developed for Ole Devil to have the greatest reluctance to feel them sink into his flesh.

Discarding the idea of making a Comanche-style rescue, Ole Devil drew the Manton pistol – mate to the one in his belt loop

– from the holster on his weapon-carrier and cocked its hammer. Already he was alongside the bear and the horse's speed was carrying them by. No sooner had they drawn ahead than he saw the youngster trip and go sprawling.

There was no time to lose!

Tossing his left leg forward and over the saddlehorn, the young Texian quit the horse at full gallop. He landed with an almost cat-like agility which told of long and arduous training. His momentum carried him onwards a few strides, until he had almost reached the youngster who had managed to break his fall and was attempting to rise. Coming to a stop, Ole Devil swung around and brought the pistol up to arm's length and eye level. Once again, he adopted the double handed grip on the butt that had served him so well in the *cantina*.

Rushing closer, the bear made an awe-inspiring sight. Its coat was bristling with rage until it seemed far larger than its already not inconsiderable size. Uttering savage, blood-chilling snarls, its open, slavering jaws were filled with long and sharp teeth. Its slightly curved, almost needle-pointed claws, tore grooves in the ground and sent dirt flying as they helped to propel it towards its intended prey. All in all, the furious three hundred pound beast was not a spectacle to inspire confidence, or even peace of mind, when one was facing it armed with nothing more than a pistol which held only a single shot and could not be re-loaded quickly.

'Lord!' Ole Devil breathed, in an attempt to control his rising tension as he looked along the nine inch, octagonal barrel at the approaching animal. 'If you can't help me, don't help the bear!'

While the young Texian found himself repeating the line from the old Negro comic song, 'The Preacher And The Bear', he was also aligning the 'V' notch of the rear- and blade of the front-sights on the centre of the approaching animal's head. An area the size of the top of the bear's skull would have been comparatively easy to hit at such close range, on a stationary paper target. However, even to a man of Ole Devil's skill, it seemed much smaller and vastly more difficult at that moment. He knew that he would have time for only the one shot. So it had to strike accurately or somebody, himself for sure and in all probability the youngster he was attempting to save, was going to be killed.

Forcing himself to remain calm and to wait until certain of

his aim, Ole Devil made allowance for the bear's forward movement and squeezed the trigger. Forty grains of powder were waiting to be ignited and turned into a mass of gas which would thrust the half-ounce ball through the barrel's rifling grooves. It was a very heavy charge and would be capable of inflicting considerable damage – providing a hit was made.

On the other hand, if the pistol should hang fire for some reason – as the youngster's rifle had – Ole Devil would be unlikely to survive. Even if he did, he would be too badly injured to carry on with his assignment.

CHAPTER NINE

HE'LL SKIN YOU ALIVE!

NEVER had the hammer of the Manton pistol seemed to be moving so slowly!

It fell, at long last, striking the brass percussion cap!

Still moving to compensate for the bear's ever changing — and nearing – position, the pistol roared!

Converging with the approaching beast, the .54 calibre bullet struck it between and slightly above the eyes to plough through into the brain. Hit while its forelegs were approaching the end of a rearwards thrust, the bear began to crumple forward.

Even as smoke partially obscured the bear and the pistol's barrel rose under the impulsion of the recoil, without waiting to discover the effect of the shot, Old Devil Hardin sprang to his right. Dropping the empty weapon, he sent his right hand curling back and around the butt of the pistol's mate. Twisting it free from the retainer loop on his belt, he was just starting to draw back the hammer with the heel of his left palm when the bear emerged from the smoke. However, it was turning a somersault and it crashed to the ground on its back. With its jaws chomping in a hideous fashion and legs flailing their death throes, it slid to a halt on the very spot Hardin had just vacated.

It was, the young Texian decided, as narrow an escape from a painful death as had ever come his way.

Suddenly, courageous as he was, Ole Devil found that he was perspiring very freely and breathing as heavily as if he had run a mile. What was more, his limbs were shaking from the reaction to the highly unnerving few seconds that he had just passed through.

Much of Ole Devil's reaction was, he realized, stemming from a belated understanding of the possible effects of the risk he had taken. If he had been killed or injured, the very important mission upon which he was engaged would have ended in ignomonious failure.

And all because of a stupid act by a boy who might even be one of the party who were trying to prevent Old Devil from completing the assignment.

'Thanks, mister. You surely saved my life.'

The youngster's voice came to Ole Devil's ears as, starting to regain control of his churning emotions, he looked from the bear's body to where the linebacked dun had been brought to a halt by its trailing reins and was standing quietly. Something about the words, perhaps the fact that they sounded so damned effeminate, brought the young Texian's temper to boiling point.

'Why the hell did you have to pull such a god-damned stupid trick as that?' Ole Devil roared swinging around, fury making his features as Mephistophelian as 'Ole Nick' forking sinners into the fiery furnaces of Hades. 'Your folks shouldn't let you out alone if—'

The angry tirade died away at the sight which met the young Texian's gaze. And it wasn't the sight of the borrowed horse, carrying his sabre on its saddle, still galloping away that stopped him.

Having apparently contrived to wriggle onwards for several feet after falling down and losing his hat, the youngster had regained his feet. Returning the knife which he had been drawing to its fringed, Indian-made sheath, he was walking towards his rescuer. An expression of mingled relief and gratitude was on his tanned and freckled face as he held out his right hand.

The reason for the falsetto, effeminate tones which had been one cause of Ole Devil's annoyance was explained. Describing the youngster as 'he', or 'him' was most inaccurate. Despite the masculine clothing, the person he had rescued was a pretty and, although her garments did only a little to emphasize it, shapely girl in her late 'teens, with shortish, fiery red, curly hair. Her reaction to his hostile words and attitude suggested that the hair was matched by a hot and explosive temper.

Coming to a halt, her features lost their friendliness which was replaced by indignation. Like a flash, she whipped up her extended right hand in a slap that met Ole Devil's right cheek hard enough to snap his head around and caused him to jerk back a pace. Rocking to a stop and, in his surprise, dropping the

93

pistol he responded almost automatically to the blow. Before he could stop himself, he was launching a backhand swing in retaliation to the attack. Although he just managed to reduce the power behind it, as a realization of what he was doing belatedly came to him, his left knuckles came up against the side of her head in a cuff of some force.

The girl had been retreating. Her expressive features were registering a change to contrition, as if she was already regretting her hasty and uncalled for behaviour towards the man who had saved her life at some risk to his own. The blow connected, knocking her off balance. Staggering back a few paces, she flopped rump-foremost on the ground. A screech burst from her as she landed and her face turned red with fury.

Like the girl, Ole Devil started to regret what he had done. Meaning to apologize and help her to rise, he began to move forward. Before he could achieve either intention, she bounded to her feet. Ducking her head, she charged at him like a big-horn ram going at a rival in the mating season.

Growling an imprecation which he would not normally have used in the presence of a member of the opposite sex, the young Texian tried to fend off the girl. Although he caught her by the shoulders, the impetus of her charge drove him backwards. Unable to stop himself, or the girl, he retreated until his legs hit the now fortunately dead and motionless bear.

With the girl toppling after him, Ole Devil sat on the corpse. Pure chance rather than a deliberate intention caused him to guide the girl so that she landed face down across his lap. Studying the situation, he decided that the opportunity was too good to miss. Holding her in position by gripping the scruff of her neck with his left hand, he applied the flat palm of his right to the tightly stretched and well-filled seat of her buckskin trousers.

Ten times in rapid succession Ole Devil's hand came into sharp and, if the girl's yelps after each slap were anything to go on, painful contact with her rump. She struggled with considerable strength and violence, twisting her body and waving her legs, but to no avail. Suddenly, her captor once again realized what he was doing. He decided to bring the spanking, well-deserved as some might have said, to an end. Coming to his feet and releasing her neck, he precipitated her from his lap. She landing, rolling across the ground, and came to her knees.

94

Tears, caused by anger and indignation over the way she had been treated more than pain, trickled down the girl's reddened cheeks. She glared furiously at the young Texian as she sprang to her feet. Spitting out a string of curses which were the equal of any he had ever heard, she crouched as if meaning to throw herself at him for a second time. However, on this occasion, her right hand flew across to close around the hilt of the clip-pointed knife sheathed at the left side of her belt.

'I'm sorry that I spanked you,' Ole Devil said quietly. His soft spoken words were anything but gentle and, taken with the savage, almost demoniac aspect of his countenance, seemed to be charged with menace. 'But if you pull that damned knife on me, I'll take it from you and paddle your *bare* hide until you've learned better sense.

For a moment, watching the girl's every move and the play of emotions on her face, the young Texian thought that she intended to force him into a position where he would have to disarm her, even if he did not carry out the rest of his threat. She was quivering with temper over the humiliation she had suffered at his hands and made as if to continue drawing the weapon. Wanting to avoid such a confrontation, he stared straight into her eyes. Almost twenty seconds dragged by before she tore her gaze from his coldly threatening scrutiny.

'Just you wait until Grandpappy Ewart hears about this!' the girl warned, without looking at her assailant, spitting out the words as if they were burning her mouth. However, her fingers left the hilt of the knife.

'Who?' Ole Devil asked before he could stop himself, with a cold feeling hitting him in the pit of the stomach.

'Ewart Brindley, *fancy pants!*' the girl elaborated viciously, sensing her combined rescuer and assailant's perturbation and drawing the wrong conclusions regarding what had caused it. 'As soon as he hears what you've done to me, he'll skin you alive!'

'Diamond-Hitch Brindley!' Ole Devil thought bitterly, recollecting General Samuel Houston's comment on the advisability of keeping on the best of terms with the girl as that would be the most certain way of winning her irascible grandfather's support and assistance. 'I've sure picked a fine way of doing *that*.'

'Happen you know what's good for you,' the girl went on, although not quite so heatedly, when her warning failed to evoke a verbal response or discernible change in the young Texian's attitude, 'you'll go catch my horse for me. Then get going to wherever you're headed and I'll forget what you did.'

Even as the wrathful words had been boiling from her lips, Charlotte Jane Martha Brindley was starting to regret that she was saying them. Always of a volatile and ebullient nature, she was quick to anger but just as ready to forgive; particularly when conscious that she herself was as much, perhaps even more, at fault than the other participant in the contretempts.

While Di had been very grateful for being saved from a very painful death, her rescuer's attitude and scathing words could not have come at a worse time. She had been churned up emotionally over her narrow escape and not a little annoyed by the realization that her perilous predicament had come about through her own reckless behaviour.

On finding the dead mule, which had strayed from the *remuda* the previous night, a girl with her experience ought to have shown greater caution. The *tobiano* gelding was not long broken to the saddle and she was riding it to further its training. So she should have known that it was not as steady as her regular horse and would be unreliable in an emergency. On top of that, when the bear had made its appearance, she had provoked a charge which could have been avoided by using her common-sense. In doing so, she had endangered her own and the stranger's lives. She could guess how he must have stopped the animal. Only a man of great courage, or a reckless fool would have attempted to do so in such a manner. Her instincts suggested that he came into the former category.

So Di's relief and gratitude had been entangled with guilt over her folly. Nor had her rescuer's behaviour on turning to face her done anything to lessen her emotional tensions. With her nerves stretched tight, his obvious anger had triggered off her unfortunate response.

Despite the way in which her rescuer had subsequently treated her, Di was sorry for the way in which she had acted. However, her pride would not permit an open apology and she hoped that he would do as she suggested.

For his part, Ole Devil could appreciate the girl's motives and, under different circumstances, he might have sympathized with her. Unfortunately, he too had been under a considerable strain and possessed a fair amount of pride. So her attitude was doing little to bring about a conciliatory situation. However, as he remembered what was at stake, he forced himself to consider how he might establish a more amicable relationship with her. He decided to explain what he was doing and hoped that she would have the good sense, sufficient gratitude for her rescue, and loyalty to Texas, to overlook the spanking.

Before Ole Devil could start putting his good intentions into practise, he saw four riders topping a ridge about half a mile away. One of them was pointing in his and the girl's direction, then they were urging their horses forward at a faster pace. He could tell that they were a Mexican and three buckskin-clad white men, two of whom were carrying rifles. While the distance was too great for him to make out further details, he was certain that they were the quartet he had been expecting to be in the vicinity. What was more, unless he was mistaken, the recognition had been mutual.

Ole Devil could have cursed the vagaries of fate. Having saved Di Brindley's life, which would have made him extremely popular with her grandfather, he had ruined the effect by giving her a not undeserved spanking. Now, before he could try to make amends, she was likely to find her life endangered because of him.

'Run and fetch my horse!' Old Devil ordered, striding forward. The urgency of the situation put an edge to his voice which, he realized too late, taken with his choice of words, would not enhance his popularity with the girl.

'Who the hell—!' Di began, once again taking umbrage at his tone.

The indignant tirade trailed off as Ole Devil hurried past the girl. Turning, she watched him picking up the pistol which he had dropped when she slapped his face. Then she noticed the approaching riders and stopped speaking.

Retrieving the weapon, Ole Devil examined it to make sure that its barrel had not become plugged up with soil when it landed. Satisfied, he replaced it in the belt loop and, after another glance at the four men, swung around. Much to his annoyance, he found that Di was still standing watching him.

'Get going!' Ole Devil commanded, bounding forward. 'Head for my horse!'

Realizing that the riders must be the cause of her rescuer's behaviour, Di did not waste time in asking questions or making protests. Turning, she started to run at his side. Any lingering doubts she might have been harbouring were wiped away when a bullet passed between them and ploughed into the ground a few feet away from the dun. She darted a glance at her rifle as she went by, but knew better than to stop and pick it up.

As Ole Devil was approaching the dun, he reached behind him with his left hand and raised the flap of the leather pouch that was attached to his belt. From it, he drew a rectangular metal bar with rounded ends. Having done so, he put on a spurt which carried him ahead of the girl. Arriving alongside his mount, he thrust his right hand towards the rifle in its saddle-boot.

'Mount up and get going!' the young Texian told the girl as he drew out the rifle and turned to face the direction from which they had come.

'Like hell I will!' Di answered, guessing what he had in mind. She pivoted to a stop by his side, reaching to haul the pistol from his belt's loop and, serious as she realized the situation must be, could not resist continuing, 'I hope whoever loaded this blasted thing for you knew what he was doing, fancy pants.'

'And I hope you know how to handle it and can shoot better than most women,' Ole Devil commented dryly, although he guessed that the girl would prove competent, accept that to try and enforce his demand for her to leave would be futile.

'I can shoot better than most *men*,' Di countered, speaking jerkily as she replenished her lungs with air. 'Don't worry, fancy pants, I'll protect you.'

While speaking, the girl was drawing back the hammer of the Manton pistol and gauging the strength of the trigger-pull that would be required from the amount of resistance she was meeting. It moved easily and the gentle clicking of the mechanism implied that the pull would be light, but not excessively so. Taken with the pistol's weight and balance, her deductions were comforting. She knew that she was holding a weapon of exceptional quality which, in capable hands, would prove extremely accurate.

Despite the danger which was threatening them, Ole Devil could not hold down an appreciative grin at Di's spirited response. A quick glance at her assured him that the breathless way she was speaking was caused by her exertions and not from fear or panic.

Having satisfied himself upon that not unimportant point,

the young Texian returned his attention to the four men. They had fanned out into a well-spaced line and were galloping closer. Although they still had at least a quarter of a mile to cover, the *vaquero* and the lanky man who had fled with him from the *cantina* were already holding pistols. Tucking his empty rifle between his left thigh and the saddle, the man who had fired the shot started to draw his handgun. However, the last of the quartet was still carrying a loaded rifle even though, as yet, he had not attempted to use it.

On meeting their companions, who had heard the shooting and were returning to the hamlet to investigate, Arnaldo Verde and Mucker had done almost exactly what Ole Devil had deduced they might.

Being aware that Al Soapy regarded every man of Mexican origin as a coward and knowing they had just as little regard for Mucker's courage, the *vaquero* had considered it advisable to stretch the truth when telling them what had happened at the *cantina*. So he, with Mucker's support, had deliberately over-estimated the size of Ole Devil's escort. They had claimed that their quarry had been accompanied by at least half a dozen men and had appeared to have been expecting trouble, which had chilled any desire the other two might have felt towards avenging their dead companions.

There had been a difference of opinion between the quartet as to what their best line of action would be in view of the changed circumstances. Soapy had suggested that they should return to their hide-out and pick up reinforcements. Verde had pointed out that there had only been six men at it when they had left, and that their leader was intending to use them to gather together the rest of the gang ready to go and intercept the shipment. The *vaquero* had also pointed out that their task was to prevent Ole Devil Hardin from reaching Ewart Brindley and they would not have sufficient time to go to the hide-out before making another try at stopping him.

After Verde had established his points and gained his companions' grudging agreement, he had declared that they ought to continue with their assignment. As none of the others could come up with a better idea, they had let him make the arrangements. Without having realized it, the *vaquero* had duplicated Ole Devil's summation of the situation. Instead of trying to lay an ambush along the trail, or attempting to locate the young Texian as he made his way across country to Gonzales, they had headed directly to the town. Learning where the Brindleys' place was situated, they had taken up a position that offered them a good view of the terrain over which he was most likely to pass.

The discovery that Ole Devil was riding alone had been the cause of considerable recriminations, with Soapy demanding to be told what had happened to the escort. Although Verde had not cared for the other's attitude and implications, he had managed to control his temper. He had suggested that the men might have been accompanying the young Texian only as far as Guadalupe, or Gonzales. Or they might even have been a patrol which just happened to be using the trail and Ole Devil was riding with them for the company. Either explanation had left a number of questions unanswered, but the urgency of the situation had prevented them from being asked. As Mucker had said, no matter what had happened to the escort, its absence made their work that much easier and safer.

Accepting Mucker's statement, the quartet had set off to intercept the young Texian. Although while using Verde's telescope to watch for Ole Devil they had noticed Di Brindley, they had been in a hollow and missed seeing her meeting with him. On coming into view, having heard the shot, they had drawn at least one incorrect conclusion from the sight which had met their eyes. As they could not see the pistol which Ole Devil had discarded after firing, they assumed he was holding an empty weapon. So they had not been surprised when Ole Devil and the 'boy' – the quartet had fallen into the same error regarding Di's sex – turned and ran towards the line-backed dun. They had expected the fleeing pair to mount the horse and try to escape in that way.

Always boastful about his ability as a marksman, Soapy had tried to prevent the Texian and the 'boy' from escaping by shooting the dun. Not unexpectedly, as the range had been close to five hundred yards and he was sitting a fast-moving horse, he missed. So, having emptied his weapon to no purpose, he felt somewhat perturbed when Ole Devil and Di turned instead of mounting the waiting dun. If the way they were arming themselves meant anything, they were going to fight rather than try to escape with the animal carrying a double load.

Watching Ole Devil holding and doing something to the rifle which he could not make out, Verde did not share Soapy's misgivings. In fact he was not displeased by the way things were turning out. True the 'boy' had armed himself with the Texian's pistol, suggesting that it might have been reloaded, but even in skilled hands it would only be a short range weapon. The rifle which Ole Devil was raising to his shoulder would be a far greater danger.

'Keep moving at long range until he fires,' Verde called to his companions. 'Then rush him before he can reload.'

Although the *vaquero's* advice did not reach Di's ears, she was aware of such a danger. Having helped to fight off more than one Indian attack, she suspected that the four men might adopt similar tactics by hovering at a distance until fired on and then attacking before the empty weapons could be replenished. Noticing that her companion was taking aim, she decided to warn him against playing into the quartet's hands.

Before the girl could speak, the rifle cracked!

Almost as if wishing to oblige his attackers, Ole Devil sighted and touched off a shot. Soapy heard the bullet passing close to his head, but was not hit.

'Come on, *amigos*!' Verde yelled, watching the Texian lowering the rifle's butt so as to start reloading. 'We've got him now!'

CHAPTER TEN

KEEP GOING, IT'S EMPTY NOW!

EAGERLY urging their horses forward Arnaldo Verde and his three white companions began to close together as they bore down on their intended victims. Each of the quartet used his spurs as an encouragement to make his mount run faster, wanting to make sure that they arrived before the young Texian could reload his rifle.

Watching the men approaching, Diamond-Hitch Brindley was very worried and her earlier annoyance returned. She had been revising her opinion about the possible capabilities of her rescuer, deciding that he might be much less of the fancily-dressed dude she had first thought. After the way in which he had discharged his weapon's only bullet, she concluded that his method of dealing with the bear must have stemmed from ignorance and reckless folly and not out of a courageous calculation of the dangers it involved. There was, Di knew, no way that he could go through the time-consuming process of reloading any type of rifle with which she was acquainted before the quartet reached them.

That was where Di and the four men were making the same mistake. It was an error caused by ignorance, although pardonable under the circumstances.

At first sight, the weapon in Ole Devil Hardin's hands appeared to be a so-called 'Kentucky' rifle* of the kind which had long been popular in the more easterly of the United States; although it was being supplanted by the heavier calibred and shorter 'Mississippi' models west of that mighty river. However, a close examination would have revealed that it possessed several features which were not incorporated in the design of the standard 'Kentucky' flintlock, or the 'Mississippi' caplock. Most noticeable difference was the hammer being set underneath the rifle, just in front of the trigger-guard. There had

* The majority of 'Kentucky' rifles were made in Pennsylvania.

been a few 'under-hammer' pieces made, but they had never been common, or popular, due to the difficulty of retaining the priming powder in the frizzen pan. Neither had any of them carried a lever on the right side of the frame, nor had an aperture cut through it. An omission which might have aroused comment was a ramrod, for it was not supplied with the means to carry one beneath the barrel. The latter item was, in fact, not needed.

The action which Verde had noticed Ole Devil carrying out, but unfortunately for his party had failed to understand, was the remarkably easy process of loading a Browning Slide Repeating rifle. Once the original preparations had been made, it did not require a powder flask, patch, ball and ramrod.

The rectangular metal bar which Ole Devil had taken from the pouch on the rear of his belt was, in reality, the rifle's magazine. Five chambers had been drilled in the front of the bar, that having been the number Jonathan Browning had considered most suitable for convenient handling; although he produced models with a greater capacity if requested. Each chamber had a hole at the rear to take a percussion cap.

After firing a shot, a thrust with the right thumb on the lever caused the magazine to move through the aperture in the receiver so that the next chamber was in place. Not only did the mechanism lock the magazine into position, but thrust it forward until a gas-tight seal was formed against the bore of the barrel. As a further aid to ease of operation, the proximity of the hammer to the right forefinger allowed it to be cocked without the need to remove the butt from the shoulder.*

So Ole Devil did not have any need to reload in the normal fashion. Lowering the rifle as if he was compelled to had been done to make the quartet believe they had nothing to fear and to lure them closer.

When Verde and the three white men were about a hundred

* Despite the difficulty of transporting it with the magazine in position, Jonathan Browning had produced a comparatively simple repeating rifle that was capable of a continuous fire unequalled by contemporary weapons. For all its advantages, it never achieved the fame which it deserved. During the period when he was manufacturing it, between 1834 and '42, he lacked the facilities for large scale production. In later years he would have been able to do so, but the development of metallic cartridges and more compact, if less simple to construct, repeating arms had rendered it obsolete.

and fifty yards away, ignoring the muttering from the girl at his side – although he could hear that it consisted of profane comments about what she assumed to have been his stupidity in 'emptying' his weapon – the Texian returned the butt to his right shoulder. He had already pressed on the operating lever and watched the magazine creeping through the aperture. With all ready for aligning the sights, he manipulated the hammer with his right forefinger.

Sighting at Al along the forty and five-sixteenths of an inch octagonal barrel, Ole Devil selected him because his rifle was most probably unfired and, at that distance he would be the most dangerous of the four. Squeezing the trigger, the Texian felt the thrust of the recoil. Although smoke swirled briefly between them, his shooting instincts told him that he had held true.

Caught in the chest by a ·45 calibre bullet, Al was knocked backwards from his saddle and the rifle pirouetted out of his hand. The other three men were surprised that their intended victim had been able to fire as they had not seen him do anything which they could identify as recharging his weapon.

'What the hell—?' Soapy ejaculated, glaring from Verde to Mucker.

'It must have two barrels!' the *vaquero* answered, although he had a suspicion that was incorrect. 'Keep going, it's empty now!'

As double-barrelled rifles were not uncommon, Soapy and Mucker were inclined to accept Verde's solution. However, they were puzzled to see Ole Devil was still lining the rifle. So was the *vaquero*, but his thoughts on the matter ended in consternation as he realized that the strange weapon was being directed towards him. Before he could do anything to save himself, it spoke again. Shot in the head, he crumpled from his horse and was dead by the time his body struck the ground.

'What the hell kind of gun's that?' Mucker wailed, trying to slow down his racing horse.

'Come on!' Soapy ordered, being made of sterner stuff than his lanky companion. 'It must be empty now.'

Seeing that the last two men were not turning aside, as he had hoped they would, Ole Devil made ready to deal with them. He took no pleasure in what he was having to do, but knew he had no other choice. Not only were the approaching pair traitors to Texas, but neither of them would hesitate to kill him, or the girl, if they were given the chance. Should they capture the girl after disposing of him, her fate was likely to be worse than a quick death.

Operating the mechanism of the Browning, Ole Devil turned its barrel towards Soapy. While Mucker was doing as his companion had ordered, he showed less resolution and was allowing the other man to draw ahead.

Finding himself the object of their intended victim's attentions, Soapy thrust out and sighted his pistol as well as he could from the back of his galloping mount. He stood up on his stirrup irons, letting the empty rifle slip from under his leg, in an attempt to form a steadier base for his efforts. Fifty yards was a long range for a hand-gun, but he had seen sufficient of the Texian's marksmanship not to chance holding his fire until he was closer. The pistol bellowed and the sound coming so close to the horse's ear caused it to swerve.

Although the bullet threw up dirt between Old Devil's feet without harming him, the shot was not entirely wasted. Squeezing the rifle's trigger, he saw his target swing aside and, being too late to prevent the discharge, knew that he had missed.

Thrusting down on the lever with his right thumb, Ole Devil switched his aim to Mucker as the magazine crept onwards to position the final chamber in front of the barrel's bore. The lanky man might be allowing his companion to take the lead, but he still held a loaded weapon. Ignoring Soapy, the Texian turned loose his last available bullet. Attempting to steer his mount so as to put Soapy between them, Mucker caught the lead in his right shoulder. Screeching in agony, he lost his balance and toppled from the saddle.

That still left Soapy!

Seeing that he had missed with his pistol, he regained control of his horse and sent it tearing onwards. Hurling the empty weapon ahead of him, he saw Ole Devil fend it off with the barrel of the rifle. Reaching for one of the pistols which were hanging in their holsters from his saddlehorn, he knew that he would need time to open the flap and draw it. Guiding the horse straight at the Texian, so as to ride him down, Soapy hoped to gain it. Just a moment too late, he realized that the 'boy' was raising a pistol in both hands and lining it at him.

'Take him, Di!' Ole Devil yelled as he threw himself aside, hoping that the girl would at least be able to create a diversion.

Even as the Texian moved and shouted, he heard the deep-throated boom of a pistol. Looking up, he saw Soapy's head slam back and the hat flying from it. The speeding horse missed Ole Devil by inches as it passed between him and the girl. Its rider's lifeless body was already starting to slide from its back as it went by.

After glancing to where Mucker was sprawled face down and motionless, having been knocked unconscious when he landed from the fall, Ole Devil turned his gaze to Di. She was lowering the smoking Manton pistol and did not appear to be distressed, or even greatly concerned, by having had to kill a man.

However, as it had been because of him that her life had been endangered, the Texian doubted whether his standing with her grandfather would be improved.

CHAPTER ELEVEN

HE WANTS 'EM AND HE CAME FIRST

'GRANDPAPPY EWART, this here's Cap'n Hardin,' Diamond-Hitch Charlotte Jane Martha Brindley announced, leading the way into the sparsely furnished main room of her home. 'He's come over from San Antone with a message from General Sam—'

The introduction came to an end as the girl realized that her grandfather was not alone.

Without having waited to discuss what had happened, Di and Ole Devil Hardin had made sure that they had nothing further to fear from their attackers. Arnaldo Verde, Soapy and Al had all been dead. However, on examining Mucker, the girl had stated that, while he was still unconscious, his wound was not too serious and he would live. Then she had requested to be told why the quartet had attacked them, only now her opinion of Ole Devil was so improved that she spoke without making it a demand.

Noticing the change which had come over the girl, Ole Devil had given a full explanation. On learning that he believed the two attacks were attempts to prevent him from reaching her grandfather and being told the purpose of the visit, she had said they should question their captive on his recovery. Ole Devil had agreed that such would be their best line of action.

Looking a trifle sheepish, Di had thanked the Texian for saving her from the bear and he had returned the compliment with regard to Soapy. Neither of them had referred to the spanking which had been the unfortunate aftermath of her rescue. Instead, she had offered to have the men she would be sending from the ranch to collect the bear's carcass bring in the three bodies for burial at the same time.

Accepting the girl's offer, Ole Devil had agreed with her further suggestion that he went to see if he could catch some of the horses while she attended to Mucker's wound. On being asked if she would be safe, she had requested the means to reload the Manton pistol and, with it done, had declared that she could 'chill the ornery son-of-a-bitch's milk happen he woke up feeling feisty.' Confident that she could do so if it should become necessary, Ole Devil had mounted the dun and set off. Neither the horse he had been riding nor Di's *tobiano* gelding were in view, so he went after and succeeded in retrieving the mounts of the three white renegades. Verde's horse had been nowhere to be seen and he had not wasted time searching for it. On his return, he had found that Mucker was still unconscious but Di had done a very competent job of bandaging the wounded shoulder.

While they were waiting for Mucker to recover so that he could be questioned, Ole Devil had searched the bodies. He had found nothing, but put off an examination of their bed-rolls until he and the girl had arrived at her home. Di had gathered up the second Manton pistol and her rifle. On checking the latter to find out why it had failed her, she had concluded that the powder in the frizzen pan must have slipped away from the vent hole so that, when it was ignited, the flame had not reached the main charge in the barrel. After she had commented on the matter to Ole Devil, they had reached an amicable agreement about how they should address each other.

When Mucker had regained consciousness – he had been in a state of shock although neither of his captors had identified it by such a name – incoherent and unable to answer questions. Di had suggested that they took him back to the ranch and let him rest until the following morning. He had been barely able to sit his horse and had had to be tied on the saddle.

During the journey, Ole Devil had satisfied the girl's curiosity regarding the Browning rifle. They had also found his borrowed horse standing with its reins tangled in a bush. On arriving at the ranch, without having seen Di's *tobiano*, they discovered the corrals and barn to be deserted. Hearing a lot of noise from the cookshack, she had decided that the hired hands were having their suppers. Having no wish to disturb the men, she had suggested they should deliver Houston's message to her grandfather. Securing their prisoner had been no problem, even if his physical condition had been less enfeebled. The Brindleys' cook, an aged Tejas Indian called Waldo, occasionally went on a drinking bout. To prevent him from causing trouble – liquor had that effect on him – they had had a storeroom in the barn fitted with a sturdy door and strong iron bars at the window. Leaving the key in the lock – having placed Mucker on Waldo's bed – so that the cook could fetch him some coffee, Di had accompanied Ole Devil to the house.

Following the girl into the room, so that she could introduce him before going to make arrangements for feeding and guarding Mucker and having the bear and bodies collected, Ole Devil looked at the two men who were sitting on the only two remaining chairs at the table. He did not need to be told which of them was the girl's grandfather. Nor did he need to seek an explanation for the meagre nature of the furnishings. According to the girl, the majority of their portable property had already been sent to the east.

Ewart Brindley was not much taller than Di's five foot seven, but made up in breadth for what he lacked in height. Despite his age, he looked as hard and fit as a man much below his years. Almost bald, with his remaining hair a grizzled white, his leathery, sun-reddened face suggested not so much a bad temper but one which, like his granddaughter's, was quick and high. He was dressed in much the same way as the girl, with a bowie knife hanging from his belt. There was a spectacle case on the table in front of him.

Matching Ole Devil in height and build, the other occupant of the room would be in his mid-thirties, had dark brown hair and was suavely handsome. He was dressed in expensive, if travel-strained, riding clothes of the style much fancied by wealthy French Creoles in Louisiana. A shining black, silver-headed walking cane lay with his white 'planter's' hat on the table and he did not appear to be armed. He had stood up when Di entered, but had turned his gaze to Ole Devil when he had heard the name she mentioned.

'Howdy there,' Brindley greeted, his voice having a kind of high and harsh tone, also subjecting the young Texian to an interested scrutiny. 'What'd you say, Di – gal?'

'Cap'n Hardin's brought you a message from General Houston,' the girl answered, daring a curious and interrogatory glance at the handsome visitor. 'Set 'n' take the weight off your feet, mister—?'

'Now what'd General Sam be wanting from me, young feller? Brindley inquired, ignoring what he had known to be his granddaughter's hint about the identity of the man at the table and the reason for his presence.

'It's a confidential matter, sir,' Ole Devil replied, flickering a look to where there other visitor was sitting.

'Happen you've come about using my mules,' Brindley drawled and jerked a thumb in the well-dressed visitor's direction. 'Mr. Galsworthy here, he wants 'em and he came first.'

Having delivered the information, the old man settled back on his chair and eyed the young Texian in a challenging fashion. Clearly he was waiting to discover how his news would be received.

Knowing that the correct response could be vital, Ole Devil thought fast. Possibly Brindley was anticipating a demand that the General's requirements should be given priority over private business. Or he might be expecting an appeal to his patriotism. Remembering Houston's comments regarding Brindley's contrary nature, Ole Devil felt certain that neither was the way to handle the situation.

'That's between you and Mr. Galsworthy, sir,' the Texian stated, meeting the old man's gaze without flinching and pleased with the opportunity to watch for evidence of how his words were being received. 'But I hope that you'll be willing to read the General's letter.'

'You couldn't ask for nothing fairer than that,' Brindley declared, although his face showed nothing of his feelings. He turned his eyes to the second visitor and went on, 'What do you reckon, Mr. Galsworthy?'

'Well, sir,' the handsome man replied and, despite his style of dress, he spoke with the accent of a well-educated citizen of Boston. There was a hint of icy arrogance in his voice, as if he was used to giving orders and having them carried out unhesitatingly. 'As I told you, my property is valuable and I'm willing to pay a high price to have it transported east. But, if General Houston needs your mules for some official purpose, I'm willing to withdraw any claim I might have on them. After all, the Republic of Texas must come first.'

'Be it official business they're wanted for, Cap'n Hardin?' Brindley asked.

'Yes, sir,' Ole Devil confirmed and gave his attention to Galsworthy, noticing that the other seemed to be avoiding looking him in the eyes. 'Thank you, sir. That's generous of you.'

'I'm merely doing my duty as I see it, captain,' Galsworthy answered and once again stood up. Taking his hat and cane from the table, he continued, 'As your business is confidential, I'll wait outside.'

'Ain't no call to sit out out on the porch, mister,' Brindley remarked. 'Hey, Di-gal, seeing's how Waldo's off feeding the boys, how's about taking this gent into the kitchen and giving him a cup of coffee while I find out what General Sam wants?'

'Sure thing,' the girl assented cheerfully. 'Come on, Mr. Galsworthy and I'll tend to it. You want I should fetch some in for you and Fancy Pants, Grandpappy Ewart?'

'How about it – cap'n?' Brindley asked, having turned a speculative gaze on the Texian when his granddaughter had used the sobriquet.

'I'd admire to take a cup, Miss Charlotte,' Ole Devil confirmed and watched the old man's head swivel rapidly between himself and Di in what would one day become known as a 'double take'. 'Black with sugar.'

'How many times do you want it stirred and shall I blow on it to cool it down?' the girl grinned. 'That's what you're used to, I'd reckon.'

'No, ma'am,' Ole Devil contradicted, watching Brindley's reaction to the by-play. 'My folks brought me up to be self-reliant and always made me blow on my own.'

'Allus did like a self-reliant feller,' Di drawled. 'Come on, Mr. Galsworthy.'

'Well I'll be hornswoggled!' Brindley ejaculated, after his granddaughter and Galsworthy had left the room closing the door behind them. 'She was like to bust the last feller's called her "Charlotte's" jaw-bone.'

'We came to an agreement soon after we met, sir,' Ole Devil explained cheerfully and truthfully, sensing that his host was impressed. 'Arranged that I wouldn't object to her calling me "Fancy Pants" once in a while and she'd let me use her given name in return.'

'Sit down, damn it, young feller,' Brindley requested and there was more than a hint of respect in his cracked old voice. 'Let's take a look at what Sam's got to be writing about.'

Reaching to the front of his shirt, as he took the seat which Galsworthy had vacated, Ole Devil produced a thin oilskin wallet from his inside pocket. Extracting the letter which Houston had given to him, he passed it to the old man. Brindley opened the flap of the envelope, took out the sheet of paper and spread it before him on the table. Then he removed the spectacles from the case and donned them. With his lips moving and silently mouthing the words, he started to read. On coming to the paragraph about Ole Devil, he lifted his eyes and looked at the object of the comments for a moment. Then he finished the letter.

'General Sam seems to set a whole lot of store on getting these rifles, young feller,' the old man commented as he removed his spectacles and leaned back.

'Yes, sir,' Ole Devil replied. 'Like he says, they could make a lot of difference when the time comes for us to take our stand against Santa Anna in open battle.'

'Likely,' Brindley grunted in a non-committal tone. 'How'd you aim to go about doing it?'

'Well, sir,' Ole Devil answered, sensing a challenge and selecting his words with care. 'Before I decide on that, I'd like to know whether you'd be willing to do as the General asks?'

'And just supposing I am?'

'Then the problem's at least partly solved, sir.'

'How do you mean, *partly* solved?' Brindley demanded. 'You reckon I can't handle it, or something?'

'No, sir,' Ole Devil assured his host, whose tone had been prickly with indignation. 'It's just that the situation has changed.'

'How?'

'The Mexicans know about the shipment.'

'The hell you say!' Brindley ejaculated. He glared at the letter, which had explained why it had not been felt necessary to send a military guard. 'How'd that happened?

'I've no idea, sir,' Ole Devil confessed. 'The General and I were alone when we made the arrangements. We thought that as only he and I – or so we assumed – knew how I was hoping to make the collection, I wouldn't need a escort if you agreed to handle it. Then I was jumped by a bunch of renegades before I'd reached Guadalupe. We downed two, but the rest got away—'

'*We?*'

'I had a man with me, sir. But I sent him back to warn the General that there's a spy at his headquarters.'

'You did right there,' Brindley praised. 'It's something he should know. Are you sure that's why they jumped you?'

'Near enough, sir,' Ole Devil replied. While speaking, he had continued to watch his host's face. The examination was not particulary fruitful, for the leathery features were showing as little of Brindley's feelings as Houston's had during the earlier stages of the interview in his office. Which did nothing to make him more at ease as he realized that he was approaching the point where he would have to admit he had already placed the old timer's granddaughter in considerable danger. However, he also guessed that it would be advisable to let Brindley learn about the incident from him. 'The four who got away were waiting and jumped me just after I'd met Di.'

'They try *real* hard to do it?' the old man growled.

'Hard enough, sir,' Ole Devil confessed and, without elaborating upon the incident with the bear, described the fight that had followed the quartet's arrival. He finished by saying, 'I'm sorry it had to happen, sir, but Di had to kill the last of them—'

'You'd rather he'd've killed you, or her?'

'No, sir, but—'

'That fancy rifle of your'n was empty, way you told me, and she'd got your pistol?'

'Yes, sir.'

'Then somebody had to stop that jasper and she was the one best suited to do it, I'd reckon.'

'I'm not gainsaying that, sir,' Ole Devil replied. 'But Di's—'

'I've never figured she was a *man*, no matter how I've raised her,' Brindley interrupted and his harsh tones were strangely gentle. 'Boy, Di had to burn down a Comanche buck when she was fourteen. Eighteen months later, she blew half the head off a drunken *Chicano* 's'd got the notion of laying hands on her. 'Tween then 'n' now, she's been in three Injun attacks and done her share to finish 'em. Maybe that wouldn't be counted lady-like, nor even proper, back in the U.S. of A., but Texas's a long ways different. I've reared her to know how to defend herself. So I'm not holding it again' you 'cause she's had to do what I taught her.'

'Thank you, sir,' Ole Devil said sincerely.

'Do you reckon there's more of them varmints?' Brindley inquired, with the air of getting down to business.

'I'm not sure, sir,' Ole Devil answered. 'If there are, I'd have expected them all to be along after the first try had failed. The wounded man would know for sure, but he's in no condition to answer questions.'

'Maybe you didn't ask him the right way,' Brindley suggested.

'Maybe, sir,' Ole Devil conceded. 'But I think we'll get more out of him when he's rested, in his right mind, and has had time to think about his position.'

'Huh!' the old man grunted, but did not pursue the matter any further. 'Way I see it, we don't have too much time to get to Santa Cristobal Bay.'

'No, sir.'

'So how're *you* planning to handle the mule train?'

'I once tried to teach my grandmother how to suck eggs, sir,' Ole Devil drawled, having detected another challenge. 'She took a hickory-switch to my hide. One thing about me, I learn fast and easily – and it sticks once I've learned it.'

'What's that mean?' Brindley asked, although his attitude suggested he knew and approved.

'I'm just the General's messenger, sir,' Ole Devil replied. 'If he hadn't considered that you were competent to handle the collection, he'd never have suggested that I came.'

At that moment, the kitchen door was opened and Di entered. She was carrying a tray, with a sugar basin, milk jug and two steaming cups of coffee.

'Where's Mr. Galsworthy?' Brindley wanted to know when the man did not follow his granddaughter into the room.

'Just now gone,' the girl replied. 'Said to tell you "Good-bye and thanks for listening." Reckoned he'd head over to Gonzales and see if there was any other way he could get his gear shifted east. When do we pull out, Grandpappy Ewart?'

'How do you know we will be?' the old man demanded, accepting the cup which – having set the tray on the table – she was offering to him.

'Five hundred rifles, say ten pounds apiece; which I'd sooner go over than under,' Di remarked, half to herself and ignoring her grandfather's question as she passed the second cup to Ole Devil. Hooking her rump on the edge of the table, she screwed up her eyes and was clearly doing some mental calculations. 'Take 'em out of their boxes 'n' wrap 'em in rawhide, we could manage twenty-six to a mule. Be better at twenty-four though, which'll mean using twenty-one knobheads* for 'em. Another twenty to tote the ammunition. Fifty ought to be enough. Which's lucky, 'cause that's all we've got on hand.' Her gaze

* Knobhead: derogatory name for a mule.

114

flickered to the younger of her audience. 'What do you say?'

'You put the sugar in,' Ole Devil drawled. 'But you forgot to blow on it.'

'That mean you agree, or you don't?' Di challenged.

'I'd say that the agreeing to how it's to be done stands between yourself and your grandfather,' Ole Devil countered. 'What I could do, sir, is go to in to Gonzales and ask Colonel Gray if he can let us have enough men to act as escort to the Bay.'

'Why'd we need them?' Di asked, just a trifle indignantly.

'Those four renegades could have friends,' Ole Devil pointed out. 'And if they have, we'll most likely have them to content with.'

'I don't recollect's how Grandpappy Ewart 'n' me's ever needed to ask Lawyer Gray to do our fighting for us,' the girl protested. 'Nor anybody else, comes right down to it.'

'I'm not gainsaying *that*,' Ole Devil assured her. 'It's one of the reasons why I didn't bring men from San Antonio. But seeing how important our mission is and that we don't know for sure what we might run up against—'

'We've got a feller close by's could maybe help us on *that*,' Brindley pointed out, with the air of having solved their problem.

'Yes, sir,' Ole Devil agreed. 'If you want to go and question him—'

'Way he is, it wouldn't do a whole heap of good,' Di warned. 'I thought we'd decided to leave him until morning.'

'Sure we did,' Ole Devil conceded. 'But if you want us to—'

'I've not seen anything to make me think you pair don't know what you're doing,' answered Brindley, to whom the words had been directed. 'So I'll go along with it.'

'Anyways, sir,' Ole Devil drawled, not a little impressed by what he knew to be a compliment. 'I'll look in on him while I'm attending to my horses. Which I'd like to make a start at, if that's all right with you.'

'Go to it,' Brindley authorized.

'Can I take it that you'll collect the shipment for me, sir?' Ole Devil asked as he came to his feet.

'You can take it,' Brindley confirmed. 'We'll talk out the details over supper.'

Leaving the house, accompanied by Di, Ole Devil noticed

Galsworthy riding along the trail through the gathering darkness. Ignoring the departing man, they went to the barn. On unlocking and opening the storeroom, they found their prisoner was laying on the bed. Mucker was covered by a blanket and apparently sleeping.

'Shall I wake him?' Ole Devil inquired.

'I wouldn't, was I you,' the girl answered. 'Fellers I've seen took like he was when they'd been hurt got over it better if we let 'em sleep.'

'That's what I've found, too,' Ole Devil agreed and closed the door.

On their arrival to carry out the interrogation the following morning, Ole Devil and Di learned that they had been in a serious error regarding Mucker's condition. Going in to rouse him, they found that he had been stabbed through the heart with a thin-bladed weapon – and had been dead for several hours.

CHAPTER TWELVE

IT WAS MY FAULT, SIR

'Son-of-a-bitch!' Diamond-Hitch Brindley ejaculated, taking an involuntary step to the rear as she stared at the lifeless body on the bed. 'How the hell did this happen?'

'I'm more interested in who did it,' Ole Devil Hardin answered, studying the wound and taking note of the small amount of blood which had oozed from it. 'Because he sure as hell didn't do it himself.'

'None of *our* boys'd do it!' Di declared.

'I never thought they had,' Ole Devil assured her.

'Galsworthy!' the girl spat the name out.

'What about him?' Ole Devil inquired, although he had been considering the handsome man as a possible suspect.

'It must have been him!' Di stated.

'How did he know about this feller?' Ole Devil challenged.

'I – I told him!' Di admitted and, as the young Texian swung to face her, took on the attitude of defiance which he remembered from the previous afternoon. 'Hell, the walls of our place're so thin that he could hear what you and Grandpappy Ewart was saying. So I figured on stopping him listening and reckoned he'd be interested in hearing about them four fellers jumping us.'

'And as soon as you'd mentioned this feller, he said he'd be going,' Ole Devil guessed.

'Not *straight* after,' the girl contradicted. 'He finished his coffee, then asked if I reckoned Grandpappy'd do what the General wanted and I told him it was likely. So he said he'd head for Gonzales and see if he could make other arrangements.'

'You weren't to know what he was planning,' Ole Devil drawled. 'I'll say one thing, though. If it *was* him, he's a cool son-of-a-bitch. He must have come straight over here, let himself in, killed and covered this feller up and left, all within about five minutes.'

'We'd best go tell Grandpappy Ewart,' Di sighed.

'What've you got to tell me about?' Ewart Brindley's cracked tones inquired from outside the storeroom.

Turning, the girl and Ole Devil saw the old timer approaching across the barn. They stood aside and let him through. Then, after he had looked at the corpse, he turned his cold gaze upon them.

Although the young Texian met Brindley's scrutiny, he was far less at ease than showed on the surface. The previous night had done much to cement the amicable relationship that had been developing. Over supper, Di had told of how she had been saved from the bear. As he had been receiving the old man's gruff thanks, Ole Devil had sensed that the matter had cut deeper than heart-felt gratitude. Unless he was mistaken, Brindley had been impressed by the fact that he had not attempted to use the rescue as a means of attaining his ends. Nor had his prestige diminished when, after having eaten and made a fruitless search of the renegades' bed-rolls – which had been fetched from the barn by two of the hired hands who had said that the prisoner was still sleeping – he had spent an enjoyable evening in the company of his host and hostess. He had taken a lively and genuine interest in their arrangements for transporting the shipment, while also making it plain that he considered it was their concern and he would be merely an official passenger. In return, they had questioned him about the bid for independence and the state of affairs to the west. As they were supporters of Houston's policies, there had been no cause for controversy between them.

All in all, Ole Devil had gone to spread his bed-roll on the floor of the guestroom with a sense of achievement. His diplomatic handling of the Brindleys had, he felt sure, established the grounds for complete co-operation based on a mutual liking, trust and respect for each other's abilities.

Finding the man murdered, when they had hoped that he would supply them with vitally important information, might easily ruin all that had been achieved. However, Ole Devil knew what must be done.

'It was my fault, sir—' the young Texian began.

'No more'n mine!' Di interrupted and told Brindley what

118

had happened between herself and Galsworthy in the kitchen. 'Hell, I never thought—'

'Nope, and neither did either of us,' Brindley put in soothingly, glancing at Ole Devil as if in search of confirmation. After he had received a nod of agreement, he went on. 'I never took to that jasper, though. He never looked me straight in the eye when we was talking.'

'I noticed that, sir,' Ole Devil admitted. 'But I've known a few gambling men who wouldn't and that's what I took him to be.'

'And me,' Brindley declared. 'But it looks like he was tied in with them other four. Which fetches up another right puzzling point.'

'Why'd he come here?' Di concluded for her grandfather.

'That's the one, gal,' Brindley confirmed. 'Either of you smart young 'n's got the answer?'

'He was counting on them getting you, Devil,' Di suggested. 'So he came here to see if he could hire our mules and us to help him collect the shipment.'

'It's possible,' Ole Devil conceded. 'Did he tell you what he wanted moving, sir, or anything about himself?'

'Not a whole heap about either,' Brindley replied. 'He reckoned he'd come up from Victoria and had some supplies's he wanted to take east afore the Mexican army got there. Wasn't nothing about him to make me think otherwise. Anyways, you pair came in afore we could do much talking.'

'He must've been with those four yahoos when they first saw you, Devil,' Di guessed. 'Then headed here after he'd sent them to get you. I'd swear that he didn't know we'd fetched one of 'em in alive until I told him.'

'His hoss wasn't lathered when he got here,' Brindley contented. 'Which it would've been had he come as fast's he'd of needed to if he had known. I reckon you could be right, Di-gal. Only, him saying he'd come from Victoria, it doesn't sound like he was after using the mules to collect the rifles.'

'He might have come to find out what he'd be up against if I should get by his men,' Ole Devil surmised. 'Or so that they could make you do what they wanted if I hadn't. You know, I couldn't help thinking yesterday that he didn't strike me as the kind of man who would give up as easily as he did when he found out that General Houston needed your mules.'

'He gave a good reason for doing it,' Brindley reminded his guest. 'A lot of folks, some's you wouldn't expect it from, are putting Texas afore themselves these days. Wasn't no reason why he shouldn't be.'

'God damn it to hell!' Di spat out furiously and indicated the body with an angry gesture. 'If we'd made him talk—'

'There was no way we could have, the state he was in,' Ole Devil pointed out.

'Even if it did come out wrong, you was both acting for the best by leaving him to sleep,' Brindley interposed. 'Anyways, there's not a whole heap of sense in crying over spilled milk. What we've got to do now is figure how we're going to play out the deal, way it's gone.'

'We could send Joe Galton and a couple of the boys after Galsworthy,' Di offered. 'A dude like him couldn't hide his sign so they can't find it.'

'He'll be long gone by now and might not be all that easy to find,' Ole Devil warned. 'Even if he is a dude, those four who were with him weren't and he could have more of them with range savvy. In fact, I'd bet on it. He must have been counting on us not finding out he'd killed the man until it was too dark for us to pick up his tracks. Which means he wasn't going to stay on the Gonzales trail. So he either knew he could find his way across country, or had somebody waiting who could.'

'I still say Joe and the boys could trail him,' Di insisted.

'Don't let me talk you out of the notion,' Ole Devil replied. 'It'll be a big help if we can find out just what we're up against.'

'I'll float my stick along of you on that, Devil,' Brindley drawled. 'Go and tell Joe, Di-gal.'

'Sure,' the girl answered, nodding to the corpse. 'I'll have him took out and buried while I'm at it.'

'Might's well,' Brindley agreed. 'It's got to be done.'

'You wouldn't change your mind about me going into Gonzales and asking Colonel Gray for an escort, would you sir?' Ole Devil inquired as he and the old man followed Di into the barn.

'That side of it's up to you, boy,' Brindley replied. 'But I'd sooner not. Like I said last night, all his men have families to move east. They'd not rest easy going off and leaving 'em to do it. Anyways, my boys've gone through Kiowa, Wichita and Comanche country 'n' come out of 'em all with their hair. So I

120

reckon we could handle anything a bunch of white fellers try to pull on us.'

All of Ole Devil's last lingering anxieties left him as he listened to the first sentence of the answer. It implied that, despite the murder of their prisoner, the old man still respected Hardin's opinion and judgement.

'What I'll do,' Brindley continued, 'is have Tom Wolf and his boys ride with the train.'

'How about your place here, sir?' Ole Devil asked, being aware that his host had intended to leave half a dozen men as guards for the property.

'They couldn't have stopped the Mexicans burning it down, happen the army comes through this way,' Brindley answered. 'And there won't be all that damned much left for anybody to steal. So they'll be more use with us than sitting on their butts here.'

'We'll forget Colonel Gray then, sir,' Ole Devil stated, being satisfied that his host would not have reached such a decision if he had had doubts over their ability to manage without a military escort. 'From what I've seen of them, your men can take care of themselves.'

'You can count on it, boy,' Brindley grinned, pleased that his guest was showing such confidence in his men. 'They're not Mission Indians. Let's drift on out and see what's doing. I want to be moving out in an hour.'

Ole Devil's acceptance had not been made merely to please his host. All of the mule-packers were Tejas Indians. However, he had noticed that they were lean, tough-looking men with an air of hardy self-reliance that made them very different from those members of their tribe who had fallen into the hands of the Spanish priests. That was one of the factors which was causing him to go along with Brindley's wishes. He also agreed with the old man that the escort soldiers from Colonel Gray would probably react unhappily at being taken away from their families at such a time.

Emerging from the barn, Ole Devil looked around. Not far away, Di was talking to Joe Galton. A tall, red-haired Texian of about twenty, dressed in buckskins, Galton was Brindley's adopted son and acted as *cargador** for the train. They had met the previous night, after Galton had returned from a successful hunt for camp meat. Ole Devil had found him quiet but

* Cargador: second-in-command and assistant pack-master.

friendly. Out of the *cargador's* hearing, Di had claimed he was not only good at his duties but was also an excellent farrier.

Turning as the girl walked away, Galton called two names and was joined by a pair of the Indians. They went to the corral, collected horses, and started to make ready for leaving. Going across to Galton, Ole Devil told him about Tommy Okasi and requested that if they met, the *cargador* would bring him to the pack train.

Having received Galton's promise on the matter, Ole Devil turned his attention to the preparations which were being made for the train's departure. While he had made use of a pack horse on more than one occasion, he had never before seen professional muleteers at work and found it interesting. There was a lot of apparently confused activity taking place, but it was all being carried out in a purposeful manner that told of long experience. Taking in all the sights, he realized that he was watching the cream of the mule-packing industry in action.

At General Houston's request, so as to prevent such fine animals from falling into the hands of the Mexican army, Brindley had sent the majority of his stock and hired hands to Washington-on-the-Brazos. It said much for the high esteem in which the normally fiercely independent old man held the General that he had retained the pick of his packers and mules in case they should be needed.

After a few minutes Old Devil became aware of Di's behaviour. Unlike her grandfather, who appeared to stay in the background and let the men carry on, she went from one group to another. Yet the Texian could see no reason for her doing it. The men were all obviously competent and did their work in a swift, capable manner. Suddenly she swung on her heel and came to stand at Ole Devil's side.

'Joe and the boys're on their way,' the girl remarked, nodding towards the corral. 'He says he'll catch up with us some time tomorrow, or later.'

'Huh huh!' Ole Devil replied, continuing to watch the work that was going on all around him. 'These men of yours are very good.'

'They should be,' Di answered, trying to sound off-handed but unable to conceal her pleasure at the compliment. 'Grandpappy Ewart trained each and every one of 'em. And don't you worry none, happen that Galsworthy *hombre* tries to jump us, you'll find they're just as good at fighting.'

'I've never doubted *that*,' Ole Devil assured her. 'Is there anything I can do to help?'

'Nope,' Di said and made as if to move away. Instead, she remained by him and went on, 'how much do you know about mule packing?'

'Not a whole heap,' Ole Devil confessed.

During the three-quarters of an hour that was needed to complete the preparations, Di told Ole Devil what was being done and why. In addition, she gave him much information about various aspects of handling a mule train when it was on the move. She talked all the time with a feverish zest, but not always in a smooth flow.

Before many minutes had passed, Ole Devil guessed what lay behind the girl's loquacity. Disturbed by the thought that she might never see her home again if the bid for independence failed or it should be destroyed by the Mexican army, she wanted something to take her mind off of leaving. So he listened and, when she showed signs of drying up, managed to find some fresh point upon which she could enlighten him.

At last everything was ready. Ole Devil noticed that Brindley's usually emotionless face showed that he too was feeling some strain over going away from his home. There was a catch in his voice as he gave the order to mount up and move out. Then, having swung astride his big *grulla** gelding, he gave his granddaughter a comforting smile. Having done so, he started the horse moving with the bell-mare stepping forward at its side. Hearing the tinkling of the bell, the mules surged into motion and the packers formed up about them.†

The day's journey was uneventful, except that Di rode ahead for a time. When Ole Devil caught up with her, there was evidence on her face that she had been crying. Neither of them ever referred to the fact that she had been in tears. However, the girl was anything but her usual cheery self as she continued to ride between Ole Devil and her grandfather.

The pack train was travelling with a scout ahead, one on each flank and two more bringing up the rear. At nightfall, Tom Wolf came in to say that he had seen nothing to suggest Galsworthy and his men were in the vicinity. Before going to sleep,

* Grulla: a bluish-grey horse much the same colour as a sandhill crane.

† The formation and organization of a mule train, including the function of the bell-mare is given in detail in: *Get Urrea*.

123

Ole Devil had the satisfaction of knowing that he was about twenty miles closer to his destination.

Moving on soon after dawn, the party progressed without incident until shortly after midday. While the animals were being rested, the Tejas packer who had been at the rear with Tom Wolf arrived with a warning that four riders were following them. Accompanied by Di, who was still disturbed and unhappy, Ole Devil returned with the man. They found there was no cause for alarm.

'It's Joe and the boys,' Di said, studying the four riders. 'Is that your man who's with them, Devil?'

'It is,' the Texian agreed, having identified the small figure who was leading a spare horse. 'That's Tommy Okasi. I wonder what he's got to tell us?'

CHAPTER THIRTEEN

I THINK SHE IS THEIR PRISONER

'TOMMY'S wig-wagging for us to catch up with him,' Diamond-Hitch Brindley remarked, pointing to where the little Oriental was sitting his bay gelding just below the top of a slope about a quarter of a mile ahead. 'Looks like there's something on the other side's he reckons we should see.'

'But we shouldn't let see us,' Ole Devil Hardin supplemented, taking notice of how Tonny Okasi was carefully avoiding showing himself to whatever – or whoever – was beyond the rim. Reaching down, he eased the Browning rifle from its saddleboot and, as he made ready to load it, nodded at the flintlock across the crook of the girl's left arm. 'Make sure that the powder hasn't shifted in the pan this time.'

'Yah!' Di scoffed, although she started to do as her companion suggested. 'At least I can carry mine ready to be used.'

Listening to the girl's response, Ole Devil was pleased to observe that she was more her usual cheerful self. She appeared to have thrown off the depression and gloom which had been caused by the thought of having left her home. It was clear that the decision to let her accompany Tommy and himself to Santa Cristobal Bay had been a wise one. It had come about because of the news which had been brought by Tommy and Joe Galton.

On learning that there must be a spy at his headquarters, General Houston had immediately started an investigation. However, the little Oriental had not waited to discover what had come of it.* Instead, armed with a written authority from the General, he had set out to rejoin Ole Devil. Riding relay

* The investigation was successful. On being told about the spy and asked if he had seen anything suspicious, First Sergeant Gladbeck remembered finding Juglares in the wine cellar and realized that it was directly beneath the General's office. Comparing the time at

125

and changing horses at Guadalupe and Gonzales, but keeping his bay with him, he had made very fast time. Meeting Galton and the Tejas, he had identified himself as the man Ole Devil was expecting and had accompanied them for the remainder of the journey.

While it had not been completely successful, Galton's mission had not proved a complete waste of time either. Without having produced definite confirmation, his findings implied that Galsworthy was not what he had pretended to be. What was more, despite his appearance, he had shown himself capable of covering his tracks along the route in which he was travelling. Even men as skilled as Galton and the two Tejas braves had had difficulty in following him. They had known that, as long as he kept moving, there was little chance of them catching up with him.

After having left the Gonzales trail about two miles from the Brindleys' ranch, Galsworthy had ridden west and met five companions at a small, deserted cabin. From there, the party had headed south. As they were swinging clear of the town, one of their number had left them to take a westerly direction. After covering about ten miles, Galton had stopped following them. They had shown no sign of altering their direction and he had considered that he would be more usefully occupied with the pack train.

Discussing Galton's information, Ole Devil and the Brindleys had decided that as long as Galsworthy had only four men with him he did not pose any direct threat to them. However, as he was travelling south, he might be making for a rendezvous with a force sent from the Mexican army. In which case, their position would be far more dangerous.

Taking into consideration the attempts upon his life and the fact that Galsworthy had sent a man to the west, Ole Devil had suggested that he might not have informed his employers about the shipment. If that should be so, he could be looking for assistance to deal with the situation. He was almost certain to

which Gladbeck had met the major domo with the information given in Ole Devil's report, Houston deduced that Juglares must be their man. So a trap had been laid. Calling Colonels Bowie and Travis in for a conference, Houston made sure that the major domo heard it would be one of considerable importance. He had been caught on top of the wine-rack and met the appropriate end for a spy.

be in possession of an identification document similar to the one which Ole Devil had taken from Halford's body. So he would have the means to enforce his request with any of Santa Anna's outfits that he came across. While it could prove serious, that possibility had not unduly alarmed Ole Devil and his companions. Unless Galsworthy or his men were fortunate enough to find the Mexicans in the next two days, he would reach Santa Cristobal Bay too late to prevent the shipment from being landed.

Having already explained the need to avoid the possibility of international repercussions, Ole Devil had warned his companions that the landing was the most critical period of the collection. Once the rifles were on shore and the ship had sailed, there was no way in which the Mexicans could prove that they had come from the United States. With that in mind, Ole Devil had proposed that he and Tommy should go ahead of the pack train at their best speed. When they reached Santa Cristobal Bay, they could make sure that there were neither Mexican troops nor Galsworthy and his renegades in the vicinity. If either should be around, they would find some way to alert the captain to the danger.

On her grandfather agreeing, Di had suggested that she should accompany Ole Devil and Tommy. Her argument had been that, if the ship arrived and there were no enemies present, she could help to prepare the rifles for being transported on the mules. They could, she had pointed out, remove the weapons from the crates and, using canvas and rope supplied by the captain of the ship, make them into bundles of a suitable size to be packed on the *aparejos*.*

While conceding that the idea had merit, Brindley had suggested Galton or one of the men should go instead of his granddaughter. She had countered by reminding him that the *cargador's* secondary, but equally important, duties as farrier made him indispensable. If there should be fighting, any of the packers would be of more use than herself. Lastly, capable as he was in other directions, Ole Devil lacked the technical knowledge required to make up the bundles.

Intelligent and logical as the girl's reasoning had been, Ole Devil and her grandfather had realized that it had had a secondary motive. Ever since they had set off from the ranch, she

* Aparejo: type of pack saddle used for carrying heavy or awkwardly-shaped loads.

had been growing increasingly restless, moody and irritable. The cause of the change in her normally merry, happy-go-lucky disposition had not been difficult to surmise. While the train was travelling, due to the capability of the Tejas packers and the excellent training which the mules had received, there had been far too little requiring her attention and occupying her active mind. So she had had very little to divert her thoughts from the possible loss of the only home she had ever known. With that in mind, Brindley had acceded to her wishes.

Once again Ole Devil had considered that he was being given evidence of Brindley's faith in him. Having made the decision, apart from requesting that he took very good care of the girl, the old man had not shown the slightest apprehension or hesitation over letting her accompany him. Even though they would be travelling alone – apart from having his very loyal servant with them – for at least two and probably three days and nights, the latter being spent of necessity under the stars and far from other human beings, Brindley had obviously accepted that the young Texian would not attempt to take advantage of the situation.

Ole Devil had fully justified the old man's faith and trust. While possessing an eye for the ladies and being far from being a monk* (although he was not a promiscuous libertine) his sense of honour and duty had been effective barriers against him making advances to the girl. While aware of her physical charms, he had treated her as he would have a well-liked tomboy cousin.

Nor had Di given her companion cause to behave differently. Despite having grown up on the ranch, she was anything but innocent and naïve where sexual matters were concerned. Accompanying her grandfather on his packing trips had allowed her to travel extensively in and around Texas. Knowing the dangers, Brindley had considered it advisable to acquaint her with the facts of life. So, although she had been aware that Ole Devil was a virile, good looking young man, she had shown no indication of it. In fact, her behaviour towards him was almost identical to his own with regards to her.

Riding a two-horse relay required too much attention and effort for Di to be able to find time to brood about the possible fate of her home. She, Ole Devil and Tommy were covering

* The full story of why Ole Devil had to leave Louisiana may be told one day.

between thirty and thirty-five miles a day as opposed to the twenty-five maximum of the pack train. Although only the cook's and farrier's mules had been carrying a full load, Brindley had wanted to conserve the animals' strength for transporting the shipment. So he was maintaining an economical pace.

Apart from when answering the calls of nature, Di, Ole Devil and Tommy had made only one concession to her sex. On reaching the Navidad River about two miles south of the town of Edna, they had found the ford over which they had planned to make their crossing was far deeper than usual due to recent heavy rain. Wanting to save their clothing from being soaked, they had decided to go over wearing as little as possible. Without debating the matter, the girl had waited behind a clump of bushes while her companions undressed and made their way to the other side. Then, after they had gone out of sight, she had disrobed and followed them.

On making their plans for the journey, Ole Devil and the Brindleys had taken into consideration that Santa Anna had spies, or supporters, in most Texas communities. So they had decided to avoid such towns as lay between the ranch and their destination. As Di, Ole Devil and Tommy had by-passed Edna, so they swung around Matagorda. They were about five miles from Santa Cristobal Bay and had not seen any other human beings since leaving the pack train. Being so close to the rendezvous, Tommy had been ranging ahead as scout and now his actions suggested that there might be some kind of danger ahead.

Advancing cautiously, after having prepared their weapons, Di and Ole Devil joined Tommy who had withdrawn a little way below the top of the slope.

'Two Mexicans with a white woman, Devil-san,' the little Oriental reported. 'I think she is their prisoner.'

'Let's take a look,' Ole Devil suggested, slipping from his saddle and allowing the dun's reins to fall free.

Joining the young Texian on the ground, Di eased back the hammer of her flintlock and Tommy nocked an arrow to his bow's string. With the girl in the centre, they edged their way towards the rim. Crouching low, they peered over the top at the riders who had attracted Tommy's attention.

Even at a distance of something over a quarter of a mile, it seemed that the small Oriental's summation was correct. The woman, who was approaching from the direction of a large post oak grove, did not appear to be a free agent. Riding side-saddle on a good-looking black horse, she wore an expensive black riding habit that was somewhat dirty and dishevelled and a frilly bosomed white blouse. The brim of her head-dress – a masculine 'planter's' instead of the more usual top hat – prevented the watchers from making out the details of her face. However, they could see that her hands were either held or tied behind her back and that the horse was being led by a man at her right side. Well-mounted, clad in the fashion of working *vaqueros*, he and his companion were hard-looking Mexicans. In addition to a pistol and a knife on their belts, each of them had a rifle cradled across his knees.

Taking in the scene, Di let out an angry sniff. Always impulsive, she started to rise.

'Let's—!' she began.

'Keep down!' Ole Devil snapped, taking his left hand from the Browning rifle to catch her by the shoulder and enforce the command

'What the—' Di protested, but the very urgency of the Texian's behaviour caused her to obey.

'Old Nipponese saying, which I've just made up,' Tommy said quietly, bringing the girl's attention to him. 'Is foolish to try to rescue lady in distress if the way you do it gets her killed.'

'Hell, yes!' Di ejaculated and swung her gaze back to Ole Devil. 'I could have hit *my* man at that range, but you—'

'I don't think they saw you,' the Texian interrupted. 'So let's—'

Whatever Ole Devil intended to suggest would never be known. Even as he started speaking, they heard a feminine yell such as was used to encourage a horse to go faster. Next there came a shouted exclamation in Spanish, followed by the crack of a rifle shot.

Realizing that something must be happening to preclude the need for remaining concealed, Di and her companions rose. They found that, in some way, the woman had pulled the lead rope from the Mexican's hand and was galloping away from her captors. Smoke was drifting from the muzzle of the rifle in the hands of the man at the left. Clearly her actions had taken him by surprise. Despite being fired at what must have been very close range, the bullet had missed. At least, she was showing no sign of having been struck by it. She was not, however, out of danger. The other man was already raising his weapon.

Whipping the butt of the Browning to his shoulder, Ole Devil was conscious of the girl duplicating his actions. He sighted fast, knowing that he had a more distant mark at which to aim than the *vaquero*. Even as his finger tightened on the trigger, Di's flintlock roared. Ole Devil's shot sounded an instant after the girl's. One of them came very close to making a hit. The man's *sombrero* was torn from his head. Startled, he jerked the barrel of his rifle out of alignment and sent his bullet into the air.

Taking her right hand from the rifle and sending it flashing towards the powder horn and bullet pouch which were hanging at her left hip, Di allowed the butt to sink to the ground so as to reload. She saw that the Mexicans were staring in their direction and thought of the surprise that Ole Devil's repeating-fire weapon would hand them if they should attack or go after the woman. They did neither.

'*Vamos, amigo!*' yelled the man who had lost his hat, reining his horse around and putting his spurs to work, an example which his companion followed.

Watching the *vaqueros* racing off in the direction from which they had come, Ole Devil thumbed down the Browning's loading lever without requiring to think. He doubted whether there would be any need for the loaded cylinder which was moving into position. There was, however, something far more urgent requiring his attention.

Turning his gaze from the fleeting pair, Ole Devil looked at the woman. Her horse was galloping at an angle in front of his party's position. Riding side-saddle, with her hands tied behind her back, she had no way of controlling or halting the fast-moving animal.

'Here, Di, take mine!' Ole Devil ordered, thrusting the Browning rifle towards the girl. 'I'll go after her!'

Realizing what was expected of her, Di let go of the powder horn and her flintlock. Ignoring the empty weapon as it fell from her hand, she accepted the Browning. Ole Devil had taught her how to use it on the first night of their journey and she understood its mysteries. A glance assured her that he had made it ready to fire, the position of the magazine bar in the aperture supplying the information.

Confident that the girl could defend herself, or give him

covering fire if the *vaqueros* returned, Ole Devil turned and ran to the waiting horses. Catching hold of the dun's saddlehorn, he vaulted astride its back. He had gathered up the reins in passing and gave a jerk which liberated those of his reserve mount. Having done so, he sent the dun bounding forward.

'Go get her, Devil!' Di whooped as the Texian went by. 'I'll stop them from billing in.'

Urging his mount to go faster, Ole Devil heard the girl's encouraging words but did not attempt to acknowledge them. Instead, he concentrated his attention upon the woman and guided the dun at an angle which would bring them together.

'Look at that damned black go!' Di ejaculated. 'She's right lucky that she can ride so good the way it's running.'

Much the same thought was passing through Ole Devil's head as he was approaching the woman. Although the black was running at a gallop and, as he could see now, there was a rope knotted around her black gauntlet covered wrists, she was retaining her seat on the side-saddle with considerable skill. The jolting which she was receiving had caused the hat to slide from her brunette head and dangle by its *barbiquejo* on her shoulders. It allowed him his first unimpeded view of her face. Flushed by the pounding she was taking from the saddle, her features were beautiful. They topped what the riding habit could not conceal, a very shapely figure. She would, he guessed, be about Di's height and in her early thirties. However, there were other matters of even greater importance than her appearance to be considered.

With each successive sequence of the dun's galloping gait bearing him closer to the woman, Ole Devil started to think about how he might bring about the rescue. He discarded the idea of trying to come alongside and lift her from the saddle. Approaching as he was from her right, she had her legs hidden from his view. Having fastened her hands behind her back, the Mexicans might also have tied her feet to the stirrup as a means of securing her to the side-saddle. If so, he could throw the horses off balance and might even bring them down. Nor would there be time for him to go around and check whether she was tied on or not.

'Help!' the woman screeched, staring at the Texian. 'Stop the horse, *m'sieur!*'

Coming alongside the black, Ole Devil did not bother to reply to the woman's plea. Instead, he reached across towards the one-piece reins which were hanging over the horse's neck. Having obtained a hold on them, he cued the dun with knee-pressure so that it began to move off to the right. Feeling the pull on its bit, the black followed without making any fuss. Guiding the two animals around and gradually reducing their speed, he brought them to a halt in front of his companions.

'Nice going, Devil!' Di praised, having laid down the Browning after the Mexicans had disappeared into the grove of post oaks.

While speaking, the girl was advancing to hold the black's head. Dropping to the ground, Ole Devil went around the horses. He found that the woman's feet were not fastened to the stirrup iron. Holding out his hands, he helped her to slide down. She stumbled into his arms, causing them to tighten about her. Pressing – almost rubbing – her well-developed bosom against him, she began to babble incoherent thanks in a voice which had a marked French accent.

'You saved my life, *m'sieur*,' the woman stated, after recovering her composure and moving away from her rescuer. 'I don't know how to thank you.'

'Here,' Di said, stepping behind the woman. 'Let's get this rope off for you.'

On reaching for the rope, the girl noticed that it was tied around the stiff cuffs of the gauntlets. She gripped their fingers and pulled, liberating the woman's hands without the need to unfasten the knot.

Having been set free, the woman introduced herself as Madeline de Moreau. She explained how she had been the only passenger on a stagecoach heading for Texas City. It had been attacked by a gang of Mexican *bandidos*. The driver and the guard were both killed, but she had been saved from the same – or a worse – fate by being able to prove that her father was wealthy and would be willing to pay a high ransom for her safe return. The leader of the band had told the two men to escort her to their hideout while the rest went in search of fresh loot.

'A bunch of *bandidos*!' Di growled. 'That's all we need!'

'I don't think they will come looking for you,' Madeline replied. 'They were afraid of meeting soldiers and I'm sure that they believe there are more of you— There are more, aren't there?'

'Not too close,' Di warned. 'But they're coming.'

'Then you will be able to see me safely to Texas City, Captain Hardin,' the woman suggested, having learned her rescuers' names after introducing herself.

'I'll make arrangements to do it as soon as possible,' Ole Devil promised, but he could not shake off the feeling that something was wrong. 'But I'm on a mission of importance and great urgency and can't turn aside from it.'

'Very well,' Madeline said, accepting the situation without argument.

'If you feel up to riding, we'll move on,' the Texian requested, then his eyes went to the black. 'Hey! Where did they get the side-saddle?'

'It's mine,' Madeline answered. 'I had it with me on the coach and my horse was fastened to the boot, Would you help me up, please. I don't want to delay you.'

Complying with the woman's request, Ole Devil mounted the dun and retrieved his second horse. The party started moving and, as before, Tommy ranged ahead. In the late afternoon, as Ole Devil and the women were approaching a deserted building, they saw the little Oriental returning. They were about a mile from Santa Cristobal Bay, but could not see it as yet.

'There's a ship in the bay, Devil-san,' Tommy announced, bringing his horses to a stop.

'Is it the one we've come to meet?' Di inquired, although she sensed that the answer would be negative.

'No,' Tommy replied, confirming her suspicions. 'It's a small warship, flying the Mexican flag.'

CHAPTER FOURTEEN

YOU COULD BE TRYING TO TRICK ME

STANDING on the quarterdeck of the Mexican navy's ten-gun brig *Destructor*, having been called from his cabin by the master's mate who had the watch, Lieutenant Tomas Grivaljo directed his telescope at the cause of the summons. Three riders were coming down the slope towards the edge of Santa Cristobal Bay. They made no attempt to conceal their presence from the ship's working party who were refilling the water barrels at the stream which flowed into the sea at that point. The lack of concern was strange. The woman and the taller of the two men were *gringos* and their companion, who rode in a subordinate position behind them, appeared to be Chinese.

Puzzled by the trio's apparent lack of fear, Grivaljo studied the white man. Tall, young, unshaven, he had on a buckskin shirt and light-coloured trousers the legs of which hung outside his boots. There was a pistol and bowie knife balancing each other on his waist belt, but they were his only visible weapons.* A closer examination of the female suggested that 'girl' would be more appropriate than 'woman'. She was wearing a black hat like the man's, and a black riding habit but was sitting astride her horse. Neither she nor the small Oriental appeared to be armed.

Seeing that the working party were grabbing up weapons, the *gringo* raised his hands. He called something which Grivaljo, watching him, could not hear. Holding a pistol in one hand and cutlass in the other, the master's mate who was commanding the men on shore advanced warily. The trio brought their mounts to a halt. Still keeping his hands level with the sides of his head, the *gringo* swung his left leg up and over his dun's neck. Although he dropped to the ground, his companions remained in their saddles. Ignoring them, Grivaljo kept the

---

* As the use of a saddleboot as a means of carrying a rifle was not yet widely practiced, Grivaljo had not noticed the Browning.

gringo under observation as he strolled to meet the master's mate.

There was nothing in the *gringo's* attitude to suggest that he had the slightest doubt about dismounting, thus leaving the means by which he might be able to make a rapid departure. Looking completely at ease, he walked a good thirty feet away from his horse and companions. Then, coming to a halt in front of the Mexican petty officer at a range where even a mediocre shot could be expected to make a hit with a pistol, he started to speak. Whatever the *gringo* was saying, he was apparently ready to back it up with some kind of document. Taking a sheet of paper from his pocket, he offered it to Master's Mate Gomez who opened it out and looked down at it. After reading whatever was on it, he pointed towards the ship. Then he handed back the document and he called to his men.

Turning to his companions, the *gringo* must have told them to dismount. Jumping from his horse, the small Oriental hurried to help the girl down. Then he held the animals reins while she joined the *gringo*. They spoke together and she seemed to be protesting. Instead of arguing, he pointed to one of the boats and she went towards it.

While the small Oriental led their horses towards the stream, the *gringo* helped the girl into the boat and then followed her in and sat by her side. Two of the sailors, looking disgruntled at having the task thrust upon them by Gomez, shoved the boat off, climbed aboard, and started to row towards *Destructor*.

Ever conscious of his dignity and having no desire to compromise it by showing his curiosity, Grivaljo lowered the telescope as the boat was approaching. Then he went to where he could watch without making his scrutiny too obvious.

On being brought alongside, the *gringo* showed that he had some knowledge of ships. Standing up, he took hold of the entering-ropes and hauled himself without any difficulty on to the deck. Several members of the crew were hovering around and, in fair Spanish, the *gringo* asked for help with the girl. There was a rush of volunteers such as Grivaljo had never seen on other occasions when the men were called upon to carry out some duty, but the bosun's bellow of displeasure drove them back. Having done so, the bosun and the *gringo* leaned over. The girl had risen nervously and, taking hold of her wrists, they heaved. With a startled yelp, she found herself being plucked from the boat. Her feet beat a tattoo against the side of the ship until she was set down on the deck.

Commanding the girl to come with him – and there was no other description for the way in which he addressed her – the *gringo* strolled nonchalantly to where Grivaljo was standing. As he approached, his eyes were darting around. Watching him, the lieutenant felt it was merely an interest in his surroundings that made him do so. There was nothing in his attitude to suggest he had any fear of coming to harm.

However, the girl did not appear to be quite so much at ease. That, Grivaljo told himself, could be caused because she was aboard a ship. Unless the lieutenant was mistaken, she was of a lower social standing than her escort. Her travel-stained riding habit was expensive, but it had been tailored to fit a woman with a somewhat more ample figure. What was more, if her tanned face and work-roughened hands were anything to go by, she had not always worn such expensive garments. Being a well-born Spanish-Creole, which accounted for his low rank and humble command, Grivaljo could guess at her relationship with the *gringo* and he dismissed her from his considerations.

Conscious of the lieutenant's scrutiny, Ole Devil Hardin forced himself to retain an outward calm and swaggering confidence. From the look of her when he told her to follow him, Diamond-Hitch Brindley was feeling the strain. Yet she had remembered to kick the sides of the ship while being lifted aboard, ensuring that if certain other sounds had been made, they would pass unnoticed. He felt sure that he could count on her to continue playing her part. If he had not been sure, he would never have allowed her to accompany him in the first place.

On hearing Tommy Okasi's news, Ole Devil had called a halt at the deserted cabin. Then he had discussed the matter with Di and the small Oriental. They had not attempted to exclude Madeline de Moreau from their council of war. While she had not been told the exact purpose of their assignment, she was aware that it was of considerable importance to the Republic of Texas. So she had taken a lively interest in what was being said.

While it had seemed likely that the brig was awaiting the arrival of the ship carrying the rifles, Ole Devil had pointed out that – as the crew were engaged in taking on water – it was

137

possible the visit had only been made for such a purpose. One thing was obvious to them all. No matter what had brought the Mexican warship to Santa Cristobal Bay, its presence called for some kind of action on their part.

From all appearances, the owners of the cabin had left hurriedly. Certainly they had not waited to pack and carry off all of their property. Noticing one of the items that remained, Ole Devil had started to concoct an audacious scheme.

Telling Tommy to unpack his war bag, Old Devil had explained what he intended to do. Making use of the document which he had taken from Halford's body, he would visit the brig and try to find out why it was there. Should it be waiting in ambush, he would find some way of warning the arms ship of its presence. On the other hand, if the reason was merely to replenish the water supply, he had something else in mind. He would attempt to persuade the Mexican captain to sail south and, if successful, hoped to make sure that the brig would not be able to interfere with the landing of the arms.

On learning of how Ole Devil hoped to achieve his intention, Di had suggested that she should accompany him and Tommy. At first he had refused to consider the idea. However, as on the issue of riding with him to the Bay, she had had her way. Her argument had been that her presence might tend to lessen the Mexican's suspicions. Also, she had claimed, if Madeline would co-operate, she could carry the means to put Ole Devil's scheme into operation. Neither of the men would be able to do so, certainly not by concealing the object, and for it to be in plain sight was sure to arouse comments and questions.

On Ole Devil yielding to Di's demands, Madeline had suggested that she too should accompany the party. The girl had replied that she did not think it would be a good idea, as there would be considerable danger involved and the need for fighting or fast movement. Di had not considered the woman capable of either, but thought she could help in another way. Madeline had accepted the girl's decision with apparent good grace. At any rate she had not hesitated to agree when the girl asked to change clothes with her. Nor had the woman shown any alarm over being left alone at the cabin. She had stated that she was a pretty good shot and would have a selection of firearms at her disposal should the need to prove it arise.

With the various points settled, the party had made their preparations. In addition to having changed his riding breeches for less military-looking trousers from his war bag, Ole Devil had left his second pistol and sabre – which had his name inscribed on the blade – at the cabin.

For the part which she would be playing, Di could not carry her rifle. Taking advantage of the riding habit's slightly loose fit, she had buckled her belt around her underwear and had concealed the secret object beneath the outer garment. She had, however, insisted upon riding astride as she had never used a side-saddle.

Wanting to appear innocuous and to be more convincing in his pose of a harmless 'Chinese' servant, Tommy had left his bow, arrows and swords behind, as well as changing his boots for a pair of sandals. He had, however, retained one weapon; but few people outside his native land would have identified it as such. Certainly Madeline, who had seen him replacing it in his trousers' pocket after having shown it to a clearly puzzled Di, had not. Nor had she heard the explanation of its purpose as that had been made while the trio were riding towards the rendezvous.

Before allowing themselves to be seen, Di, Ole Devil and Tommy had studied the brig as it lay at anchor. It was, the Texian had told the girl, well-situated for ambushing any vessel that entered. Due to the way in which the land rose on three sides, it could only be seen from the sea when the mouth of the bay was being approached. At night, provided that the brig was properly darkened, it would be practically invisible against such a background. However, the precautions which Hardin expected had not been taken. There was no lookout on either of the mastheads. The breechings and side-tackles had not been cast off, nor the guns run out. Neither was there a spring attached to the anchor's cable to facilitate turning the brig and bringing one of its broadsides to bear.

Ole Devil had regarded the lack of preparations as a good sign. Unless he was mistaken, the omissions were not the result of incompetence. To his eyes, the brig showed no signs of being poorly commanded. In fact he had concluded it was just the opposite. Although the party on shore had been working in a somewhat dilatory fashion, he believed that could be the fault of the master's mate who was in charge rather than the captain.

The lieutenant, whom Ole Devil was approaching, seemed old for such a low rank, particularly as he had the appearance of being a capable seaman. There was a bitter expression on his lean, aquiline face that the Texian recognized as common to officers in other navies who had, for some reason, been passed over for promotion.

'*Saludos, senor*,' Ole Devil greeted, taking out the 'proof' of his identity. His bearing suggested that he was merely going through an unnecessary formality. 'This will tell you who I am.'

'Well, *Senor* Halford,' Grivaljo said, after reading the document and introducing himself. 'What brings you to my ship?'

The voice suggested to Ole Devil why Grivaljo was still only a lieutenant. Some of the Spanish warships and their crews had gone over to the Mexicans during the struggle for independence, as had military units. According to rumours, officers of Spanish-Creole birth were discriminated against by their Mexican superiors. If that was so in Grivaljo's case, dealing with him could be easier.

'Information, lieutenant,' Ole Devil replied, accepting and refolding the document. 'Something you'll be pleased to hear about.'

'Will I?' Grivaljo asked.

'If you've a mind to make some prize money, you will,' Ole Devil answered in a louder voice than was necessary.

'Prize money?' Grivaljo repeated. Then, hearing his words echoed in a number of voices, he realized that the conversation was being listened to by almost every man on deck. Angrily, he raised his voice in a bellow. 'Bosun! Put the hands to work, damn you!'

'Like I said, if you've a mind for prize money, you'll be pleased to hear what we've found out,' Ole Devil stated, as the cursing bosun chased the sailors away.

'*We, senor?*' Grivaljo said quietly, keeping his eyes on the Texian's face. 'And who might "*we*" be?'

'The people I work with.'

'Who are they?'

'Friends of Mexico,' Ole Devil countered. 'I don't give names. Right now, I'm taking a pretty important message to General Rovira. But my boss told me to keep close to the coast and get word to any Mexican warship I saw going by that there's a ship expected during the next three days at Port Lavaca.' He paused dramatically, then continued, 'It's carrying supplies for Houston — including ten thousand Yankee dollars.'

140

'How do you know of this?' Grivaljo demanded, trying, and not entirely succeeding, to sound disinterested.

'Come on now! A man of your intelligence doesn't really expect me to give the answer to *that*,' Ole Devil scoffed, with the air of one who had done his duty. 'Well, I've told you. The news I've got for General Rovira's important, so I'll be on my way and let him have it.'

'Just a moment, *senor*!' Grivaljo barked as his visitor went to turn away. 'It's not as easy as all that. You could be trying to trick me.'

'Even if *I'd* come out here instead of just sending a message with one of your men,' Ole Devil countered calmly. 'Would I have brought my girl along if that's what I had in mind?'

'Perhaps not,' Grivaljo answered, although a similar thought had occurred to him. 'But—'

'There are no "buts" about it where I'm concerned!' Ole Devil interrupted, bristling with well-simulated indignation. 'Damn it all, I've told you something that any naval officer ought to be pleased to know. If you don't want to believe me and act on it, that's up to you. I'll be going—'

'Not so fast!' Grivaljo snapped. Although he was not armed, he felt sure that the *gringo* would have more sense than to attempt resistance. 'Being, as you said, a man of intelligence, I think it would be better if you stayed on board until after I've seen this ship which you *say* is bound for Port Lavaca.'

'As I'm here, and seeing that the boat which brought me's gone back, I'd be a fool to try and stop you,' Ole Devil declared, giving a resigned shrug. He showed nothing of the elation that he was feeling. From the way he had spoken, the lieutenant was contemplating acting upon Hardin's information, which suggested that he was not awaiting the arrival of the consignment of rifles. Looking Grivaljo straight in the eye, he went on, 'But I want what you're doing put in writing, so that I can show General Rovira what's made me late getting to him.'

'What do you mean?' the lieutenant asked uneasily, showing that he had a pretty fair idea of the answer.

'Like I told you,' Ole Devil drawled. 'I've some *very* important news for the General. Getting it to him, even with her—' He indicated the girl with a disparaging jerk of his left thumb, 'and my "Chink" servant along to make folks less suspicious – don't worry, she's so stupid she barely speaks English and doesn't know a word of Spanish – it's going to be dangerous to deliver. So, if I'm going to be delayed maybe two or three days – there's no way of knowing just when that ship will arrive – I want to be able to prove *I* wasn't responsible.'

Listening to the conversation, Di – who spoke sufficient Spanish to follow it – silently swore that she would raise lumps on a certain Texian's head for his comment about her. However, impressed as she was by the way Ole Devil was manipulating the officer, she did not forget her part. Standing with a partially open mouth and an expression that suggested a complete lack of comprehension, she showed none of her admiration for Ole Devil's acting. Everything about him implied that he was completely content to be delayed – as long as he could lay the blame on somebody else.

Watching Grivaljo's reactions, Ole Devil could guess at the cause of his perturbation. While one part of the lieutentnat advised taking the precaution of keeping Hardin on board, another was warning him of the consequences if he should do so and be proven wrong. General Rovira was one of the new breed of Mexican – as opposed to Spanish-*Creole* – officers. The kind of man, in fact, who had probably blocked Grivaljo's promotion because of his birth and upbringing. If Rovira learned that vital information had been prevented from reaching him as quickly as possible, he would have no mercy on the man – especially upon a *Creole* – who had caused the delay.

'Don't get any ideas about holding me until you're sure, then having me disappear and saying you've never seen me,' Ole Devil warned, seeing from Grivaljo's expression that such an idea was at that moment being contemplated. 'For one thing, some of the crew would talk. And even if they didn't, unless that "Chink" of mine gets a signal from me that all's well in about a minute, he'll be on his horse and heading back to tell my boss where I am. Maybe he's only a heathen Chinese, but he could do it.'

An angry scowl creased the lieutenant's face and his fingers drummed against his thighs. He had already considered the first objection – that of an indiscreet crew suggested by the *gringo*. While he did not believe it to be insurmountable, the second point put his plan beyond any hope of accomplishment. Even if he clapped his visitors below hatches immediately and sent a flag signal to the shore party, the 'Chinaman' would almost certainly take fright and flee. He was far enough away from the sailors to mount and be reasonably safe from their pistols. For the *gringo* to have adopted such a high-handed attitude implied that he had very influential superiors. In all probablity, they would be men who could cause a great deal of trouble over his disappearance. It would go badly for any officer who was suspected of being involved, particularly if he was a Spanish-*Creole*.

Unpalatable as the thought might be, Grivaljo had to accept that he could not impose his will upon the sardonic-looking young white man.

'Very well, signal your man that all is well,' the lieutenant requested, almost spitting each word out in the bitterness of defeat. 'I'll have you put ashore as soon as the boats come back.'

'*Gracias*,' Ole Devil replied, although the latter part of the officer's speech did not fit into his plans. 'And you'll go after that ship?'

'I'll sail with the morning tide,' Grivaljo promised and could not stop himself from adding, 'For a "friend of Mexico", you don't have much faith in your friends.'

'I was born careful,' Ole Devil answered. 'Which is why I like to choose the winning side. Especially when it's the side who can pay best.'

'How do you mean?' the lieutenant wanted to know.

'I'm not so *loco* that I believe *el Presidente* will let any *gringo*, even those who have stood by him, stay on in Texas,' Ole Devil explained. 'So I'm making sure I don't leave with empty pockets.'

'Hey, honey,' Di put in, speaking English with a whining tone. 'How much longer you going to stand a-jawing? I'm hungry 'n' tired, although I'm damned if I know what we'll eat tonight. You ain't shot noth—'

'Shut your mouth, damn you!' Ole Devil snarled in the same tongue, swinging around to face the girl, and she backed off a couple of steps registering right in a convincing manner. He turned back to the officer and, although he sensed that the other understood sufficient of the language to have followed the brief conversation, he reverted to Spanish. 'She's right, though. We've been travelling so hard I haven't had time to shoot anything. How about trading a meal for the news I've brought?'

'Very well,' Grivaljo answered, after a pause during which

143

he revised his original inclination to refuse. It might, he realized, be impolitic to antagonize a man with possible influential connections, one who could maybe supply information in the future. 'I was just going to ask you to be my guest.'

'That's good of you,' Ole Devil declared, adopting a more friendly tone and feeling delighted at the way the officer had played into his hands. There was one more thing which had to be arranged. 'Can I have my "Chink" come out and eat?'

'Of course. I'll pass the word for the shore party to bring him,' Grivaljo assented and nodded up at the rapidly darkening sky. 'It looks like rain. Perhaps you and your – wife – would like to spend the night on board and shelter from it?'

'We'd be pleased to,' Ole Devil replied, showing nothing of his delight at the suggestion – upon which the success of his plan depended – having come from the other man. 'Just so long as we can get off again *before* you sail.'

'I'll have you put ashore at first light,' Grivaljo promised. 'You have my word of honour as an officer and gentleman.'

The acceptance was made with almost good grace. As far as the lieutenant could tell, he had nothing to lose by being amiable to his *gringo* visitors.

In that, Grivaljo was making a very serious mistake!

It was one which was to have a severe effect on his career!

CHAPTER FIFTEEN

IF YOU DON'T WANT TO GET HER KILLED

'WHEN do you reckon it'll happen, Devil?' Diamond-Hitch Brindley inquired as she sat her horse between her companions and watched the *Destructor* brig sailing out of Santa Cristobal Bay shortly after dawn on a cold, miserable and – although the rain had stopped – damp morning.

'Not until they set all sail and hit the rough water,' Ole Devil Hardin replied. 'Unless they find out what's happened before then.'

'If they do,' Di said, turning a sympathetic eye on the other member of their party. 'You'll have had a wet night for nothing.'

Even though the girl spoke lightly she knew that the failure of their plan might have more serious repercussions than the waste of Tommy's night in considerable discomfort and not a little danger.

On receiving Ole Devil's message, which Lieutenant Grivaljo had sent ashore, Tommy had off-saddled and hobbled the horses. When he had reached the brig, he was given a meal. As the vessel was already crowded, he had been told to make himself a shelter between two of the starboard side's twenty-four pounder carronades.* That had been ideal for his purpose, having given him a legitimate reason for staying on deck. He could keep watch in case the ship carrying the rifles should arrive and, if it had, contrive to give a warning of the danger. More important, it had allowed him to carry out another task.

Despite the discomfort it had caused, the rain which had fallen steadily for most of the night had been of great help to Tommy. On the pretense of collecting something from her saddlebags, their property having been brought on board by the

* Carronade: a short-barrelled, large calibre, compact cannon with a limited range used as a broadside weapon on some classes of warship.

brig's shore party, Di had given him the saw which they had found at the cabin. She had been carrying it suspended from her belt and under the borrowed riding habit.

Once satisfied that Grivaljo had turned in, the master's mate who had the watch did not remain on deck. He went below to shelter from the rain. So, once he had left, so had the other members of the watch. In their absence, working with more freedom than would have been possible if they had attended to their duties Tommy had started to work. Using the saw, which was practically new, he had cut into the breeching, side-tackles and the lashing which held the muzzle of each carronade against the top of its gun-port.

The departure of the sailors had allowed Tommy to work with less immediate danger of being caught. Taking his time, he had worked on the inner sides of the various ropes so as to lessen the chances of his tampering being discovered prematurely. He had not, of course, sawn all the way through. To have done so would have made the damage so obvious that it could not be missed. Instead, he had weakened the ropes. He had sought for the happy medium of cutting just deep enough to ensure that they would not start breaking until the brig was well clear of the bay. So well had he done the preliminary work that he and his company had been put ashore and the brig had set sail without it having been noticed.

Although just as interested as the girl, Ole Devil and Tommy hid their feelings better. She was wriggling impatiently in her saddle and staring at the brig with grim concentration. While she had little knowledge of ships, when she saw the additional sails being unfurled as it passed beyond the mouth of the bay, she turned her head and grinned expectantly at her companions before resuming her scrutiny.

Nothing untoward happened.

Carried onwards by the shore-breeze, *Destructor* heeled over and turned to the south. Despite being rolled by the waves, it kept going without showing any evidence of distress.

'Damn it!' Di ejaculated after about five restless minutes had dragged by, 'They must have found out!'

'I don't think so,' Ole Devil contradicted, trying to conceal his disappointment. 'They'd be reducing sail if they had, or turning back so that they could make repairs in the bay.'

'Those ropes must have been of better quality than I

thought,' Tommy commented in tones of contrition. 'Or I didn't saw into them as deeply as I thought I was doing.'

Whatever the reason, the brig was still under all sail and clearly not in any difficulties when it disappeared beyond the horizon. The only slight satisfaction Ole Devil could find was that it had not shown any signs of returning.

Di could not hide her disappointment as she turned her horses. However, being a good natured girl, she felt that she should prove to Tommy that she did not hold the failure against him.

'You wouldn't be able to see in the dark and sure as hell couldn't've started lighting matches even if it hadn't been raining,' Di stated as they rode away from the rim overlooking the bay. 'Anyways, we got the damned thing headed south and that's almost worth having to wear this son-of-a-bitching riding habit for. What do you reckon Grivaljo'll do when he finds out, Devil?'

'That depends,' the Texian answered, having given the matter some consideration. 'He may think we went aboard just to do the damage and put the brig out of action, But, if he decides that we'd need a better inducement than *that* before taking such a risk, he could guess we wanted him gone because we're expecting a ship to arrive.'

'And if he does,' Di said bitterly, 'he'll be headed right back.' Then her face showed relief and she went on, 'Hey though. He can't. The wind's blowing him south.'

'That won't stop him,' Ole Devil warned, but he did not attempt to explain how a sailing ship could beat back against the wind. Instead, he gave a shrug. 'Well, there's nothing we can do about it right now. So we might as well go back and let you get into your own clothes.'

'I sure as hell won't be sorry about *that*!' Di spat out, trying to pass off her unrealized hopes and present anxieties as lightly as possible

All in all, it was a dejected trio who rode towards the cabin. Yet, although they did not learn of it for many weeks, their plan met with complete – if belated – success.*

In spite of their gloomy forebodings, Di, Ole Devil and Tommy did not forget to be cautious. However, they saw nothing to disturb or perturb them as they approached the

* Details of how this came about are given at the end of this chapter.

building. It had been erected in the centre of a fair-sized hollow, with plenty of open ground on every side to counteract the clumps of trees and bushes which grew thickly in a number of places. There was no sign of life, but that was neither surprising nor alarming. To prevent drawing attention to the fact that the cabin was occupied, they had taken Madeline de Moreau's black gelding with them. Ole Devil had also asked the woman to stay indoors as much as possible.

Taking the horses to the small corral, the trio dismounted. They were about to start attending to the animals' welfare when the side door of the cabin opened. Expecting no more than Madeline coming out to greet them, Ole Devil glanced over his shoulder. He stiffened and his right hand went towards the butt of the Manton pistol. Hearing Di's low and startled exclamation, he knew without turning his head that she was also looking. There was a very good reason for their reactions.

Although Madeline was emerging, clad in Di's shirt and trousers – which were tight enough to show off her full figure to its best advantage – she was not alone. Walking close behind her, with the muzzle of a pistol held against the side of her head, was the man who had called himself 'Galsworthy' when he had visited the Brindleys' ranch. His other hand, holding the walking-cane which Ole Devil had already suspected was concealing the blade of the sword that had murdered the wounded prisoner, was resting on her shoulder and urging her onwards.

'Come away from those horses!' Galsworthy barked, pushing Madeline forward.

'D – Do it, please!' Madeline gasped in a frightened voice.

'You'd better, if you don't want to get her killed,' Galsworthy supplemented. 'And don't think I – wouldn't shoot a woman.'

'Do as he says!' Ole Devil ordered, having no doubt that the man was not making an idle threat.

Even as he spoke, the young Texian was trying to locate Galsworthy's companions. It was unlikely that he had left the other men with their horses. The nearest point at which they and the animals could be concealed was almost two hundred yards away, too far for them to be of use in an emergency. So, in all probability, they would be in the cabin. They were either positioned so as to be able to cover their leader, or were waiting to follow him out.

148

'Stop there!' Galsworthy commanded when the trio had moved far enough for them to be unable to use the horses as a shield. They did as they were told and he went on, 'Now throw down your weapons. Do it carefully and no tricks, or she's dead.'

Knowing that he had no other choice without costing Madeline her life, Ole Devil extracted the pistol from his belt loop. He tossed it in front of him so that it landed on its left side with the hammer uppermost. Having done so, he slid the bowie knife from its sheath and flipped it point first into the ground alongside the other weapon.

'How about you and the "Chink"?' Galsworthy asked, looking at Di.

'Neither of them are armed, Randy,' Madeline said, before the girl could reply. Then she stepped away from the man.

'What the—?' Di spluttered, then realization struck and her voice rose like the squall of an angry bobcat. 'Why you—!'

'Easy!' Ole Devil snapped, catching the furious girl by the arm as she was about to spring forward. 'That won't do any good!'

Much to Ole Devil's relief, Di restrained her impulse. She might be hot-tempered, but she had enough sense to recognize sound advice when she heard it. Now she realized that the way in which Madeline's clenched fists had been raised was not that of a frightened woman, and she also saw the two men who were coming out of the cabin. Although she had not had a close acquaintance with them, she identified them as the Mexicans who had been Madeline's 'captors'. Grinning at each other, they went to flank Galsworthy and the woman. Clearly the pair were satisfied that the situation was under control. While each was holding a pistol, the muzzles were dangling towards the ground.

'It's lucky for you that you stopped,' Galsworthy told the girl with a grin. Then he swung his pistol, which had been pointing towards Ole Devil, in Tommy's direction and snarled, 'Bring it out empty, damn you!'

'Very sorry, sir!' the little Oriental yelped, snatching his right hand from his trousers' pocket into which he had slipped it. However, his hand did not emerge quite as had been instructed. 'Don't shoot humble self, excellent and honourable sir.'

'What's that you're holding?' Galsworthy demanded.

Although Tommy had created something of a diversion,

causing Galsworthy to take his pistol out of alignment on Ole Devil, there was no hope of it being turned to the trio's advantage. The Mexicans had brought up their weapons and we're covering the Texian.

'Don't shoot him!' Old Devil called urgently. 'It's only his *kongo*.'

'His *what*?' Galsworthy asked, refraining from squeezing the trigger as he saw the thing Tommy was holding and decided that it could do him no harm.

'A *kongo*, mister,' Ole Devil repeated. 'It's his *yawara* prayer stick.'

Laying across Tommy's left palm, the *kongo* looked harmless. It was a rod of some kind of hard wood, rounded at the ends and with grooves carved around its six inch length.

'If I am to join honourable ancestors,' Tommy went on, displaying the *kongo*. 'I must make *yawara* prayer.'

'We'll give you a chance to do it before we kill you, if you behave,' Galsworthy promised, grinning sardonically and dismissing both Tommy and the *kongo* as of no importance.

The handsome man considered that he had every right to feel satisfied with the way things had turned out. When Arnaldo Verde had first come to him for help, he had seen a way in which he might make a lot of money. Loyalty to the Mexican citizenship he had adopted was not his motive for serving Santa Anna. In fact, his were much the same motives that Ole Devil had given Grivaljo. Five hundred new caplock rifles and a plentiful supply of ammunition were very valuable commodities. They would command a high price whether sold in bulk or individually. He had no intention of turning them over to the Mexicans if they should fall into his hands. So, while he was willing to destroy the shipment if necessary, he had been determined to gain possession of it if possible.

With his band scattered, looting the properties which had already been deserted by their owners or pillaging such as were still occupied but only lightly defended, Galsworthy had lacked sufficient strength to attack the Brindleys and take over the means to transport the shipment. So, having sent Halford and four men with Verde to intercept General Houston's messenger, he had tried without success to gather reinforcements. Failing to do so, he had left word for any of his band who arrived at their headquarters to come after him and had taken the remainder, including his wife, to Gonzales. He had not known that the remnants of Halford's party were in the vicinity when he had visited the Brindleys' ranch to size up the opposition.

The meeting with Ole Devil had informed Galsworthy that Halford had failed in his assignment. When he had learned of Mucker's capture, he had known that he must not allow an interrogation to be carried out. Mucker was neither brave nor staunch and would talk. He had known too much to be left alive. So Galsworthy had excused himself and gone to the barn. Finding it deserted and the key in the storeroom's door, he had availed himself of the opportunity with which he was being presented. Entering, he had killed Mucker with his sword-cane. Having laid the body on the bed and covered it with a blanket, he had locked the door and rejoined his party.

Still determined to try and take the shipment, Galsworthy had realized that he could not hope to do so unless he had more men. So he had reduced the number of his already small party by dispatching one of them in search of other members of his band. Having done so, he had brought the rest to the coast. He had known that the mule train would have to come to Santa Cristobal Bay and had wanted to study its strength with the idea of taking it over. Instead of staying in sight of the Bay, he had taken his party to a hill which offered a good view of the surrounding country and had set a watch against the train's arrival.

Learning that Di was approaching accompanied by Ole Devil and Tommy much earlier than he had anticipated, Galsworthy had guessed that they were travelling a long way ahead of the mule train. He had also seen he was being given a chance to outwit them. With the girl in his hands, he could force her grandfather to transport the shipment and, as long as he held her hostage, he could ensure that there would be no trouble from the old man or the Tejas Indian mule-packers.

Knowing that Halford had been a better than fair fighting man, Galsworthy had acquired considerable respect for Ole Devil's capabilities in that line. Any man who could get by Halford – who had been with Galsworthy for several years and was second-in-command of the band – with the backing that he had was far too dangerous to be treated with anything other than great care. So, with Madeline's approval, Galsworthy had formulated a plan to get her into his potential victims' company. He had not been worried about asking his wife to take on the task. In spite of her elegant appearance and air of being a well-bred lady, she was tough, ruthless and able to take care of herself.* As long as her true purpose was not suspected, having her attached to the Texian's party would be a great advantage.

Realizing that there would be a certain amount of danger involved if they were to make the woman's 'rescue' appear genuine, the conspirators had planned it carefully. Although Galsworthy's warning had probably not been necessary, the Mexican 'captors' had been instructed to allow Madeline to 'escape' at some distance away from her 'rescuers' so as to lessen the chances of being shot by them. The precautions had been justified. However, due to the nature of the terrain, they had been nearer than they had intended before Di's hasty actions had allowed them to locate the trio and put the scheme into action.

On the other hand, Madeline's part of the plan had gone without a hitch. She was an excellent rider and had been mounted upon a well-trained horse which she had been confident she could trust. While she had been sitting side-saddle with her hands fastened behind her back, her bonds had been tied around the thick leather gauntlets. So, as an experiment had proved, she could have freed herself if necessary. As a further air, should she have needed to regain control of the black gelding, its reins were dangling across its neck and the Mexican was leading it by a rope that was too short to have entangled its legs when he had released it.

Everything had gone to plan. In fact, Madeline considered that her worst moment had been when Ole Devil had questioned her about the side-saddle. Fortunately, she had been sufficiently quick witted to have thought up a plausible excuse.

When Madeline had heard about the presence of the Mexican brig in the bay, she had recognized that it was posing a serious threat to her husband's hopes. It would either frighten away, or capture, the ship that was delivering the rifles. No matter

---

* Before their conduct had made the United States too hot to hold them and they had fled to Texas, Madeline and her husband – whose full name was Randolph Galsworthy Buttolph – had operated a high-class combined brothel and gambling house in New York. While there, Madeline had earned a well-deserved reputation for being able to quell – by physical means if necessary – the toughest and most recalcitrant of their female employees or competitors.

which happened, the consignment would be lost to them. Listening to her 'rescuers' discussing the situation, she had been faced with another dilemma. She was aware of Galsworthy's desire to capture and use the girl as a hostage. With that in mind, she had tried to talk Di out of accompanying the men. Discovering that the girl was adamant, Madeline had offered to participate in a more active manner than had been suggested. Although not entirely displeased at being refused – for she considered the chances of failure were high – she had been irritated by the way in which Di had turned down her suggestion. Clearly the girl had considered that she would be more of a liability than an asset on such a hazardous mission. Being proud of her reputation for competence and toughness, she had resented being treated that way by a poorly educated country yokel even though she should have regarded it as a tribute to her acting ability. However, she had managed to conceal her resentment and, apparently yielding to Di's greater experience, had even consented to the exchange of clothing.

Shortly before nightfall, having followed the tracks of his wife and her 'rescuers', Galsworthy had found his wife at the cabin. On being told why she was alone and dressed in such an outlandish fashion (although he had regarded the clothing as very fetching due to the way in which she filled them) he had expressed his approval of her actions.

Then, in case the attempt to get rid of the brig should be successful, Galsworthy and his wife had made plans to capture the trio on their return. Wanting to take them alive if possible and having heard nothing to diminish his regard for Ole Devil's abilities, Galsworthy had told his party what he wanted them to do. There were now only three men with him, the fourth having been sent back to look for and speed the arrival of such other members of the band whom he should meet.

Although Galsworthy had known that it would most likely be after dawn before his victims arrived, he had been disinclined to take chances. So, while he and his wife had spent the night making love in the cabin, their horses had been picketed beyond the nearest clump of bushes. The three very disgruntled men had been compelled to occupy a draughty and poorly constructed barn, being under orders to ensure that at least one of them remained awake and alert at all times.

Galsworthy had had no way of knowing how well, or otherwise, his order had been carried out. With his passions aroused by Madeline's sensual appearance, he had been too occupied in sating them to check up on the trio. Certainly he had not found any of them asleep, although all looked damp, depressed and miserable, when he visited them at the first hint of daybreak. The party had eaten a cold breakfast as he had refused to allow a fire to be lit in case their victims should see the smoke and become suspicious. After that, it had only been a question of waiting. One of the men had been sent to keep the horses hidden and quiet. The other two had been warned against letting themselves be seen before the Texian and his companions were disarmed.

There had been no doubt in Galsworthy's mind that the plan would succeed. A man of Ole Devil Hardin's background would do nothing to endanger the life of a woman, especially as she had apparently been helpful and was, as far as he knew, a loyal Texian.

The gamble had paid off. All that remained for Galsworthy to do was secure his prisoners and, provided they had done the work of removing the Mexican ship, await the arrival of the arms and the means to transport them.

[Note from page 147: The damage had gone unnoticed and unsuspected until late that afternoon. On running into a squall, the *Destructor* brig's violent motions had completed the work which had been done by Tommy Okasi's saw. First one of the carronades, then the others in rapid succession, broke free. Careering about the heeling deck, the angle of which had altered with sudden and unexpected speed as the weight upon it kept shifting, the guns created havoc and chaos. In addition to killing and injuring several members of the crew, one of them collided with and brought down the forward mast.

No fool, Lieutenant Givaljo realized that he had been tricked and drew fairly accurate conclusions as to why it had been done. However, in view of the fact that considerable damage had been inflicted upon the brig – not the least of which was the loss overboard of all the broadsides' armament – he had accepted that it would be impossible for him to return in the hope of intercepting the ship which he suspected the Texians were awaiting at Santa Cristobal Bay.

Being aware of what his fate would be when his superiors heard of what had happened, Grivaljo took the battered brig into a small, deserted bay on the coast of Texas under the pretence of making sufficient repairs to let them reach Matamoros. While the work was being carried out, he deserted and, later, surrendered to the garrison at a Texian town. On discovering that he had gone, the rest of the crew followed his example.]

CHAPTER SIXTEEN

YOU NEED A LESSON, MY GIRL

ANGER, resentment and annoyance at having fallen for the trick that had been played by the woman whom she knew as Madeline de Moreau, was boiling through Diamond-Hitch Brindley. It grew rather than diminished as the girl was watching the woman walking confidently towards her. There was an arrogant mockery and more than a hint of smug self-satisfaction on Madeline's beautiful features that Di was finding particularly infuriating. However, having no wish to endanger the lives of her two companions, the girl managed to hold her temper in check.

On reaching the place where Ole Devil Hardin had tossed the bowie knife and Manton pistol, Galsworthy halted with the intention of picking them up. Having studied them while he was approaching, he knew that each weapon was far too valuable to be allowed to fall into his men's hands. The rest of the party stopped when he did and stood awaiting his instructions. Instead of speaking, he thrust the uncocked pistol with which he had 'threatened' his wife through his waist-band.

Measuring with his eyes the distance which was separating him from his captors, Ole Devil accepted that it would be futile to take any action at that moment. Although Galsworthy was putting away his weapon and had not yet removed the sword from its cane-sheath, the two Mexicans still held their flintlock pistols in their hands. Before he could reach and tackle their leader, unless something happened to divert their attention, one or the other of them was sure to have thrown down on him. At such a short range, it was highly unlikely that they both would miss.

'The Mexican brig's gone, *hombre,* but we did what we planned before it sailed,' Ole Devil warned, playing for time. 'Which means it won't be coming back. There's no way *you* can take the ship when it arrives.'

'Seeing that I've got *you*, I don't even have to *try* to take it,' Galsworthy replied, so delighted by the success of his planning that he could not resist boasting. Respecting the young Texian as he did was such an unusual sensation that he wanted to impress the other in return. 'All I have to do is use the authorization Houston gave to you and the captain will hand over the consignment.'

'Like hell he will,' Ole Devil contradicted, with an air of complete assurance.

'Why not?' Galsworthy demanded, having no wish to fail because of some error in his thinking.

'My Uncle Marsden arranged the shipment and is coming with it,' Ole Devil explained, so convincingly that he might have been telling the full truth. 'He won't turn it over to anybody but *me*. Try thinking about that before you kill us.'

'Don't kill humble self, honourable and excellent gentleman!' Tommy Okasi wailed, throwing himself to his knees and closing the fingers of his right hand around the *kongo* stick.

Raising both hands above his head as if in supplication, the small Oriental shuffled forward on his knees and started to howl something in his native tongue.

'What the hell's he doing?' Galsworthy growled, straightening up without having retrieved either of the weapons on the ground. He eyed Tommy with contempt.

'Praying to his ancestors to protect him,' the Texian replied, raising his right hand slowly. Removing his hat, he laid it reverently across his chest and went on in Spanish, 'May the Good Lord forgive him for being a heathen.'

The gesture was so touching that one of the Mexicans, being religiously indoctrinated like so many of his race and creed, crossed himself with his left hand. He did not, however, turn his pistol from its alignment on the young Texian. Being either less impressed, or not so pious as his companion, the other Mexican continued to point his weapon in the small Oriental's direction.

Seeing the way Tommy was acting, Di might have felt disgusted if she had not recollected the things Ole Devil had told her about him. Remembering that he had willingly and without hesitation agreed to handle a potentially dangerous task aboard the brig – even though he had apparently failed in his purpose, she found his present cowardly behaviour puzzling.

Then enlightenment struck the girl!

With it came the realization that Tommy was only being partially successful in his deception. Although the Mexican whom he was approaching appeared to be amused by his 'terrified' grovelling, the pistol was still aiming straight at the centre of his chest. Before he could get close enough to do whatever he was planning, the man might become suspicious and squeeze the trigger.

What was needed, Di concluded, was something to distract the men's attention away from her friends.

The next question the girl decided was, how could she do it?

Turning her gaze along the line of her enemies, Di brought it back to Madeline. The woman was standing with her hands on her hips, and looking at Tommy with something between amusement and contempt. Becoming aware of the girl's eyes on her, she returned the scrutiny.

Having gained some considerable proficiency at playing poker, it being a favourite pastime of her grandfather and all their employees regardless of race, Di possessed a fair ability to read human emotions if they were shown. Taking in Madeline's obvious delight and pleasure over their predicament, the girl guessed what was causing it.

Although Di had thought nothing of it at the time, having had more important issues demanding her attention, she had sensed on the previous afternoon that – no matter how Madeline was reacting on the surface – there had been an undercurrent of animosity because Di had refused her assistance. The girl now realized what had brought it about. Clearly Madeline – who must be possessed of considerable courage, determination and confidence to have accepted her role in the fake rescue – had resented a much younger and far less worldly-wise member of her sex snubbing her. She was obviously incensed that Di believed she lacked the kind of qualities which would be required during the proposed deception of the Mexican naval officer.

The experienced and confident way in which the woman had put up her fists when Di appeared to be on the point of attacking her, taken with Galsworthy's comment that she had been fortunate not to have done so, suggested that Madeline might not be a pampered, delicate and well-bred lady. She could, in

157

fact, be a whole heap tougher than the girl had anticipated. What was more, while she filled the borrowed garments a mite snugly, there was little or no flabby fat on her gorgeous body.

Watching Madeline's face all the time, Di gripped the lapels of the riding habit's jacket. With a sudden jerk that popped off the buttons, she peeled it from her and flung it on to the ground. Anger replaced the mockery on the woman's beautiful features. Nor did it diminish as Di unfastened and released the shirt. Letting the garment slide down, the girl stepped backwards from it. She stood clad in her hat, the borrowed blouse, a pair of men's red woollen combinations and her moccasins.

'Here,' Di said, as she kicked the riding habit contemptuously in its owner's direction. 'Now you get the hell out of my duds, you fat bladder of cow-shit, afore you bust 'em at the seams.'

'You lousy little bitch!' Madeline hissed. Then she became calmer and started to move forward. Clenching and lifting her fists, she went on with malicious delight, 'You need a lesson, my girl.'

Almost before the woman had finished speaking, while Galsworthy was opening his mouth to yell at her to keep back, Di went into action. However, although the girl passed in front of Ole Devil, neither she nor Madeline came between him and the Mexican who was covering him

Seeing the girl darting to meet her, Madeline eagerly and briefly savoured the thought of what she was going to do. She wished that she was wearing some of her rings, as they had been of considerable use in other brawls. Having removed and left them in her husband's possession, as an added 'proof' that she had been robbed by her 'captors', she had not replaced them in case they should be noticed before the Texian was disarmed, warning him of what was really happening. However, she did not doubt that she could give the girl a thorough thrashing without such artificial aids.

Preparing to throw a punch into the girl's belly when close enough Madeline was expecting Di's hands to grab for her hair. Such had almost invariably been the tactics used by other women with whom she had come into conflict and it had given her a decided advantage. So it was an unpleasant surprise when, instead of obliging, the girl rammed a left jab into Madeline's right breast. What was more, the blow was far from being a wildly-thrown, unscientific feminine swing. Directed with masculine precision, the hard knuckles came in contact with the ultra-sensitive region.

Despite being almost at the end of its flight, Di's punch still caused enough pain to turn Madeline's advance into a retreat. Going back a couple of steps, the woman caught her balance and, as the girl followed, whipped up her right leg in a kick. Once again, the girl demonstrated that she was far more skilled than any of Madeline's earlier opponents. Stabbing out her hands, she caught the rising ankle with the right and cupped the left under the calf. Giving a heaving, circular twist, she turned the woman to her right and heaved. Screeching in mingled anger and alarm, Madeline went down and rolled over twice before coming to a halt on her back. Eager to make the most of her advantage, Di went after the woman.

Guessing what the girl was planning to do when he saw her disrobing, Ole Devil was ready to take advantage of any situation that might arise. The chance did not come immediately. However, as Madeline was pitched by him and Di followed her, the Mexican swung his gaze to watch them. In doing so, he allowed the barrel of his pistol to turn to the left.

Instantly, the Texian acted as he had planned to do if Tommy had succeeded in creating a diversion. Taking advantage of the fact that his three male enemies were watching the women, he sent his hat skimming through the air. It struck the Mexican on the left in the face, arriving with sufficient force to bring a yelping profane word of protest. Going back an involuntary pace, his forefinger jerked at the pistol's trigger. In doing so, he inadvertently caused the barrel to resume its alignment on Ole Devil.

The hammer fell, with the muzzle pointing straight at the centre of the Texian's chest!

Hitting and tilting forward the frizzen, the flint caused sparks which fell into the priming pan!

Like Ole Devil, Tommy had been alert for any chance to turn the tables on their adversaries. Seeing that the man in front of him was turning his head to stare at Di and Madeline, he stopped his lamentations and brought down his hands. If his captors had been more observant, they might have noticed that he had ended his crawling with the left knee on the ground and the right leg bent. It was a posture which allowed rapidity of movement.

Even as Ole Devil threw the hat, Tommy thrust himself

erect and forward all in one movement. There was need for every bit of speed he could muster. Catching the movement from the corner of his eye, the Mexican was starting to return his attention to the small Oriental.

Reaching Madeline, it became Di's turn to grow over-confident. Standing on her right leg, she raised her left foot with the intention of stamping on the woman. While Madeline had been taken by surprise, she was a skilled rider and had learned how to reduce the force of even an unexpected fall. So she was far from being as helpless as the girl imagined.

Rolling on to her side, Madeline let the downwards-thrusting foot strike her right shoulder. She was hurt by doing so, but not as badly as she would have been if she had taken the attack on the bust or stomach. Ignoring the pain, she grabbed for and jerked Di's right leg from under her. Losing her hat as she landed, the girl proved to be just as capable at breaking a fall. However, before she could recover, the woman was on top of her and two strong hands closed around her throat.

Moving like lightning, Tommy used his left hand in a scooping, outwards motion to deflect his victim's – and, under the circumstances, there could be no other term for the Mexican – weapon. Having turned the pistol so that it was no longer a threat to his well-being, the small Oriental demonstrated the true purpose of the *kongo* – and proved in no uncertain fashion that it was anything but a harmless piece of wood used as an aid to prayer.

A *kongo* was, in fact, a deadly weapon when wielded by a student of *yawara*.*

Even as his left hand came into contact with the pistol, Tommy was twisting his upper body in the opposite direction to the way he was pushing the weapon. He raised his right arm outwards, bending the elbow and turning the hand so that the knuckles were uppermost. Then he pivoted his torso to the front

* The self-defence system known as *yawara* had its origins in Okinawa over a thousand years ago. Having been forbidden by the invaders who had conquered their home land to own or carry weapons of any kind, the Okinawans had developed and perfected the use of the innocuous-looking *kongo* stick which became known as the 'six inches of death' because of its lethal capabilities. It was so simple to manufacture that, if one had to be discarded for any reason, there would be no difficulty in replacing it. The *kongo*'s small size made concealment easy and carrying had been no problem.

and snapped the right fist forward so that the rounded point*
of the *kongo* was carried towards its target.

The small Oriental's attack was delivered before its recipient
could even start to appreciate his terrible predicament. Nor was
he given a chance to try and avert it. Driving upwards with
speed and power, the *kongo*'s point ended its propulsion against
the *jinchu*; the collection of nerves which came together in the
centre of the top lip. Blood spurted as the wood ground into the
flesh and an unimaginable agony detonated through the Mexican. Everything seemed to disintegrate around him into a cata-
clysm of roaring flame. Slipping from his fingers, the pistol fell
to the ground.

From delivering the blow, Tommy let his hand continue to
rise until it was above his left shoulder. Once again he whipped
it forward. This time, it was the butt of the *kongo* that connected. There was a sharp crack as it impacted on the centre of
the man's forehead. Already being driven to the rear, he pitched
over on to his back. He would never rise again, dying of con-
cussion without regaining consciousness.

Leaping forward to tackle Galsworthy, Ole Devil saw the
hammer of the Mexican's pistol swinging around and was
aware of where its barrel was pointing. There was, he realized,
nothing that he could do to save himself.

When Madeline rolled on to her, Di reacted instinctively and
in a completely feminine manner. Even as the hands started to
tighten and the woman raised her head from the ground, the
girl's fingers sank deep into the brunette locks. It was not the
first time that Madeline had had her hair pulled, but never with
such strength and savage violence. Screeching a pain-filled protest, she felt as if the top of her skull was being torn off. She
reared back and released the girl's neck with the idea of grabbing the wrists to try and relieve the agony. Instantly Di un-
tangled the right hand, folded and struck out with it. Caught
on the nose, Madeline's head snapped back and blood flowed
from her nostrils. The girl gave a surging heave which toppled
the woman from the upper position and twisted to gain it herself. Straddling Madeline's waist with her knees, Di sat up and
started to assail the beautiful, anger and pain distorted, features
with fore and backhand slaps.

Ole Devil should have been killed only one thing saved his

* The end of the *kongo* which protruded from between the thumb
and forefinger was the 'point' and the other end, the 'butt'.

life. The basic and often fatal flow of the flintlock system.

Having been out in the cold, damp air, the powder in the priming pan failed to ignite. Letting out a startled exclamation, the Mexican stared down at his weapon. Then, allowing it to fall from his hand, he grabbed at the knife that was sheathed on the left side of his belt.

Furious at his wife for her behaviour, Galsworthy saw Ole Devil approaching. At the same moment, he became aware of the change that had come over Tommy. Snapping a quick glance to his right, he saw the little Oriental delivering the attack. Hearing the dead click of a pistol and its user's exclamation, he swung his gaze in the other direction. What he saw filled him with alarm and he guessed what had caused the weapon to misfire. In all probability, his own pistol would fail to function for the same reason.

Ignoring the weapon that was thrust into his belt and those which were just in front of him, Galsworthy sprang backwards. His actions were motivated by a desire to gain sufficient time to unsheath his sword from inside the cane. Even as he moved, he realized that he was committing an error in tactics. If he had stood his ground, he might have been able to prevent the Texian from arming himself. It was, however, too late to change his mind. So he gripped the cane, twisted and started to draw from it the shining, razor-sharp blade.

'Dodd!' Galsworthy bellowed as the sword was coming free. 'Dodd! Get here!'

Reaching his weapons, Ole Devil grabbed for the one which he felt was most suited to his needs. He had watched Galsworthy's hurried retreat and guessed what was the reason for it even before he saw the unsheathing of the sword. To his right, the Mexican was already moving forward and pulling out a knife. While the pistol was percussion-fired and relatively impervious to damp, it held only a single shot. So Ole Devil's right hand closed around the concave ivory handle of the bowie knife.

Plucking the weapon from the ground, with Galsworthy's yell ringing in his ears, Ole Devil swung it around and out to the right. Seeing the great knife rushing at him, the Mexican arched his stomach to the rear and, with his body bent like a bow, flung himself away from its arc. Nor was he a moment too soon. The convex curve of the blade's point barely missed him. Continuing to withdraw and sliding free his own weapon, which suddenly seemed very puny and fragile in comparison to that held by the Texian, he was relieved when his assailant did not favour him with any further attentions, but went straight by.

Without waiting to see if there was any response to his yell, Galsworthy hurled the empty cane so that it went spinning parallel to the ground and at the Texian's head. Still moving forward, Ole Devil threw up his left hand to knock the missile aside. Galsworthy sprang forward, going into an almost classical lunge which sent the point of his sword flashing towards the young man's stomach.

After taking two slaps in each direction, which had rocked her head from side to side, Madeline responded. She was being held down by the girl's weight and knew what to do about it. Leaving the left wrist, as she realized that all she was doing was adding to the pain its hand was inflicting on her hair, she sent her fingers to the girl's bust. Sinking like talons into the firm mounds under the flimsy cover of the woollen combinations, they crushed and squeezed. Shrieking, Di tried to jerk away. As the pressure upon her was relieved, Madeline tipped Di over and regained the upper position. She was not there for long. Using all her strength, Di contrived to reverse their roles. Tearing at hair, slapping, punching, scrabbling and gripping with their hands, they rolled along the ground oblivious of everything except their hatred for each other.

Taking no notice of the squealing of the embattled women, Ole Devil skidded to a stop. Like many young men of his class and generation, he had been a regular attendant at a *salle des armes*. Not only had he learned fencing with the sabre and *epee de combat*, but his instructions had included fighting with a bowie knife against a similar weapon or a sword. The training stood him in good stead at that moment. Swinging the knife around in a circular motion, he used the flat of the blade to strike and deflect the sword to his left. Once it was clear of him, he disengaged and attempted a backhand slash to his opponent's neck. Galsworthy's rapid stride to the rear saved him. The razor-sharp false edge hissed by and, as he was about to advance, the knife returned in a swing that would have laid its edge across his throat if he had begun to move. Stepping further back, almost involuntarily, he made a rapid cut across with the sword only to be thwarted by the Texian's equally swift withdrawal.

On the point of going to his leader's assistance, the Mexican became aware that Tommy was coming towards him. A glance at the bloody face of his companion, who was sprawled supine and motionless, gave a warning that the small Oriental might be far more dangerous than his earlier behaviour had suggested. However, as the Mexican held a knife and was skilled in its use, he did not feel particularly perturbed. He failed to notice the *kongo*. Even if he had seen it, having been watching the women when his *amigo* was attacked, he probably would not have appreciated its true purpose. Darting to meet Tommy, he put his faith in a low thrust that curved inwards towards the stomach.

Protecting himself with a backhand and downwards blow, Tommy miscalculated a little. His wrist struck the Mexican's forward driving forearm. While the knife was turned to his left and in front of him, the defence was less damaging than it would have been if it had been delivered by the rounded butt of the *kongo*. Instead of having his arm numbed, if not more seriously injured, the Mexican was able to snatch it clear of the small Oriental's wrist. Then he whipped the knife back and up in the direction of Tommy's throat.

Having heard the commotion, and also seeing something which had been a source of pleasure and satisfaction, the last member of Galsworthy's party ran from behind the clump of bushes which was being used to hide the horses. Taking in the sight a good hundred and fifty yards away, he cocked and whipped the rifle that he was carrying to his shoulder. At the same time, he gave advice and some news which he felt sure his leader would find most acceptable under the circumstances.

'Get clear of him, boss!' the man yelled, trying to line his weapon but not caring to attempt a shot at that distance with the Texian so near to Galsworthy. 'It's all right. Some of the boys're coming.'

CHAPTER SEVENTEEN

I'LL KILL YOU FOR THIS, HARDIN!

HEARING his man's yell, Galsworthy tried to do as he had been requested. However, Ole Devil Hardin had also heard and appreciated the danger. So, when Galsworthy leapt backwards, he followed and tried to crowd in closer. Even though retreating, Galsworthy continued to wield his sword defensively. The extra length of his enemy's blade forced the Texian to keep at a distance from which his bowie knife could not make contact. Yet, if the man was speaking the truth – and there did not appear to be any reason why he should lie – there was urgent need for Ole Devil to act quickly. He had to deal with Galsworthy, separate the fighting women and get his party into the shelter of the cabin before the reinforcements arrived.

Crouching swiftly, Tommy Okasi allowed the Mexican's knife to pass just above his head. Having done so, he lunged forward with his right arm. Rising rapidly, the point of the *kongo* took his assailant in the *solar plexus* with all the driving force of his muscular frame behind it. Such a blow was deadly in the extreme. Letting go of the knife, as the sudden onrush of pain caused paralysis and loss of consciousness, the man crumpled. He went down like a pole-axed steer and with just as permanent results.

Even as the Mexican was falling, Tommy sprang clear and turned his attention to his companions. Diamond-Hitch Brindley and Madeline de Moreau were rolling over and over, screeching like a pair of enraged bobcats. In a tangle of wildly thrashing and waving limbs. Deciding that they were the least of his worries at the moment, for he too had heard Dodd's shouted advice, he swung his gaze to where Galsworthy was trying to put it into effect.

Lining his rifle, Dodd saw what he felt would be his chance. Galsworthy had retired fast enough to put just sufficient distrance between him and the Texian for the man to be willing to act. His forefinger tightened on the trigger and, unlike the Mexican, he had contrived to keep the powder in his priming pan dry. So, after the inevitable brief delay while the priming charge ignited, reached and detonated the powder in the chamber, the rifle roared.

Hit in the upper part of the crown by Dodd's bullet, Ole Devil's hat that was snatched from his head. While he realized what must have happened, the narrow escape caused him to duck involuntarily. Like a flash, Galsworthy turned his retreat into an attack. He saw that he had passed beyond the point where a lunge would serve his purpose. So, despite being aware of the basic flaw in its use, he went into a *flèche*. Bounding forward, he drove ahead with the sword at shoulder height and his torso leaning towards his potential victim.

With the needle-sharp point of the sword rushing in his direction, Ole Devil halted on spread apart feet and slightly bent knees. Just – and only just – in time, he swivelled himself at the hips and inclined his torso to the rear. As his assailant's weapon went by, its edge slicing a couple of the buckskin fringe's thongs from his shirt, he reversed his direction and the bowie knife swung in a glistening arc.

With a sickening sensation of horror, Galsworthy saw that his attack had failed. The worse feature of the *flèche* was that, if it did not succeed, the almost invariable result was a complete loss of balance and control from which, particularly against such an able opponent, there was no hope of recovery. So it proved. Carried onwards by the impetus of his movements, he watched the great knife passing under his sword arm. Then a sudden numbing sensation drove all coherent thought from his head. Biting in through his shirt, the blade sank deep and tore across his belly. There was a rush of blood and his intestines poured from the hideous wound as he stumbled by the Texian. Sinking to his knees, he toppled forward on to his face.

Having disposed of his attacker, Ole Devil straightened up and looked around. He found that Tommy had already succeeded in rendering the second Mexican *hors-de-combat*, which did not come as any surprise. However, the danger was far from over. The man whose bullet had nearly ended the fight in Galsworthy's favour had turned and was yelling for the group of about ten riders who were approaching to get a move

166

on. Having seen and heard, Ole Devil swung his eyes to the two women.

'Grab my pistol, Tommy!' the Texian ordered, knowing that an extra weapon might be very useful. 'Then get Di into the cabin.'

'Can do!' the little Oriental answered as Ole Devil swung around and started to run to where their horses were standing.

Going forward, Tommy returned the *kongo* to his trousers' pocket. He picked up the Manton pistol and, guessing that he was going to need both hands to separate the women, thrust it through his waist belt. Waiting until Di came on top, he bent and catching her under the armpits, heaved. The girl let out a startled shriek as she felt herself plucked from her rival and sent staggering backwards. Sitting up, Madeline tried to rise. Before she could do so, Tommy delivered a *tegatana* chop to the top of her head. Stunned, she flopped limply on to her back.

Wild with rage, Di managed to keep on her feet and came to a stop. The blouse had gone and the combinations had been torn from her left shoulder, leaving that side of her torso bare to the waist. Oblivious of her appearance, she charged forward so as to resume the attack on her recumbent opponent.

Realizing that trying to reason with the girl in her present frame of mind would be a waste of time, Tommy made no attempt to do so. Darting to meet her, he caught her right wrist with his left hand as she tried to hit him. Bending forward, he thrust his other hand between her legs and, turning, jerked her across his shoulders. To the accompaniment of blistering invective from the furious girl, while her legs waved wildly and her free hand beat a tattoo on his back, he started to run towards the cabin. On entering, he dumped Di to the floor hard enough to jolt the wind out of her. Satisfied that he could leave her untended for the moment and hoping that, on recovering her breath, she would also come to her senses, he returned to the door. As he did so, he pulled out and cocked the pistol. From what he could hear, the weapon was likely to be needed in the near future.

Reaching his dun, Ole Devil slid the Browning rifle from its sheath with his left hand. Keeping the riders under observation, he noticed that one of them was better mounted than the rest and had already passed Dodd. Like his companions, who were coming as fast as they could manage, the leader had already

167

drawn and cocked a pistol. Deciding to wait until he was indoors before loading the Browning, Ole Devil sprinted towards the cabin. As he was approaching the half-way point, he realized that the leading rider would have reached him before he could attain the safety of the building.

Seeing his employer's predicament, Tommy Okasi sprang outside. He swung up the Manton in both hands, sighted and fired. Struck in the chest by the bullet, the man slid sideways from his saddle. Slowing down to let the horse race by, Ole Devil increased his pace as it did so. Several shots were fired at him. With lead flying around him, he flung himself the last few feet. Stepping aside to let Ole Devil enter, Tommy followed him in and slammed the door.

Dropping the bowie knife, the Texian hurried to the nearest window. As he went, he reached behind him to pull a magazine bar from the pouch on the back of his belt. He eased it into the aperture, guiding it home and thumbing down the lever to seat it correctly. Then, drawing down the under-hammer, he thrust the barrel through the window to line it at the approaching men. Although he was aware that the pistol in his hand was empty, Tommy went to the other window and duplicated Ole Devil's actions.

Seeing the two weapons emerging and pointing in their direction, the remainder of Galsworthy's men veered away. While the pistol and the rifle held only a single shot each, or so they assumed in the latter's case, every man was aware that he had only one life. With that sobering thought in mind, not one of them was willing to press home the attack as he might become selected as a target. Instead, they galloped by the building, those who had not already done so firing in passing. The rest took in the sight of their companions who had already fallen to the defenders.

Galsworthy and the two Mexicans lay without movement, the former in an ever-growing pool of his own blood. Sitting up and feeling at her head, Madeline gazed about her dazedly. The buckskin shirt had come out of her borrowed trousers, which were now burst open along the seams. Her underclothing had been torn apart in the tussle, leaving her magnificent bosom exposed. Such a sight would have warranted the men's attention and study under less demanding circumstances, despite her once immaculate hair now resembling a woollen mop and her slap-reddened face being smeared by gore from her own and Di's bleeding noses. Sobbing as she fought to replenish her lungs, she started to rise.

In the cabin, the girl was also recovering. Gasping in air, she managed to get to her feet. For a moment she stood swaying and glaring about her as if ready to attack the first thing that moved. Then the wild light faded from her eyes as she realized where she was and, from her companions' positions at the windows, what must be happening outside. Ignoring the blood which was running out of her nostrils to splash from her chin on to her heaving and only partially covered breasts, she staggered to where her rifle was standing in the corner. Grabbing it up, she crossed to where Ole Devil was standing and cocked back the hammer as she went.

Standing up and swaying in exhaustion, Madeline had acted in much the same way as Di was doing in the building. Then she too became aware that the situation had changed. Staring around, her eyes came to rest on her husband's body. For a moment, she looked at the gory corpse. A shudder shook her and she swung away from it.

'I'll kill you for this, Hardin!' the woman shrieked, glaring and shaking her fists at the cabin.

Even if she had tried, Madeline could hardly have selected a worse – or – in one way, better – moment to make the threat. Even as she spoke, Di reached the window of the cabin. Before Ole Devil could stop her, the girl had lined the rifle and was squeezing its trigger. Although the weapon roared, Madeline was lucky. Still feeling the effects of being dropped on to the floor, Di was not controlling her breathing and caused the barrel of her rifle to waver up and down. So the bullet passed just over, instead of through, the woman's head. The narrow escape from death served as a warning to Madeline. Turning, she fled as fast as her exhausted condition would allow to where her men had halted their horses about a hundred and fifty yards from the building. One of them returned, guiding his mount around and, scooping her up, he carried her to their companions.

'Wh – What now?' Di gasped, lowering the rifle.

'Get loaded before they come at us,' Ole Devil answered. 'Tommy, string your bow. I'll try to keep them back while you're doing it.'

Holding the Browning ready for use while his orders were being carried out, the Texian watched the woman's rescuer set her down by the rest of the men. They were recharging their pistols, but she started to order – or try to persuade – them to attack the cabin. Ole Devil guessed that they would take some action – although he doubted if it would be a frontal assault – once the weapons were ready.

Everything depended upon whether Di could reload her rifle and Tommy string the bow before the men had made their preparations. Even if they did, the odds were still in their assailants' favour.

Suddenly Dodd, who had joined his companions leading the woman's and dead men's horses, let out a yell and pointed to the west. Although Ole Devil could not see what had attracted his attention, clearly the other men found it a cause for alarm. Their horses milled as they stared in the direction Dodd had indicated and consternation reigned amongst them.

'Rush the house!' Madeline howled. 'You can do it before they get here!'

'Like hell we can!' a man answered and set his horse into motion. 'I'm going!'

Panic was always infectious. Given such guidance, the rest of the men followed their companion's example. Splitting up, they scattered in every direction except the west. Only Dodd remained, saying something urgently to the raging woman and pointing to the horse with two bed-rolls fastened to the cantle of its saddle. When she showed no sign of taking his advice, Dodd dropped the reins of the animals he was leading and sent his own mount bounding forward. The final desertion appeared to have a sobering effect on the woman. Going to the horse which the man had indicated, she hauled herself on to its saddle and followed him.

Puzzled by the departure, Ole Devil wondered if it might be a trick to lure his party into the open. Two minutes went by and, as Di joined him holding the reloaded rifle, he saw something that informed him there was no further danger from Madeline and her men.

On his return to the Texas Light Cavalry, Mannen Blaze had given Colonel Fog a report and a request from Ole Devil. The latter having been granted, Mannen had set off to join his cousin, accompanied by the whole of Company 'C'. Fifty strong, they had arrived in time to chase away their commanding officer's enemies.

Next day, just before noon, the ship glided into Santa

Cristobal Bay. Standing on the rim and watching the anchor go down, Ole Devil and Di exchanged glances. The girl had tidied up her appearance and donned clothes from her warbag. Apart from a black eye and swollen top lip, she showed no evidence of the fight. With his men tired from their long, hard ride, Ole Devil had not sent them after Madeline. He had doubted whether she would cause any more trouble.

Going down the slope towards the water's edge, young Ole Devil Hardin felt a sense of elation. The ship had brought the rifles. Now it was up to him to see that they reached General Houston.

OLE DEVIL AND THE CAPLOCKS

*To Chuck and Ellen Kurtzman of Fort Worth, Texas
with fond memories of many a filling of Ubert with
'Limpopo Water'.*

AUTHOR'S NOTE

Whilst complete in itself, events in this book continue from those recorded in YOUNG OLE DEVIL. Although readers have been promised more information about the composition and operation of a Mule Train, regretfully space has not permitted me to include it in this book, but I promise it will be given in THE DEVIL AND THE MULE TRAIN (not as stated in various footnotes in OLE DEVIL AT SAN JACINTO).

Chapter One

THEY COULD CHANGE HISTORY

HAVING been carried in by the sea breeze and flowing tide shortly before noon on February the 26th, 1836, the two masted trading brig *Bostonian Lady* was rocking gently at its anchor. There was an air of urgency about the actions of the sailors who were starting to transfer some of the cargo from the forward hold to the boats which had been lowered. Although Captain Adams had not offered any explanation, they realized that only exceptional circumstances could have caused him to accept the navigational hazards of bringing his vessel into the small, landlocked, Santa Cristóbal Bay. Situated about ten miles north of the Matagorda Peninsula, it was in what was usually an unpopulated region. The nearest human habitation was the tiny port of San Phillipe, which they had passed on their southbound course some fifteen miles further up the Texas coast.

From all appearances, the captain had not been surprised to find human beings at the bay. In fact, his behaviour had suggested that he was expecting to find somebody in what should have been a deserted area. On approaching the coastline, he had studied the mouth of the bay through his telescope. Although they did not have similar aids to vision, a couple of the hands claimed they had seen a man waving what appeared to be a blanket from the cliffs above the entrance. Despite this signal, Adams had not entered immediately. Instead, the *Bostonian Lady* had hove to off-shore for almost an hour. During that period he had climbed the main mast and searched the horizon; presumably to satisfy himself that there were no other vessels within visual distance. When sure that they were unobserved, he had descended and given orders to go in.

On entering the bay, there had been indisputable evidence that the visit was prearranged. Several men were gathered on the beach and the brig's sole passenger had been sent ashore in the jolly boat. As soon as he had landed, orders had been given that had set the crew to work.

Few of the sailors took much interest in current affairs unless the issues involved were such as might affect them personally, but even the most disinterested of them could not help being aware that at that time there was some kind of serious trouble taking place in Texas. It had been the main topic of conversation around New Orleans for several months past. None of the fo'c's'le hands had extensive knowledge of why the Anglo-Saxon colonists and not a few *Chicanos** had elected to sever all connections with Mexico and establish a self-governing Republic under the Lone Star flag.† Nor did they particularly care. What did concern them was an uneasy feeling that the local authorities would not approve, to put it mildly, of their visit.

The suspicion had been strengthened when the sailors were told which items of the cargo to extract from the hold. The designated boxes had caused comment and speculation after they had been loaded at New Orleans. Some were oblong, about five foot in length, three wide, three deep, and heavy. The rest were lighter and roughly three foot square. All had one significant point in common. There was nothing on them to say what their contents might be, from whence they had come, nor to where and whom they were to be delivered.

However, the hands knew better than to mention their misgivings openly. Captain Nathaniel Adams was a

* Chicano: *a Mexican, or Spanish born citizen of Texas.*
† *The reason for the colonists' decision is explained at length in:* YOUNG OLE DEVIL.

12

humane, tolerant and easy-going man—in comparison with many of his class—but he would not—could not—permit the members of his crew to question his actions. So they set to work as quickly as possible in order to reduce the length of time they must spend in such a potentially precarious location.

Fortunately for the crew, none of them stopped to think too deeply about their situation. Having arrived at their destination at the commencement of the incoming tide and with the breeze blowing from the sea towards the land, the *Bostonian Lady* would have difficulty in leaving before the ebb. Even after the tide had turned, it might be necessary to tow the brig out to sea with her boats. Going out before the ebb would be a slow and laborious task. Too slow, in all probability, for them to escape if anything should go wrong.

Captain Adams had a better appreciation of the position. While he was not fully cognizant with the causes of the strife which was embroiling Texas, he knew that carrying out the mission which had brought him to Santa Cristóbal Bay was placing himself and his vessel in considerable jeopardy. If he should be caught, the very least he could expect was for the *Bostonian Lady* to be impounded. From what he knew of Latin officials—and he had seen plenty of them during his years of trading from the *Rio Bravo** in the north, via Cuba and Puerto Rico, as far as the *Rio de la Plata* in South America—his fate was likely to be far worse than that. He had been well paid, with the certainty of other and less risky cargoes in the future. Arrangements which appeared to be working, had been made to reduce the risks, but he knew that there was still danger and he would not be sorry when he could get under way. Once he was out at sea, it would be very difficult for the Mexican authorities to prove that he had been connected with the unmarked consignment.

* Rio Bravo: *the Mexicans' name for the Rio Grande.*

13

'I've got the cargo broken out and am having it put into the boats, cap'n,' announced the mate, having come from the forward hold to where his superior was standing amidships studying the beach through a telescope. 'So I hope yon fancy dressed supercargo* knows what he's talking about.'

'He said he knew the party who were waiting, Mr. Shrift,' Adams pointed out. 'And he wouldn't be fool enough to go ashore unless he was certain that everything's all right. You can start sending his consignment across.'

'Aye aye, sir,' the mate assented and returned to supervise the work.

For all the captain's comment, he felt perturbed. The men who had hired him had laid great emphasis upon the need for secrecy and that their consignment must not be permitted to fall into the wrong hands. In spite of having received the correct signal from the cliffs and his passenger's assurance that all was well, he was uneasy when he thought of the reception committee. While none of the quartet who had come to the water's edge looked like Mexicans, neither did they appear to be a delegation from the Republic of Texas; particularly when something so important was involved.

While the man at the left of the party most assuredly was not of Latin origin, neither did he spring from Anglo-Saxon stock. In fact, despite Adams' entire sea service having been confined to the eastern side of the American continent and its off shore islands, he was able to recognize that the man was a native of the Orient.

Not quite five foot six in height, but with a sturdy build, the Oriental was young. Bare headed, his black hair was close cropped and he had sallow, almond-eyed, cheerful features. His garments were a loose fitting black shirt hanging outside trousers of a similar material which were

* Supercargo: an agent placed on board a ship to be in charge of the purchase, sale, or safe delivery of a consignment. Often used as a derogatory term by sailors.

14

tucked into matching Hessian boots.† Apart from his foot-wear and the lack of a pigtail, he might have been a Chinese coolie such as could be seen in most of the United States' major seaports. However, one rarely saw a coolie carrying weapons and he appeared to be well, if primitively, armed. A pair of long hilted, slightly curved swords with small circular guards hung—the shorter at the right—with their sheaths attached by slings to his leather waistbelt. In addition, he held a long bow in his left hand and a quiver hanging across his right shoulder pointed the flights of several arrows so they would be readily accessible when required.

Adams found the second member of the quartet equally puzzling, but in a different way. About three or four inches taller than the Oriental, the snug fit of a fringed buckskin shirt, trousers and rawhide moccasins left no doubt that—in spite of a pistol thrust through the right side of a belt which also had a knife hanging at the left in an Indian-made sheath—it was a girl in her late 'teens and fast approaching the full bloom of woman-hood. Her fiery red and curly hair had been cut fairly short. For all that the right eye was blackened and the top lip swollen, her pretty, freckled face expressed a happy-go-lucky zest for life. While the attire was uncon-ventional to say the least for a member of her sex, it seemed to suit her personality, and, somehow, the weap-ons she was carrying did not appear incongruous in her possession.

From the similarity of their clothing, the remaining pair were apparently clad in some type of uniform. Hanging on their shoulders by *barbiquejo* chinstraps, they had black hats of the low crowned, wide brimmed pattern which had become popular as *Presidente* Antonio Lopez de Santa Anna's repressive and obstructive policies had

---

† *Hessian boots: designed for riding, with legs extending to just below the knee and having a 'V' shaped notch at the front, orig-inally used by light cavalry such as Hussars.*

caused a growing antipathy among young Texians*
towards everything of Mexican origin. Their buckskin
shirts were tucked into tight legged fawn riding breeches
and they had on Hessian boots. A pistol carried in a
broad, slanting leather loop on the right side of the belt
had its butt turned forward so as to be available to either
hand. It was balanced by a massive knife of the kind
which had already acquired the name 'bowie'† in honour
of the man who was credited with designing the original
weapon. There was only one noticeable difference in the
pair's attire. The man next to the girl sported a long,
tightly rolled bandana that was a riot of clashing colours
while his companion's was plain scarlet.

At least six foot tall, the man with the scarlet bandana
appeared to be in his early twenties. Bulky of build, he
conveyed an impression of well padded, contented lethargy. He had curly auburn hair and there was an amiable
expression on his sun-reddened face.

Unless Adams missed his guess, the remaining member
of the group was its leader. Matching his Anglo-Saxon
companion's size and about the same age, he had a whipcord lean physique. He stood with a straight-backed alertness that was emphasised by the other's almost slouching
posture. However, it was his features which the captain
found most interesting. Combed back above the temples,
his black hair seemed to form two small, curved horns.
Taken with eyebrows like inverted 'V's', a neatly trimmed
moustache and a short, sharp pointed chin beard, either
accidentally or deliberately the protuberances made his
lean, tanned, otherwise handsome face look like the
accepted conception of the Devil's physiognomy.

---

* Texian: an Anglo-U.S.-born citizen of Texas, the 'i' being
dropped from general usage after annexation by the United States
and the Mexican War of 1846-48.
† What happened to James Bowie's knife after his death at the
conclusion of the siege of the Alamo Mission—at San Antonio
de Bexar, Texas, on March the 6th, 1836—is told in: THE QUEST
FOR BOWIE'S BLADE.

Even from a distance of close to a quarter of a mile, aided by the magnification of his powerful telescope, Adams' shrewd judgement of human nature led him to determine that the slender young man bore the undefinable and yet recognizable aura of a born leader. He comported himself with assurance, but there was no trace of self-conscious arrogance which frequently marked a less competent person who had been placed in a position of authority. In spite of that, he struck the captain as being an unusual choice for so important a task as collecting and delivering the consignment.

Despite appreciating how vital the goods in his charge might prove to be in the Texians' struggle for independence, the 'supercargo' had not shared Adams' qualms. In fact, Beauregard Rassendyll had been delighted when—using a borrowed telescope as the brig was approaching its anchorage—he had discovered who was to be his escort. He had not hesitated to request that he be taken ashore, or in confirming that the consignment could be landed. What was more, his only slight misgivings were relieved by the conversation which took place shortly after he had stepped from the jolly boat.

'Beau!' greeted the slender young man, striding forward with his right hand held out. 'I thought it was you, but Cousin Mannen said Uncle Marsden couldn't be so short of reliable help that he'd need to send *you*.'

'Huh!' Rassendyll sniffed, looking all around the bay with an over-exaggerated care. 'I was told I'd have a suitable escort waiting. You wouldn't have seen them, would you, Devil?'

In spite of the comments, there was pleasure on the two young men's faces as their hands met and shook. Then they studied each other as friends would when meeting after a lengthy separation.

Studying the most obvious change in Jackson Baines Hardin's appearance, Rassendyll felt puzzled. There had always been a slightly Mephistophelian aspect to his features, which in part had produced his nickname 'Ole

17

Devil',* but the horn-like effect caused by the way his hair was combed, the moustache and beard, tended to emphasise it. Being aware of the circumstances which had compelled him to come to Texas, the supercargo would have expected him to avoid anything that made him easily identifiable.

Returning the scrutiny, Ole Devil found little change in Rassendyll. His senior by four years, the supercargo topped him by about three inches and, although not as bulky as Mannen Blaze, was more heavily built. Red haired, clean shaven and handsome, clad in a white 'planter's' hat and riding clothes cut in the latest fashion popular among the wealthy young Southrons of Louisiana, he looked as hard and fit as when they had served together on a merchant ship commanded by Ole Devil's father.

'They've sent you *the* best,' the Mephistophelian-featured Texian declared, releasing his right hand so that he could indicate a group of about twenty well armed men in similar attire to his own. They were standing about two hundred yards away, with a number of excellent quality horses. 'Isn't that right, Cousin Mannen?'

'You've never been righter, Cousin Devil,' confirmed Mannen Blaze, in a sleepy drawl that matched his lethargic attitude, having ambled forward to his kinsman's side. However, there was nothing weak or tired in his grip as he shook the supercargo's hand. 'You ask most anybody, Beau, and see what they say about Company 'C' of the Texas Light Cavalry.'

'I'd hate to, if there were ladies present,' Rassendyll stated, glancing past the Texans in a pointed manner. 'Hello there, Tommy—ma'am.'

'This is an old friend of ours, Beauregard Rassendyll, from New Orleans, Di,' Ole Devil introduced, taking the hint and presenting the supercargo to the girl and the lit-

---

* *A more important cause of Jackson Baines Hardin's nickname was his well deserved reputation for being a 'lil ole devil' in a fight.*

18

tle Oriental. 'I wish I could say he was kin, you can't pick them. Beau, I'd like you to meet Diamond-Hitch Brindley. She and her grandfather are handling the transportation of the consignment.'

A keen student of women, Rassendyll had been examining the girl with interest. While she was not yet twenty and dressed in a most unusual manner, there was little of the shy, naive, backwoods maiden about her. Nor, despite the revealing nature of her garments, did she appear brazen and wanton. Instead, her whole attitude was redolent of self confident competence. It implied that she was used to the company of men and dealing with them as equals, neither ignoring nor playing upon the fact that she was an attractive member of the opposite sex.

The supercargo was aware that he was being studied and analysed just as thoroughly, and he found the sensation a trifle disconcerting. Normally he would have enjoyed being stared at by such a good looking and shapely person, but on this occasion he deduced that it was not for the usual flattering reasons. She was not contemplating him with a view to a possible romance. Rather she was considering him as a man would consider another member of his sex who would be accompanying him upon a hazardous endeavour. He was as yet an unknown quantity who might prove more of a liability than an asset. From her attitude it appeared that while she was willing to accept him as the friend of somebody for whom she had considerable respect, he would have to win her approbation on his own merits.

'I'm not *so* old, Miss Brindley,' Rassendyll corrected, offering his hand. He wondered how the girl had come by such a strange Christian name and how she had received the injuries to her face. 'It's just that knowing this pair has aged me.'

'Likely,' Charlotte Jane Martha Brindley admitted, shaking hands. 'Only the name's "Di", which's short for

19

"Diamond-Hitch" and I'm called that because I can throw one faster, tighter 'n' better than anybody, man, woman, or child. How soon'll we be getting 'em over here, Beau?'

'The crew should be fetching the first of them in the next few minutes,' Rassendyll replied, having been impressed by the strength and hardness of her hand. 'Are your wagons coming down?'

'We're using mules, not wagons,' Ole Devil put in. 'It was decided that they'd be quicker and better suited to our needs.'

'Grandpappy Ewart's fetching 'em along,' Di went on. 'But we figured's how we'd best come ahead to make sure it'd be safe for them to be landed.'

'And I presume that it is safe,' Rassendyll remarked, making the words a statement rather than a question.

'It is,' Di confirmed. 'Now.'

'Did you run into trouble, Devil?' Rassendyll inquired, swinging around to look at the Texian.

'Some,' Ole Devil admitted, but nothing could be read from his Mesphistophelian features to suggest just how serious the trouble might have been. 'With any luck, it's all over now.'

'Huh!' snorted Di. 'The way those damned renegades lit out, they won't dare come back and, after what Tommy did to it, that blasted Mexican ship'll not be able to.'

'Renegades,' the supercargo repeated. *'Ship!'*

'There were a bunch of renegades around,' Ole Devil explained. 'But Cousin Mannen arrived with Company "C" and drove them off. We found a ten gun brig taking on water in the bay, but we tricked its captain into leaving. It went south and, provided we don't have any delays, we should have finished here and the ship'll be gone before it could beat back.'

'If I know Captain Adams, there won't be any delays. He knows too well what will happen to him if he's caught,' Rassendyll stated, then glanced at the men with the

20

horses. Knowing something of the Republic of Texas's newly formed Army, he continued, 'Is that your full Company?'

'Less than half of it,' Ole Devil answered in a reassuring manner. 'I've sent twenty-five men to the mule train in case they should be needed. The rest are beyond the rim, some keeping watch from the cliffs in case that Mexican brig comes back, the rest acting as pickets on the range.'

'Good,' Rassendyll praised, finding that his misgivings about the small size of the escort were groundless. 'If you'll bring the mules down, we can start loading them as soon as the consignment arrives from the brig.'

'It's not that easy,' Di warned. 'You can't move pack mules as quickly as riding hosses. So Grandpappy Ewart won't be able to get 'em here afore sundown at the soonest.'

'*Sundown*?' Rassendyll repeated, glancing at the sky as if to estimate how much longer they would have to wait. 'Adams won't agree to stay in the bay until then.'

'He doesn't need to,' Ole Devil replied. 'In fact, he can leave as soon as he's sent the consignment ashore. One of the reasons we came on ahead of the mule train was so he could land it and set sail again with the minimum of delay.'

'On top of that,' Di went on, bristling a little at what she regarded as the supercargo's implied criticism of their arrangements. 'We figure on having the rifles packed ready for moving when Grandpappy Ewart gets here.'

'There's no need for *that*,' Rassendyll protested. 'We aren't carrying them loose, they're in boxes of twenty-four.'

'Our mules can tote twenty-four a-piece all right, but not while they're in a wooden box,' Di countered, and the supercargo could sense that the conversation was doing nothing to improve her opinion of him. 'So we aim to take 'em out and put 'em in bundles of twelve.'

'Can you get us enough canvas from the ship to wrap

21

them in, Beau?' Ole Devil inquired, hiding the amusement he was feeling over having noticed the girl's attitude towards his friend and recollecting that she had treated him in a similar fashion on their first meeting. 'We were travelling fast and couldn't bring anything with us to make up the bundles.'

'I'll ask the captain to send some over,' Rassendyll promised. 'I was told that I could make any purchases which might be necessary.'

'*Bueno*,' Ole Devil drawled.

'You called it right, Beau,' Mannen put in, before his cousin could continue. 'They're surely not wasting any time. Here comes the first load.'

Propelled by four sailors, a boat was making a swift passage between the *Bostonian Lady* and the shore. At Ole Devil's signal, the men of his Company left their horses standing ground-hitched by allowing the split-ended reins to dangle and walked to the beach. Without needing orders, they waded to where the boat had been brought to a halt. Taking hold of an oblong box's rope handles, two of them lifted and carried it on to dry land.

'Open them up, Sergeant Grayne,' Ole Devil instructed to a stocky, bearded man who had no insignia of rank but was standing aside with a short crowbar in his hand.

'Yo!' the non-com replied, giving what was already the accepted cavalryman's response to an order.

Prying open the box's lid, Grayne exposed its contents to view. Twenty-four rifles lay inside, their butts in alternating directions. Lifting one out, the girl examined it without worrying about the grease with which it was coated. About four foot in length, with a barrel thirty-six inches long and .53 in calibre, it looked a typical 'plains' rifle developed with the needs of travellers west of the Mississippi River in mind. However, she noticed that there were three main differences between it and the weapons to which she was accustomed. Most obvious, at the breech, the hammer had a flattened head with no jaws for holding a flint and, instead of a frizzen-pan,

22

there was only a small protuberance with a nipple on top as a means of igniting the powder charge in the chamber. The third difference was a metal stud on the side of the barrel slightly over an inch from the muzzle.

'It's a fair piece,' Di stated with the air of a connoisseur after several seconds, and she indicated the stud. 'But I've never seen a doohickey like this afore.'

'It's to fix a bayonet on, there's one for each of them in the bottom of the boxes,' Rassendyll explained. 'A company in the United States made them, hoping to sell them to the Army, but the generals didn't want anything as new-fangled as caplocks.'

'Which is lucky for Texas,' Ole Devil declared. 'Provided we can get them to General Houston, they could change history.'

'Then we'd best be getting to doing something more than standing and talking,' Di announced, replacing the rifle and wiping her hands on her thighs.

'I'll go and make arrangements for the canvas,' Rassendyll offered.

'*Bueno*,' the girl replied. 'We can start splitting 'em into twelves, Devil.'

Crossing to the *Bostonian Lady* in the jolly boat, Rassendyll bought sufficient canvas for Di's purpose. On his return to the shore, he found the work of making the consignment ready for onwards transportation was being carried out. So he took the opportunity to pass on some private information which he was sure Ole Devil would be very pleased to receive.

'Kerry Vanderlyne has proved who killed Saul Beaucoup, Devil,' the supercargo said, having taken his friend beyond the hearing of the rest of the party. 'That clears your name. There's nothing to stop you going back to Louisiana.'

Chapter Two

THERE COULD BE *NO* GOING BACK!

'THAT clears your name. There's nothing to stop you going back to Louisiana.'

Beauregard Rassendyll's words still seemed to be keeping time with the big linebacked dun gelding's two-beat gait—wherein the off fore and near hind and the near fore and off hind alternately struck the ground at the same time—and Ole Devil Hardin tried to shake them from his thoughts as he rode 'posting the trot'* into an area of woodland some five miles south-west of Santa Cristóbal Bay. They had been so perturbing that, wanting to consider them without distraction, he had left Diamond-Hitch Brindley, Mannen Blaze and the supercargo to attend to the consignment of caplock rifles while he, ostensibly, made the rounds of the pickets.

While Rassendyll's news had been very welcome in one respect, from another it had presented its recipient with the making of a very difficult decision.

From the beginning of the affair which had caused Ole Devil to come to Texas, but he could have proved that he was innocent of Saul Beaucoup's murder but for one vitally important detail. He had had a perfect alibi, except that he could only use it by besmirching the honour of the woman he loved and creating a situation which could have had grave repercussions throughout the whole State of Louisiana.

Not that Melissa Cornforth would have objected, or refused to help Ole Devil. In fact, she had begged him to ignore the consequences and allow her to do so. Despite the precarious nature of his position, he had declined to accept her suggestion. He had appreciated the ramifications of permitting her to compromise herself. They went

* *A detailed description of how to ride 'posting the trot' is given in the 'The Scout' episode of:* UNDER THE STARS AND BARS.

far beyond the disastrous effect which such an action would have had upon her social standing and future.

As was frequently done by upper class Southrons, Melissa's parents had arranged what they considered to be a suitable and mutually advantageous marriage for her. Apart from one factor, she would have been content to conform with their wishes. The man in question was Kerry Vanderlyne, whom she had known since they were children. He was handsome and, while there had been no romantic feeling between them, she had always been on the best of terms with him. Unfortunately, shortly before their betrothal was announced, she had met and fallen in love with his best friend—Jackson Baines Hardin.

Hoping to find some way of resolving the situation without hurting or embarrassing Vanderlyne, of whom they were both fond, Melissa and Ole Devil had met secretly to discuss it in an unoccupied cabin on the boundary separating her parents' and his uncle's plantations. Caught by an unexpected and violent thunderstorm, they were compelled to spend the night there. Although Melissa had contrived to return home the following morning without anybody discovering what had happened, a serious complication had arisen.

During the night, a wealthy Iberville Parish* bully and trouble-causer, Saul Beaucoup had been murdered in Crown Bayou.

In spite of his family's social prominence, Kerry Vanderlyne, having become interested in law enforcement, was serving as town constable and deputy sheriff in Crown Bayou. So it had fallen upon him to conduct the investigation. All the available evidence had suggested that Ole Devil was the culprit. There was known to be ill will between him and Beaucoup and a sword belonging to him was buried in the other's back. What was more, while unable to make a positive identification, a witness claimed to have seen a man answering to Ole Devil's

* *The State of Louisiana uses the term 'parish' instead of 'county'.*

25

general description hurrying away from the scene of the crime at about eleven o'clock the previous evening.

When questioned by Vanderlyne, Ole Devil had stated he was innocent. The sword was one of half a dozen he had brought with him and had been in the *salle de armes* at the Blaze plantation from where it could easily have been removed without the loss being noticed. However, he had refused to account for his movements at the time that the murder was being committed.

There had been excellent reasons for Ole Devil's reticence and refusal to let Melissa speak on his behalf. When her parents heard what had happened, they would never forgive him even if he married her. Nor, no matter how Vanderlyne accepted the loss of his fiance, would the rest of his kin. As the two families formed a powerful support for the Hardin, Fog and Blaze clan in the State's affairs, he had no desire to bring such an advantageous alliance to an end if it could be avoided.

Although convinced of Ole Devil's innocence, Vanderlyne had been forced to take him into custody. Failure to have done so would have been contrary to the oath the young man had sworn on becoming a peace officer. In addition, it would have antagonized the Beaucoup family and their friends who were hinting that justice would not be done. So a refusal would have embroiled the citizens of Crown Bayou and the parish seat, Plaguemine, in the controversy. With so many influential people involved, most of Louisiana's population would probably have taken sides. Once that had happened, a feud of State-wide proportions and costing many lives was almost certain to have developed.

Being an intelligent girl, Melissa had not blamed Vanderlyne for arresting Ole Devil. She had also understood the latter's reason for insisting that she did not become involved, even to prove his innocence. Yet, with so much of the evidence suggesting that he was guilty, she was determined to save him. Taking Mannen Blaze into her confidence, she had found that he was willing to help her.

26

However, neither of them had been able to decide what to do. The arrival of one of Melissa's cousins had provided them with a solution. Telling Rezin Pleasant Bowie* the full story, she had obtained his support. A shrewd man, he had produced a plan. Aided by Mannen, he had broken Ole Devil out of jail. No suspicion of his part had fallen upon Bowie. The cousins had fled to Texas, joining others of their kin who had already settled there and were taking an active interest in that area of Mexico's affairs.†

While the Beaucoup faction had been furious when they heard of the escape and had offered a large reward for the capture of Ole Devil and Mannen, nothing worse had happened. Tactfully, as the bounty said 'Alive Only', the Hardin, Fog and Blaze clan had not protested at its issue. So, having no desire to antagonize such a powerful confederation, the Beaucoups had announced publicly that they accepted that the jail-delivery had been engineered by the two young men without the knowledge, authority or assistance of their family. With an apology from Ole Devil's and Mannen's fathers, made without any admission that the former might have been guilty, the affair had been allowed come to a peaceful end.**

As Vanderlyne had been handling a matter of law enforcement on the Beaucoups' behalf some distance from Crown Bayou at the time of the escape, one of the factors which Bowie had taken into consideration, his career as a peace officer, had not suffered on account of

* *Rezin Pleasant Bowie, elder brother of James, q.v., and believed by many authorities to have been the actual designer of the 'bowie' knife.*

† *During the period in question, Texas was regarded by the Mexican Government as being a Territory of the State of Coahuila. Santa Anna's refusal to make it a State in its own right, with full representation in the national Government, was one of the reasons for the Texians' resentment and bitterness.*

** *In the author's opinion, the fact that the Beaucoup family did not take the matter any further suggests they suspected—or knew—the wrong man was being blamed.*

27

it. Not only was he retained in office—much to the annoyance of his father, who did not approve of him carrying out such work—but two years later he had been elected sheriff of Iberville Parish. He had continued to search for the truth about the killing, believing that—in spite of Ole Devil's escape and flight—some other person was responsible.

The discovery that he had finally been proven innocent was a great relief to Ole Devil. Not only had his conscience been troubled by his having escaped from jail, although he had had more than his own welfare in mind when agreeing, but he had hated the stigma which he felt his actions had put upon his name. On learning of the price which had been put on his head by the Beaucoups, he had adopted the horn-like style for his hair and cultivated the moustache and beard. He had always been aware of his features' somewhat Mephistophelian characteristics. So he had sought to emphasise them in spite of warnings from others of his family that they would draw attention and remind people of his nickname. It had not been a mere act of braggodocio, but was a subconscious wish to prove that—although he might have 'gone to Texas'*—he had no reason to conceal his true identity.

However, the rest of Rassendyll's news had caused the young Texian considerable mental turmoil and heart-searching.

Being aware of the consequences if he should return to Louisiana with the murder charge still hanging over him and having had no hope that his name would be cleared by the discovery of the real culprit's identity, Ole Devil had reconciled himself to making his home in Texas. Nor was there any chance of Melissa joining him. They had decided that at their last meeting, on the road west out of Crown Bayou just after he had made his escape

* 'Gone to Texas': at odds with the law in the United States. Many wanted men entered Texas in the period before annexation, knowing that there was little danger of them being caught and extradited by the Mexican authorities.

28

from the town's jail. For her to have followed him would have meant the end of her engagement with Vanderlyne and the creation of the dissension between their respective families which they were trying to prevent. So they had put their duty to their kinfolk before their love for each other and had parted. Nor had they made any attempt to communicate and he had heard little about her until Rassendyll's arrival.

While far from being promiscuous, having accepted that Melissa was in all probability lost to him, Ole Devil had not entirely shunned contact with members of the opposite sex since settling in Texas. Nor had the opportunity to meet them been lacking. Despite knowing why he had been compelled to leave Louisiana, or at least such of the facts as had been made public, he was still considered an eligible bachelor by virtue of his influential connections. More than one family had sought to interest him in its unmarried daughters, cousins or nieces. However, not one of the young ladies with whom he had become acquainted had drawn even close to replacing Melissa in his affections. What was more, according to the supercargo's story, there was a chance that she reciprocated his feelings.

Although Melissa and Vanderlyne were still engaged, it had been announced that they did not intend to marry until he was in a position to support her in something close to the manner to which she was accustomed. The reason for the delay was that he had become estranged from his father by his insistence on remaining a peace officer and refusing to accept financial assistance from her parents. He had been so successful during his period in the capacity of sheriff of Iberville Parish that he was to be appointed U.S. Marshal for the State of Louisiana. Such an important post had brought a reconciliation with his father and would also allow him to take Melissa for his bride.

The date set for Vanderlyne's appointment was the Thirty-First of March!

Everybody who knew the couple was expecting that their wedding would follow shortly, probably before the end of April!

With his innocence established, Ole Devil was free to return to Louisiana and renew his relationship with the only woman he had ever loved. However, apart from any other consideration, he would have to leave Texas as soon as possible if he wanted to arrive before she was lost to him forever by becoming Vanderlyne's wife.

Unfortunately, Ole Devil had appreciated that there were a number of obstacles in the path of his desire. One of the most important was the realization that he now owed an additional debt to Vanderlyne. Thinking about his and Mannen's flight, he had always suspected the peace officer had failed to act with his usual diligence and efficiency when organizing the pursuit after the jail-delivery. Now it was clear that he had continued to devote time and effort to clearing his friend's name.

Such an obligation was not to be taken lightly by a man of Ole Devil's character, background and upbringing.

What was more, there were others to whom the young Texian was under a debt of gratitude.

The Bowie family had a claim upon Ole Devil for the part one of them had played in his escape. Not only had Rezin Pleasant Bowie planned how it was to be done, he had risked his liberty and reputation by helping Mannen Blaze to implement the far from danger-free scheme.

Being members of the Hardin, Fog and Blaze clan had done much to smooth the two young fugitives' path across Louisiana, as had the money and other aids to the flight which had been supplied without question when Mannen had requested them. Other kinsmen, accepting Ole Devil's word that he was innocent, had helped the cousins to establish themselves in Texas. He knew and shared their sentiments on the matter of breaking free from the tyrannical yoke of *Presidente* Antonio Lopez de Santa Anna and had committed himself, without pressure from them to do so, to the cause.

30

Bearing the latter point in mind, Ole Devil had his well developed sense of duty to contend with. He was all too aware of how badly the hurriedly formed, greatly outnumbered Army of the Republic of Texas needed every man. Harassed by internal friction as much as from the enemy, Major General Samuel Houston could ill afford to lose the services of a loyal, disciplined and competent officer, which Ole Devil knew he had proved himself to be.

In addition, there was Melissa's feelings for Ole Devil to consider. While the delay in the marriage might have been at her instigation and caused by the hope that circumstances might allow him to return and resume their love affair, it could also be for the reason given by Rassendyll. It was in keeping with Vanderlyne's character that he would want to support his wife and by his own efforts rather than relying upon the bounty of his, or her, parents, and yet refuse to allow her standards of living to be lowered to any great extent.

So, in spite of his assumption that he could go back and take up where he had left off with Melissa, Ole Devil was realistic enough to concede that he might be wrong. In the years which had elapsed since his departure, she could have changed her attitude towards him. It was possible that she had come to love Vanderlyne and put Ole Devil from her thoughts as being unattainable. If he returned, he might stir up an emotional conflict which would be better avoided.

What was more, a successful resumption of their love affair would produce the friction between their respective families which Ole Devil's refusal to allow Melissa to prove his innocence in the first place had been intended to avert. The need to prevent it was even greater now than it had been when the incident occurred. The Cornforths and Vanderlynes were backing the Hardins, Fogs and Blazes in the bitter controversy over whether the United States' Congress should continue to allow support to be given to the Texians in their struggle for independence.

The continuation of the powerful alliance between the families would be of far greater importance in the future. Many prominent Texians, Ole Devil's kin among them, accepted that the forming of an independent Republic was only a short term policy. However, their ambition to see Texas become a part of the United States did not meet with complete approval in that country. The anti-slavery lobby was utterly, almost rabidly, opposed to what threatened to be the creation of further 'Slave-States'.* Others could not see any profit in the acquisition of such a vast, thinly populated, and, as far as they could tell, unproductive wilderness; particularly when obtaining it would antagonize and probably have an adverse effect upon trade with Mexico.

Taking all the facts into consideration, Ole Devil realized that his decision could have far reaching effects. If Melissa was being forced against her wishes into an unwanted marriage with a man she hated, he would not have hesitated to return and take her regardless of the consequences. However, he knew that such was not the case. She had always felt warmth and affection, if not love, for Vanderlyne. In fact, her only misgivings over her feelings towards Ole Devil had been caused by a wish to avoid hurting her fiance.

Being an intelligent young man, with a well developed sense of responsibility, Ole Devil had known at the bottom of his heart from the moment he had heard Rassendyll's news that there was only one course he could take with honour. He must continue to adhere to the arrangement which Melissa and he had made that night on the outskirts of Crown Bayou.

There could be *no* going back!

* The Texians had suggested that, considering the enormous area of land which would be involved, after annexation Texas could be divided into three or four separate States.

Knowing it had been one thing, accepting it was less easy!

Although Ole Devil was normally too well adjusted to be plagued by self doubts, the receipt of the news and the understanding of its implications had been a traumatic experience. So much so that he had felt an irresistable desire to be alone and give the matter his undivided attention. Certainly the noise and activity on the beach at Santa Cristóbal Bay had been too distracting and disturbing for him to concentrate upon the various conflicting issues which were involved. Knowing that he could count upon Mannen, Di Brindley and Rassendyll as on himself, he had collected the gelding and, ostensibly, set off to inspect the pickets whom he had positioned earlier that morning.

None of the men Ole Devil had visited so far had had anything to report. However, in spite of approaching the most distant of the remaining pickets and knowing that it was the direction from which an enemy force might be expected to come, his emotional condition was making him far less alert and watchful than would normally have been the case.

An excellent horseman, the young Texian guided his horse through the woodland with hardly any need for conscious thought. He was following a trail which had been made either by wild animals or free-ranging longhorn cattle. Being well trained, the gelding kept far enough away from the trees to save him from banging his legs against the trunks or being swept from the saddle by low hanging branches.

Approaching a massive old cottonwood tree, the dun saw nothing to prevent it passing underneath the lowest branches. They were high enough for there to be no danger of them touching its rider. Still engrossed in his thoughts, Ole Devil was giving little attention to his surroundings. So the man who, having been concealed by the thick foliage, dropped off of an overhanging limb took him completely unawares.

Before the Texian could react, he was being half knocked and half dragged from his low horned, double girthed 'slick fork' saddle.* Trying to struggle, his head struck the tree's trunk a glancing blow. For a brief instant, it seemed that bright lights were exploding inside his head. Then everything went black.

Chapter Three

THEY'LL MAKE YOU TALK

'He's beginning to show signs of life at last. By the Holy Mother, that's fortunate for you. If you'd killed him, I would have made you wish you'd never been born.'

The words, spoken in Spanish with the accent of an upper class Mexican, seemed to be coming from a long way off. Yet for all his dazed and bewildered condition, Ole Devil Hardin could detect their hard and imperious timbre. Whoever was speaking appeared to be addressing his social inferiors.

'I'm pleased to see that you're recovering, *senor*,' the voice continued, changing to English and picking the words carefully, as if the language was familiar but had not been used recently. 'I was concerned when I first saw you, thinking you were more seriously injured by my man's attack.'

Hearing his native tongue helped Ole Devil to clear his head of the mists which seemed to be swirling around in it, but nothing could dispel the nagging ache that was emanating from the back of his skull. However, with his faculties returning, he was able to appreciate that there

* *'Slick fork' saddle: one with little bulge, or roll, at the fork. Because of its Spanish connotations, the Texians preferred to use the word 'girth' instead of 'cinch'.*

was an underlying hardness to the polite and almost solicitous tones.

'Your hat cushioned at least some of the force with which your head struck the trunk of the tree,' the speaker went on, 'otherwise the result would have been far worse. As it is, you have been unconscious for some minutes.'

Gradually, the Texian's vision began to clear. From the sight which met his eyes and what he could feel, he was lying supine and far from comfortably on the ground. Above him spread the branches of the massive old cottonwood tree in which his unknown and, as yet, unseen assailant must have been concealed before dropping upon him.

Wanting to feel at his throbbing head in the hope that doing so would reduce the pain, Ole Devil tried to bring his hands from beneath his body. He found that he could not move them. For a few seconds, such was his befuddled state, that he was unable to think why they were failing to respond to his will.

Then understanding struck him!

His wrists were bound together behind his back!

On experimenting, Ole Devil discovered that his ankles were also secured.

The Texian was not too surprised by the discovery. Already his brain was functioning sufficiently for him to deduce that, no matter how amiable the speaker might sound on the surface, he was unlikely to be an ally.

Shaking his head and gritting his teeth, Ole Devil raised his shoulders until he could examine his surroundings. As soon as his gaze was focused upon the speaker, he knew that the conclusions he had formed were correct. Standing with his legs apart, just clear of the Texian's feet, the man's attire was military in cut. It was not the uniform of any Mexican regiment with which Ole Devil was acquainted. Nor, despite there being a number of high born *Chicanos* fighting against Santa Anna, did he believe the other was a member of the Republic of Texas's Army.

35

Slightly over medium height, the man's physique—emphasised by the cut of his expensive and well tailored garments—was reasonable if not exceptional. In his late twenties, his deeply bronzed and handsome face had hazel eyes with somewhat drooping lids and a Hapsburg* lip such as frequently occurred among members of high class Spanish families. A Hussar-style black astrakhan† busby, with a silver grey bag hanging out of its top behind a long, flowing plume made of several emerald-green tail feathers from a cock Quetzal,** had a golden cord passing around his neck from the back. His form-fitting, waist long light green tunic was elaborately frogged with black silk and the matching, tight legged breeches sported broad stripes of gold braid. The latter ended in black Wellington-legboots†† with dangling gold tassels at the front and large-rowelled 'chihuahua' spurs on the low heels. A silver-grey coat, trimmed with black astrakhan, its sleeves empty, was draped across his shoulders. However, instead of a cavalry sabre, there was a magnificent Toledo steel *épée-de-combat* attached to its slings on the left side of his black leather waistbelt. As his hands—encased in white gauntlets—were occupied, a heavy riding quirt dangled by its strap from his left wrist.

In spite of the way that the elegant—if somewhat travel-stained—young man had spoken, Ole Devil sensed

* *Hapsburg: an ancient German family from which were descended rulers of Austria, Hungary and Bohemia, the Holy Roman Empire and Spain.*

† *Astrakhan: originally the pelts of very young lambs, with tightly curled wool, from the district around the Russian city of that name. Later a fabric with a curled pile in imitation of such pelts.*

** *Quetzal: Pharomachrus Mocino, one of the* Trogoniformes *birds, found in the mountain forests of Central and South America regarded as sacred by the Ancient Aztecs and Incas. Two of the cock's fringed tail covert feathers may reach a length of over three feet, making them much sought after for decorative purposes.*

†† *Wellington-leg boots: not the modern waterproofed rubber variety, but the knee-length leather pattern made popular by the Duke of Wellington.*

36

there was something menacing about him. His dress and appearance marked him as being from a wealthy family of pure Spanish blood. Since arriving in Texas, Ole Devil had met many of his class. Some he had found to be gentlemen, even when judged under the exacting standards by which he had been raised. Others were race-proud, arrogant and vicious bullies. He guessed that his captor was of the latter kind. Behind the veneer of culture was a cold blooded sadistic nature which would take pleasure in inflicting pain.

Looking past the Mexican, Ole Devil discovered that they were on the edge of a fair-sized clearing fringed with bushes and trees.

And they were not alone!

Some twenty feet away, squatting on their heels in a rough half circle and gazing at the Texian with coldly impassive dark brown faces, were five tall, lean, and muscular Indians. They had shoulder long black hair held back by cloth head bands which had no decoration such as feathers. Loose fitting, multi-coloured trade shirts hung outside deerskin breech cloths and the legs of their moccasins extended almost to knee level.

Only one of the quintet possessed a firearm, the others having either a knife in a sheath or a tomahawk's handle thrust through the leather belts which encircled their shirts. A couple nursed short bows and had quivers of arrows on their backs. Three had flattish, slightly curved, sturdy pieces of wood about twenty-four inches in length, which Ole Devil identified as throwing sticks—simple, yet effective and deadly weapons in skilled hands—by their sides. From all appearances, the remaining member of the group was its leader. Eldest and best dressed, with a red head band, he not only had a knife, but there was a flintlock pistol tucked into his belt and a nine foot long war lance standing with its head spiked into the ground within easy reach of his right hand.

Although Ole Devil could not claim to be an authority on such matters, he had always been a good listener,

37

and he remembered what he was told. From the information given by men with more extensive knowledge, he decided that the Indians were Hopis. Hailing from the region of North-West Sonora known as 'Arizona', they were one of the few tribes to employ throwing sticks as weapons.

There were a number of horses in the centre of the clearing beyond the men, including the Texian's line-backed dun gelding which was ground hitched by its dangling, split-ended reins. The magnificent *palomino* gelding, with a floral patterned single girth saddle that had a swollen fork and a horn almost the size of a dinnerplate, obviously belonged to the Mexican. It was standing a few feet away from the other animals, its one piece reins held by an unarmed, barefooted Indian boy—who was shorter and more stocky than the Hopis, if that was their identity—clad in a battered straw *sombrero*, torn white cotton shirt and trousers with ragged legs.

With one exception, the rest of the animals were wiry Indian ponies of various colours. The latter had saddles with simple wooden trees covered by rawhide and war bridles made from a single length of rope fastened to the lower jaw by two half hitches. They were positioned so that Ole Devil could not see enough of the exception to make out how it was rigged. Nor did he waste time trying to find out.

Having given the Indians and the horses a quick examination, Ole Devil returned his attention to their Mexican companion and, almost certainly, superior. What he saw was not calculated to increase his peace of mind. Just the opposite, in fact.

The man was holding what at first glance appeared to be a so called 'Kentucky'* rifle, except that it had some unusual features. One of the differences was that the hammer was underneath the frame, just ahead of the

* *The majority of the 'Kentucky' rifles were actually made in Pennsylvania.*

triggerguard. Although a few 'underhammer' pieces had been made, they were never popular due to the difficulty of retaining the priming powder in the frizzen pan. There would be no such problem with the weapon in his hands. It did not have a frizzen pan, nor even a nipple to take a percussion cap. Another omission was a ramrod, and there was no provision made to carry what was normally an indispensible aid to reloading. However, the most noticeable departure from the standard 'Kentucky's' fittings was a rectangular metal bar with rounded ends which passed through an aperture in the frame and a lever-like device behind it on the right side.

There was no need for Ole Devil to wonder what the weapon might be. It was his Browning Slide Repeating rifle, which had been in the leather boot—still something of an innovation—attached to the left side of the dun's saddle. What was more, as one of the three five-shot magazines that had been in a leather pouch on the back of his waistbelt was now positioned in the aperture on the piece's frame, the Mexican either knew, or had deduced, its purpose.

The other two magazines, Ole Devil's sabre, matched pair of pistols—one of which was carried in a holster that, along with the sword, hung over his saddlehorn—lay at his captor's feet.

'That's better, *senor*,' the Mexican remarked, taking his eyes from the weapon and looking at the Texian. 'Are you sufficiently recovered to understand me?'

'Just about,' Ole Devil admitted. 'But I'm as uncomfortable as hell. Can I sit up, please?'

'If you wish,' the Mexican authorized, with an air of friendly magnanimity, but he made no offer to help. Instead, he continued to study the rifle while the Texian shuffled laboriously to sit propped against the trunk of the tree. Then he went on, 'This is a remarkable weapon —if it works.'

'It works well enough,' Ole Devil declared, puzzled by his captor's attitude and playing for time almost instinctively; although he did not know what good gaining it might do.

'Then it's a great pity that it will only fire five shots in succession,' the Mexican remarked, cradling the butt against his shoulder and sighting along the forty and five-sixteenths of an inch long octagonal barrel so that its .45 calibre muzzle was directed at the centre of its owner's chest. 'Of course, under certain conditions, *one* would be sufficient.'

'When Jonathan Browning* saw how difficult it was to carry with the slide in place, he decided that five was the number that could be handled most conveniently,' Ole Devil explained, noticing that the hammer had not been drawn down into the fully cocked position and guessing that his captor was merely playing a cat-and-mouse game with him. So he was able to show no concern and spoke as if making nothing more than casual conversation. 'He'll make slides to take greater numbers as a special order.'

'That's interesting,' the Mexican said thoughtfully, his right forefinger caressing the trigger. Seeing no trace of alarm on his captive's face, he turned the barrel out of its alignment with an air of annoyance and disappointment. 'Does he make many rifles like this?'

'I don't know,' Ole Devil admitted, deciding against claiming that the majority of the Republic of Texas's Army were supplied with similar weapons. 'It's the only one I've come across, but I expect he's made and sold more.'†

* *Jonathan Browning was the father and tutor of the master firearms' designer, John Moses Browning, who appears in:* CALAMITY SPELLS TROUBLE.

† *Despite the difficulty of transporting it with the magazine in position, Jonathan Browning had produced a comparatively simple repeating rifle which was capable of a continuous fire unequalled by any contemporary weapon. However, during the period when he was manufacturing it, between 1834 and '42, he lacked the facilities to go into large scale production. He would have been able to do so in later years, but the development of self contained metallic cartridges and more compact, if less simple, repeating arms had rendered it obsolete.*

40

'I've never heard of a weapon like this,' the Mexican stated. 'An Army equipped with them would be a formidable thing.'

'Except that the Generals would never accept anything so new,' Ole Devil pointed out, wondering what the conversation was leading up to.

'That's true enough,' the Mexican conceded and gave a shrug. Laying the rifle down carefully alongside the other weapons, he straightened with an attitude of being ready to get to business. 'Enough of this small talk, *senor*. The time has come for us to introduce ourselves. I am Major Abrahan Phillipe Gonzales *de* Villena y Danvila, of the Arizona Hopi *Activos* Regiment, at your service.'

The introduction accounted for the man being clad in a uniform with which Ole Devil was not acquainted. *Activos* were not members of the regular Army, but reservists and local militia commanded by influential civilians from the districts in which they were raised. Coming from wealthy families, the majority of such officers selected whatever type of attire they fancied.

As, in general, the *Activos* regiments were formed of *peons* who were poorly trained, armed and equipped and who had little desire to become soldiers, they were not regarded as dangerous by the Texians. However, Ole Devil realized that his captors might prove to be an exception to the rule. Although the Hopi Indians, being a nation of settled pastoral agriculturalists, did not have a reputation as raiders and warriors like the Apaches, Yaquis and Comanches, they were said to be tough and capable fighting men. So being a prisoner in their hands was not a thing to be taken lightly.

'May I ask who you are, *senor?*' Villena went on, when the Texian did not offer to respond to the introduction. 'You will pardon me for doing so, but my curiosity has been aroused by meeting with a member of the Texas Light Cavalry in this part of the country——.' He raised his hand in a mockingly prohibitive gesture as Ole Devil

41

was about to speak. 'Please, *senor, don't* try to deny it. I'm not one of those regular Army clodhoppers. I've made a thorough study of—if you will excuse the use of the term—the enemy. The way you are dressed tells me that you serve in Colonel Edward Fog's *"regiment"*.'

'In that case, I won't deny it,' the Texian promised, impressed by the extent of the Mexican's knowledge and hiding his annoyance over the note of derision with which the word "regiment" had been said.

'Then perhaps you will be good enough to answer my question,' Villena suggested, still speaking politely, but the underlying threat in his voice was growing more noticeable.

'I decided that I didn't like the idea of being a soldier any more,' Ole Devil explained. 'So I deserted.'

'*You* are a deserter?' the Mexican purred, exuding disbelief and waved his hand almost languidly towards the weapons at his feet. 'I very much doubt *that, senor.* A matched pair of percussion-fired pistols made by Joseph Manton of London, England, a "bowie" knife inscribed with the name "James Black, Little Rock, Arkansas", a sabre from L. Haiman and Brother, this remarkable rifle. They are not the arms supplied to an ordinary enlisted man. *You* are a *caballero*, like myself, *senor*. Men of our class do not desert.'

Considering he was on dangerous ground, Ole Devil did not reply. Instead, he looked around the clearing again. He was no more fortunate than on the first occasion in finding something which might offer the slightest hope of escaping from his desperate situation. Certainly there was no help anywhere close at hand, unless the picket whom he had been on his way to visit——

'I must confess that I am puzzled, *senor*,' Villena stated, breaking into his captive's train of thought. 'According to the information I was given, the Texas Light Cavalry are forming part of the screen for General Houston's flight. And yet I find *two* members of it over here near the coast.'

42

Try as he might, Ole Devil could not prevent himself from giving some slight indication of how disturbing that news was. Yet, when he came to think of it, Villena had suggested that he had already met with another member of the Texas Light Cavalry. Which meant that he must have come across the picket. Even as Ole Devil regained control and halted the stiffening movement he was making, he knew that it had not gone unnoticed.

'*Two* of you, *senor*,' the Mexican confirmed, clearly delighted at having evoked even so small a response. 'My scouts came upon the other at the edge of the woodland. But you know what these damned savages are like. Instead of taking him a prisoner, so that I could question him, one of them caved his skull in with a throwing stick.'

The mocking timbre in the Mexican's voice filled Ole Devil with anger. Like any good officer, he took an interest in the men under his command. Although well qualified to handle the duty, having spent several years on the frontier, the picket was also a married man with two children. No matter how he had allowed the Hopis to come near enough to kill him, his death was a tragedy. However, the Texian controlled his emotions. Displaying them would serve no other purpose than to give amusement and pleasure to his sadistic captor.

'So you see my predicament, *senor*,' Villena went on, but he was clearly growing irritated by Ole Devil's continued refusal to respond to his goading. 'My colonel has sent me on a scouting mission and I come across a member of the Texas Light Cavalry far from where he should be. But he is killed before I can question him. At first I tell myself he must be a deserter. Then I am told that one of his officers has been captured. So, being a man of intelligence, I ask myself, "Why are they in *this* vicinity?" and find I cannot supply the answer.'

Despite his distress over the death of the picket, Ole Devil was listening with growing relief. Up until then he had been afraid that, having learned about the consignment of caplocks, Santa Anna had sent a regiment to

43

help the renegades who had tried to prevent their collection. Now he was sure that Villena's presence was no more than an unfortunate coincidence. In addition to the Mexicans' main force, which was marching towards San Antonio de Bexar, there were said to be two other columns on their way to invade Texas. In all probability, the Arizona Hopi *Activos* Regiment were the advance party from one of the latter.

'Perhaps *you* would care to supply me with the answer, *senor*?' Villena suggested. 'I'd advise you to do so. These Indians of mine can be most brutal. Much as I would dislike to have to give the order, they'll make you talk whether you want to or not.'

'I've nothing to say,' Ole Devil replied.

'That is a foolish attitude, *senor*,' Villena warned. 'And one which will avail you nothing. Much as I would regret the necessity, my sense of duty would compel me to employ even barbarous and painful means if that is the only way in which I can get the information I require from you. Tell me what I want to know and I give you my word that I will set you free.'

'You will?' Ole Devil gasped, with well simulated eagerness.

'I will,' Villena confirmed. 'You have my word on it.'

An experienced poker player, Ole Devil had become experienced at reading facial expressions. As the Mexican was giving the assurance, a malicious glint came to his eyes and his lips twisted into a derisive sneer. It was obvious to the Texian that his captor was still playing the cat-and-mouse game by making such an offer. Even if he supplied the information, it would not save him from torture and death. Yet he also had to concede that Villena was playing the game in a clever fashion. The pretended amiability and reluctance to employ painful methods was calculated to lessen his resistance when the latter were being applied.

'Is *your* word worth as much as that of General Cós?'

44

Ole Devil inquired, dropping his former attitude and eyeing the Mexican in open derision.

Anger darkened Villena's features, wiping away every trace of amiability and showing that the thrust had gone home. He had had no intention of keeping his word, but had been convinced that the Texian believed he would do so. Knowing what was implied by the question,* he realized that he was wrong.

'Very well, *gringo!*' Villena spat out, dropping all his pretence. 'We'll see how long you will refuse to talk.' Looking over his shoulder, he barked in Spanish, 'Many Plantings, make this one tell me everything I want to know. Do it slowly. I want to hear him scream and beg me to make you stop.'

Chapter Four

I'LL MAKE SURE OF YOU!

WATCHING the five Hopi Indians standing up and starting to walk in his direction, Ole Devil Hardin stiffened slightly. No coward, he was also far from being a reckless fool. So he did not try to delude himself regarding the predicament he was in. Bound hand and foot, there was little enough he could do in his own defense. Nor could he expect any mercy from his captors. Even if he gave Major Abrahan Phillipe Gonzales *de* Villena y Danvila the required information, it would not save him.

* *On December the 6th, 1835, at the end of a battle lasting for six days, General Martin Perfecto* de *Cós and his force of eleven hundred men had surrendered to the Texians at San Antonio de Bexar. On Cós giving his parole that he and his men would refrain from further military action against the Republic of Texas, they were allowed to return unharmed to Mexico. As Cós was accompanying the army which was marching north, it was apparent that he did not intend to honour the terms of his parole.*

Not that Ole Devil even considered taking such a course. He knew how much the consignment of caplock rifles could mean to the Army of the Republic of Texas in the struggle which was still to come. Yet he could also see one disadvantage in refusing to speak. Villena was already curious over having found two members of the Texas Light Cavalry so far from their regiment's recorded position. If he did not receive an answer of some kind, he was certain to investigate.

By going along the route taken by Ole Devil, who had not troubled to try and conceal his tracks, the Mexican would eventually arrive at Santa Cristóbal Bay. Of course there was a chance that one of the pickets visited by the Texian would not be taken by surprise and deliver a warning to Mannen Blaze. In that case, preparations could be made to protect the consignment. The snag to that was, while Villena was accompanied only by a small party, there was almost certain to be a larger force from the Arizona Hopi *Activos* Regiment not too far away. Even if the reinforcements were not sufficient in numbers to defeat Company 'C', they could harass the mule train and at least slow down the delivery even if they were unable to stop it.

'Come on!' Villena commanded in Spanish, stepping back a few paces, his face ugly with sadistic anticipation. 'Get to work on him!'

Understanding the Mexican's words, Ole Devil brought his thoughts on the situation to an end. The Hopi with the red head band snapped something in his own tongue. Darting forward, the two youngest of the other braves—who, like their companions, were advancing empty handed—grabbed the Texian by the feet. Giving him no chance to resist, they dragged him away from the tree. Although he managed to avoid having his head banged against the trunk, he could do nothing to prevent himself from being hauled along the ground.

Releasing the boot he was grasping, the shorter of the braves drew his knife. Stepping into position, he dug the

46

fingers of his other hand into Ole Devil's` hair. With a savage jerk, he snatched the Texian into a sitting position. Searing pain which seemed to be setting the top of his skull on fire brought tears involuntarily to Ole Devil's eyes, but he managed to hold back the yelp of torment that the sensation almost caused. At any moment, he expected to feel the knife's blade biting into his flesh. It would not be a mortal thrust, but merely designed to hurt.

Sucking in a breath, Ole Devil prepared to resist any inclination to cry out. If possible, he meant to die well. However, before he did, he must give Villena some satisfactory yet untrue explanation for his presence. Not only would it have to be believable, but it would have to send the Mexican as far away as possible from Santa Cristóbal Bay and the route to be taken by the mule train.

The expected cut from the knife did not materialize!

Instead, there was a hissing sound which every man present recognized!

Even Ole Devil could hardly believe the evidence of his ears!

Passing between the other braves, having flown from among the bushes at the northern edge of the clearing, an arrow struck the Texian's assailant just below the left armpit. It arrived with such a velocity that the shaft sank in to the fletching and sent the stricken brave reeling. Spinning around helplessly on buckling legs, he measured his length on the ground.

Startled exclamations burst from the Mexican and the rest of the warriors. Swivelling around with hands grabbing for the *épée-de-combat*, knives, tomahawks, or—in the eldest brave's case—a pistol, Villena and the Hopis stared in the direction from which the arrow had come. What they saw was cause for concern and relief; particularly for those warriors who realized that they were some distance from weapons which offered a greater range than those they carried.

Only a single man was standing among the bushes. Small, bare-headed, clad in black garments, he did not look like a Texian. In fact he was unlike anybody, Indian, Mexican, or *gringo*, the Hopis had ever seen. Nor was Villena any better informed as to what nationality he might belong.

Experienced warriors, the Indians recognized one thing!

In spite of the newcomer's lack of inches—he was barely as tall as the *mozo** holding Villena's *palomino* gelding—he could not be dismissed as harmless. In his left hand was—compared with his stature—a remarkably long bow, its handle set two thirds of the way down the stave instead of centrally. His stance for shooting appeared strange to the Indians' eyes,† but that clearly did not make it any the less effective. Already, moving with the smoothly flowing speed of a highly trained archer, his right hand was plucking another arrow from the quiver on his back.

'Get-him, *pronto*!' Villena screeched furiously, starting to slide the *épée-de-combat* from its sheath.

Nocking the arrow to the string and laying its shaft on the shallow 'V' formed by the base of his left thumb and the bow's stave, the newcomer made his draw with what appeared to be a circling motion of his arms.

The Hopi braves were starting to move forward without waiting for their Mexican superior's order. Although their people did not have the cult of the warrior so highly developed as in the nomadic nations who lived by hunting and raiding, they too were taught to regard a coup taken by personal contact as more estimable than making a kill from a distance. What was more, they considered that they would have a better chance of dealing with the diminutive foreigner at close quarters than by taking the time—brief as it would be—to go and retrieve their bows

---

* Mozo: *a man-servant, particularly one serving in a menial capacity.*

† *A description of Tommy Okasi's archery technique is given in:* YOUNG OLE DEVIL

48

or throwing sticks. The speed with which he was moving warned them that every second's delay would be deadly dangerous.

Tugging to liberate the pistol which he had taken from the dead *gringo's* body, Chief Many Plantings became aware that he was in peril. He saw the little man's left index finger, which was extended instead of being coiled around the bow's handle with its mates, pointing straight at him from just below the arrow. However, he refused to be deterred by the discovery that he was selected as the next target. A warrior who elected to carry a war lance was expected to set an example by having a complete disregard for his personal safety. So he continued to step forward and, as the weapon came free, his left hand went towards it with the intention of cocking the hammer. If he was to die, he would give his younger companions—to the parents of whom he had a responsibility for their welfare—an improved chance of survival.

Even as the chief was commencing his second stride, before his left hand could reach the pistol, the small man had completed his draw and taken sight. Loosing his hold on the string, he allowed the flexed limbs of the bow to return to their original curves. Propelled across the intervening space so swiftly that the eye could barely follow its movements, the arrow reached its mark. The needle sharp, razor edged steel point, set horizontally on the shaft, passed between Many Plantings's left ribs and through his heart. He stumbled backwards, dying as he would have wished, with a weapon in his hand and facing an enemy.

'Kill the little devil!' Villena shrieked as the chief went down, but he did not offer to go and help carry out his command.

Nor was the Mexican's exhortation needed by the remaining braves. The sight of their leader receiving a fatal wound gave them an added inducement to reach and deal with the man who had inflicted it. What was more, they felt sure that they could make contact with

49

him before he was able to take out, nock, draw, and aim another arrow.

Obviously the newcomer shared the Hopi warriors' summation of the situation. He made no attempt to recharge his bow. Instead, he tossed it aside. Having done so, his left hand flashed upwards at an angle. The quiver's shoulder strap was joined together by a knot which disintegrated as he grasped and tugged sharply at one protruding end. Having released the quiver from restraint, he allowed it to fall behind him and out of his way. Then he bounded rapidly towards the advancing trio.

Despite the small man's display of competence up to that point, both in having reached his position without being detected and in the way he had handled the bow, his latest actions appeared to be a serious error in tactics. Although a pair of swords swung in sheaths from his waistbelt, he was darting forward with empty hands to meet three larger, heavier enemies—each of whom was already grasping a weapon ready for use.

Still seated, as he had been since the Indian had dragged him into that position by his hair, Ole Devil watched. He recognized his rescuer and was far from perturbed at seeing what Villena and the braves regarded as a fatal mistake on the small newcomer's part. In fact, he had no doubt that it was the three Hopis who were going to suffer for their over-confidence and ignorance of the truth about the man they were rushing to attack.

The ignorance was understandable, Ole Devil realized. At that period, there were few people in the Western world who would have anticipated Tommy Okasi's potential as a highly skilled fighting man. The Chinese coolies and merchants—and their number was far from extensive —with whom the majority of Occidentals came into contact were, in general, a passive race who rarely displayed any knowledge of armed, or unarmed, combat.

However, Tommy was not Chinese.

Some five years earlier, the merchant ship commanded by Ole Devil's father had come across a derelict Oriental

50

vessel drifting in the China Sea. Half dead from hunger and thirst, Tommy had been the sole survivor. He had had no possessions apart from the clothing on his back, his *daisho,** a bow six foot in length and a quiver of arrows.

On recovering, it had been found that Tommy spoke a little English. When questioned, while he had described what had happened to the rest of the crew, he had not explained his reason for being aboard the stricken vessel. Nor had he evinced any desire to return to his as yet little known native land, Japan.† Instead, he had made a request to be allowed to stay on Captain Hardin's ship. When this had been granted, he had attached himself to his rescuer's son who had help persuade Captain Hardin to keep the little Oriental.

Whatever had been the cause of Tommy's disinclination to go home, it had proved to be most beneficial as far as Ole Devil was concerned by providing him with a loyal and useful friend. Although Ole Devil did not acquire the proficiency of another—as yet unborn—member of the Hardin, Fog and Blaze clan,* he had learned a number of useful unarmed fighting tricks from the little Oriental. However, while highly adept in his nation's very effective martial arts, Tommy had insisted upon serving in the capacity of Ole Devil's valet.

In spite of his passive occupation, the little Oriental had never hesitated to participate in any hazardous activity upon which his employer had become engaged. Not only had he played an important part in Ole Devil's escape from jail in Crown Bayou, he had willingly joined in the

---

* Daisho: *a matched pair of swords, comprising of a* tachi *with a thirty inch long blade and a* wakizashi, *the blade of which was eighteen inches in length.*

† *Until the visits in 1853-'54 of a flotilla commanded by Commodore Perry, U.S.N., there was little contact between the Western World and Japan.*

* *How Dustine Edward Marsden 'Dusty' Fog made use of the tuition which he received from Tommy Okasi is told in the author's 'Civil War' and 'Floating Outfit' stories.*

51

missions carried out by his companions since their arrival in Texas. Tommy had helped Ole Devil to deal with the renegades who had tried to prevent them reaching Santa Cristóbal Bay and had also done much to ensure that, having left, the Mexican warship which had been there would be unable to return.

So, all in all, Tommy Okasi was well able to take care of himself.

Nor was the little Oriental acting in as reckless a manner as it appeared to Villena and the Hopis.

Having saved Ole Devil from the knife of the first brave and dealt with the man whom he had calculated was posing the most immediate threat to himself, Tommy had realized that the affair was far from at an end. The rest of the Indians clearly intended to attack him and there was also the Mexican to be taken into consideration. So, thinking fast, he had decided how he could best deal with the situation. Having reached his conclusions, he did not waste time in putting them into practise. Going to meet the trio without holding a weapon was part of his plan, designed to lull them into a sense of false security.

Although they were trained warriors, the three Hopis had never come into contact with a man like Tommy. So they attached no greater throught to his apparently foolhardy behaviour than to consider that it would make him an easy victim for whichever of them reached him first.

In their individual eagerness to be the one who counted coup, each brave was running at his best speed. Before they had covered half of the distance, they had attained a rough arrowhead formation with the youngest of them at its point. Waving his tomahawk over his head and whooping his delight, he charged onwards. Still the strange looking little foreigner was showing no sign of arming himself. Nor was he slackening his pace. To the brave, it seemed that he intended to do neither but meant to come to grips with his bare hands. Having drawn his conclusion, the Hopi made ready to strike without bothering to guard himself against possible reprisals.

For all the seeming disregard of danger which Tommy was showing, he was calculating the distance between himself and the leading brave with great care and studying the relative positions of the other two. When he estimated that the time was right, he made his moves and they proved to be devastatingly effective.

One of the martial subjects in which the little Oriental had acquired considerable proficiency was *laijitsu*, fast sword drawing. Although he no longer carried his *daisho* in the manner of his forefathers,* he could still produce either of the weapons with remarkable speed.

Darting across in a flickering blur of motion, Tommy's right hand closed around the hilt of the *tachi* just above the three and three-eighths of an inch diameter circular *tsuba*, hand guard. Even as he was whipping the thirty inch long, reverse-Wharncliffe point† blade from its bamboo sheath, he weaved to his left. Nor did he act a moment too soon.

Launching a swing with sufficient power to sink the tomahawk deep into the top of its recipient's skull, the young brave was taken completely unawares by Tommy's change of direction. With a sensation of horror, he saw that his blow was going to miss. Then, just a fraction of a second too late, he realized that he was in terrible danger. However, there was neither the time nor the opportunity for him to take any evasive action.

* *Traditionally, the* daisho *was carried through the girdle. However, as he had had to spend long periods on horseback since arriving in the United States, Tommy Okasi had found it was more convenient to equip the sheaths with slings which could be attached to his waist belt.*

† *Reverse-Wharncliffe point: where the cutting edge joins the back of the blade in a convex arc. The normal Wharncliffe, also called a 'beak', point—said to have been developed by the Earl of Wharncliffe in the sixteenth century, although variations of it had been in use since Roman times—is mainly used on pocket-knives and has the back of the blade making a convex arc to the cutting edge.*

53

'*Kiai!*' Tommy shouted, giving the traditional cry of self-assertion, as the sword came clear of the sheath and, making a glistening arc, continued to sweep around to the right.

Such was the little Oriental's skill at *laijitsu* that the *tachi* reached its destination before the brave's tomahawk-filled right hand had descended far enough to impede it.

The steel from which the *tachi* had been forged was as fine as could be found anywhere in the world. Produced by a master swordsmith with generations of experience behind him and involving techniques unknown outside of Japan,* its cutting edge had been ground and honed until it was as sharp as a barber's razor, but it was more pliant and far stronger. Nor had Tommy ever neglected it for it was still in the same excellent condition as it had been on the day it was presented to him by his father. So, in his hands, it was a weapon of terrifyingly lethal efficiency.

Just how lethal and efficient was soon evident.

Reaching the brave, even as his shocked mind was beginning to register the full horror of his predicament, the hardened cutting edge of the *tachi's* blade performed one of the functions for which it had been designed. Slitting into the unprotected region below the rib-cage, it passed through as if the living tissues were incapable of

---

* After the blade had been shaped by fusing together numerous layers of steel, it was ready to be tempered. A clay-like material, for which every master swordsmith had his own secret recipe, was applied to the whole of the blade apart from an inch or so at the tip and the entire cutting edge. After heating the blade to the correct temperature—traditionally this was commenced in the half light of the early morning—it was plunged into a tub of cold water. The exposed metal cooled instantly and became very hard. Being encased in the clay sheath, the rest of the blade lost its heat gradually and, remaining comparatively soft, was given a greater pliancy. To prove that the finished article was capable of carrying out the work for which it was intended, the smith beat it against a sheet of iron and hacked to pieces the body of a dead criminal before handing it over to its owner. This is, of course, only a simplified description of the process.

54

offering any resistance. Having disembowelled him, it emerged and rose until its point was directed away from the little Oriental. Releasing the tomahawk, the stricken brave's hands went to the wound in an unavailing attempt to close it. He blundered past his would-be victim on buckling legs, falling first to his knees and then face downwards.

Having avoided being struck by his leading assailant, Tommy was confronting the remaining pair of braves. As he advanced so as to pass between them, his right fist rotated until its knuckles were pointing at the ground and the left hand went to the handle of the sword. Taking hold above its mate, it acted as a pivot for the other's leverage. Driving to the left with a similar deadly speed to that of the first blow, the blade met the side of the second brave's neck and sliced onwards. The Hopi's head parted company with his shoulders, toppling to the ground as nervous reactions caused his decapitated body to continue its forward movement.

On the point of making an attack with his tomahawk, the last of the braves saw what was happening to his companion. The sheer horror of the sight, intensified by the fact that the havoc had been created by such a small man as Tommy, caused him to hesitate. Nor was he permitted to regain his wits.

Taking away his left hand and ignoring the headless Hopi, Tommy curled the *tachi* around in a half circular motion. His right knuckles swivelled until they were upwards and the weapon swept at its next target in a whip-like motion which no other type of sword could duplicate. Although only the last three inches of the blade made contact, they were sufficient. Passing under the brave's chin, the steel laid his throat open to the bone and he crumpled dying to the ground.

With the unsheathed *épée-de-combat* in his right hand, Villena was staring across the clearing. Although reluctant to believe his eyes, he accepted that they were not playing him false. When he saw the third of the braves

55

being struck down, he realized that there was nobody left between himself and the strange, yet deadly, little foreigner. For all that, the Mexican believed he had one advantage over his subordinates. They had rushed recklessly into the attack on the assumption that the newcomer would be easy meat. Having seen how fatally wrong such deductions were, he had no intention of duplicating their mistakes. A skilled fencer, used to fighting against a man armed with a sword—which none of the Hopis had been—he was confident that he could more than hold his own.

Another thought struck Villena as he was reaching his conclusions regarding Tommy. From his actions, if not his attire and armament, it seemed likely that the small man was another member of the Texas Light Cavalry. It was possible that there were more of them close by and they could arrive before he was able to dispatch the little swordsman. In which case, he would be advised to withdraw if he wanted to stay alive and avoid capture.

However, Villena's every instinct told him that the uncommunicative Texian prisoner was more than a mere enlisted man and could be engaged upon a mission of importance. If that should be so, duty demanded that he must be prevented from carrying it out.

There was only one way to ensure that the Texian did not continue with whatever duty had brought him to the east of his regiment's reported position. Killing him would not only deprive the rebels of a capable fighting man, but would satisfy Villena's sadistic pleasure in inflicting pain.

'I'll make sure of you!'

Shouting the words, the Mexican sprang forward with the intention of killing his prisoner.

Chapter Five

IF HE COMES, HE WON'T BE ALONE

HEARING the words yelled by Major Abrahan Phillipe Gonzales *de* Villena *y* Danvila, Ole Devil Hardin's attention was drawn from the brief fight that had taken place at the side of the clearing. Instantly he realized that his life was still in as great a danger as it had been prior to Tommy Okasi's fortunate arrival. With a good forty yards to cover, there was no hope of the little Oriental being able to reach them quickly enough to save him.

Having drawn a similar conclusion, the Mexican did not anticipate any difficulty in dispatching his prisoner. Seated on the ground, with his hands bound behind his back, and ankles lashed together, he was in no position to defend himself. So Villena went into a lunge, aiming the point of his *épée-de-combat* at the Texian's left breast.

Watching the needle-sharp point of the Toledo steel blade darting in his direction, Ole Devil was grateful for one thing. The conversation he had had with Villena had allowed him to clear his head. While he had not thrown off all the effects of being knocked unconscious when the Hopi Indian had dragged him from his saddle, his condition was much improved.

Thinking fast and taking into consideration that Tommy was already running towards them, Ole Devil decided that there was something he could do about his predicament. While it would be risky in the extreme, it offered him his only slender hope of salvation.

Waiting until Villena's sword was within inches of him, Ole Devil threw himself backwards. So accurately had he timed the evasion that the weapon passed above him—but only just. Instead of piercing his heart, the point brushed the lobe of his left ear as it went by. While his shoulders were descending, he raised and bent his legs until his knees were above his chest.

The Mexican was expecting to meet with some resistance

as his blade sank into flesh. When it did not, his momentum carried him onwards and his torso was inclined forward. Up thrust the Texian's feet, taking him in the centre of his chest. While Ole Devil was unable to exert his full power, he had no reason to despise the result of his efforts.

Shoved backwards, Villena staggered and, in his determination to retain his balance, lost his hold on the sword. As soon as he felt the hilt leaving his grasp, he appreciated just how badly his situation had changed. He was unarmed against an assailant who was carrying an effective and deadly weapon. So he took the only course that was left to him. Putting aside any notion of trying to retrieve his *épée-de-combat*, or collecting one of the Texian's arms, he managed to turn and run to where the frightened-looking *mozo* was holding his *palomino* gelding.

Snatching the reins and knocking the youngster aside, Villena vaulted astride the *palomino*. A pair of pistols were hanging in holsters from his saddlehorn, loaded and ready for use. However, even as he was reaching for one with his right hand, he glanced in the direction from which he had fled. What he saw caused him to change his mind about drawing the weapon.

Being a shrewd fighting man, Tommy was aware that the loss of the *épée-de-combat* did not mean the Mexican was completely unarmed or defenseless. In fact, he had seen the pair of pistols carried by the gelding and realized that they could be a potent factor in the continuation of the fight. So he did not offer to go any closer to Villena.

Instead, Tommy swerved to where Ole Devil's weapons were lying. He noticed that there was a magazine attached to the Browning Slide Repeating rifle and decided it would be most suitable for his needs. Dropping the *tachi*, he bent to scoop it up.

Cursing himself for having made the rifle ready for firing, Villena could appreciate how it changed the situation. While he did not know how skilled the little foreigner might be in the use of firearms, he was disinclined to taking the chance of finding out. A fair pistol shot, but not exceptional, he was sitting on a horse already made restless by his hurried and far from gentle arrival astride its back. So its movements were not making a steady base from which to take aim, particularly when he would be opposed by a man holding a weapon which had a greater potential so far as accuracy was concerned. Putting discretion before valour, the Mexican clapped his spurs against the gelding's flanks and set it into motion.

'Don't let him get away, Tommy!' Ole Devil commanded, but he was not acting out of a desire for revenge against his captor. 'He knows too much!'

Swinging the butt of the rifle to his shoulder without acknowledging the order, the little Oriental took aim. His right forefinger drew down the underhammer to fully cocked and returned to the trigger. It tightened as the sights were aligned on the fleeing Mexican's back.

Although the hammer rose, nothing else happened!

Surprised, for the weapon had previously never misfired, Tommy stared at it.

'Work the lever!' Ole Devil instructed, glancing around and guessing what had gone wrong.

Although Villena had deduced enough to fit the magazine through the aperture, he had not completed the simple loading process. Thumbing down the lever on the right side of the frame set the mechanism into operation. Not only was the chamber aligned, it was cammed forward and held so that the face of the magazine formed a gas-tight connection against the bore of the barrel.

In his ignorance, the Mexican had saved his life.

Carrying out his employer's advice, Tommy manipulated the lever and felt the magazine move into position. However, by the time he had done so and pulled down the hammer again, Villena was approaching the edge of the clearing. For all that, before he could enter the woodland, the little Oriental had the rifle's barrel pointing at the centre of his back. Satisfied that he was holding true, Tommy started to squeeze the trigger.

Having been knocked on to his rump by the force of his employer's shove, the *mozo* let out a wail of alarm as he realized that he was being deserted. The sound distracted Tommy at the worst possible moment, with the hammer just liberated from the sear. There was the crack of detonating black powder, but the muzzle had wavered out of alignment. He missed, but not by much.

In passing, the bullet snipped through one of the *quetzal's* plumes which dangled from the top of Villena's busby. Before Tommy could go through the Browning's reloading process, brief as it might be in comparison with contemporary single-shot arms, the Mexican was urging the *palomino* to greater speed and was partially concealed among the trees.

'Get after him!' Ole Devil barked, appreciating how difficult trying to shoot the swiftly moving Villena would be under the circumstances.

'Best I set you free first,' Tommy replied, lowering the rifle. 'I don't think he will be turning back, but if he comes, he won't be alone.'

Accepting the wisdom of the little Oriental's comment, Ole Devil did not argue. In fact, he was considerably relieved by the prospect of being released from his bonds. He realized that it was his earlier preoccupation with his private affairs which had resulted in him being taken prisoner, at a time when he should have been devoting his entire attention to the needs of the Republic of Texas. The thought was far from pleasing. It was, he told himself grimly, the first time he had made such an error for that reason and he promised himself it would be the last.

Setting down the Browning rifle, after a glance to make sure that the wailing and still seated *mozo* was not planning to take any hostile action, Tommy drew his *wakizashi*. Bending, he used its eighteen inch long, razor-sharp blade to sever the rawhide thongs holding Ole Devil's ankles. Then, stepping behind his employer, he liberated the wrists.

'*Gracias!*' Ole Devil gritted, trying to conceal the pain

which the renewal of his impeded circulation was causing. 'How the hell did you come to be here so conveniently when I needed you?'

'Old Nipponese saying———,' Tommy began.

'Which you've just made up,' Ole Devil put in through clenched lips, making what had become an accepted response to such a statement by the little Oriental.

'Man with great personal problem on his mind less capable of taking care of himself,' Tommy went on, as if the interruption had never taken place, returning the *wakizashi* to its sheath. There was, although he would not have admitted it, complete justification for his employer's comment and he continued, 'So Di and Mannen-san sent humble and unworthy self to watch over you.'

'Why that was right neighbourly and considerate of you-all, I'm sure,' Ole Devil declared and thrust himself to his feet. 'And thank you 'most to death. Come on, I want to find out what happened to Ilkey.'

'I already have,' Tommy replied, as the Texian went towards his weapons. 'That's why I didn't get here sooner. I didn't want you to know I was following, so I wasn't too close and I lost sight of you. So I went straight to where we'd left Ilkey. When I found his body and you weren't there, I came looking for you. I heard you talking and moved in on foot.'

While the little Oriental was speaking, Ole Devil picked up one of the Manton pistols. After checking that it had not been tampered with and was still capable of being fired, he thrust its barrel through the loop on his belt. Then he retrieved the bowie knife and slid its eleven inches long, two and a quarter inches wide, three-eighths of an inch thick clip point blade* into the sheath. Collecting the rifle's two spare magazines, he returned them to the pouch on the back of his belt. By the time he had

---

* *Clip point: where the back of the blade curves to meet the main cutting edge in a concave arc five and a quarter inches in length. It is sharpened and forms an extension of the cutting edge.*

done so, Tommy was holding the second pistol and the sabre.

'Are there any more of them around?' Tommy inquired, nodding towards the dead Indians.

'I'd say "yes" to that,' Ole Devil replied and picked up his rifle. 'Let's find out how many and how near they are.'

Although the *mozo* was no longer wailing, he had not attempted to rise. Instead, he had remained crouching on the ground, hoping to avoid drawing attention to himself. He stared in horror as the two men began to walk in his direction. Nor could he decide which was the more frightening. The smaller had killed Many Plantings and the other Hopi braves, three of them with his sword, taking one's head off with a single blow. However, despite having seen the taller as a bound and helpless prisoner, his appearance aroused a sense of superstitious dread in the youngster. His hair and face made him look like the pictures of *el Diablo*, the Devil, which the *mozo* had been shown many times by the fathers at his local mission.

'Have mercy, *senores*,' the youngster screeched in Spanish, crossing himself with great vigour. 'It wasn't me who attacked you. I had to come with my *patrón* to——.'

'Don't be frightened,' Ole Devil put in gently, employing the same language. 'We won't harm you if you answer our questions truthfully.'

'Wh—What do you want to know, *senor*?' the *mozo* whimpered, gazing up as the two young men halted before him.

'Where are the rest of your regiment?' Ole Devil asked.

'F—Far off, *senor*,' the youngster replied, waving his right hand vaguely to the south-west. 'D—Don Abrahan left the camp early yesterday morning and we've been travelling ever since.'

'How many more men did he have with him?'

'N—None, *senor*.'

'*None*?' Ole Devil challenged.

'None, *senor*,' the *mozo* confirmed. 'I was told that the rest of the regiment were staying where they are until we returned and then it would be decided which way we will march. I hope that it is back home.'

'I think he's speaking the truth,' Ole Devil stated, having reverted to English so that he could translate the conversation for his companion's benefit. 'In which case, we've some time in hand to get the consignment on the move.'

'Do the Mexicans know about it?' Tommy inquired.

'Not from the way that Villena spoke when he was questioning me.'

'Then he might not come back.'

'I don't intend to count on it,' Ole Devil declared. 'He was no fool and finding members of the Texas Light Cavalry this far east's aroused his curiosity. So he could persuade his colonel that investigating things might be worthwhile.'

'How many men do they have?' Tommy wanted to know.

'He can't say for sure,' Ole Devil replied, after putting further questions to the *mozo*. 'Over a hundred, but only a few of them have firearms.'

'Even with that few, they still have us outnumbered,' Tommy pointed out. 'And they can travel faster than we'll be doing with the mule train.'

'That's for sure,' Ole Devil agreed. 'So the more miles we can put between us and them, the better I'll like it. I'll go back to the bay and tell Di what's happened. Keep watch here until I send a couple of men to relieve you.'

'What about him?' Tommy asked, indicating the *mozo*.

'We'd better keep him with us for the time being,' Ole Devil decided. 'Let him bury Ilkey and fetch him in with you when you're relieved.'

'I'll see to it,' Tommy promised. 'Are you all right?'

'It's mainly my pride that's hurt,' Ole Devil admitted wryly. 'Shall I leave you my rifle?'

'I'd rather rely on my bow,' Tommy replied and his next words were more of a statement than a question. 'We won't be going back to Crown Bayou?'

'No,' Ole Devil answered quietly, removing the magazine from his rifle and returning it to the vacant space in the pouch. 'We won't be going back. Provided we can hold on to it, Texas's our home from now on.'

'I'll go and fetch my horse before you leave,' Tommy suggested, guessing what reaching such a decision must have cost his employer and refraining from further discussion.

'That'd be advisable,' Ole Devil agreed, knowing that the little Oriental might have need of the animal.

While waiting for his companion to return with his horse, Ole Devil made preparations for his own departure. Going to the horses, he discovered—as he had suspected —that the one he had not been able to see clearly earlier belonged to the dead picket. He examined his linebacked dun gelding to ensure that it had not been injured when he was dragged from its back. Satisfied that it had not, he slid the rifle into the saddleboot. Then he replaced the second pistol and sabre in the holster and scabbard which were suspended on either side of the rig's low horn. All the time he was working, he kept the *mozo* under observation and was watched fearfully in return.

Telling the youngster to fetch his hat, which lay under the tree where it had fallen, Ole Devil donned it. Retrieving the pistol dropped by the chief of the Hopis, he took it to the picket's horse and tucked it into the bed roll on the cantle of the saddle. When an opportunity presented itself, he intended to send the animal and property to Ilkey's widow.

'I'll take Ilkey's horse with me and ride relay,' Ole Devil announced, when Tommy joined him leading a powerful roan gelding and carrying the long bow and quiver of arrows. 'You and the *mozo* there can bring the Hopis' mounts when you come. And don't take any chances. If the Mexican shows up with reinforcements, get away fast.'

'I will,' Tommy promised. 'And you be watchful.'

'Count on it,' Ole Devil replied. 'I don't make the same mistake twice.'

'Old Nipponese saying, which I've just made up,' Tommy said. 'Wise man does not make the same mistake *once*.'

'I'll keep it in mind for the future,' Ole Devil promised and, telling the *mozo* what was expected of him, swung astride the dun. Taking the reins of Ilkey's mount, which the little Oriental handed to him, he went on, 'I'll see you back at the bay, Tommy.'

Holding his mount at a steady trot, with the other horse following obediently as it had been trained to do, the Texian guided them into the woodland. He had decided against alerting the rest of his pickets by returning over the route he had taken on the outwards' journey. If the *mozo* had told the truth—and Ole Devil felt sure that he had been too frightened to lie—there was no immediate danger from the Arizona Hopi *Activos* Regiment. So he considered that he would be more usefully employed in rejoining his companions at Santa Cristóbal Bay with the minimum of delay.

Although Ole Devil was still disturbed by the news he had received via Beauregard Rassendyll and his decision regarding the future, he remembered the result of having become engrossed in his thoughts and he pushed the matter resolutely to the back of his mind. So he was far more alert than he had been on his way out from the bay. He saw nothing to disturb him, but did not regret his vigilance.

On his arrival, Ole Devil found that a considerable amount of work had already been completed. Not that he had expected anything else. For all Mannen Blaze's appearance of being half asleep, he was a reliable subordinate and could be counted upon to keep the men at any work to which they were assigned.

All of the consignment was on the beach and, from what Ole Devil could see, the vessel which had delivered it was already being made ready to leave. Looking around, he noticed that the oblong boxes were missing. The rifles were split into bundles of twelve and were being wrapped in pieces of sailcloth under Diamond-Hitch Brindley's supervision. Fortunately, the paper cart-ridges and percussion caps were in containers of a suitable size to be carried on the mules and did not require repacking.

'That looks like one of our boys' horses, Cousin Devil,' Mannen remarked, indicating the animal alongside the dun as he, Di and Rassendyll came to meet the Texian.

'It was Ilkey's,' Ole Devil replied and swung from the saddle.

'*Was* Ilkey's?' Mannen prompted.

'He's dead,' Ole Devil said and explained what had happened.

'Hopis, huh?' Di growled at the end of the narrative. 'I've never had any doings with 'em, but from what I've heard tell, they're tolerable tough *hombres*. Anyways, even if they come, we ought to be long gone by the time they get here.'

'We'd better be,' Ole Devil warned. 'They'll have us outnumbered.'

'Only we'll have 'em out gunned,' Di pointed out. 'Say one thing, though. It's right lucky for us all that we let ole Tommy go after you, Devil.'

'Couldn't rightly figure any way to stop him once he got to figuring on doing it,' Mannen supplemented indolently. 'You know how he is. He's mighty set in his ways.'

'Could be he had help to decide on following me,' Ole Devil drawled, eyeing the girl and his cousin sardonically. Then he jerked his left thumb in the direction of the brig and went on, 'Captain Adams isn't wasting any time in getting under way.'

'We can't blame him for *that*,' Rassendyll pointed out, studying the Texian without learning anything from the Mephistophelian features and wondering why the news he had brought had not produced the response he had anticipated. It almost seemed that Ole Devil was more distressed and perturbed than delighted in learning that his name was cleared and that he was free to go back to

Louisiana. However, there were matters of more pressing importance to be taken care of. 'I've let him take the rifle boxes for firewood.'

'We'd only have had to burn them ourselves if you hadn't,' Ole Devil answered.

'Riders coming, Cap'n Hardin!' called the nearest of the watchers posted on the top of the slope. 'It looks like the rest of our boys headed back.'

'What the——?' Di ejaculated, for the report implied that the riders were returning alone.

'Come on!' Ole Devil interrupted, having drawn a similar conclusion, mounting the dun.

Darting forward, Di just beat Mannen Blaze to the dead picket's mount. Like the burly Texian, she had removed her horse's saddle. By appropriating Ilkey's animal, she was able to accompany Ole Devil. They ascended the slope swiftly and, on reaching the top, she found that her assumption had been correct. Although the approaching riders were the remainder of Company 'C', there was no sign of her grandfather and the mule train.

'Howdy, Di, Cap'n Hardin,' greeted the lanky sergeant, after looking around, as the two riders converged with his party. 'Seems like them two fellers was wrong.'

'Which two fellers?' Di inquired.

'They met up with us on the trail,' the sergeant elaborated. 'Allowed they seed a fair-sized bunch of *hombres* led by a right fine looking, but somewhat mussed up woman headed this way.'

'That sounds like that blasted de Moreau bitch and her renegades, Devil,' Di spat out.

'Which's what your grandpappy figured,' the sergeant admitted. 'So he told us to head back here and find out if you needed a hand. Reckoned us coming up from behind, we'd get 'em boxed in and whup 'em good.'

'It's a pity they never came,' Di declared. 'We could have settled——.'

'Turn your men, sergeant!' Ole Devil barked.

'What's up?' Di asked, startled by the vehemence with which the order had been given.

'They haven't come here,' Ole Devil replied. 'So it must have been a trick to draw off the escort and let them attack the mule train. If they can stop it, they'll have us pinned down here until they can raise enough help to come and take the consignment from us.'

Chapter Six

THEY WON'T MOVE WITHOUT HER

ALTHOUGH Ole Devil Hardin was extremely perturbed by the thought that Ewart Brindley might have been tricked, he also realized that he could not set off immediately to satisfy himself upon the matter. First, taking into consideration the other development which had arisen to threaten the safety of the consignment, he had to organize additional protection for it. There was a chance that the *mozo* had been lying, or was mistaken, and the Arizona Hopi *Activos* Regiment could be much closer than he had claimed. So the circle of pickets had to be reinforced, thereby lessening the possibility of another lone man suffering the same fate as Ilkey; or, worse still, falling alive into the enemies' hands and being made to answer their questions. Unfortunately, the only way in which the pickets could be strengthened was by reducing the already small force who were at Santa Cristóbal Bay.

Under different circumstances, the arrival of Sergeant Maxime and his detail would have been a blessing. However, with the possible danger to the mule train, Ole Devil did not dare take the chance of adding the newcomers to his defenders. Instead, he told them to return as quickly as possible while he rejoined the rest of Company 'C' and, after he had made his arrangements, he would follow.

Appreciating the difficulty the young Texian was having in deciding upon the best line of action, Diamond-Hitch Brindley did not attempt to influence him. Despite being aware of how tough her grandfather and his men were, she shared Ole Devil's concern for the safety of the consignment. However, she also knew that mentioning the matter would do nothing to lessen the burden of his responsibility.

'Shucks, Devil,' the girl remarked, turning her borrowed mount at the Texian's side as Sergeant Maxime led the detail in the direction from which they had come. 'Grandpappy Ewart's been taking good care of his-self for a heap of years. And I reckon him 'n' our Tejas packers can look out for themselves until your boys get back. Anyway, de Moreau don't have all that many men with her.'

'That's the thing I'm counting on most,' Ole Devil replied, 'But, if she sent those men to tell your grandfather about seeing her and her men coming this way, she must have had a reason for doing it. I wish I could think what it was.'

Throughout the short ride back to his waiting companions, the Texian tried to console himself with the thought that Di's final comment had been valid. The arrival of Mannen Blaze and Company 'C' the previous day had scattered the renegades who were with Madeline de Moreau. Nor, even if she had managed to gather them again, were there so many as to have a great numerical supremacy over Brindley and his Tejas Indian employees.

In spite of the latter point, Ole Devil could not dispel his perturbation. He felt sure that the two men who had met the mule train were acting under Madeline de Moreau's orders. In which case, she must have had a good reason for sending them. Nothing he had seen of her led him to assume she was foolish. In fact, he had found her to be intelligent and unscrupulous. So, if he was cor-

69

rect in his assumptions, she was planning mischief of some kind. He wished that he could guess what it might be.

Swinging from the dun's saddle near to the other horses, Ole Devil put aside his speculations so as to give his instructions to his cousin and Beauregard Rassendyll. Each picket was to be given a companion and warned about the Hopis, with orders to report to the bay immediately if any of them were seen. Fifty of the new caplocks were to be cleaned—all were coated in grease—ready for use and would be loaded as soon as word was received that the Indians were coming.

'I'll see to it,' Mannen promised, after his cousin had explained the reason why he was being left in command. 'And I've got something that will help. Uncle Ben Blaze sent me a Browning and three slides.'

'That could come in handy all right,' Ole Devil admitted. 'But I hope that you don't need it.'

'Tell you though,' Di went on. 'You might not be able to stop them Hopis a-coming, but with the caplocks and your lil ole Browning, you ought to be able to make 'em limp a mite going back.'

'Like Cousin Devil says,' Mannen drawled, his tones suggesting that he was having difficulty in staying awake. 'I hope it doesn't come to that.'

While the conversation had been taking place, Ole Devil was transferring his saddle and bridle to the big, powerful black gelding which was his second mount. Being fresh, it would travel at a better speed than the dun. As Di was equally aware of the need to move fast, she had been making her sorrel gelding ready instead of relying upon the mount belonging to the dead picket.

Satisfied that he had done all he could to safeguard the consignment and confident he could rely upon Mannen to do everything necessary, Ole Devil set off with the girl. They made good time, but the sun was going down before they arrived at their destination.

Topping a ridge which gave them their first view of the mule train, Di and the Texian could sense that their fears

70

had been justified. The animals, still saddled and under the watchful gaze of the Tejas Indian packers were standing in a bunch just beyond some bushes on the bank of a small stream. Forming a rough circle around them were a number of the Texian soldiers, positioned as if waiting to repel an attack. However, only half of Maxime's detail were present. Nor was there any sign of Brindley and his *cargador*.* A further suggestion that something had happened was given by a grey horse which lay unmoving on its side a short way from the other animals. The sight of it brought a furious exclamation from the girl.

'Hell's teeth!' Di ejaculated, reining in the sorrel. 'Something's happened to ole Whitey!'

The words were directed at Ole Devil's back. Disturbed by what he was seeing, he signalled with his hands and heels for the black gelding to increase its pace. Nor, despite the shock she had received and appreciating what the loss of the white horse could mean, did the girl delay. Even as she stopped speaking, she urged her mount forward at a better speed and followed her grim-faced companion. Galloping across the intervening distance, they were almost neck and neck as they passed between two members of his Company.

'Go in there, Cap'n Hardin!' called one of the soldiers, pointing towards the bushes.

Acting upon the somewhat inadequate advice, with the girl still at his side, Ole Devil went in the direction indicated by the man. Before they had gone many feet, he began to get an inkling of what the soldier had meant. At least two other members of his Company were partially concealed by the foliage and it was impossible to tell what they were doing. Recognizing one as possessing a reasonable knowledge of medical and surgical matters, he felt an ever growing sense of alarm.

Sliding the black to a halt on the edge of the bushes, Ole Devil was quitting the saddle and allowing the reins

* Cargador: *assistant pack master and second-in-command of a mule train.*

71

to fall free even before it was fully at a stop. Responding with an equal alacrity, Di dismounted and accompanied him as he advanced on foot.

'Grandpappy!' the girl shrieked, as she and the Texian passed between some of the bushes to enter a small patch of open ground. 'Joe!'

Ewart Brindley was lying on his back. About the same height as his granddaughter, he made up in breadth what he lacked in height. Stripped to the waist, his buckskin shirt having been cut off so that 'Doc' Kimberley could get at the wound in the right side of his chest, he was well muscled and looked as hard and fit as a much younger man. Almost bald, with what little hair that remained a grizzled white, his leathery and sun-reddened features showed that, although he was trying to hide it, he was in considerable pain. He had on buckskin trousers, encircled by a belt with a big knife in an Indian sheath, and moccasins which extended to just below the knee.

Not far away, propped in a sitting position against the bent leg of a kneeling soldier, Brindley's *cargador* was having what appeared to be a wound on his forehead bandaged. About twenty years of age, Joe Galton was tall, red haired, good looking in a freckled and, usually, cheerful way. He too wore buckskins and carried a knife on his belt.

To give her full credit, regardless of the discovery she had just made, Di did not go into a display of hysteria. Raised by her grandfather in a predominantly male society since her parents had been killed during her early childhood, she had seen much of life—and death. So she was able to restrain her external emotions after the initial reaction. Going forward, her body trembling slightly with the strain of acting in an impassive manner, she watched the tall, lean, unshaven, yet clean looking soldier who was attending to Brindley. Deciding that he was competent to handle the task, she halted and looked down. However, when she tried to speak, the question she wanted to ask would not come.

72

'How is he, Doc?' Ole Devil inquired, having moved forward and stopped at the girl's side. His left hand gave her right bicep a gentle squeeze of encouragement.

'He'll pull through, but it's bad enough to keep him off his feet for a while,' Kimberley answered, in the accent of a well-educated Englishman, without taking his attention from his work. 'Joe's got a bad graze on his forehead. The bullet just touched and glanced off. It knocked him from his horse and stunned him, but he was lucky. Another inch, or less——Lie still, sir.'

The last words were directed at Brindley. Having opened his eyes, the old man was stirring and tried to sit up.

'God damn it!' Brindley gritted, as Kimberley enforced the request by pushing at his shoulders. 'Get your cotton-picking hands offen——.'

'You hush your mouth and do like he says, blast it!' Di yelped, springing forward and dropping to her knees at the other side of her grandfather. Spitting the words out almost breathlessly in her anxiety, she continued, 'This gent knows what he's about and there's nothing you can do yet a-whiles.'

'That's better,' Kimberley went on, when his patient subsided more from agony-induced weakness than through any desire to be co-operative. He indicated a bulky, open saddlebag by his side, 'I've got something in here will ease the pain.'

'N—No—drugs for me!' Brindley protested feebly and managed to focus his eyes upon his granddaughter. 'Damn it, Di-gal, they shot ole Whitey——.'

'I saw,' the girl admitted bitterly.

'Y—You—kn—know—what—that means?' the old man demanded.

'If I don't, you've sure as hell wasted a heap of time raising me,' Di replied. 'Which you haven't. So you just lie still while I go tend to things.'

'Lemme come and——,' Galton put in.

'I don't reckon you'd be a whole heap of help right

73

now,' Di answered, looking at the speaker. 'So stay put, blast you. Ain't nothing you can do that I can't, not's needs tending to right now anyways. I'll see to things and the boys'll tell me what's happened.'

'Hell, I'm not hurt all that bad!' the *cargador* objected, but his voice lacked conviction and his attempt to force himself away from the support given by the soldier's knee achieved nothing. Giving a low groan, he sank down again and raised a hand to his head, trying to speak lightly, he went on, 'I feel like I've just woke up after a night at Mama Rosa's *cantina*. So I wouldn't be a heap of help. Damned if you wasn't right, Di-gal.'

'*I* never figured's I wasn't,' the girl pointed out, returning her attention to Brindley and wagging her right forefinger in front of his face. 'You do what the doc here says, mind. And that goes for you, Joe Galton.' Having delivered her instructions, she looked at Kimberley and continued in milder tones, 'Happen this pair of worthless goats give you any trouble, doc, treat 'em like I do when they make fuss for me.'

'How would that be, young lady?' the Englishman inquired, removing some of the contents from his saddle-bag.

'Same thing's I do with the mules, which there's not a whole heap of difference 'tween 'em,' Di elaborated. 'Whomp 'em over the head with something heavy and's won't matter happen it gets busted.'

'By jove! That strikes me as being a sound piece of medical advice,' Kimberley declared, darting a glance filled with approbation at the girl. He could sense the deep emotional stress that she was experiencing and felt admiration for the way in which she kept it under control.

'Like they say,' Di replied, straightening up. 'You can do most anything with kindness, 'less you're dealing with mules—or men.' Her gaze swung to Ole Devil. 'You fixing to stand here jawing for the rest of the day?'

'It's a thought,' the Texian answered. 'But I wouldn't

74

get any peace from you if I did, so I'll go and do some work.'

'And not before time,' Di sniffed.

'I don't know why he left England,' Ole Devil remarked to the girl as they were walking through the bushes. 'But he's a damned good doctor.'

'I could see that, or you'd have heard me yelling,' the girl stated and glared at the dead horse. 'God damn it, Devil, if——!'

'I'll be talking to Maxime about coming away from the train,' Ole Devil promised and, in spite of the gentle way that he was speaking, his face became even more Satanic.

'It wasn't *his* fault, damn it,' Di protested, realizing that her comment had been misinterpreted and her sense of fair play demanded that the error must be corrected. 'You put those boys you sent under Grandpappy Ewart's orders and it was him, not ole Charlie Maxime's said they should head back to the bay and try to trap the renegades a-'tween us.'

'Yes,' Ole Devil conceded. 'But——!'

'There's no son-of-a-bitching "but" about it!' the girl interrupted. 'What in hell's use is it you giving a feller orders to take orders from somebody, then expecting him to pick and choose which of 'em he takes?'

'You're right,' Ole Devil admitted, his lips twitching into a smile that he did not feel like giving. Again he gave Di's arm a gentle squeeze, for he shared Kimberley's feelings about her. 'And saying what should have been, or laying blame, isn't going to change what happened. It's how we're affected and what's going to need doing now that counts. First, though, we better find out how it came about.' He raised his voice, 'Corporal Anchor!'

'Yo!' responded a medium-sized and thickset soldier, rising and ambling swiftly towards his superior.

'What happened?' Ole Devil inquired, acknowledging the other's salute.

'I don't know, cap'n,' Anchor replied. 'We heard

75

shooting's we was coming back. But by the time we came into sight, it was all over. Ewart and young Joe Galton were down and the fellers who'd done it had lit out like the devil after a yearling. So Charlie Maxime sent me with Doc Kimberley and half of the boys to stand guard, then went after 'em with the rest.'

While the brief conversation was taking place, a tall, well-made and middle-aged Tejas Indian approached from where he and his companions were attending to the mules. Dressed in buckskins and knee-high moccasins like the rest of the mule packers, he had on a high crowned, wide brimmed black hat with an eagle's tail feather in its band. He was armed with a big knife on his belt and had a 'Plains' rifle across the crook of his left arm. There was something dignified and commanding about him and he showed none of the servility or debauchery which characterized many of his tribe who lived and worked in close contact with Mexicans or Anglo-Saxon colonists.

The same applied to all of Brindley's Indian employees, even Waldo, the aged cook, who occasionally went on a drinking spree. All had avoided the 'civilizing' influence of the missions. Tough, hardy and capable, the old man, his granddaughter and *cargador* treated them with respect and they reciprocated by being loyal and hard working.

'How Ewart 'n' Joe?' the man asked in a guttural voice. 'I see white feller know what him doing and tell him take them in bushes in case bad *hombres* come back.'

'They will both be all right,' Di answered, speaking Tejas fluently. 'What happened, Tom?'

'We were tricked,' replied Tom Wolf, the chief of the mule packers, reverting to his native tongue.

'Tell me about it, please,' the girl requested.

Keeping his face impassive, but speaking with a vehemence that was obvious to Ole Devil even though he did not understand the language, Tom Wolf complied. He could speak passable English, but felt—as did Di—that he could make a more thorough explanation in his own

76

tongue. So Di listened and translated for the young Texian's benefit.

According to Tom Wolf, Sergeant Maxime had not been to blame for leaving the mule train. The non-com had been reluctant to do so, but Brindley insisted. On the face of it, the decision had been correct; or at least justifiable under the circumstances as they had known them. There was nothing suspicious about the way that the two strangers had divulged their information. In fact, it had come up in what seemed a natural manner. They claimed to have seen a woman, who looked to have been in a fight, leading a group of men towards the coast. Not having cared for the appearance of the party, they had kept out of sight and made their examination with the aid of a telescope. On coming into view of the train, they had concluded that—as its escort were soldiers—they would be advised to ride over and give a warning. They were, they had said, on their way west to join Houston and the Republic of Texas's Army.

Although Brindley had dispatched his military escort, in the hope of trapping the renegades, he did not accept his informants at face value. After they had ridden away, he told Tom Wolf to follow them. If they were working in cahoots with the woman and her band, such a possibility had been anticipated. Certainly they had neither turned back nor acted in a suspicious fashion up to the time that the sound of shooting from the rear had caused the Tejas chief to give up his observation and return.

Like the soldiers, Tom Wolf had arrived too late to participate in the fighting. Nor, much as he had wished to do so, was he able to go after his employer's assailants. Instead, he had remained with the mules and left the other task to Sergeant Maxime. In addition to attending to his duties, he had learned how the attack had taken place. The mule train was approaching the stream when a packer had seen a number of riders on a rim about half a mile to the south.

77

While the newcomers had behaved in a menacing fashion, they were only acting as a diversion. Four of their number had been concealed in a grove of post oaks less than a quarter of a mile to the north. As the exposed group approached, but before they had come into range of the defenders' weapons, the hidden men opened fire to hit Brindley, the *cargador* and the grey mare. Having done so, they withdrew and the threat of a charge, which was not launched, by their companions prevented the packers from giving chase.

'The men would have gone after them when the others rode away, but I stopped them,' Tom Wolf concluded. 'I could see the soldiers coming and knew we must look after Ewart, Joe and the mules.'

'You acted with wisdom, chief,' declared Ole Devil, to whom the words had been directed in English. 'I don't doubt the courage of your braves, or that you would have preferred to avenge the shooting of your friends.'

'Do you want us to make camp here, Di?' asked the Indian, but the girl could see he was appreciative of and relieved by the young Texian's statement.

'It's all we can do,' Di sighed, anger clouding her expressive face. After Tom Wolf had turned to go and give the necessary orders, she swung towards Ole Devil. 'God damn it, even though they didn't scatter the mules like they was hoping, they couldn't have done worse to us than they did.'

'They did just what they meant to do,' the Texian answered.

'You mean all they was fixing to do was down Grand-pappy Ewart and Joe?' the girl demanded.

'That was the idea, but they were told to shoot the bell mare as well,' Ole Devil replied. 'Whoever planned the ambush must have been around mules enough to know that, especially with a well trained team like this, they'd bunch and balk, but wouldn't scatter under fire, particularly with old Whitey down. From what you've told me, they won't move without her to lead them.'

78

'They won't,' Di confirmed, realizing what her companion was driving at.

Being hybrids, resulting from the crossing of a male donkey with a female horse, mules were only rarely capable of breeding. For all that, they tended to find the company of a mare irresistible. It was a trait which packers, handling large numbers of the animals, turned to their advantage. The mules would follow a mare all day without needing to be fastened together and, apparently soothed by a bell fastened around her neck, were content to remain close to her all night instead of requiring tying when on the trail.

'So, by dropping her, they've prevented us from collecting the consignment,' Ole Devil continued. 'There weren't enough of the renegades to tackle the train, especially if their *amigos* didn't manage to persuade at least part of the escort to leave it. Even with all of Sergeant Maxime's detail headed for the bay, they wouldn't be willing to risk their lives making a straightforward attack. They're fighting for what they can get out of it, not because of patriotism, and wouldn't take too many chances. I'll say one thing, though, Madeline de Moreau must be *very* persuasive to get them to do as much as they did.'

'I'll "persuasive" her if I get my hands on her!' Di spat out, with such pent up fury that Ole Devil began to have a greater appreciation of just how great a strain she was under. Then, with a visible effort, she regained control of her emotions and her voice became almost normal as she continued, 'What do you reckon she aims to do now she's got us stopped?'

'Either she's got more of her own band coming to attack us, or she's going to look for help from the Mexican Army to do it,' Ole Devil guessed. 'She's hoping that with your grandfather, Joe and the bell mare dead——or so she assumes——we'll not be able to move before she can get reinforcements.'

79

'Which we won't,' Di warned, 'unless we can replace ole Whitey.'

'Will the mules accept another mare?' Ole Devil asked.

'Shucks, yes. Just so long as she's got a bell on, they'll follow her. Do any of your boys ride a mare?'

'I'm afraid not. We've only geldings.'

'That figures,' Di sighed, being aware that having a mixed bunch of horses created problems which a military unit would wish to avoid.

'The nearest place we might find one is San Phillipe,' Ole Devil remarked.

'Sure,' the girl agreed, but showed a noticeable lack of enthusiasm. 'You know the kind of folks who live there?'

'I do,' Ole Devil admitted and his tone proved that he understood the cause of the girl's reaction. 'They're just about as bad a bunch of cut-throats as can be found in Texas. But they're the quickest chance we have of laying hands on a mare. And without one, we'll never be able to move the consignment.'

Chapter Seven

WE'LL BE ALL RIGHT—I HOPE!

ACCOMPANIED by Diamond-Hitch Brindley and Tommy Okasi, Ole Devil Hardin was travelling through the darkness towards the cluster of lights and the various sounds which marked the locations of the fifty or so dwellings and business premises that comprised the town of San Phillipe. They rode in line abreast, with the girl in the centre, their attitudes suggestive of extreme wary alertness. She and the Texian were nursing their rifles, fully cocked and, in the latter's case, with a five-shot slide magazine in the frame. The little Oriental was carrying his bow with an arrow nocked to the string. Nor, despite being close to their destination, did they place the weapons in less accessible positions. In fact, they grew even more watchful.

Few people who knew Texas would have blamed the trio for such behaviour.

Even judged by the most tolerant standards, San Phillipe was far from an attractive place. For a number of reasons, particularly the presence of several dangerous reefs and shoals off shore, it was not even a success as a port and served mainly as a point at which small vessels could put in with illicit cargoes. However, it had not been considered a suitable location for the *Bostonian Lady* to land the consignment of caplock rifles. There were ugly rumours that a number of the wrecks which had occurred in the vicinity might not have been accidental, but were caused through the ships being lured to destruction by the local inhabitants.

Although the time was close to midnight, most of the houses still had lamps burning and people moving about in them. Laughter, shouts, a rumble of conversation and music sounded from the largest building in the centre of the town. However, while there did not appear to be anybody on the single street, the girl and the two young men were conscious of being watched.

'Blast it!' Di muttered, nodding towards the noisy and well illuminated building, but holding her voice down to little more than a whisper. 'I was hoping that Cole Turtle'd be closed down afore we got here.'

'The trouble with you is that you want everything too easy,' Ole Devil replied, just as quietly and without relaxing his vigilance any more than the girl had while speaking. 'What would this life of ours be without a little challenge or two and a few difficulties?'

'A damned sight easier,' Di stated, *sotto voce*. 'Which I'd sooner it son-of-bitching was, but don't reckon it's ever likely to get to be. And I don't want any old Nipponese sayings that *you've* just made up!'

'Humble self was not going to say a word,' Tommy

81

answered, the girl's last sentence having been addressed to him. 'Let honourable and illustrious companions make foolish conversation while I keep watch over them.'

'Why thank you 'most to death,' Di sniffed, then went on as if to herself. 'Damned if I know which of 'em's the worst. Ain't neither the one to improve on the other.'

Glancing quickly at Di, Ole Devil found nothing to lessen his admiration for the way in which she was bearing up under what had been—and still was—a period of dire tribulation and anxiety.

Doc Kimberley had done everything in his power, but Ewart Brindley's condition was still critical. Nor could moving him have been achieved without much pain and the risk of aggravating his injury still further. Yet there was a definite limit to how long he could be allowed to stay where he was. Not only was the weather far from ideal for a badly wounded man to be out of doors, even though a shelter had been made for him, the area he was in might—in fact, probably would—be unsafe in the near future. Even accepting that Major Abrahan Phillipe Gonzales *de* Villena *y* Danvila's deserted *mozo* had spoken the truth, it would only be a matter of a few days before the Arizona Hopi *Activos* Regiment put in an appearance. There was also the possibility that Madeline de Moreau might gather sufficient assistance, either from renegades or the Mexican Army, to make another bid at capturing the assignment. So the old man would have to be taken somewhere beyond their reach.

For all the great concern she was feeling over the welfare of her grandfather and Joe Galton, who was her adoptive brother and companion since they had been children, the girl had neither said nor done anything that would have interfered with the work in which she was involved. Instead, she had accepted that both were receiving the best possible care and had given her full attention to dealing with the urgent problem of transporting the consignment.

With time of such vital importance, and there having

been nowhere else close by from which a mare might be obtained, Ole Devil had set out for the town as soon as it was possible. Being aware of the inhabitants well-deserved unsavoury reputation, he had realized that the visit would entail a .considerable element of danger. He had doubted that, even though it might be to their advantage to gain independence from the rule of *Presidente* Antonio Lopez de Santa Anna, they would allow thoughts of how useful the five hundred caplock rifles would be in their fellow Texians' struggle against the numerical superiority of the Mexican Army to override their predatory instincts. The weapons were too tempting a prize for them to ignore and he had sufficient worries on his hands already without creating more.

However, with Company 'C' of the Texas Light Cavalry already sub-divided by the need to maintain a circle of pickets around Santa Cristóbal Bay as well as guarding the consignment and the mule train, he was unable to bring a strong enough force to ensure his safety. In fact, but for one detail, he would have restricted his party to himself and the little Oriental.

There was a man in San Phillipe, no more law abiding than his neighbours, who owed Ewart Brindley a debt of gratitude and could be counted upon to repay it. As he was, or had been, a leader of the community, his support could spell the difference between success and failure. However, being of a suspicious nature, he would not have accepted either a verbal or a written request from the wounded pack master if it was delivered by someone with whom he was not acquainted. Galton was still too weakened by his injury to make the hard and fast ride which the situation required. So Di, who Cole Turtle knew and liked, had been given the task of enlisting his aid.

In spite of their hopes that they might find an ally at San Phillipe, the girl and her companions had made certain preparations which they believed would improve their chances of survival.

83

Di had on a long and bulky wolfskin jacket and it did much to conceal her well rounded feminine curves as well as the pistol and knife on her waistbelt. By drawing down the wide brim of her low crowned, fawn coloured hat—which had been hanging with the coat on her saddle when the *Bostonian Lady's* captain had studied her on his arrival at Santa Cristóbal Bay—she could partially hide her features and her hair was short enough to attract no attention.

For his part, Ole Devil had retained his armament—with the exception of the sabre—which he had left in Mannen Blaze's care—but exchanged his riding breeches for a pair of yellowish-brown civilian Nankeen trousers from his warbag.

However, apart from donning a hat to be used for the same purpose as the girl's head gear, lessening the chances of his Oriental features being noticed, Tommy had not made any alterations to his attire, weapons, or appearance.

As an added precaution, in case they should be seen arriving—which Di had claimed was practically inevitable—the trio had made a wide detour around the town and were approaching it along the trail from the north. From what they could see and hear, taken with the sensation of being watched, they decided that the additional distance which they had been compelled to cover so as to mislead such observers was worthwhile.

Drawing closer to the large building without being challenged or molested, Di and the two young men became aware of a shape on the porch at the right of the open front door. Conveying an impression of considerable size and bulk, but wearing a high crowned black *sombrero* and a *serape* which covered it from head to foot, the figure was squatting with its back against the wall and appeared to be asleep.

'Could be's good ole Cole Turtle's still the head he-hooper around these parts,' the girl hissed, relief plain in her voice. 'That there's his man, Charlie Slow-Down,

84

's I telled you about. There's a full loaded and cocked blunderbus under his *serape*, which he's never been slow to use it. But do and say like I told you and we'll be all right—I hope!'

'That's what I like,' Ole Devil answered, studying the motionless shape. 'A girl with confidence in her own advice.'

'Ancient and wise Nipponese saying——,' Tommy began.

'That's all we need!' Di groaned.

'Woman seldom speaks with wisdom,' the little Oriental continued blandly. 'And when she does, it is by accident.'

'If things go wrong,' the girl whispered. 'I know who I hope gets shot first—and where he's hit.'

For all their quietly spoken banter, Di, Ole Devil and Tommy appreciated that, far from being over, their problems could soon reach a crisis. The conversation was a way of reducing the tension which all of them were experiencing.

While confident that Cole Turtle would do what he could to help, Di had never minimized the risks involved by going to ask him for it. Strangers had never been made welcome in San Phillipe, unless they were sufficiently well armed and tough enough to make expressions of disapproval from the population inadvisable. What was more, almost two years had elapsed since her last visit. Turtle might have left during that time, or have lost his position of authority. Should either have happened, the trio might find it impossible to achieve their purpose. It could even prove difficult for them to escape with their lives.

Unfortunately, as the girl and her companions realized, the presence of Charlie Slow-Down in his usual position could not be regarded as conclusive evidence that the man whom they were hoping to contact was available. While the big Kaddo Indian had acted as Turtle's bodyguard, he could have transferred his loyalties to the new owner if the San Phillipe Hotel—by which grandiloquent name the establishment was known—had changed hands.

85

However, they were aware that it was too late for them to turn back and attempt to satisfy their curiosity by some other, safer, means.

Neither increasing nor slowing their pace, although Tommy returned the arrow to his quiver, the trio brought their mounts to a halt in front of the building and at the unoccupied half of the hitching rail. While doing so, they looked across at the half a dozen horses tethered on the other side. There was nothing significant about the various styles of saddles on the animals. It would be many years before the low horned, double girthed rig—designed for the specialized needs of the cattle industry as it would be practised in the Lone Star State*—became almost *de rigueur* for Texians. Many colonists still used the outfits which they had brought with them, or sat Mexican saddles purchased locally.

On dismounting, Tommy hung the bow and quiver over his saddlehorn. Effective as they would have been in the event of attempts to molest his party during the ride through the town, he preferred to rely upon his *daisho* of swords when on foot and at close quarters. However, Di and Ole Devil retained their rifles. Nor did they set the hammers at half cock before, having hung their reins over the hitching rail, they stepped on to the sidewalk.

'*Saludos*, Charlie Slow-Down,' Ole Devil greeted, as he had been instructed by the girl, taking a buckskin pouch from the inside pocket of his shirt. 'Ewart Brindley sent this snuff and said he'd be obliged if you'd keep an eye on our horses and gear while we're inside.'

There was no verbal response to the request. However, a thick left wrist emerged from beneath the *serape*. Deciding that—with the possible exception of Mannen

---

* *The double girths were necessary because Texas cowhands scorned the use of a 'dally', a half hitch which could be released immediately in an emergency, when roping. Instead, being determined to retain anything upon which they dropped a loop, they fastened the rope to the saddlehorn.*

Blaze's hands—the upturned palm was the largest he had ever seen, Ole Devil dropped the pouch into it. Closing, the fist disappeared and the mound of humanity became as motionless as before.

Satisfied that he had carried out and been accepted in a proscribed ritual, the Texian wished he had been given some indication of the state of affairs which was awaiting his party inside the hotel. Not that he gave any sign of his feelings. In fact, he had a Gasconading swagger in his walk as, with the Browning rifle cradled on the crook of his left arm, he led the way across the porch. With the girl and the little Oriental following on either side and about a pace to the rear, he paused to let his eyes grow accustomed to the glare of the well lit interior. Then he stepped through the double doors and his friends followed him.

The lateness of the hour did not appear to be having any adverse effect upon trade in the hotel's barroom. There were a number of men in various styles of clothing ranging from Eastern suits to buckskins and Mexican *charro* garments, but all had one thing in common. Every one was well armed, with pistols, knives, or both. A number of white, Latin and Indian girls in garish costumes circulated among the customers and helped to ensure that the two bartenders behind the counter—made from planks set on empty barrels—were kept occupied in dispensing their wares. Although the band, which was comprised of a piano, two fiddlers and a trumpeter, continued to play with no reduction of volume, conversations died away. Cold, hard, watchful eyes turned in the newcomers' direction.

Advancing to Ole Devil's right, with enough room for her to turn the rifle she was carrying into a firing position if the need arose, Di tried to walk in a cockily masculine fashion. She also scanned the room from beneath the drawn down brim of her hat, searching for the man who could mean the trio would achieve their purpose and be allowed to go without hindrance. Reaching a table in the

87

right hand rear corner, she was hard put to hold down an exclamation of relief.

There were many people in Texas and along the lower reaches of the Mississippi River who would not have shared the girl's satisfaction over seeing the man who was responsible for it. In fact, they would have regarded such an emotion as peculiar when it was directed at Cole Turtle.

Even sitting down, Turtle was obviously tall and built on a massive scale. Completely bald, his fat and from a distance (but not when close enough to notice his hard eyes) jovial face sported an enormous black moustache. He wore an expensive grey cutaway coat, white shirt with a ruffed front and Nankeen trousers tucked into riding boots. Evidence of his prosperity was given by a couple of diamond rings and the pearl stickpin in his scarlet silk cravat. A good quality percussion-fired pistol lay close to his big right fist and there were four stacks of gold coins in front of him. Tossing down his cards, he let out a thunderous guffaw of laughter and scooped in the money which had formed the pot in the hand of poker which had just ended.

None of the other five players in the game appeared to find their heavily built host's actions amusing. Instead, they scowled at him and one angrily gathered the cards ready to continue. Ignoring his companions, Turtle glanced at the newcomers. After one quick look, he neither moved nor gave any indication of being aware that the trio had entered. For all that, he felt uneasy.

One of Charlie Slow-Down's functions was to prevent unauthorized visitors from coming in with such readily accessible weapons as the rifles carried by two of the new arrivals. Nor had he ever failed in the duty. Yet despite there being something which seemed vaguely familiar about the tall young man, Turtle could not remember having met him. Nor, due to the positions of their hats, could the hotelkeeper identify the other two.

Conscious of Turtle's scrutiny, brief as it had been, Di

wished that she could inform her companions that this was the man they had come to meet. However, such was her faith in Ole Devil and Tommy, she felt sure that such an explanation would not be necessary. She had described Turtle for their benefit while riding to the town. Men of their ability could be counted upon to keep their eyes open and wits about them under such trying conditions. So they were sure to have already seen him and made a correct identification.

While the Texian and the little Oriental were justifying the girl's faith in their powers of observation, having noticed that Turtle was present, they were not devoting their entire attention to him. Instead, once they had seen and recognized him, they were studying the other occupants of the room.

Some of the furnishings of the barroom, particularly the counter, left much to be desired in style and elegance and made one fitting seem out of place. Taken from a wrecked vessel—which had gone aground on a local reef —having survived the impact and being brought ashore in a small boat, a large mirror was attached to the wall behind the bar. It was a fixture regarded with mixed feelings by the customers. However, as three men had already been killed because their behaviour had been considered a menace to its existence and safety, it was now an accepted feature of the hotel.

While crossing the room, Ole Devil and Tommy were taking advantage of the mirror's most controversial and, to some of the clientele's way of thinking, objectionable qualities. Looking at the reflections on its surface, which was cleaned daily even though other parts of the establishment might not be, they were able to watch the people to their rear as well as keeping those in front and to either side under observation. They could tell that their arrival was a source of considerable interest and speculation, but that was only to have been expected. Strangers must be even rarer in San Phillipe since the struggle for independence had commenced than they had been in more peaceful times.

However, in spite of their curiosity, the majority of the customers had no intention of attempting to satisfy it. Many of them were residents of the town and most of the remainder had visited the hotel often enough to be aware of its most stringently enforced rule. Not only did the tall young man look as mean as hell and might prove dangerous if riled, but the fact that he and one of his companions carried rifles was significant. It suggested that they were sufficiently trusted by Cole Turtle to have the right to be armed in such a manner. Visitors who were less favoured were compelled by Charlie Slow-Down to leave outside all but the weapons upon their persons.

Four men, who were occupying a table to the left of the door, struck Ole Devil as being more than casually interested in his party's arrival. Dressed in the kind of clothing which would evolve into the attire of the Texas cowhand, they were unshaven and travel-stained. Empty plates, a coffee pot and cups in front of them implied that they had not been present for long. In fact, even as the Texian gave the quartet his attention, a girl with a tray arrived and cleared the table.

Although Ole Devil could not recollect the circumstances, he was certain that he had come into contact with at least one of the quartet recently. However, he was unable to make a more extensive examination. Seated with his back to the trio, the man had been looking over his shoulder. Then, turning his head to the front, he began to speak to his companions.

Before the Texian could decide whether he was correct in his assumption, he saw certain disturbing movements by the rest of the quartet. The man nearest to the door and the one at the far side of the table dropped their hands out of his range of vision. However, the behaviour of the last man supplied a clue to what they might be doing. He reached across with his right hand and grasped the butt of the pistol which was thrust through the left side of his belt. Before he could draw the weapon, an angry comment from the first to have attracted Ole Devil's attention caused him to refrain. If the way in which he glared at the mirror was any guide, he had been warned that his actions might have been seen via its reflection. He did not appear to be too pleased with what he was told next, but scowled and spoke heatedly.

After a brief discussion, the man with his back to Ole Devil shoved aside his chair and stood up. The rest also rose, with the second and third of them taking care to keep their right hands concealed behind their backs. Throwing another brief look across the room, the first man strode out of the door.

Suddenly, Ole Devil's memory clicked. Unless he was mistaken, the man had been a member of Madeline de Moreau's gang of renegades and had fled with her when Company 'C' had put in its appearance to rout them.

Even as Ole Devil was reaching his conclusions regarding the identity of the man who was leaving the San Phillipe Hotel, he became aware of something else. Instead of following Dodd, as he remembered having heard their companion called, the other three from the table were walking towards the bar. They might merely be intending to buy drinks, but he doubted it.

In fact, the young Texian felt sure that two of the approaching men were holding cocked pistols concealed behind their backs!

If that was so, there could be only one reason for the three renegades' actions!

Chapter Eight

YOU *COULD* SAY THEY'RE ON OUR SIDE

'WHAT do you make of it, Mr. Blaze?' asked the sentry who was posted on top of the slope overlooking Santa Cristóbal Bay, at about the time that—some fifteen miles to the north—Ole Devil Hardin was identifying the member of Madeline de Moreau's band of renegades in the San Phillipe Hotel. Holding his voice down, he peered through the darkness in an attempt to see the approaching riders who, as yet, he could only hear. Failing to do so, he went on, 'It can't be Cap'n Devil, Di 'n' Tommy. There's more 'n three of 'em and they're coming from the south-west.'

'That's the living truth,' Mannen Blaze conceded, sounding as if he was still more than half asleep. He had, however, been sufficiently awake to pick up and fit a five shot magazine into his Browning slide repeater rifle before leaving his blankets. 'It's not them. You did right to call me.'

'It might be some of your men from the mule train,' Beauregard Rassendyll suggested, having been disturbed when the sentry had arrived to report to his superior that he had heard riders in the distance and had accompanied them to investigate.

'Only they ain't coming from the right direction for that, neither,' the enlisted man pointed out, wondering somewhat irascibly why the dude—whom he had not bothered to waken—had come with them. 'On top of which, they've been told to stay put 'n' guard the mules. And Cap'n Devil don't take kindly to folks going again' his orders.'

'Who do you think it can be, Mannen?' Rassendyll inquired, far from pleased at the sentry's faintly derisive attitude; which had not been in evidence while the man was addressing the burly red head.

'I wouldn't know and couldn't even start to guess,' Mannen admitted, in tones redolent of disinterest. From the way in which he was speaking, his only desire was to get back to his blankets and interrupted sleep. 'Whoever they are, they're not trying to sneak up on us.'

'Could be they're just passing by, Mr. Blaze,' the sentry offered, far from being fooled by the other's air of lethargy. 'We haven't got no fire, nor nothing else to show we're here.'

'Could be,' Mannen grunted, still with nothing to show he found the subject other than a boring interference with the more important business of resting. 'I only hope's that's all there is to it.'

'You haven't heard anything to suggest they've come across the pickets in that direction, have you?' Rassendyll asked, holding his Croodlom and Co. 'Duck Foot' Mob Pistol in his right hand and wondering if he would find use for its special qualities.*

'A thing like that's not real likely to slip my remembering, *mister*,' the sentry answered indignantly.

'By the Lord!' Rassendyll began furiously, being accustomed to more respectful treatment from members of the lower social orders. 'I've had ab——!"

'Might be's well if we all talk softer,' Mannen put in almost sleepily, but there was a hard timbre underlying his words.

'Sorry, Mr. Blaze, sir,' the sentry grunted, his attitude vastly different from when he had addressed the former supercargo of the *Bostonian Lady*. 'What do *you* want for us to do?'

Rassendyll had been on the point of directing some of his wrath and indignation at the burly red head, but

---

* *The Croodlom & Co. 'Duck Foot' Mob Pistol and similar weapons had four barrels fixed side by side and splayed out in the form of a fan, so that its bullets would spread when leaving the muzzles. They were popular with prison guards and the officers of merchant ships as a means of quelling an unruly crowd at close quarters.*

common sense took control. Instead, he refrained from speaking and looked at the other with considerable interest. Up to that moment, he had always regarded Mannen as an amiable, exceptionally strong, yet—if not exactly slow witted—dull and lazy young man who took little notice of what was going on around him.

Suddenly, Rassendyll realized that he had been comparing the burly red head with Ole Devil and other more obviously competent members of the Hardin, Fog and Blaze clan. Since being left alone with Mannen, he had grown increasingly aware that he might have made an incorrect judgement. Certainly, none of the detail who were guarding the consignment had shown any concern over Ole Devil's departure, or hesitated to carry out Mannen's orders. The sentry's attitude was further evidence that there was more to the red head than met the eye. Such respect had to be earned and was not given merely because the recipient had had the good fortune to be born into the right circles.

Having noticed the way Rassendyll had stiffened, then relaxed, but was still continuing to gaze at him in a speculative fashion, Mannen guessed what had caused the behaviour. He was more amused than annoyed by the Louisianan's reaction. If it came to a point, he felt just a mite flattered. While he had never imagined himself to be as brilliant as his Cousin Devil, he knew that he was competent enough to carry out his duties without needing to have somebody hold his hand. Yet it was satisfying when others, particularly a smart and capable person like Rassendyll also appreciated his good qualities.

However, there were more important matters than self congratulation demanding Mannen's attention. As yet, the approaching riders were still only noises which came ever closer.

The questions which the burly Texian had to answer were, who they might be and, more important, how to deal with them?

Although Mannen did not reply to the sentry's request

for orders immediately, indecision was not keeping him silent. Knowing the vitally important issues which were at stake, he wanted to consider the matter before committing himself and his men to any line of action.

Firstly, before any plans could be made, or orders given, there was the matter of the riders' identity to be taken into consideration.

The direction from which the party was coming suggested that they might be members of the Arizona Hopi *Activos* Regiment, but their apparent disregard for the need to travel silently argued against such a solution. Suspecting that there might be an enemy force in the vicinity, they would not be likely to move through the darkness with so much noise. Unless, of course, they had learned of the consignment and its location, so hoped their behaviour would lull the guards into a sense of false security.

Other Mexican soldiers could also be expected to come from the south-west. If they had not made contact with the *Activos*, they might believe that there were no Texians around and therefore see no need to take precautions.

Or they could be renegades. Not Madeline de Moreau's band, who would know better than attempt such a subterfuge. There were other gangs, any of whom would be only too willing to make a stab at snatching off such valuable loot if they learned about it.

On the other hand, the riders could be members of the Republic of Texas's Army who had been sent to reinforce Company 'C' and increase the chances of delivering the consignment safely. They could even be engaged upon some unconnected mission. Knowing how certain sections of the Army were conducting themselves, Mannen felt that the arrival of a party who were on the latter kind of assignment might prove a mixed blessing and could even be a disadvantage.

Lastly, they could be no more than a bunch of ordinary civilians running away from the advancing Mexican Army. Such people were likely to make for the coast so as to join the north-bound trail. Except that did not

95

explain why they were travelling after nightfall. If the need to do so had been caused by the presence of a hostile force near by, they should at least have been attempting to move in a quieter fashion.

The fact that there had been no warning from the pickets was not such a good sign as it might appear on the surface. There had not been sufficient men available to set out a ring of them through which it would be impossible for anybody to pass undetected. However, especially as the approaching party were not even trying to conceal their presence, they should have attracted at least one of the pairs of lookouts' attention. Once that had happened, following the orders they had been given, a man should have returned to announce that riders were coming. That such a message had not been received aroused disturbing possibilities. If a picket had fallen into hostile hands, they might have been tortured into betraying their companions. In which case, the men who were coming might act in such a way to lessen the chances of their true purpose being suspected.

All in all, Mannen found himself faced with one hell of a difficult problem.

'Damn it all!' the burly red head told himself, with a certain doleful satisfaction which he had found helpful as a means of reducing his tension in times of stress. 'Whatever I do about them is bound to come out wrong.'

However, there was no sign of indecision in the way that Mannen addressed his companions. From various slight sounds beyond the rim, he guessed that Sergeant Dale had also been aroused when the sentry came to tell him about the riders and was acting in a sensible fashion.

'Head back and fetch half of the men up here, Beau,' Mannen ordered and, for all the lethargic way in which he was speaking, the words were a command rather than a request to a social equal. 'Hold them just below the rim. Have Sergeant Dale keep the rest ready to fetch up the spare rifles if they're needed.'

'Aye aye!' Rassendyll replied, giving the traditional seafarer's response to an order with an alacrity which he would not have shown five minutes earlier.

'Hey there!' yelled an unmistakably Anglo-Saxon voice, which had the tones of a poorly educated Southron's drawl in it. 'Thishere's Sammy Cope 'n' I'm fetching in some fellers.'

'That's young Sammy for sure,' the sentry declared quietly. 'And he don't sound like he's got a knife shoved again' his back to make him say it.'

'It doesn't,' Mannen conceded, although he also realized that—while competent to handle their duty—neither of the pickets to which the man in question belonged could be termed the most intelligent and discerning members of Company "C". They were, in fact, probably the two most likely to be duped by an enemy. So he went on, in what could only be described as a languid commanding hiss, 'Challenge them!'

'You-all stay put a-whiles!' called the sentry, which might fall short of a formal, "Halt, who goes there?", but proved adequate for the situation. 'Who've you got with you, Sammy?'

'They're a bunch of fellers——!' the original speaker commenced, still sounding unperturbed, as he and whoever was with him came to a halt while still beyond the trio on the rim's range of vision.

'I'm Major von Lowenbrau, with a patrol of the Red River Volunteer Dragoons!' interrupted a harder and more decisive voice, which—although speaking English fluently—held just a trace of a German accent. 'We're coming to speak with your officers!'

'They're all right!' Rassendyll breathed, having guessed at the cause of the red head's perturbation and sounding relieved.

'Sure,' Mannen replied. 'You *could* say they're on our side. Go fetch those fellers up here.'

'But——!' Rassendyll began, then remembered what the red head had told him about one aspect of the current situation in Texas.

97

'Figure on them being a guard of honour to show our respect for such an important visitor,' Mannen suggested, before the supercargo could comment upon the matter, his somnolent tones charged with grim urgency. 'Only get them up here *pronto*, but quietly and have them keep out of sight below the rim.'

'Very good!' Rassendyll assented and turned to hurry away.

'Damn it, man, what's wrong with you?' the Germanic voice of von Lowenbrau barked irritably. 'Can we advance?'

'Tell them to come ahead real slow and easy,' Mannen ordered *sotto voce*, as the man by his side looked to him for guidance. 'And make them think I'm just helping you stand guard.'

'Yo!' responded the sentry, showing no surprise at his superior's behaviour.

One of the better informed members of Company 'C', the enlisted man was aware of certain conditions which were prevailing. So he understood why Mannen was taking precautions which seemed more suitable for dealing with enemies than greeting men who were serving on the same side in the Texians' struggle for independence.

Among the many problems with which Major General Samuel Houston was having to contend was the way that a few senior officers in the Republic of Texas's Army were refusing to accept orders and abusing their positions of authority. Instead of conforming to the sound tactics he was advocating—which consisted of withdrawing to the east until the time, place and conditions were suitable for making a stand—two in particular were taking advantage of the lack of an effective disciplinary system and insisted upon conducting their own private campaigns.

Having declared that he had no intention of retreating and would hold the town of Goliad under his control, Colonel James W. Fannin was retaining his force of four hundred of the Army's best equipped soldiers who would

98

have been infinitely more useful serving under Houston's direct command.*

Another of the dissidents, Colonel Frank Johnson, was making preparations for—as he grandiloquently put it— carrying the war to the enemy by invading Mexico along the coast road. Using the prospect of the loot which was waiting to be collected, he was gathering supporters for the venture. Nor did he care from where they came, or how they might affect the overall campaign. In fact, Ole Devil and Mannen had been responsible for the disruption of an attempt by one of his officers to persuade members of the regiments loyal to Houston that they would be better off in his service.

The Red River Volunteer Dragoons were a regiment— although, like most of the others in the Republic of Texas's newly formed and privately recruited Army, its strength was not much over one hundred and fifty officers and men—who were prominent as adherents to Johnson's force. So the sentry could appreciate his superior's disinclination to trust its members.

'Come ahead, gents,' the enlisted man requested. 'Only do it real slow 'n' easy. We've had trouble with renegades and aim to make sure of who you are before you get too close.'

'Good thinking!' Mannen praised, knowing that such a precaution would be understandable when taken for the reason which had been given.

'I hope Sammy's got enough sense not to give you away when he sees you're with me,' the sentry replied. 'I wouldn't think him and his amigo know how things stand 'tween General Sam and Johnson, so they've probably already told that major about the rifles.'

That was a point which Mannen had also anticipated. While loyal enough, Cope and the man who was with him had never struck the red head as being the kind to

---

* *The tragic consequences of Colonel James W. Fannin's decision are told in*: GET URREA.

take an interest in something as remote as their superiors' policies beyond how they would be involved personally. Having no wish to emphasise the dissension amongst the senior officers, Ole Devil had advised Mannen and his non-coms to avoid referring to Johnson's plans. Some of the shrewder of the other ranks might have heard of it, but he doubted whether that would apply to the pair in question. So, seeing no harm in it and proud that their Company had been selected to handle such an important assignment, they would not be likely to speak other than the truth if asked by von Lowenbrau—as they were certain to have been—why they were on picket duty so far from the area in which the Texas Light Cavalry should be serving.

'Damn it, man!' bellowed the Dragoon major, but without setting his horse into motion. 'I've told you who I am!'

'So did them renegades, 'cepting *they* wasn't who they claimed and I'm not about to take no chances,' the sentry answered, once again supplying an understandable explanation for his behaviour and went on to give a further demonstration of his intelligence. 'I'd be a heap happier happen I knowed you'd let Sammy go back to his *amigo* on picket duty.'

'Aw hell, Smithie—!' Cope began, identifying the sentry's voice and seeing his chance of rejoining his companions by the bay.

'Get going!' von Lowenbrau interrupted, with anything but good grace.

'But——!' Cope commenced.

'Do as you're told, blast you!' the major thundered, furious that his plans were suffering such a disruption.

'Call out when you're well on your way, Sammy-boy!' the sentry advised.

'You'll have rank as corporal comes Cousin Devil getting back,' Mannen promised, nodding his approval.

'*Gracias*,' the enlisted man replied and, as they heard a

100

horse moving away, he went on, 'I hope he doesn't yell too soon. Once he has, I can't keep on stalling them.'

Looking over his shoulder, Mannen blessed his good fortune in having subordinates who were capable of intelligent thought. Clearly Sergeant Dale appreciated the situation without the need for lengthy explanations. He was personally leading the men up the slope and they were holding the noise of their ascent to the minimum.

From the bottom of the slope came a sudden, tiny red glow accompanied by a shower of minute sparks and barely audible—at that distance—popping sounds. A low curse burst from Mannen and he wondered what Rassendyll, the most likely culprit, was doing. Clearly he had lit one of those new-fangled friction matches* which were starting to replace the 'Instantaneous Light Box'† and similar devices as a means of producing a fire. The matches were as yet not readily available in Texas, but could be obtained in the more civilized parts of the United States.

'Seems like Sammy's smarter'n we figured, Mr. Blaze,' remarked the sentry, whose name was Smith even before he had arrived in Texas, bringing the red head's attention from the bottom of the valley. 'He's not yelled and those fellers aren't moving in yet either.'

By the time Cope declared that he had taken his departure without hindrance and, somewhat saractically, von Lowerbrau had requested permission to approach, Sergeant Dale had brought his men to positions just below the rim. Whatever had caused Rassendyll to strike a

---

* The first practicable friction matches were marketed in 1827 by, among others, John Walker of Stockton-on-Tees, England, who called his product the '100 Sulphurata Hyperoxegenta Frict' match.

† 'Instantaneous Light Box': consisting of a bottle containing sulphuric acid which was used to ignite wooden slivers—known as 'splints'—tipped with a potassium chlorate, sugar and gum arabic compound. In the United States of America, a box with fifty 'splints' retailed for two dollars, or four cents a light.

match still was not apparent to Mannen, but he could see the supercargo coming from the bottom of the valley at a swift but quiet run.

However, the red head had things other than the supercargo's behaviour to demand his attention. In a few seconds, as they began to come into sight, he was able to confirm what he had already suspected. Major von Lowembrau's party was around thirty strong. While there were fifty non-coms and men in Company 'C', half had been assigned to protect the halted mule train and were too far away to hear shooting at the bay. Putting out the seven two-men pickets had been a sensible precaution, but it had seriously depleted the numbers of the guard on the consignment. Even though Dale had exceeded the half which he had been ordered to bring, that still only put eight men—including Dale, but not counting Rassendyll and Mannen—on the upper reaches of the slope. However, every one was carrying three loaded caplock rifles as well as his personal weapons.

'Hold it there until you're identified 'n' Cap'n Hardin says you can come on!' Smith ordered, without the need for prompting, when the foremost of the riders was about thirty feet away, and he emphasised his words by cocking his rifle.

'Halt——!' snorted von Lowenbrau, although his military training secretly approved of the precaution and he wished that the men under his command would display an equal efficiency when carrying out their duties.

'Come on up here, you fellers!' called Mannen, adopting a coarse tone more suitable to an enlisted man than an officer, when the command did not meet with instant obedience. 'They ain't doing it!'

Immediately, Dale's detail advanced into view and the red head discovered why Rassendyll had struck the match. What was more, he heartily approved of what he had previously regarded as an inexplicable and possibly ill-advised action.

A beam of light stabbed from the bull's eye lantern,

102

which had been part of the supercargo's luggage along
with the Mob Pistol that he was still holding, as his left
hand shook open its front shield. While it did not have
the brilliance of later electric battery powered flashlights,
it was still sufficient to illuminate the man who was leading the newcomers and, if his annoyed reaction proved
anything, it at least partly dazzled him.

Tall, well built, sitting a fine looking horse with a stiff-
backed military carriage, Major Ludwig won Lowenbrau
wore clothes more suitable to a professional gambler from
a Mississippi riverboat than a former officer—if of two
grades lower rank than he now laid claim to—in the
Prussian Army. However, his close-cropped blond hair,
moustache drawn to spikes and held there by wax, and
the duelling scars on his cheeks were indications of his
background to those who knew the signs.

No matter why he had 'gone to Texas,' von Lowenbrau—who had once borne an even more distinguished
name preceded by the honorific '*Freiherr*', Baron—was
far from being a reckless fool. Sent by his colonel, for
whom he had little respect as an officer or a man, to take
possession of the consignment of caplock rifles which a
spy on Houston's staff had reported would be arriving at
Santa Cristóbal Bay, he was aware of what he would be
up against. Even without the support of Ewart Brindley's
Tejas Indian mule packers, who had a reputation for
salty toughness and the ability to protect any property
under their care, Company 'C' of the Texas Light Cavalry outnumbered the small force which had grudgingly
been given to him.

Having met Ole Devil Hardin in the early days of the
conflict, von Lowenbrau regarded him as being a potentially capable and efficient officer. Nor had anything he
had seen so far caused him to revise the opinion. Travelling through the darkness in the hope of reaching his
destination and moving in shortly before the escort woke
up in the morning, he had been intercepted by the picket.
Although he had satisfied its members that he was an

ally, neither had told him of their exact reason for being so far away from their regiment. They had been equally uncommunicative about the other details which he had hoped to learn. Clearly they had been ordered to keep their mission a secret, even from other members of the Republic of Texas's Army, and they had insisted that their officers would answer all the questions. He had been too wise to force the issue. Nor had he been able to dissuade Cope from accompanying his party, to 'show them the best way'. The soldier's presence had ruined any chance of taking the rest of the escort unawares. From what he could see, they were alert and ready to take any action which might be necessary.

'Who's command is this?' the major asked, halting his horse and signalling for his men to stop as he realized that the light from the lantern would make him an easy target.

'Captain Hardin's Company "C", Texas Light Cavalry,' Mannen replied, although he suspected that the information was unnecessary. 'He's taken a detail to change the pickets.'

'Can we make camp with you for the night?' von Lowenbrau inquired.

'If you're so minded,' Mannen answered. 'But we've got six men down there with what could be yellow fever, so we'd be obliged if you'd stand watch up here for us.'

'Yellow fever!' several voices repeated from the major's rear, showing alarm.

'Quiet!' von Lowenbrau roared, checking the undisciplined chatter instinctively, but he knew the damage was done. Fear of the dreaded disease would make his men reluctant to enter the hollow. 'Are you sure of it?'

'We've a man who knows enough about medical matters to know it when he sees it,' Mannen declared, which was true as far as it went. 'So you could help us plenty if you'd stand guard up here. We drove those renegades off, but they might be back.'

For a moment, von Lowenbrau stood in silence. Having made **Mannen's** acquaintance also, he had formed a less favourable impression than that which Ole Devil had made upon him. So he did not believe that the red head would have sufficient intelligence to make up such a story, nor to command that kind of disciplined obedience from the men of their Company. What was more, the sentry had implied that Hardin was close at hand.

Another thought came to the major. A man as shrewd as young Hardin would know of Johnson's activities and about the Red River Volunteer Dragoons' support for them. So he would be wary of its members. In which case, he might have made up the story about the yellow fever to keep von Lowenbrau's party away from the consignment. Trying to ignore the request to stand guard could be very dangerous in that case.

'Of course we'll do as you ask, Mr. Blaze,' the major declared.

Although Mannen had hoped to bring about such a result, he knew that the trouble was far from over. Once the sun came up, von Lowenbrau would know how few men he had at his disposal to protect the consignment.

Chapter Nine

I WANT HIM ALIVE AND TALKING

CLEARLY Madeline de Moreau had been even more intelligent in her planning than Ole Devil Hardin had imagined. Not only had she selected a way to delay the mule train whilst she gained additional reinforcements to capture it, she had anticipated how he would react to the situation. Guessing that he would try to obtain a replacement for the dead bell mare from the nearest source, she must have sent some of her men to intercept whoever came. Possibly, being aware of the town's unsavoury reputation, she had even deduced that he would take the risks involved by coming himself. If so, hating him for having killed her husband, she could have made arrangements to ensure her vengeance.

Having drawn his conclusions, Ole Devil diverted his full attention to solving the problems which he envisaged would arise from them. Much as he would have liked to do so, there was no safe way in which he could warn Diamond-Hitch Brindley and Tommy Okasi of the latest developments. Nor, with the brims of their hats drawn down to hide their features, could he tell if they realized the danger. To have spoken, as might have seemed the most obvious way, would have informed the three men that their purpose had been suspected and might have made them launch their attack immediately instead of waiting until they were nearer. The trouble with that was they were still well beyond the distance where the little Oriental could hope to protect himself with his swords. So, in addition to lulling them into a sense of false security, allowing them to come closer would increase Tommy's chances of survival. It would also make dealing with them much easier—but only if the Texian's companions were alerted to the situation.

Taking one factor into consideration as he watched the three men without allowing his scrutiny to become obvious, Ole Devil decided that he could delay warning his companions for a little while longer. The renegade who had been prevented from drawing his pistol was following the girl. From what he knew of her, the Texian was confident that she was capable of taking care of herself for at least sufficient length of time to let him render his assailant *hors-de-combat* and go to her aid.

Apparently the trio did not intend to take any action until the empty handed man was within reaching distance of his victim. Ole Devil decided that must have been what the final, brief, discussion with Dodd was about. Having

106

been denied an opportunity to draw his pistol, the renegade would not want the attack to be launched before he was close enough to avoid being shot. No matter why they had elected to deal with the situation in such a manner, the Texian felt that it was improving his friends' chances of survival.

Provided, of course, that Di and Tommy were aware of what was happening!

Ole Devil wished that he could tell whether they were or not.

However, the Texian realized that the question would very soon be answered.

Having advanced at a faster pace than their intended victims, the renegades were only about three paces behind the girl and the little Oriental. Although a number of the customers were able to see the pistols held by the centre and left hand men, it was typical of the type of people who came to San Phillipe that nobody gave a warning. For all that, the interest which some of the crowd were displaying served to notify the Texian that something was amiss, even if he had not already been aware of it.

In one respect, the attitudes of the onlookers raised another problem for Ole Devil. Were any of them in cahoots with the renegades?

The Texian was inclined to think that they were not. As Dodds' party had been alone at the table and, apparently, had only been there for a short time, they might have come in for a meal. In all probability, they had not expected him and his companions to arrive and were merely trying to take advantage of the situation.

At which point, Ole Devil was compelled to turn his attention from such speculations. As there was still nothing to inform him of Di's and Tommy's state of readiness, he tensed and prepared to warn them. Even as he was reaching the decision, the little Oriental's right hand rose as if to thrust back his hat.

Before Ole Devil could speak, Tommy demonstrated

107

that he—for one—appreciated the situation and had made plans to deal with it. Raising his right hand had been a ploy to distract attention from his other actions. Closing his left fingers and thumb around the hilt of the *tachi*, he pulled forward and up until the blade was clear of the scabbard. At the same time, instead of continuing to walk forward, he stepped to the rear.

'*Kiai!*' the little Oriental yelled, bringing down his left arm with the same rapidity that it had risen.

Driving his left hand rearwards, with the *tachi's* blade extending below its heel instead of ahead of the thumb and forefinger, Tommy sent the inverted 'beak' point into his would be assailant's *solar plexus*. The speed with which the little Oriental had drawn the sword and the unconventional manner in which he was wielding it, aided by his unexpected change of direction, gave the renegade no chance to take evasive action. Nor, although the man had just started to bring the pistol from behind his back, was he able to use it and save himself. Pain numbed him and, as he stiffened involuntarily, the weapon slipped from his fingers.

Like his companion, the second pistol-toting renegade was commencing to bring the firearm into use. While he was clearly startled by the discovery that at least one of their proposed victims had guessed what they were planning to do, he refused to become flustered. In fact, the urgency created by the changed conditions gave an added speed to his movements. Without giving a thought to avenging his stricken fellow conspirator, he devoted all his energies to the task to which he had been assigned, killing the young Texian.

When Dodd had refused to let the third man draw his pistol, he had insisted that he should be allowed to tackle the least dangerous member of the trio. Agreeing, Dodd had ordered that the girl must be taken alive. She would make a useful hostage and, even if her grandfather was dead, the Texians might turn over the consignment as the price for her liberation.

With that in mind, the renegade had decided how he would capture Di. Six foot tall and muscular, he had size, weight, strength and the element of surprise in his favour. So he meant to step up and enfold her in his arms from behind. Wanting to avoid a premature attack, he had allowed his companions to draw slightly ahead. Doing so had allowed him to watch for a signal from them and had also enabled him to keep the girl under observation.

Seeing the other two's pistols beginning to move forward, the man knew that the moment for action had come. So he lunged in the apparently unsuspecting girl's direction and his big hands reached out to grab her. He was already in motion before he realized that things were not going exactly as had been anticipated.

Despite having hoped for such a result, Ole Devil was surprised by the way in which the little Oriental was handling the situation. The left handed draw was a trick that he had never seen before. Not that he gave the matter any thought. There was something of far greater importance demanding his complete attention.

In the interests of preventing the renegades from realizing that he had recognized them for what they were, Ole Devil had allowed his right hand to dangle at his side. It flashed on to the Browning rifle's stock as he swivelled from the hips to his left. Although the hand took hold and its forefinger entered the triggerguard, he made no attempt to lift the weapon from the crook of his left elbow. With the man's pistol swinging in his direction, he knew there would not be time for him to do so.

Unlike Ole Devil and Tommy, Di had not noticed the renegades. Instead, she had been watching the customers ahead and to her right. As these had not been able to see the pistols in the renegades' hands, they were doing nothing to alert her of the danger. Hearing Tommy's spiritual cry, which she identified for what it was, caused her to lift her head. It was her intention to look around and find what, or whom, the little Oriental was attacking. Instead, as her gaze reached the reflection in the bar's mirror, she discovered that there was a big man approaching, clearly intending to catch hold of her.

The sight came as one hell of a shock to the girl!

The Texian realized that the little Oriental had his part in the affair under control, which did not come as any surprise. However, he was equally aware that the danger was still far from ended. Nor, much as he would have liked, could he devote any attention to how the girl was faring. The renegade to his rear had to be stopped—and fast!

Swivelling to the left at the hips, Ole Devil pointed the Browning by instinctive alignment. At such close range, he felt that it would be sufficiently accurate for his needs and, of infinitely greater importance under the circumstances, faster than any other method. With the barrel directed in what he believed to be the required area, his forefinger squeezed the trigger. If he missed, there would not be time for him to carry out the simple manipulation of his rifle's mechanism which would allow him to fire again.

With the blade of his *tachi* sinking into its recipient's flesh like a hot knife passing through butter, Tommy flashed a glance to discover how his companions—the girl in particular—were faring. He realized that, due to the attacks having been launched almost simultaneously, she would have to fend for herself until either he or Ole Devil was able to go to her aid. Twisting and starting to step to the right so as to avoid the stricken renegade and draw free his weapon, he watched the third man rushing towards Di and realized that she had not equalled his speed in becoming aware of the danger.

Even as Tommy came to his disturbing conclusion, Di looked up. Conditioned by her way of life to react swiftly and sensibly in the face of danger, she displayed remarkable presence of mind. Accepting that there would not be time to turn and defend herself with the rifle, she made no attempt to do so. Nor did she try to avoid her assailant by leaping forward or aside. With his hands

110

almost upon her, she dropped into a crouching posture with her right knee on the floor.

Much to his mortification, the burly renegade found that his objective was disappearing from his range of vision just as he was confident that he had her at his mercy. Carried onwards by his momentum, he tripped over her and, turning a half somersault, alighted supine and with a bone jolting impact.

Up flicked the hammer of Ole Devil's rifle, setting off the chain reaction which it was designed to create. There was a crack and flame gushed from the muzzle, followed by a swirling mass of white powder smoke. Before the renegade's pistol could point at the Texian, a conical .45 calibre bullet slammed into the centre of his chest. There was an audible crack as it broke the breast bone and passed through to reach the vital organs of the torso. Slipping from its owner's hand, the pistol landed on the floor and fired, but its ball flew harmlessly to hit one of the barrels which were supporting the counter.

Although the man's collision with Di had not been gentle, she had braced herself in anticipation of it. So, despite having her hat knocked off, she was able to retain her equilibrium. Straightening up almost as soon as her assailant struck the floor, she threw a quick look which assured her that there was no cause for alarm so far as her companions were concerned. Smoke was still curling out of the barrel of Ole Devil's Browning and his right thumb was operating the lever on the side of the frame so as to cause the next chamber of the magazine to move into alignment with the bore. Twirling around, the man he had shot was going down. Beyond them, Tommy had withdrawn his *tachi* and, clutching at the wound, the stricken renegade was collapsing to his knees with his face showing horror and agony.

Startled expressions were bursting from all sides. Chairs rasped, or were thrown over, as their occupants began to rise hurriedly. Every non-participating person in the bar-room stared at the group which was the centre of attraction. The fact that one of the involved parties had proved to be a good looking girl, who showed herself to be as capable as either of her companions, gave added spice to the drama.

Cole Turtle had been an interested onlooker from his place at the big stake poker game over which he was presiding. While he had noticed that one of the men who was following the newcomers carried a concealed pistol, he had not offered to intervene. He was puzzled by how the trio, none of whom he had been able to identify, managed to pass Charlie Slow-Down with two of their number carrying rifles. However, he had felt that it was not his place to intrude upon what was clearly a private matter. His curiosity could be satisfied after the affair had run its course.

'Well I'm damned!' Turtle spat out, his eyes focussing on the girl.

Before the hotelkeeper could say or do anything more, there was an interruption.

When Dodd had sent his companions to deal with Ole Devil's party, using the valid excuse that he might be remembered from the previous day's fighting, whereas they had not arrived until long after it was over, he had promised to support them from outside if necessary. Leaving the building, he had done no more than glance at and dismiss as of no importance the motionless and, apparently, fast asleep Kaddo Indian. Instead, he had drawn and cocked his pistol. Then he waited to see if he would be required to take a hand.

Watching what was happening, the renegade felt no remorse over his companion's failure and fate. His whole attention was being devoted to considering what would be the most advisable line of action, concluding that discretion was of far greater value than valour under the circumstances. According to Madeline de Moreau, Ole Devil Hardin's rifle could be fired a number of times without needing to be recharged in the normal manner. Even if she had misunderstood its qualities, or was exaggerating for some reason, the girl held what was almost certain to be a loaded rifle. So, to Dodd's way of thinking, the most sensible thing to do was withdraw.

On the point of departing, Dodd saw an objection to doing so until he had taken care of another matter. While two of his companions were either dead or close to it, the third had survived. He had toppled over the girl's back when she had ducked to avoid his hands, but was already trying to sit up and did not appear to be too seriously injured.

For a moment, Dodd thought that the problem would be solved without the need for any action on his part. Seeing the man was still capable of movement, the girl took the rifle from across her left arm. Grasping it in both hands, she raised it ready to drive its butt against his head. Such an attack could easily prove fatal, particularly when it was being delivered in the heat of anger by somebody as quick tempered as Di Brindley.

Unfortunately for Dodd, Ole Devil was equally aware of the possibility.

'Hold it, Di!' the Texian snapped. 'I want him alive and talking!'

Hearing his employer's words, Tommy Okasi transferred the *tachi* to his right hand and bounded forward. He angled the blade so that its point, coated with the blood of the man he had stabbed, was in an ideal position to be driven into the renegade's chest.

'D—Don't!' the man yelped, staring at the *tachi* with horror and making no further attempt to rise. 'I—I quit!'

Although the renegade did not know it, he was in far greater danger from the girl whom he had tried to attack than the grim-faced 'Chinaman' as he assumed Tommy to be. There were *very* few people who could have prevented her from smashing the butt of the rifle on his head by speaking. However, such was the respect in which she now held Ole Devil that she was willing to yield to his demand.

113

'Aw shucks, Devil!' Di protested, lowering the weapon. 'You don't let a gal have any fun at a——.'

A commotion just outside the building brought the girl's words to an end.

Realizing that the Mephistophelian-featured Texian intended to take a living and, given suitable inducements, information supplying prisoner, Dodd knew what must be done. So he lifted his pistol to shoulder level and with both hands. He was about to take aim into the room when there was a movement to his left. Glancing in that direction, he received a shock.

Either the man who was squatting by the entrance had woken up, or——which seemed more likely——he had not been asleep!

A savage face showed from below the brim of the *sombrero*, but that was not the main cause of alarm for Dodd. Looking as large as a cannon under the circumstances, the bell mouth of a blunderbus was pointing in his direction from beneath the *serape*.

Even as the renegade was taking in the sight, there was a puff of white smoke from the priming pan of the Indian's weapon. Then, with a thunderous roar, it vomited a spray of buckshot balls which encompassed him and ripped his torso into gory dollrags. Thrust sideways by their impact, he twirled and measured his length face down on the sidewalk.

As always, Charlie Slow-Down had done his duty. Noticing Dodd's furtive behaviour on leaving the building, he had been alert for the possibility of trouble. On hearing the crack of Ole Devil's rifle, he had drawn the correct conclusion as to who was involved. He also remembered that the newcomers had given the name of one of his employer's friends. So he had prevented the renegade from taking any part in the affair.

Chapter Ten

HOW MANY OF YOU WANT TO DIE

DESPITE the urgency of dealing with his assailant, Ole Devil Hardin had not forgotten that Dodd was somewhere outside the San Phillipe Hotel. Even as the man he had shot was going down, he had seen the renegade standing on the sidewalk. However, before he could take any more positive action than completing his turn instead of remaining swivelled at the hips, Charlie Slow-Down's blunderbus had removed any need for him to do so.

Satisfied that Dodd no longer posed a problem, the Texian swung his gaze around the barroom. The majority of the customers were on their feet and, although as yet none of them were making out-and-out threatening gestures, most were reaching for weapons. So he could not be sure of what their sentiments might be over the interruption to their pleasure.

Alert for the possibility that there were other renegades, or people in sympathy with them, present, Ole Devil kept his Browning Slide Repeating rifle in a position of readiness. He did not worry about the surviving member of the quartet who had tried to attack his party, being confident that Tommy Okasi could keep the man under control. Knowing the kind of customer Cole Turtle's establishment attracted, he wished they had not discovered that Diamond-Hitch Brindley was a girl.

For her part, although just as appreciative of the situation, Di was much less perturbed than the Texian. In fact, she believed that the loss of her hat and exposure of her features had reduced rather than added to the danger. Provided, of course, that Turtle recognized her.

'Why howdy there, Di,' the hotelkeeper boomed, his voice that of a well educated Southron, rising with considerable alacrity despite his bulk. 'It's good to see you again. Is your grandfather with you?'

115

Carrying around the room, Turtle's words were as much an announcement as a greeting, Ole Devil decided as he watched the effect they were having. They were stating that he not only knew the girl, but was showing his support for her and her companions. Taking notice, the customers realized that it would be unwise—to say the least—to become involved. Not that any of them had cause to do so. As far as they were concerned, the affair had been between two parties of strangers and was none of their concern.

'Sorry about causing the fuss, Cole, although it wasn't our fault's it happened,' the girl replied, returning the rifle to the crook of her left elbow after setting its hammer at half cock. As Ole Devil duplicated the actions and Tommy wiped the blade of his *tachi* on his victim's shirt, she went on, 'You saw the way it was, they didn't leave us any other choice.'

'They didn't,' Turtle conceded, sitting down again. 'Are there likely to be any more of them looking for you?'

'Couldn't rightly say off hand,' Di admitted and made a contemptuous gesture with her right thumb at the seated and frightened-looking renegade. 'Maybe this yahoo'd like to tell us. What do you reckon, Devil?'

'I reckon he might feel obliging,' the Texian replied, wishing that the girl had been more careful in the selection of her words. However, although the crowd were listening, nobody appeared to have noticed the clue to his identity which she had given. Scowling at the man, his voice hardened as he continued, 'On your feet and shed your weapons, *hombre. Pronto!*'

Aided by a threatening gesture from Tommy's *tachi*, which looked no less deadly despite having had the blood cleaned from its blade, the order was obeyed with promptitude. Hurriedly scrambling up the man discarded his pistol and knife in a manner which left no doubt that he did not intend to use either as a means of resisting his captors. Returning the sword almost as swiftly as it

116

had been drawn, the little Oriental gathered up the weapons.

'Yes sir,' Di grinned, noticing how the renegade was staring with awe-stricken fascination at the smaller of her male companions. Clearly the man had been impressed by the demonstration of *lai jitsu* in reverse and realized that, swiftly as the *tachi* had been returned to its sheath, it could be produced with an equal or possibly even greater speed. 'He just might at that.'

'Bring him over so that he can answer Mr. Turtle's question, Tommy,' Ole Devil commanded.

Having delivered his instructions, the Texian turned around. His whole bearing was redolent of confidence that he would be obeyed. Not only did the girl share his conviction that the little Oriental could handle their prisoner, but she knew why Ole Devil was acting in such a manner. He meant to impress the onlookers and warn them that he was a man with whom it would be dangerous to meddle. So she accompanied him as he strode across the room.

Approaching their host's table, Di gave the other men at it more of her attention than she was devoting to Turtle. All had an air of prosperity, but that was only to be expected. A player needed to have plenty of money, or negotiatable property, to sit in on a game with the kind of stakes for which they had been playing. Three were prominent members of the community, with only slightly lower social standing than the hotelkeeper, whom she knew slightly and did not care for. Nor did the other two, one in the attire of a civilian ship's officer and the other dressed in the fashion of a Mississippi riverboat gambler, strike her as being any more likeable. She noticed that the latter was studying Ole Devil with considerable interest.

'Go after Devil-San!' ordered the little Oriental, picking up the pistol and knife without taking his eyes off the renegade.

117

Gulping nervously, despite having an even greater size and weight advantage than he had had over the girl, the man showed no inclination to refuse. Instead, he turned to scuttle after Di and Ole Devil. Tucking the pistol into his belt, Tommy followed at a more leisurely pace.

'All right, *hombre*,' the Texian said, his face taking on its most Satanic expression as the man came up. 'You heard Mr. Turtle. How many more of your outfit are there and how close might they be?'

'I—!' the prisoner began, torn between fear of his captors and the knowledge of the way a betrayal would be regarded by his fellow renegades no matter how it had been extracted from him. 'Augh!'

The last exclamation had been involuntary and was one of agony. It was caused by Tommy driving his right hand, with the fingers extended and the thumb bent across the palm, in a *hira-nukite*—four finger piercing—thrust against the man's kidney region. It was a most painful form of treatment, as its recipient might have testified if he had not had more urgent matters on his mind.

'You'll find it's a whole heap easier on yourself if you answer,' Ole Devil remarked. 'That was only for starters.'

'There's a dozen more of us,' the renegade croaked, having reached a similar conclusion. 'The—They're about three miles out, on the trail south.'

'Are they likely to come here?' Ole Devil asked.

'N—No!' the man yelped. 'Honest to Gawd! Mrs. de Moreau allowed that you'd be sure to come that way and didn't even want us four to come in. How the hell did they miss——.'

'*We're* asking the questions,' Ole Devil pointed out.

'N—No offense!' the prisoner squawked, drawing in his spine as he anticipated the arrival of another painful blow from what had felt like a blunt steel spike.

'What're you laying for these folks over?' asked the gambler, who had been sharing his attention between the girl and the Texian.

118

'With respect, sir,' Ole Devil put in before the renegade could answer, having no wish for the other occupants of the barroom to learn about the consignment of caplock rifles. 'But that's between *them* and *us*.'

'Is that so?' the gambler growled, for the way in which the statement had been made was less polite than the words themselves.

'That's how *I* see it!' Ole Devil declared, his voice and attitude showing he considered the matter to be closed.

'Well I don'——!' the gambler began.

'I'm not acquainted with either of these gentlemen, *Mister* Trellis,' Cole Turtle interrupted, laying his big right hand on the butt of the pistol in what some people might have regarded as a casual, or even accidental, manner. 'But Di Brindley and her grandfather are my friends.'

'It seems I've the advantage over you in one respect,' Wade Trellis replied, without making any great effort to hide his resentment over the hotelkeeper's intervention. He indicated the young Texian. 'He's Ole Devil Hardin——.'

'I'd an idea that he might be,' Turtle admitted with a sardonic smile. 'You're travelling in distinguished and influential company, Di.'

'There's some's'd say better your'n, Cole,' the girl answered, darting a hostile glare at the gambler.

'And what the nut-man* here's going to say next, sir,' Ole Devil went on, 'is that there used to be a price on my head in Louisiana.'

'Used to be?' Trellis repeated, his cheeks reddening although he tried to keep from showing his resentment at having been classified as a "nut-man".

'Used to be,' Ole Devil confirmed. 'I've been told that

---

* *Nut-man: operator of a 'shell game', using a dried pea and three walnut shells or thimbles, such as is described in* THE LAW OF THE GUN. *As the game is purely a swindle, despite requiring considerable manipulative skill, a nut-man was not regarded very highly in gambling circles.*

my name's been cleared and the charge which brought me here no longer applies.'

'So that's what you've heard, huh?' Trellis sneered.

'Di's here as your guest and under your protection, sir,' Ole Devil said, ignoring the gambler and addressing the hotelkeeper in tones intended to carry around the room. He was aided by the silence which had descended upon the employees and customers alike. 'But I can protect myself.'

'That's understood, Captain Hardin,' Turtle replied, speaking just as loudly and, as was obvious to everybody present, once again giving what amounted to his seal of approval for the Texian.

'Take this, Tommy,' Ole Devil ordered, handing his rifle to the little Oriental. Then he swung his cold, Satanic gaze to Trellis. 'The news was brought by a friend, whose word I trust, so *I* believe it, *nut-man*. If *you'd* care to dispute the story, pick up Mr. Turtle's pistol and start to do it.'

Looking from the grim-faced young Texian to the gambler and back, a broad grin twisted the hotelkeeper's lips. After a glance at Di, who neither moved nor spoke, he set the hammer of the pistol at half cock and pushed across the table until it was just within the gambler's reach. Then, taking his hand away, he sat back with an air of eager anticipation. His whole attitude showed that he expected, hoped even, that the challenge would be accepted. Knowing Trellis, he did not doubt it would.

Nor was Turtle particularly surprised that Ole Devil should be adopting such a high handed attitude. It was typical of an arrogant, hot tempered young Southron blood that he would be quick to respond to any suggestion which might affect his honour. Or even merely because he had, for some reason, taken a dislike to another person.

For all the apparently impassive way in which Di was looking on, she felt deeply perturbed by the latest turn of events. However, she held different views from those of her host regarding Ole Devil's behaviour. Knowing him very well, in spite of their brief acquaintance, she felt sure that he was not acting out of a kind of glory in the *code duello* which caused many young men of his class to issue a challenge to fight under the most flimsy of excuses.

In her summation, the girl was doing less injustice than Turtle to the Texian's motives.

Originally Ole Devil had hoped to arrive in San Phillipe, carry out his business with the hotelkeeper and depart without attracting attention. Due to the intervention of the renegades, there was no longer any hope of doing so. The revelation of Di's identity would, as Trellis's words had proved, be sure to arouse speculation among the customers. Even if they could be prevented from discovering the reason for the visit, knowing who the girl was and the nature of the business with which her family was connected, they would be eager to learn if something of value was being transported in their vicinity.

While Turtle wielded considerable authority in the town, he was not its absolute and unchallenged ruler. Any of the three citizens in the game possessed the means to go against his desires provided they considered there was sufficient inducement. With that in mind, Ole Devil had decided to give them an object lesson. His every instinct warned him that the gambler was posing the most immediate threat. With his curiosity aroused, Trellis would be willing to satisfy it even at the risk of offending the hotelkeeper. Having drawn his conclusion, the young Texian did not hesitate to act upon it.

'There's one thing you'd better know, *nut-man*,' Ole Devil drawled, making no attempt to arm himself. 'Down here in Texas, we don't waste time by following the Clonmel Code.* So you can either admit that you accept my word, or pick up that pistol and *try* to use it.'

* Clonmel Code: twenty-six 'commandments' laying down the rules to be followed when fighting a duel, particularly with pistols, adopted by the Summer Assizes at Clonmel, Tipperary County, Ireland, in 1770.

'And have that damned "Chink" of yours shoot me as soon as I touch it?' Trellis countered, his face's expression ugly in its anger but his inborn caution warning him that he might be approaching a trap.

'With an *empty* rifle?' Turtle commented, darting a glance pregnant with meaning at the other men around the table. He did not say, 'He's trying to avoid fighting', but they and the gambler knew it was implied.

'Like hell it's empty!' Trellis spat out, although he guessed that his host was equally aware of the fact. 'That thing fires more than one time without reloading.'

'The nut-man's right,' Ole Devil confirmed, seeing the advantage of allowing his audience to appreciate the Browning's potential. 'But to show that *I* don't need any help, one of you gentleman can cover my man and shoot him if he offers to turn the rifle this way.'

'Maybe one of 'em'd best throw down on me, too, Devil,' Di suggested, still unaware of why the Texian was determined to force a showdown with the gambler but willing to help. 'Seeing's that *hombre's* so all fired scared somebody'll take advantage of him.'

'I don't think that *even* Mr. Trellis would go that far,' Turtle remarked, running a coldly prohibitive gaze at his fellow influential citizens in case any of them should be contemplating taking up Ole Devil's suggestion. 'Will your man obey you, Captain Hardin?'

'He will,' the Texian declared. 'Tommy, take the prisoner and Di's rifle across the room and wait there until I call for you.'

'You heard Devil-san,' the little Oriental told the captive, tossing down the knife he had been carrying in his left hand and accepting the girl's rifle. 'Get going and keep your mouth closed.'

Watching Tommy carrying out the first part of the orders, Trellis became aware that other eyes were being turned in his own direction. So he realized that he must decide upon what action to take. Not that he had any real choice. If he backed down, he would be finished in

San Phillipe. What was more, he had guessed that only a matter of the greatest importance would bring Di Brindley to the town at that hour of the night. That she was accompanied by a person of Ole Devil Hardin's prominence was further proof of the supposition. If he could dispose of the young Texian, he would be in a better position to satisfy his curiosity. Then, should his belief that the girl's mule train was transporting something of exceptional value be confirmed, he could easily gather sufficient help to take what ever it might be by force.

There was only one problem to be solved.

Disposing of Ole Devil Hardin!

Studying the situation, the gambler felt that he had discovered a way to do it.

'All right,' Trellis growled, thrusting back his chair and coming to his feet. 'You've asked for it. We'll step outside and I'll give you satisfact——.'

In spite of making his suggestion, the gambler had no intention of carrying it out. Not when he had decided that there was a much safer and more certain way to deal with the matter than by facing Ole Devil in a fair fight. Nor would any of the local citizens other than Turtle be inclined to object about his methods. More likely the hotelkeeper's rivals at the table, all of whom had been losers in the poker game, would be only too willing to oppose him. Especially when Trellis had told them of his suspicions over the reason for the girl's arrival.

So, while still speaking, the gambler grabbed for Turtle's pistol. It had been placed barely within reach when he was sitting down and with the barrel pointing towards him. Having stood up had put him even further from the weapon, but not enough to be detrimental to his chances. The Texian had not made any attempt to arm himself. Nor would he be expecting that there would be any need for him to do so until after they had left the building.

All in all, the scheme appeared sound and certain to succeed.

Unfortunately for Trellis, it was doomed to fail because of his ignorance.

To be fair to the gambler, his error was understandable. While he had been in Texas long enough to have heard of the Brindleys and their business, his only knowledge of Ole Devil had come from Louisiana. Nor had his information been complete.

Even before circumstances had caused Ole Devil to leave the United States, he had developed a very effective method of handling a pistol. While it was not one which would have been permissible under the rigid rules of the Clonmel Code, he had perfected it in the more demanding conditions of his new home.

Alert for treachery, Ole Devil was ready to counter it with deadly efficiency. Turning palm out, his right hand flashed up to coil around the butt of his Manton pistol. In a single motion, he slid the barrel from his belt loop and turned it forward after the fashion gun fighters of a later era would call the 'high cavalry twist' draw.* However, unlike the men who would use it in years to come, the shape of his weapon did not permit him to fire one-handed. As he could not cock the hammer with his right thumb, he had trained himself to do it with the heel of his left hand.

Shock twisted at Trellis's face as he was raising the pistol with his left hand on the barrel and the right reaching for the butt. He saw the Texian's weapon was swinging rapidly in his direction and having its hammer cocked at the same time. Then it roared and something which felt like a hot iron bored into the right side of his chest. Slammed backwards, agony depriving him of any further conscious thought, he struck the wall and lost his hold on the pistol. Bouncing off, he crumpled and fell.

'Well, gentlemen,' Ole Devil said, raking the other participants in the game—apart from Turtle—with coldly menacing eyes. 'How do you see it?'

* *A more detailed account of the 'high cavalry twist' draw is given in*: SLIP GUN

'You did the right thing,' the owner of the town's general store declared with only a momentary hesitation. Then, after the other players had stated their concurrence and Turtle's men were removing the unconscious gambler, he went on, 'Trellis had no call to doubt your word, captain.'

'That wasn't why I called him down and shot him,' Ole Devil warned and signalled for Tommy to return with the prisoner. Replacing the pistol in its belt loop, he took back the Browning rifle, continuing, 'Most of you are wondering what has brought us here. Trellis guessed that the Ewarts might be moving something of value and had notions of taking it from them. And he was guessing right. They're transporting a consignment for General Houston —and it *is* valuable.'

A low hiss of astonishment burst from the girl as she listened, but could hardly believe her ears. From the beginning, Ole Devil had insisted that they must keep their business with Turtle a secret. Yet he was announcing it openly to as mean and ornery a bunch of cut-throats as could be found in—or outside, Texas.

'That's why I forced a fight with him and he's lucky to be alive, I wasn't trying merely to wound him,' the Texian elaborated, conscious of Di's restless movements and guessing what was causing them. However, he gave his full attention to the men at Turtle's table while speaking so that his words carried to everybody in the room. 'The consignment is so important to General Houston and the future of Texas that anybody with the idea of trying to take it from us had better ask his helpers, "How many of you want to die?". Because, you have my word on it, that's what any attempt will mean. I've got Company "C" of the Texas Light Cavalry, fifty strong and fighting men from soda to hock,* backing Ewart

* The 'soda' and the 'hock' were the top and bottom cards of the deck when playing at faro, a description of which is given in: RANGELAND HERCULES. *So the term 'from soda to hock' meant all the way, from the beginning to the end.*

Brindley and his Tejas packers. That mule train is going through, gentlemen, and I don't give a damn how many I have to kill to see it reaches General Houston intact.'

Studying the grim lines of Ole Devil's Mephistophelian features and the way in which he stood holding the rifle, nobody doubted that he meant every word he said.

Chapter Eleven

DON'T SHOOT, FELLERS!

'THISHERE'S a no good, stupid son-of-a-bitching notion, was you to ask me!' muttered one of the five men who were squatting on their heels in a group under the spreading branches of a big old white oak tree. 'Riding all this damned way to lay an ambush for somebody's most likely won't come don't strike me's making real good sense.'

'Nor me, neither,' declared another member of the quintet, also holding down the level of his voice and darting a glance at a figure which was standing a short distance away. 'I don't see nobody's knows sic 'em about Texas being *loco* enough to go to San Phillipe looking for help.'

'That's for sure,' confirmed a third of the group, speaking no louder than his companions. The mention of the town brought something else to his attention and he went on, 'What in hell's keeping Dodd 'n' the others? They sure's hell aren't rushing back, are they?'

Listening to the muted rumble of agreement from the other four men, Madeline de Moreau struggled to keep a check on her normally imperious and demanding nature. Before her husband had been killed by Ole Devil Hardin, the members of the band of renegades which

126

they had gathered would not have dared to display opposition to orders in such an open fashion. Although she felt anger surging through her, she was aware of her position at that moment, and was too wise to show it.

Madeline was sufficiently intelligent to appreciate just how slender a hold she had over the remnants of the band. Serving *Presidente* Antonio Lopez de Santa Anna for profit, as she and her husband had been, she was all too aware of the type of men they had enlisted into their organization. Every one of them had 'gone to Texas' to evade the consequences of criminal activities in the United States of America, and they were only willing to accept the leadership of a more ruthless, cold blooded and dominant personality than their own. So she had been fortunate in preventing them from scattering after the fight at the cabin had left her a widow, and even more so in that they had, albeit reluctantly, agreed to act upon the plans which she had formulated for making another attempt to capture the consignment of caplock rifles. Certainly they did not consider her as the natural successor to her late husband as head of the band. They had only gone along with her suggestions out of greed and because nobody else had been able to think up an alternative scheme.

About five foot eight inches in height and in her early thirties, Madeline had a full bosomed, slender waisted and curvaceous figure which was not created by artificial aids. Despite the marks left by her fight with Diamond-Hitch Brindley—in which she had been coming off a bad second-best when it was brought to an end—she was a very beautiful woman. A grey 'planter's' hat covered her brunette hair and her black two-piece riding habit—spare clothing which had been in her warbag on the cantle of her saddle—was supplemented by the warm man's cloak-coat that she had donned.

Despite her physical attractions, there had always been a hard and superior air about Madeline which—when they remembered how she and her husband had

127

earned a living before coming to Texas*——repelled and annoyed the male members of the band. Nor, feeling nothing but contempt for what she regarded as the hired help, would she have had it any other way. As far as she was concerned, even before her bereavement, they were nothing better than dull witted, uncouth animals. Although necessary for Randolph and her purposes, they were expendable; to be used as long as there was a need for their services and then discarded. Nor had her thinking about them changed. Provided things went as she hoped, she would soon be leaving their company permanently. The kind of life she had been leading recently no longer had anything to offer, or to hold her in it.

Regardless of her faults, which were many, Madeline had loved Randolph Galsworthy Buttolph† deeply and sincerely. Distressed, grieving and enraged by his death, she had sworn to be avenged upon the man who had killed him. That had been her main reason for gathering together the men who had fled from the cabin. Nor could she have hoped to achieve anything with them, but others of the band—having been summoned by a message left at one of their hideouts—arrived. Even with the reinforcements, it had taken all her persuasive powers before they would agree to carry on with the task which her husband had started. Nor would she have succeeded without Dodd's backing. He had always been infatuated by her and had hopes of taking Buttolph's place in her affections as well as becoming the new leader of the band.

Conceding that any direct attack upon the well guarded

* Before their activities had made the United States of America too hot to hold them, Madeline and her husband had been actively involved in a white slavery ring as well as operating a high class, but notorious, brothel and gambling house in New York.

† Although Ole Devil Hardin had known Madeline as 'de Moreau' and believed her husband's surname to be 'Galsworthy', they were Mr. and Mrs. Buttolph. However, to avoid confusion, the author will continue to refer to her by her maiden name, which she and her husband had elected to use since arriving in Texas.

consignment, or the mule train, was out of the question, the woman had realized it would become even more difficult to deal with them after they had come together at Santa Cristóbal Bay. However, Dodd's explanation of how the pack mules were handled had shown her a way in which she might be able to attain her desire for profit and revenge. There had been added inducement in the thought of how the shooting of Ewart Brindley would affect his granddaughter, for whom she was nursing a hatred which almost equalled her antipathy towards Ole Devil Hardin.

Although Madeline would not have been averse to capturing the consignment, that was far from being her primary consideration. She had been too appreciative of the difficulties involved in taking and disposing of it—as well as retaining the lion's share of the profits it would bring—with her husband dead to feel sanguine over the chances of success. So her main objective had been vengeance.

Basing her plan upon a shrewd summation of Ole Devil's character, formed whilst in his company as part of her husband's scheme to gain possession of the caplocks, the woman had guessed how he would respond to the loss of the bell-mare. Feeling sure that he would personally lead the detail sent to obtain a replacement, and as he would not wish to reduce the guards on the consignment or the mules to any great extent, she knew it would consist of only a few men despite the unsavoury nature of the town's population. She had argued that catching him would place a useful hostage in their hands. Even if his men refused to exchange the rifles for him, or he should be killed, they would be left leaderless and consequently much easier to deal with.

None of the men, not even Dodd, had suspected Madeline's true motive for bringing them to the San Phillipe area. Being shrewd as well as intelligent, she knew that she could not hope to retain her former position of authority in the band now that her husband was dead. Nor was

129

she willing to act in a subordinate capacity to any other man, particularly those who were with her. So she planned to break away from them and return to the United States, where she felt certain that she could re-establish herself without difficulty, as soon as they had helped her to take revenge upon Buttolph's killer.

On arriving in the vicinity of San Phillipe, Madeline and the men had sought for the best place to establish their ambush. Doing so had only been a matter of selecting the most suitable of several locations, any one of which would have filled their needs adequately. Concluding that their victims would in all probability follow the trail which ran parallel to the coast had made their task easier. However, they had not wanted to be too near to the town in case any shooting that was necessary should be heard and bring some of the citizens to investigate. Being aware of the kind of people who lived there, the renegades had considered it most inadvisable to let them learn about the valuable consignment. With that in mind, they had settled upon a bend with a number of bushes on either side to offer concealment for themselves and their horses. It was in fairly thick woodland and about three miles from the nearest human habitation.

In spite of having agreed to carry out the ambush, a difficulty had arisen. While the men had been willing to take the precaution of eating the food which they were carrying without warming it and to do without lighting a fire, they had started to complain about the lack of liquid refreshment. Finally, to keep the peace, Dodd had taken three companions and set off to purchase a supply of liquor from the town. As he had pointed out to the woman before leaving, some of the others were sure to slip away for it if he did not go and, by taking charge of the party himself, he could make sure that it returned as quickly as possible.

From the way in which her companions had been and still were behaving, Madeline could tell that they were growing less enarmoured of the scheme. While fine and dry, there was a chill in the air which did nothing to make the waiting more pleasant and comfortable. If the Texian failed to act as she had anticipated, or there should be any other setback, she would lose what little control she had over them. In view of the kind of men they were, especially without Dodd to stand by her, she might suffer an even worse fate than merely being deserted.

'Maybe something's happened to 'em,' suggested the fourth of the renegades who were with Madeline on the right side of the trail. 'You know what kind of a place San Phillipe is.'

'Or it could be they've changed their minds and don't conclude to come back,' suggested the man who had started the latest outburst of complaints.

'There's some's wouldn't blame 'em if they have,' commented the second speaker. 'Hell's teeth, we ain't going to do no son-of-a-bitching good here. Happen Hardin knows about San Phillipe, which 'most everybody in Texas does, he'll not be *loco* enough to come there fixing to get another mare.'

'It don't strike *me's* he would,' admitted the last of the quintet.

As the woman heard the trend being taken in the conversation, she began to grow increasingly perturbed. Up to that point, she had drawn some slight comfort from the way in which the men had been speaking. Several feet were separating her from them, which was nothing unusual as she had never mingled closely in their company. Up until that point, she could only just hear their words and had felt sure that they were not aware she could do so. The fact that they were no longer attempting to hold their voices down implied that they might be contemplating a revolt against continuing the ambush.

Worried by the possibility, Madeline slipped her right hand into the side pocket of what had been her husband's cloak-coat. Closing her fingers about the butt of the weapon which was inside, she found herself wishing, not for the first time, that he had had it in his possession when he was confronting Ole Devil Hardin. However, for some reason, he had failed to take the precaution. In view of the latest development, she was not sorry to have it available and unsuspected by her companions. It had a potential which could be of great use if they were considering more than merely deserting her.

Even as the woman was drawing her conclusions, she began to walk in a casual seeming fashion to where her section of the party had left their horses. Although she was alert for any hint that her actions were arousing the men's suspicions, she did not take out the multi-barrelled Maybury 'Pepperbox'* handgun. It offered her the advantage of being able to fire no less than eight shots without needing to be reloaded, but was only .34 in calibre and lacked accuracy at anything except close quarters. If there should be trouble, she planned to stop at least one of her assailants before they were near enough for it to be effective. Her husband had taught her to shoot and she had attained a fair proficiency at it even before her arrival in Texas.

Coming to a halt, as if she had merely gone to check on the animals, Madeline glanced at the group beneath the white oak tree. First one, then another began to stand up and all were gazing in her direction. Alarm and anger gripped her, but not to the extent of rendering her unable to think. The situation was bad, but not desperate. As a precaution in case a hurried departure should become necessary, all the horses were saddled and had the girth tight enough to let them be ridden with the minimum of delay. So she could mount and be gone long before any of them could reach her. Especially if she caused some confusion by shooting one of their number. With that in mind, she lifted one of a brace of pistols from the holsters attached to her saddle's horn. If the men

* Pepperbox: a multi-barrel repeating firearm where all the barrels rotate around an axis instead of, as on a revolver, only the cylinder holding the firing charges.

132

had noticed what she was doing, they made no comment. However, when they heard her drawing the hammer to full cock, they might suspect why she had armed herself.

Even as the woman's left hand went to the hammer, she heard a low whistle from where the sixth member of her group was keeping watch on the trail.

'Hey, Mrs. de Moreau!' hissed the first complainant and, although more softly spoken than his last words, his tones were sullen as he continued, 'There's somebody coming!'

Taking advantage of the news as an excuse, Madeline cocked the pistol while returning to the men. They were reaching for rifles, or pistols when the sound of the approaching horses reached their ears.

'Not from the south,' the woman said, a touch bitterly. 'It's probably only Mr. Dodd's party coming back from town.'

'It's taken 'em long enough to do it!' commented another of the quintet, just as quietly as the first and sounding equally resentful. 'This sitting around waiting's surely hell without a drink to help pass the time.'

'I know's I can use one,' declared a third speaker, turning towards the trail. 'There's no saying how long we'll be here. Or if anybody'll come after we've waited.'

With that, the renegade walked in the look-out's direction. Leaving their rifles behind and handguns in their belts, his companions followed. Setting after them, still carrying her pistol, Madeline could see and hear enough to inform her that the other group across the trail were behaving in a similar manner.

Taking the recent events into consideration, the woman was not sorry to hear the approaching riders despite them coming from the wrong direction. While Dodd lacked the masterful personality of her late husband, he was tougher than the others and still a force to be reckoned with in the band. His presence would offer her considerable protection if things should go wrong.

Suddenly a thought struck Madeline and it drove the

133

relief from her mind as she felt sure it had not occurred to any of the men. The riders might not be Dodd's party, but somebody else who had been in San Phillipe and were using the trail. Travellers from the town were likely to be engaged in a way of earning a living which would make them wary and mistrusting. Riding into such a situation, they would be inclined to shoot first and ask questions later.

'Hey there!' yelled a voice, almost quavering with urgency and alarm, to the accompaniment of several bottles clinking against each other, before the woman could put her thoughts into speech. 'Don't shoot, fellers! It's only us 'n' we've brought the liquor!'

Having given a startled gasp at the first shouted word, a snort of annoyance burst from Madeline as the explanation continued. From the way in which the approaching rider was carrying on, he considered that he was taking a most sensible and necessary precaution. In fact, his tones suggested that he was very nervous.

For all the woman's relief at discovering the identity of the men on the trail, she silently cursed Dodd for not having kept him quiet. If Ole Devil Hardin—or whoever had been sent to obtain a replacement for the slaughtered bell-mare—was close enough to have heard what was said, he would know that somebody was lurking in the vicinity and ready to start shooting at passers-by. While he was unlikely to guess who the ambushers might be, he was certain to take steps to avoid them. Obviously Dodd's party had failed to take that point into consideration. Nor were the rest of the band showing any better grasp of the situation.

'You was right, ma'am!' announced the look-out, no longer bothering to speak quietly. 'That's ole Pudsey. I'd know his voice anywheres.'

'Sounds like they ain't coming back empty handed, neither,' another renegade went on in normal tones. 'Which a drink's what I'm needing right now.'

Before Madeline could suggest that they remembered

134

what they had come to try to do, the second speaker
started to walk from the bushes and the others followed
his example. They were joined by the men from the
other side. An ever growing anger filled her as she listened to the commotion her irresponsible companions
were making, but she doubted whether they would take
any notice if she attempted to make them behave in a
more sensible manner. What was more, there was a likelihood that they would become even more noisy. With the
mood her group of the ambushers had been in, they
could also do worse to her than just alerting anybody who
might be in the vicinity of their presence.

A bitter sense of resentment against Dodd began to
assail the woman. She wished that he had given more
thought to what they hoped to achieve and had restricted
the quantity of liquor his party were bringing from San
Phillipe. If the clinking was anything to go by, there
were sufficient bottles to let them all get drunk and she
was all too aware of how dangerous that could be for
her. There were men present who had little cause to be
kindly disposed towards her. Under the influence of the
cheap whiskey, they could decide to repay her for the
arrogance she had always shown to them.

Appreciating the peril from the renegades, either if she
tried to prevent the issue of the liquor or after they had
finished it, Madeline did not follow them. Instead, remaining amongst the bushes, she peered through the darkness
at the four returning members of the band. Although she
could only make out their shapes, she concluded from
the steady way in which they sat their horses that none of
them had imbibed an excessive amount of liquor while
they were in town. Clearly Dodd had restrained any
desire the other three might have had to over-indulge.

Even as the thought came, Madeline grew puzzled.
While nowhere near the man her husband had been,
Dodd was tough, experienced and not unintelligent. What
was more, he had proven himself capable of enforcing
his will upon the other members of the band even before

he had made his party refrain from getting drunk in San Phillipe.

So why had Dodd allowed Pudsey to call out the warning of their arrival instead of announcing it himself in a more suitable manner?

Or, if it had been done without Dodd's knowledge and authority, why was he keeping silent when he ought to be remonstrating with his indiscrete companion?

With the two points raised, Madeline began to sense that something was very, *very,* wrong. However, for a few seconds, she could not decide what it might be.

Then certain significant, frightening even, factors started to emerge!

Dodd and his companions had all been approximately the same height and build, clad in low crowned hats and range clothes. While the woman could identify the man in the lead as Pudsey, there was considerable disparity between the shapes of himself and two of his companions. What was more, even the fourth of the party —who was behind the other three—struck her as being wrong. After a moment, she realized why.

Pudsey had been marginally the largest of the quartet, yet the man who was following him looked even more massive. In addition, he appeared to have changed his clothes while in the town. At least, there was now a Mexican *sombrero* on his head and he had not been wearing a *serape* when they set off.

Even as Madeline was noticing the fourth rider's change of attire, she became aware of how the horses of the men on either side of Pudsey were behaving. While his mount was walking normally, they seemed restless and reminded her of something. Just what it was struck her an instant later. They looked like a couple of racehorses being restrained, yet ready to hurtle forward when they received the signal to start a race.

Other thoughts crowded into the woman's mind. The rider on the left and slightly behind Pudsey was far smaller than any member of the band.

136

However, it was the man who was closest to Madeline's position who attracted the majority of her attention. Tall and slender, his right hand hung by his side and the left was also hidden from her view. However, he was sitting his horse with the straight backed poise which reminded her of an officer in a first class cavalry regiment riding in a parade.

Or of somebody whom Madeline had come to know —and hate!

With a sensation like an icy cold hand running along her spine, the woman realized what must have happened!

Possibly because Ole Devil Hardin had guessed how she had anticipated his reaction to the shooting of the bell-mare, he had selected a route which had avoided the ambush. In addition, he must have recognized and dealt with Dodd's party in San Phillipe. Pudsey would not hesitate to betray the rest of the band if it would save his own skin.

Suddenly an even greater appreciation of the situation burst upon the woman. Her men were walking towards the riders completely oblivious of their peril. Taken unawares and attacked by three effective fighters, which she did not doubt the Texian's party would be, some of them were certain to be killed.

Apart from one consideration, Madeline would not have worried over what fate had in store for her companions, regarding it as being no more than their stupidity warranted. However, coming in their disgruntled frame of mind, such an event would be all the inducement they needed to flee. Even if she went with them, they would never trust her judgement again. In fact, especially as she could no longer count upon Dodd for protection, they were likely to turn on her and she was all too cognizant with what *that* would mean.

Once again, Madeline was finding her schemes thwarted and her life endangered by the man who had killed her husband!

All the woman's virulent temper erupted!

'It's Hardin!' Madeline shrieked, raising and, confident that she could hit her intended mark, sighting the pistol. Her finger began to tighten on the trigger and she went on, 'Kill him!'

Chapter Twelve

I'LL NEVER REST UNTIL HE'S DEAD!

SITTING his horse with the reins tied to the saddlehorn, but restraining its eagerness to move—by holding the near side ribbon with his pistol-filled left hand—Tommy Okasi watched the renegades. They were emerging from their places of concealment in response to Pudsey's call and the clinking of the empty bottles supplied by Cole Turtle. None of them gave the slightest sign of suspecting that anything was wrong, even their betrayer's understandably nervous tones had passed unnoticed. As far as the little Oriental could make out, they had left their rifles and were approaching with empty hands. For his part, he was holding his *tachi*—its blade blackened by smoke to avoid any glitter from the steel giving the game away —and the Manton pistol which he had borrowed from his employer. His unstrung bow was suspended in the loops on the left side skirt of his saddle, but he had left the quiver of arrows in Diamond-Hitch Brindley's care.

Studying the situation, Tommy was impressed—as he had been on other occasions—by Ole Devil Hardin's shrewd assessment of human nature. It had already been displayed earlier that night, by the way in which he had turned the events at the San Phillipe Hotel to their advantage.

Despite Tommy's—and, the little Oriental suspected,

Di's—original unspoken misgivings as to the wisdom of the Texian's decision to tell the crowd that they were transporting items of considerable value, only good had accrued from it. Supporting his grim warning with a demonstration of his Browning Slide Repeating rifle's potential, by shattering nine bottles in a rapid succession, which would have been beyond the capability of any single shot firearm no matter how well handled, he had increased his audience's awareness that he was a man with whom it would be *very* dangerous to trifle. They had already seen him provoke a fight and cripple one of their number whom he had suspected might pose a threat to the goods in his care. Nor did they doubt that he had sufficient force at his command to back up his statement of intentions.

Always quick to grasp and willing to benefit from any situation, Cole Turtle had reached a decision which was —and would continue to be—of the greatest help to Ole Devil. He had announced that, with the consignment being of such importance to the future of Texas, he meant to do everything in his power to ensure its safe delivery and anybody from the town who attempted to interfere would incur his grave displeasure. All who had heard him knew exactly what he meant.

Having made his position clear, and supported by the hotelkeeper, Ole Devil had turned his attention to the business which had brought them to San Phillipe, and also to removing the threat posed by Madeline de Moreau and her renegades. Once again, Turtle had shown his good faith. In addition to presenting Di with a mare from his stable, he had offered his assistance in dealing with the ambush.

Badly frightened by his predicament, the surviving renegade had done more than tell his captors that his name was Pudsey. He had described the place where his companions were waiting. With the added inducement of being told that he could go free after the ambush had been broken provided that he got the hell out of Texas by

139

the shortest and quickest route, he had agreed to lure the rest of the band from where they would be hiding.

Hearing what the young Texian intended to do, Turtle had warned that the woman and her party would be expecting four riders. Although Di had pointed out that she was on hand to make up the required number, Ole Devil had refused to let her participate. As he had pointed out, if things should go·wrong, somebody had to deliver the mare and warn Mannen Blaze of what had happened. Once again, Turtle had supplied the answer. Not only had he promised to give the girl an escort to Santa Cristóbal Bay in such an eventuality, but he had offered the services of Charlie Slow-Down to fill the remaining vacancy in the quartet. Di had reluctantly gone along with Ole Devil's wishes.

Satisfied that he had achieved his original purpose in visiting San Phillipe and, in spite of having failed to keep it a secret, having prevented the citizens from causing him trouble on account of it, Ole Devil wasted no time in leaving. Nor had Tommy blamed him for being disinclined to linger any longer than was necessary in such a location. There was considerable urgency in returning to the mule train with the replacement bell-mare. What was more, given time, some of the inhabitants' avaricious natures might override their fear of opposing Turtle's will. Regaining their courage, they might start contemplating means by which they could take possession of the consignment.

Once the mare had been handed over to Di and various other preparations had been completed, Ole Devil, Tommy and Charlie Slow-Down had set out with Pudsey. Escorted by Turtle's fifteen year's old son, Rameses—who was, at a later date, to achieve even greater prominence than his father in the law breaking circles of Texas*—and four trusted, well armed men, the girl was following Ole Devil at a safe distance.

* Some details of 'Ram' Turtle's later career are given in: SET TEXAS BACK ON HER FEET

140

When Pudsey had told the Texian that they were drawing close to the curve where the ambush was to take place, the trio had made ready for action. In the Kaddo Indian's case, that had entailed no more than cocking the pair of blunderbus handguns he was relying upon. Nor had Ole Devil and the little Oriental needed to do much more, but they had a somewhat different problem to contend with. Each was astride a horse trained for cavalry duties. There was only one kind of situation in which such mounts would have their reins fastened to the saddlehorn. Their reaction would be to dash forward without any guidance other than the rider's movements on the back, and knee pressure. However, this tendency must be restrained until the most advantageous moment if they were to benefit fully from the element of surprise. So, once the reins had been secured, Ole Devil and Tommy kept hold of one rein with the hand grasping the pistols. These were to augment the swords they were already carrying to ensure that the prisoner did not try to betray them. Although the spirited mounts were restless and eager to move faster, their riders were able to keep them under control, knowing that they would bound forward on being allowed to do so.

Too frightened to be treacherous, even though he was aware of what would happen to at least some of his former companions, Pudsey had carried out his instructions and the perturbed agitation in his voice had failed to warn them that all was far from well. As Ole Devil had hoped, the clinking of the bottles had drawn the waiting renegades from their places of concealment. What was more, as they walked along the trail, they were not so closely bunched together as to create an extra hazard to what he was planning to do. In fact, they could hardly have positioned themselves more suitably if he had explained what he wanted from them.

However, another problem which the Texian had envisaged had failed to materialize and he did not care for its omission. Sitting his impatient mount, with his right hand held so that his sabre—suitably treated like Tommy's *tachi*—was concealed behind his leg, he studied the approaching figures. Although Madeline de Moreau must have been aware of the threat to the ambush, she had made no attempt to halt the exodus of the men from the bushes. Nor could he see her amongst them. He guessed that she was close by and must be furious at their undisciplined, rowdy behaviour.

Measuring the distance separating them from the rene- gades, Tommy glanced at Ole Devil. Making just as care- ful an estimate, the Texian decided to hold off until they were a little closer. The nearer they were when they launched their attack, the greater effect it would have and the more damage it would inflict. Nor did he have any qualms over assaulting the men who were walking towards him under the misapprehension that they were approaching friends. In fact, his only regret was that he did not hold a firearm capable of discharging more than one shot, either in succession or as a volley. To have carried his Browning Slide Repeating rifle would have prevented him from using the sabre and might have aroused the renegades' suspicions. Nor was there any handgun in production at that time which he felt would have filled his requirements if he had purchased it.*

Although Ole Devil had seen a Collier Repeating Pistol† on his travels, the fact that it was a flintlock and

* *Although the Patent Arms Manufacturing Company was being established by Samuel Colt, with Elias B.D. Ogden (later Judge) as President, and Colt's cousin, Dudley Selden, as Secretary and General Manager, at Paterson, Passaic County, New Jersey, early in 1836 and would receive its charter on March the 5th—and have it amended twice in 1839—it would be another year before the first of the 'Paterson' revolving cylinder rifles and pistols—the name of the latter becoming shortened to 'revolver'—were available to the public.*

† *Invented in 1813 by Elisha H. Collier at Boston, Massachu- setts. An early and comparatively successful attempt to create a firearm, utilizing a single barrel and a hand-operated cylinder rotating with the firing charges, which could fire several shots in succession. Lack of patronage and production facilities in the*

142

had more than forty separate parts in the lock alone—not counting the lock-plate, attaching screws, stock and barrel-cylinder pin—in his opinion made it far too delicate and complicated to handle the work it was now called upon to perform.

Much the same considerations had caused Ole Devil to reject the various types of multi-barrelled 'pepperboxes' which were on sale. None of them, even those designed as caplocks—particularly as the latter possessed what he regarded as a lethal failing—had struck him as being sufficiently rugged and reliable to stand up to the rigours of conditions in Texas.

However, at that moment and under the prevailing circumstances, the Texian would even have settled for the loan of the Croodlom & Co. 'Duck Foot' Mob Pistol—which would have allowed him to discharge four .45 calibre bullets simultaneously and not in the same direction—that Beauregard Rassendyll had brought as a personal sidearm. Such a weapon would have served his purpose better than his single-shot Manton pistol.

Ole Devil's yearning for a repeating—or multi-shot—firearm was not activated by blood lust, but he refused to be influenced by the knowledge that some of the men before him were going to die without a chance to defend themselves. Not one of them would have hesitated to murder him if they were presented with an opportunity. In fact, some of them had already tried during the fighting at the cabin and they had been waiting in

---

United States of America caused him to cross the Atlantic and manufacture his arms in England. In spite of Ole Devil's misgivings, a number of the weapons were purchased for use by the British Army in the Colonies. Although there is no evidence of the fact, it has been suggested by some authorities that—having seen examples while serving as a seaman on a ship which put in at Calcutta, India, then a part of the British Empire—Samuel Colt, q.v., used the Collier Repeating Pistol as the basis for the mechanism of his first 'revolving cylinder' firearms.

143

ambush with similar intentions. What was more, some of their number had shot her grandfather, Joe Galton, and the bell-mare while the rest were creating the diversion which had made it possible for them—in part, at least— to achieve their purpose. He knew that they had not even the excuse of patriotism to condone their actions. They were cold-blooded opportunists, traitors to their own kind who were serving a tyrannical dictator for what they could get out of it.

However, revenge was not Ole Devil's primary consideration. First and foremost in his thoughts was the fact that he was up against renegades who were a serious threat to the security of the Republic of Texas. So, he was prepared to be as ruthless as necessary whilst contending with whoever, or whatever, might be menacing it.

With the latter thought in mind, Ole Devil decided to hold off the attack for a couple or so more yards.

For all that everything appeared to be going in his party's favour, with the renegades failing to grow alarmed when Ole Devil's party did not answer the shouted greetings. But Ole Devil was perturbed by the woman's absence and silence. Such behaviour seemed most unlike her and he wondered where she might be.

Even as the thought came, it was answered in no uncertain manner!

At the first sound of Madeline's voice, which solved the mystery of her whereabouts to the Texian's satisfaction if not relief, he knew that he could not delay the attack any longer.

'Yeeagh!' Ole Devil roared before Madeline had finished speaking, releasing the rein from his left hand and jabbing his heels against his horse's flanks.

'*Banzai!*' Tommy bellowed at almost the same instant, having duplicated his employer's summation of the situation and giving his mount a similar indication of his wishes.

Unfortunately for Madeline and her companions, the

144

warning she was shrieking—like her realization that the ambush was to be a failure—came just a little too late. Nor did she achieve her intentions by raising the alarm in such a manner. Startled exclamations began to burst from the renegades, but they were not to be granted an opportunity to recover their wits and act upon her advice.

Well trained and knowing what was expected of them, on receiving the awaited signals the two horses lunged forward willingly. The sudden change in the pace of the big dun gelding, to which the Texian had transferred before setting out from Santa Cristóbal Bay, saved its master's life.

Lining her pistol, the woman had completed the pressure on its trigger and the hammer was beginning to fall when the horse obeyed its master's command. Even as the percussion cap was crushed and, in turn, ignited the main charge, she saw her target was passing from in front of the barrel. Nor was there anything she could do to correct the mishap. Being momentarily dazzled by the flames which gushed from the muzzle, she did not see the result of her shot. However, her efforts had not been entirely wasted. She might have missed her intended mark, but the bullet ended its flight in the chest of the man who had betrayed the ambush.

Even as Ole Devil felt the powerful thrust with which the bay responded to his instructions, the sound of the woman's pistol reached his ears to be followed an instant later by the eerie 'splat!' which told him that a bullet had passed *very* close behind him. It was succeeded by the unmistakable soggy thud of lead driving into human flesh.

A quick glance to his left satisfied the Texian that the little Oriental was not the woman's victim. He also felt sure that the same applied to Charlie Slow-Down. Judging from the angle the bullets had come, there was only one other alternative, but he did not bother to investigate it. Nothing he had seen of Pudsey caused him to have even the remotest interest in the renegade's well being.

Not that Ole Devil had the time to ponder extensively upon the identity of whoever it was who had been shot. Almost as soon as he had turned his gaze to the front after checking that Tommy was not the victim, the dun was about to carry him between the foremost of his enemies.

Remembering the advice he had been given by the *maitre des armes* who had taught him to wield a sabre, Ole Devil did not attempt to slash. Instead, he drove out his weapon with a thrusting motion. Its point entered the mouth of the man on the right, turning his yell of alarm into a strangled gurgle. A moment later, seeming to have responded of its own volition, the Manton pistol boomed awesomely and propelled its ball into the face of the left hand renegade. The muzzle-blast illuminated Ole Devil's features and its fiery glow made them appear even more Mephistophelian than usual.

Keeping level with his employer, Tommy launched his attack almost simultaneously. Using the point of his *tachi*, he aimed badly and did no more than cut open a man's right shoulder in passing. However, the pistol was more successful and avenged Ewart Brindley by sending its ball into the throat of the man who had shot him.

Pudsey gave a screech of pain as Madeline's bullet found him and he went sideways from the horse. Startled by the commotion, it gave a leap which helped to unseat him and he went crashing to the ground. Nor were his troubles at an end. Alert for the first suggestion that his companions were commencing the attack, Charlie Slow-Down let out a Kaddo war whoop which caused his mount to run. Its hooves struck the injured man as he sprawled helplessly in front of it.

Pandemonium and chaos was reigning unchecked on the trail.

Seeing the pair of riders bearing down upon them, the remaining members of the woman's band made no attempt to draw weapons and defend themselves. Instead, as Ole Devil had anticipated when making his plans for

146

breaking the ambush, they began to scatter so as to avoid their assailants. Not all of them succeeded.

Spinning around, the man who had erroneously reported the return of Dodd's party tried to retire in the direction from which he had come. It proved to be a disastrous choice. Coming up behind him, Ole Devil elevated and brought down the sabre in a 'cut when chasing' blow which split open his skull and tumbled him lifeless on the trail.

Another renegade might have counted himself more fortunate in that he had been on the left flank of the ambush while waiting for their would-be victims to put in an appearance. Turning and darting towards where his horse was tethered, he went in a direction which kept him clear of the little Oriental's *tachi*. Satisfied that he had escaped death or injury, he continued to flee as fast as his legs could carry him.

Two more of the band were less lucky. Passed by Ole Devil and Tommy, they became the targets for the Kaddo Indian's right hand blunderbuss. One caught the majority of the sprayed out lead and the other received a couple of the surplus buckshot balls. Although the latter was injured, he managed to run away. His companion went down, as dead as Dodd had been under similar circumstances.

Within a minute from starting out to greet what they had imagined to be friends carrying liquid refreshment, Madeline de Moreau's band of renegades had ceased to exist as such. Shouting curses, or going in silence and saving their breath, all who could rushed away from the trail with only one aim in mind. To collect a mount and put as much distance between themselves and their assailants as swiftly as possible.

Not that the woman was giving any thought to the disastrous fate into which she had led her male companions. The moment she had realized that Ole Devil Hardin had escaped unscathed from her bullet, she had also known

147

that the time had come to quit their company. Without even waiting to discover how the men might be faring, she lowered the empty pistol and, pivoting on her heels, ran away from the trail.

Reaching her horse, Madeline snatched its reins free from the bush to which it was tied. An excellent rider, she contrived to swing astride the restless animal without relinquishing her hold of the pistol and despite the encumbrance of the cloak-coat. Having done so, she urged it into motion.

From the various sounds to her rear, the woman could tell that her men were not fighting back. So there was no hope that, in some miraculous way, they might turn the tables on their attackers. Any remote chance that they would rally and, possibly, succeed in the purpose of the ambush was dashed by yells of encouragement and the drumming of several horses' hooves originating from the north. Riders coming from that point of the compass were almost certain to be the Texian's friends, particularly as one voice was feminine in timbre and she felt sure she recognized it. Anybody who was accompanying Diamond-Hitch Brindley would only add to the renegades' troubles.

Accepting the inevitable, although she was in a searing rage, the woman guided her horse through the trees at a very fast pace. Furious as she was, she did not ride blindly. Rather the violence of her emotions seemed to increase her perceptions and equestrian skill so that she was travelling much more swiftly than she would have done if she had been in a calmer frame of mind.

Madeline had two objectives as she was allowing her horse to gallop through the woodland.

Firstly, there was the very urgent necessity to get far beyond the reach of the proposed victims of the abortive ambush.

During the time the woman had spent in Di Brindley's and Ole Devil Hardin's company, she had formed a shrewd assessment of their characters. Neither had showed hesitation in risking their lives to ensure the

148

safety of the caplock rifles. So neither would be inclined to show compassion to anybody who had done as much as she to prevent the delivery of the weapons to Major General Samuel Houston and the Republic of Texas's Army. While the Texian *might* be held back from taking extreme measures out of considerations for her sex, the girl most assuredly would not; particularly since the shooting of her grandfather and the pack train's *cargador*.

Secondly and of equal importance, Madeline had no wish to come into further contact with the men she was deserting. After the perilous situation into which she had led them, her fate at their hands would be as bad—probably even worse in some respects—than if the two young people she had been hoping to kill were to capture her. At least, no matter how the girl might wish to act, the Texian would ensure that her end would be quick.

So, while she was riding, Madeline tried to hear if she was being followed. Her instincts warned her that if she was, her pursuers were most likely to be members of her band who were also fleeing from the wrath which had descended upon them. That would not make them any less a menace to her safety. Let them catch up with her and they might shoot her in their rage over their narrow escape from death. However, the noise made by her passage through the woodland prevented her from gaining any information and she had no intention of stopping to listen.

After covering something over a mile in the same reckless fashion, common sense dictated that Madeline should slow down. There was, she realized, a danger that she might ride the horse into the ground if she continued her flight in such a manner. If that happened, she was all too aware of how slim her chances of survival would be.

Taking the sensible line of action, the woman caused her lathered mount to reduce its pace. Struggling to control her own breathing, for riding at a gallop was hard work especially under such demanding conditions, she brought the animal to a halt. She could not hear anything

149

to suggest that the men she had deserted were fighting with their assailants, nor had she expected it. If she knew them, all who were able would already be making good their escape.

Necessity rather than any sense of kindness or responsibility had caused Madeline to become proficient in horse management. So she dismounted and, loosening the girth of her eastern rig, she moved the saddle backwards and forwards to help cool the animal's back. Having done so, she decided against reloading the pistol—which she had contrived to return to the holster on mounting, leaving her hands free to hold the reins—and resumed her journey on foot.

Violent emotions churned through the woman as, leading the horse by its reins, she walked in a south-westerly direction. She was obsessed by the realization of how close she had been to death, if nothing worse, that night. Instead of admitting that she had brought all her misfortunes on herself, she laid the blame for her past and present predicaments upon the young Texian who had thwarted her and killed the only man she had ever loved.

'Damn Hardin!' Madeline hissed. 'I'll never rest until he's dead!'

However, the woman appreciated the difficulties which stood in the way of her quest for vengeance. She could not hope to obtain it unaided. Nor did the answer lie in gathering together such members of the band as had not yet responded to the message left by her late husband at their hideout. They were the same kind of men as those whom she had deserted and she had no desire to put herself in their power.

As far as Madeline could see, there was only one solution. Continue travelling to the south and search for official assistance. She had in her possession a document signed by *Presidente* Antonio Lopez de Santa Anna, demanding that all members of the Mexican Army render her protection or support if either was required. If she could find a unit of suitable strength, its commanding officer would be only too pleased to learn about the consignment of caplock rifles and she might yet bring about the destruction of Ole Devil Hardin. In fact, that would be her price for supplying the information.

Chapter Thirteen

LOOKS LIKE *YOU* WAS HORNSWOGGLED

'GOTT in himmel!' ejaculated Major Ludwig von Lowenbrau, commanding Company 'B' of the Red River Volunteer Dragoons, as the rising sun allowed him his first unimpeded view into the hollow which surrounded Santa Cristóbal Bay. In the stress of his emotion, he continued to speak with his native tongue. 'If I'd known last night——!'

Realizing that there were some of his subordinates also studying the terrain and its occupants below, von Lowenbrau made an almost visible effort to restrain his display of anger and surprise. It would never do for them to suspect, even if they had not understood his words, just how badly he had been mistaken in his summation of the situation. Discipline in his regiment was slack enough without him behaving in a manner likely to increase their disrespect. However, while outwardly he resumed his hard and expressionless demeanour, internally he was boiling with rage and mortification.

No man, particularly a proud and arrogant former Prussian officer who also considered himself a capable gambler, enjoyed learning that he had been tricked. Yet, taking in the sight which was spread beneath him, von Lowenbrau knew that he had fallen for a bluff. Realizing who was responsible for it did nothing to improve his feelings.

It was, the major concluded bitterly, all too easy to be wise *after* the event!

Everything the previous night had suggested that von Lowenbrau might be leading his men into a situation which they could not handle and from which they were likely to suffer heavy losses. From all appearances, his purpose had been suspected, and very effective measures taken to circumvent it. The disparity between the references made by Mannen Blaze and the sentry regarding Ole Devil Hardin's whereabouts had suggested that he was close at hand instead of being away relieving the pickets. Such would have been a task assigned to a subordinate, for it did not require the services of the Company's commanding officer. Of course, Hardin might have been reluctant to trust it to such an incompetent second-in-command, but he would have been even more reluctant to leave Blaze in charge of the consignment of caplocks.

All in all, von Lowenbrau had been convinced that there was too much organization about his reception for it to have been arranged by Hardin's dull-witted lieutenant. So, he had decided it was wise not to enter the hollow. And Blaze's mention of yellow fever made his men unwilling to approach the source of such a virulently infectious disease.

Having been well trained in an officer's duties, von Lowenbrau had decided to wait for daylight to reassess the situation and form a better impression of it. Once he had seen the exact strength of the opposition, he could estimate the chances of being able to carry out his assignment by force if necessary.

With that in mind, the major had ordered his company to make camp on the rim. Although Blaze had withdrawn the majority of his men, he had left two sentries at the top of the slope. Nor had there been a time when they, or their reliefs, relaxed their vigilance and most of it had been directed at the Prussian and his subordinates. However, much to his surprise, they had rejoined their

152

companions as soon as his men had shown signs of rising.

Dawn's grey light showed von Lowenbrau just how he had been misled!

One of the first things to strike the major on commencing his examination was the absence of Ewart Brindley's mules. He had wondered why the animals were so quiet during the night and had finally concluded that, having been pushed hard on the journey to the bay, they were sleeping.

However, the matter of the missing mule train struck von Lowenbrau as being a minor issue. Once he had taken charge of the consignment, he would wait until Brindley arrived and then commandeer the animals for his own use. From what he could see, gaining possession of the caplocks would not be as difficult as he had anticipated.

On counting the men in the hollow, von Lowenbrau found there were nowhere near as many as he had anticipated. In fact, his contingent had the consignment's guards outnumbered by close to three to one. However, Hardin's men—although he did not appear to be present —were ensconced in pits which had been sited so as to offer protection against assailants who were descending from the rim. Each of them had no less than five rifles close at hand.

'Looks like *you* was hornswoggled, *major*,' remarked Lou Benn, a burly and sullen featured man who held rank as sergeant and had ambitions to become an officer. He had given the situation a similar evaluation and drawing much the same conclusions as the Major. 'What're *you* fixing to have us do now?'

The words came to von Lowenbrau like the thrust of a sharp-rowelled spur. All too well he could imagine how the story of his failure would be received if they returned empty-handed to the regiment. There were many, including the speaker, who hated him and would be delighted

153

to see him humbled. In fact, the colonel might even use it to remove him from his position of command.

'Have the men saddle up,' the major ordered, goaded by the need to take some kind of action and thinking about the consequences of going back a failure. 'We're going down for the rifles and ammunition.'

'Ole Devil Hardin's not the man to give——,' Benn began.

'Hardin's not there!' von Lowenbrau pointed out, snapping shut the telescope through which he had been conducting his scrutiny. 'And, even if he was, I out rank him. So saddle up, damn you. We have them out numbered and, as they've only got Blaze in command, there won't be any trouble from them.'

While the sergeant felt that his superior might be somewhat over-confident, he did not announce his misgivings. Fancy-dressed and high-toned the Prussian—like many of his race, he grew indignant if called a German—might be, but he had gained the reputation for being bad medicine when crossed. What was more, Benn had to concede that he had been correct on two points.

Firstly, the numerical odds were well in the Dragoons' favour.

Secondly, as far as Benn could make out—and he too had used a telescope to look *very* carefully—Ole Devil Hardin was not present. One did not easily forget such a man and the sergeant was confident that he could have made the required identification if its subject had been available.

Sharing von Lowenbrau's low opinion of Mannen Blaze's personality and capability, Benn also considered that it would be possible to commandeer—he disliked the more accurate term 'steal'—the consignment. The Texas Light Cavalry's enlisted men were unlikely to resist with their commanding officer absent and while they were being led by a numbskull who acted most of the time like he was about to fall asleep. Especially when they found

154

themselves confronted by a determined force of nearly three times their numbers.

Nor, if it came to a point, did the sergeant relish the notion of reporting to Colonel Johnson without having successfully accomplished the mission. He had his eyes set upon promotion to and the status—plus benefits—gained by being an officer. So delivering the caplocks would be a big step towards attaining his ambition. Turning, he barked orders which sent the rest of the Dragoons hurrying to saddle their horses.

'Bring the pack animals too,' von Lowenbrau commanded. 'I want every man going down there with us.'

'Here they come, Mannen,' Beauregard Rassendyll remarked, looking at the rim and wishing he could draw the sword he was wearing to supplement the Croodlom & Co. 'Duck Foot' Mob Pistol which dangled in his right hand. However, the burly red head had said that he must not and—no matter what his earlier opinion of the other had been—the events of the previous night had made him willing to bow to what he now accepted as superior wisdom. 'And, was I asked, I'd say they were ready to make trouble.'

'Yep,' Mannen Blaze conceded, still sounding as if he might fall asleep at any moment. Standing by the supercargo, with the Browning Slide Repeating rifle across the crook of his left arm, he studied the approaching riders as they spread out to descend the slope in line abreast. 'They're loaded for b'ar, not squirrel, I'd say.'

Which was, the burly red head told himself silently, pretty well what he had expected would happen once Major Ludwig won Lowenbrau discovered the exact strength—or lack of it—of the force at his disposal.

There were, Mannen conceded, a few consolations. His ruse and the intelligent backing of the men under his command had bought him some valuable time. Unless Smith—who had been replaced by another sentry on

155

the rim—had been prevented from departing, help should already be on its way from the mule train.

The big question was, would it arrive in time?

Mannen had hoped that the reinforcements would have put in an appearance before von Lowenbrau could find out that he had been tricked. Unfortunately, the hope had not materialized. Nor, from what Mannen could remember of the major, would he be likely to turn aside after he had been seen by his men to have fallen for a bluff. In fact, going by the way each of his men was nursing a rifle, it had made him even more determined to carry out his intentions—

And a man did not need to be a mind reader to work out what they must be!

Sweeping a quick glance at the few members of Company 'C' who were at his disposal, Mannen could find no traces of alarm and despondency as they watched the thirty or so Dragoons. He did not doubt that they were ready and willing to fight despite the disparity of their numbers, but that was a mixed blessing. Even if they should be victorious, he could imagine how the rest of the Republic of Texas's Army would react to the news— which was sure to leak out—that two outfits had done battle with each other. Morale was low enough already without giving Major General Samuel Houston that sort of a situation to contend with.

'Don't any of you make what could be called a hostile, or even threatening, move,' Mannen warned, in tones more suggestive that he was complaining over having had a nap disturbed and which fooled none of his audience. 'And stay put in those holes you volunteered to dig.'

'*That* was volunteering?' asked one of the enlisted men, with a grin, for the red head had insisted that the pits were dug as a precaution the previous evening.

'You 'n' Mr. Rassendyll get into your'n *pronto* comes trouble, Mr. Blaze,' Sergeant Dale requested, after the chuckles had ended, for the two young men alone were standing exposed to their visitors. 'We'd hate for him to

156

get killed afore we've seen if that danged thing he's holding really can shoot.'

'I'll do my best not to disappoint you, sergeant,' Rassendyll promised, delighted by the evidence that his status had improved where his comrades-in-arms were concerned.

Up until the supercargo's collection and use of the bull's eye lantern the previous night, he had been annoyed to find that the Texians did not hold him in very high esteem. Partly it had been his own fault. His earlier attitude was not calculated to be acceptable to such fiercely independent souls. So his assumption that he would automatically be accorded the same respect as Ole Devil and Mannen had antagonized them. However, having demonstrated that he was good for something more than dressing fancy, handling the easiest part of the consignment's delivery, and toting a mighty peculiar kind of handgun, he was being treated as an equal.

Conscious of his companion's elation, Mannen did not allow it to distract him. Instead, he continued to keep the Dragoons under observation and waited to see what would develop. He felt satisfied that he had done everything he could to receive them.

'Halt the men here, sergeant!' von Lowenbrau ordered, while a good fifty yards still separated them from their objective.

'Huh?' grunted Benn.

'You heard!' the major snarled, glancing back and finding that the men were already obeying without the non-com's orders. 'Come up when I signal.'

Riding onwards, von Lowenbrau studied the Texians. Noticing the disciplined manner in which they were behaving, he could not help wishing that the Red River Volunteer Dragoons could be counted upon to act in such a fashion. However, he put the thought from his mind. Bringing his horse to a stop about thirty feet from the closest rifle pit, he dismounted.

'Your men seem to have recovered rapidly, Mr. Blaze,'

157

the major commented dryly, leaving the animal and walking—marching in review would be a better description—forward.

While advancing, von Lowenbrau studied Rassendyll and made an accurate guess at his reason for being present. Briefly, the Prussian wondered if he had been the brains behind the preparations and bluff. It was possible, but for one thing. All too well, from his own experiences shortly after his arrival in Texas, von Lowenbrau knew the ruggedly individualistic spirit of the colonists. They would never have accepted the leadership of a newcomer in such a short time.

'Must have only been a touch of the grippe, major,' Mannen replied blandly. 'Anyways, they're over it now, no matter what it was, so I'm giving them a mite of training to stop them thinking about it.'

'Is this your entire command?' von Lowenbrau demanded.

'The rest of them are off someplace with Cousin Dev—Captain Hardin,' Mannen replied, looking and sounding exceptionally somnolent. 'They *should* be back some—any time now.'

'And until they return, this valuable consignment of arms has been left with completely inadequate protection!' the Prussian barked, barely able to restrain himself from bellowing at the red head to wake up. Then he glanced at Rassendyll as if expecting some comment. When it did not come, he continued, 'That won't do. I'll take it in my charge.'

'Well now, major,' Mannen drawled and, although he seemed to be finding it difficult to stay awake, he sounded both grateful and perturbed. 'Grateful as I am for you offering, I couldn't rightly let you do that.'

'I'm not making a friendly *request*, mister!' von Lowenbrau warned, still wondering why the other young man did not intervene. 'I'm ordering you to hand it over.'

While speaking, the major made a beckoning motion with his lowered left hand. Seeing the signal, Benn growled at the Dragoons to advance. However, conscious of the menace from the rifles of the soldiers in the pits, he held the pace to a walk and issued a warning that nobody had to even look like raising a weapon.

'Isn't there some rule or other's calls it mutiny if I don't obey an order from a superior officer?' Mannen inquired worriedly, raising his eyes to look at the approaching Dragoons as if wishing to avoid meeting the Prussian's gaze.

'There is,' von Lowenbrau confirmed with grim satisfaction, deciding that his task was growing easier. 'And the punishment for mutiny is death.'

For all his feeling that the burly red head would yield to his demand, the major became conscious of how the men in the rifle pits were reacting. None seemed alarmed, or disturbed by the sight of his Dragoons riding nearer. Instead, they seemed to be finding the affair interesting and even amusing. There was something vaguely familiar about their attitudes, but he was unable to decide what it might be.

'And so, Mr. Blaze,' von Lowenbrau went on, as Benn brought the Dragoons to a halt near his horse. 'I am ordering you to hand over the consignment to me. If you refuse, I will have to regard it as an act of mutiny and you will suffer the consequences.'

Chapter Fourteen

I CAN REPAY YOU FOR SAVING ME!

WITHOUT realizing that some six miles to the north-east another threat had arisen to the safety of the consignment of arms which had caused her husband's death, tiredness and the knowledge that she must allow her horse to rest brought Madeline de Moreau to a halt.

Once her mount had recovered its breath after the mad dash through the woodland, the woman had mounted and pushed on with all the speed she could muster. Using the training she had received from her husband, she had continued to travel south-west. While she had known that the most simple way to find members of the Mexican Army would be to follow the coast road, she had also seen the objections to doing so. The trail did not go into Santa Cristóbal Bay, but went sufficiently close to it for there to be the danger of meeting with pickets set out by Ole Devil Hardin before he had left for San Phillipe. He was too intelligent, damn him, to have overlooked such a precaution.

What was more, before Madeline could reach territory under Mexican control, she would have to pass areas occupied by other Texian outfits. Probably they would not molest her, but she would be expected to give an account of her presence and had no wish to attract such undesirable attention. There was no way in which she could be sure that Hardin had not passed word of her activities. It would not have surprised her if he had. So she was disinclined to take the chance.

So Madeline had kept moving across country. It said much for her physical condition that she had got so far during the hours of darkness. Furthermore, she might have counted herself fortunate that she was such a skilled horsewoman and astride an exceptionally reliable mount. Exhausted by the strain which she had been under, she had found herself repeatedly threatened with dropping off to sleep as she was riding. In fact, she had been dozing and almost fallen from the saddle before she woke up and, taking the warning, concluded that she must grab some rest.

Gazing ahead with eyes glazed by fatigue, the woman located a place where she could satisfy her craving for sleep. The terrain was once more fairly dense woodland, with plenty of undergrowth. However, she was approaching a clearing through which a small stream was flowing.

If Madeline had been in a more alert frame of mind, she might have heard and been alarmed by certain noises from not too far behind her. Barely able to keep her eyes open, she was only conscious of one thing. That she had found a reasonably safe haven in which she could rest.

Entering the clearing and finding it deserted, the brunette allowed her horse to reach the bank of the stream before halting it and dismounting. Its pace had been slow enough for the last hour for it to be able to drink without harmful effects. Removing the bit, she allowed it to do so.

In spite of her tiredness, Madeline knew that there were things which she must do before she dared to succumb to sleep. First, she had to make sure that her mount would still be available when she woke up. Removing the cloak-coat, she laid it on the ground without removing the 'Pepperbox' from its pocket. Then she took a set of hobbles from her saddlepouch and applied them to the pasterns* of the animal's fore legs. With that done, she removed the rig. There was one more essential task to be attended to, she told herself, and she would do it as soon as she had set her burden down.

'Well dog my cats, Nippy, you was right,' declared a hard masculine voice, coming from the bushes through which the woman had passed on her way into the clearing. 'It air that high-toned Mrs. "dee" Moreau.'

'Only she don't look nowheres near's high-toned now as when her and that stinking mac was treating us like dirt,' answered a second set of male tones. 'Nor when her damned fool notions was getting some of the boys killed.'

Letting the saddle slip from her fingers, Madeline stared at the speakers. Even if she had not recognized their voices, the words would have informed her that they were members of her husband's band of renegades. Not that she took any pleasure from finding them striding towards her. Rather the opposite. In addition to insulting

* Pastern: part of the horse's leg immediately above the hoof.

his memory by referring to Randolph as a 'mac', which meant a pimp, they had been two of the more vocal malcontents in her party before the disastrously abortive ambush. Nor, judging from their comments and expressions, were they coming with friendly intentions.

Bending, the woman snatched the upper of the brace of pistols from the holsters on her saddlehorn. Knowing how capable she was, the men started to run towards her. Even as her brain began to scream a warning, she cocked and raised the weapon to aim at Nippy. However, although she realized the futility of the gesture, she could not stop herself snatching at the trigger. The hammer fell, but there was only a click. In her haste, she had selected the pistol with which she had tried to kill Ole Devil Hardin.

Letting out a shriek of combined rage and fear, Madeline flung the empty weapon at Nippy. She missed, but was already grabbing for its mate when she saw each man's face registering alarm and fright.

Something passed through the air close above the woman and struck Nippy between the eyes with considerable force. His head snapped to the rear and he pitched over backwards. Bouncing off after the impact, the missile proved to be a sturdy piece of curved wood.

An instant after the renegade was hit, there was a different kind of hiss and the second man, trying to stop running, gave a convulsive jerk. With his hands rising to claw ineffectually at the fletching of the arrow which had buried itself in his chest, he spun around and collapsed.

Looking over her shoulder with her fingers closing on the butt of the loaded pistol, Madeline did not know whether to be pleased or terrified. While they had rescued her from the renegades, her fate at the hands of the two Indians across the stream might not be different to that which Nippy and his companion had intended. It could, however, result in a quicker death. Nippy's killer no longer held a weapon, but the second brave was already reaching for another arrow from his quiver.

162

'Don't kill her!' yelled a voice in Spanish.

Another man appeared, striding from behind a bush. At the sight of him, Madeline straightened up without drawing the pistol. Although she did not know to which regiment he belonged, the newcomer was an officer in the Mexican Army. His black busby, which had lost part of its Quetzal's tail feathers' plume, and light green Hussar-type uniform suggested he served in a volunteer unit. There was an air of breeding about him which she found comforting. Such a man would be more willing to honour her identification pass from *Presidente* Antonio Lopes de Santa Anna than either of the Indians.

'*Gracias, senor,*' Madeline said, also employing Spanish. 'I can repay you for saving me.'

Five minutes later, Major Abrahan Phillipe Gonzales *de* Villena *y* Danvila of the Arizona Hopi *Activos* Regiment had solved the mystery which had brought him back accompanied by a small party of braves who had been sent to locate him. He knew why two members of the Texas Light Cavalry were so far from their regiment's last reported position.

'Dang it all!' Mannen Blaze almost wailed, in a sleepily petulant tone, after Major Ludwig von Lowenbrau had delivered the ultimatum. 'It looks like one way or the other I'm forced and bound to become a mutineer and get shot. Because Captain Hardin, who's my superior officer, *ordered* me to hold on to the consignment until he comes back.'

'Damn it, man,' the Prussian thundered, all his military background and upbringing revolting at such a display of stupidity from an officer. 'I'm a major and that's senior to a captain. So, in Captain Hardin's absence, I'm countermanding his order and assuming authority for——.'

'Excuse me for interrupting, major,' the red head put in, exuding a slothfully apologetic aura. 'But before you can

163

countermand an order in Captain Hardin's absence, he had to be absent—doesn't he?'

'Of course——!' von Lowenbrau commenced, before he could stop himself. 'What do you mean, damn it?'

'It's just that I can't see how he can be absent,' Mannen explained, 'when he's walking down the slope behind you.'

Looking over his shoulder, the Prussian let out a guttural and explosive oath in his native tongue. Unnoticed by the rest of the Red River Volunteer Dragoons' contingent, three men were advancing on foot and had almost reached them.

Von Lowenbrau recognized all the trio. At the right, carrying a strange looking rifle, was the man who had departed during the night. Apparently he had partly told the truth about his reason for going. On the left, with an arrow nocked to the string of the remarkably long bow he was carrying and armed with two swords, was Hardin's 'Chinese' servant.

However, the Prussian's main attention was focussed upon Tommy Okasi's employer. Unshaven, showing signs of having ridden hard and fast, clearly very tired, Ole Devil Hardin still contrived to stride out with a smart, almost Gasconading, swagger. Unlike his escort, he had no weapon in his hands.

Suddenly, von Lowenbrau realized what the attitudes of the Texians in the rifle pits had reminded him of. It had been the look of men who knew that somebody they disliked was shortly to be given an unpleasant shock. Obviously they had seen their captain coming even though their other officer had not.

Or had Mannen Blaze been aware of his cousin's arrival?

Considering the behaviour of the man who had accompanied the consignment from New Orleans and who had remained silent when he should have been protesting or trying to take control from the bumbling, incompetent, red head, the Prussian was puzzled. Either the burly lieu-

164

tenant had been exceptionally lucky, or he was far from the dullard he appeared.

However, there was no time for von Lowenbrau to ponder on the question. Glancing at the rim, he stiffened. There were several men armed with rifles advancing from it. They had not been there when he had led his Dragoons into the hollow. The members of his Company were not yet aware of the new and very dangerous factor which had arisen.

'Good morning, Captain Hardin,' the Prussian greeted, hoping that none of his Dragoons did anything stupid. While the man he was addressing kept walking, the other two had halted to their rear. 'I'm pleased to see that you have brought more men to help guard the consignment.'

'Good morning, Major von Lowenbrau,' Ole Devil replied, knowing that the second sentence had been a warning to the Dragoons, but he passed without as much as a glance in their direction.

On arriving at the mule train, having found Smith there and learning of Mannen's problem, the Texian had wasted no time. Borrowing fresh mounts, he, Tommy, Smith and fifteen members of Sergeant Maxime's detail had set out to give support to his cousin. Reaching the vicinity just as the major was leading the Dragoons into the hollow and realizing that they were unaware of his party's presence, he had gambled upon Mannen being able to keep the Prussian occupied until he was ready to take over. From all appearances, the red head had—as on other occasions—fully justified his cousin's faith in him.

'Anything to report, Mr. Blaze?' Ole Devil asked, halting in between von Lowenbrau and the Dragoons, but looking by the major and still ignoring his men.

'Everything's set up ready for moving as soon as the mules arrive, sir, except for the rifles you told me to have loaded and held in reserve in case of an emergency,' Mannen reported, with slightly greater animation than he had shown so far and using the honorific which he had

165

not employed when addressing the Prussian. 'The major was good enough to have his men stand watch last night, so I called in our sentries.'

'*Bueno*,' Ole Devil praised, then turned his attention to von Lowenbrau. 'Thank you, major. The safety of this consignment is of the greatest importance.'

'You seem to have been taking its safe keeping lightly,' the Prussian answered. 'I arrived to find you absent and your second-in-command with insufficient men to ensure its protection. If that's—!'

'Damn it—!' Beauregard Rassendyll ejaculated, filled with indignation at such an unjust criticism of his friend.

'You're at attention, Mr. Rassendyll!' Ole Devil interrupted, without taking his eyes from von Lowenbrau. 'It appears that they've protected it adequately regardless of their numbers, major. May I ask what brings you hereabouts?'

'I've been sent to take charge of this consignment,' von Lowenbrau replied.

'On whose orders?'

'*Colonel* Frank Johnson's. He has given me written authority—.'

'With respect, sir,' Ole Devil put in, although his tones were far from apologetic. 'My orders come from *Major General* Houston. They are that I'm to deliver the arms to him and, unless I receive *written* instructions to the contrary from *him*, that's exactly what I intend to do.'

There von Lowenbrau had it, just as plainly as anybody could have asked for.

Being close enough to hear the conversation, the Dragoons waited—the majority with bated breath—to discover what their officer meant to do. They were not unmindful of the danger to themselves if he tried to enforce his demand. While outnumbering the contingent from the Texas Light Cavalry, they offered a better target to the men in the rifle pits than vice versa.

'The primary purpose of an officer is to obey his superior's orders, *Captain* Hardin!' von Lowenbrau pointed out, sharing his men's awareness of the situation and playing for time in the hope that he might find a way to gain ascendancy over the tall, ramrod straight young Texian. One thing was for sure, unlike his cousin, he would not be frightened by the prospects of committing mutiny by refusing to obey.

'Yes, sir,' Ole Devil replied, chopping off the other's thought train. 'Which is why the Texas Light Cavalry and other regiments are withdrawing to the east as General Houston ordered.'

Just as the Texian had anticipated, from what he remembered of von Lowenbrau's character from their meetings, the comment was not well received. No matter what had caused the Prussian to have 'gone to Texas', he still retained much of the training which was instilled since his early childhood. *'Befehl is befehl'*, orders are orders, was the creed by which he had been raised. So he had never been completely reconciled to serving Johnson. He was honest enough to admit to himself that loot rather than patriotism, or even strategy, was the main purpose behind the proposed invasion of Mexico. What was more, it went against the commanding general of the Republic of Texas's Army's policies and instructions.

'And what does *that* mean?' von Lowenbrau demanded, his face struggling to remain as impassive as Ole Devil's Mephistophelian features.

'Looky here now!' called the Dragoons' sergeant, seeing what he regarded as his opportunity and appreciating how his words would sound when reported to their superiors on rejoining the regiment. 'All this talk's fine, but it ain't getting us them rifles.'

'You're not having them, *hombre*!' Ole Devil stated flatly, turning to face the speaker and seeing how he might turn the interruption to his advantage.

'Now you just listen to me!' Sergeant Benn growled, the Texian's obvious disdain causing him to forget that the

167

odds were no longer in his Company's favour. 'We've been told by Colonel Johnson to take 'em and that's what *I'm* fixing to do.'

'*You* are?' Ole Devil challenged, noticing that the Prussian was not offering to intervene and, while guessing why, pleased that he had not.

'Me 'n' these fellers here,' Benn corrected, having understood the implications of the Texian's emphasis on the word "*you*" but oblivious of the consternation being shown by the majority of "these fellers here".

'You'll have to kill all of *us* first,' Ole Devil warned. 'And we'll try to stop you. And we're in a better position to stop you than you are to kill us.'

'You don't reckon's them boys back of you'd throw lead us's is good 'n' loyal Texians same's them,' Benn countered. 'Now do you?'

'*Hombre!*' Sergeant Dale called, before his superior could reply. 'We'd throw lead at our own mothers happen Cap'n Hardin gave the word and we knowed he was in the right.'

'Which we-all concludes he's in the right just now,' announced a grizzled old timer from another pit.

'So, happen you jaspers want it,' went on the youngest member of Company "C", in the belief that he too would be helping out. 'Just come on ahead and try to take it from us.'

While Ole Devil had been delighted by the first two comments, he was less enarmoured of the third remark. It was too like a direct challenge and there looked to be a few equally young hot heads among the Dragoons who, despite their companions appreciation of the danger, would want to pick up the gauntlet. If that happened, blood was sure to flow and, like Mannen, he was equally aware of the subsidiary consequences of such a fight.

'There's no call for men who're needed to help fight Santa Anna to get killed,' the Texian pointed out, still keeping his gaze on Benn. 'If *you*'re so set on having the consignment, *hombre, I'll* fight *you* for it.'

'What——?' gasped the sergeant, conscious of the muted rumble of conversation to his rear.

'It should be plain enough, even for *you*,' Ole Devil replied dryly, walking forward. 'If *you* can kill *me, just us two, nobody else* involved, Mr. Blaze has my orders to give it to you.'

'Stay put, major,' advised Mannen, as von Lowenbrau began to move. 'You've let it get this far, now see it through. That way, a whole slew of lives will be saved.'

Assessing the red head's comment and the situation with a gambler's cool calculation rather than an officer's training, the Prussian knew he was hearing the truth. Having set the stakes in the game, Hardin would have to face the consequences. If he lost, his own men would insist that the forfeit be paid. So von Lowenbrau stood still, allowing the events to run their course without his participation.

As with the case of most of his regiment's non-coms, the sergeant had been promoted through his connections and toughness rather than military qualities and intelligence. However, he was smart enough to duplicate his superior's summation of how his victory would be received.

And Benn also knew that there was only one way in which the prize could be won!

Studying the man who had made the offer, the sergeant found that he did not care for what he was seeing.

Although Ole Devil had never heard the term, he appreciated the psychological effect produced by his horn-like hair style and features in times of trouble. So he had shoved back his hat and allowed it to dangle on his shoulders by its *barbiquejo*. Unshaven, haggard from lack of sleep, even without the savage challenge that it bore, his face had never appeared more Satanic.

To Benn, whose childhood religious instruction had instilled a hearty fear for the possible wrath of the here-after——although it had been many years since he last saw the inside of a confession box——it seemed that he was

169

confronted by Old Nick himself all ready, willing and out-and-out eager to pitchfork him into a fiery furnace.

'Let's take——!' the sergeant began, just managing to control a desire to make the sign of the cross as he had been taught by the Fathers and looking to his rear in the hope of enlisting support.

'This is between just you and I, *hombre*!' Ole Devil snapped, bringing the other's head to the front and ending his words. 'So either get down from that horse and make your play, or turn it and ride out of this hollow.'

'But——!' Benn commenced, staring as if mesmerised at the Mephistophelian face.

'Count to five, Mr. Blaze,' Ole Devil ordered, still staring with awesome intensity at the sergeant. 'And, *hombre*, if you haven't done one or the other by the time it's reached, I'll kill you where you sit.'

'One!' Mannen said, as soon as his cousin had stopped speaking.

'Hey now——!' Benn growled, realizing the position in which he had been placed.

'Two!' Mannen went on unhurriedly, but ignoring the interjection.

While the red head was counting, he knew without needing to be told what his cousin wanted. So he did not hurry his words. While Mannen did not doubt that Ole Devil would carry out the threat, he guessed that the other would prefer that the need to do so did not arise. So he intended to give the sergeant time to back off.

Waiting for the count to continue, Benn considered his position faster than he was used to thinking. On the face of it, he held the advantage. His rifle lay across his knees, not yet cocked but more available than any weapon carried by the empty handed young man in front of him. However, even as he was on the point of turning the barrel forward, doubts began to assail him.

Would Hardin be taking such a chance unless he was completely confident of surviving?

170

Knowing that he personally would not, the sergeant based his answer upon his own standards.

If the young Texian had accepted the risk when making the challenge, he must be certain that he would win!

'Three!' Mannen drawled, seeing the perturbation on the sergeant's face.

Would Hardin kill another member of the Republic of Texas's Army?

Ben did not doubt that, under the circumstances, the answer was 'yes!'

'Four!'

Inexorably, if unhurriedly, the count was going on!

Standing as rigidly as if waiting to be inspected by the Emperor of Prussia, von Lowenbrau watched and waited without offering to intercede. Like his sergeant, he felt certain that Ole Devil would carry out the threat. Faced by something which was endangering the consignment he had been entrusted to deliver and aware that it might make all the difference when the time came for the Texians to make their stand against Santa Anna's Army, he would deal ruthlessly with anybody who tried to stop him.

As far as von Lowenbrau could see, he stood to benefit in one of two ways dependent on the result. Should Benn succeed, the consignment would be in their hands and his own moral dominance would soon put him back in full command of the Company. If Hardin won, he would be rid of a troublesome subordinate who was too well connected in the regiment for his demotion or removal in any other way.

For his part, Benn had been counting upon the backing of the other Dragoons, but he now knew that it would not be forthcoming. So he would have to stand—or fall— alone.

Suddenly the sergeant experienced a sense of overwhelming fear. The motionless figure with the face of the Devil was something beyond his comprehension. Despite his empty hands, he seemed as grimly inevitable as death

171

and just as permanent. Although he was making no attempt to arm himself, the sergeant knew that somehow he had the means to do what he had said he would.

Seeing Mannen's mouth starting to open for what would be the last digit of the count, Benn's courage—always more bravado than bravery—broke. Reining his horse around and dropping his rifle, he rode up the slope at an ever increasing pace.

'Don't you say a word!' Sergeant Dale snarled at the youngest member of Company "C", who was on the point of making a derisive comment, and his order was obeyed.

Von Lowenbrau watched his ex-sergeant's flight with mixed emotions. Two things he knew were sure. After such behaviour, Benn was through. However, having seen the non-com routed, the rest of the Dragoons would refuse to attempt anything he wanted to try and carry out the assignment.

'Any of you who want to go with him may do so,' the Prussian announced, raking his men with cold eyes. 'Whoever stays will ride with me.'

'Where are you going, major?' Ole Devil inquired, turning to look at the speaker.

'With you, if you let me, captain,' von Lowenbrau replied. 'My men and I may be of assistance until you've delivered the arms to General Houston.'

'How about Colonel Johnson?' Ole Devil asked.

'I'm going to serve a better man,' the Prussian stated. 'And we'll be riding in better company than any under Johnson's command. If *you'll* permit us to accompany you that is.'

Chapter Fifteen

I'LL COME AND HOLD YOUR HANDS

OLD DEVIL HARDIN had an active and inquiring mind which would always take an interest in anything he believed might one day be of service to him. While he had no intention of going into business competition with Ewart Brindley, he knew that the time might come when a knowledge of mule packing could prove advantageous. So, leaving the organization of the escort to his subordinates, he was standing and watching the main preparations for the start of the return journey.

Taking everything into consideration, the Texian felt that he was entitled to grant himself a brief period of relaxation after the events of the past few days. Not only had he dealt with one positive and one potential threat to the consignment of caplocks, he had almost doubled the strength of its escort. Only time would tell whether the latter would be beneficial or not. He refused to worry about it at that moment.

Not one of the Red River Volunteer Dragoons had elected to follow Sergeant Benn, who had kept riding once he passed beyond the rim. Nor had a problem envisaged by Ole Devil arisen. Major Ludwig von Lowenbrau had waived the matter of his rank, stating that he placed himself and his men under the young captain's command until the delivery of the caplocks was completed. After which, the Prussian had gone on, he intended to offer to transfer himself and his Company to the Texas Light Cavalry.

While von Lowenbrau had sounded sincere, Ole Devil had continued to be wary of him. However, there had been nothing about his behaviour, or that of his men, to which exception could be taken. Not knowing how long they might have to wait for the mule train and wishing to

173

keep the Dragoons out of mischief, Ole Devil had put them to work strengthening the defences. While he was taking some well earned and badly needed sleep, watched surreptitiously by Mannen Blaze, they had dug more rifle pits at the top of the hollow. The red head had reported that, although there was some grumbling, they had carried out the duty in a satisfactory manner. By the middle of the afternoon, the chance of treachery had been greatly reduced.

Diamond-Hitch Brindley had wasted little time in utilizing the replacement bell-mare. Although her grandfather was being transported on a *travois** made by the Tejas packers, Joe Galton was sufficiently recovered to ride a horse. However, they had arrived at Santa Cristóbal Bay too late for there to be any point in loading the mules and moving out that day. So the girl and Ole Devil had agreed to bed down in the hollow for the night and set off early the following morning.

Looking around, Ole Devil could tell that what appeared to be a lot of confused activity taking place was all being carried out in a swift and purposeful manner which called for no action on his part. He was on the point of watching the nearest mule packer, merely to find out how the work was performed, when something happened which prevented him from doing so.

'Riders coming, Cousin Devil!' Mannen Blaze called, speaking in what—for him—was considerable haste, having noticed the sentry on the rim giving one of the pre-arranged signals. Waving his hat from left to right in a series of double circular motions gave additional information. 'Could be some of Tom Wolf's scouts headed in.'

Partly to strengthen his force in case von Lowenbrau might still be contemplating treachery and knowing that

---

* Travois: *a primitive form of sledge, although not restricted to use on snow, constructed of two poles for shafts with a frame upon which the load is carried and drawn by a single animal.*

the Tejas Indians would be even better at the duty than his own men, Ole Devil had sent Tom Wolf's scouts out to replace his pickets. As there was nobody else belonging to the party outside the hollow, in all probability the riders had been sent by Tom Wolf with urgent news. So the Texian wanted as little delay as possible in learning what it might be.

'I'll go up and meet them,' Ole Devil decided, striding to where his linebacked dun gelding was standing saddled and ready for use. 'Will you come with me, major?'

'Thank you, captain,' von Lowenbrau answered, making just as quickly for his bay which was in an equal state of readiness.

Glancing around as he mounted, Ole Devil noticed that —like himself—all of the soldiers wore either cloak-coats or some other form of protective clothing. While fine, the weather was cold and damp. So he decided against telling them to remove the garments until he found out what the returning scouts had to say.

'Hey, Di!' the Texian called as he swung astride the dun's saddle, looking to where the girl was standing by her grandfather's *travois* and supervising the packers' work without needing to tell them anything. 'Can you come with us, please?'

While the Tejas could speak a certain amount of English and some Spanish, only their leader was fluent in either and the Texian wanted a fuller report than he felt he could obtain by using those languages. Knowing that the girl was able to speak their tongue, in fact it could be termed her second language as she had been cared for by Wolf's squaw after the death of her parents, her presence would be of the greatest assistance.

'Be right with you,' Di promised, knowing what Ole Devil had in mind. She directed a glare at her grandfather, who was trying to sit up, and went on, 'Stay put, you're not going no place. Anyways, he wants somebody's can "interpretate" Tejas for him properly. If you have to

175

do anything, make sure the boys's *you* taught don't put the *aparejos** on upside down or backwards.'

Ignoring Brindley's spluttered response, the girl ran to her horse. Mounting, she set off after the two men. Catching up, she accompanied them towards the rim. On reaching it, they all gazed in the direction indicated by the sentry.

'Son-of-a-bitch!' Di ejaculated. 'That's Tom Wolf. So whatever's fetched 'em must be real important.'

'It would have to be for Tom to be doing it himself,' Ole Devil admitted, taking note of the direction from which the two Indians were galloping. 'Like the Comanches say, "Bad news rides a fast horse". And I'll take bets that I can guess what it is.'

'Not with me!' Di stated emphatically.

'Or I,' von Lowenbrau seconded, but was pleased by the thought that—although he had acted with efficiency up to that point—the Texian had omitted to take a basic military precaution before ascending to the rim.

'Damn it,' the girl went on indignantly. 'After us feeding him and him putting the victuals down like they was going out of fashion, that son-of-a-bitching *mozo*'d lied to us.'

'Or he was wrong about how far off they were,' Ole Devil pointed out, thinking of the fear shown by Major Abrahan Phillipe Gonzales *de* Villena *y* Danvila's deserted servant—who was in the hollow and probably being better treated than in all his life—when first questioned. Stopping the dun, he dismounted and continued, 'It doesn't matter which, but I go for my guess.'

'*You* would,' Di sniffed, joining the Texian on the ground. 'Might just's well wait here 'n' find out just how bad it is.'

'Let's hope it isn't as bad as you believe, Miss Brindley,' von Lowenbrau suggested, also quitting his saddle.

'It'll likely be *worse*!' guessed the girl, knowing that they would have the answer within seconds.

* *Aparejos: a type of pack saddle designed for heavy or awkwardly shaped loads.*

'Them house-Indians* coming, *Diablo Viejo!*' announced Tom Wolf, translating Ole Devil's name into Spanish as he and the younger brave brought their mounts to rumpscraping halts before the trio. 'Plenty of em. Maybe so twenty, thirty hands, with Mexican officers.'

'How far off are they, chief?' Di inquired, speaking Tejas.

'Except for their scouts, they're about two miles away,' the Indian replied in the same language. 'I collected Little Foot here on my way back and sent Son Of The Wind to fetch in the rest of our men if there was time. I didn't figure *Diablo Viejo* would want them to know for sure I'd seen them and didn't wait to kill their scouts.'

'Good thinking, chief. That way there's just a chance they might go by without coming near enough to find us, although they're probably following my trail,' Ole Devil remarked, when the girl had translated the report and, as Wolf started speaking again, he could see the next information was displeasing her. 'What is it, Di?'

'You don't need to count on 'em missing us, even if they wouldn't've seen the mule train's sign,' the girl warned, anger flashing in her eyes. 'That bitch de Moreau's with 'em, Tom recognized her from when they hit at Grand-pappy Ewart 'n' Joe. She'll've been able to tell 'em just smack where we'll be.'

'There's nothing more certain than *that*!' von Lowenbrau agreed, having heard of the abortive ambush and the escape of the woman in question. 'It's a pity you didn't get her, Captain Hardin. She's probably the only one of them who would get a chance to tell the Mexicans what she knows.'

'Blast it, Devil did all any man could and better'n many——!' Di protested.

'The major's right, though, they'd probably have shot

---

* *House-Indians: unlike the nomadic tribes, the Hopi, Zuni and kindred nations tended to make and live in permanent homes instead of transportable lodges or tipis.*

any of the men they'd come across on sight,' Ole Devil interrupted. 'But, as she's sure to have told them, maybe we can turn it to our advantage. In fact, I think it already is!'

'How the hell do you make *that* out?' Di demanded and the Prussian showed just as great a lack of comprehension. 'She'll bring 'em straight here, without them even having to do a mite of work cutting for sign.'

'Yes,' Ole Devil conceded. 'But she doesn't know how many of us there are.'

'She knows your whole Company's here—!' the girl began, then understanding came as it had with von Lowenbrau if the way he was nodding his head meant anything. 'But she won't be taking your fellers into account, major.'

'Not unless they come across our tracks,' the Prussian pointed out.

'That they not do, soldier-coat,' Wolf put in, having been able to follow the conversation without difficulty and using it. He could speak good English if the need arose, but preferred to use his native tongue particularly when addressing white strangers.* 'Coming way they are, they won't see 'em until they're out on this open ground here.'

Listening to the Indian, Ole Devil had his own thoughts on the matter confirmed by an expert. While there were a fair amount of bushes, trees and other cover in the vicinity, through which even a large body of the enemy could pass undetected provided that they took precautions —which Wolf and his companion had not troubled to do —none of any consequence was available for a strip

* *Warrant and non-commissioned officers of the King's African Rifles also frequently had this trait. One with whom I worked for several months during the Mau Mau Uprising had been to England and taken the Drill Instructor's Course at the Brigade of Guards' Depot, Pirbright, Surrey, shortly after World War II. He could read and understand verbal instructions which were in English, but would only speak Swahili, the* lingua franca *of most race in Kenya, unless he knew the person he was addressing very well. J.T.E.*

about two hundred yards wide extending from the cliffs and the rim of the bay. Having come in at a more acute angle than the Arizona Hopi *Activos* Regiment would be approaching, the tracks of the Red River Volunteer Dragoons were unlikely to be noticed until the more open terrain was entered. By then, if things could be arranged properly, it would be too late for the attackers to appreciate the danger.

'Whereabouts are their scouts, Tom?' Ole Devil asked.

'Maybe a mile back,' Wolf replied, employing better English than when he had spoken to von Lowenbrau. 'Not much more.'

'Will they find your sign?' the Texian wanted to know.

'If they're any good, they will—and I think they are good,' the Indian answered and, knowing that many settlers had small respect for his tribe's fighting qualities, went on, 'We came back too fast to hide our tracks.'

'I know,' Ole Devil said, with a grin.

'I figured *you* did,' Wolf stated, flickering a brief glance at the Prussian although his words had been directed at the Texian.

'I hope they are good,' Ole Devil declared, before the indignant von Lowenbrau could comment. 'It'll be a help to us if they do cut your sign. They'll move even slower and give us more time to get ready. But we'd still better go down straight away and get started at it, major.'

'Little Foot says do you want us to go and deal with their scouts?' Wolf translated after the younger brave had asked a question in tones of eager anticipation.

'Tell him I apologise for making him miss the chance to count coup, but they must be let come, see what we want them to see, then go to report,' Ole Devil requested, mounting the dun. 'But if they arrive before we're ready, they must be killed. Will you stay here, chief, and attend to that for me, please?'

'You're leading this war party with Ewart and Joe shot,' the Indian replied. 'You tell us what you want doing and that is what we do.'

179

'*Gracias*,' Ole Devil answered, aware that he had been granted what amounted to an unqualified accolade, then he looked at the Prussian and, setting his horse moving, continued, 'I hope your men see it the same way, major.'

Without elaborating upon his cryptic utterance, the Texian sent his dun loping down the slope. The girl and the Prussian followed him. Straight away, von Lowenbrau discovered that he had not forgotten to take what would have been a necessary precaution when dealing with the Dragoons. Obviously he had known that he could count upon Mannen Blaze to assemble and form up the men ready to be put to whatever use the situation demanded. The two Companies stood in separate groups and each man had a pair of the new caplocks to supplement their own arms.

'All right,' Ole Devil said, leaping to the ground before his mount had stopped and looking at the Dragoons. 'I want all of you in the rifle pits you dug on top of the rim.'

'Why *us*?' growled the man whom von Lowenbrau had promoted to replace Sergeant Benn, and there was a mumble of agreement from the other Dragoons.

'Because Captain Hardin has told you to do it!' the Prussian thundered, taking note of his men's reactions and seeing an opportunity to build up their resentment against the Texian.

'Yeah, but you're——,' Sergeant Otis began, realizing that he and his companions would be in the forefront if —as seemed almost certain from what was happening— an enemy force was approaching.

'The protection of the arms is Captain Hardin's responsibility,' von Lowenbrau interrupted, picking his words with care. 'It is *he* who decides how it can best be carried out.'

'Why that——!' Beauregard Rassendyll hissed and was on the point of going to support his friend.

'Stay put, Beau!' Mannen Blaze commanded, lounging in his usual fashion at the supercargo's side.

180

'Damn it, Mannen!' Rassendyll replied, glaring at the red head. 'Don't you see what he's trying to do?'

'I do,' Mannen admitted languidly. 'Only I reckon that Cousin Devil's eyesight's as good—and most likely better.'

While the two young men had been speaking, another factor had entered the affair. Less perceptive than either with regard to the Prussian's motives, Di had listened to Otis's response to Ole Devil's orders. She found herself comparing their new helpers with Company 'C' of the Texas Light Cavalry—and not to the former's advantage.

'There ain't no son-of-a-bitching time to stand arguing,' the girl yelled angrily, glaring around the Dragoons. 'But, happen you-all too scared to go up there, *I'll* come and hold your hands!'

'There'll be no need for that, Di,' Ole Devil contradicted, although he was pleased by her spirited words. He could see that she had annoyed and, to a certain extent, shamed the Dragoons. 'Mr. Blaze, Tommy and I'll be with them.'

'And I, captain,' von Lowenbrau stated, having no desire to lose the slight advantage he had gained from the sergeant's objections. 'They're *my* Company and as their commanding officer, it is my place to be with them.'

'I'd agree, sir, but for one thing,' Ole Devil countered politely. 'You and your Company aren't supposed to be here. Most of your men are wearing buckskin shirts like mine, so they'll pass as they won't be seen below the waist until it's too late. But having a strange officer could ruin everything.'

'May I know what you have in mind, captain?' the Prussian requested, neither making agreement nor refusal to the instructions.

'Certainly,' Ole Devil replied. 'Mr. Blaze, Mr. Rassendyll, Di, Joe, Sergeant Otis, Sergeant Dale, Corporal Smith, come and listen.'

'By cracky, it could work!' Di enthused and could see

181

that the men shared her sentiments, after the Texian had explained what he wanted to be done.

'You won't get no more arguments from me on that,' Otis stated, although he was still aware that he and his men would be the first upon whom the attackers concentrated.

'I'll tell you something else there ain't going to be no son-of-a-bitching argument on either,' Di declared, her expressive face set in lines of grim determination. 'I'm going to be up there with you. De Moreau's with the greasers and, after all she's done to us, I figure me and her've got things to settle happen she comes close enough.'

Chapter Sixteen

GIVE THEM THE CAPLOCKS

COLONEL OTÓN EUGENIO ALARCÓN *DE* REUDA had one advantage over the officers under his command. While a wealthy *haciendero*, with a vast estate in Arizona, he had been a regular soldier for ten years in his youth. So he had felt that he was emminently qualified to make the most of the information which he had received from Madeline de Moreau.

Nor, on listening to the reports of his advance scouts, had the colonel been told anything to make him believe his summation of the situation was other than correct. Although he had had hardly any contact with the *gringo* rebels, few of whom had travelled so far west as his home, the stories he had heard of their traits and conduct had not left him with a high regard for their skill as fighting *soldiers*. Thosè who were guarding the consignment

182

of arms might have taken a few precautions and they might know that the Arizona Hopi *Activos* Regiment were coming, but he still saw no cause for alarm.

Advancing with care and pondering upon how much better the terrain of East Texas was adapted to such tactics—although the cold and damp weather was less pleasant—than most of the land in Arizona, Alarcón studied the state of the enemies' defenses. They were obviously aware that his Regiment was in the vicinity and were positioned to fight back. However, he felt sure that he could exploit their weakness. It stemmed from the climatic conditions' effect upon their weapons. It was something which would not have such repercussions upon his men. Few, apart from the Mexican officers, had firearms. Even the latter, appreciating the serious fault which inflicted such weapons under the circumstances, would be placing their reliance upon swords or sabres. Nor would the lack of discipline which his military colleagues had declared was a characteristic of the *gringo* rebels make them as effective as might otherwise have been the case.

Looking through his telescope at the figures assembled in the rifle pits, the colonel made a rough estimate of their numbers. Then he picked out their officers from the descriptions he had been given by the woman who had been brought to him by Major Abrahan Phillipe Gonzales *de* Villena *y* Danvila. The tall, slim one with the face like *el Diablo* and the burly red head would be the primary targets for his men, but he decided that the *gringo* in the well cut civilian clothing and the small, yellow-skinned foreigner holding a bow and arrows must also be regarded as of an equal priority. Possibly the red haired girl standing alongside the civilian could be considered in a similar fashion, for Madeline de Moreau had warned that she was as dangerous as any of her male companions. While the colonel was inclined to doubt the statement, he saw no reason to take chances. Nor did he want a female prisoner, who might cause dissension

183

among his soldiers. Whether she was taken alive or not, the four men he had selected must die as quickly as possible. Killing the leaders had always been sound strategy. With them gone, their subordinates would have no guidance and be that much easier meat.

Satisfied with his examination, Alarcón closed the telescope and glanced at the Hopi Indian who had brought him to the point of observation. They withdrew with a care equal to that displayed as they moved in and he was confident that they had come and gone without the Texians being aware of their visit. Collecting their horses, they rode back to where the rest of the Regiment were waiting. He was confident of success and pleased with the thought of the acclaim which would be forthcoming in its wake.

Not that the colonel underestimated the fighting qualities of individual *gringos*, having heard of what had happened in San Antonio de Bexar the previous year.* Of course, the Texians who were involved then had been more numerous and commanded by older, more experienced leaders. However, the rebels had also appeared to have scored a number of minor victories in skirmishes during the early days of the rebellion. What was more, although they were withdrawing from the west, he could understand and even approve of Major General Samuel Houston's reluctance to meet a larger army in an open confrontation unless on favourable terms.

For all that, unlike their fellow rebels in the earlier victories—who were fighting hit-and-run on the offensive —the men he had been studying were outnumbered and acting in a defensive capacity. Alarcón felt sure that the rank and file of the Company would appreciate that their inexperienced commanding officer had not even left them with the means for rapid flight if their position should prove untenable. There had been no sign of their horses, which therefore could not be closer than fifty

* *This is the incident referred to in the footnote on page 25.*

yards away and below the rim overlooking Santa Cristóbal Bay. The officer might even have arranged it that way, as the colonel knew he personally would in similar circumstances, to ensure that the men stood their ground to the bitter end.

'Very well, gentlemen—and you, *Senora* de Moreau,' Alarcón announced, looking at the three majors and nine lieutenants who were gathered about the woman. His gaze went next to the leaders of the Hopi Indians who were serving as non-commissioned officers over the rest of the braves. 'All is as Chief Jesus† told us. We can follow the kind of action which I outlined when I heard our first scouts' reports.'

There was a brief rumble of interest and delight at the colonel's news. The commanding officers of the three Companies who were present had approved of the tentative plan which he had made, provided that it should be workable. Nor could the Hopi war leaders, who were practical and experienced tacticians, find fault with the reasoning behind it. However, none of the lieutenants gave the tactics a great deal of thought. Each was more interested in the prospect of going into action, with the attendant possibility of outdoing the others and winning Madeline de Moreau's approbation.

The one person who might have shown the main flaws in the scheme failed to do so.

Having been admitted into the councils of war which were caused by her arrival and news, although noticing that she had been kept under observation at all times, the woman had approved of all she had heard. She had warned that the Mexicans should not take the Texians' leader too lightly, without being too determined in stressing just how competent he had proved to be. While the Regiment consisted of ten fifty-strong Companies, a useful system in that it allowed a greater number of promotions, seven had been left three days' ride to the south.

† *Pronounced 'Hey-Soos'*

185

So she had not wished to have her revenge delayed while reinforcements could be summoned because Alarcón decided the enemy was too dangerous for his force to handle.

'You were correct about the mule train having been brought here, *senora*,' the colonel went on, causing the junior officers to scatter like flies frightened from a pool of honey. 'Or at least, the number of men in the rifle pits indicates that it is.'

On telling how her ambush had failed, laying all the blame on her now scattered or dead associates, Madeline had warned that there was a possibility that the two sections of the enemies' party were reunited. Although she had not lingered in the vicinity of San Phillipe, she had felt sure that the bell-mare had been replaced. In which case, she could count upon Ole Devil Hardin and Diamond-Hitch Brindley to waste no time in putting the new animal to use. For all that, it rankled to learn that the young couple had once again proved to be so capable and efficient. However, the woman found some consolation in considering that both of them would be at Santa Cristóbal Bay, and the full strength of Company 'C' of the Texas Light Cavalry and the Brindleys' Tejas mule packers were less than half the number of the Arizona Hopi *Activos* Regiment.

'That will save us going looking for them,' Villena called out and the other officers mumbled their agreement.

'The time has come for us to ride, gentlemen,' Alarcón stated. 'But I don't need to warn any of you to use cold steel and not to fall into *their* error.'

'May I accompany you, colonel?' Madeline inquired.

'It won't be any place for a lady, *senora*,' Alarcón pointed out.

'Nor do I expect it to be,' the woman declared and her emotions turned her face ugly. 'But they murdered my husband and I have a score to settle with them.'

For a few seconds, Alarcón did not offer to reply.

186

While he had read the woman's identification pass, he was not familiar with *Presidente* Antonio Lopez de Santa Anna's signature. So he could not tell whether the document was genuine or not. However, he was aware of what his fate would be if it should be authentic and he had not honoured it. Nor would his future career be improved if he allowed a friend of el *Presidente* to be harmed.

'Very well, *senora*,' the colonel finally said. 'You may come. But it must be on the understanding that you do so at your own risk and knowing there will be a very great element of danger.'

'That is fully understood and accepted, colonel,' Madeline replied, her hatred for the girl and the Texian driving out any thought of the perils she would be facing. She nodded to the listening officers, going on, 'These gentlemen are witnesses that I insisted upon going and that no blame shall attach itself to *you* in the event of my being killed or injured.'

'My thanks, *senora*, and well said,' Alarcón answered, but decided that precautions might still be in order. 'I must only ask that you stay close to me—.'

'Perhaps you'd be good enough to put me under Major Villena *y* Danvila's care, *senor*,' the woman suggested, guessing that—having captured the leader of the Texians and allowing him to escape—the officer in question would be the best choice for her purpose. He would want to remove the stain on his reputation by killing Ole Devil Hardin and would put her in the best position to achieve the same end. 'If he doesn't object, that is.'

'It will be my privilege, *senora*,' Villena stated.

'Very well,' the colonel authorized, realizing that the major could be made to bear the brunt of the recriminations if anything should befall the female renegade. 'I trust you will take no unnecessary chances, *senora*?'

'I've no wish to be killed, Colonel,' Madeline replied.

On rejoining their men, the officers removed the outer clothing which they had donned to combat the inclement

187

weather. Although travel-stained, their uniforms looked martial and impressive; particularly when compared with the way the men under their command were dressed.

Wanting a greater freedom of movement, Madeline peeled off her cloak-coat. Taking the 'Pepperbox' from the pocket, she tucked its barrel into her waist band. Then she handed the heavy outer garment to one of the small party of *mozos* who were waiting to take care of the officers' property. Having done so, she joined Villena and his lieutenants.

With his force mounted, Alarcón gave the order to advance. Following his plan, each Company formed into three ranks. The youngest braves and the lieutenants were in front, with the older warriors and senior officers bringing up the rear. Nor had either the junior officers nor the Hopis seen anything unusual in the formation. To the Indians' way of thinking, such an arrangement was not only logical but honourable* and such of the lieutenants as bothered to give it any consideration accepted that it was being done to satisfy the preferences of the men under their command.

Madeline de Moreau was not alone in feeling that such an arrangement had merit. Seeing the advantages, the colonel and the three majors had been only too happy to go along with the Hopis' tradition. It gave them a greater chance of survival and the woman saw it in the same light.

Although the colonel and Chief Jesus had contrived to reach a point of vantage from which they could study the enemy without being detected, they had realized that there was no chance of such a large body of men meeting with equal success. Nor did he mean for them to waste time trying. Instead, they were heading straight for their

---

* As with the majority of Indian tribes, the Hopis considered that the older and more experienced warriors had already had many opportunities to earn acclaim and loot. So they could allow those who were less fortunate to have the first opportunities by leading the attack.

objective. Once the Texians saw them coming, he would be able to find out if a very important aspect of his strategy was correct. He hoped that it would be, for he had used it as a major argument when the dangers of a frontal attack upon what would probably be prepared positions had been raised.

Before the Hopis were within a hundred yards of the strip of almost open land, the defenders had seen them. Finding themselves located, the front rank let out whoops and urged their horses forward at an increased pace.

Looking between the men ahead of him, Alarcón gave a sigh of relief. Just as he had anticipated, instead of waiting to deliver volley firing when the Indians reached the fringe of the sheltered terrain—which would have proved advantageous to him, provided the other factor happened —first one and then many of the other men in the pits began to open fire.

Or tried to!

Only a few of the rifles spoke!

The remainder proved to be suffering from a terribly dangerous fault of the flintlock mechanism under such climatic conditions.† Having been affected by the damp air, the powder in the priming pans was failing to ignite and set off the main charges in the barrels.

Seeing that their colonel's prediction was justified even the more cautious of the older braves cast aside their doubts. When rifle after rifle misfired, they added their war whoops to those of the leading ranks and signalled for their mounts to go faster.

Dashing through the bushes and other cover, the three Companies were prepared to launch a determined and, what they felt sure would be, an unstoppable charge. With the way the Texians' weapons were failing to function, they could have done little to save themselves even

_____

† *Another example of just how serious the flintlocks' fault could be is given in*: OLE DEVIL AT SAN JACINTO.

if they had been sufficiently well disciplined to wait and deliver a volley.

Or so thought the attacking force.

Although the attackers did not realize it, they were being lured into a trap!

Ole Devil Hardin had been counting upon the Red River Volunteer Dragoons contingent's lack of discipline to help him spring it. That was why he had selected them to occupy the rifle pits. For the success of his scheme, he needed men upon whom he could rely implicitly below the rim and concealed from the enemies' view.

However, while guessing that any attempt at volley firing would be doomed to failure where the Dragoons were concerned, Ole Devil had given one command to them. Only a few owned percussion-fired weapons and he had insisted that they employed their personal arms before bringing the caplocks he had loaned to them into action. He had also threatened to shoot any man who attempted to touch the new rifles before he gave permission. It said much for the respect, or fear, which he inspired among them that not one had offered to go against his orders even after their pieces failed to function.

Knowing what was at stake, Di, Mannen, Tommy Okasi, Rassendyll and Joe Galton had not fired so much as a shot between them. While the discovery of a rifle which could keep on pumping out lead without apparently needing to be reloaded might have had a salutary effect upon the Indians,* from the defenders' point of view, Mannen doubted whether any of them would notice it in the excitement and confusion of the mass charge. So he was saving the five bullets until they could be put to a more useful purpose. Nor was the little Oriental using his bow, preferring to economize where the arrows were concerned.

Reaching the open ground, the Hopis and their Mexican officers made an awesome sight. Brandishing lances,

---

* *Just how great an effect the fire power of the Browning Slide Repeating Rifles had under suitable conditions is told in:* GET URREA.

throwing sticks, bows and arrows, or in the lieutenants' cases, some kind of a sword, they swept onwards.

'Now!' Ole Devil roared, swinging the butt of his Browning Slide Repeating rifle to his shoulder. 'Give them the caplocks, Dragoons!'

Eagerly and with great relief, the enlisted men in the pits discarded their own arms to snatch up the first of their reserve rifles. Every one of them hoped that the caplocks would prove more effective than the weapons which had failed to function.

However, the sight of the Dragoons changing rifles was not the attackers' main source of consternation. To their amazement, many more *gringos* began to appear over what the majority of the Mexicans and Indians had assumed to be the edge of the cliff. Each of the newcomers was holding a rifle ready for use and had a second, with a bayonet attached, suspended by an improvised sling across his back.

Shock and alarm burst through Alarcón as he realized that he had been tricked into greatly underestimating the number of the enemy. There was, however, no time for him to wonder if his informant had been a party to the deception.* Other matters of more immediate importance were demanding his undivided attention, particularly the way in which the newcomers were behaving. From all appearances, they were far better disciplined than the occupants of the pits. Although they might not be acting with the puppet-like precision of some of the crack European regiments he had heard and read about, they advanced from the rim and, halting in a fairly straight line, lifted their rifles to the aiming position so nearly simultaneously as to be impressive—

* *Madeline de Moreau had not deliberately misled Colonel Alarcón about the Texians' armament. The information which she and her husband had received was merely that a shipment of new rifles was to arrive and the nature of their mechanisms had not been mentioned.*

191

And, but for the lethal fault of the flintlock mechanism, frightening.

Alarcón and his men doubted whether more than a fraction of the weapons being pointed at them would perform in a more satisfactory manner than those of their previous assailants.

'Fire!' bellowed Major Ludwig von Lowenbrau, having been assigned to perform the duty as he could see when the men from below the rim were ready whereas Ole Devil could not without looking away from the enemy.

Over sixty rifles roared and Tommy Okasi's long bow twanged in a ragged, but adequately concentrated volley. It was followed by the shots from those of the Dragoons who had been less speedy in exchanging weapons.

Already half way across the open strip, the tightly packed ranks of the Arizona Hopi *Activos* Regiment's three Companies were ideally positioned to be caught by the holocaust, and they suffered grievously. Horses and men went down like wheat before a mower's scythe.

Being in the forefront of the attackers, not one of the Mexican lieutenants survived the onslaught. Their colonel had not been alone in appreciating the tactical and moral value of removing officers and the Texians had acted accordingly. What was more, practically every member of the front rank felt the effects of the volley. Although they bore the brunt of the casualties, some of the bullets found billets in the men who were following them after having passed between—or through—their bodies. In fact, those who were behind horses which were struck down might have counted themselves fortunate. At something around a hundred yards, the lead could not pass through the length of the animal's body and emerge to fly on with sufficient velocity to claim a second victim.

Just how well Ole Devil had laid his plans was shown by the success which his party had attained. With the single, well delivered volley, the assault by the much larger force had been disrupted and brought to a halt. What was more, the effect went even further than he had anticipated. He had not suspected that the Mexican colonel would have counted upon his men being armed with flintlocks and that these would misfire in the damp air.

Nor were the Texians finished!

Without waiting for or needing orders, the members of Company 'C' dropped the empty rifles and began to liberate the second weapons from across their backs. The Dragoons were also making the necessary adjustments to allow them to continue the bombardment. While they were doing so, Ole Devil, Mannen and Tommy made use of the Brownings' and the bow's capabilities for rapid reloading and sought to select the best targets among the mill of rearing, swerving, hopelessly entangled and confused riders.

Ole Devil toppled one of the majors. A brave passing between them saved Alarcón's life by intercepting the bullet which Mannen had thrown at him. However, Chief Jesus was less fortunate. Having contrived to keep some kind of control over his war pony, he emerged through the scattered dead or wounded animals and men to try and rally the rest. Before he could do so, he was transfixed by the little Oriental's arrow and joined many of his braves on the ground.

To give the Hopis their due, while realizing that their war medicine—the belief in which no amount of Christian mission indoctrination succeeded in wiping out—had failed, some of them tried to fight back.

Before the Texians could fire a second time, a throwing stick* spun through the air and struck von Lowenbrau's head and he went down.

* The throwing stick of the Hopi and related tribes of North American Indians is a similar device to the war and hunting boomerang of the Australian aborigines, but is neither designed nor expected to return to the thrower if it misses its target. This does not make it any less effective as a weapon. American author, Daniel Mannix—who, in Chapter 7, 'The Boomerang—The Stick That Kills' of his book A SPORTING CHANCE covers the subject thoroughly—has thrown one a distance of five hundred and forty feet and it still retained sufficient force at the end to crack an inch-thick limb of a tree.

Holding her second rifle cocked and ready, Di was scanning the confused mass before her in the hope of locating Madeline de Moreau when she heard a cry of pain from alongside her.

Having emptied both his rifles, Rassendyll had set down the second where it would be readily available if he required the bayonet that was attached to it and was reaching for the Croodlom & Co. 'Duck Foot' Mob Pistol which was laying close by. Before his fingers could grasp the butt, an arrow struck him in the shoulder. He could not restrain his agonized exclamation. Grabbing ineffectually at the shaft which was protruding from his flesh, he spun around to stumble against the rear of the pit.

Two of the Dragoons and four members of Company 'C' were also struck by the Hopis' missiles, while others had narrow escapes as arrows or throwing sticks whizzed by them. However, such reprisals—only one member of each party received a fatal injury—were nothing compared to the slaughter which had been dealt out already—

And that which was about to be inflicted!

Less than twenty seconds after the supercargo had been wounded, although too late to prevent it from happening, Sergeant Dale gave the order and Company 'C' turned loose their second fusilade. Nor had the slight delay while the non-com had waited—being unaware that von Lowenbrau was indisposed—reduced its effectiveness. In fact, it proved to be just as devastating and even more potent than its predecessor.

Once again, the deadly tempest of lead assailed the Hopis. Any who had managed to evade the confusion and were trying to continue the attack were selected as targets. The others were hit, or missed, by random shooting as the fates directed. Many fell, including the second major who had come to the fore and was heading towards the rifle pits.

However, Madeline and Villena survived both of the vollies. Being cautious and knowing that his uniform made him an easily distinguishable target, the major had

194

contrived to keep as many bodies as possible between himself and the enemy. He did not wish to let his former captive or the strange little foreigner pick him out for revenge. On her part, the woman was aware that Di Brindley would not hesitate to kill her. So she had allowed the men to draw ahead and had followed ready to grab any opportunity which was presented, or let them take care of the objects of her hatred.

While the Hopis were far from being cowards, there was a limit to how much punishment they were willing to take when there seemed little hope of returning it. What was more, a number of the leaders had fallen and the rest saw no reason to throw their lives away. So they turned and fled, scattering in every direction save towards their assailants.

Seeing what was happening, the woman and Villena followed the Hopis' example. They went independently, neither giving even a thought to the other or to the men whom each had helped send to their deaths.

At the sight of Madeline dashing away, Di threw a shot after her and missed. Growling a curse, the girl dropped her empty weapon and looked at Rassendyll. Experienced in such matters, she knew that the wound was not desperately dangerous.

'I'll send the doc to you, Beau!' Di promised, grabbing up the mob pistol. 'And I'll borrow this seeing's you'll not be needing it.'

With that, the girl bounded up the rear slope of the pit, which had been dug at such an angle as to facilitate a rapid departure. Already the men of Company 'C' were charging forward to use their bayonets and deal with the unhorsed, but uninjured Hopis. So she knew that she was not leaving the supercargo defenseless while she pursued the urgent matter demanding her attention.

The Tejas had been left to look after the mules and, if need be, to destroy the consignment by blowing it up. However, half a dozen of them stood just below the rim holding several saddled horses. One was Ewart Brindley's

195

big *grulla** gelding, selected by the girl as her own mount was tired from the strenuous activity of the previous few days. Running to it, she used her empty hand to grab the reins from the young brave. Swinging astride the saddle, she set the spirited animal into motion and went like a bat out of hell in the direction from which she had come.

Chapter Seventeen

THAT'S ANOTHER I OWE YOU, DE MOREAU

MADELINE DE MOREAU was travelling at a good rate, but she was not afraid of being followed by the Texians after her original near panic had subsided. From various noises which had reached her ears, she had concluded that close-quarters fighting was taking place. So her enemies would be too occupied in dealing with the surviving Hopis to pursue her. Having made her deduction, she saw no reason to keep on pushing her horse at such a speed. It had seen much use recently and she wished to conserve its energy in case of emergency. What was more, she needed it to carry her to safety.

After what had happened on the cliffs above Santa Cristóbal Bay, the woman felt it would be advisable to avoid further contact with the Arizona Hopi *Activos* Regiment. Once the remaining Companies heard of their companions' fate, they might believe she had brought it about deliberately. Nor would any of the survivors who had fled be more inclined to regard her favourably. So she

* Grulla: *a bluish-grey horse much the same colour as a sandhill crane.*

must seek out some other Mexican force and try to persuade its officers to offer her protection from the Indians in addition to striking at the consignment of caplocks.

Bitter rage surged through the woman as she realized that the objects of her hatred had not only survived her wrath, but had once again got the better of her. The emotion was so intense that, at first, she took no notice of the sound of a horse approaching rapidly from her rear. Becoming aware of it, she looked back expecting to find one of the Hopis was following. Dangerous as that might have been under the circumstances, she learned she was wrong in her assumption; but the pursuer posed an even greater threat.

Perhaps an Indian would have been more interested in escaping than repaying her for what she had helped to bring about, but that did not apply to Diamond-Hitch Brindley.

The pistol in the girl's right hand was grim evidence of her intentions!

Letting out a shriek of combined fury and fright, the woman turned her gaze to the front and slammed her heels savagely against the flanks of her mount. Jabbed by her spurs' sharp rowells, it bounded forward with a force which almost caused her to drop the single-barrelled pistol she had drawn at the start of the charge and had not yet replaced in its saddle holster. However, she contrived to retain her grip on the butt and started to urge her horse to go even faster.

Having set off in the general direction taken by Madeline, ignoring the hand-to-hand fighting by the men, Di had soon caught sight of her. Excellently mounted on a horse which was comparatively fresh, the girl had not doubted that she could overtake the woman. However, in case there might be shooting at other than close quarters, she had decided against depending upon the weapon she had borrowed from Beauregard Rassendyll. Taking advantage of a refinement he had had applied, she hung it on her saddlehorn by the rawhide loop which was

197

threaded through a ring on the butt. Then she had drawn a pistol from the brace which were holstered on her rig. With the heavy calibre flintlock in her hand, she felt that she could deal with any situation that might arise.

Oblivious of everything except one another, guiding their mounts almost instinctively through fairly open bush speckled country, the girl and the woman galloped in a south-westerly direction. The latter was fleeing with the fear of death as her goad and the former rode just as recklessly, spurred on by a desire to kill.

Almost a mile fell behind the pursued and the pursuer!

Slowly, but inexorably, Di's big *grulla* was closing the gap between them!

Having noticed this, in rapid glances taken to her rear whenever the opportunity had arisen, Madeline tried desperately to improve the situation. Gallantly as her flagging and lathered mount responded to the punishment she was inflicting with her spurs, it failed to draw away.

Driving the horse up a gentle slope, with slightly less than a hundred yards separating it and the *grulla*, the woman felt it reeling. Just as it reached the top, it stumbled and almost threw her. This time, she lost her hold on the pistol and, as it flew from her fingers, the exhausted animal started to collapse. Sobbing in alarm, she flung herself from the saddle. Not until her momentum had carried her several steps forward did she realize that she had left the weapon's mate in its holster on her saddle. Nor did she feel that the 'Pepperbox' would serve her needs under the circumstances.

Turning around, Madeline almost hurled herself towards the stricken animal. She could see Di charging through the bushes and the sight gave her an inducement for extra speed. Snatching out the pistol, she prepared to fight for her life. Cocking and sighting it, she squeezed the trigger. With a crack, it vomitted out its load. Although the bullet failed to contact the girl, it drove into the *grulla's* chest.

A superb rider, Di felt the lead's impact and her mount

going down. She knew what she must do. Liberating her feet from the stirrup irons, she kicked her right leg forward and over the *grulla's* head. Jumping clear, she alighted without being trapped by the falling animal. Unfortunately, she landed upon a piece of uneven ground. While it threw her off balance, she neither fell nor lost her pistol. However, before she had recovered her equilibrium, she saw that her troubles were far from over.

Hurling the empty pistol aside, the woman looked for its mate. She discovered that it had buried the tip of its barrel into the ground. So there was a chance that the muzzle was plugged and it would not be usable. Instead of wasting time in checking, she snatched the 'Pepperbox' from her waist band. It was one of the best models available, percussion fired and double action in operation. While its mechanism did not allow for such rapid shooting as would later and better designed revolvers,* it still permitted a rate of fire far in excess of any contemporary handgun.

'That's another I owe you, de Moreau!' Di shrieked, glancing at the dying *grulla*.

Spitting out obscenities in French and English, Madeline brought up the 'Pepperbox' with both hands. However, she knew its limitations and started to move closer. For all her knowledge, she could not refrain from chancing a shot when she saw the girl was drawing a bead on her. Not surprisingly, considering her weapon's rudimentary sights, she missed. At first, rage caused her to overlook her peril. Even as the realization struck her, she

---

The fastest recorded rate of fire for a manually operated double action mechanism occurred on January the 23rd, 1834, at the Company 'K', 163rd Infantry's Armoury, Lewiston, Montana. Using a .38 calibre Smith & Wesson Model 1899 revolver, No. 640792, Ed. McGivern fired five shots into a playing card at eighteen feet in two-fifths of a second; not, of course, starting with it holstered.

could tell—although they were still too far apart to make out the actual movements—that Di was squeezing the pistol's trigger.

Confident that she was holding true on the centre of the woman's breast, the girl sensed rather than noticed that the flintlock's hammer was pivoting towards the frizzen plate. It struck, striking sparks that fell into the pan as the plate hinged back under the impact.

There was no other result!

In her eagerness to settle accounts with Madeline, Di had fallen into the error which Colonel Alarcón had hoped would afflict her companions. Either that, or the roughness of her landing when quitting the falling horse had jolted the priming powder from the pan. Whichever it might be, she was in dire and deadly peril.

Again the woman's weapon cracked, its comparatively light powder charge ejecting a .34 calibre ball which stirred the girl's red locks in passing. Continuing her advance, Madeline drew back the trigger, which turned the next barrel into battery and cocked the hammer. Despite being taken on the move, the third shot came even closer to achieving her purpose.

Di saw the puff of white smoke well from the uppermost muzzle of her assailant's weapon, then felt as if a red hot iron had been pressed lightly against her left shoulder. Pain slammed her into a fuller awareness of her predicament. She had heard of 'Pepperboxes' and guessed that the woman must be using something of the kind.

What was more, de Moreau did not intend to miss, or merely score a flesh wound, next time!

Coming to a halt, the woman took a more careful aim than would be possible—even employing both hands —while on the move. After the first three attempts, Di had developed a *very* healthy respect for her marksmanship.

Accepting that there was only one hope for her, the girl spun around and ran towards her horse. With each step, she expected to feel lead driving into or flying past her.

Sighting at the middle of the girl's back, Madeline was confident that she could send the bullet into it. Set free by the rearwards' movement of the sear, the hammer descended—

And produced no better result than Di had achieved with the flintlock!

But for a different reason!

Madeline had fallen foul of the deadly flaw to which Ole Devil Hardin had known percussion-fired 'Pepper-boxes' were prone. Unlike the revolvers that would soon succeed and eventually replace them, which had the caps situated horizontally at the rear of the cylinder, the formation of the barrels caused the cap-nipples to be placed on top and vertically. So, unless seated very firmly, when a barrel was at the lowest point of the axis around which it revolved the cap frequently fell off.

To give the woman credit, she realized what had caused the misfire and understood how to correct it. Unfortunately, neither realization nor understanding came quite quickly enough. Even as she started to press at the trigger, she saw the girl diving over the horse.

Although Di was wondering what had prevented Madeline from shooting, she made no attempt to find out before she had re-armed herself. Remembering what had happened with its mate, she ignored her second pistol. Instead, she jerked free Rassendyll's weapon. The Mob Pistol had started its life as a flintlock, but he had had it altered to handle percussion caps by a master gunsmith in Louisiana.

Praying that the artisan had carried out the modification satisfactorily, although she did not put it into those exact words, the girl drew back the single hammer which served the quadruple barrels. Even as she noticed the brass cap sitting so comfortably on its nipple, she heard footsteps drawing rapidly closer to the horse behind which she was crouching. Obviously the woman was gambling upon her second pistol producing no better result than its mate and was approaching for the kill.

201

'Have you got a surprise——!' Di began, but the thought was cut off when she came very near to death.

Once again, Madeline was firing on the move. However, her bullet did no more than nick the lobe of the girl's ear; which was only a matter of pure chance. She had aimed with all possible care, but her heavy breathing had spoiled what should have been a fatal shot.

Thrusting herself into a kneeling posture, Di swung around the Mob Pistol in both her hands. Even so, Madeline was already squeezing at the 'Pepperbox's' trigger and looming at such a proximity that she would not be likely to miss again.

There was no time for the girl to take a careful aim, but the weapon she held had been designed to remove the need for that. Slanting it in the woman's general direction, she cut loose.

Touched off by the impact of the hammer, the percussion cap ignited the priming charge in the chamber which was connected to all four barrels. There was a sullen roar louder than any other pistol or rifle could produce and a quartet of .45 calibre balls spread fan-like through the air from their respective muzzles. Madeline was so close that she took three of them in a line across her bosom. Shock and agony slammed her backwards, with the 'Pepperbox' flying from her grasp as she went down.

Hooves thundered from behind the girl. With a cold sensation of apprehension, she realized that she did not have a firearm with which to defend herself if the riders —she knew that there must be at least two—were enemies. Swinging around and driving herself erect, she dropped the Mob Pistol which had saved her life and sent her right hand flying to the knife sheathed upon her belt. The gesture proved to be unnecessary. A sigh of relief broke from her as she recognized the three men who were bearing down so rapidly upon her.

'See you got her, Di,' Mannen Blaze remarked, in his invariable languid manner.

'That's what I come out here for,' the girl answered,

throwing a glance at the lifeless body of the woman who had caused them so much trouble and danger. Then she turned her gaze to Ole Devil and Tommy Okasi, both of whom were displaying—if only a good friend could have seen it—satisfaction and pleasure at finding her alive. 'I'd say you boys've handed them Hopis their needings.'

'We have,' Ole Devil Hardin confirmed. 'So now perhaps we can get the caplocks on their way to General Houston.'

OLE DEVIL AND THE MULE TRAIN

For William D. 'Bo' Randall Jr and his son Gary of
Orlando, Florida, makers of damned fine knives.

Author's note

While complete in itself, this book continues the story which has been told so far in YOUNG OLE DEVIL and OLE DEVIL AND THE CAPLOCKS. It also gives the information of how a mule train operates which various footnotes in the earlier stories said would appear in OLE DEVIL AT SAN JACINTO.

CHAPTER ONE

HOW THE HELL DID THEY LET IT HAPPEN?

THERE had been death in plenty at the top of the hollow which surrounded Santa Cristóbal Bay, some ten miles north of the Matagorda Peninsula, Texas, on the morning of February the 28th, 1836. The bodies of many horses and men lay in a mass some fifty or so yards from the rim, their life blood thickly upon the ground.

A few of the corpses were Mexicans, clad in fancy light green uniforms of the style worn by Hussars and other light cavalry regiments in Europe. The remainder were Indians, but not of the kind who might have been expected in East Texas. Tall and lean for the most part, their garments were multi-hued cotton shirts hanging outside trousers which were tucked into the knee-high leggings of moccasins. Weapons of various types were scattered about, discarded by their lifeless owners. There were the officers' swords, the enlisted men's tomahawks, lances, primitive yet effective curved wooden throwing-sticks, bows and arrows, but few firearms.

The commanding officer of the Arizona Hopi *Activos* Regiment, who lay with a large proportion of the three Companies which he had sent into the attack, had based his strategy upon the fact that there was always a serious failing of flintlock rifles and pistols in chilly and damp weather conditions.[1] He had stated that the Regiment would rely upon cold steel. Shattered open by one of the defender's bullets, the state of his skull was testimony to the fact that he had made a terrible miscalculation.

In spite of all the slaughter they had inflicted that morning, it seemed the victors still had not become sated by fighting and wanted to see more killing.

Gathered in a rough circle around a pair of young men who

[1] Another and even more serious example of the effect of inclement weather conditions on firearms using the flintlock system is given in: OLE DEVIL AT SAN JACINTO.

9

were facing each other and holding bared knives, it was plain that those responsible for the corpses belonged to two separate parties. They were, in fact, members of the Texas Light Cavalry, and the Red River Volunteer Dragoons; both part of the recently organized Army of the Republic of Texas.

Like the majority of the other Texians[2] and *Chicanos*[3] who were fighting to obtain freedom from Mexican domination,[4] the two groups of men who had defeated the attack by a much larger force – the purpose of which was to capture a valuable shipment of arms – belonged to privately raised outfits.

The Texas Light Cavalry showed the greatest uniformity in attire and weapons. Its members wore low-crowned, wide-brimmed black hats of a pattern which had become popular among the Anglo-U.S. colonists, particularly as the oppressive policies of *Presidente* Antonio Lopez *de* Santa Anna had caused an increasing antipathy towards everything of Mexican origin. Their fringed buckskin shirts were tucked into fawn riding breeches which ended in black Hessian boots.[5] Each of them had a pistol carried butt forward on a broad, slanting leather loop at the right side of the waist belt, so that it would be accessible to either hand, and had a knife of some kind sheathed on the left. While their garments were stained and untidy, it was from hard usage and long travelling rather than neglect.

However, while the Red River Volunteer Dragoons also sported buckskin shirts, they had retained whatever style of head dress, trousers, footwear and armament they had had in their possession at the time of enlistment. In most cases, their dirty and dishevelled aspect stemmed from a complete disinterest in their personal appearance.

The combatants in the centre of the circle were about the same age, in their early twenties. At close to six foot, they were evenly matched in height and weight. From all appearances, there was little between them where skill was concerned. Crouching slightly, with the knives' blades extended in front

    [2] Texian: an Anglo-U.S.-born citizen of Mexico, the 'i' being dropped from general usage after annexation by the United States of America and the conclusion of the 1846–48 war with Mexico.
    [3] *Chicano:* a Mexican-born citizen of Texas.
    [4] The reasons why the colonists of both races had been driven to rebel are given in: YOUNG OLE DEVIL.
    [5] Hessian boots: originally designed for use by light cavalry such as Hussars, having legs which extend to just below the knee and with a 'V'-shaped notch at the front.

of the thumb and forefinger of the right hand – a grip permitting a variety of cuts or thrusts – each used his left as an aid to his balance as well as to try and distract or grab hold of the other. Moving warily around, they watched for their chances and launched or evaded attacks.

'Go get him, Wilkie!' yelled one of the Dragoons, as the representative of his outfit made a fast stride rearwards to avoid a low thrust.

'Keep after him, Stepin!' encouraged one of the cavalrymen, watching the fighter in the fawn breeches press forward to make another attempt at driving home his weapon. 'You've got him on the run!'

There were other pieces of advice, some similar and others conflicting, supplied by various members of the crowd. Being so engrossed in watching and exhorting, none of them noticed the two groups of riders who were approaching. The first, consisting of three young men, was coming at a gallop and was about a quarter of a mile ahead of the second, larger – elevenstrong – party.

If the Texas Light Cavalry's contingent around the fight had been aware of the leading trio's presence, particularly that of the man in front, not even their excitement would have prevented them from realizing that they were behaving in a most unsatisfactory and undesirable fashion. They would also have realized that they were likely to have the point brought home to them, aware or otherwise, in no uncertain fashion.

Having seen and heard the commotion, as he and his companions were returning from the successful pursuit of the person who had been responsible for the Arizona Hopi *Activos* Regiment's attack, Captain Jackson Baines Hardin – commanding officer of Company 'C', Texas Light Cavalry – acted with his usual promptitude, but also showed the kind of forethought and understanding which made him one of the regiment's most successful fighting leaders.

Those same qualities had caused Captain Hardin to be given responsibility for handling his present assignment. It was one upon which the future of Texas might be hinged. So the last thing he wanted was further trouble and difficulties, particularly such as might accrue from a fight between his men and the other group who had been thrown into their company at such an opportune moment.

Since circumstances had caused Captain Hardin to leave

11

Louisiana and would make it impossible for him to return,[6] he had become deeply involved in the Texians' struggle for independence. That was only to have been expected. Other members of the wealthy and influential Hardin, Fog and Blaze clan had already made their homes in what was at that time a Territory of the State of Coahuila[7] and had welcomed him to their midst. When it had become obvious that open conflict with Mexico was unavoidable, they had financed, recruited and equipped the small regiment in which he was now serving.

The Hardin, Fog and Blaze clan were stout supporters of the strategy proposed by Major General Samuel Houston, who had been given command of the Republic of Texas's[8] hastily assembled Army. They had willingly accepted his decision to withdraw to the east. They had shared his understanding that it would be disastrous to make a stand against the vastly superior numbers of the force which Santa Anna was already marching north to quell their uprising, unless it was at a time and in a place of their own choosing. Whilst retiring, they were to harass the Mexicans with hit-and-run tactics calculated to create as much havoc as possible.

However, Captain Hardin had been taken away from the regiment and was handling an important mission. A consignment of five hundred new, percussion-fired, caplock rifles and a large supply of ammunition had been donated by sympathizers and had been dispatched by sea from New Orleans. Due to the delicate political situation in the United States of America, where feelings were sharply divided over the rebellion,[9] it had been considered advisable to keep the consignment a secret. So

[6] The circumstances are explained in: OLE DEVIL AND THE CAPLOCKS.

[7] *Presidente* Santa Anna's repeated refusals to make Texas a separate State with full representation in the Mexican Government had been a major cause of the rebellion.

[8] Although it would not be until March the 2nd, 1836, that a Convention at Washington-on-the-Brazos declared Texas a free and independent Republic under the Lone Star flag, many Texians had been referring to it in such a manner since the previous year's conflict with the Mexican authorities had ended all hopes of a peaceful settlement.

[9] Knowing many prominent Texians believed their only secure future lay in annexation of the Republic by the United States of America, the liberal anti-slavery factions were afraid that doing so would increase the power of the pro-slavery lobby. The Texians had suggested that, in view of the vast area of land which was involved, Texas could be divided into three or four separate States. The Abolitionists claimed that these would join the others which already supported the continuance of slavery.

12

it was landed at Santa Cristóbal Bay, instead of being delivered through one of the seaports which were in the Texians' hands. Company 'C' were under orders to collect the consignment and, transporting it by Ewart Brindley's mule train, take it to wherever General Houston and the rest of the Army might be.

A band of renegades led by Madeline de Moreau and her husband had learned of the shipment. Before they could be disposed of, in addition to wounding Ewart Brindley and his cargador, assistant pack master, Joe Galton, they had killed the train's bell mare. However, Brindley's grand-daughter, Charlotte Martha Jane – who was more usually referred to as 'Diamond-Hitch', shortened to 'Di', because of her speed and efficiency in 'throwing'[10] such a fastening on a mule's pack – was fully capable of handling the train.

With her husband already dead, Madeline de Moreau's last fling had been to guide the three Companies of the Arizona Hopi *Activos* Regiment – also a volunteer outfit consisting of Mexican officers and Indian enlisted men – to the bay. Having learned that they were coming, Captain Hardin had conceived a most effective defensive plan. The attack had been driven off with heavy losses ending in the deaths of the woman, all but one of the officers, and many of the Hopis' chiefs and war leaders who were serving as non-coms.

Whilst it had still left them outnumbered by almost two to one, the arrival of a Major Ludwig von Lowenbrau and thirty members of the Red River Volunteer Dragoons had given Captain Hardin the means by which he could defeat the larger enemy force. However, there had been a time when the new-comers' presence had appeared to be anything but a blessing.

Having found out about the shipment of arms and ammunition, Colonel Frank Johnson – the founder of the Red River Volunteer Dragoons – had seen how it could be put to his private use. Ignoring Houston's strategy and orders to the contrary, he was planning to – as he put it – carry the war to the enemy by invading Mexico along the coast road. Not knowing that Captain Hardin had arranged for Company 'C' to act as an escort for the mule train, he had sent von Lowenbrau to confiscate the consignment. Nor had he given a thought to how the loss might affect the rest of the Republic of Texas' Army. He was solely concerned with the loot and acclaim which would accrue from the successful conclusion of his

[10] A mule packer never used the word 'tied', but always said he was 'throwing' a diamond-hitch on his animal's load.

13

scheme. Being foiled in the attempt, the Prussian had elected to desert Johnson and transfer with his men to the Texas Light Cavalry.

On seeing and realizing what must be causing the commotion at the top of the rim, Captain Hardin began to doubt the wisdom of having agreed to von Lowenbrau's suggestion. He was also furious that such a situation had been allowed to develop and take place in his temporary absence. Not that he could blame von Lowenbrau, who had been knocked unconscious by a Hopi throwing stick and had not yet recovered. In addition, Sergeant Maxime of Company 'C' had been killed by an arrow and Corporal Anchor wounded in the hand-to-hand fighting. Sergeant Dale had led the party which had followed ready to support himself and his two companions when they had gone after Diamond Hitch Brindley in pursuit of Madeline de Moreau.

However, that had still left all of the Dragoons' non-coms, and Corporal Smith, who had earned his promotion for the part he had played in preventing the confiscation of the consignment. While none of the former would have attained their ranks in Company 'C', the latter ought to have been intelligent enough to have seen the trouble brewing and tried to avert it.

'God damn it to hell and back!' the young captain had raged. 'How the hell did they let it happen?'

In spite of his anger and desire to bring the potentially explosive situation to an end, Captain Hardin had appreciated the disadvantages of charging up at the head of the party who were with him. Veterans all, disciplined and obedient as they were, the enlisted men if used to quell the disturbance would be likely to side with the other members of Company 'C'. Even if they had no such intention, the Dragoons would have expected it of them and acted accordingly.

With that in mind, the captain had ordered Sergeant Dale to return at a slower pace and take care of Di, who had lost her horse and was riding double with him. Then having transferred the girl to the non-com's mount, he had set off at a gallop accompanied by only two companions. However, he was confident that the pair were adequate for his needs, each having special qualities which made him particularly suited to the task. With their assistance, he hoped to break up the crowd before they got completely out of hand. Even so, he knew it was not going to be easy.

Six foot in height, First Lieutenant Mannen Blaze was

dressed in a somewhat better quality version of the enlisted men's uniform, but with a scarlet silk bandana tight rolled and knotted around his throat. He had a .54 calibre Manton[11] caplock pistol and a massive, ivory handled knife of the kind which had already acquired the name 'bowie' in honour of the man credited with the design of the original weapon.[12] Although he was bulky in build and generally conveyed an impression of well padded, contented lassitude, the men under his command – and others who had been fooled until they had learned the error of their ways – realized that his demeanour was deceptive. For all his size, he was not clumsy. He could move fast when necessary, and possessed great strength. Some indication of the former was shown by the way in which he sat his powerful brown gelding, being a light rider for all his weight.

So, while on the surface the burly red haired young man appeared somnolent to the point of being a dullard, in reality he was a smart and capable officer. It had been his quick grasp of the situation and his adroit manipulations which, in Captain Hardin's absence, had bluffed von Lowenbrau out of attempting to gain possession of the consignment.

On the face of it, the second of the young captain's assistants seemed to warrant even less confidence than Mannen Blaze. Not quite five foot six inches in height, but with a sturdy physique, his almond-eyed and cheerful features were those of a native of the Orient. Bare headed, he had closely cropped black hair. His garments were a loose fitting and wide sleeved black shirt hanging outside trousers of the same material which were tucked into matching Hessian boots.

Apart from his footwear and the lack of a pigtail, the man could have been a Chinese coolie who might be found in any of the United States' major seaports. However, one rarely saw a coolie carrying weapons and he appeared to be well armed if in a somewhat primitive fashion. A pair of long handled, slightly curved swords with small, circular guards, balanced each other – the shorter at the right – in lacquered bamboo

[11] Joseph 'Old Joe' Manton, a gunsmith of London, England, who was an early maker of fine quality percussion fired rifles and pistols.
[12] What happened to James Bowie's knife after he was killed at the conclusion of the Siege of the Alamo Mission – at San Antonio de Bexar, Texas – on March the 6th, 1836, is told in: THE QUEST FOR BOWIE'S BLADE. Some authorities have claimed that Bowie's eldest brother, Rezin Pleasant, was the actual designer of the knife, which was made by the Arkansas blacksmith and master cutler, James Black.

sheaths attached by slings to his leather waist belt.[13] In addition, he grasped a bow at least six foot in length in his left fist and there was a quiver suspended across his back so that its arrows would be readily accessible to his right hand.[14]

As with Mannen Blaze, Tommy Okasi's looks were deceptive. There was little contact between his homeland and the Western Hemisphere – nor would there be until after the visits in 1853–54 of a flotilla of warships commanded by Commodore Perry, United States' Navy – so few people knew that he had originated from the group of islands known collectively as Japan. They believed him to be Chinese. He was reticent about his reasons for leaving and, being exceptionally capable in his nation's highly effective martial arts, for the most part his privacy was respected. Those who tried to invade it never repeated the attempt.

For all his undoubted skill as a warrior, the little Oriental was content to act as Captain Hardin's valet. He had always proved to be a cheerful, loyal, courageous and dependable companion, being willing to take any risk which became necessary. These admirable traits had been displayed many times, even before accompanying his employer to Texas and taking an active part in the present assignment.

Matching Mannen Blaze in height, attire – with the exception that his tight rolled silk bandana was a riot of clashing, multi-hued colours – age (in the mid-twenties) and armament, Jackson Baines Hardin was slender without being skinny or puny. Even while riding at a good speed across uneven terrain, he sat his linebacked dun gelding with a ramrod straight erectness. Although travel-stained and somewhat dishevelled, his clothing showed signs that he had endeavoured to keep it as clean as possible.

The most remarkable feature about the young commanding

[13] Traditionally a Japanese *samurai* warrior's *daisho* – a matched pair of swords comprised of the *tachi*, with a thirty-inch blade and the *wakizashi*, about half the former's blade length – were carried thrust through the girdle. As Tommy Okasi had had to spend long hours on horseback since arriving in the United States and accompanying Ole Devil Hardin to Texas, he had found it more convenient to equip the sheaths with slings and carry them on either side of his belt.

[14] To permit men of such small stature to wield bows of that length, the handle was positioned two thirds of the way down the stave instead of, as is the case with the majority of Occidental bows, centrally. One Japanese system of drawing, aiming and loosing an arrow is given in: YOUNG OLE DEVIL and, for comparison, descriptions of two Occidental archery techniques are to be found in: BUNDUKI.

16

officer of Company 'C', especially at such a moment, was his face. Combed back and exposed by having his hat hanging on his shoulders by its *barbiquejo* chinstrap, his coal black hair formed what looked like small, curved horns above his temples. Taken with eyebrows like inverted 'V's', lean cheeks, an aquiline nose, a neatly trimmed moustache – he had shaved that morning – and a short, sharply pointed chin beard, they created a Satanic aspect which, in part, had produced his nickname, 'Ole Devil'.[15]

Bringing the dun to a rump-sliding halt about thirty feet from the still unsuspecting and rowdy mob, the young captain quit its low horned, double-girthed[16] saddle and released its split-ended reins. Doing so ensured that the animal would not stray. It had been trained to stand still when 'ground hitched' by the dangling strands of leather and would only move under the direst of provocation.

Without even so much as a glance at his two companions, knowing that he could rely implicitly upon their judgment, Ole Devil Hardin strode forward with sharp and angry strides. Since taking on the mission, he had had to deal ruthlessly with several situations and was willing to do so on this occasion. Nor would the fact that his own men were involved prevent him from taking whatever steps he considered necessary. For all that, he knew a single mistake on his part could blow the whole affair up into something which neither he nor anybody else could handle.

[15] Another cause of Jackson Baines Hardin's nickname was his well-deserved reputation for being a 'lil ole devil for a fight'.
[16] Because of its Mexican derivation, from the word 'cincha', Texians tended to use the term 'girth' rather than 'cinch'.

CHAPTER TWO

I'LL MAKE YOU SORRY YOU WERE BORN!

SELECTING a portion of the onlookers comprised of his own men, from whom he felt he could produce the most desired effect, Ole Devil Hardin headed straight for it. He heard footsteps on either side and a few paces to his rear. So he knew that Mannen Blaze and Tommy Okasi were following in the same rough arrowhead formation in which they had been riding. Although he did not see that the little Oriental no longer carried the bow and, by tugging at the quick-release knot of the carrying strap, had removed and left both it and the quiver near the horses, he would have felt no qualms if he had. Even without wearing his *daisho*, Tommy's ability in the little publicized – outside his homeland – unarmed combat techniques of *ju-jitsu* and *karate* made him more than a match for most bigger, heavier and stronger assailants.

Two of the spectators, who were clad in fawn riding breeches, felt themselves being pushed roughly from the rear by somebody who clearly wanted to pass between them. Turning, bristling with indignation and ready to take reprisals, they found themselves confronted by a figure whose features were meaner than – and very much like the pictures they had seen of – Old Nick as he was stoking up the fiery furnaces to roast another bunch of miserable sinners. Although they realized that the owner of the face was considerably more earthly and mundane, the effect was pretty near the same.

In fact, the pair were aware that somebody was sure as hell going to find themselves pretty close to being roasted in the *very* near future. Assuming expressions which they hoped showed indifference, trying to appear innocent, they lost all their hostility. Once their commanding officer had stalked by, they began to edge backwards with the intention of disassociating themselves from a situation that they felt sure would *not* meet with his approval.

18

Glancing at Tommy, Mannen diverged from the line being taken by his cousin and passed around the circle to the right. Without needing advice, the little Oriental hurried in the opposite direction until he reached the dividing line between the Dragoons and the left flank of Company 'C'. It was, he concluded as he entered the gap, fortunate that he had demonstrated his skill at *lai jitsu*, the fast withdrawal of the *tachi*, during the final stages of the fight and also how deadly effective such a weapon could be in his trained hands. It would be a fine inducement towards compliance with orders and a warning that any attempt to extend the hostilities would be extremely dangerous.

For his part, the burly red-haired lieutenant seemed to be almost on the point of falling asleep as he elbowed his way through the other narrow space separating the two factions. A few from each group turned with angry protests on their lips, but none of them continued with their complaints. All of them were aware of his true potential and were not fooled by his languid exterior. However, before he could emerge beyond them, he saw something which demanded his immediate attention.

On arriving at the forefront of the circle, Ole Devil took in the situation with a swift look. He found some slight relief in noticing that, as yet, there was no mingling between the members of the two Companies. That made things just a little more stable, provided the Dragoons did not attempt to take their representative's part. He was counting upon his companions and the speed with which he must now act to prevent trouble.

Although Ole Devil had never heard of psychology, he realized that the more spectacularly he dealt with the situation, the greater its effect would be upon the onlookers. In this, he would be aided by his knowledge of *savate*; the foot and fist fighting practised by French Creoles in Louisiana. Furthermore, while he did not possess the skill which would be acquired by another – as yet unborn – member of the Hardin, Fog and Blaze clan,[1] Tommy had taught him several useful *ju-jitsu* and *karate* tricks. Utilizing his combined lessons in the art of self defense, he felt he could achieve his purpose. Particularly as, seeming to wish to help him, the combatants were close together. Each having grasped the other's right

[1] The member in question was Dustine Edward Marsden 'Dusty' Fog, whose history and fighting abilities are recorded in the author's 'Civil War' and 'floating outfit' series of biographies.

wrist with the left hand, they were straining to gain the advantage.

Thrusting himself forward without waiting for Mannen or Tommy to emerge from the crowd, the captain darted towards the two young men. He bounded into the air, rotating his body until it was parallel to the ground. Unfortunately, an instant before he reached them, they decided their position was at a deadlock and, as if by mutual consent – or realizing another factor was entering the game – shoved each other away. So they were just too far separated to receive the full impact of the collision.

While Ole Devil still struck the fighters and sent them staggering, his attack lacked the force to incapacitate them. They went reeling at angles away from each other, but without losing their holds on the knives. Having been hit slightly the harder, the cavalryman sprawled to his hands and knees. Blundering onwards for a few more paces, the Dragoon contrived to remain erect. Alighting on his feet, Ole Devil glared from one to the other, knowing the affair was not yet over.

Muttering an oath, one of von Lowenbrau's men standing at the edge of their group reached for the pistol which was thrust into his belt. A friend of the knife fighter, he felt it was incumbent upon him to register a protest over such an unfair intervention by a man clad in the fashion of the opposition. Before he could do so, or identify the interloper – not that he would have been influenced towards wisdom by the discovery – he experienced a sensation such as might have resulted if he had allowed his right shoulder to come between the jaws of an exceptionally powerful bear trap.

'Now you just leave that be and stay out of it, *please*,' requested a drawling and lethargic voice, which somehow sounded as chilling as if it had been snarled ferociously. The last word of the sentence were accompanied by an even greater crushing pressure on the shoulder. 'Because, if you don't, I'll make you sorry you were born!'

Numbed with agony, the Dragoon glanced behind him. Maybe some folks would have regarded the bland features which met his gaze as belonging to a dull-witted simpleton, but he was not among their number. Recognizing his captor, he would have obeyed even if the excruciating torment being inflicted by the largest thumb and fingers he had ever seen were leaving him with a second choice.

Noticing that several members of both factions appeared to

be contemplating hostile action, either for or against his employer, Tommy Okasi sprang to confront them. In a flickering blur of motion which would only be matched by top grade gun fighters – employing much shorter weapons – using techniques developed from the late 1860's to the present day,[2] he whipped the thirty inch long, razor sharp blade of the *tachi* from its sheath.

'Ancient Nipponese saying, which I've just made up,' the little Oriental announced, in sibilant tones and employing very good English, as he brandished the sword in both hands. 'Man who pokes his nose into thing which must be stopped for good of all could end up walking on his knees, having lost all that is below them.'

As in Mannen's case, there were those alive who might have regarded such behaviour, coming as it did from so short a person in the presence of many larger men, as being foolhardy to say the least.

However, several of Tommy's audience had seen and told the majority of the rest how he had practically decapitated – although that was not the term used by those who described the incident – a large Hopi brave who was trying to gut him with a war lance. Then, even before the corpse had struck the ground, he had pivoted through a good ninety degrees to fell a second warrior harbouring similar intentions towards him.

So the listeners did not regard the little Oriental's politely phrased words as other than a serious warning of the action he was willing to take if necessary.

Without being aware of the way in which his companions were supporting and protecting him, although neither of their tactics would have been a surprise, Ole Devil prepared to bring the fight to an end.

Being on his feet, the Dragoon posed the greater and more pressing threat.

Unfortunately, the problem was not so simple as there was the future to consider.

The man's companions would be resentful of anything which they regarded as a show of favouritism on the young captain's part.

Accepting what could be the only solution, Ole Devil started to put it into effect. His conscience was soothed by knowing

[2] Just how competent the present day combat shooting experts can be is described in: THE ¼ SECOND DRAW and the rest of the author's Rockabye County biographies.

21

the nature of his Company's representative in the fight. Stepin had always shown considerable reluctance to accept discipline, despite being loyal to his outfit and proud to be serving in it, and in the past his behaviour on a number of occasions had come very close to warranting punishment.

Leaping forward, as the cursing cavalryman began to rise, Ole Devil swung up his right leg. Well versed in *savate*, he sent the toe of his boot with carefully calculated force under Stepin's chin. Back snapped the head of the recipient of the attack. Lifted upwards a few inches, he released his knife's hilt and collapsed limply to the ground. It was obvious that he would not be taking any further interest in the proceedings for a few minutes at least.

However, the Dragoon was already rushing to the attack. He hoped that he would take his second assailant by surprise and repay the unprovoked assault upon him.

The hope did not materialize!

Instead of waiting for his assailant to reach him, Ole Devil glided forward on what appeared to be a converging course.

Intending to drive his knife 'up to the "Green River" '[3] into the intruder's belly, the Dragoon became aware of how his would-be victim looked. Studying the savage, Mephistophelian features, he could not help glancing down. It came almost as a surprise and relief to discover that the other did not have cloven hooves or a forked tail, but was clad in the attire of the Texas Light Cavalry.

The understanding came a trifle too late.

Swinging to face his attacker, Ole Devil watched the knife as it was driven towards his midsection. At the last moment, he rotated his torso clear by swinging his left foot in a circular motion to his rear. Simultaneously, he raised both hands to shoulder height, palm downwards. Bringing them together, he sent them to clamp hold of Alvin's right wrist and force it downwards away from him. Taking his weight on the right foot, the captain bent his left knee until its thigh was parallel to the ground. Still guiding the point of the knife in a harmless direction, he pulled with his hands and snapped around the raised limb so that the knee took his attacker in the pit of the

[3] First produced on the Green River, at Greenfield, Massachusetts, in 1834, a very popular type of knife had the following inscription on its blade just below the hilt, 'J. Russell & Co./Green River Works'. Any knife thrust into an enemy 'up to the "Green River" ' – whether it bore the inscription or not – would be fatal.

22

stomach. Then, with a surging heave, he flung the winded, folded over, and helpless young man with a flipping motion. Turning a half somersault, Alvin alighted supine and with a bone jarring thud which drove all the air from his lungs and stunned him. Like Stepin, he was no longer in any condition to resume hostilities.

Having ended the main source of dissension, Ole Devil wasted no time in setting about removing the rest. Glancing quickly at the two recumbent soldiers, to ensure that neither was going to make further trouble, he turned and raked the crowd with his cold black eyes. Noticing in passing that Mannen and Tommy had fully justified his confidence in them, he sought for the means to put into operation his father's advice upon how to handle such a situation.

'When you're dealing with an unruly mob, particularly if the men in it are subject to some form of discipline,' Captain Jeremiah Hardin, master of the trading ship *Star of the Southland* – which had brought Tommy Okasi to the United States – had counselled, 'Pick out one of them and make it look like you hold *him* responsible for what's happening.'

Few of the Dragoons and none of Company 'C' would meet the grim-faced young captain's angry scrutiny. Fortunately, the one he had selected to be his target did so.

'All right, *Sergeant* Otis!' Ole Devil growled, staring at the burly man who was standing in the centre of the Dragoons. 'How did *you* let it start?'

'M-*Me*?' the designated soldier began, becoming aware that the men on either side of him had begun to edge away furtively.

'Hell, Cap'n, all young—' commenced a member of Company 'C', but the words trailed away as his superior's Satanic face turned in his direction.

'Just how the hell long have *you* been Sergeant Otis?' Ole Devil demanded, with cold and savage fury which caused its recipient to back off and put aside all notions of making an explanation. On returning his gaze to its original subject, he found to his satisfaction that the non-com was no longer eyeing him defiantly, but was looking at the ground as if finding it of absorbing interest. 'Well, *sergeant*?'

'It was all the fault of them damned fly-slicers[4] of your'n,'

---

[4] Fly-slicers: derogatory name for members of the cavalry as opposed to Dragoons, who although mounted for the purpose of travelling, usually fought on foot.

Otis mumbled, jerking an indignant thumb towards the cavalryman. 'They reckoned—'

'I don't know how it is in the Red River Volunteer Dragoons, *sergeant!*' Ole Devil interrupted, after having silenced his men's muttered protests with a glare. 'But in *my* regiment, which *you're* figuring on joining, you address an officer by his rank, or call him "sir".'

'Well – sir,' Otis went on, the honorific popping like a cork from a bottle as the captain's right foot tapped on the ground in warning. 'It was – They reckoned's how us Dragoons didn't do our share of the fighting.'

'Hell, cap'n!' yelled one of Stepin's boon companions. 'They took their time—'

'Mr. Blaze!' Ole Devil thundered, above the growls of objection from the Dragoons. 'Put that man to the hardest, dirtiest job you can find – and look for some more that need doing!'

'Yo!' Mannen boomed, giving the traditional cavalry acknowledgment. Having anticipated how his cousin would react to the interference, he was already ambling in the required direction with what could only be described as leisurely alacrity. 'Get the hell into the hollow and ask Joe Galton to give you something to start digging with.'

Satisfied that his second-in-command could deal with that aspect of the situation, Ole Devil returned his attention to the discomforted sergeant.

'Hell – sir!' Otis spat out. 'We done our fair share and we was on top here in them rifle pits right from the start. And we got out of 'em's quick's we could when you yelled for us to charge. So why—?'

'I wasn't asking for a debate upon our action against the enemy, sergeant,' Ole Devil pointed out coldly. 'My question to you, the only one to which I require an answer, is how did *you* let the fight start?'

Nothing about the young captain's Mephistophelian features suggested that he too had noticed that the Dragoons had been slow in quitting the rifle pits when he had given the order to engage the Hopis at close quarters. He could see what had happened. Always arrogant and hot headed, Stepin must have commented upon their dilatoriness. Being of a similar disposition, Alvin had taken offense. However, the last thing Ole Devil wanted was to have the matter retained as part of the conversation.

24

'Hell, cap'n,' Otis began, 'we was all just standing around—'

'Why?' Ole Devil asked.

'Huh?' the sergeant grunted, showing puzzlement.

'Why were you all just *standing* around?' Ole Devil elaborated, wondering where Corporal Smith had been and why he had not organized some kind of work to keep at least Company 'C' occupied.

'You'd all gone after the Brindley gal,' Otis explained. 'Von Low – the major was unconscious and that Rassendyll feller'd got an arrow in his shoul—'

'I don't need a casualty list, sergeant,' the captain interrupted and, realizing that he had not seen any of the wounded as he was returning, deduced that his missing corporal had organized their removal into the hollow so that they could receive medical attention. 'What you're trying to say is that nobody had given *you* any orders and *you* didn't have enough damned sense to put the men to work without them.'

'Well— That is—!' Otis mumbled, hanging his head and shuffling his feet.

'You're not under *my* command,' Ole Devil stated and, although he did not say "Thank god", the words were there. 'And I'll leave it to Major von Lowenbrau as to what action he takes against you. However, in his absence, *sergeant*, I'd be obliged if you would put yourself and your men at Mr. Blaze's disposal so that *he* can tell you what needs to be done.'

'Yes, sir,' Otis responded, throwing angry glares at his companions rather than towards the man who was delivering the tongue-lashing.

'You men of Company "C" get started throwing the Mexicans' and Indians' bodies into the sea,' Mannen commanded, having heard what was being said. Shrewdly, he realized that his cousin was expecting him to act without waiting for instructions so as to emphasize the point made to Otis. 'Put *your* Dragoons to helping them, sergeant. I'll leave you in charge of the burial detail. Take those two yacks lying there, as soon as they can stand. Have the one I sent to fetch shovels and a man from your Company. I'd say the one rubbing his shoulder, but that's up to *you*. Then get graves for our dead dug up here.'

'Yes, sir,' Otis answered, showing as little hesitation in giving the honorific to the red head as he had to the captain.

Not for the first time, Ole Devil blessed his good fortune in having such an excellent second-in-command. Mannen had done exactly the right thing by putting their own men to work

25

before dealing with the Dragoons and in letting Otis be responsible for the way in which the latter carried it out. The division of labour and the choice of personnel for the grave-digging detail had also been as expertly handled as the captain could have wished it. While he had no idea why the Dragoon was rubbing his shoulder, he felt sure that his cousin had had a sound reason for making that selection. Certainly the behaviour of the other three had been bad enough to warrant the punishment. What was more, putting Otis in direct charge of them was an equally shrewd move. Smarting with humiliation, he was likely to pay greater attention than he had done previously in performing his duties and keeping them hard at work.

Despite his satisfaction with Mannen's handling of the situation and his belief that he could rely upon Otis, Ole Devil decided to stay on the rim. By reminding them that retribution was close at hand, his presence would tend to act as a calming influence on any recalcitrant spirits.

'I've let Di take my horse and ride down to see Doc Kimberley so that she can tell her grandpappy she's all right, sir,' Sergeant Dale reported, striding up at that moment. Being just as good a judge of the situation as Mannen, he delivered a very smart salute. 'Looks like you've quietened them down for a spell.'

'Yes,' Ole Devil agreed. 'For a spell.'

'You reckon they'll be *loco* enough to get to fussing again, cap'n?' Dale inquired.

'There's always that danger once it's been started,' Ole Devil warned. 'So we'll have to—'

At that moment, Corporal Smith appeared from the hollow. A big, blond haired man in his early thirties, he moved with an erect carriage which suggested that he had had military training. Glancing around, he seemed both pleased and relieved with what he saw. Then he strode forward, but halted a short distance away from where his three superiors were standing.

'Yes, corporal?' Ole Devil asked.

'I'm sorry I didn't get here before, sir,' Smith answered, after he had advanced and saluted. 'By the time I'd heard the ruckus and started up, you must have come back and stopped it.'

'That's all right, I don't blame you,' Ole Devil replied. 'How're things down in the hollow.'

'Major von Lowenbrau's recovered, but won't be in any

26

shape to ride today, Doc Kimberley says, sir,' Smith replied. 'Mr. Rassendyll's as well as can be expected and none of the others are too serious. Two of them'll need to ride a *travois* and the Tejas'll be making one apiece for them as soon as they can.'

'*Bueno*,' Ole Devil praised, feeling sure that the arrangements had been made at Smith's instigation and liking the corporal all the more for not having mentioned the fact. 'Take rank of sergeant in Sergeant Maxime's place.'

'*Gracias*, Captain,' Smith said, showing his pleasure at the promotion. 'Thing is though, sir, Doc asked me to tell you he'd like to get Ewart Brindley and the other two to Washington-on-the-Brazos as quickly as possible, so he can get them attended to properly. Like he says, he hasn't the gear to do it himself.'

'It'll be noon at least before we'll be ready to pull out,' Mannen put in thoughtfully.

'If then,' Ole Devil went on, then looked to where Stepin and Alvin were on their feet and scowling at each other. 'Mr. Blaze, give Sergeant Otis my compliments and tell him that I intend to hold the burial services on our dead in ninety minutes so the graves had better be ready by then.'

'Yo!' the red head answered, and turned to deliver the message without waiting to find out why there was such urgency.

CHAPTER THREE

VON LOWENBRAU'S UP TO SOMETHING

PRAYS LOUDLY, SOMETIMES, the Tejas Indian mule packer, had been in old Ewart Brindley's employment for close to ten years. During that time, he had become competent in his work and could be trusted to carry out every part of it without needing to be supervised. So, but for one *very* important detail, he might have taken grave exception to having somebody – particularly a person who knew little or nothing about the finer points of his specialized trade – standing close by watching him. What was more, in spite of the low regard which many Texians and *Chicanos* had for members of his nation as warriors, he was tough enough and possessed sufficient weapon savvy to back up any protests that he cared to make.

However, bearing in mind various recent events, Prays Loudly, Sometimes felt that the man in question had earned the right to carry out an unchallenged scrutiny. In fact, guessing the reason for it, he even experienced a sense of pride that he had been selected from all his fellow workers to be watched. It was most flattering that a war chief of *Diablo Viejo's* well deserved reputation should consider that he, of all the mule train's experienced and accomplished packets, was the one most worthy of being watched and learned from.

As the late February weather tended to be chilly and damp, particularly so soon after dawn, Ole Devil Hardin had his black cloak-coat – its front open and sleeves empty – draped across his squared shoulders. However, despite the inclement conditions, his black hat was still hanging on his back.

Possessing an active and inquiring mind, Ole Devil invariably took an interest in anything he believed might one day be of service to him. He had neither the desire nor the intention of going into active business competition with Ewart Brindley, but he did consider that the time might come when having a knowledge of mule packing could prove advantageous. So,

28

having made all his own arrangements, he was grabbing the opportunity to watch some of the preparations which were being carried out for the most important aspect of the return journey. He was hoping that he would not be interrupted before he had satisfied his curiosity, as had happened the day before while they had been getting ready to leave Santa Cristóbal Bay.

Nothing had happened so far and Ole Devil was waiting with eager anticipation to see what would be done. As on the previous morning, before the arrival of the Arizona Hopi *Activos* Regiment had ended it, the seemingly confused activity taking place before him was nothing of the kind. It was being carried out by the pick of the cream of the mule packing profession. So the men concerned went about their work with a speed and purpose which told of years of practical experience.

Although Major General Samuel Houston had requested that Brindley sent the majority of his stock to Washington-on-the-Brazos, to help with the evacuation of what was regarded as the Republic of Texas's capital city[1] and, more important, to lessen the chance of them falling into the hands of the enemy, he had retained the best of his men and mules to collect and deliver the consignment.

The train consisted of fifty pack and fourteen riding mules plus the indispensable bell-mare. From Ole Devil's examination of the pack animals, he could tell that all were of excellent quality and had been specially selected – in fact were bred – for their respective duties.

Each of the pack mules was just over fourteen hands in height,[2] with a well-muscled back that was straight, or had a slight roach,[3] from the withers to the croup; being broad and level at the top, but having only sufficient length for it to carry its burden without injury to the point of the hip. Wide chested, with a good breadth at the shoulders, it had the well developed and powerful quarters so vitally important when traversing hilly terrain whilst fully loaded. Shortish, clean and straight at the front, although some tended to be a trifle cow-hocked at the

[1] The capital was transferred to Austin – named in honour of Stephen Fuller Austin, 1793–1836, one of the first of the Anglo-U.S. colonizers – after the Texians had won their independence.
[2] Measured at the withers, the highest part of the back between the shoulder blades, a 'hand' being equivalent to four inches.
[3] Roach-backed: slightly arched.

rear,[4] – which was no disadvantage as the limbs were free from disease – the legs appeared to be slender when compared with those of a horse. They were between six and eighteen years of age, fully trained and in the peak of physical condition.

Standing at least a hand taller, longer backed and with a somewhat lower shoulder to give a better reach when walking, the packers' riding mules were equally well conditioned animals.

Every packer was in charge of five mules, not counting his personal mount. The cook and Joe Galton, who acted as farrier as well as *cargador*, had an animal apiece assigned to them to carry their respective equipment. On the trail, working with a portable outfit and a selection of ready-made shoes, the farrier had to ensure that the stock were kept well shod at all times. The cook's implements – a sheet iron stove, several camp kettles packed one inside another, a Dutch oven, a coffee-mill, a bread pan, a couple of skillets, butcher's knives and a sharpening steel – were transported in two mess boxes of a suitable size and shape to be attached to a pack saddle.

When deciding to watch one of the packers in action, Ole Devil had asked Diamond-Hitch Brindley – who because of her grandfather's indisposition was in the position of pack master – whom she would suggest. Having been directed to Prays Loudly, Sometimes, he had wondered how the brave would regard being under observation. From what the captain could see, he concluded that the other was pleased to have been selected.

Highly skilled at his duties, Prays Loudly, Sometimes was working fast and making the task seem a lot easier than it really was. Taking one of the ready-made cloth blindfolds which were fastened around his arms, he used it to cover the mule's eyes. Doing so ensured that the animal would stand still through the saddling and attaching of its load. It would also be re-applied if there should be any need to adjust the rig and burden during the day's travel. Like most of its kind, while well trained and experienced in its work, the mule was inclined to be highly strung and quick tempered. Any sudden, unexpected sound or movement could cause it to shy and might end with it kicking and plunging in a dangerous fashion if it was able to see what

[4] Cow-hocked: where the legs are curved inwards at the hocks – the joints which correspond with the human ankle – so that they are closer together at the pasterns – the part of the leg between hock and hoof – and the stifles, the upper joints of the limbs.

it was doing; when its eyes were covered it was inclined to be more passive.

Having taken the precaution, the packer set the sheepskin pad marked with the mule's number – the cook's and farrier's animals were identified by the letters 'C' and 'F' – and known as a *corona* in position on its back. Next, he took the folded blanket which had formed part of his bedding the previous night and laid it carefully upon the *corona*. This was followed by the *aparejo* type of pack saddle. Specifically designed for the transporting of heavy, or awkwardly shaped loads which could not be carried on a conventional pack saddle, it consisted of a pad about twenty-eight inches wide by thirty-six inches long and stuffed with dry, coarse grass to a thickness of three inches. Attached to it was a wide girth and an exceptionally broad – twelve inches in this case – breeching strap which fitted under the animal's tail like a crupper. Adjusted to the appropriate length for that particular beast, being laced to the *aparejo* and padded where it came into contact with the tail, the latter's purpose was to prevent the load from slipping forward over its wearer's shoulders when going down hill. So important was the correct fit and positioning of the *aparejo* that the line of the mule's back was marked by stitching exactly along its centre.

With the breeching in place and the girth drawn tight, Prays Loudly, Sometimes affixed the *sobre-jalma*[5] on the *aparejo* and coupled them together with the thongs at the ends of the latter's centre line. Made of sturdy tarpaulin, cut to cover the *aparejo* exactly and completely, it was faced at the sides and ends with leather. The ends were protected from wrinkling or gathering by having twenty inches long sticks – known as 'shoes' – held in place by leather 'caps', across the bottoms.

Finally, all was tied together with a strong bellyband and a latigo strap. All that remained for Prays Loudly, Sometimes to have done was to have the load – two sets of twelve caplock rifles and their bayonets, which had been taken from their shipping boxes and wrapped in sailcloth supplied by the vessel that had delivered them, on being brought ashore – placed upon the assembly. These would then be wrapped in a pack cover and lashed by having a forty to fifty foot length of rope 'throwed' around, drawn tight each time and lashed in the diamond-hitch fastening from which the girl had received her nickname.

[5] Mule packers in the United States' Army called the *sobre-jalma* a 'hammer cloth'.

But once again, it seemed that fate was about to decree against Ole Devil seeing the final preparations of a packer.

Leaving her place by the dead embers of the previous night's fire – it had been put out before daybreak to prevent smoke rising and attracting unwanted attention – Diamond-Hitch Brindley was strolling towards the young captain in what some people might have considered a casual fashion. Having come to know her very well during the time that they had been acquainted, he knew differently. Unless he missed his guess, she was approaching him on a matter of some importance.

About five foot seven inches in height and in her late 'teens, Di was possessed of a shapely body which was blossoming into full womanhood, a fact the snug fit of her buckskin shirt and trousers, under an open black wolfskin jacket, did little to conceal. She had rawhide moccasins on her feet. There was a pistol thrust through the right side of her waist belt and a knife hung in an Indian sheath at its left. Somehow, neither they, nor the powder horn and bullet bag swinging from her left shoulder, seemed incongruous in spite of her obvious femininity. Fiery, fairly short and curly red hair framed a pretty freckled face. Nor did having a swollen top lip, a blackened right eye and a piece of sticking plaster attached to the lobe of her left ear – gained in the course of two fights, the first bare-handed and the second using firearms, against Madeline de Moreau – detract from its charm. Normally her features showed a merry zest for life and a quick, although not bad, temper. Now they held a sober, worried and annoyed expression.

'What's up, Di?' Ole Devil inquired.

'That high-toned 'n' fancy von Lowenbrau jasper's got all his fellers together,' the girl answered, throwing a malevolent glare towards the man she had mentioned. 'And, was I asked – which I don't expect to be – I wouldn't count on it being just to tell 'em how his lil pumpkin head's still hurting.'

Glancing in the direction indicated by the girl, Ole Devil stiffened slightly. He had been so engrossed in watching the packer's preparations that he had paid no attention to anything else that was happening. So he had failed to notice that Major Ludwig von Lowenbrau had gathered the men of the Red River Volunteer Dragoons some distance away and was talking to them. Remembering the decision he had reached and implemented the previous afternoon, the captain wondered if the girl had cause for her alarm.

Matching Ole Devil in height, von Lowenbrau was a few

years older and slightly heavier in build. Although there was still a bandage around his close-cropped blond head, he appeared to have thrown off the effects of the injury he had sustained during the fighting. He had been fortunate in that the Hopi's throwing stick had only caught him a glancing blow and stunned him. A direct hit from it would have been fatal.

Despite being attired after the fashion of a successful Mississippi riverboat gambler, except that his footwear was more suited to riding than walking a deck and that he had a sabre hanging from the slings of a well polished waistbelt, von Lowenbrau had an even more militaristic bearing than the young captain. Nor was his conception of discipline tempered by the other's sense of humour. He was handsome in a harsh, Teutonic way, with his moustache's tips waxed to sharp points. He also sported the small duelling scars on his cheeks which some students – particularly those who had attended Heidelberg's University – allowed themselves to be marked by as a sign of belonging to a certain class of society.

He had been an officer in his country's Army before some unspecified trouble had caused him – like Ole Devil – to have 'gone to Texas'.[6] Although he had been two grades lower in rank than that to which he now laid claim, he was trained after the fashion of his race. Competent in military matters, skilled in the use of weapons, authoritative if unimaginative where formal tactics were concerned, his kind were men to be feared, obeyed, but were rarely liked by the soldiers under their command.

That had certainly been the case with von Lowenbrau. He had soon found that his Prussian inspired notions of what soldiering should be had availed him little when tried upon the kind of men who were enlisting in the Red River Volunteer Dragoons. It said much for his prowess as a tough and ruthless hardcase that he had attained the rank of major. In fact, that had been one of his arguments when he had offered to transfer his services from Colonel Frank Johnson to the Texas Light Cavalry. To have joined his superior under the stigma of having

---

[6] 'Gone to Texas': at odds with the law, usually in the United States of America. Many fugitives from justice and wanted men had entered Texas during the colonization period – which had commenced in the early 1820's – and would continue to do so until annexation on February the 16th, 1846. Until the latter became a fact, they had known there was little danger of being arrested and extradited by the local authorities. In fact, like Kenya from the 1920's until the outbreak of World War II, Texas had gained a reputation for being 'a place in the sun for shady people'.

failed to confiscate the consignment would have given his rivals the lever they needed to bring about his demotion.

Although the Prussian had appeared sincere enough when making the proposal, Ole Devil had soon had cause for misgivings. While he had been making his arrangements for meeting yesterday's attack, von Lowenbrau had acted in a manner which might have been constructed as trying to undermine the captain's authority over the Dragoons. Or he could have been – as he had claimed after he had recovered and was congratulating Ole Devil on the successful outcome – merely concerned for the welfare of the men under his command who had been placed in the forefront of the fighting. The declaration had been made in a loud voice, with most of his men close enough to hear it. For all that, nothing in his subsequent behaviour had suggested he might be contemplating a further attempt to carry out the assignment which had brought him to Santa Cristóbal Bay.

So, on the face of it, Ole Devil had only slight reasons for being suspicious. He had left von Lowenbrau in command of the Dragoons, having no authority to do otherwise. In return, the Prussian had placed himself under Ole Devil's orders. Knowing that the captain wanted to set off without delay, he could be ensuring his men were ready. Yet there was something furtive in the way they were acting. Formed into three ragged ranks, they were displaying considerable interest in whatever it was their superior was telling them.

Judging from the surreptitious glances being thrown in his direction, Ole Devil concluded that he could be the topic under discussion. If so, the situation might require delicate handling. There was nothing to be gained by allowing von Lowenbrau to guess that he was arousing suspicions.

'Perhaps he's pointing out what a fine, upstanding figure of a man I am, 'Ole Devil suggested, turning his gaze to the girl. 'And how they should take me as an example and smarten themselves up so they'll be a credit to us when we take them to join the Texas Light Cavalry.'

'Oh sure!' Di snorted derisively. 'And if my Grandmammy Brindley's stood up, 'stead of squatting, when she was having a pee, it'd've been her 'n' not Grandpappy Ewart's took lead back there.'

'I didn't know your grandmother was with us,' Ole Devil remarked and gave the impression that he was going to resume watching Prays Loudly, Sometimes.

34

'God damn it, Fancy Pants!' the girl began, employing a name for him which she had not used since early in their acquaintance. 'That son-of-a-bitch's up—!'

'Pull your horns in, *Miss Charlotte*!' Ole Devil interrupted, his tone causing Di to stop as she was on the point of gesturing towards the subject of their conversation and bringing her full attention back to him.

'What the—?' the girl spluttered.

'I don't claim to be *real* smart like you,' Ole Devil put in, with as much calm as Di was displaying indignation. 'So I can't see what benefit – if any – there'd be in rushing over and saying, "Excuse me, Major von Lowenbrau, sir, we haven't noticed that you might be up to some shennanigans, but if you are, perhaps you'd be good enough to let us in on them."'

Finding that he was no longer the centre of attraction, the Tejas packer was watching and listening. Even though he spoke only a little English, he was aware that Di took very strenuous exception to being addressed by any of her Christian names. That *Diablo Viejo* could do so in such a manner, indeed employing the one she hated most, without her landing her fist in his mouth was, in the opinion of Prays Loudly, Sometimes, further evidence of his capability.

'Ancient Nipponese saying—' commenced Tommy Okasi's polite voice from behind the girl.

'Which you've just made up,' Di groaned, her attitude changing so that she directed a look of mock exasperation at the speaker. 'That's *all* I son-of-a-bitching need right now.'

To give Di her due, despite her quick temper, she was always willing to listen to sound advice when it was given by someone for whom she had respect. The young Texian and the little Oriental rated highly in her estimation. Having already seen that the former was making good sense and did not take the situation as lightly as his first comment suggested, she welcomed the latter's intervention as it allowed her to yield without openly surrendering.

'Woman's place is in home, or *geisha* teahouse,' Tommy continued. 'Not trying to tell men what to do.'

'It's a pity your mammy ever went home,' Di answered.

'She *never* left it,' the little Oriental countered blandly. 'Nipponese woman—'

'What do *you* reckon von Lowenbrau's up to, Devil?' the girl asked, turning her back on Tommy.

'His duty, maybe,' the Texian replied.

35

'Who for?' Di demanded, restraining her impulse to look at the man in question as both her companions were apparently ignoring him.

'There are some who might say the best way to find out is to go over and ask,' Ole Devil stated. 'Shall I do just that, Tommy?'

'Humble self considers it would be best,' the little Oriental agreed.

'Now just you hold hard there for a teensy minute!' Di ordered. 'Leave us not forget's how you've sent off half of your boys to help get Grandpappy Ewart and them other wounded fellers' hurts tended to. Top of that, all of Tom Wolf's scouts didn't go with 'em are standing guard too far off to get back 'n' help us very quick.'

Having questioned the *mozos*[7] of two Mexican officers who had been taken prisoner during the fighting, Ole Devil had learned that the remaining seven companies of the Arizona Hopi *Activos* Regiment were camped about two days' ride to the south awaiting their colonel's return. Which had meant that they would be unable to put in an appearance for some considerable time.

Faced with the possibility of further trouble and dissension between the two outfits, Ole Devil had seen how the information would allow him to prevent it. Selecting the hot-heads from Company 'C', he had sent them under Lieutenant Mannen Blaze to escort the wounded as far as Washington-on-the-Brazos. A protesting Beauregard Rassendyll had been dispatched with the others, along with four of the Tejas Indians who were serving as scouts for the mule train. This had solved one problem. However, even counting the packers, the force at his command and upon which he could certainly depend was now smaller than the Company of Dragoons.

'I haven't forgotten,' Ole Devil said quietly. 'But I was hoping that von Lowenbrau might have.'

[7] *Mozo:* a man servant, particularly one employed in a menial capacity.

CHAPTER FOUR

I'M ASSUMING COMMAND, CAPTAIN HARDIN

MAJOR LUDWIG VON LOWENBRAU scanned the faces of the Red River Volunteer Dragoons' contingent as he addressed them, and sought for signs as to how they were receiving his comments. All in all, their response was about what he had anticipated.

Knowing his subordinates to be typical of the kind of men who had joined Colonel Frank Johnson's enterprise, the Prussian had selected arguments which he believed would appeal to them. Like himself, the majority were hard bitten opportunists and regarded the proposed invasion as a chance to obtain loot while they were with the Republic of Texas's main body. So he reminded them of the wealthy seaports which were their objectives on their march south along the coast road. The rest of the men were similar in nature and attitude to the participant of the previous day's knife fight, who was still resentful over his treatment at Ole Devil Hardin's hands. Fiercely patriotic in a misguided way, made over confident by the Texians' earlier victories, they regarded General Samuel Houston's strategic withdrawal as a cowardly and needless flight.

By playing upon the greed of the opportunists, and the desire for more positive action on behalf of the patriots, von Lowenbrau hoped that he would sway them to his purpose. However, being a fair judge of human nature, he was aware that there could be one major obstacle to achieving control of the consignment. Having anticipated it, he had also taken steps to circumvent it.

'Talking about Hardin – major,' Sergeant Otis remarked, at the conclusion of his superior's reminder that the Dragoons and not the men of the Texas Light Cavalry had been placed in the position of greatest danger during the fighting. 'What'll *he* do when you tell him's you're fixing to take the rifles?'

'*Do !*' von Lowenbrau repeated, scowling at the interruption and its maker's somewhat mocking demeanour. 'What can he do?'

'Could be we'll soon find out,' the non-com declared, before the Prussian could repeat an earlier reminder that he was not only the senior officer present but also had the greater number of men to enforce his orders. 'He's headed this way right now.'

Letting out a short, savage hiss, von Lowenbrau stiffened slightly. For a moment, controlling his anger with an effort, he glared at Otis's surly features. Then he directed a quick glance around at the faces of the other Dragoons, confirming something which he had envisaged from the beginning.

Silently promising himself that he would repay the non-com's disrespectful actions later, the Prussian turned almost as smartly as if he was on a parade ground. He gave the ramrod straight figure who was approaching only a brief look before sweeping the surrounding area with his gaze. From all appearances, Hardin had not attached any special significance to the Dragoons assembling. Standing with her back to the Prussian, Di Brindley was talking to the mule packer Hardin had been watching. Although the little 'Chinaman' was walking away, it was not in the direction of the cavalrymen who were making preparations to move out. Instead, he appeared to be heading for the fire around which the girl, both officers, and he had slept the previous night.

Returning his attention to the Satanic-faced young Texian, von Lowenbrau could find nothing to suggest his motives might have been suspected. Hardin advanced with the somewhat Gasconading swagger which characterized his normal movements. He still had the cloak-coat hanging from his shoulders. Satisfied with what he saw, the Prussian dipped his right hand into his jacket's pocket and it emerged holding a large key.

Although noticing von Lowenbrau's action, Ole Devil was more interested in the men behind him. They had gathered in three closely packed ranks. Every one of them held his rifle, but the weapons were neither in positions of threat nor even readiness. Instead, the Dragoons lounged in attitudes of those awaiting developments.

'Di says her men will be ready to move out in fifteen minutes, major,' Ole Devil announced as he came to a halt about twenty feet in front of the Prussian.

'That's good!' von Lowenbrau replied, tapping the key against his left palm as if doing so was nothing more than a nervous habit. 'I am assuming command, Captain Hardin. You will consider yourself under my orders.'

'I see,' Ole Devil drawled, his eyes on the Prussian's face. 'And what might your orders be?'

'They are those which brought me here,' von Lowenbrau answered, searching the other's face in the hope of learning the thoughts behind it. 'To take the consignment of arms to where they will be most usefully employed.'

'Where would that be?' Ole Devil challenged.

'In the hands of men who are willing and ready to fight against the enemy,' the Prussian stated, pitching his voice so it reached the men to his rear as well as the slim young Texian. 'Not being carried by an Army which is running away and may discard them if pressed too hard.'

'I thought that you'd decided to do your duty to Texas and join General Houston?' Ole Devil remarked, showing no emotion at what had obviously been an insult.

'I might have considered it until I saw how you placed my men's life in jeopardy to save casualties among your own,' von Lowenbrau replied, once again hoping to prod the Texian into a hostile response. 'That is the kind of action which one might expect from an officer who is willing to run instead of stand and fight.'

'With respect, major, I hardly think you're in a position to judge my conduct in action,' Ole Devil countered and his attitude was still one of deadly calm. 'Your injury occurred too early in the action for you to have been able to form any opinion of how I comported myself under fire.'

'That is neither here nor there!' von Lowenbrau barked, glaring in an attempt to stare the Texian down. 'I am taking charge of the consignment!'

There were, as the Prussian appreciated, disadvantages in continuing a discussion on the previous day's attack. He had made the insulting comments with the object of producing a response which would justify the measures he was contemplating. However, the answer he had received could cost him more than he might gain. Despite his reminders of how they had been placed in the forefront of the battle, he knew his men were still impressed by its successful outcome. So he had no wish to let them hear further references about how he had been incapacitated shortly after the commencement of hostilities, while Hardin had taken a prominent part from the beginning to the end.

'On whose authority?' Ole Devil challenged, using tones of icy politeness and meeting the other's eyes without flinching.

'On the authority granted by my commission as a major in the Army of the Republic of Texas,' von Lowenbrau explained, grateful for the opportunity to establish that he had what could be regarded as a legitimate right to make the demand. 'Which makes me your superior in rank. What is more, *Captain* Hardin, as you have seen fit to send off more than half of your Company, my men form the bulk of the escort and that places the responsibility for the consignment's safe delivery on their shoulders.' He paused for a few seconds to let the Dragoons absorb his words and wished he could look back to find out how they were being received. 'You can have a choice, *captain*. Come with us and play a part in carrying the war to the enemy, or take your men and join General Houston in his flight.'

'Leaving the caplocks with you?'

'Of course!'

'You realize that they were purchased by our supporters in the United States to help us establish our right to form an independent republic?'

'I do,' von Lowenbrau admitted. 'And I'm sure that our supporters will want them put to the purpose for which they were intended, used to fight against the enemy and not given to men who are running away. Colonel Johnson—'

'Is acting contrary to General Houston's orders,' Ole Devil interrupted. 'If you wish to continue serving him, that is your affair. But I intend to carry out the duty to which I've been assigned and deliver the consignment.'

'Do you know the consequences of refusing to obey the orders of a lawfully appointed superior whilst on active service?' von Lowenbrau demanded, stepping two militarily smart paces nearer to the Texian and keeping all his attention upon him.

'I do,' Ole Devil admitted, standing as motionless as if he was made of stone.

'You know that you can be shot, without the need for a court martial to pronounce sentence, if you refuse to obey?'

'Yes.'

'Then, Captain Hardin!' the Prussian barked, standing at a rigid brace so that his right hand – holding the bulky key with its oval grip on his palm and its stem between the first and second fingers – was pointing to the ground. 'By the authority granted from my commission as a major of the Republic of Texas, I *order* you to place yourself and the consignment of arms under my command.'

'I refuse,' Ole Devil answered, with no greater show of emotion than if he had been involved in a casual and innocuous conversation.

'Got you!' von Lowenbrau thought exultantly and, without taking his gaze from the Mephistophelian features, he started to raise his right hand.

Considering himself an excellent tactician, the Prussian was delighted at the way he had led his victim into his trap. He had realized from the beginning that talk alone would not gain the Dragoons' support. In fact, he had appreciated that he must deal with the other officer before he could hope to achieve his ends. So he had conceived his strategy accordingly. Killing Hardin would present the Dragoons with a *fait accompli*. They would be even more willing to back him up against the cavalrymen now he had established, at least to their satisfaction, that he had the authority and legal right to carry out the 'execution'.

The means by which von Lowenbrau intended to implement his plan had served him most satisfactorily on four previous occasions. Made by a master firearms' manufacturer in Germany, the device was a refinement on the key-pistols of earlier generations; which had been produced for jailers and others who might require a dual purpose, unsuspected weapon. Designed to operate on the percussion system, it was more compact than its predecessors and was lethal at the distance which separated him from his victim. What was more, as he had not shown it to anybody who was present, he felt sure that he alone appreciated its deadly purpose.

Unfortunately for the Prussian, Ole Devil had come across references to key-pistols in various books about firearms he had read. So he had guessed what the other had in mind when he had seen the device emerging from the pocket. In addition, the trend taken by the conversation had suggested how von Lowenbrau was meaning to kill him. With the safety of the consignment as an added inducement, he had decided how he would counter the attempt.

Just as the Prussian had not been required to produce the disguised weapon during the battle with the Hopis, there had been no cause for Ole Devil to demonstrate a fighting technique which he had developed. Even before he had come to Texas, he had considered that the *defensive* qualities of a pistol were not being fully utilized by the accepted methods of the day. So, after considerable thought and experimentation, he had found a means by which such a weapon could be carried upon the person, then produced and fired with considerable speed.

Realizing that his refusal would present von Lowenbrau with an excuse to use the key-pistol, Ole Devil did not need to watch for it being elevated in his direction. Instead, an instant after he had spoken, he sprang to his left. Simultaneously, his right hand turned palm outwards and enfolded the butt of the Manton pistol. Then, employing similar actions to those which would be used by a later generation of gun fighters when performing a high cavalry-twist draw,[1] he started to slide the barrel from the retaining loop of his belt.

With the key-pistol rising into alignment, the Prussian became aware that his would-be victim was moving aside. Furious over the discovery that he had been over confident, he tried to correct his aim. However, he was unable to halt the pressure he had begun to exert upon the stud on the back of the grip which served as a trigger. There was a sharp crack and a .41 calibre round lead ball passed through the disguised weapon's short barrel.

In spite of having made the correct deductions, Ole Devil had almost left his evasion too late. Von Lowenbrau's ball passed through the material of his cloak-coat beneath the bent right arm as it was turning the muzzle of the Manton outwards. Despite feeling the slight tug, he refused to let himself become flustered by the narrow escape. Already his left hand was crossing to hook over and draw the hammer.

Held at waist level, aimed by instinct and without the need to look along the sights, the pistol bellowed almost as soon as Ole Devil landed from the leap that had saved his life. For all that, guided by the skill acquired through long hours of practice, the heavy bullet flew true. Rising, it entered beneath the Prussian's jaw and retained sufficient power to smash its way out of the top of his skull. Killed instantly, the key-pistol slipped from his grasp. The men behind him jumped hurriedly out of the way as he crashed backwards to the ground.

Startled exclamations burst from the Dragoons. Even when

[1] A detailed description of the later technique for performing the high cavalry-twist draw, the major difference being that the hammer was cocked by the thumb of the hand holding the weapon, is given in: SLIP GUN.

they had seen Ole Devil approaching without showing any signs of suspecting the purpose of their gathering, none of them had expected that he would yield to von Lowenbrau's commands. Nor had they anticipated how the Prussian was meaning to terminate the affair. So the sudden eruption of violence caught them unawares.

'All right, Sergeant Otis,' Ole Devil said, before any of the startled men could recover their wits, as he allowed the smoking pistol to dangle downwards at his side, 'the matter's settled and the consignment is going to General Houston. Have the major buried and be ready to move out as soon as the mules are loaded.'

For all the calm and apparently assured manner in which he was speaking, the Texian was studying the Dragoons' reactions with well concealed anxiety. Like von Lowenbrau, he believed that the enlisted men were content to allow their officers to settle the matter of who was in command between themselves, and would go along with the winner. If he was wrong, the threat to the consignment was still far from ended and the danger to his own life was even greater than when he had confronted the Prussian. Not only had he lost the element of surprise, but he was holding an empty pistol and, if his instructions had been carried out by Di and Tommy, his friends were in no position to come to his aid quickly enough to save him.

Listening to the crisply delivered and seemingly confident orders, the Dragoons' attention ceased to centre around the Texian and his victim. Up to that point, as Ole Devil had hoped, they had been too engrossed in him and the Prussian to watch what the other occupants of the hollow were doing. Although the latter were all looking towards them, none were making any attempt to approach or even draw weapons. In fact, with three exceptions, they began to carry on with their work as if satisfied that the situation was under control.

Even the exceptions were neither displaying concern nor offering to arm themselves. The girl was standing with her hands on her hips, but had moved until she was at the centre of the packers' activities. Although Tommy had collected his bow in passing and had joined Sergeant Smith at the Texas Light Cavalry's horse lines, there was no arrow nocked to its string. Instead, he and the non-com's attitudes conveyed the impression that they considered the trouble was over and that no action on their part would be required.

43

Bringing back his gaze to Ole Devil, Sergeant Otis sucked in a deep breath. Of all his party, he was the most perturbed by the way the situation had developed. Once again he had been singled out and put into a position of responsibility. He did not like the sensation any more than he had on the previous occasion.

Although Otis felt no personal loyalty towards Colonel Johnson, he could see the advantages of carrying out the orders which had caused von Lowenbrau's death. Not only would taking part in the invasion be less dangerous than joining the main body of the Army, but it was certain to be a much more lucrative proposition. Considering the latter point, he knew that promotion would come his way if he delivered the cap-locks, and he felt sure the officers would receive the pick of the loot.

With the major dead, Otis knew that the rest of the Dragoons would follow his lead. So, if he was to make a bid for control of the consignment, the numerical odds were still in his favour. In addition, his companions had weapons more readily available than those of the cavalrymen. All he had to do was give the order—

And contend with Captain Hardin's opposition to accepting it.

That, the burly non-com warned himself, was the main snag in attempting to take over von Lowenbrau's assignment. He remembered all too well how the young captain had circumvented other schemes to acquire the caplocks.

Despite Hardin clearly having suspected treachery, the cavalrymen and the Tejas packers were not making any preparations to defend the consignment. He would not have overlooked such a basic precaution unless he had organized some other means of protecting it.

What if, having mistrusted the Prussian's offer to accompany him, Hardin had only pretended to send half of his men away?

Were the absent party waiting on the rim, ready to take action if the need arose?

Or had Hardin something else in mind?

Watching the sergeant's surly face, which was more expressive than von Lowenbrau's had been, Ole Devil could read his indecision. In spite of it, the Texian's gamble was far from being won. Guessing that the Prussian would have tried to stir up rivalry between the Dragoons and his own men, he had told Di and Tommy to prevent the latter from making anything

44

which might be interpreted as a hostile gesture. Concentrating upon Otis, he could not look around and find out if he had kept the conversation with von Lowenbrau going for long enough to let them pass on his instructions. However, if the Dragoons' lack of activity was any guide, the girl and the little Oriental had succeeded. Which meant his men were not holding weapons, whereas the Dragoons had rifles in their hands.

Everything depended upon Otis. If he accepted Ole Devil's orders, his companions would do the same.

A good thirty seconds went by in silence and, although nothing showed on his features, Ole Devil appreciated the problem which was confronting him. The longer the delay, the greater the risk that the sergeant would conclude he had too much in his favour to yield. Yet to try and force the issue before Otis had reached a decision might make him fight out of stubbornness.

'We don't have all day, sergeant!' Ole Devil stated, knowing that a continued hesitation on his part could be construed as a sign of weakness. 'I'd be obliged if you'll put your men to work.'

While speaking, the Texian was alert for Otis's first warning flicker of expression. He was ready to drop the empty pistol and draw the bowie knife as swiftly as possible, but hoped the need to do so would not arise. If it did, the affair was likely – in fact, would almost certainly – erupt into a clash between the two factions.

There was an interruption before Otis could make his choice.

'Riders coming down, Cap'n Hardin!' Sergeant Smith called.

With a sensation of relief, Otis watched the coldly Satanic features – which had been holding his eyes like iron filings drawn to a magnet – turn away. Looking in the direction indicated by Smith, he let out a startled exclamation. The three men who were approaching along the path from the rim were acquaintances and showed signs of having pushed their horses very hard. One of them was his predecessor as sergeant who had been driven away by Ole Devil during von Lowenbrau's first abortive attempt to take possession of the consignment. It was unlikely that he would have dared to return unless confident that it was safe for him to do so.

'What do you make of them, Sergeant Otis?' Ole Devil inquired, having matched the other's identification and summation.

45

'They belong to our outfit – sir,' the non-com answered, continuing to study the trio as they came closer, and drawing a conclusion from their attitudes which suggested he might be advised to use the honorific.

'Hey, fellers!' yelled the former sergeant, before any more could be said. 'The Mexican Army's jumped Colonel Johnson down at San Patricio. They've wiped him 'n' all his men out.'

CHAPTER FIVE

HELL, WE CAN DO WITHOUT YOU

'IT's this way, Cap'n,' Sergeant Otis said hesitantly, throwing a glance over his shoulder as if to ensure that the rest of the Red River Volunteer Dragoons' contingent were still standing behind him. 'Most of these fellers've got homes down San Patricio way and they're worried about their families.'

'That's to be expected,' Ole Devil Hardin replied in a non-committal tone.

Knowing the request he was going to make, and having learned the nature of the man to whom it would be addressed, the burly non-com sought for some indication of how his words were being received. He met with little success. Standing ramrod straight, legs apart and hands behind his back, the young officer's Satanic features revealed nothing of his thoughts.

For all his impassive exterior, Ole Devil had a very good idea of what was coming. Over the past few minutes, despite having been occupied in another matter, he had noticed certain things which had helped him to draw his conclusions.

Although the news which was received too late to save Major Ludwig von Lowenbrau from death had removed the most immediate threat to Ole Devil's mission, he would have preferred it to have been delivered in a more discreet fashion. Not unexpectedly, learning of their companions' misfortunes had had a disturbing and demoralizing effect upon the Dragoons and he had appreciated that, far from removing the problems with which he was faced, the tiding had added to them.

Passing on the information to Diamond-Hitch Brindley, Tommy Okasi and Sergeant Smith, Ole Devil had sent them to continue with the preparations for moving out. Then he had given his attention to the newcomers. The presence of a second Mexican column north of the Rio Grande, particularly as it was coming from an unanticipated quarter, could pose a very

47

serious threat to Major General Samuel Houston's policy of withdrawal. So Ole Devil wanted to have a better understanding of the situation before he took any action.

Unfortunately, in spite of having subjected the two Dragoons to a lengthy questioning, Ole Devil had not improved his knowledge of what had happened at San Patricio to any great extent. It had soon become apparent that the pair had thought only of saving their own skins. Neither had been able to say which, or even how many, Mexican regiments had been employed to defeat Colonel Frank Johnson's command. Even the number of attackers they had claimed to be involved had struck him as being wildly exaggerated. What was more, unless he was mistaken, their arrival at Santa Cristóbal Bay had come about more through a chance meeting with Otis's predecessor than from a desire to do their duty by delivering a warning. About the only positive information they could give was that, to the best of their knowledge, they had not been pursued in their flight.

Throughout the interrogation, Ole Devil had been aware that the other Dragoons were not making ready to leave. Instead, they had gathered around Otis and his predecessor, talking volubly and quietly with many glances at him. Nor had he been surprised when, having dismissed the survivors, the non-com had approached him displaying a somewhat apprehensive demeanour.

'Then you'll likely see's how we don't feel it'd be right for us to go heading off away from 'em when they're going to be in danger,' Otis went on, wishing that the other's cold black eyes would look away from him. 'It's— Well— We— They're—!'

'Get to the point, sergeant,' Ole Devil requested, giving no indication that he knew what it would be. 'There's still plenty to be done before we can pull out.'

'Th – that's what I want to talk to you about, sir,' Otis replied, shuffling his feet and dropping his gaze to the ground. 'Us fellers— Well, we're all of a mind to go back and take care of our families. All of us feel tolerable strong about it – sir. So, happen it's all right with you—?'

'Very well, sergeant,' Ole Devil drawled, when the non-com's words trailed to a halt. Apparently paying no attention to the group of Dragoons who hovered with sullenly menacing attitudes in the background, he continued, 'You can go!'

'It's not that we wan—!' Otis began, before an understanding of how his request had been treated sank in. 'Huh?'

48

'I said that you can go back, instead of coming with us,' Ole Devil explained. 'There's only one thing I'd like you to do for me. Wait until after we've gone, bury Major von Lowenbrau and make sure that we haven't left anything down here that would tell the Mexicans what we've been doing.'

'Sure thing, Cap'n!' Otis replied, so relieved at having received permission to leave the escort duty that he gave the agreement without hesitation. A quicker thinker might have wondered why the request had been made. The boxes in which the caplocks were delivered had been burned and the Mexicans already knew they had arrived. 'We'll tend to everything here for you. I'm right sorry to be leaving you short handed this ways, but—'

'Don't let *that* bother you, sergeant,' Ole Devil interrupted. 'I told Mr. Blaze to come back as soon as they'd seen the wounded safely across the San Berhard River. They'll be meeting us before we've gone much more than a mile.'

'I'm right pleased to hear it, Cap'n,' Otis declared, having suspected that such an arrangement had been made and believing the second party of the Texas Light Cavalry were even closer so as to help deal with any treachery his late superior had been contemplating. 'Looks like you won't have any trouble getting them caplocks to General Houston even with us gone.'

'*You* can count on it that we won't, sergeant,' Ole Devil stated, with an air of grimly determined finality. 'And I hope that you all find your families safe when you reach San Patricio.'

With that, the young officer strode past the Dragoons. For all the notice he took of them, they might not have existed. Showing relief, mingled with puzzlement, Otis swung around and watched him go.

'What'd he say?' demanded the former sergeant, as his replacement walked up.

'We can go,' Otis replied.

'I told you he wouldn't dare try to stop us,' scoffed the former non-com.

'I wouldn't want to count on it,' Otis warned. 'He wants us to stay on, bury von Lowenbrau and clean up after the mule train's pulled out and I said's we would.'

'Why should we?' protested one of the Dragoons.

'Because that's what *he* wants and I don't figure to rile him by saying "no",' Otis answered, scowling at his companions. 'Like I warned you, the rest of his Company's close enough by

49

to take cards real fast should they be needed. So we're staying down here until after they've gone well out of sight and won't find out which way we're really heading.'

'Aw hell!' objected Wilkie, fingering the hilt of his knife sulkily. 'This don't set right with me. We ain't doing nothing to pay them greasers back for what happened to the rest of our boys.'

'It might not set right to some, but it makes right good sense to me,' growled the taller of the survivors. 'I know what happened down to San Patricio. Them greasers who wiped out our fellers'll be headed up here foot, hoss 'n' artillery. 'Twixt them and Santa Anna, we don't stand a snowball in hell's chance. The only way out's to head for the good ole U.S. of A. afore we gets caught in the middle.'

'Thing being,' put in another of the original Dragoons' Company, 'I'm like you 'n' most of the others, Wilkie, got folks up along the Red. So I aims to see 'em safe instead of trying to get evens for somebody's already dead, 'specially when there ain't enough of us to do nothing should we try.'

'All right then,' Otis put in, after a rumble of agreement had died down. 'We're headed north. Only, seeing's how we've got Hardin fooled, let's keep him that way by doing what he's asked. Hell, we can rest up until noon at least and still be on our way afore there's any chance of the greasers catching up with us.'

Sharing the non-com's opinion of how dangerous the Mephistophelian-faced young officer could be when roused or crossed, the rest of the Dragoons were willing to accept his suggestions. They all felt that their flight would be much easier to accomplish now they had tricked Ole Devil Hardin over their true purpose for leaving the mule train.

If the Dragoons had overheard the conversation which took place between the Texian when he had joined Di Brindley and Tommy Okasi, they would have discovered that they had been far from successful in their deception.

Crossing to where Di was talking to Tommy, Ole Devil noticed with satisfaction that the various preparations for departure were progressing. His men and the mule packers had been interested in the newcomers, but Sergeant Smith and Joe Galton had not let them be diverted from their respective tasks.

For her part, the girl had watched the interview between Ole Devil and Otis. She also noticed that, although it had ended, the latter and his men were still standing in a group. However, her main attention was upon the young Texian. During the time they had been together and shared a number of dangers, she had learned a lot about him. Sufficient for her to wonder why he was allowing the Dragoons to behave in such a manner instead of insisting that they got on with their work.

'Likely it's none of my never-mind,' Di remarked, as Ole Devil joined her. 'But happen those butt-trailing yahoos don't right soon start to saddling up, they'll not be ready to move out with us.'

'It doesn't matter if they aren't,' the Texian answered, with no more emotion than he had shown while talking to Otis. 'We're leaving them here.'

'Huh!' the girl snorted, and the glance she directed at the Dragoons showed anything but faith in their abilities. 'I can't say's it makes me feel a whole heap safer knowing it's them's'll be 'tween us and any Mexicans's're coming.'

'I wouldn't let *that* worry you,' Ole Devil replied. 'They won't be. Sergeant Otis told me that they're all so worried about the folks they've left behind that they're heading down to San Patricio to effect a rescue. So I wished them the best of luck with it and said they could go.'

'You *believed* them?' Di yelped.

'If you must know,' Ole Devil said calmly, 'I didn't.'

'Then why in hell—?' the girl spluttered.

'Because, with the mood they're in, they'd desert *en masse* if I'd said they couldn't go,' Ole Devil explained, seeming to grow calmer as Di's indignation increased. 'And I've neither the time nor the inclination to stop them, even if it could be done. The frame of mind they're in, we couldn't count on them to stand by us if the Mexicans catch up with the train.'

'You could be right at that,' the girl conceded, considering the alarm being shown by the Dragoons. Then she glared at Tommy, who was clearly about to speak, warning, 'And I don't want any of them son-of-a-bitching wise old whatever they are sayings that you've just made up from *you.*'

'Humble self was only going to point out how, when danger threatens, it is wiser to depend upon a few warriors who are steadfast than to have many who will run at the sight of the enemy,' the little Oriental commented, exuding patience and forebearance. 'Fear is like a contagious sickness. It goes from one who has it to those who have not and infects them.'

'Them's a right fancy heap of words to say nothing,' the girl sniffed with well simulated disdain, although she had

51

understood and agreed with all Tommy had said. However, having no intention of admitting that she did, she returned her attention to the third member of their group. 'Just how bad are things down to San Patricio?'

'I wish I knew for sure,' Ole Devil answered and something in his voice confirmed Di's suspicions that he regarded the news as exceedingly grave. 'According to the two men who came here, all of Johnson's command have gone under except for themselves.'

'That being the case, we'd best send off word to General Sam,' the girl suggested, despite feeling certain the point had already occurred to her companion. 'If all of 'em have been made wolf-bait, neither him nor Fannin's boys over to Goliad'll have heard what's happened.'

'Sending a message based on the little I've learned could do more harm than good,' Ole Devil said quietly, but still giving Di an inkling of the problem with which he was faced. 'I might be doing those two an injustice, but I think they ran away from San Patricio before the fighting was over. Things might not be as bad as they've made out.'

'You mean that Johnson's bunch could've fought off the Mexicans after they'd run away?' Di asked.

'It's a possibility,' Ole Devil replied. 'And even if they were beaten, those two might not be the only survivors. In which case, somebody could already have taken the news to Goliad.'

'Somebody *might* have,' Di admitted, instinctively appreciating the misgivings which were plaguing the Texian. 'Only, from what I've seen of Johnson's bunch so far, I'd sooner bet's anybody who got clear'd be running north as fast as they could rather than was headed to where the Mexicans'd be likely to go next.'

'That's the problem,' Ole Devil conceded. 'But, if I send word based on just what those two told me, there'll be some in the garrison at Goliad and with the General who won't wait to learn how serious the situation might be.'

'There's some's won't, happen the way those Red River yahoos've let it spook 'em is anything to go on,' the girl admitted, favouring the Dragoons with a disgusted look. 'And once a few start pulling out, more'll follow. Couldn't you send word to General Sam and make sure that nobody but him gets it?'

'I could try, but doing it wouldn't be advisable,' Ole Devil answered. 'The effect would be a whole lot worse if it slipped out. That's why I'm going to tell my men all I know before we set off.'

Such was the faith that Di had developed where Ole Devil was concerned, it had never occurred to her to wonder how the members of the Texas Light Cavalry who were present might be affected by the news from Goliad and the Dragoons' behaviour. On the other hand, she could imagine how the tidings would be received by Houston's retreating army and the garrison under Colonel James W. Fannin's indecisive command at Goliad. Morale was already low, and finding themselves threatened with encirclement by the Mexicans might prove the breaking point.

Swinging her gaze in the cavalrymen's direction, the girl saw that they were talking among themselves and pointing at the Dragoons. However, for all their interest, they had not allowed it to impede them in the work of saddling the horses ready to move out with the mule train. Nor were any of them offering to go over and satisfy their curiosity by questioning members of the other outfit.

'I'd say's how you don't need to worry about them,' Di stated. 'And, to a half smart lil country girl like me, seems like the easiest way to find out what's happened at San Patricio'd be send somebody to take a look.'

'Some such idea had crossed my mind,' Ole Devil admitted.

'Only you're not sure who to send,' the girl went on.

'I'm not.'

'Sergeant Smith's a pretty smart *hombre*.'

'He's also married with a young family, and there's no safe way of gathering the kind of information that's needed.'

'On top of which, you figure that *you're* the one who's best suited to get it,' Di went on, once again making a shrewd guess at the Texian's thoughts. 'And, much as I hate to have to say it, you're right. Only you've got these caplocks on your hands.'

'I have.'

'And even if somebody from Johnson's crowd's was took prisoner and trying to save his skin hasn't told about 'em, them Hopis will have?'

'It's possible.'

'Well, knowing's the Hopis're already after 'em, they'll not be likely to send anybody else, will they?' Di went on, before Ole Devil could finish his comment.

'Probably not,' the Texian answered. 'Except that they mightn't know the Hopis are after us.'

'Why wouldn't they know?' Di challenged.

'According to the *mozos*, the Hopis came from the west,' Ole Devil explained. 'Nothing they said suggested they knew there were any other Mexican troops nearer than Santa Anna's army. If so, they don't belong to the column which took San Patricio.'

'Then them fellers's whupped Johnson's bunch could figure they're the only Mexicans hereabouts,' Di remarked. 'And they're likely to send somebody to take the caplocks from us.'

'It's more than likely,' Ole Devil declared. 'They're a tempting prize.'

'And if they send,' the girl continued, more in a statement than a question. 'They'll use enough men to make sure of taking 'em and getting 'em back.'

'It's not likely they'll send less than half a regiment of cavalry,' Ole Devil admitted.

'Well then,' Di said, with the air of having reached a decisive point. 'I don't see's how we're all that much worse off. With that many, same's with the Hopis, we've a good head start and we'll be heading away from them near on's fast as they can move.'

'That's true,' Ole Devil concurred.

'Then it'll be three days, at the very least, afore they could catch up with us,' the girl declared. 'And by then, we'll be close enough to Thompson's Ferry to count on getting enough help to stand 'em off. So, way I see it, there's nothing to stop you 'n' Tommy heading down towards San Patricio and finding out for yourselves what's happening. Hell, we don't need you pair along to hold our hands and you won't rest easy until you know.'

'I wish it was that easy, Di,' Ole Devil said. 'But there are more than just the Mexicans and the Hopis for us to consider.'

'You mean *that* bunch?' Di snorted, indicating the Dragoons with a contempt-filled jerk of a thumb. 'Huh! You've got the Injun sign on them—'

'Only I won't be along to make sure it stays on,' Ole Devil countered. 'And they still have us outnumbered.'

'Why not just tell 'em straight that we'll start shooting without waiting to find who-all's coming happen anybody comes once we're on our way?' the girl asked.

'If I did, they'd know I didn't believe they meant to go south,' Ole Devil replied. 'And one lesson I learned real early

54

was never to give a horse, dog or man cause to think I was scared of him. Which is how they'd regard it and that could give them bad ideas. No, Di. It's not them I'm worrying over. They'll be too busy running for safety to trouble us. But there're the folks at San Phillipe. If they learn how small an escort is left—'

Although the replacement for the dead bell-mare had been obtained in the small sea port of San Phillipe, Di knew why Ole Devil had misgivings. The population were notorious as unscrupulous cut-throats, some of whom would be only to willing to snap up such valuable loot as the consignment.

'You know something, Devil,' the girl said quietly, with a mischievous grin. 'After the news they're going to get, I don't reckon's they'll cause us any fuss.'

'Which news ?'

'Well now,' Di answered, contriving to give off an aura of innocence. 'I've just got me a feeling that they're going to get told the same's we've heard about what happened at San Patricio— Except that they'll hear's how the Mexicans's whupped Johnson're already headed north along the coast trail. And, once they've been told that, I'm game to bet that the only thing's'll get them away from the boats' there'd be to put all they own in a wagon and head for the U.S. line like the devil after a yearling.'

'Would it be too much to ask who is going to do this "telling" ?' Ole Devil inquired, hearing Tommy giving a delighted chuckle.

'Tom Wolf,' Di answered, naming the chief of her Tejas employees. 'And everybody *knows*'s Injuns don't *never* tell lies. Which it's sure lucky ole Tom's been round us white folks long enough to've learned how.'

'Around *you* white folks,' Ole Devil corrected. 'I don't want to be blamed for corrupting him.'

Despite the light way in which he had just spoken, the Texian was all too aware that he was in a very difficult position. He was torn between two conflicting duties; the one to which he had been assigned by his Commanding General, and that of an officer in a light cavalry regiment, a major task of which was the gathering of military information. The situation at San Patricio called for investigation by somebody who was capable of assessing its full potential and, without being immodest, he knew that he was the man best suited to carry out the task. However, the safe delivery of the caplocks and ammunition

55

could make the difference between victory and defeat when Houston made his stand. As in the previous case, he knew that he was the man best suited to ensure the consignment reached its destination.

So Ole Devil had to decide what to do.

And the decision must be correct!

Either way, the future of the Republic of Texas might depend upon it!

CHAPTER SIX

IT DON'T PAY TO LAG BEHIND

'WE'RE all ready to go, happen you are, Devil,' Diamond-Hitch Brindley announced, riding up as the young Texian was walking away from the Red River Volunteer Dragoons after having taken part in an impromptu funeral service for Major Ludwig von Lowenbrau.

'So are we, Di,' Ole Devil Hardin replied, neither his tone nor expression supplying any hint as to how he was feeling with regard to the line of action to which he had committed himself. Raising his voice, he called, 'Mount the Company, Sergeant Smith.'

'Yo!' the non-com answered and gave the requisite order.

Darting a glance filled with disgust at the men who were gathered around the grave, Di needed all her self control to hold back the comments she felt bubbling inside her. None of the men met her scornful gaze and, remembering Ole Devil's desire to avoid letting them know that their true purpose was suspected, she turned her horse away without addressing them.

'All right, Joe!' the girl yelled, keeping pace with the Satanic-featured Texian and waving a hand to the *cargador*. 'I've got the soldier-boys woke up. Now you can start *our* knob-heads moving.'

Turning her gaze to the ramrod straight figure striding alongside her, Di found he was watching what was going on around him. Although she noticed that his attention was directed towards the activities of her men rather than his own she felt no resentment. She knew why he was taking such interest.

Fortunately for Ole Devil, in the course of his far from uneventful young life he had cultivated a fatalistic outlook. When faced with problems, even the most demanding upon which important issues might depend, he had learned to give them careful consideration before taking action. However, once having reached a decision and taken whatever precautions he believed would contribute to success – making the fullest use of such resources as he had available – he was aware of the danger of indulging in self-doubt. And he did his best to avoid fretting over the consequences if it was proved that his judgment had been at fault. He had always been helped in this by being blessed with an inquiring mind, which would never cease trying to add to its fund of knowledge, and he could generally find something of interest to help divert his attention from whatever cares might be assailing him.

So, having planned how to cope with his current difficulties, the young Texian was finding that travelling with the Brindleys' mule train was proving to be something of a blessing. While fully cognizant of how vitally important it was for him to ensure that the consignment did not fall into the wrong hands, at the same time the means by which it was being transported served to prevent him from being plagued by concern over the various perturbing aspects arising from the decision he had taken. He believed that he was acting in the most suitable manner, but he also realized that he was relying upon insufficient and possibly inaccurate information.

Like every officer carrying out an independent assignment in the days before the invention of rapid means of communication – such as, for example, the radio – Ole Devil appreciated that he was out of touch with the current situation elsewhere.[1] So he was compelled to rely upon his own initiative and summations based upon the last known state of affairs.

When Ole Devil had set off with orders to collect and deliver the consignment, the main body of the Republic of Texas's Army had been about to fall back to the town of Gonzales on the Guadalupe River. However, as *Presidente* Antonio Lopez de Santa Anna had already crossed the Rio Grande, a detachment of one hundred and eighty-two volunteers under the joint command of Colonels William Barrett Travis, James Bowie and David 'Davey' Crockett had insisted

[1] A classic example of the effect of slow communications occurred during the final stages of the American Civil War. The last engagement, ironically won by a unit of the Confederate States' Army under the command of Colonel John Salmon 'Rip' Ford, took place at Palmitto Hill, about fifteen miles east of Brownsville, Cameron County, Texas, on May the 13th, 1865; more than a month *after* the surrender of General Robert E. Lee at the Appamattox Courthouse in Virginia – on April the 9th – should have brought an end to military hostilities.

upon staying in the Alamo Mission at San Antonio de Bexar. It was their intention to try and delay *el Presidente* for long enough to allow Major General Samuel Houston to consolidate the rest of the Texians' forces. They were to be reinforced by some of the four hundred well armed and equipped men, under the command of Colonel James Walker Fannin, occupying Fort Defiance at Goliad.

Although that was practically the sum of Ole Devil's knowledge, he was working on the assumption that no news from the main body was good news. He felt sure that, if some major catastrophe had befallen them, General Houston would have found a way of notifying him so that he could dispose of the consignment and prevent embarrassment to their supporters in the United States. For all that, the information which had arrived from San Patricio was adding a new dimension to his problems and he had taken it into account when selecting his future movements.

While approving of Di's suggestion for reducing the possibility of trouble from the less scrupulous citizens of San Phillipe, Ole Devil had also been aware that in all probability any attempt they might be contemplating would already have been set into motion. In addition, after having been deprived of the chance of loot from other sources, the surviving members of Colonel Frank Johnson's ill-fated command might try to compensate themselves by gaining possession of at least some of the valuable caplock rifles and ammunition.

Without being egotistical, the Texian had appreciated that he had established a very healthy respect for himself among the members of both factions. His presence with the mule train was likely to serve as a strong deterrent to any plans they might be considering. In the event of an attack by either group, his planning ability and guidance would do much to offset whatever disparity in numbers there was between his party and the attackers.

Taking everything into account, Ole Devil was inclined to regard the enemy as being the least pressing factor as far as the protection of the consignment was concerned. Di had made a sound point when stating that the mules could, even if unable to outrun any pursuers, at least make the chase such a lengthy affair that there would be a good chance of them reaching an area in which reinforcements could be obtained before they were overtaken.

Against that, the Texian was faced with the problem of

finding out exactly what had happened at San Patricio, and learning everything possible about the strength and intentions of the second column. On thinking about it, he concluded that there might not be any extreme urgency for an investigation. From what he had seen of Mexicans, and Di – whose knowledge of them was even more extensive – had agreed, he doubted whether the victors could resist celebrating their success over Johnson's command. In which case, they were unlikely to take any further military action until the festivities were at an end. Even then, their soundest tactics – and probably their orders – would be to move westwards and, having dealt with the garrison at Fort Defiance, try to trap the main body of Houston's Army between themselves and Santa Anna's force.

In that case, unless the second column sent a detachment north in the hope of snapping up such a tempting prize, they did not pose too great a threat to the consignment. Nor, even if there were no other survivors from the fighting at San Patricio, were they likely to catch the garrison at Fort Defiance unawares. Fannin might not be an efficient and energetic commanding officer, but his instinct for self-preservation was such that he would have patrols operating in his immediate vicinity. Even if he did not, he had officers serving with him – such as Captain James Butler Bonham[2] – who would ensure that such a basic military precaution was carried out.

Despite his conclusion, Ole Devil had known he would have no peace of mind until he had personally reviewed the situation. So he had reached what he regarded as a satisfactory compromise to deal with his dilemma. He would accompany the mule train as far as the San Berhard River, beyond which he had felt sure there would be no danger from either the Dragoons or the citizens of San Phillipe. Then, providing nothing else had come up, he and Tommy Okasi would return and carry out a reconnaissance in the direction of San Patricio.

Once Ole Devil had made up his mind, he informed his companions of his decision. Then, while the packers were completing the preparations for departure, he told his men about the news from San Patricio and that the Dragoons would no longer be accompanying them. As he had anticipated, the men

[2] After failing to persuade Colonel Fannin to reinforce the Alamo Mission and, penetrating the surrounding Mexican lines, delivering a warning that no help would be forthcoming, Captain James Butler Bonham (1807–1836) elected to remain and perished with the other defenders on March the 6th.

of the Texas Light Cavalry were not distressed to learn of
Johnson's downfall. Nor were they perturbed to discover that
the size of the escort would be drastically reduced. Their view
was that the Dragoons would be no great loss. Although none
of them had mentioned it, he could tell that they were sharing
his own suspicions over the reason Sergeant Otis had given for
leaving.

Having had a grave dug, Otis had requested that Ole Devil
perform the burial service over the dead Prussian. Wanting to
convince the Dragoons that he had no doubts about them, the
young officer agreed. With that task completed and having
nothing further demanding his immediate attention, he was
looking forward with eager anticipation to the commencement
of the journey. Not only did he want to have the consignment
on the move, he wished to learn more about the way in which
the mule train was handled.

In the past when Ole Devil had had occasion to make use of
pack animals, they had always been horses. Mostly he had
employed them singly and he had never had more than half a
dozen to contend with.

When conditions called for a number of horses to be used,
they could be led individually or, providing they were trained
for the work and traversing a good trail which had few ob-
structions such as fallen trees or deep streams, fastened one behind the other. The latter arrangement was carried out by
either securing the lead rope to the 'back buck' of the pack
saddle of the horse in front, or by 'tailing' them in line. Whichever method was selected, each led animal had to be far enough
behind the horse it was following so that it could not be kicked,
but sufficiently close to prevent it from stepping over a dangling
lead rope and becoming entangled. This limited the number of
of animals which could be coupled up to form a string and it
was inadvisable to secure more than four together.

Where possible, 'tailing' was the more satisfactory method.
This was carried out by having half-hitched a metal ring to the
preceding horse's tail, the next in line's lead rope was attached
to it by a short length of $\frac{1}{4}$-inch cord, or a double thickness of
hay-bale twine; either of which would break easily in an emergency. On the other hand, wherein lay 'tailing's' main advantage, if something happened to startle a horse which was
being led by the 'back buck', its struggles might snatch off its
predecessor's saddle, or even bring them both down.

Effective as leading by the 'back buck' or tailing method

might be when dealing with no more than a handful of horses, Ole Devil realized that neither method was feasible when travelling with the large number of animals required to transport the consignment. However, as Di had explained, over the centuries packers had learned to take advantage of a peculiar trait in the nature of the creatures which they had found most suitable for their purposes.

Despite being hybrids – produced by crossing a male donkey with a female horse[3] – which meant that they were rarely able to procreate and never produced fertile offspring on the rare occasions when they succeeded, mules tended to find the company of a mare irresistible. Packers had discovered that, recalcitrant though they might be in some circumstances, they would follow a female horse all day without the need to be led or 'tailed'. Furthermore, when a bell was carried by the mare, its sound apparently produced a soothing effect upon them. In fact, under its comforting influence, they were content to remain close to her through the hours of darkness while on a journey without requiring to be hobbled or secured in any other fashion.

On receiving Di's order, Joe Galton set about utilizing the mules' obsession with the opposite sex. Starting his mount moving, a gentle tug on the hackamore's lead rope caused the horse which was fastened to his saddlehorn to accompany him as he rode towards the slope.

The replacement which had been obtained by Di, Ole Devil and Tommy – at some considerable risk to themselves[4] – was a much finer looking animal than the Brindleys's original bell-mare. However, appearances and physical conformation were not of great importance in the performance of her duties. Her predecessor had been a most unprepossessing creature, unsuitable for either comfortable riding or even the lightest draught work; but this had never detracted from her worth as an essential part of the mule train. When on the move, her only burden had been the hackamore by which she was led and the bell that was suspended from the leather collar around her

[3] The result of a cross between a horse stallion and a female donkey is called a 'hinny'. Always smaller than a mule, the hinny bears an even closer resemblance to its dam. Inheriting the donkey's obstinate disposition to an even greater degree, which combines with its smaller size to make it a less useful beast of burden, the hinny has never been bred to the same extent as have mules.

[4] The events referred to are related in: OLE DEVIL AND THE CAP-LOCKS.

neck. Fortunately, the new animal was of a placid disposition and did not raise any objection to having the clonking of the bell's clapper so close to her. In fact, she had already settled down to her duties in a satisfactory manner.

Hearing the mare's bell and having learned by long experience what to expect when the heavy loads had been placed in position, the majority of the mules began walking after the departing mare. One of the exceptions, a mean looking, washy brown animal bearing the number '28' on its *corona* continued to stand as if engrossed in deepest meditation not far from where Ole Devil was passing. Wanting to find out what would happen, he came to a halt and watched. It was one of Prays Loudly, Sometimes's string and the packer had clearly anticipated something of the sort would take place. Setting his riding mule into motion, he guided it behind the stationary beast. Swinging the doubled-over length of rope he was now carrying, he delivered a couple of hearty whacks to 'Twenty-Eight's' rump and accompanied them with a couple of loudly spoken Anglo-Saxon 'cuss-words'. Giving a snort and shake of its head, but showing neither alarm nor resentment over such treatment, the mule started to amble after its companions.

Looking around, Ole Devil found that some of the other packers were engaged in encouraging such of their charges as were displaying a similar tardiness over joining the march. Not all of the laggards needed blows to stimulate a willingness to co-operate. A few responded to verbal abuse, either in Tejas or with English vilifications picked up by the user without his having troubled to learn more of the language. The means of physical inducement varied between those who shared Prays Loudly, Sometimes' faith in a length of rope, to those who favoured a bare-handed slap or a kick. However, the Texian noticed that the target was invariably either the rump or the ribs. Nor, he also observed, was any punishment given unless it was warranted and in every case four blows at the most, backed where necessary by a volley of obscene threats, were required to produce the desired result.

'It looks like most of them are as eager as I am to be getting under way,' Ole Devil remarked, glancing up at Di as she lounged on the saddle of her big bay gelding by his side.

'Shucks,' the girl replied, without interrupting her examination of the way things were progressing. 'They all know it don't pay to lag behind so's they'd have to run afore they catch up. Only, way some mules act, you've got to sort of jog their

63

memories afore they remember it. Grandpappy Ewart allus allows it's them long ears's makes 'em go a touch absent-minded now and then.'

For all the Texian's lack of practical experience at packing, by studying the departing animals he could guess why it was essential to prevent any of them from being left too far behind at the start of the march. Once they had commenced moving, the mules adopted an ambling 'fox trot' gait which allowed them to travel without unduly rocking their loads. Any other pace, whether a fast walk, a jogging trot, or running, would transmit a troublesome motion to the packs.

'I'll say one thing, they weren't any trouble to get moving,' Ole Devil commented, recollecting all the stories he had heard about the awkward, stubborn and unco-operative natures of the species *mulus*. 'I've always been told that the only treatment a mule understood was with a firm hand and that the hand should be used to take a grip on a good stout club.'

'Not all of 'em,' Di contradicted, looking at the Texian. 'Mules're like people. Some you can ask polite and they'll do it, others you need to whomp a mite afore they'll oblige. Only, happen you have to work with a club, wham his butt end and not over his head. Mules ain't like you menfolks, you can hurt 'em bad and do damage by whomping 'em between the ears.'

'My Grandfather Baines always told me that the only time a gentleman should strike a woman is when she's not wearing corsets,' Ole Devil stated, as if imparting very important information, meeting the girl's challenging gaze without flinching.

'Why?' Di asked, before she could stop herself.

'It's dangerous to kick her in the stomach when she is,' the Texian replied, his demeanour implying that the girl should remember the advice. 'He claimed that the one time he forgot and did it, he broke his big toe.'

'It's a son-of-a-bitching pity he didn't break his fool neck *afore* he met your Grandmammy Baines!' Di snorted. Then, noticing Tommy approaching with Ole Devil's line-backed dun gelding, she pulled a wry face and went on, 'I'm going afore *he* gets to spouting some more of them son-of-a-bitching wise old what in hell he calls 'em sayings. *Some* folks around here've got better things to do than just standing jawing about nothing 'n' looking pretty.'

'Well,' Ole Devil drawled, as the girl started to rein her

mount around. 'That's one thing nobody could accuse *you* of doing.'

'That's for su—!' Di commenced, but a sudden realization of how the comment had been worded caused her to bring the bay to a halt and glare at the speaker. 'Just which son-of-a-bitch of 'em did you mean?'

'I'll leave *that* for *you* to decide,' Ole Devil replied, his attitude conveying a belief that the matter was beneath his attention. He strolled over to meet the little Oriental.

A smile came to the Texian's lips as he listened to the profane prediction which followed him about his most likely future. The light hearted exchange of banter had helped divert both Di's and his thoughts from their problems. That was useful. In spite of believing that he was carrying out his duties in the best possible manner, he could not help feeling disturbed by the way he would be doing it.

Knowing how anxious the girl was over her grandfather's well-being, Ole Devil had the greatest admiration for her courage and the manner in which she was conducting their family's affairs. She was different from any other member of her sex with whom he was acquainted. However, while anything but a misogynist, he harboured no romantic notions where she was concerned. He belonged to an age and generation which had sound moral standards and a sense of purpose, so did not need to use sexual prowess – which, after all, was within the reach of even the most primitive form of mammal – in an attempt to excuse or replace a lack of more desirable qualities. So, although conscious of her physical attractions, he was equally aware that Ewart Brindley had entrusted her into his care. As far as a man of his upbringing was concerned, that trust was inviolate.

For her part, Di had a greater appreciation of the young Texian's feelings than he suspected. She knew the heavy burden of responsibility he was bearing and realized that she had helped him to forget it, even if only for a few seconds.

Watching Ole Devil striding away, the girl found herself considering how her feelings towards him had changed. Although she had had misgivings about him on their first meeting, they no longer troubled her. At that time, she had wondered if he might be nothing more than an arrogant and spoiled young man who held his rank by virtue of a wealthy family's influence. Now she knew better. What was more, she had discerned the humanity beneath his grim and apparently ruthless exterior.

Being a realist, despite Tommy having told her why Ole Devil had left Louisiana and could not return, Di had no visions of them falling in love and spending the rest of their lives in a state of marital bliss. She did not doubt that they would go their separate ways once the consignment was delivered and suspected how, no matter which way the struggle for independence ended, he would be unlikely to settle down in matrimony for several years.

Giving a sigh, the girl nudged the horse with her heels. The time for levity and day-dreaming was over. There was work demanding her attention. Maybe there was no immediate threat to the consignment, but she knew that transporting it was the task for which she was responsible. Leaving Ole Devil to his affairs, she rode after the mule train.

CHAPTER SEVEN

THEY'RE SMARTER THAN I REALIZED

'SERGEANT SMITH said that I should tell you the Company is ready for your inspection, Devil-san,' Tommy Okasi reported as his employer strolled up to him.

Looking around the hollow, Ole Devil Hardin was once more filled with gratitude for being blessed with intelligent and capable subordinates who could draw conclusions of what was required and act upon them. Showing the kind of initiative which had earned him very rapid and well-deserved promotion (he had in fact been a private on his arrival at Santa Cristóbal Bay) the non-com had not moved out after the departing mule train. Instead, he had formed up the twenty enlisted men of the Texas Light Cavalry's Company C in a single file. Each of them was standing holding his horse with the right hand and his rifle across the crook of his left arm. They were ideally positioned to counter treachery, if the remnants of the Red River Volunteer Dragoons should be contemplating it. Furthermore, the reason which had been given for their action would provide an excuse for them to stay behind until the consignment had passed over the rim.

'*Bueno!*' the Texian enthused, taking the reins of his line-backed dun gelding from the little Oriental. Conscious that he was being watched by the Dragoons, he went on louder than was necessary. 'You can get going while I inspect the men, Tommy.'

Leading his horse, while the little Oriental rode away, Ole Devil joined his men. He allowed his reins to fall from his grasp, ground-hitching the animal, then walked along the file. By pausing before each man and subjecting him to a careful scrutiny, he contrived to stretch out the period of the subterfuge.

'Look at the son-of-a-bitch playing soldiers,' sniffed one of the survivors from San Patricio, watching the "inspection" without any inclination of its true purpose.

'Mister,' Sergeant Otis growled, speaking no louder but with savage emphasis. 'He's not playing. There's the best god-damned soldier you'll ever see.'

'Happen you're so all-fired fond of him,' the survivor spat out, 'maybe you should be going with him 'stead of us.'

'You could be right!' Otis stated.

'Like hell you do, Otis!' another of the Dragoons put in. 'That could tell him we ain't fixing to go back to San Patricio.'

'They'll do, Sergeant Smith,' Ole Devil declared, unaware of the discussion that was taking place among the other party. 'Mount up and move out in column of twos.'

'Yo!' the newly promoted non-com responded and gave the necessary orders, reading the unspoken approbation for the way he had acted in his superior's tone and nod of approval.

Instead of accompanying his men as they started to carry out Smith's commands, Ole Devil swung astride but kept his gelding motionless. From this point of vantage, he turned his attention to the Dragoons. They were still all clustered around the grave of their deceased, if unlamented officer. Although a few of them tried to look defiantly at him, not one continued to do so when they found themselves the subject of his Mephisto-phelian-faced scrutiny.

'I'll leave you to take care of things here, Sergeant Otis,' Ole Devil announced, satisfied that there would be no attempt at a last minute interference. '*Adios.*'

'*Adios*, Cap'n,' the burly non-com replied, stiffening to a brace and delivering the smartest salute he had ever managed.

Riding up the slope after his men, Ole Devil saw that Diamond-Hitch Brindley and Tommy were waiting for him on the rim.

'It's allus handy to have a climb like this at the start,' the girl commented, as the Texian reached her, knowing that he was interested in every aspect of the mule train's operation. 'Happen there's anything wrong, it'll show up a whole heap sooner than on level ground.'

Ole Devil did not need to have the point clarified. Some horses and, he assumed, mules developed an annoying habit of filling their lungs to capacity, which caused the body to expand, when being saddled. The subsequent expulsion of the air allowed the girths, belly-band and latigo strap to become slack. Of course, with packers of the Tejas Indians' calibre, each man knew the habits of the individual members of his string too well to have been tricked by such a basic subterfuge.

However, there were other problems that might result from the rig having been fitted incorrectly. Once on the move, particularly when climbing or going down a slope, any such deficiencies would soon become obvious.

Before the Texian could comment, he saw a further example of Sergeant Smith's forethought. A number of horses belonging to the Arizona Hopi *Activos* Regiment, including several excellent mounts from the officers who had been killed, had been collected after the battle. Along with the reserve animals of Company C and the Dragoons, they had been grazing on top of the rim under the care of three cavalrymen. Without needing instructions from his superior, the non-com had caused the Dragoons' horses to be cut out of the *remuda*[1] and they were being driven to their owners. As the mule train had already gone by, the remainder were set into motion to follow them.

Not only had Smith dealt with the matter of the *remuda* – and removed a possible cause for the Dragoons to harbour resentment – but also, to Ole Devil's satisfaction, he could find no fault in the way that the positioning of the escort had been arranged. Five men were going out on each flank, but all of the remainder were staying behind the *remuda*.

'I had a word with Tom Wolf afore he lit out for San Phillipe, Cap'n,' the non-com explained on reporting to Ole Devil. 'He's sent two of his boys on ahead and one out beyond our flank riders. But I figured, what with that bunch back there—' he gestured with a thumb towards the rim, 'and all, we'd best have a good strong rearguard.'

'I agree, sergeant,' the Texian answered, well pleased with his subordinate's shrewd assessment of the situation's needs. 'If there should be any trouble, it's most likely to come from behind.'

Satisfied that all was under control, needing no further attention or action on his part, Ole Devil settled down to continue his study of the art of handling a large pack train.

With each flank party varying their distance so that they were always just within sight and a Tejas scout further off beyond them, the concourse of animals and riders headed north. Under the ever watchful eyes of the packers, but picking their

[1] *Remuda:* the Spanish word meaning 'replacement' which was adopted by the Texians to describe a collection of spare mounts herded together and not at the time under saddle. Also occasionally called a 'remotha', pronounced 'remootha', a corruption of the Spanish word for remounts, *remonta*. In later years, cowhands in the Northwest used the terms 'cavvy' or 'saddle band'.

own routes along the line of march instead of being made to travel one behind another, the mules ambled at a steady pace that covered five to six miles an hour. There was, Ole Devil observed, little confusion and no jostling or pushing among them. Like all animals with well-developed herd-living instincts, they had acquired a hierarchy in which each knew and, unless capable of changing it by bluff or physical means, was kept in its place. For all their individual desire to get as close as possible to the bell-mare, only the most dominant of them could do so. Those lower down the social scale had learned by painful experience that it did not pay to try and usurp the places of their betters.

Apart from the climb out of Santa Cristóbal Bay, the first few hours of the journey were spent traversing terrain which allowed easy travel and presented no problems. It was fairly open, if rolling, range with no steep slopes or other obstacles to be negotiated. There were a few streams, but none was more than twenty feet wide nor deeper than about a foot. In addition, there was plenty of rich and nutritious grazing of which, like the water, the mules availed themselves. They snatched up mouthfuls of liquid or the hock deep grass whilst on the move and without causing delays.

With each passing mile, Ole Devil grew more impressed by the packers' skill at attending to their duties. They were constantly on the alert, watching their charges and ready to cope with any emergency. On the few occasions when a load needed adjusting for any reason, the animal would be led clear of its companions, the blindfold affixed and the correction carried out without hindrance to the rest.

Ole Devil could soon see why Di had been so confident that they could make any pursuit a long process. What was more, he realized that a pack mule might be at a disadvantage in the earlier stages of a journey if they started together, but – as Di had claimed – by the time thirty miles were covered, it would be pushing any horse. The girl also explained that mules had great endurance, tolerated thirst well, could put up with changes in food and climate, and was not fastidious regarding the former. So, on a march of from seventy-five to a hundred miles – particularly in barren and rugged country – they could have even the best of horses at their mercy. In addition, as he was seeing, when cared for by attendants who understood them and gave them proper handling, they were not troublesome, being easy to look after and keep in condition. A further good quality was their ability, due to a keen sense of smell, to keep together when on the move through the night. Against that, they had a resentment of violence. This, along with a shyness towards strangers and being touchy about the head and ears, could make them free kickers and had done much to give them their reputation for truculence.

Towards noon, as Di, Ole Devil and Tommy were preceding the rest of the party in the ascent of a gentle incline, the first serious obstacle came into view from its top.

'I'm damned if I can make out where the son-of-a-bitch ends,' the girl told her companions, standing in her stirrups and gazing from under her right hand at the distant woodland across their proposed line of march. 'If I could and it wasn't too far, I'd say we start to go so's we'd swing around. Trouble being, we might have to yet, comes to that.'

'Ancient and wise Nipponese saying, which I've just made up,' Tommy remarked, from his place at Di's right. Ignoring her well-simulated moan of anguish, he went on, 'When a person is in doubt, he should always look carefully before making up his mind how to act. That way, he will know before it's too late that he's not doing the wrong thing.'

'Well dog my cats from now to then and back!' the girl ejaculated, slapping a hand on her thigh and turning an expression of wonderment to the Texian. '*I'd* never've thought of *that*.'

'Which is why humble and unworthy self mentioned it,' the the little Oriental pointed out imperturbably.

'Well, I'll tell you something, Tommy,' Ole Devil drawled, giving the girl no chance to get another word in. 'You just beat *me* to suggesting it.'

'I'll be eternally damned if one of 'em's not's bad's the other!' Di almost wailed, turning her face upwards as if in search of strength and guidance from the heavens. Then she snapped her fingers as if a thought had struck her and continued, 'Hey though, I've just now had an idea—!'

'I *knew* it would have to happen one day,' Ole Devil declared. 'Why don't we push on ahead and find out if we can take the mules through?'

'That's what I was aiming to say,' Di protested indignantly. 'How'd you get to figuring it out?'

'Just fortunate, I reckon,' Ole Devil replied.

'I suppose one or the other of you varmints had to get lucky and say something right some time,' the girl sniffed. 'Let's go.'

71

Without allowing either of her companions an opportunity to reply, or bothering to tell Joe Galton – who had almost caught up with them – what she was doing, Di urged her mount to increase its speed. She knew that the *cargador* was aware of the need to examine the woodland and would not require an explanation. Tall, well built, in his early twenties, with red hair and a ruggedly good looking face, the buckskin-clad Galton was Ewart Brindley's adopted son and, like her, fully conversant with every aspect of their family's business.

Holding their horses to a fast trot, the girl, the Texian and the little Oriental were soon approaching the two Tejas forward scouts, who had halted at the edge of the trees. The woodland stretched as far as they could see in either direction and, if it should prove unsuitable for the mules to pass through, would involve them in a lengthy and time-consuming detour.

'Mannen's detail went in,' Ole Devil remarked, indicating the tracks left by his cousin's party which they had been following since leaving the Bay. He swung a challenging glare in Di's direction. 'But, before *anybody* tells me, I know that they only had horses and not mules carrying packs.'

'Now me, I've give up on trying to tell either of you smarty britches anything,' the girl declared in tones of deepest disgust, studying the trees. 'Anyways, unless it gets thicker further in, we'll not have any trouble getting through.'

Joined by the scouts, the trio rode onwards still following the route taken by Mannen Blaze and his detail. At first there were massive live oaks, pecan-hickories, black walnuts and Eastern cottonwoods, interspersed, although not too thickly, with a variety of bushes and Carolina buckthorn shrubs through which wound paths made by wild animals or the semi-domesticated longhorn cattle that would eventually become a major fact in the economy of Texas.[2] However, after having advanced for about three quarters of a mile, they came across boxelders, silver maples and American hornbeams[3] which warned them what to expect. So they were not surprised when they emerged from the trees to find themselves looking across about fifty yards of open ground at a river. While it was narrow, compared with the San Berhard, which they would have to cross on their way to Washington-on-the-Brazos, it was

[2] How this came about is told in: GOODNIGHT'S DREAM and FROM HIDE AND HORN.
[3] American hornbeam: *carpinus caroliniana*, a small tree with birch-like leaves, also known as the 'blue-' or 'water-beech'.

considerably wider than any of the streams they had already come over that day.

'Afore I get told, I know *they* went over here,' Di announced, indicating the tracks of the previous party and riding forward to scan the muddy water in a futile attempt to discover what lay beneath the surface. 'Only that don't mean the mules can tote packs across. It looks like it might be all right, but I suppose I'll be the one who has to make sure.'

'I've always been taught it's polite to let a lady go first,' Ole Devil replied, but he knew that the girl was far better qualified than himself to make the decision.

Having told the scouts in their own language – which she spoke fluently – to go along the banks and see if there was anywhere more suitable for a crossing, Di rode into the water. For all her levity when addressing Ole Devil, she was in deadly earnest as she pressed onwards. She watched the level of the water as it crept higher and reached the *tapaderos*[4] of her stirrups so she was compelled to raise her feet to avoid it. Much to her relief, it did not get much deeper. What was more, the current was not too fast and there was a bed of firm gravel with no rocks protruding from it.

However, the girl did not restrict herself to making a single crossing. Instead, she waded back and forth on different lines until she had covered an area about fifty yards in width. Satisfied with the results of her examination, she waved for Ole Devil and Tommy to join her. When they had done so, the trio continued until the woodland ended. If anything, the terrain was slightly better – although forward visibility was still restricted – on the western bank.

'We can get through all right,' Di declared. 'Let's go back and do it.'

Retracing the route they had taken while conducting their examination, the trio did not wait for the scouts to return and report. On reaching the point at which they had entered the woodland, they found that the leaders of the mule train were about a hundred yards away. Di signalled with a beckoning motion and Galton kept coming.

'We've been through better places, Joe,' the girl stated. 'And worse.'

---

[4] *Tapadero:* in speech usually shortened to 'taps', a wedge-shaped piece of leather covering the stirrup at the front and sides, but open at the rear. Made from heavy cow hide, often carved decoratively, it is used to protect the rider's feet.

'Likely,' replied the *cargador*, who had a reputation for never using two words when one would suffice.

Moving aside, while Di accompanied Galton, Ole Devil and Tommy watched the mules going by. After about half of them had passed, Prays Loudly, Sometimes came along. Wanting to see what kind of problems might be met under such conditions, the Texian rode alongside the packer.

Much to Ole Devil's surprise, although Prays Loudly, Sometimes and his companions were clearly exercising extra vigilance, the passage through the trees was being accomplished without any great difficulty. Wending their individual ways along, the mules displayed an awareness of where they could or could not go. They never tried to pass between a gap that was too narrow for themselves and their burdens.

Remembering some of the comments he had heard Di make, the Texian only stayed with the packer for half a mile. Then he went forward to catch up with her and Galton. By the time he reached them, they were on the banks of the river and he knew that he was going to witness another important part of a mule train's activities.

The first thing to strike Ole Devil's notice was that the four leading packers had already joined the girl and the *cargador*. Leading the bell-mare into the water, Galton started to cross. Looking back, he found that the foremost mules were hesitating and, leaning over, he took hold of the leather collar to give the bell a vigorous shake. After a moment, the sound and a reluctance to be parted from the mare produced the desired effect without the need for action on the part of Di and the packers.

As the animals entered the water, the packers accompanied them. More of the Tejas came up, following their companions. However, none of them went straight to the other side. Ole Devil could understand why they halted to form a double line through which their charges were passing. If one of the heavily loaded mules should stumble and go down, the weight of its pack would prevent it from rising. Unless it was helped quickly, it would drown. What was more, its struggles might frighten the others and make them refuse to go on.

No such tragedy occurred and the crossing went by uneventfully. Before going over himself, Ole Devil waited for the *remuda* and the rear guard to pass. Wisely, as the horses lacked the mules' incentive to stick together, Sergeant Smith had reinforced their herders on reaching the woodland. The non-com also told him that there was no sign of anybody following them, nor had the flank parties reported anything of interest.

With the woodland behind them, Di called a halt. Once again, Ole Devil became aware of the apparent intelligence of what he had previously regarded as stubborn and somewhat stupid animals. Each mule stood patiently until its packer could fasten on its blindfold, remove its burden and examine its back and hooves. Not until that had been done and its eyes uncovered did it attempt to first enjoy a good roll and then start to graze. In addition to the grass they consumed, each was given a feed of grain from the packs carried by the reserve mules.

'You know something, Di?' Ole Devil remarked as he and the girl were strolling around watching the work being carried out. 'I've been wrong about mules. They're smarter than I realized.'

'Figuring 'em's being stupid's a mistake most folks's haven't been around 'em much make,' Di replied. 'Mules're as smart and in some ways even smarter'n hosses. All you have to do is treat 'em right and train 'em properly.'

'There's a rider coming, Cap'n Hardin!' Smith called, before the discussion could be continued. 'Can't make out who it is yet, but he's waving.'

'It must be to us,' Di guessed. 'If he wasn't somebody's they figured was all right, the scouts would've let us know afore now.'

Putting the matter of the mules from his mind temporarily, Ole Devil gazed in the direction indicated by the non-com. He watched the horseman coming towards them at a gallop. Although he too failed to make an identification at first, he was in agreement with the girl's assumption. It proved to be correct. In a short while, the rider was close enough to be recognized.

'It's young Sammy Cope, Cap'n,' Smith decided, having joined his superior and Di so as to be ready if any action had to be taken. 'Mr. Blaze must've sent him back to report, unless something's wrong.'

A few seconds later, they could all tell that the sergeant's doubts were unfounded. Although showing signs of having ridden a long distance at speed, the lanky young enlisted man displayed nothing but a cheerful satisfaction at having reached his destination.

'Come and walk his horse until it cools down, one of you

men!' Ole Devil called, as the newcomer brought his lathered mount to a halt and dismounted.

'Gracias, Cap'n,' Cope said gratefully, handing the reins to the man who hurried forward. 'He's been running plenty. Mr. Blaze told me to get back here and meet you's fast's I could 'n' that's what I've done.'

'Is everything all right with him?' Ole Devil asked.

'Sure is, Cap'n,' Cope replied and looked at the girl. 'Your grandpappy's doing right well, Di. He was cussing fit to bust and said I should tell you that he'll take a switch to your hide happen you lose any of them knobheads.'

'Is the ferry at Hickert's Landing still in use?' Ole Devil inquired, guessing why his cousin had sent the man.

'Yes sir, Cap'n,' Cope answered.

'I told you's ole Mose' Hickert 'n' his boys wouldn't've pulled out,' Di put in, but there was relief in her voice.

The girl's emotion did not entirely stem from learning that her grandfather was making the far from comfortable trip with no worsening of his condition. She had known that they were faced with crossing the San Berhard River. It would be a different, much more difficult, proposition than the one they had forded in the woodland unless the services of the ferry at Hickert's Landing were still available. While mules were excellent swimmers, they could not do so when they were carrying such heavy weights. Nor was there anywhere along the San Berhard that was sufficiently shallow at this time of the year for them to be able to wade across. They could ride on the ferry, having been trained to do so. However, if it had gone, her men would have to make rafts and float the consignment over, allowing the unburdened animals to swim without impediment.

'Mr. Blaze said for me to tell you he's left half of our fellers at the Landing, Cap'n,' Cope went on. 'He figured it'd be best in case them San Phillipe varmints come around with notions of making fuss for you there.'

'Good for ole Mannen,' Di ejaculated, darting a mischievous grin at the Satanic-looking Texian. She was delighted to hear they had reinforcements waiting, even if it was only twelve men, but she was unable to resist the temptation to strike back at her occasional tormentor. 'It's lucky there's *one* right smart *hombre* in your family, Devil.'

'Hey!' Cope almost yelped, having been looking around, before his superior could think up a suitable reply. 'Where at's all them Dragoons?'

76

'They're pulled out 'n' gone home,' Di replied.

'They won't be no loss, wasn't one of 'em worth a cuss any way at all,' Cope declared, displaying no more concern than the other members of his Company had over the departure of the Dragoons. 'You want for me to head back after Mr. Blaze, Cap'n.'

'No,' Ole Devil decided. 'You can stay with us from here on. Go grab something to eat, then pick yourself a fresh horse from the *remuda*.'

'It's about time things started to go smoother for us,' Di commented, as the enlisted man ambled away. 'You could head for San Patricio now, if you're so minded.'

'I've considered it,' Ole Devil admitted. 'But I think I can go easier in my mind after I've seen you safe across the San Berhard.'

Although the Texian and the girl did not realize it, he had made what was to prove a most fortuitous decision.

CHAPTER EIGHT

WE'LL HAVE TO FIND OUT THE HARD WAY

'WHAT do you think, Tommy?' Ole Devil Hardin inquired as, bringing their four horses to a halt while still partially concealed among the trees, he and the little Orientai studied the opposite bank of the small river they had forded about twenty-four hours earlier. 'Did I see something over there?'

The crossing of the San Berhard River had been accomplished, due to the help given willingly by the Hickert family, without any great difficulty. However, darkness had fallen before the consignment and everybody concerned in its protection were on the eastern shore. So, eager as he was to set off on the reconnaissance mission, Ole Devil had realized that Diamond-Hitch Brindley was making her usual good sense when she had suggested he and Tommy Okasi took a night's rest before leaving. They were going to need all their wits about them, which would not be the case if they were tired. Nor would they be able to sleep with such a measure of safety once they had parted company from their companions.

While Ole Devil and Tommy were returning to the south, the remainder of the party were to make their way to the Brazos River. Once there, despite it making a large curve to the east above the lower reaches' most westerly bend, they would stay on the banks instead of following Mannen Blaze and the injured men who had gone straight overland to Thompson's Ferry. When discussing the proposed route with Di and Joe Galton, Ole Devil had envisaged one difficulty which might arise. The girl had assured him that, with the mules she was employing, it would not present any problem and he had bowed to her superior knowledge in such matters. One further point had been settled. Although the other citizens of Hickert's Landing had already fled, the family were remaining to continue operating the ferry until there was danger from the approaching Mexican forces.

Being aware of the need to travel fast, Ole Devil and the little Oriental had made careful preparations. To conserve their personal mounts, all of which had been worked very hard over the past few days, they had selected the best two of the dead Mexican officers' horses to ride during the earlier stages of the journey. The animals' burdens had been reduced to the bare necessities; a telescope, arms and a small supply of ammunition, cloak-coats, but neither a change of clothing nor blankets, some jerky and pemmican – easily transported and nutritious – for food. Superbly mounted and excellent riders, they were capable of covering at least fifty miles a day. However, once they were drawing near to their destination, they would be compelled to take precautions which would require a reduction of their speed. So they intended to make the best possible time before they were required to go more slowly.

For all the urgency of their mission and in spite of believing they would be unlikely to come into contact with any of the enemy before the following day at the earliest, the Texian and his companion were too experienced campaigners to take any unnecessary chances. Instead of sticking to the trail which they had traversed with the mule train, they had made their way out of sight and parallel to it. However, on reaching the area of thick woodland, they had accepted that they would have to make use of the same ford at which they had crossed the small river. According to the flanking parties, this was the only point at which they could go over without considerable effort and difficulty.

As he and Tommy were approaching the ford, Ole Devil thought that he detected something moving among the undergrowth on the other side. Although he had received only a very brief glimpse and it was not repeated, they had come to a halt while still in at least partial concealment. There was close to fifty yards of completely open ground on either side of the river and they wanted to make sure they could cross it in safety.

'I can't see anything,' the little Oriental answered, having completed his scrutiny. 'But there are many places for anybody who wants to be able to hide.'

'That's for sure,' Ole Devil declared and began to unfasten the reins of his reserve mount from the saddlehorn of the horse he was sitting. 'So it looks as if we'll have to find out the hard way. I'll go first.'

'Let me get ready, just in case,' Tommy requested, swinging to the ground.

While he had been alert and watchful, the little Oriental was not holding his bow. As its length would have made it too unwieldy to be used with any great effect in the woodland, he had preferred to leave his hands free for manipulating his sword. So the bow was hanging unstrung on the loops of his saddle's skirts and the quiver of arrows was suspended from the horn instead of across his shoulders. However, the circumstances might have changed and, if he needed to support his employer, archery would provide him with the best means of doing so.

'Very old and wise Louisiana saying, which *I've* just made up,' Ole Devil drawled, delighted at having an opportunity to do so. 'A man should always be ready, then he wouldn't have to get ready.'

Unlike his companion, who looked pained at the comment, the young Texian was already armed in a suitable manner to cope with whatever emergency should arise. With an overall length of fifty-eight and seven-eighths inches, the weapon resting across the crook of his left elbow had a similar general appearance to that of a so-called 'Kentucky'[1] rifle. A closer examination would have disclosed that it was a far more sophisticated device. It was, in fact, an invention of the Mormon gunsmith, Jonathan Browning,[2] designed to meet the requirement for a firearm which could discharge several shots in succession and without the need for each to be loaded individually.[3] So the Browning Slide Repeating rifle[4] possessed

---

[1] The majority of what have come to be known as 'Kentucky' rifles were manufactured in Pennsylvania.

[2] Jonathan Browning (1805–79) was the father of John Moses Browning, the world's greatest firearms designer and who appears in: CALAMITY SPELLS TROUBLE.

[3] For the benefit of those who have not read YOUNG OLE DEVIL, OLE DEVIL AND THE CAPLOCKS or GET URREA, the Browning Slide Repeating rifle was one of the earliest successful American designed multiple-firing weapons. The 'Slide' magazine – generally with a capacity of five shoots, although greater numbers could be had if requested – was a rectangular iron bar, drilled to take percussion caps and the main firing charge, which passed through an aperture at the rifle's breech. When operated by the thumb, a lever at the right side of the frame moved each successive chamber into position and cammed the Slide forward to form a gas-tight connection against the bore. Because of its proximity to the front of the triggerguard, the under-hammer could easily be cocked by the right forefinger without taking the rifle's butt from the shoulder. Despite the difficulty of transporting it for any length of time with the magazine in position, the rifle was simple in operation and capable of a continuous fire unequalled by any other firearm available in 1836.

qualities which Ole Devil had considered more than compensated for the inconvenience of carrying it by hand, as opposed to in the leather 'boot' – an innovation of a young saddler, Joe Gaylin, who would in later years attain considerable acclaim as a maker of superlative gunbelts – attached to the left side of his saddle, while travelling through such difficult terrain.

'If you're going to start making up ancient and wise sayings,' Tommy declared, as he tied the reins of his borrowed horse to a bush and, lifting free the quiver, slung it across his shoulder. 'I think I'll face the *Shogun's* wrath and go home.'

The bow stave which the little Oriental drew from its loops on the skirt of his saddle was constructed in the classical Japanese fashion. It was built of three strips of bamboo, sheathed on two sides by mulberry wood, forming a core which was encased by two further lengths of bamboo and pasted with fish glue, the whole being painted with lacquer. By laminating the bamboo and the softer, more pliable, mulberry wood, a greater strength and flexibility was achieved than if a 'self' bow was manufactured from either material.

Taking the bow's coiled *tsuru* hemp string from a pocket of his tunic, Tommy shook it straight. Then he slipped the appropriate loop into the *urahazu* upper nock groove of the stave. Holding the lower end of the *tsuru* between his teeth, he wedged the top of the bow under a branch of the nearest tree and supported the bottom with his right hand against the top of his slightly bent left leg. Grasping the *nigiri* handle with his left hand and pushing at it, he flexed the bow. Removing the *tsuru* from his teeth with his right thumb and forefinger, he

---

However, during the period of its manufacture, between 1834 and '42, Browning lacked the facilities for large scale manufacture. He would have been able to do so in later years, but the development of self-contained metal-cased cartridges and more compact, if less simple, weapons had rendered it obsolete.

4 Whilst engaged in manufacturing the Slide Repeating rifle, Jonathan Browning, q.v., also developed a rifle which could be fired six times in succession. The charges were held in a cylinder, but there was no mechanism and it had to be rotated manually after each shot. While the same calibre – roughly .45 – and almost ten inches shorter, it was more bulky and weighed twelve pounds, two ounces as opposed to the Slide Repeating rifle's nine pounds, fourteen ounces. It was not offered for sale until Browning had settled at Council Bluffs, Utah, in 1852. However, by that time, it too had become redundant due to the ever increasing availability of Samuel Colt's mechanically superior rifles and revolvers.

gave it the traditional three outwards twists before applying the second loop to the *motohazu* bottom nock.[5] Although he did not bother to check, as the bow was properly strung, the distance between the handle and the *nakishikake* nocking binding of the *tsuru* could have been spanned by his fist with its thumb extended and was approximately the same width as that between his cheekbones.

Having completed his preparations, Tommy removed the top of the bow from beneath the branch and took two arrows from the quiver with his right hand. Although he had made them since his arrival in Texas, he had used the methods learned in his homeland.[6] Holding one by its head, so that the shaft was pointing to his rear, he nocked the other to the *nakishikake*. Then, adopting a position of readiness which was somewhat different to that of an Occidental archer,[7] he gave a low, sibilant hiss which drew Ole Devil's attention from the other side of the river, then he gave a nod.

While the little Oriental had been making ready to cover him if the need should arise, the Texian had tried without avail to locate any sign of danger. Having failed to do so, he allowed his dun's split-ended reins to fall free thus ground-hitching it. Easing down the rifle's under-hammer to full cock, he set the Mexican's bay between his legs moving at a walk. On leaving the shelter of the trees, he continued to keep the terrain ahead under constant observation.

Still without seeing anything to disturb him, the Texian guided his mount into the river. As it advanced, he removed his feet from the stirrups and raised his legs to avoid the water which was soon lapping at the horse's belly. If there had been the slightest suggestion that enemies were lurking in concealment, he would not have acted in such a manner. Believing that there was no cause for alarm and knowing he had neither the time nor the means to dry his footwear, he wanted to save it from getting wet.

[5] One method of stringing a modern recurved hunting bow is given in SACRIFICE FOR THE QUAGGA GOD.

[6] The traditional Japanese arrow was made from *mashino-dake*, a very straight, hard and thin species of bamboo. After being cut in the winter, the bamboo was left to dry out of doors until spring. Having been further dried and hardened by being placed close to a fire, the joints were carefully smoothed down. When the shaft had been polished with emery powder and water, it was once more exposed to the fire. Finally, it was fletched with three feathers from a hawk, falcon or eagle and had its metal arrowhead and nock affixed.

[7] See the first footnote on page 16.

'Look out down there!' yelled a voice from among the foliage of a large silver maple tree, as Ole Devil was about three-quarters of the way across and contemplating returning his feet to the stirrups. 'Indians!'

Even as the warning was given, a young Hopi brave lunged out of the undergrowth some thirty yards to the right of the speaker. Leaping forward, he raised and propelled his curved throwing stick through the air. What was more, it had left his hand before the words could affect his aim.

Just after the weapon had left the brave's hand, three somewhat older warriors followed him into the open ground. One held a short wooden 'self' bow with an arrow nocked to its string but not yet drawn. The second grasped a flintlock rifle and the last was carrying a lance. While his companions followed the first of their number to appear, the man with the firearm turned towards the tree from which the warning had originated. For all that it had been in English, he guessed its meaning and knew it must have been uttered by an enemy. Peering at the thick canopy of leaves that covered the branches as he advanced, he came to a halt before he had taken half a dozen steps. Snapping the rifle's butt to his shoulder, he lined the barrel upwards.

Watching the missile as it was approaching, Ole Devil could tell that it was flying straight towards him and not so as to pass by him. Nor did he underestimate the danger it presented. In fact, he realized that it could prove even more effective than an arrow or a bullet under the circumstances.[8] Spinning towards him at chest height and parallel to the ground, the three foot long throwing stick – made from a carefully selected and shaped branch of a Gambel's oak tree (*Quercus Gambelii*) – stood far less chance of missing than either of the comparatively narrow missiles and was capable of striking even harder.

Although neither he nor Tommy had come into contact with throwing sticks before their meeting with the Hopis, Ole Devil

[8] The throwing-stick of the Hopi and related tribes of North American Indians is a similar device to the war and hunting boomerangs of the Australian aborigines, but is neither designed nor expected to return to the thrower if it should miss its target. This does not make it any less lethal as a weapon. American author, Daniel Mannix described in Chapter 7, 'The Boomerang, the Stick that Kills', of his book, A SPORTING CHANCE – which covers the subject thoroughly, along with other unusual methods of hunting – how he has thrown one a distance of five hundred and forty feet and it still retained sufficient momentum to crack an inch thick branch of a tree.

was all too aware of his peril. Having an affinity for primitive weapons, the little Oriental had been able to assess the device's potential. What was more, while waiting for the mule train to move out of Santa Cristóbal Bay, they had taken an opportunity to experiment and confirm his summations.

In spite of Ole Devil's left hand shaking his mount's one piece Mexican pattern reins from between his second and third fingers, so that they fell on to the saddlehorn, he knew that trying to raise the rifle and shoot would avail him nothing. He might kill the young brave, but the weapon had already been thrown at him. Nor, from what he had seen and Tommy had told him, would trying to deflect the missile serve his purpose any better. On coming into contact with the Browning's barrel, even if no other damage was inflicted, the stick would not be halted. It would either knock the rifle from his grasp or, failing that, spin around the barrel and retain sufficient impetus to reach and strike him with considerable force.

Accepting that there was only one course left open to him, the Texian took it. Grasping the rifle firmly with both hands, he quit the horse's back. There was no time for him to try and throw a leg forward and jump clear in the hope of landing on his feet. Instead, he toppled sideways to the left out of the saddle. Even as he was going down, he heard the hissing of the throwing stick as it twirled rapidly by not a foot above him. Then, as he plunged into the river, he thrust up the rifle in an attempt to prevent it from accompanying him below the surface.

Annoyance filled the young Hopi as he saw that he had missed his target. The missile was an old favourite which could be counted upon always to fly in the same fashion when thrown correctly and he might not be able to find it in the woods across the river. However, he derived consolation from the thought that he could obtain some even more satisfactory and modern weapons from the Texian. As the first to count coup,[9] he would be entitled to the pick of the dismounted victim's property. So, snatching the knife from its sheath on his belt, he continued to run towards the water's edge.

Having seen Ole Devil evade the throwing stick, Tommy

[9] Unlike the Comanches, who allowed only the first arrival to count the coup – which was done by touching preferably a living enemy, or a corpse, and saying, '*A:he !*', meaning 'I claim it!' – the Hopis and some other tribes permitted the second and third warrior to take lesser shares in the credit.

returned his attention to the Indians. Commencing his draw, he knew that he must decide – and very quickly – which of the braves to aim at.

What was more, the answer must be correct!

For all his comparatively modern weapon, Tommy concluded that the man with the rifle could be ignored. He was concentrating upon whoever had called the warning from among the foliage of the silver maple.

Being closest, the youngest brave was posing the most immediate threat. With that in mind, Tommy selected and started to take aim at him.

The action was not completed!

Slower than the lance carrier, who still ran on, the fourth warrior skidded to a halt. Raising his bow, he began to pull back on the string and sight the arrow. When it was released, it would fly much faster than either of his companions were capable of moving. So, no matter who counted the first coup, the honour of killing the paleface would be his.

As soon as he struck the river's bed, Ole Devil twisted himself upwards until he was sitting slightly less than chest deep in the water. Seeing the young brave approaching, with the lance carrier following about fifteen feet to the rear, he snapped the Browning's butt to his shoulder. Noticing the man with the bow preparing to shoot at him, he guessed at what Tommy was doing and knew that he must handle his nearest attackers himself. So he squinted along the forty and five-sixteenths of an inch octagonal barrel rather than the V-shaped notch of the rear right.

Although the young Hopi saw he was being covered, he was not especially perturbed. He had never used a firearm, but knew enough about the shortcomings of those owned by other members of his nation to feel he was in no danger. What he failed to appreciate was that he did not face a flintlock, the powder in the priming pan of which would almost certainly have been ruined when its owner fell into the river.

The Browning rifle was not impervious to water, but it was less susceptible to its effects than the older type of mechanism. For all that, Ole Devil knew a misfire would put him in a desperate situation. Squeezing the trigger, he felt the hammer being liberated and start to snap upwards.

Even as Tommy was altering the alignment of his weapon, a shot crashed from the other side of the river. It was the sharp detonation of a fairly light calibre handgun, probably a duelling pistol, and not the deeper roar of a shoulder arm. Back jerked the head of the brave with the rifle. A blue-rimmed hole appeared in the centre of his brow and the base of his skull burst open as the bullet emerged. Toppling over, he fired his weapon harmlessly into the air and it fell from his grasp.

Refusing to let himself be distracted by the shooting, Tommy made sure of his aim and loosed the arrow. It flashed across the intervening space, but not quite to the mark at which it had been directed. Going past the youngest brave as he was being struck in the left breast by Ole Devil's bullet, it hit and sliced through the upper limb of the warrior's bow. For all that, the effect of the shot served the little Oriental's purpose. It snatched the ruined weapon from the Hopi's hands before he could release his own shaft. Letting out a startled yelp, he staggered backwards.

Sharing the younger brave's summation of the situation, the lance-carrier was surprised when Ole Devil's rifle went off. To his annoyance, he saw his stricken companion spin around and, dropping the knife, blunder into his path. Swerving around the falling youngster, he hardly noticed that the bay was startled by the shot and beginning to lope away. He found the behaviour of the paleface of greater interest. Not only was he still sitting down, but he made no attempt to take the rifle from his shoulder and yet its single barrel must now be empty.

Not for the first time, Ole Devil's life was depending upon the reliability of Jonathan Browning's inventive genius and skilled craftsmanship. Thrusting down the lever with his thumb, he watched the magazine creeping slowly through the aperture. Nearer rushed the Hopi, his lance held ready for use and savage determination etched in the lines of his face.

CHAPTER NINE

THEY'RE CLOSER THAN WE EXPECTED

EVEN as the Browning Slide Repeating rifle's magazine halted and was cammed into position against the barrel's bore, Ole Devil Hardin's right forefinger reached around the front of the triggerguard to cock the under-hammer. Although he had been watching the slide to make sure that it was operating correctly, the sound of water splashing warned him that his assailant was drawing ever closer. Looking up, he found that the Hopi brave was already lifting back the lance ready to strike.

On the eastern bank, Tommy Okasi had lowered his right hand and was allowing the second arrow to slide through it until he could take hold of the nock. He was such a highly skilled archer that he had no need to look down and made the movements instinctively. Affixing the slot of the nock on the *nakashikake*, he rested the shaft in the shallow 'V' formed by his left thumb and the bow's handle. While doing so, he continued to keep the other side of the river under observation. In spite of knowing the rifle's potential, he saw enough to warn him that his employer was still in deadly peril. What was more, there might not be sufficient time for him to draw and aim the arrow with the accuracy that was needed if he was to help.

With the hammer at full cock, Ole Devil returned his finger to the Browning's trigger. There was no need for him to bother about making sure of his aim. Dashing onwards recklessly, the Hopi was so near that it would be practically impossible to miss. Nor was he showing the slightest alarm over having the rifle directed at him. Clearly he believed it was empty and that he had nothing to fear.

Pressure on the Browning's trigger set the firing cycle into motion. Much to Ole Devil's relief, he heard the slight pop as the hammer ignited the percussion cap. Even as flame and white powder smoke was erupting from the barrel in the wake

87

of the .45 calibre round soft lead ball, with the lance driving straight at him and almost level with the rifle's muzzle, he tipped himself to the left.

Shock mingled with the agony that came to the Hopi's face as the bullet ploughed into the base of his throat and broke his neck. Although he was mortally wounded, his momentum carried him onwards and the lance was still grasped firmly enough in his hand for it to have achieved his purpose.

Ole Devil's hat had slipped sideways when he fell from his horse, being arrested on his right shoulder by its *barbiquejo* chinstrap. The tip of the lance brushed its brim in passing and, tripping over him, the dying brave plunged face forward into the river.

Watching along the shaft of his arrow, which he had just drawn until it was at its anchor point ready to be aimed, Tommy let out a hiss of relief as he saw it would not be needed to save his employer. So he began to turn it in search of another target and had no trouble in finding one.

Seeing the fates which had overtaken the rest of his companions, the last Hopi brave decided that discretion was the better part of valour. He regarded the loss of his bow with mixed feelings. While he had been deprived of his main weapon, its destruction had also prevented him from being injured. On the other hand, he now had no way of either killing the Texian in the river or defending himself against the man on the opposite bank and who was preparing to launch another arrow at him. Furthermore, his party were on a scouting mission and he now had something of importance to report to his superiors.

Even as he was drawing his conclusions, the brave saw that the means for escape were at hand. Frightened by the shooting, the horse from which the paleface had fallen was approaching. Darting to meet it, the brave heard the whistle of an arrow passing close behind him. Grabbing the horse's saddlehorn as it went by, he vaulted on to its back. Then, flattening himself along its neck to offer a smaller target, he gave a yell that caused the animal to bound forward even faster.

Muttering imprecations in English, which he had found offered a more satisfactory breadth than his native tongue for expressing annoyance and anger, Tommy reached up to extract another arrow from his quiver. He realized that he was unlikely to be able to use it, but intended to try in the hope of bringing down the fleeing Indian.

The little Oriental discovered, while nocking the shaft into position, that whoever was concealed up the silver maple tree had a similar idea. Either the pistol was double barrelled, or its user had its mate. No matter which, a second shot – sounding like its predecessor – came from the foliage. However, the bullet failed to take effect. Before Tommy could draw and aim the arrow, the brave had passed beyond his range of vision amongst the trees.

Watching the departing warrior as he was coming to his feet and starting to press the Browning's reloading lever, Ole Devil spat out a few choice Anglo-Saxon obscenities. Not only was he soaked to the skin, with no dry clothing into which he could change, but he had lost one of his horses. There was some slight consolation to be drawn from the latter. The animal was carrying nothing except its former owner's saddle and bridle, to which it was accustomed and which Ole Devil had used rather than replace it with his second set of Texas-style rigging. Against that small benefit, he would be unable to travel as quickly now that he was reduced to the services of a single mount.

Wading ashore, after having glanced behind him to make sure there was nothing further to be feared from his lance-carrying assailant, Ole Devil saw the deeply cut and indented leaves – their dull yellow winter hue just start to change to the colours of spring – pale green on the outer surface and whitish on the inner – of the silver maple being agitated. However, remembering how the person hidden by the foliage had acted, he concluded that there was no cause for concern.

A pair of mud-smeared black Hessian boots, with stained white trousers tucked into them, appeared below one of the silver maple's lowest branches. Even as a tall, slim man dressed in the fashion of a professional gambler swung downwards, there was a movement in the same clump of bushes on the left of the tree from which Ole Devil had received his first intimation of danger.

'Don't shoot!' the man yelled, as the Texian's Browning began to rise, and he dropped to the ground showing alarm.

The warning had not been necessary. Before the butt of the rifle had reached his shoulder, Ole Devil was able to study the small figure emerging from the bushes. What he had seen was sufficient to tell him that he would not need the weapon. So he did not complete the movement.

Despite all the hair being tucked out of sight beneath the

crown of a wide brimmed hat and having on a dirt be-spattered brown cloak-coat over masculine attire, the newcomer was definitely *not* a man.

Although somewhat haggard and showing signs of considerable strain, the young woman's face was exceptionally pretty and struck Ole Devil as being familiar. She was walking slowly, showing every evidence of feeling extremely tired. For all that, there was something of what would have been a graceful and even slightly seductive carriage in more favourable conditions. A bell-mouthed blunderbus was hanging muzzle downwards in her right hand.

'It's Captain Hardin, isn't it?' asked the man, striding forward with an attitude of relief. He had a fine-looking double barrelled, percussion fired pistol thrust into the silk sash around his waist and an *épée-de-combat* hung sheathed on the slings of his belt. 'I thought – and hoped – it might be when I saw you crossing the river, sir, but I couldn't be sure.'

Even if seeing the young woman had not supplied him with a clue, Ole Devil would have identified the voice before turning towards the speaker. Its tones were resonant and unforgettable, having been trained to reach the furthest seat of the largest theatre without artificial aids and allowing every word to be understood by its occupant.

Clearly in the peak of physical condition, despite having reached his middle forties, the man was impressively handsome. His normally immaculate shoulder long black hair, which had no covering and was uncombed and unkempt, was still luxuriant and had no traces of grey. Like the young woman, he was showing signs of considerable exertion and much hard travelling. All in all, he was looking far less debonair, elegant and composed than during his previous meetings with the Texian.

'It is,' Ole Devil admitted, somewhat coldly, lowering the Browning and returning its under-hammer to the position of safety at half-cock.

'*Et tu, Brute?*'[1] the man sighed, his welcoming smile wavering. Then he shrugged his shoulders and went on half to him-

---

[1] '*Et tu, Brute?*', 'And you also, Brutus?': said to have been Gaius Julius Caeser's reproachful dying comment on discovering that his friend Marcus Junius Brutus, was one of the assassins who had attacked him at the foot of Pompey's statue in the Senate Building, Rome, on the 15th 'The Ides' of March, 44 B.C., and quoted by the British playwright, William Shakespeare (1564–1616) in Act Three, Scene One of: JULIUS CAESAR.

self, 'I suppose it's only to be unexpected, though hard.'

Considering that his life had been saved by the speaker's timely warning, the young Texian was behaving in a far less cordial fashion than most people would have expected of him. However, while he was grateful, circumstances had caused him to have misgivings where his saviour was concerned.

Prior to his having left the United States, Mangrove Hallistead had appeared with great success at every major theatre in that country. Such was his fame, popularity and general behaviour that, in spite of the normally marked reluctance shown by many wealthy Southern families towards accepting members of the theatrical profession as social equals, he had gained access to the homes of almost every influential Texian family – the majority of whom had their origins south of the Mason–Dixon line[2] – since arriving in Texas.

Ole Devil had met Hallistead on a few occasions and, being of a tolerant nature, had had no scruples in accepting him as a social equal. He had found the entertainer to be well-educated, cultured, intelligent, well-informed about current events and a gentlemen even by the exacting Southern interpretation of the word. They had never been more than acquaintances. So, although he had wondered why such an obviously talented person – to whom not even the slightest taint of a public scandal had attached itself – should have given up a successful and profitable career to make a home in Texas, convention would not allow him to satisfy his curiosity.

The cause of the young Texian's apparent ingratitude had arisen a few mouths earlier. After having seemed to be a supporter of Major General Samuel Houston's policies, the entertainer had been one of the first to go and join Colonel Frank W. Johnson at San Patricio.

'My thanks for your warning, sir,' Ole Devil said stiffly, puzzled by the other's comment and suspecting that it had implied he was behaving in a churlish manner unbecoming a gentleman.

'I would have called out sooner, but I thought you to be aware of the Indians' presence and, somewhat ill-advisedly in my opinion, were acting as a decoy to lure them into exposing

---

[2] Mason–Dixon line, sometimes called the 'Mason–Dixie' line; the boundary between Pennsylvania and Maryland, as surveyed in 1763–'67 by the Englishmen Charles Mason and Jeremiah Dixon, which came to be regarded as the dividing line between the Southern 'Slave' and the Northern 'Free' States of America.

themselves,' Hallistead explained, his speech returning to the flamboyance gained in a lifetime on the stage. 'And I must tender a further apology for not being able to send an earlier warning. Although, from all I've seen, you managed very well without it.'

'I don't understand,' Ole Devil stated and glanced over his shoulder to find that Tommy, riding with feet raised as he had done, was bringing all the horses across the river.

'Manny!' the young woman put in, preventing the conversation from continuing. Her voice had a melodious Southern drawl, but was also pitched so that it could carry around the auditorium of a large theatre. 'Mist— Captain Hardin's soaked through to the skin. Surely you-all can let him change into something dry before you start asking questions?'

'Egad, my dove, I concur,' Hallistead replied, giving a courtly bow to his wife. 'However, the proximity of these noble aborigines—' he gestured towards the nearest of the Hopi Indians' bodies, 'presupposes that they have confederates in the offing. I may be reaching an erroneous conclusion, Captain Hardin, but I assume that they are merely a marauding band of indigenous natives and not a portion of the Mexican Army.'

'They're members of the Arizona Hopi *Activos* Regiment, Mr. Hallistead,' Ole Devil corrected. 'Forward scouts, most likely. We've had trouble with them before, but I thought the main body were at least two days' ride away. If those four mean what I suspect, they're closer than we thought.'

'I can't claim that I was aware that they formed part of the force—' the entertainer began.

'Now, Manny!' Corrinne Hallistead interrupted, indignantly stamping a dainty – despite being encased in an unfeminine boot – right foot and looking the Satanic-featured young Texian over from head to toe. 'Why the poor Captain's just running with water and like to catch a mortal chill. Surely you can let him change into something dry before you go on with your talk?'

'A most level-headed suggestion, as always, light of my very existence,' Hallistead conceded, reaching out to take the woman's left hand and kiss it. Then he glanced to where Tommy was dismounting and, returning his gaze to Ole Devil, went on, 'Your worthy Oriental factotum has arrived, sir. I trust that you have the vestments suitable for your needs?'

'I haven't,' the Texian admitted wryly, knowing that even though the situation might have changed so that he could not

92

continue with his present assignment, he was still faced with a long ride in wet clothing.

'I suspected as much from the paucity of impedimentia attached to your saddles,' Hallistead admitted. 'Being aware that you are possessed of a strong sense of duty, sir, I can only conclude that you have heard of the happenings at San Patricio and, having seen the consignment of caplocks well on their way to safety, you are returning hot-foot to ascertain—'

'Manny!' Corrinne put in and her tone took on a sharper, more demanding note.

'Of course, my love,' the entertainer answered soothingly. 'I'm afraid that I can't help you in the matter of alternative raiment, sir. As you can doubtless envisage, our departure from the scene of our recent labours was of necessity hurried and—'

'Why don't you go back over the river and light a fire to dry your clothes, Devil-san?' Tommy suggested. 'I'll go after the Indian who escaped and try to fetch your horse back.'

'That's the first intelligent suggestion I've heard,' Corrinne declared. 'And it's what we're going to do.'

'I warn you that we may as well accede, sir,' Hallistead told the Texian. 'When my dear lady makes up her mind, nothing we mere men can do or say will shake her.'

'Whatever you say then, ma'am,' Ole Devil drawled, favouring the woman with a courtly bow. 'Go to it, Tommy. And you'd better find out how far away the rest of the Hopis are while you're at it.'

'I wonder, sir, if we could have the loan of transportation?' Hallistead inquired, before the little Oriental could turn away. 'We've lost our horses and are a-foot.'

'I'll leave this one for you,' Tommy offered, swinging from his borrowed mount.

Having collected the telescope from the pocket of Ole Devil's clock-coat, which was strapped to the cantle of the line-backed dun gelding's saddle, the little Oriental mounted his horse and rode away. After the entertainer had fetched two sets of bulky saddlebags from the bushes in which his wife had hidden, they both climbed on the animal that had been left for them and accompanied Ole Devil to the eastern bank of the river. Knowing that there would no longer be any purpose in trying to conceal their presence, the two men gathered wood and managed to set it on fire. Standing close, so the flames would warm him and, if time was permitted, dry his garments,

93

Ole Devil requested a continuation of the explanation that Hallistead had started to give before Corrinne's intervention.

'Firstly, sir,' the entertainer commenced, having seated his wife on the saddlebags after removing the means to reload his pistol. 'Although I can only give you my word that what I am going to tell you is the truth, I joined Johnson at my own request and with General Houston's wholehearted approval. Of course, the very nature of the task I was performing precluded a truthful explanation of my motives.'

'The General needed to find out just exactly what Johnson was up to,' Corrinne stated, wanting to ensure that there was no doubt in the young Texian's mind regarding her husband's behaviour. 'And, if it hadn't been for Manny, the invasion of Mexico would have been made weeks ago.'

'I did my modest best, sir,' the entertainer continued, throwing a look filled with gratitude at the woman who had endured so much for him without complaint or protest. 'Without allowing myself to be identified as the culprit, I commenced by starting rumours that a large number of volunteers would soon be forthcoming and their assistance would greatly enhance our chances of success. When these failed to materialize, I hoped to capitalize upon the general disappointment, persuade them to give up the ill-conceived venture and attach themselves to the rest of the Army, even if only to the extent of joining the garrison at Fort Defiance. Regrettably, I learned of von Lowenbrau's mission too late to send a message warning the consignment's escort that he was coming. However, on hearing that *you*, sir, were in command, I was sanguine that it would not succeed. If it had, nothing further could have prevented the invasion from being launched. On the other hand, a failure would in all probability have resulted in what I was striving to achieve, the abandonment of the scheme.'

'It failed, but not before I'd had to kill von Lowenbrau,' Ole Devil said flatly. 'And, if he'd held off for another five minutes, that needn't have happened.'

'I doubt if anybody of consequence and perception will hold his death against you, sir,' Hallistead replied and his wife nodded vigorous agreement. 'Knowing him, I'm certain that he left you with no other choice but to do what you did.'

'How about the attack?' Ole Devil wanted to know, his every instinct suggesting that the entertainer had been speaking the truth and was sincere. 'I was told that Johnson and all his command, or just about, had been wiped out.'

'A gross exaggeration, sir,' Hallistead corrected. 'I'd be surprised if more than fifty of them were killed or have fallen into the enemy's hands.[3] We were, I admit, very nearly taken by surprise. Johnson's men were growing disenchanted by his leadership – or lack of it – and discipline was practically non-existent. So word that a large Mexican force was in the offing arrived much later than would have been the case if the few patrols which had been sent out were performing their duties correctly. When the attack came, all was confusion. There was some resistance, but the majority of those present cut and ran. I—'

'Manny only left as soon as he did because of me and to make sure that you were warned,' Corrinne interrupted, once again wanting to set the record straight on her husband's behalf. 'Before that, what little resistance there was had been organized by him. Johnson had gone and—'

'I don't question Mr. Hallistead's courage, ma'am,' Ole Devil assured the woman, smiling warmly. 'And I'm satisfied that he acted throughout with the best interests of Texas in mind.'

'My thanks, sir,' the entertainer boomed and, as he noticed with relief that there was a distinct improvement in the young Texian's attitude towards him, his own tone showed his thanks were more than just a formal response. 'We remained unnoticed in the vicinity while I was ascertaining something of the enemies' strength. I regret that my knowledge of matters material is insufficient for me to go into greater detail, but there appeared to be one regiment each of regular artillery, cavalry and infantry, the cavalry being Lancers. In addition, there were one foot and one mounted *Activos* or some other form of volunteer regiments. After I had despatched one of my men to alert Fannin to the danger and sent the other to General Houston with a full report of what had taken place, Corrinne and I made our way towards Santa Cristóbal Bay. We intended to turn back von Lowenbrau if he should have succeeded in his purpose, or to warn you in the more than likely – in our opinions – event that you had thwarted him.'

'*Gracias*, sir,' Ole Devil drawled, pleased with the

[3] The actual figure proved to have been sixteen killed and twenty-one – who were subsequently executed by a firing squad – taken prisoner. Colonel Johnson was among those who made good their escape, arriving at Fort Defiance, Goliad, q.v. on February the 29th, 1836.

compliment. He turned to let his rear side receive the benefit of the fire and glanced at the woman. 'Please excuse my back, ma'am.'

'Think nothing of it, Captain, I only hope that you'll have time to get properly dried,' Corrinne answered, showing more grace now that she was satisfied the Texian was regarding her husband favourably. 'Tell him the rest, Manny darling.'

'With the greatest of pleasure, my dove,' Hallistead assented. 'We arrived just in time to see von Lowenbrau's party taking their departure. From his and your absence, we concluded, correctly as has been proven, that you had circumvented his schemes and dispensed with their dubious services. So we sought out the tracks left by your party, not a difficult task in itself, and followed. Unfortunately, first Corrinne's and then my mount foundered and we were left a-foot, but we kept on undaunted.'

'You had bad luck,' Ole Devil commiserated, with a sympathetic glance at the exhausted-looking woman, but he was also seeing how the loss of their horses added to his difficulties.

'It had its compensations,' Corrinne replied.

'Very true, light of my life,' Hallistead agreed. 'And there was one consolation, sir. My dear lady wife was attired for walking, a precaution we had both considered advisable before taking our leave of San Patricio. What was more, as we appreciated the necessity of travelling light, we brought away little apart from our invaluable make-up equipment and a change of raiment for her. All our possessions are in the saddlebags.'

'I'm sorry to hear you lost everything else, ma'am,' Ole Devil remarked, knowing that the couple's fame had been founded on their excellent disguise, quick-change and impersonation act involving numerous wigs and sets of appropriate clothing.

'It's not as bad as that,' Corrinne smiled, being far from displeased by the Texian's obvious concern. 'We left the majority of our costumes in General Houston's care and brought away all that mattered.'

'Knowing the precarious nature of what we were intending to do, I considered the course to be judicious,' Hallistead elaborated. 'Then, if we needed to flee, all would not be lost.'

Amused by the entertainer's pedantic and bombastic way of speaking, Ole Devil allowed him to carry on with the explanation in his own fashion. On reaching the stream, the couple had heard horses beyond it. Telling his wife to hide with their property and leaving her the blunderbus for protection, Hallistead had climbed into the silver maple meaning to discover who was coming. Before he could satisfy his curiosity, he had seen the Hopis approaching on foot and realized that they were stalking the men whose appearance he was awaiting. The Texian knew the rest of the story.

While listening, Ole Devil was considering the latest developments. The fact that the Arizona Hopi *Activos* Regiment was almost certainly much closer than he had anticipated meant he must return to the mule train as quickly as possible.

Doing so with only three horses between four people was going to be difficult.

CHAPTER TEN

THE TEXIAN WITH THE FACE OF *EL DIABLO*

ALTHOUGH a person who had only been acquainted with
Tommy Okasi in his capacity of valet might have questioned
the wisdom of the decision, Ole Devil Hardin had not had the
slightest qualms over sending him in search of the Arizona
Hopi *Activos* Regiment. In fact, the Texian was confident that
he was more than equal to the task.

Before he had been compelled to leave his homeland with no
possibility of ever returning,[1] the little Oriental had been a
fully qualified *samurai*.[2] The power and authority of the
formerly highly influential warrior class was already on the
wane,[3] but its members still received a very thorough education
in many aspects of the martial arts. Not only was he well able to
take care of himself in any kind of fight – whether it should be
with his nation's traditional weapons, bare-handed employing

[1] While attending the 21st Annual Convention of Western Writers
of America at Fort Worth, Texas, in 1974 and during a second visit
the following year, the author tried to discover what had caused
Tommy Okasi – this was not his real name, but an Americanized
corruption of the one he gave when picked up by Captain Jeremiah
Hardin's ship – to leave his native land. The members of the Hardin,
Fog and Blaze clan to whom I spoke were adamant that, because of the
circumstances and the high social standing of the families involved –
all of whom have descendants holding positions of influence and
importance in Japan at the time of writing – it is inadvisable even at
this late date to make the facts public.

[2] *Samurai:* a member of the lower nobility's elite warrior class,
usually acting as a retainer of the *Daimyos*, the hereditary Japanese
feudal barons.

[3] During the mid-nineteenth century, an increasing contact with
the Western World was bringing an ever growing realization that the
retention of an hereditary and privileged warrior class was incompatible with the formation of a modern and industrialized society.
Various edicts issued by the Emperor between 1873 and '76 abolished
the special rights of the *samurai* and, although some of their traditions
and concepts were retained, they ceased to exist as such.

ju-jitsu and *karate*, or to a lesser extent, firearms⁴ – he was equally competent at performing the exacting duties of a scout.

Holding his big blue-roan⁵ gelding at the fastest pace that was compatible with following the tracks of the fleeing Hopi brave and carrying the long bow by hand through the woodland, Tommy kept constantly on the alert. He did not know if his quarry had companions in the vicinity, other than those who had been killed at the small river. So he listened carefully as well as scrutinizing the surrounding trees and bushes for signs of possible danger. Before he had covered much more than a hundred yards, he heard the sounds of several horses moving away; but he was far too experienced a warrior to be lulled into a sense of complacency.

From the signs he observed, Tommy deduced that one of the braves had been in advance of the other three as they were coming through the woodland. Either he had seen or heard something to make him suspicious, for he had returned to fetch his companions on foot. Further evidence of this was given when the little Oriental came to a spot where four horses had been tethered to a clump of bushes. There were torn off leaves, broken twigs and other signs to suggest that the fleeing man had paused to snatch free the securing ropes. He was still riding the dead Mexican officer's mount which he had acquired from Ole Devil, and was apparently leading one of the remainder. Impelled by herd instinct, training, or an open plains dwelling creature's distaste for wooded country, the other three horses were following.

In spite of the fact that everything he saw suggested that the quartet had comprised the entire scouting party, Tommy pressed onwards without any relaxation of his vigilance. He hoped that he would be able to catch up with his quarry and recover at least his employer's reserve horse before going too far. If he could do so, he would deliver it – or them, should he be fortunate enough to obtain more than the one – to Ole Devil for use by the Hallisteads, who were in urgent need of transportation. With that done, he could resume his search for the enemy.

⁴ Although primitive kinds of firearms had been known in Japan since the arrival of Portuguese explorers in 1543, the *samurai* had small regard for them and little time was devoted to learning how to use them.

⁵ Blue-roan: a horse with a more or less uniform mixture of white and black, or deep mahogany bay coloured hairs over the entire body. If the darker hairs are sorrel – yellowish to red-golden – it is a strawberry roan, if an ordinary bay, a red-roan.

Much to Tommy's unspoken annoyance, the hope did not materialize.

On reaching the fringe of the woodland, the little Oriental saw the Hopi a good three hundred yards ahead. He was travelling in the manner suggested by the tracks. What was more, he clearly had not overlooked the possibility of pursuit. Even as Tommy was emerging from the last of the trees, he gazed over his shoulder. Snapping his head to the front, he immediately encouraged the horse he was sitting and the one he was leading to increase their pace. To add to Tommy's sense of vexation, the three animals which were running free, stimulated by a yell from the brave continued to keep pace with their companions.

An expert *kyudoka*, archer, Tommy appreciated the limitations as well as the qualifications of his weapon and skill. Even if an arrow would carry that far and he was fortunate enough to make a hit, it would not retain sufficient impetus to kill, or disable, the brave or the horse he was sitting. So the only alternative would be to try and ride into a lethal range. Once that had been attained, there would be no need for him to dismount before drawing and loosing a shaft. In spite of the bow's length, it could be used effectively at *yabusame*. [6]

Instead of setting off immediately to make the attempt, Tommy gave rapid thought to the other aspects involved. It was, he realized, impossible for him to reach a shooting distance without a long chase. Nor was there any certainty that he would be able to do so. The Hopi had the advantage of riding a two-mount relay. If – as everything so far had indicated – he was an accomplished horseman, he could transfer from the newly acquired animal to the other while on the move and with little reduction of speed. Against that, Tommy would have to push his solitary animal without respite. At the end of the chase, and it was quite possible that he might fail to catch up, or be led to the rest of the *Activos*, he was faced with the

[6] *Yabusame:* translated literally, 'shooting from a running horse'. In competition, the mounted *kyudoka* rides at a gallop over a course two *cho* – roughly two hundred and thirty-eight yards – in length, along which are placed at approximately thirty-eight, one hundred and eighteen, and one hundred and ninety-three yards, two foot square wooden targets on posts between thirty-six and forty-eight inches high. Traditionally, the *kyudoka* discharges – from a distance of around thirty feet –an arrow with a forked head that shatters under the impact of a hit.

necessity of returning as quickly as possible to pass on the information to his employer.

Reluctantly, for he still retained the *samurai*'s distaste towards admitting any task was beyond his capabilities, Tommy conceded that he would be unable to obtain the horses unless something unforeseen should occur. Being a realist, he was unwilling to rely upon such an uncertain eventuality to serve his purpose. So he concluded that the only course left open to him was to carry out the secondary mission of locating the rest of their enemies.

Waiting until the rapidly departing Hopi looked behind again, Tommy shook his bow-filled fist in the air and, with a gesture of disgust, turned his horse and retreated into the woodland. Halting when he was satisfied that he would be concealed by the trees, he saw nothing to suggest his true purpose had been suspected. Showing no sign of slowing down, much less coming back, the brave was disappearing over a distant fold of the ground.

Setting his roan into motion, the little Oriental once more took up the pursuit. However, he travelled in a vastly different manner. Now his purpose was to follow undetected rather than to catch up and attack. For all that, while he had not done so earlier, now he nocked an arrow to the bow's string. If he had need of the weapon, it would be quickly, and there might not be time for him to remove and set it up when trouble came.

Advancing cautiously, Tommy studied the terrain ahead with great care. As he followed in the general direction taken by the Hopi, he took advantage of every available scrap of cover. When he had to cross a sky-line, he first ensured that he could do so without running the risk of being seen by his would-be quarry. At intervals, he caught glimpses of the brave. However, from the other's behaviour, he was confident that he had not been seen in return.

After having covered about six miles in such a fashion, Tommy was treated to a suggestion that he was approaching the rest of the *Activos*. Halting behind a clump of bushes, he watched the scout talking with half a dozen more Hopi braves and pointing towards him. For a moment, he wondered if he had been less successful in avoiding being noticed than he believed. One of the warriors seemed to be urging the rest to advance. However, another – the oldest, if his grey hair was any guide – declined. Turning their horses, they accompanied the scout towards where more riders were appearing on the horizon.

Employing an even greater stealth and care, the little Oriental followed the latest party of Hopis. Noticing a small knoll that seemed well suited to his needs, he headed towards it. Leaving his roan concealed and ground-hitched behind the knoll, he returned the arrow to his quiver. Taking the telescope from his saddlebags, he carried it and the bow with him as he made the ascent. On reaching the top, he found he had an ideal point of vantage. Flattening on his stomach behind a rock, he laid the bow at his side and opened the telescope.

Half a mile from Tommy's hiding place, halted on the banks of a stream, were a mass of men and horses. Using the telescope, he gave them a closer examination than was possible with the naked eye. One glance was sufficient to stifle any slight hopes he might have cherished. He had found the main body of the Arizona Hopi *Activos* Regiment.

What was more, there was a much greater number than Ole Devil had anticipated!

At least three hundred braves and twenty or more Mexicans, Tommy estimated as he scanned them through the powerful magnification of the telescope. His employer had assumed there would be two hundred at the most.

From what the little Oriental could make out, based on his experiences with the Texas Light Cavalry, the return of the scout and advance party had caused a halt to be called. While the majority of the Hopis were attending to the horses, some of their chiefs – who acted as non-coms and could be identified by the necklaces and bracelets of silver inlaid with turquoise blue gemstones they sported – and all the Mexicans were gathered around the survivor. Among them, he could recognize the man who had captured and been on the point of torturing his employer when he had intervened and effected a rescue. The man had escaped then, and again after the battle at Santa Cristóbal Bay. From what Tommy could make out, it was he who was doing most of the talking.

'It was the Texian with the face of *el Diablo, senores*!' the surviving scout announced dramatically, making the sign of the cross as he had been taught to do when mentioning the Devil by the mission fathers.

Although the words were addressed to the whole group assembled around him, the brave was looking straight into the face of the Arizona Hopi *Activos* Regiment's current commanding officer. He had just completed a description of the events at the small river which confirmed the summations that Tommy Okasi had formed from reading their tracks.

A low and furious snarl burst from Major – recently promoted by virtue of his skill with a sword and willingness to demonstrate it, to the unofficial rank of colonel – Abrahan Phillipe Gonzales *de* Villena *y* Danvila's prominent Hapsburg lips; which stemmed from the result of an indiscretion on the part of a female ancestor. Unconsciously, his right hand rose to touch the severed end of one of the long, flowing plumes of emerald green tail feathers from a cock Quetzal[7] attached to the top of his black astrakhan Hussar-style busby.

All too well Villena remembered how the damage had been inflicted by a bullet from the remarkable rifle belonging to the 'Texian with the face of *el Diablo*', although it had been in the hands of the strange little foreigner who had proved to be such a terribly efficient and deadly warrior. He should have been grateful for having had a narrow escape, but he was not. In addition to having to flee from them, he had left behind his magnificent Toledo steel *épée de combat* that he carried instead of the more cumbersome cavalry sabre. While he had subsequently retrieved the weapon, which they had not carried off for some reason,[8] he would never forgive either of them for inflicting such a humiliation. Nor would he cease to hate them as long as they lived.

Slightly over medium height, with a physique that was reasonable without being exceptional, Villena was in his late twenties. Scion of an extremely wealthy family, he was truculent, proud and overbearing. His deeply bronzed and handsome face was marred by cold hazel eyes with somewhat drooping lids and an arrogant expression. Apart from being light green instead of yellow and having a few other minor differences, his uniform – which had been accepted as the official attire for the officers because his father had financed the

[7] Quetzal: *Pharomachrus Mocino*, one of the *Trogoniformes* group of birds, found in the mountain forests of Central and South America and regarded as sacred by various Indian nations in those regions. Two of the cock's fringed tail covert feathers may attain a length of over three feet each, making them much sought after for decorative purposes.
[8] Being in a hurry to rejoin the mule train, Ole Devil Hardin and Tommy Okasi had not taken the *épée de combat* as neither had wished to be encumbered by carrying it without a sheath.

formation of the Regiment[9] – was modelled upon the late eighteenth-century Spanish Army's Olivenza Hussars; in which, during the Napoleonic Wars, one of his forebears had been a colonel.[10]

'Well, *gentlemen*,' Villena purred, in the icily polite yet mockingly impolite way he always adopted to those he regarded as his inferiors. 'It appears that *I* was correct about the actions of the rebel scum.'

On rejoining the surviving seven Companies after the defeat of the three which had made the disastrous attack at Santa Cristóbal Bay, Villena had announced that he was taking command and intended to avenge their dead comrades-in-arms. Using a chance comment that might have been construed as implying he had shown cowardice as an excuse, he had killed the only officer senior to him in a duel. That had served as a warning to any other potential dissidents. Knowing his quick and savage temper, as well as his deadly skill with a sword or a pistol, they had taken the hint and there had been no further objections to his proposals.

However, some slight demur had been expressed when Villena called for comments upon the proposals he had outlined for achieving vengeance. The general concensus of opinion had been divided on the matter of where the Texians might be located. Although it had been accepted they could no longer be found at the Bay, that was the only point upon which there had been unanimous agreement. Some of the officers had believed they would take a route to the north-west and deliver the consignment of rifles to the retreating main body of the Republic of Texas's Army. Others had considered that they would travel in a south-westerly direction with the garrison at Fort Defiance as their destination.

Showing a surprising forethought, Villena had disagreed with both schools of thought. He had the advantage of knowing the nature of the man who had briefly been his prisoner and who appeared to be in command of the consignment. So he had decided that neither was likely to be the true objective. Or, even if Goliad had been the Satanic-faced Texian's original

[9] Possibly so that, in the event of anything going wrong, there would be a scapegoat other than his son, Villena's father had appointed an older man with military training – who had subsequently fallen during the battle at Santa Cristóbal Bay – to be the commanding officer of the Arizona Hopi *Activos* Regiment.

[10] Colonel José Gonzales *de* Villena *y* Danvila, see Chapter XIII of A SHIP OF THE LINE by C. S. Forester.

goal, knowing that the *Activos* were likely to be between him and it, he would not take the most direct route. On the other hand, it was improbable that Major General Samuel Houston would want the rifles taken to him while he was withdrawing. Rather, he would have arranged for them to be transported to a prearranged rendezvous. The most likely point, in Villena's opinion, would be the 'capital' city of the so-called Republic; Washington-on-the-Brazos. With that in mind, he had led his Regiment in the appropriate direction.

'But, if – as that is the case, M – Colonel,' the major commanding Company Five put in, making the corrections to his phrasing of the question and the honorific as he remembered how touchy the other was on such points. 'Why was the Texian coming in this direction?'

'He has left his command to carry out a scouting mission once before,' Villena explained, having no idea that a second and larger force of the Mexican Army was operating not too far away.[11] Swinging a threatening gaze upon them which dared the rest of the officers to comment upon how he had gained his information regarding the Texian, he turned his attention to the scout, 'Did either of them follow you?'

'No, *senor*,' the brave replied and, having failed to see Tommy Okasi on the occasions when he had looked behind him, believed he was speaking the truth.

'They'll be going back to the mule train as quickly as they can now they know we're so close,' Company Five's commanding officer suggested.

'Then we'll go after them as soon as the horses are rested, *if* that meets with your approval, *Major* Santoval,' Villena answered, his tone and attitude filled with menace and offence. Once again, there was no response to his challenge and he looked at the group of Hopi war leaders. 'Chief Tomas, send twelve of your best men ahead to find the rebels. Tell the rest that we will soon catch those who killed their brothers and they will soon be able to extract a terrible revenge.'

---

[11] The second Mexican column was the Tamaulipa Brigade under the command of General José Urrea, who was to gain notoriety for his inhuman treatment of prisoners. In addition to having the twenty-one surrenderees executed at San Patricio, he later ordered the cold-blooded slaughter of almost four hundred Texians who had fallen into his hands at Goliad.

CHAPTER ELEVEN

YOU'LL HAVE TO LEAVE NOW

'WELL, there's Hickert's Landing and the ferry,' Ole Devil Hardin remarked, pointing down the long and gentle slope that he and his companions were about to descend. He paused and turned to gaze back for several seconds in the direction from which they had come. To anybody who knew him well, there was a noticeable anxiety in the apparently unemotional words with which he went on, 'But no sign of Tommy yet.'

'Would the continued absence of your worthy Oriental factotum be advantageous, or otherwise, Devil?' Mangrove Hallistead inquired – having dropped the formal 'sir' during the long and arduous hours of travelling in the young Texian's company; but, even tired though he was, retaining his usual verbosity – as he and his wife trudged alongside the lathered and leg-weary horse that had been left for them by Tommy Okasi.

'It could be good,' Ole Devil admitted. 'The longer he's away, the further he's had to go to find the Hopis and the more time we'll have before they can reach us.'

'In that eventuality, finding themselves faced with a lengthy and extended pursuit, might they not turn back?' Hallistead suggested, without mentioning the possibility that Tommy might be unable to return.

'They might,' Ole Devil conceded, grasping his linebacked dun gelding's saddle-horn and reaching for the stirrup iron with his left foot. 'But I don't mean to count on it. Let's get down to the landing stage and over the river.'

'Does that mean I get to ride again?' Corrinne Hallistead asked.

'Unless you'd rather run alongside,' Ole Devil replied with a grin, swinging astride the dun.

'I'm not sure which would be most preferable right now,' the little woman sighed, waiting for her husband to mount the borrowed horse so she could get on behind him. 'But knowing you pair, I'll probably be expected to dance for your entertainment when we get to the other side. Do you know something, Devil? My mother actually warned me against marrying into the "thittuh".'

'Up you come, light of my life,' Hallistead boomed, helping his wife to board the animal. 'Didn't I promise you would travel extensively and see strange and exotic places of interest?'

'Yes, dear,' Corrinne agreed, wrapping her arms around the entertainer's waist. 'But you didn't say I'd have to do it *this* way. I don't know which is most sore, my feet or my – well, somewhere else.'

Glancing at the little woman, Ole Devil felt nothing but the greatest admiration for her. Once his clothes had dried, he had decided against waiting for Tommy to rejoin them. So he had fastened the Hallisteads' belongings to the cantle of the dun's saddle, reducing some of the weight to be carried by the horse which they would both have to ride. They had set the best pace possible, while also conserving sufficient energy to leave the couple's heavily ladened mount particularly with something in hand to be used if there should be a need for greater speed. It had entailed them walking and leading the animals for long periods. Despite clearly being very tired, Corrinne had refused to continue riding on such occasions. Instead, not only had she trudged mile after weary mile at her husband's side, but she had also managed to keep her spirits up and had never complained.

Apart from the effort that it required, the journey from the woodland had gone by uneventfully. Throughout it, especially in the later stages, Ole Devil had expected Tommy to catch up with them. However, with about two more hours of daylight left, they had come into sight of Hickert's Landing and he still had not put in an appearance. In spite of being aware of the little Oriental's ability as a fighting man and appreciating the possible benefits from it, the Texian had grown increasingly perturbed by his continued absence.

Wanting to take his thoughts from Tommy, Ole Devil studied their destination about three quarters of a mile ahead. Because of the flow of traffic attracted by the ferry, a small community had grown up around its owner's premises on the eastern bank of the San Berhard River. However, as Ole Devil knew from his earlier visit, with one exception all of the population other than the Hickert family had already taken their departure.

From what the young Texian could see, Moses Hickert had taken to heart his warning that the second Mexican column – or at least a force from it – might already be moving north from San Patricio and, even if they were not, the Arizona Hopi *Activos* Regiment was almost certain to come in search of the mule train. A couple of wagons, which had been under the lean-to when he and Tommy had left that morning, were now standing in front of the house. He regarded the sight as a good sign. The owner of the ferry had stated an intention of continuing to operate it for as long as possible in case it should be needed to carry refugees fleeing to safety from the Mexicans. However, as he had obviously taken the precaution of making ready to leave, he was likely to be willing to accept that the time for departure had come.

There was, however, something just as important as the preparations for departure from Ole Devil's point of view. Several saddle-mounts, hopefully more than the family would consider necessary for their requirements, were mingling with the draught horses in the large corral. Provided that Hickert could be persuaded to part with some of the surplus, one of his problems would be eased.

As he and his companions were drawing nearer, Ole Devil turned his attention to the means by which they would go across the two hundred and fifty yards wide and deep river. Not only must he convince the Hickerts that the time had come for them to leave, but he must induce them to destroy their source of income. All too well, he knew that he must employ persuasion. He would be dealing with a man who possessed a full measure of the typical Texian's spirit of rugged individualism and disinclination to take orders. So any attempt to dictate orders to Hickert would end in failure.

The ferry was a flat bottomed boat, completely decked over with stout planks and having sturdy guard rails along each side. Provided that their teams were unhitched, it could accommodate two fully loaded twenty-six foot long Conestoga-pattern[1] freight wagons. However, as the river's current along that section was exceedingly sluggish, it could not be operated

---

[1] Conestoga wagon: one that is large, very heavily built, with its bed higher at each end than in the middle so that its contents would not spill out when going up and down hills. Its dull white canvas cover had a similar curve, but to a more pronounced degree. The wheels were broad, as an aid to going across country where there were no trails. Also called a 'scoop' wagon.

on the more economical 'compass' system.[2] Instead, a powerful cable of rope passed under the deck – being secured at the bow and stern – and very tightly around a massive pulley wheel on each bank. The wheel at the eastern side was equipped with a long, thick cross bar and had a ramp over the two portions of the cable, so that a pair of draught oxen could be hitched on and supply the motive power.

Noticing that the boat was alongside the opposite landing stage and wanting to avoid any delay in going over, Ole Devil drew the Manton pistol from its loop on his belt and fired a shot into the air. The two male figures working in the corral stared, then one of them pointed across the river and shouted something that did not reach the approaching riders' ears. Clearly he had announced their coming. Two more men stepped from the porch of the house and a woman appeared at the end of the wagons.

Even at that distance, Ole Devil could identify the people on the other bank. The two men who were already leaving the corral were, as might be expected, big and bulky. Their parents, Maw and Moses Hickert, stood respectively six foot and six foot two in height and weighed over four hundred pounds between them. While he was pleased to see the members of the family, he was less enamoured of the fifth person who was present.

Nothing Ole Devil had seen of Abel Ferris the previous evening had been calculated to produce a feeling of liking. Somewhat smaller than any of the Hickerts, which did not make him anywhere close to being classed as a midget, he had struck the Texian as being a bullying hard-case and potential troublemaker. Unlike the male members of the Hickert family, who wore town bought shirts, trousers and heavy boots, he had on smoke-blackened and greasy buckskins. A cheap bowie knife, even larger than the far superior James Black's product carried by Ole Devil, hung in a fancy Indian sheath on his belt.

Giving a wave, Hickert returned to the porch and collected two ox-goads. He handed one to his wife and they went to where two big draught oxen were standing patiently in harness.

[2] Compass system ferry: instead of being hauled across the river in a straight line, the boat was held at the required angle by guy ropes at each end and utilized the pressure of the current against the sides to swing it in an arc from one bank to the other. It could only be used on comparatively narrow rivers, but was cheaper as it did not need any other form of motive power.

At his command, without needing inducement from the steel tipped poles, the animals began to plod ponderously in a circle around the wheel. As it turned and the cable began to pay out, the boat moved forward. Before Ole Devil and his party had arrived, it was waiting for them at the western landing stage. Already the Hickerts were making preparations for the return trip. He observed that, although Ferris had accompanied the couple, they alone set about the task of uncoupling and turning the oxen around. Nor did the surly hard-case offer to help as they set about refastening the beasts' harnesses to the wheel's cross-bar. Instead, he stood scowling across the river. Once the passengers had led their mounts aboard, the oxen were started walking in the opposite direction and the boat reversed its course towards the eastern bank.

'Howdy, Cap'n Hardin,' Hickert greeted, as the Texian walked from the landing stage with the dun following on his feels like a well trained hound dog. 'You're back a whole heap sooner'n you counted on.'

'With cause, sir,' Ole Devil replied, conscious of the way that the owner of the ferry was looking at the Hallisteads but wanting to establish the urgency of his return before satisfying his curiosity. 'We found the Hopis are much closer than I'd been led to assume. In fact, they're likely to be here before noon tomorrow.'

'As soon's that?' Hickert asked, rubbing a huge hand across his bristle-stubbled chin and looking at his boat.

'I don't think it will be much longer,' Ole Devil replied, doubting whether the scouts with whom he had come into contact would be more than ten miles ahead of the main body. Then he turned his gaze to the big, buxom and, in spite of being in her early fifties, still handsome wife of the ferry's owner, continuing, 'Mr. and Mrs. Hallistead here have been trav—'

'Misiz—?' Maw Hickert repeated, staring at the small figure alongside the entertainer with first surprise, then enlightenment and pity. 'Land-sakes! So you are. Come on up to the house, gal. You look 'most dead on your feet.'

'I feel it,' Corrinne admitted with a wry smile, sensing and appreciating the larger woman's feeling of compassion for her condition, as she walked forward slowly. 'But I'd rather just *feel* it than be it, which could have happened if we'd stayed at San Patricio.'

'San Patri—!' Maw began, eyes raking Corrinne from head

to toe and, being sufficiently experienced to read the signs correctly she could tell the whole story without needing to take the hard-used condition of the horses into consideration. Raising her voice in a bellow which, Ole Devil decided, would not have shamed Stentor,[3] she called, 'Henry! Clyde! Get on down here *pronto* and take care of these good folks's hosses.' Then, moderating her tone she went on, 'You come along with me and rest whatever you figure needs resting, gel. We can leave the talking to the menfolks. Only don't you go wasting too much time on it, Mose. These folks've been travelling fast 'n' hard, so they could likely do with a rest.'

'Go ahead, my dove,' Hallistead prompted, when his wife looked at him for guidance. 'I'll follow you eftsoons with these gentlemen.'

'So you reckon's it's as bad as all that, huh, Cap'n?' Hickert asked, as the women were walking away.

'I do, sir,' Ole Devil confirmed. 'You'll have to move out now.'

'Have to?' Ferris repeated, before Hickert could speak. He advanced to stand by the owner of the ferry's side and eyed the young Texian truculently. 'Well now, soldier-boy, I can't say's how Mose' 'n' me've ever took kindly to letting *nobody* tell *us* 's we *have* to do anything.'

Listening to the harsh Louisiana drawl, Ole Devil decided that Ferris must have understood his meaning. When making the statement, he had had no intention of giving orders to Hickert. He was merely making a comment based upon the conversation they had had the previous night.

'Just how soon do you conclude they'll be getting here, Cap'n?' Hickert inquired, before the Texian could attempt to clear up Ferris's misapprehension.

'It could be tonight, or some time tomorrow, sir,' Ole Devil guessed, wishing he could give a more positive reply. 'I won't know for sure until—'

'Have you seen 'em?' Ferris demanded, with an air of challenge.

'We had a run in with their scouts, killed three and one got away,' Ole Devil answered, speaking in a polite way which would have warned anybody who had had much contact with him that he was growing annoyed by the interruptions. 'I sent

[3] Stentor: according to Grecian mythology and Homer's *Iliad*, a Greek herald in the Trojan War whose voice had the volume of fifty men.

my man after him, with orders to find the rest of them.'

'Your man!' Ferris snorted, his whole attitude redolent of contempt. 'You hear that, Mose'. The soldier-boy's sent that heathen "Chinese" and's counting on him to find out how close them Injuns be.'

'Tommy's as good a scout as any man I know,' Ole Devil declared, but he appreciated that, unless seen in action, the little Oriental was not an impressive figure. He was also aware that the kind of Chinese with whom either of the men had come into contact with before were not noted for ability in the martial arts. 'I'm satisfied that he'll find them if anybody can.'

'*You* might be, soldier-boy,' Ferris sneered, his voice oozing offence and disdain. 'But that don't mean's how anybody else has to.'

Listening to the challenge in the derisive words, Ole Devil realized that the burly hard-case was bent on causing trouble and wondered why this should be. To the best of his knowledge, they had never met before the previous evening and the name 'Ferris' meant nothing to him. Although he had been conscious of the other eyeing him malevolently yesterday evening, he had thought little of it. During his life, he had come across men who harboured a deep and bitter resentment against anybody in a position of authority, or who was better favoured in wealth, social standing and possessions than themselves. So he had been inclined to regard Ferris as such a person and had ignored him. Now he was wondering if the hardcase had some other reason for trying to pick a fight. He also appreciated that, under the circumstances, it was up to him to avoid becoming involved in one if possible.

While there were those who believed differently, Ole Devil was neither quick tempered nor the kind of hot head who went out of his way to seek trouble. He had been born and raised in the State of Louisiana, which was notorious as being a hotbed for adherents of the '*code duello*', but he had been taught that fighting and killing were matters to be taken seriously. They should never be indulged in on the flimsy pretences used by many wealthy young Southrons as excuses to issue challenges to duels. So he refused to allow his resentment over the doubts which Ferris was casting upon his veracity, or Tommy's abilities, to make him lose his temper.

For all his resolve, Ole Devil realized that avoiding a contretempts with the hard-case would not be easy. A shrewd judge of character, he had formed an accurate assessment of the other's nature. What was more, experience had taught him that there was only one way to deal with such a man. Any suggestion of hesitation, or attempts at temporizing, were likely to be regarded as a sign of weakness and would probably lead to further abuses.

There was, however, a further factor for the young Texian to take into consideration. If he tried to evade the issue, apart from the likelihood of causing additional aggression on Ferris's part, he might forfeit Hickert's respect. In which case, his advice and wishes would be ignored. Or at least there could be such a delay in acting upon them that it might result in the ferry falling into the enemies' hands. That would endanger the lives of everybody present, as well as lessening the time needed by the Hopis to catch up with the mule train. He was counting upon the destruction of the boat to allow him to rejoin the consignment and prepare for the fight which he believed was sure to come. Nor could he order that the wrecking of the family's business be carried out. The only way he could achieve his purpose was by gaining their support.

A glance at Moses Hickert warned Ole Devil that his assumption was correct. While he sensed a disapproval of Ferris's behaviour behind the seamed, tanned and expressionless face, he knew there would be no help out of his predicament from that source. According to the code by which the ferry boat's owner lived, any personal matter must be settled between the two main participants and without outside interference.

Even as Ole Devil accepted that he must take some kind of action, he was all too aware of what doing so would entail. He would be contending with a man who matched him in height, but was heavier. Furthermore, while he was tired from the exertions of the past day, Ferris was fresh and rested.

In spite of all that, the young Texian knew he must do something.

And soon!

CHAPTER TWELVE

ISN'T THIS JUST LIKE *MEN*?

'COULDN'T be sure this far off, Cap'n,' Moses Hickert remarked, almost casually, as the grim faced young Texian was about to release the linebacked dun gelding's reins as a prelude to tackling his tormentor. 'But it sure looks like the lil "Chinee" feller of your'n coming.'

'It *is* Tommy,' Mangrove Hallistead confirmed, having been standing silently but experiencing a growing concern over what was developing. He had heard of his companion's reputation of being a 'lil ole devil for a fight' and doubted whether the other would have sufficient self control to avoid one in spite of being on an important mission. However, he had not been able to think of a way in which he could intervene and prevent it. 'He'll soon be here, the way he's riding.'

'*Bueno*,' Ole Devil Hardin replied, without taking his eyes from Abel Ferris's surly face, but directing the words at the other men. 'Once he arrives and we hear what he has to say, we'll know what has to be done.'

'Yeah?' the hard-case growled, eager to cause a fight but also wanting to have what would pass as a reason for doing so. Remembering the stories he had heard about his proposed victim, he did not doubt that he could achieve this. 'Only we'll make up our own minds. This here ain't Iberville Parish,[1] Louisiana, where everybody has to jump when one of you Hardin, Fog and Blaze bunch beckons.'

At the mention of the region in the United States where his clan had their most extensive holdings, Ole Devil realized that he might be wrong regarding the cause of Ferris's hostility. Up until then, he had put it down to either stemming from just a bad tempered desire to make trouble or – as when a man deliberately sought out and challenged a successful duellist – a matter of wanting to prove himself better than somebody who

[1] The State of Louisiana uses the word 'Parish' instead of 'County'.

had earned a reputation for being a tough and capable fighter.

Other possibilities now sprang to Ole Devil's mind. Given so much of a clue, Ferris's Louisiana accent suggested what might be a solution. He could be nursing a grudge against the members of the Hardin, Fog and Blaze clan for some real, or fancied, wrong and was hoping for an opportunity to repay it.

It was also feasible, the young Texian decided, that the hard-case might have an even more sinister intent. After Ole Devil had left Louisiana, a reward had been offered for his arrest and return.[2] However, it had been for a comparatively small amount and would only be paid if he was taken back alive. So, particularly with Texas in such a state of turmoil, Ferris was unlikely to be considering making such an attempt. He could have something else in mind, believing that if he could kill Ole Devil the people who had put up the reward – and whose son he had been falsely accused of murdering – might be generous out of gratitude for having such a service rendered when they had no other means of taking revenge.

No matter what Ferris's actual motives might be, Ole Devil knew that nothing was changing in the situation he was trying to bring about. Except that, if the latter eventuality should be correct, he would be meaning to kill rather than merely assert his superiority by physical means.

The possibility that the hard-case was hoping to earn the Beaucoup family's appreciation and financial support made dealing with him more difficult. Although Ole Devil had not envisaged that he might need one, on the way to the ferry he had instinctively exchanged the pistol used to signal their coming for the loaded weapon in his saddle-holster. So he had the means to defend himself and in a fashion that would in all probability come as a complete surprise to his antagonist.

Unfortunately, the issue was not as simple as that.

Ole Devil realized that he could be making the wrong assumption. Perhaps Ferris was only a bully trying to assert himself; or at the worst, wanted to work off some ill feeling towards the Hardin, Fog and Blaze clan in general by picking a fist fight with one of its members who had crossed his path. In that case, he would not be contemplating a murderous assault, but merely a rough house brawl.

While Ole Devil was willing to be completely ruthless where the protection of the consignment was concerned, he had never regarded lightly the taking of another human being's life for

[2] See the first footnote on page 12.

personal reasons. So he could not adopt the most obvious course of drawing his pistol and ending the matter with a bullet.

'I'd be obliged if you'd have the ferry across there when my man arrives, Mr. Hickert,' Ole Devil requested, giving no sign of his thoughts or even that he had heard Ferris's comment.

'Sure, Cap'n,' Hickert assented, without showing the slightest indication of how he felt about what was happening. 'I'll tend to it.'

'Now me,' Ferris said, advancing a pace. 'I'm wondering why, with you being so concerned about them Hopis 'n' all, you didn't go look for 'em yourself instead of sending that heathen "Chinee".'

'We can only hope that they're not too close,' Ole Devil drawled, dropping the dun's reins and starting to turn towards the river, still apparently refusing to acknowledge his challenger's presence. 'The further they're away—'

'God damn it!' the burly hard-cased bellowed, continuing to advance and his face darkening with anger at being subjected to such cavalier treatment, 'I'm talking to you, you fancy dressed son—'

Instantly, satisfied that the other was behaving as he had anticipated and had sought to bring about, Ole Devil pivoted around with such violence that his hat was dislodged to fall back on his shoulders and he sprang to meet Ferris.

Taken completely unawares, the hard-case was further disconcerted by the exposure of the horn-like tufts of hair on the sides of the young Texian's head. They added to the already savage Mephistophelian aspect of his face that was enhanced by the strain of the exertions he had endured during his present assignment. For the first time, Ferris began to realize what was portended by the second part of Ole Devil's sobriquet. Although far from religious, he was sufficiently superstitious for the shock to numb his responses at a moment when they should have been working at their fastest.

Up lashed Ole Devil's right arm, delivering a backhand blow with wicked force to the side of the burly man's left cheek. Alarm as much as pain caused Ferris to snatch his forward leg to the rear so as to carry himself away from his Satanic-featured assailant. Almost before the foot had touched the ground, the flat palm whipped across to meet his head as it was turned by the force of the blow and reversed its direction with an equal violence. Once again, the recipient of the attack was driven to make an involuntary withdrawal and with even more disastrous results. Lashing around, driven by the full power and fury of a wiry and whipcord strong body, the knuckles repeated their contact with no loss of velocity for all the speed that they were moving.

Coming so rapidly and hard, the blows completely destroyed Ferris's equilibrium. Trying to back away with sufficient haste to avoid further punishment and not a little frightened by the almost demoniac rage which he had caused to be released, he lost his footing. Going down, he alighted on his rump with a bone jarring thud. For a few seconds, he sat dazed and winded. Then, although his vision was still blurred, he spat out an obscenity and his right hand went towards the hilt of his knife.

'Go ahead!' a savage voice challenged, cutting like the blast of an icy cold wind into the mists of anger, pain and humiliation that were tearing through the discomforted hard-case. 'Take it out – if you think you can.'

Before the final part of the speech was completed, Ferris's vision cleared and the sight that met his eyes was one he would never forget. Crouching slightly, the tall figure before him was charged with a grim and terrible menace. What frightened him was not the way in which the right arm was extended and bent so that the hand, turned palm outwards, was close to the butt of the pistol in the loop of the waist belt. The day of the fast-drawing gun fighter and his methods was yet to come, so he had no conception what the posture indicated.

It was the sheer magnetic driving force of Ole Devil's personality that produced the reaction!

Staring at him, the hard-case did not doubt for a single instant that he was ready, willing and completely able to kill without mercy.

So the young Texian was, but he hoped that the necessity would not arise!

Almost a minute dragged by on leaden feet, or so it seemed to Ferris. Much as he hated to admit it even to himself, he did not dare to attempt pulling out the knife although he had no idea of how Ole Devil proposed to stop him. He was aware that the only alternative was to back down and eat crow. He could not hope for intervention on the part of the other men. Although his main attention was riveted upon the menacing figure confronting him, he was conscious of the second male arrival's dispassionate gaze and sensed that Hickert was also studying him,

117

awaiting whatever came next with no great display of emotion.

Attracted by the commotion from their rear, Corrinne Hallistead and Maw Hickert had turned around. Neither of them knew exactly what had caused the trouble, but both suspected that it was not of Ole Devil's making. Knowing the hard-case, Maw had a solid basis for her belief. Corrinne had had considerable experience of men and had deduced correctly the natures of the protagonists in the little drama. So she felt sure that the young Texian had been provoked and guessed that he had no wish to take the matter further if it could be avoided.

Although the men had no intention of mediating, the same did not apply to the women. There was one difference in their attitudes. Maw had duplicated the little actress's summations, but was unable to decide what would be the best way to ease the situation. Seeing Tommy Okasi approaching, Corrinne realized how she could achieve her purpose; at least as far as Ole Devil was concerned.

'Really, Maw!' the actress snorted, in tones of exasperation, starting to retrace her footsteps. 'Isn't this just like *men*? There's poor little Tommy Okasi needing to be brought over the river and they're playing foolish games.'

'Danged if it don't make you want to give up on 'em,' the big woman supported, stepping out to catch up and keep pace with the other member of her sex. 'Mose' Hickert, you get them blasted oxen unhitched and turned around. And, happen you're so all-fired eager to hear what that feller's got to say, you pair want to lend him a hand to do it.'

'A most astute and commendable suggestion, my dear lady,' Hallistead admitted, showing a trace of relief as he realized what the women were hoping to do. 'And one which I, with all promptitude, would advise that we apply ourselves to carrying out, Devil.'

'I don't know what most of that was about,' Maw growled. 'But, happen it means "yes", get to it.'

'With alacrity, although I am but slightly acquainted with such a task,' the entertainer assented. 'Perhaps you would, having more experience possibly, care to instruct me, Devil.'

'Why sure,' the Texian replied, but he did not turn away immediately. Instead, he addressed the hard-case in a quiet, matter of fact, yet somehow coldly threatening manner. 'One thing, *hombre*. The Beaucoups have found out that I didn't kill Saul. So there'd be no bounty if you'd tried to claim it.'

118

'Wha—?' gasped Ferris, but Ole Devil had swung on his heel and was walking with Hallistead towards the oxen.

To give the hard-case his due, he had never heard of the reward offered by the Beaucoup family for Ole Devil's arrest and return. His animosity had arisen out of a *share-cropper arrangement*[3] he had made in Iberville Parish with Colonel Marsden Fog.

In spite of given several opportunities to change his ways, always shiftless and idle, his continued failure to uphold his end of the bargain had caused him to be evicted. As a result, his long-suffering wife had deserted him and he had drifted to Texas in search of a way of earning a living that was not burdened with the need to do much work. When he had failed to achieve his goal, never being one to admit he was at fault, he had put the blame on the owner of the property he had been mismanaging. Brooding over it, he had extended his hatred to the whole of the Hardin, Fog and Blaze clan. Ole Devil was the first of them with whom he had come into contact and that alone was the reason why he had picked the fight.

Although Ferris did not realize it, he had had a very narrow escape. Many a man, especially when labouring under the strains that Ole Devil was enduring while at the same time possessing such effective fighting techniques, would not have thought twice about killing him.

Watching the straight-backed young Texian striding away, the hard-case muttered under his breath. Fear and resentment warred with each other inside him. The latter emotion cried for revenge, but the former cautioned against trying to obtain it. For once in his worthless life, he was ready to listen to the dictates of prudence and wisdom. Which showed good sense. If he had offered to cause further trouble, Ole Devil could not have refrained from killing him.

'*Mr.* Ferris,' Maw Hickert said, as the hard-case started to rise.

'Yeah?' Ferris asked, looking over his shoulder.

'I hope you ain't fixing to make no more fuss for young Cap'n Hardin,' the big woman went on, tapping the heavy ox-goad she was still holding against the palm of her left hand as if it weighed no more than a slender willow switch. ''Cause *I* wouldn't like it if you do. Fact being, I reckon's you had a right smart notion when you was talking about pulling out and going

---

[3] Share-cropper: a tenant farmer who contracts to pay a share of his produce as his rent instead of money.

to find General Sam 'n' enlist in the Army. Why'n't you go and do it?'

'I reckon I will,' Ferris replied, refusing to meet either woman's gaze. He knew better than to antagonize Maw and also was aware that she had never cared for him. So he doubted if he would be welcome to stay in Hickert's Landing even if the news that the little Oriental was bringing in such haste should – which was not likely – be favourable. 'Yeah. I reckon I'll go and collect my gear 'n' head out now.'

'Good luck to you,' Maw grunted, then swung towards her bulky sons who were hovering in the background. 'Take care of them two hosses, Henry, and you see to that other when its gets across, Clyde. Come on, gal. I reckon's you and me can leave them shiftless menfolks to do the rest.'

Oblivious of what had taken place behind them, but confident that one of the women would give a warning if the hardcase was contemplating further hostilities, Ole Devil and Hallistead helped Hickert to unhitch and turn the oxen. With the animals on the move, the Texian watched the boat creeping forward. As he did so, he began to think how useful it had been to travellers in the past and what an asset it would be if the struggle for independence was successful. However, it was also dangerous to the safety of the consignment if the enemy were allowed to capture and utilize it as a means of a rapid crossing of the San Berhard River.

'I'll be right sorry to lose this old boat, Cap'n,' Hickert remarked, almost as if he was reading the Texian's mind.

'Yes, sir,' Ole Devil answered. 'But there's no way you could hold on to it if the Hopis are coming. Even if they passed you by, they'll want it should they come back with the consignment.'

'That's for sure,' Hickert admitted, then gave a fatalistic shrug. 'Anyways, happen ole Santa Anna wins this fuss, which he could do a whole heap easier without General Sam having them caplocks, ain't no chance of him leaving us here to keep running her.'

'You're right, sir,' Ole Devil agreed. 'He's sworn that he won't allow a single *gringo* to own land on Mexican soil in future. But, if we win, your ferry will be needed more than ever.'

'Likely,' Hickert conceded, knowing that in all probability there would be an influx of colonists from the United States if the security of an independent Republic could be attained. He darted a glance of curiosity at the younger man's Satanic face. 'Only *I* can't see's how we can have it both ways?'

'What do you have in mind, Devil?' Hallistead put in, having followed the conversation with interest and sharing the owner of the ferry's belief that the Texian was not merely making idle chatter.

'The Hopis would be willing to use the ferry,' Ole Devil replied, watching the boat reach the western bank where Tommy was already waiting on the landing stage. 'But, coming from Arizona, I don't think they would know how to refloat and repair it, even if they'd be willing to take the time.'

'You're right!' Hallistead ejaculated, so impressed that he forgot to employ his usual verbose flow of words. 'If the boat was sunk, trained men would be required to raise and repair it.'

'Whoa!' Hickert bawled at the oxen, having been keeping the boat under observation. Realizing what the young Texian was driving at, he continued as soon as the order had been obeyed, 'How about that bunch from San Patricio, could they do it?'

'From what I saw, there's a full Brigade there,' Hallistead answered, as Ole Devil looked at him. 'While I couldn't swear to their presence, my rudimentary knowledge of military organization leads me to presuppose they have engineers accompanying them. However, as I mentioned while we were coming here, Devil, there was no sign of pursuit. Furthermore, all the reconnaissance activity which I observed in the, I admit limited time they were subjected to my scrutiny, was directed to the west. I would be inclined to suggest it will be in that direction, rather than northwards they are intending to devote their energies.'

A faint grin flickered across the Texian's face as he watched Tommy leading the blue roan gelding on to the boat. For all the entertainer's diffuse manner of speaking, he was no fool. What was more, in spite of his claim to know little about the subject, his summations on military matters were worth considering.

'You mean they'll go to Goliad to take care of Fannin's bunch afore they head out to join up with Santa Anna?' Hickert asked, remembering what Ole Devil had told him about the state of affairs elsewhere in Texas, and the fact that he directed the question at Hallistead showed he too accepted the entertainer was worth listening to.

'That would be my considered supposition, sir,' Hallistead declared.

While talking, the three men had started to change the oxen.

'Santa Anna's sure to have engineers along, even if that bunch at San Patricio don't,' Hickert guessed, stepping back after the completion of the work and setting the animals into motion. 'I'd hate like hell for him to be able to use old Nellie there.'

'It's not likely he'll come this far south,' Ole Devil pointed out. 'He'll be following General Houston, who's falling back towards Washington-on-the-Brazos and will go over thereabouts.[4] So they'll go by well to the north.'

'What do you reckon'd be the best thing for us to do, Cap'n?' Hickert asked. 'Sink her in midstream.'

'That *would* be the safest way, sir,' Ole Devil replied. 'Or you could beach her somewhere downstream. Take out some of her bottom planks, load the cable on to one of your wagons and drive the oxen along with you when you leave. I think that the Hopis will come after us, not you, so you'll be all right.'

'Huh huh!' Hickert grunted non-committally, but he liked the solution he had been offered. Many a young man would not have troubled to think of such a thing. 'How long do you conclude it'll be afore General Sam's ready for the showdown with 'em, Cap'n?'

'A month, or two at the most,' Ole Devil decided, after a moment's thought. 'He's falling back until he's certain our people are close enough to be able to escape over the U.S. line if things go badly.'

'Was that all she'd be under, she wouldn't take no hurt,' Hickert said quietly. 'And, happen we get run out, I'm such an ornery cuss that I'd sooner not have some greaser taking her over unless he's had a heap of work to do.'

'I'll leave how you handle it up to you, sir,' Ole Devil stated, satisfied that he had achieved his purpose. 'And, of course, there might not be any need for you to do anything at all.'

Even as he was speaking, Ole Devil and the other two men were looking at the approaching boat. Studying the condition of the little Oriental and his horse, the coat of which was white

---

[4] Due to an inspired piece of trickery causing a change in both sides' strategy, the Texians finally crossed the Brazos River some miles south of Washington-on-the-Brazos, at what was then known as Groce's Place, on April the 12th and 13th, 1836. Having captured two canoes and a flatboat at Thompson's Ferry – which later became the town of Richmond, seat of Fort Bend County, Texas – the Mexicans went over on April the 14th, paving the way for the final battle. Further details of how all this came about and the result are given in: OLE DEVIL AT SAN JACINTO.

with lather to such an extent that its true colour was almost completely hidden, they all realized the Texian was raising a false hope. Tommy would only have driven his mount to such a state if the matter was extremely urgent. There was no chance of the Hopis having given up the pursuit. In fact, from all appearances, they could be very close at hand.

CHAPTER THIRTEEN

IF I CAN ASK THEM TO DIE,
I CAN ASK YOU TO LIVE

SITTING with his back propped against a rock and fighting to stave off the tiredness that threatened to make him fall asleep, Ole Devil Hardin was once again waiting for Tommy Okasi to catch up and deliver a report. He hoped, but did not expect, that it would be one that would relieve his anxiety over the safety of the consignment. From what the little Oriental had told him on the previous occasion, he knew that he had at least bought himself a respite by his activities at Hickert's Landing, but he doubted whether he had seen the last of the Arizona Hopi *Activos* Regiment.

Taking sufficient time only for a drink of water and to compose himself on leaving the ferry boat, Tommy had told of his activities since parting company from his employer. One important point had been his suspicion that the Mexican officer with whom they had originally been in contact appeared to have assumed command of the Regiment following the death of its previous colonel. If that was the case, unless Ole Devil was mistaken, he would be more determined than any of his fellow officers to continue the pursuit and have a reckoning with them.

Having seen the party of braves setting off, while the remainder of the Regiment were making preparations to march, Tommy had guessed their purpose. Returning to his horse he had ridden in the direction from which he had come. Smaller, lighter and better mounted than any of the men he was seeking to avoid, he had increased his lead over them and, to the best of his knowledge, his presence ahead had not been discovered by the time he was at the river in the woodland.

Although, Tommy said, he had considered trying to delay the scouting party at the crossing, he had decided against putting his idea into effect. Prudence had dictated this decision.

His supply of arrows was rapidly diminishing. While he had retrieved the shaft that had ruined the Hopi's bow and could use it again, the second that he had discharged had disappeared into the woodland and he could not delay moving on to search for it. Nor was there any other way in which he could obtain a fresh supply until he had rejoined the main body of the Texas Light Cavalry and replenished his quiver from the stock he had left with the baggage train. As his own were forty inches in length and had points peculiar to Japanese archery[1] to influence their weight and balance, he could not substitute them with the shorter and – in his opinion – vastly inferior arrows both in construction and utility which he could have taken from the dead warriors at Santa Cristóbal Bay.

As an added inducement to caution, the little Oriental had realized that his employer must be informed as quickly as possible that the enemy were so close and in much greater strength than had been anticipated. With that in mind, he had continued to travel at the best speed his mount could produce. The big blue roan gelding had *brio escondido*[2] and needed it to cover the miles separating him from his destination.

Shortly before reaching Hickert's Landing, Tommy had climbed to the top of a hill. Searching his back trail with the aid of the telescope, he had not seen the Hopis' advance party. That had meant they were at least three miles away.

Accepting the little Oriental's summation, Moses Hickert had set about making preparations for departure. However, at his suggestion, Ole Devil had not waited until the work was completed. Leaving the owner and his family to carry out what was hopefully only the temporary disablement of the ferry, he had set off to rejoin the mule train. Fortunately, they had had sufficient saddles horses to supply Tommy, Mangrove Hallistead and himself with fresh mounts. The entertainer had offered his services in the defense of the consignment, but Ole Devil had convinced him that he would be better employed in ensuring that Major General Samuel Houston was informed of what had happened at San Patricio. So he was to accompany the Hickerts, with his wife riding in one of their wagons, when they set off to the north-west in search of the Republic of Texas's Army. Tommy had also stayed behind, so that he could

[1] Details of the special Japanese archery points and their use is given in: OLE DEVIL AT SAN JACINTO.

[2] *Brio escondido:* 'hidden vigour', stamina and endurance of an exceptional standard.

get some badly needed rest and keep watch at the San Berhard River.

Travelling hard, in spite of the fatigue that assailed him, Ole Devil had taken only sufficient pauses to allow his three horse relay – two from the Hickerts and his linebacked dun gelding, which he had not ridden – to rest. He had caught up with the mule train shortly before noon that day. After telling Diamond-Hitch Brindley, Sergeant Smith and Joe Galton of the latest developments, he had sent Tom Wolf – who had returned from a successful visit to San Phillipe – and three more of the Tejas Indian scouts to relieve the little Oriental. That had been three hours ago. Now, having ridden one of his borrowed horses into the ground and reduced the second to a state of near ex-haustion, Tommy was coming to where the Texian was waiting. The tidings he brought were a mixture of good and bad.

Shortly before night had fallen, the Hopis' advance party had come into sight of Hickert's Landing. However, by that time the owner and his sons had taken and sunk the boat in the middle of the river. Although they had still been removing the cable, having no firearms, the braves had not attempted to interfere in any way. The Hickerts and the Hallisteads had taken their departure in the darkness, but the warriors had not offered to try and cross the river. Instead, they had waited on the western bank until the rest of their Regiment arrived the following morning.

Once he had come on the scene, the self appointed Colonel Abrahan Phillipe Gonzales *de* Villena *y* Danvila had wasted no time in setting about the task of going over the water. For all that, there had been a considerable delay before his Regiment could accomplish the crossing. Watched by Tommy from a distance, a party had swam to the eastern bank and, using timber wrested from the buildings, had started to construct rafts. However, once over, they had followed the consignment and ignored the tracks of the Hickerts' small party.

'They're after us,' the little Oriental finished, looking at his audience of Ole Devil, Di, Smith and Galton. 'And they coming faster than the mules are moving.'

'That figures, with Villena in command,' the Texian re-plied. 'A man like him won't easily forget, or forgive, us for making him leave his sword when he ran away.'

'What'll we do, Devil?' Di asked. 'The Brazos's only a couple of miles on, but I don't see how we can get across it hereabouts. There's no timber for us to make rafts and float the consignment over and she's sure's hell too deep and wide to take it across on the mules.'

'There isn't any chance of finding a boat we could use?' Ole Devil asked, although he could guess what the answer was going to be.

'Not's I know of,' the girl replied. 'We could maybe go and take a look.'

'That's what we'll do,' Ole Devil agreed, getting to his feet. 'You'd best come with me, Sergeant Smith.'

'Yo!' the non-com answered.

'And you, if you will, Di,' Ole Devil continued.

'Sure,' the girl assented.

Tired as he was, the young Texian knew that there was an urgent need to survey the situation and he was the one best equipped to carry it out. They had no hope of outrunning their pursuers. Nor could they reach safety before being overtaken. So, unless they could find some means of crossing the Brazos River, they would have no choice but to stop and fight. If that was the only choice, he wanted to select the best place for them to do it.

The mule train had been kept moving while the council of war had taken place. Catching up with it, Ole Devil left Galton in charge and pushed on with Di, Tommy and Smith. Studying the terrain as they were riding along, he concluded that the girl was correct. Although there were a few scattered trees, he could not see sufficient for them to be able to make rafts. However, on reaching the river, he decided that luck had not entirely deserted them.

Having passed through a deep gorge, some freak of nature caused the river on merging to make a U-shaped bend to the east forming a sizeable basin of land on the inside of the curve. There was a high and sheer cliff at the upstream arm of the 'U' and steeply sloping, rocky but otherwise fairly open ground on the lower side over which horses could only gallop with great difficulty and at considerable risk to their riders.

Gazing around, Ole Devil knew that no body of horsemen as large as the seven Companies of the Arizona Hopi *Activos* Regiment would be able to come closer than half a mile from the edge of the river without being detected. Furthermore, any mass attack down the sole means of easy access would have to be launched from a front slightly less than five hundred yards in width.

Against those advantages, there was only scanty natural cover for the defenders and the hard, rocky nature of the soil at the bottom of the basin, where they must take up their position, precluded the digging of other than very shallow rifle pits. In addition, unlike on the previous occasion when they had fought against the Hopis, not only was the size of their force drastically reduced but they would not have any element of surprise in their favour. Sufficient of the former attackers had survived and rejoined their companions to prevent a similar mistake being made. They would have been warned that the tactics upon which they had relied had failed due to the unexpected ability of the proposed victims' weapons to fire in what should have been adverse, or at least, unfavourable, weather conditions.

Although there had been and might still be one possibility of salvation for the consignment, he did not intend to rely upon it materializing. He decided that, more in hope than expectancy, he would ask Tom Wolf – if the chief returned in time – or Di, for permission to send one of the Tejas scouts in each direction to seek and bring it to him if it should be available.

'You've been along here before, haven't you, Di?' Ole Devil inquired, after he had explained the good and bad points of the hollow.

'More'n once,' the girl admitted.

'Is there anywhere else that would be better that we could reach before the Hopis catch us?' Smith asked, guessing what his superior was considering.

'Nope, not's comes to mind off hand,' Di decided, having screwed up her pretty face in concentration and visualized what she could remember of that particular section of the Brazos River. 'There's nothing but open and level ground both ways from here on for maybe two days' travel.'

'They'll be on to us before then,' Ole Devil warned, and glanced into the hollow. 'So *this's* where we make our stand. Let's go back and fetch the train up.

'Shucks!' the girl sniffed, studying the Texian's and the little Oriental's haggard and tired faces. 'Ain't no call for us all going. I reckon Smithie 'n' me can 'tend to that. You pair stay here and rest up until we get back.'

'You do that, Tommy,' Ole Devil began.

'And *you*, damn it!' Di injected.

'If I stop and sit down, I'm likely to fall asleep,' Ole Devil protested. 'And there's too much to be done before I can let that happen.'

'All right then,' the girl answered, with an air of brooking no interference or refusal, but realizing that she had heard the truth. 'You head back, Smithie. I'll stop here 'n' help you keep awake, Devil.'

'Sure, Di,' the sergeant agreed, for once not looking to his superior for guidance. 'Have you any orders before I go, sir?'

'Only one,' Ole Devil replied, noticing that the non-com had said 'before I go' instead of asking if he could leave, but making no comment or protest. Knowing that the other was acting with his best interests at heart, he decided it was not the time to stand on the formalities that should be due to his rank. Having received permission from Di to use the scouts as he had envisaged, he went on, 'And *gracias*, the pair of you.'

'*Es nada*,' Di drawled. 'I'm used to having to talk sense to fool menfolks.' Her gaze swung to Tommy and she continued, 'And here's an old 'n' wise Texian saying's *I've* just now made up. A feller's looks as dad-blasted tired's you do'd best get down and take some rest afore he falls down.'

'Now I *know* it's time for me to brave the *Shogun*'s[3] wrath and go home,' the little Oriental informed his employer.

'Get some rest afore you go,' the girl advised, apparently unmoved by the baleful glance at her that had accompanied Tommy's words. 'If you don't, you'll never make it.'

'She's right, *amigo*, much as I hate to have to say it,' Ole Devil went on. 'Go and have some sleep. I wish I could.'

'How'd you fix to handle things, Devil?' Di asked, watching the slump-shouldered and swaying little Oriental riding away and realizing just how close to complete exhaustion he must be. If anything, his exertions recently had been even greater than those of his employer.

'Like I said, make a stand on the banks down there,' the Texian replied, speaking slowly as he struggled to remain awake and thinking. 'We'll make the Hopis suffer the heaviest casualties possible and still stop them taking the consignment.'

'How do you figure on doing that, take it across the river?'

'I doubt if there's any way we could do that in the time. Nor is there much chance of us moving the ammunition over without it getting ruined by the water. Even if we did, with the

---

[3] *Shogun:* the hereditary commander-in-chief of the Japanese Army until the post was rescinded in 1868. Corrupted by foreigners to 'tycoon', the name added another word to the English language.

hatred he has for us, Villena would keep after us. No. I intend
to stop him here— Or make him believe there's no point in
continuing the pursuit.'

'How?' Di demanded.

'As soon as the mules get here, I want you to have them unloaded and moved across the river,' Ole Devil explained, being
aware that at least one of his subsequent proposals was going
to meet with considerable opposition when the girl heard it but
equally determined it would be carried out. 'We'll move over
as many of the caplocks as we can. They'll not take any harm if
they get wet, greased up as they are. I'll keep, say four, loaded
and ready to be used for every man who volunteers to stay
with me—'

'*Volunteers?*' Di repeated.

'There'll be no way that anybody who stays with me can
escape,' Ole Devil elaborated. 'I won't *order* my men to do it on
those terms.'

'Knowing them, there's not one who'll say "no",' Di stated.

'It will be their choice,' Ole Devil replied and felt sure that
the girl was correct in her assumption. 'We'll stack up all the
remaining ammunition behind our positions and cover it with
a tarpaulin so that it looks as if the whole consignment's there
ready to be taken.'

'Only it'll be fixed so's they can't lay their cotton-picking
hands on it happen they whup us,' Di guessed, although –
having already seen several examples of the young Texian's
skill at making plans to take care of possible contingencies – the
words came out more as a statement.

'There'll be a powder flask in the middle, with a piece of
quick-match fixed down its nozzle and taken to the back of the
pile,' Ole Devil confirmed. 'When there's no further hope of
holding them off, Sergeant Smith will set fire to it and take
some more of them with us.'

'There's some's might say that's a real sneaky trick to pull
on them poor Injuns,' Di commented dryly, but she was even
more impressed by the further evidence of her companion's
forethought. Realizing that the need might arise to prevent the
consignment from falling into the wrong hands, he had the
presence of mind to procure a length of 'quick-match'[4] fuse cord
from General Houston's headquarters and carry it with him.

---

[4] 'Quick-match': a cord impregnated with black powder to produce
an exceptionally fast burning fuse for igniting flares, fireworks and
explosive charges.

'We'll sure teach them varmints a lesson they'll not soon forget.'

'Yes,' Ole Devil agreed, and he dismounted, ready for the storm which he knew would soon be breaking. 'You can count on my men and I to do that.'

Swinging from her saddle, so as to join the Texian on the ground, Di suddenly realized how his comment had been worded.

'What's all this about you and your men?' the girl asked grimly, stepping to confront the young man. 'Just where in hell do you reckon me 'n' my boys'll be at while you're doing it?'

'Across the river, with the mules,' Ole Devil replied.

'Like hell we will!' Di blazed. 'If you reckon we're going to sit on our butts over there while you and those boys of your'n're getting killed—'

'That's the way it has to be,' Ole Devil said, seeming to grow calmer as the girl became more heated and indignant.

'If you think because I'm a woman—!' Di burst out.

'That's got nothing to do with it,' Ole Devil interrupted, placing his hands on her shoulders. 'And you know it.'

'God damn it, Devil!' Di almost shouted, feeling his grasp tighten slightly as she tried to step away. Seeing the tension on his face, she refrained from continuing the attempt and her voice became milder as she went on, 'You can't ask *me* to leave you and your boys— Not with what you're asking *them* to do.'

'You're wrong, Di,' Ole Devil contradicted, but gently, looking straight into her eyes. 'If I can ask them to die, I can ask you to live.'

'But—!' the girl began, wishing she could turn her head and avoid his disconcerting gaze.

'My men and I are soldiers,' Ole Devil went on. 'It's our duty to fight and, if need be, get killed—'

'You let me side them at the top of Santa Cristóbal Bay,' the girl protested, but with far less vehemence than previously.

'That was to shame the Dragoons into doing things the way I wanted,' Ole Devil pointed out, and his voice took on a slightly harder edge. 'I'd not take kindly to you thinking *my men* needed *that* sort of inducement to make them fight.'

'Such a thought never entered my head!' Di object indignantly. 'Those boys of your'n—'

'Will do their duty,' Ole Devil finished for her, resuming his previous almost emotionless drawl. 'And I'm counting on *you* to do yours.'

'Then let—'

'Even if you didn't have to deliver all the caplocks we can get across the river to General Houston, those trained packers an mules are too valuable to him for you to lose them here.'

'But with me and my boys helping you—' the girl commenced hopefully.

'The result would be just the same,' Ole Devil interrupted and took his hands from her shoulders. Glancing down the slope, he found that Tommy was already lying on the ground, wrapped in a blanket and, using his saddle for a pillow, asleep. 'I'm not selling your men short as fighters, Di. With them at our side, we'll delay and kill more of the Hopis, but the rest will swamp us under by sheer weight of numbers. Believe me, I don't want to do it this way. But there's no other. So will you do as I'm asking – please?'

For several seconds, the girl did not reply. Instead, she first stared long and hard at the Satanic features she had come to know so well. She had the same high regard for Ole Devil as she had for her grandfather and Joe Galton, but acceding to his request did not come easily. With a long and heartfelt sigh, she swung her gaze to the approaching mule train. As before, the cavalrymen were bringing up the rear. From the beginning, they had treated her with an easy-going respect that neither ignored nor played upon her sex. Leaving them to fight and, almost certainly, die was not a thing she could contemplate lightly.

Although Ole Devil did not speak again after making the request, Di knew she must not delay with her reply. The mule train would have reached them in three more minutes and there was little enough time to spare for all the work that must be carried out. What was more, unpalatable as the thought might be she had to admit he was making good sense when he mentioned the value of the mules and their packers. Nor could she see any alternative action he might take to safeguard even a portion of the consignment.

'All right,' Di said, her voice just a trifle hoarse. Then she made a not entirely unsuccessful attempt to resume the kind of banter she usually employed with the Texian. 'There's only one thing, Ole Devil Hardin. Happen you go and get killed for being so cussed, I'll never speak to you again.'

'I don't suppose you will,' Ole Devil answered, also speaking more lightly than throughout the conversation. 'Because, where I'll be going, they'll never let *you* in.'

CHAPTER FOURTEEN

THIS TIME, THERE WON'T BE *ANY* MISTAKES

'AND that's how it stands, gentlemen,' Ole Devil Hardin warned, looking at the tanned faces of the remaining members of the Company under his command. Young, middle-aged and old, he knew every one of them and was all too aware of the enormity of the thing he would be asking them to do. 'I want volunteers to stay with me.'

Beyond the group of men who had been gathered around their commanding officer by Sergeant Smith, the bottom of the U-shaped basin formed by a curve in the Brazos River was alive with feverish, yet organized and purposeful activity. Working as quickly as they could under Joe Galton's super-vision, Diamond-Hitch Brindley's Tejas Indian mule packers were unloading their charges and stacking the caplock rifles separately from the boxes of ready-made paper cartridges and percussion caps. However, having explained to the *cargador* very briefly what needed to be done, the girl was leaving him to attend to it so that she could watch how the soldiers responded to their superior's request.

Having told Smith to leave the remaining Tejas scout to keep watch from the rim and assemble the remnants of Company 'C' at the foot of the slope, Ole Devil had seen to his line-backed dun gelding. Then, without attempting to belittle the danger, or raising false hopes of the possibility of survival, he had told them how he was planning to deal with their desperate predicament. He had pointed out the importance of inflicting the greatest possible number of casualties on the Arizona Hopi *Activos* Regiment; not only to enhance the chances of safety for the caplocks and mule train, but to lessen their effectiveness as a fighting unit which could be thrown against the Republic of Texas's already greatly outnumbered Army. He had also pointed out that, in order to make sure no more loot than was absolutely necessary fell into their attackers' clutches, he would be sending all the Company's horses across the river with the mules, and restrict the defenders' arms to, at the most, four extra rifles each from the consignment. And having told them all this, he waited to discover how they would respond to the call he was making upon them.

Standing a few feet away, Di clenched her hands until the knuckles showed white. She waited with bated breath to see how many of the men would do as Ole Devil asked.

Would any of them be willing to sacrifice themselves?

There was a scuffling of feet and an interplay of exchanged glances, but for several seconds – which seemed to drag on far longer to the watching girl – none of the soldiers spoke or moved from their positions. It seemed that, faced with making a decision, every one of them was waiting for somebody else to take the initiative.

Never had Di experienced such a sensation of suspense. It was all she could do to hold back from screaming a demand that some, *any*, response must be made.

At last, there was a movement!

'Well now, Cap'n,' drawled a white haired and leathery featured old timer, whose military service had commenced by fighting the British at the – as was subsequently proved unnecessary – Battle of New Orleans.[1] He advanced a pace. 'One thing I promised me-self when I left the good ole U.S. of A. was that I'd only vo-lunteer just one more time in my wicked 'n' ornery life. Which same, I done it when I joined the Texas Light Cavalry.'

'Go on, Jube,' Ole Devil prompted, wondering what was coming next.

'It be this way with me, Cap'n,' the old timer obliged, neither his expression nor the timbre of his voice supplying the slightest clue as to his sentiments. 'I'm knowed's a man of me word, 'mongst other things. So, I can't speak for none of

[1] The Battle of New Orleans: the final engagement of the U.S. War of 1812, fought on January the 8th, 1815, ending in a decisive victory for the United States. For a loss of seventy-one casualties, they killed almost two thousand troops including Major-General Sir Edward Pakenham, who had commanded the ill-fated expedition. This is an even more glaring example than is given in the Footnote on page 58 of the effect of slow communications. Peace had been signed in Ghent, Belgium, fifteen days earlier, but the news of this had not been received by the combatants.

the others mind, but the only way I'll stay – or *go*, comes to that – is if *you-all* up 'n' orders me to do it.'

'What Jube means, Cap'n Hardin,' Smith elaborated, stepping with military precision to the old timer's side. 'is, happen you want us along, we'll tick here, root, hawg, or die.'

'Shucks, I can't see's there's all that much for us to worry about,' Sammy Cope went on cheerfully, aligning himself with the two previous speakers. 'There might be a fair slew of 'em coming, but they ain't but greasers 'n' house-Injuns.'[2]

'Damn it, yes,' another of the enlisted men continued. 'Was they Comanch' it'd be some different, dangerous even. But *this* bunch – well, blast it, we've close to got 'em outnumbered.'

'Bad luck, Cap'n,' Smith said with a grin. 'It looks like you haven't got rid of this worthless bunch. So, happen you tell me what you want done, I'll set 'em to doing it for you.'

'*Gracias*, gentlemen,' Ole Devil stated, his voice husky as he fought to keep from showing his emotions.

'Danged if I can ever ree-member being called *that* afore,' grinned Jube. 'And I don't conclude's how I'll ever get called it ag'in.'

'You'll get called something more apt happen you keep butting in when the Cap'n's trying to tell us something,' Smith warned the old timer.

Utilizing the brief respite gained by the two men's comments to regain his composure, Ole Devil stiffened as well as his tired condition would allow. They had won a few hours grace by the destruction of the ferry at Hickert's Landing. So it must be utilized to the best possible advantage. Forcing his weary brain to function, he began to formulate the arrangements which would allow the defenders to inflict the greatest damage on their assailants before the inevitable conclusion. Having done so, he made a change in his intentions with regard to the consignment. While Houston had powder and lead to make balls for the caplocks, the percussion caps were not a commodity readily available in Texas. So, as they were less susceptible to damage by water than the paper cartridges would be, he asked Di to try to take them with her.

'I'll tend to it,' the girl promised and turned her gaze to the

---

[2] House-Indians: unlike the nomadic, hunting and raiding tribes, the predominantly pastoral and agriculturalist Hopi, Zuni and kindred nations tended to build and live in permanent houses instead of using transportable lodges and tipis.

sergeant. 'Hey, Smithie, do you ever get the feeling's how you could get along just fine once you've been told what to do and don't need somebody looking over your shoulder.'

'I've had it now and again,' the non-com replied, guessing what Di had in mind. 'Do you need Cap'n Hardin any more?'

'*Me?*' the girl ejaculated. 'The hell I do. I've got more'n enough worthless and shiftless loafers on my hands now without taking another's looks like he's fixing to fall asleep on his feet.'

'All right. *All right!*' Ole Devil sighed, but darting a look of gratitude at the two speakers. 'Let it never be said that I can't take a hint. Have a couple of pickets posted on the rim, ser—'

'With respect, sir,' Smith interrupted politely. 'I reckon if I didn't have enough sense to think *some* things out for myself, you'd never have made me a segeant.'

'You could be right at that,' Ole Devil conceded. 'So you can take command while I have some rest.'

'Yo!' Smith responded. 'And, again respectfully, sir, don't tell me to wake you if anything happens.'

'Very well, sergeant,' Ole Devil promised with a wry grin. 'I won't. But, if you need me, I'll be over there with Tommy.'

Collecting his blankets, the young Texian went to where the little Oriental was already deep in the arms of Morpheus.[3] After a final and quick look around, deciding that he could count on Smith to do everything necessary without further assistance on his part, he wrapped himself in his blankets and lay alongside his employee. Within seconds of his head touching the saddle – which had already been taken from his dun by Galton's Indian assistant farrier – having covered his face with his hat, he had fallen into a deep, badly needed and well earned sleep. Nor did the work that was being carried on not too far away disturb his or Tommy's slumbers.

Leaving Smith to attend to the military side of their affairs, Di supervised the work being carried out by her men. Realizing just how much work had to be done, the non-com decided to use his initiative in regard to the posting of pickets. While explaining his strategy, Ole Devil had said that – as before the battle at Santa Cristóbal Bay – the Hopis' scouts could be allowed to see the arrangements being made for their Regiment's reception. So Smith let the Tejas keep watch and retain the services of two extra pairs of hands.

[3] Morpheus: in Grecian mythology the son of Hypnos, God of Sleep and God of Dreams in his own right.

With the mules unloaded, the business of getting them to the eastern bank of the Brazos was commenced. This was a vastly different proposition to the crossing of the ford in the woodland. There, the distance had not been anywhere near as great and the water was much shallower. So the mules, being unable to see the opposite shore, would be far more reluctant to enter even with the inducement of following the bell-mare. On top of that, there was the matter of transporting over the rifles and boxes of percussion caps.

Bearing in mind all the experience she had gathered in the years she had spent at the business of mule packing, Di knew that, while difficult, the latter task was not insurmountable. The mules could not swim with the bulky loads, but would be able to carry five of the rifles on each side of their *aparejo*; the whole being covered by tarpaulin and roped into position. She had brought along fifty mules, excluding the animals assigned to carry the cook's and farrier's equipment, which meant she had sufficient for her needs. However, the supply of grain would have to be left behind and she ordered that it was to be placed with the ammunition. Not only would it help to convey the impression that the full consignment had been abandoned, but the subsequent explosion would ensure that it was lost to the Hopis as well as herself.

Sharing his superior's summation about the unsuitability of the ground for digging adequate rifle pits, Smith assigned only half of his men to that job. The rest were to help break down the bundles of caplocks, or stack the ammunition and sacks of grain behind the defensive positions.

About half an hour later, the Tejas scout on the rim attracted Di's attention. Joining him, accompanied by Smith, she found that three Hopis had come into view. However, they were still a good half a mile away and keeping at that distance. Nor was there sufficient cover for them to ride closer. Telling her man to continue keeping them under observation, she and the non-com returned to the bottom of the basin.

Shortly after nightfall, the crossing commenced. Going over in daylight would have been easier, but there were practical and tactical objections to this. Not the least was the discovery that, while his three companions were holding the attention of the Tejas lookout, a fourth Hopi scout had slipped around and was studying the basin from the top of the sheer cliff on the upstream side. Instead of having him dislodged, Smith allowed him to carry out his scrutiny undisturbed.

There was a sound reason for the non-com's decision. The pastoral Hopis did not have the raiding tradition as highly developed as the more warlike nomadic Indian nations, but he believed a desire to gather booty rather than patriotic fervour had brought them to Texas. If they learned that the mule train and *remuda* had gone, they might insist on following instead of trying to capture the consignment. Nor could the evacuation of the animals be left until dawn, as this was the time their attack was most likely to be launched.

At Di's suggestion, the *remuda* was sent over first. Then the bell-mare was led into the cold and uninviting water by Galton, who had removed and was carrying her bell's harness. As he swam, supported by holding his horse's saddle with one hand, he used the other to shake the bell and increase the volume of its sound. The mules set off after her and some followed without needing urging. However, in the urgency of the situation, no stubborn refusals could be tolerated. Any animal trying to balk was roped around the neck and hauled in until it was compelled to swim. Once started in this fashion, the dissidents followed their more compliant companions.

On reaching the eastern bank, the *remuda* and the mules were kept moving to a hollow about half a mile away. It had been found earlier by Prays Loudly, Sometimes. In the absence of the regular scouts, he had been sent over to select a location in which they could bed down for the night and would be hidden from their enemies. Such was the high standard of the packers that, in spite of the darkness, when the halt was called each found and unloaded his five-strong string. However, there was still work to be done. Several of the *remuda* were still saddled and these had to be sought out and attended to. In addition, a further crossing of the river was required to bring back the dismantled equipment of the carrier and cook. Lastly, some of the drftwood that had accumulated on the banks – none of which had been suitable for making rafts – was collected. A couple of fires were lit in the hollow, allowing Di and her men to dry their clothing and warm themselves. When all that was done, they settled down to await the coming of the fateful dawn.

Returning from their scouting mission, having located the camp of the Arizona Hopi *Activos* Regiment, Tom Wolf and his three companions heard the sound of horses coming towards them. Stopping their own mounts, the fact that whoever was riding their way did not duplicate their actions suggested their presence had not been detected. A low hiss of annoyance left the chief's lips. The riders were not heading straight at them, but would pass some distance off to the right. There was no cover of any consequence in that direction and it would be impossible to go any closer on horseback – unlike the packers, he and his men did not use mules – without being located.

Tall, well made, exuding an aura of quiet dignity and strength, Tom Wolf was an impressive figure. In spite of wearing a white man's style of buckskins and a round topped black hat with an eagle's feather in its band, he had all the majesty of a war leader belonging to one of the free-ranging Plains Indians' nations. Dressed in a similar fashion, his scouts also looked what they were; tough and hardy braves, competent at their duties and ready to give their best in battle.

Many colonists had small regards for the Tejas Indians as warriors. Nor, in general, did members of the nation deserve it. That did not apply to Ewart Brindley's employees. They belonged to a band which had never been subdued by the Mexicans, or suffered exposure to the 'civilizing' influence of the Spanish missions. What was more, the old man had shielded them from the more corrosive aspects of contact with much of the Anglo-Saxon population. So, instead of being dissolute and dissipated – the fate of most others of their tribe – they retained the best qualities of the Indian people.

Following their chief's example, the braves slipped from their horses and allowed the reins to dangle free. Easing back the hammer of the caplock rifle presented to him by Ole Devil Hardin for his services at the battle of Santa Cristóbal Bay, he listened to the clicks which told him his men were taking the same precaution. However, there was nothing to suggest the other riders in the darkness had heard the sounds.

Leaving their horses ground hitched by the dangling reins, the Tejas' party advanced. They crouched low, feeling out the ground ahead with their feet and doing all they could to avoid making any noise. Before long, they could make out the shapes of the riders. The nearest, as they rode in single file, was about forty yards away.

'Four!' Wolf counted silently and started to raise his rifle, knowing there was no hope of going closer than they now were without being seen.

There was, the chief realized as he aimed at the second rider,

139

no way he could warn his companions of his intentions. However, they were all experienced warriors and would select the correct victims. So he must rely upon Jimmy-Whoop at his right to take the leading Hopi – which the quartet undoubtedly were, no doubt a scouting party who were returning from a similar mission to their own – while Eats Grasshoppers and Bad Breath respectively dealt with the third and fourth in line.

Making sure of his aim, Wolf squeezed the caplock's trigger. Even as the hammer began to descend, he was conscious of the brief flicker of sparks as the flint struck and pushed aside the frizzen of Jimmy-Whoop's rifle so they could fall into the pan.[4] There was a 'whoosh' and glow of flame as the priming powder ignited, mingling with the slight pop of the exploding percussion cap and deeper crack from the main charge in the breech of the caplock as it was detonated. Almost simultaneously, a similar reaction on the other side of the chief informed him that the men there had touched off their flintlocks.

Although Eats Grasshoppers' and Bad Breath's rifles vomitted out their loads like echoes to Wolf's shot, Jimmy-Whoop's weapon misfired. Except for the flash in the pan, there was no discharge from it.

With that exception, the Tejas' impromptu volley was successful. Dazzled by the glare of the muzzle blasts from their firearms, none of them was able to see Wolf's and Eats Grasshoppers' victims struck and knocked from the horses. Letting out a screech of pain as Bad Breath's bullet tore into him, the fourth rider was in no condition to cope with the behaviour of his startled mount. As it made a bounding plunge and bolted, he was pitched from its back.

Unscathed, due to the failure of Jimmy-Whoop's rifle, the leading Hopi was able to avoid being dislodged when his mount displayed a similar alarm to that shown by its companions. Retaining his seat as it started a bucking run to get away from the commotion, he did not attempt to slow the animal down. In fact, being able to guess who had attacked his party – although uncertain of how many of the enemy were involved – he was determined to make good his escape and deliver the information he had collected.

Allowing a good two miles to fall behind him before he

---

[4] Ole Devil Hardin could not present all of the scouts with a caplock rifle as, in their eyes, this would have lessened the honour and respect he was paying to the chief by making the gift.

brought his horse to a halt, the Hopi paused for long enough to satisfy himself that he was not being followed. Deciding that none of his companions had escaped and he was not being pursued by any of their assailants, he set the animal into motion and directed it towards the red glow in the sky which marked the site of his Regiment's camp.

Half an hour later, the surviving scout was standing in the presence of the Mexican officers and his fellow Hopi chiefs. Although he had deserted his companions, he made no attempt to hide or excuse his actions. They had been on a reconnaissance, not a raiding or fighting mission. So it had been his duty to save himself and report his findings to his superiors, not to try to avenge or rescue those who had fallen in the ambush.

Freshly awakened, 'Colonel' Abrahan Phillipe Gonzales *de* Villena *y* Danvila stood scowling and huddled against the chill of the night in the blankets which had formed his bed. Before he had heard many of the newcomer's words, he lost all of his resentment over having had his sleep disturbed.

Using the point of his knife to draw an accurate map of the area in which their quarry was located, employing a piece of bare ground for the purpose, the scout delivered a thorough description of their activities.

'So you think they've taken at least the majority of the rifles across the river, chief?' asked Major Santoval, at the conclusion of the report.

'*Si, senor,*' the scout replied. 'They took off the loads, but not the saddles and I saw them fastening on rifles as the light was fading.'

'But you think some of them will be staying on this side?' Villena inquired, darting a malevolent scowl at the commanding officer of Company Five for having anticipated his question.

'*Si, senor,*' the scout agreed. 'They made a pile with many small, square boxes and sacks of grain. And the palefaces were digging the kind of holes from which they fought us the last time. They also sent more men to help the Indian who watched from the top of the hollow.'

'That means they'll be waiting for us,' guessed the sycophantic Major Mendez-Castillo who commanded Company Eight, guessing his superior would welcome such a comment.

'Or want us to think they are,' Santoval pointed out, 'when they've all crossed and are marching through the night.'

'They're waiting!' Villena stated. 'The boxes will contain

ammunition which, as they've no boats, they can't take over without it being ruined by the water. And, if I know that damned Texian, he won't leave it for us. So we'll go and fetch it in the morning. And this time, there won't be any mistakes.'

Listening to the plan that their self-appointed 'colonel' was outlining, not even the normally critical Major Santoval could find a fault with it. Carried out the way Villena intended, they would not only deal with whoever was waiting but could resume their pursuit of the mule train and capture the rifles it was transporting.

CHAPTER FIFTEEN

THERE WILL BE *NO* QUARTER

'WELL, it won't be long now,' Sergeant Smith said quietly, as he stood with Ole Devil Hardin, Tommy Okasi and Tom Wolf in the centre of the Texas Light Cavalry detachment's all too small defensive perimeter and looked at the rim of the basin. 'I reckon it's too late now to start wishing I'd lived a better life.'

'This's the kind of time when most folks get to thinking it,' Ole Devil replied, without taking his attention from the sight which was holding all their interest. 'But at least they're playing the way we want and haven't passed us by to go after the mule train.'

'The scout we took alive said their Mexican leader had a great hatred for you, *Diablo Viejo*,' Wolf remarked, speaking English for once. 'And that it was a desire to take revenge on you that made him keep after you when others wanted to turn back.'

Although fluent in their tongue, unless he respected the white men he was addressing, the chief of the Tejas Indians employed by Ewart Brindley would usually speak in either Spanish or his own language.[1]

After interrogating the dying scout, Wolf had sent two of his men to tell Ole Devil what they had seen and done so far. Accompanied by the third, he had returned to where they had

---

[1] This is a trait shared by warrant and non-commissioned officers who served in the now disbanded Kings African Rifles Regiments. One with whom I worked for several months during the Mau Mau Uprising in Kenya had been to England and taken the Drill Instructors' Course at the Brigade of Guards Depot, Pirbright, Surrey, shortly after World War II – during which he had served with distinction in, among other places, Burma. Although he could understand verbal instructions and read in English, it was only with reluctance that he would speak anything other than his tribal language, Wa-Kamba or the simplified form of Swahili that was the *lingua franca* of East Africa. J.T.E.

already seen the Arizona Hopi *Activos* Regiment making camp. Leaving Bad Breath to take care of their horses, he had gone forward on foot. Although he had been successful in penetrating the ring of pickets, the Hopis had picked a site for their camp which would not allow a surprise attack against them to succeed. Nor was there any way he could get close enough to their horse-lines to try and delay the pursuit by scattering the animals.

Watching from as close as he could reach while still remaining undetected, the chief had not been able to hear what was said by the surviving Hopi scout to the assembled Mexican officers and Indian war leaders. However, he had deduced that the man had succeeded in studying Ole Devil's defensive arrangements and a plan of campaign was being made. Then the Hopis had aroused their men and commenced making what he assumed to be their war medicine. Shortly before sun up, a group of braves about twenty strong had made ready to leave. Concluding that they were to be an advance scouting party, who would be followed at a more leisurely pace – to conserve the horses' energy for the assault – by the rest of the Regiment, he had withdrawn.

Travelling fast, Wolf and Bad Breath had found the small defending force awake and in position when they arrived at the basin. Without satisfying his curiosity over the absence of the mule train, having in fact made an accurate guess at why it had been sent away, he had informed Ole Devil of what he had seen and been told. Knowing him to be a man of shrewd judgment, the Texian had accepted his summation of the situation. Ole Devil had also accepted his offer that he and the other scouts remained instead of going after their employer. With the assurance that he could return, Eats Grasshoppers had taken his companions' horses across the river. Wanting to prevent such a valuable item as the Browning Slide Repeating rifle from being taken by the enemy, Ole Devil had sent it and the pouch of reserve magazines with the scout, retaining his two pistols and the bowie knife with which to do his share of the fighting.

With all the preparations made, there had been nothing for the defenders to do except wait. Yet that had been the hardest part of all for them. Every one had appreciated what a desperate situation they were facing. They might each have four loaded firearms available – with the exception of Tommy Okasi, who preferred to depend upon his *samurai*'s weapons –

but even with the addition of the Tejas scouts they would be outnumbered by almost ten to one. If the Hopis pressed home a charge with sufficient determination – and none of them expected otherwise – they were sure to swamp all resistance by the sheer weight of their numbers.

Although Wolf had stated that, from what he had seen while returning, the attack would not happen for some time, none of the defenders could relax. In fact, it had almost been a relief when Jube – who was in command of the pickets on the rim – reported that the Hopis' advance party were in view. Following their orders, the eight men had fallen back to their companions without offering to resist. Shortly after, the braves had appeared at the top of the slope. Holding a brief consultation, they had obviously decided that the Texians were too strong for them to tackle unaided. So, apart from a warrior who had been sent to inform their superiors, they had done no more than keep the basin under surveillance. Almost an hour later, a Mexican officer had joined them. He had studied the defensive positions and scanned the opposite side of the river through a telescope, probably trying to locate the mule train, then departed to inform his superiors of the situation. Yet another ninety minutes had dragged by before the rumble of many hooves had heralded the arrival of the main body.

'Then he will soon have his chance to get revenge,' Ole Devil declared, watching the numbers of the enemy increasing until they formed an almost solid mass across the front down which they would be moving if they wanted to ride into the attack.

'Very soon I would say,' Wolf replied, gripping the caplock rifle appreciatively and glancing around. 'Ah, *Diablo Viejo*, this will be a remembered fight.'

'It's an honour to have you at our side, chief,' the Texian replied.

'My thanks,' Wolf said quietly, but sincerely. Then he raised his voice and addressed the rest of the defenders with the traditional exhortation of a war leader who knew that a hard battle would soon commence. 'Brave up, brothers. This is a good day to die.'

Almost as if to challenge the chief's inspiring and defiant words, the martial notes of a bugle rang out from the top of the slope. Listening to them, every member of the pitifully small defending force took a firmer grasp on the weapon he was holding and looked upwards.

As the sound died away, there was a movement among the

massed ranks who were sitting their horses on the rim!

Even before the bugle call had ended, Ole Devil became aware that he was not hearing the Mexican Army's usual signal for a charge. However, knowing that the Arizona Hopi *Activos* Regiment were privately recruited and equipped volunteers, he considered it likely that they had instituted their own system of passing commands in such a manner.

Yet there was no concerted advance when the bugle ceased to blow!

Instead, only one Mexican officer and a single Hopi brave, the latter carrying a lance with something white flapping from its head, rode forward.

'Hold your fire, men!' the young Texian called, realizing what was happening although he was puzzled by the development.

Over the centuries, in Europe particularly, a conventional means of requesting a parlay had been formulated and generally accepted. It had been brought to the New World in the course of colonization by members of various nations to whom it was known. First calls from a bugle gave notice that no surprise was intended. Then the displaying of a white flag announced a desire for a truce and conversation.

Studying the approaching pair, Ole Devil was disturbed. The Mexican was in his early thirties and his formerly well fleshed figure had lost considerable weight since he had been fitted for his uniform. There was a wary expression on his face, which showed signs of his recent exertion, but that was understandable under the circumstances. However, he showed that he had a sound knowledge of the procedure for calling a parlay.

'Good morning, gentlemen,' the Mexican greeted, in good English, halting about thirty yards away from the nearest rifle pit. 'I am Major Ramon Mendez-Castillo, commanding Company Eight of the Arizona Hopi *Activos* Regiment and I speak with the authority of Colonel Abrahan Phillipe Gonzales *de* Villena *y* Danvila.'

'Good morning, Major,' Ole Devil replied, meeting politeness with politeness. 'I am Captain Jackson Baines Hardin, commanding Company "C", Texas Light Cavalry.'

'Colonel Villena is a humane man and he has no wish to shed blood unnecessarily, gentlemen. So he has sent you this ultimatum,' Mendez-Castillo went on, studying the grim faces of the defenders and deciding there was no point in extending the formalities. 'If you lay down your arms and give your parole to

146

leave Mexican territory immediately, you will be permitted to do so. If you refuse, he will – with great reluctance – be compelled to order an attack. In that event, no prisoners will be taken and there will be no quarter given.'

'My thanks to Colonel Villena for his consideration, Major,' Ole Devil answered, without glancing to see how the offer might be affecting his companions. 'And assure him that I regard his word as being as binding as that of General Cós.' He saw Mendez-Castillo's fleshy lips tighten and knew that his meaning was understood,[2] so continued, 'And will you also tell him that I too am a humane man. So I will send him *my* terms. If he will order his men to lay down their arms and *surrender* to *us*, we will take a chance and accept *his* parole to leave the Republic of Texas and take no further military action within its boundaries.'

A scowl creased the Mexican officer's surly features as the Texians chuckled at their superior's counter proposal. However, guessing why it had been made, he retained control of his temper. He was helped in this by knowing that Villena had never expected the offer to be accepted and, in fact, had made plans which would be carried out whether it was or not. Realizing that his work was not yet ended, he went on with it.

'You have no chance, not even the slightest, of survival, gentlemen,' Mendez-Castillo warned, hating to use the honorific but willing to do so if it served to bring about his superior's wishes. He was directing the words at the defenders rather than to their leader. 'Why throw your lives away on such a futile venture when you can leave in safety?'

'Shall I shoot him now, Cap'n Hardin,' Jube inquired, in a matter of fact tone. 'Or do I have to wait until he comes back with his men?'

'I'll have you court martialled if you shoot him while he's here under a flag of truce, blast it!' Ole Devil declared, noticing that alarm had replaced the somewhat smug condescension with which the Mexican had been watching them. He felt himself grow increasingly perturbed, but did not show

[2] On December the 6th, 1835, at the end of a battle lasting for six days, General Martin Perfecto *de Cós* – brother-in-law of *Presidente* Antonio Lopez *de* Santa Anna – and his force of eleven hundred men had surrendered to the Texians at San Antonio de Bexar. Although Cós had accepted similar terms to those Ole Devil Hardin had been offered by Major Mendez-Castillo, he had broken his parole and was accompanying the Mexican Army which *el Presidente* was leading to crush the rebellion.

it and continued, keeping his unwavering gaze fixed upon Mendez-Castillo's face. 'You have had *my* answer, Major. And I think that I had better point out your flag does not give you the right to try to seduce my men from their duty.'

That might, the young Texian realized, be the real reason behind the request for a parley. Yet he could not convince himself it was anything so simple.

No matter what else Villena might be, he was no fool. He would realize that there was little chance of persuading the defenders to surrender on such terms. Even before news of Cós's perfidy had become known, the Anglo-Saxon colonists had learned to be very wary of Mexican promises.

So why had Mendez-Castillo been sent on such an errand?

There had to be some other, more definite reason!

Finding out went far beyond merely satisfying curiosity!

It could be a matter of life or death!

Everything about the Mexican's bearing and attitude struck Ole Devil as being wrong. Partly it was suggestive of a man who held a royal straight flush[3] at stud poker when the up-cards[4] proved no other could be out and he would not fail to win the pot. Yet there was also something furtive, nervous even, about him, as if he considered that he was in, or very close to, some serious danger.

Had the latter sentiment been in evidence before Jube had injected his comment?

Did the Mexican fear that his flag of truce would not be respected?

Or was there another and more serious cause for his perturbation?

On the face of it, almost everything was in the attackers' favour. They had a vast numerical superiority and, although they could not avoid a certain amount of losses, careful management could restrict these to the younger and more headstrong Hopi braves who would be all too eager to lead the assault. So, once Mendez-Castillo had rejoined his companions, there would be only minimal danger. Only something completely unexpected and untowards could turn the scales in the Texians' favour under the circumstances.

[3] Royal straight flush: ace, king, queen, jack and ten all of the same suit.

[4] Up-cards: in stud poker, each player's first or 'hole' card is dealt face down and the remainder – usually four, but there can be more depending upon the variation being played – are exposed.

Yet Ole Devil grew ever more convinced that the Major believed – or was afraid – something might go wrong.

The young Texian wished that he could take his eyes from Mendez-Castillo and find out if anything was happening on the rim. However, he knew that his companions were watching and would warn him immediately if there was any sign of the enemy setting their mounts into motion.

Even as Ole Devil was reaching that point in his conclusions, he felt as if he had been touched by an icy hand. A thought, alarming in its portent, drove into him. It was one, he told himself bitterly, that should have occurred to him straight away. In exculpation, despite having slept soundly and woken considerably refreshed, there had been so many other things demanding his attention that he might be excused for having failed to take such a contingency into consideration.

Except that the lapse might cost the defenders their lives more quickly than would otherwise have been the case!

While the steeply sloping ground on the downstream side of the U-shaped basin would be impassable, at least with any speed, on horseback, men could walk – or even run – over its uneven surface without too much difficulty. Certainly they would have a better chance of approaching unseen than riders. Especially when the attention of their proposed victims was being diverted and held in another direction.

'Very well!' Mendez-Castillo said, disturbed by the Satanic-faced Texian's unremitting scrutiny – which was beginning to induce a sensation of religious-inspired superstitious dread – and wanting to remove himself from it. Starting to rein his horse around, he spoke louder than was necessary. 'Colonel Villena is not an unreasonable or impatient man. He will give you an hour in which to consider his proposal and make up your minds. But, I must warn you, if at the end of that time you still persist in this foolish and futile defiance, we will strike you down without mercy.'

'My thanks to Colonel Villena for his consideration,' Ole Devil replied, addressing the words to the Mexican officer's back as he had completed the turning of his mount and started it moving while speaking. 'And tell him that we apologize to the widows of the brave men he will be sending to their deaths.'

'The stupid fool!' the commanding officer of Company Five spat out, as he sat his horse with the other senior Mexicans on the rim and watched Major Mendez-Castillo bringing the

149

parley to an end. 'He hasn't kept them talking nearly long enough!'

While the words echoed Villena's sentiments, the fact that they had been uttered by his greatest rival made him stiffen and glare around.

'I didn't notice you showing any willingness to volunteer for the task, *Major* Santoval!' the self appointed colonel snorted back.

Santoval could not have disputed the comment, even if he had wished to do so. Although approving – even if only silently and to himself – of his superior's strategy, he had been all too aware of the danger involved in carrying out a most important aspect of it. So he had studiously refused to meet Villena's eyes, or respond in any other way to the call for a volunteer to take on the precarious assignment.

From the scout's description of the Texians' defensive positions and their surroundings, Villena had concluded that attaining his desire for revenge would be anything but a sinecure. He was all too aware that success, or failure, hinged entirely upon the Hopis' willingness to fight. They had not been sufficiently exposed to the influences of Christianity to have discarded their belief in the primitive superstitions of their nation. So, remembering that the previous failure had been in a similar location at Santa Cristóbal Bay, meeting a determined resistance at this site could cause them to assume that their war medicine was bad. Once that happened, they would lose heart and be grudging of their lives to such an extent that they were unlikely to press home an attack.

With that in mind, the 'colonel' had decided to employ trickery. It was his intention, he had explained to his subordinates, to have two Companies move on foot down the steeply sloping ground over which it would be impossible for them to ride horses at speed. To prevent the impromptu infantry from being discovered prematurely, he would cause the defenders to be distracted by sending an officer under a flag of truce ostensibly to deliver terms for a surrender.

The first snag to Villena's plan had been persuading one of his majors, whose rank made them the obvious choice, to perform the vitally important part in the proceedings. In all fairness, Santoval had not been alone in evading the duty. Like him, all but Mendez-Castillo had excused themselves on the grounds that they could not speak sufficient English to conduct negotiations. Their obvious reluctance had infected and brought an equal lack of co-operation from their juniors. Nor had the 'colonel's' attempts at minimizing the risks produced the desired results. While they had been willing to concede that the leader of the Texians might be a *caballero* close to their own social standing and, as such, imbued with the well born Anglo-Saxon's respect for a flag of truce, the same could not be said of the men who would be with him.

Fear of the consequences, rather than any moral objections to the betrayal of the rules governing the conducting of a formally requested parley, had been responsible for the majors' reluctance to come forward. Their easy consciences had dismissed the latter as excusable on the grounds that they were dealing with rebels and not fighting an enemy. From their limited acquaintance and what they had been told, they considered the majority of Texians to be complete barbarians with small regard for civilized conventions and less where the sanctity of human life was concerned. Even if such men could be trusted to remain passive while their superior was talking, they would open fire upon whoever was conducting the parlay if the foot party should be seen approaching before he had withdrawn. What was more, if the plot succeeded, before they were wiped out the defenders would make him a prime target in revenge for his betrayal.

It had only been when, dark with barely controlled anger, the 'colonel' had hinted at dire consequences in the future if the plan fell through and they were compelled to retire empty handed that Mendez-Castillo had reluctantly offered his services. Of all the officers present, he was the least able to refuse. Not only was he fluent in English but his formerly wealthy family had suffered serious business reverses and were to a great extent dependent upon the charity of Villena's father. So he had volunteered with what grace he could muster.

Although Mendez-Castillo's bearing and attitude had not been calculated to induce wild optimism among his fellow officers, he had appeared to be carrying out his duty in a satisfactory fashion. For the plan to succeed, he had to hold the Texians' attention. At first, despite his somewhat nervous manner, it had seemed that he would do so. The *gringo* enlisted men had remained in their shallow rifle pits, which formed a half circle around the tarpaulin covered mound of ammunition boxes, but they had watched him instead of their fronts. Majors Pina and Gomez had already started their respective Companies advancing on foot, but they were still far from an advantageous distance when Mendez-Castillo terminated the parley by turning away.

Cold rage boiled through Villena. Because of the Hopi braves' growing disenchantment with the pursuit through terrain so vastly different to that in which they had been born and raised, he had been compelled to let their chiefs tell them of his 'medicine' for ensuring victory. The strength of his authority had been further weakened among them by the realization that much of the valuable loot they were anticipating had gone over the river and would require a further chase. If it was seen that his present scheme was not going according to plan, they might refuse to fight and certainly would not give of their best if they did.

There was, the 'colonel' concluded, only one thing to do.

'Charge!' Villena thundered, sending his restlessly moving horse bounding forward.

Realizing the danger of any further delay, the rest of the Mexicans repeated the order and followed their superior. Letting out their war whoops, the Hopis obeyed and the mass of riders began to swoop downwards towards the small band of Texians who must stand and fight as they had no means of doing anything else.

CHAPTER SIXTEEN

GOOD OLD *YELLOW STONE*

'WATCH that slope!' Ole Devil Hardin shouted, following the advice himself as he noticed Major Ramon Mendez-Castillo throw a quick look in that direction and then encourage the horse to move faster.

Only the briefest inspection was needed to inform the young Texian that his summation had been correct. However, he could also take some small comfort from the realization that the enemy's treacherous plot had gone amiss because of the major's premature departure. While a number of Hopis and their Mexican officers were approaching on foot, making the most of what little cover was available, they were still much too far away to pose the threat they would have been if the trick had not miscarried.

Startled exclamations told Ole Devil that his instructions had been carried out by the men in the rifle pits closest to the sloping ground. However, they were all experienced fighters and did not waste powder and shot by opening fire at such a long range.

Listening to Ole Devil's warning, Mendez-Castillo knew that his superior's ploy had failed. His glance had shown him that Companies Four and Nine were still much too far away to play their part. Even as he was returning his gaze to the front, he heard 'Colonel' Abrahan Phillipe Gonzales *de* Villena *y* Danvila's word of command and saw the remaining Companies of the Arizona Hopi *Activos* Regiment commencing the attack. So he applied his spurs to his mount's flanks, causing it to increase its pace, in the hope of avoiding the wrath which he felt sure the defenders would direct upon him in repayment for his treachery.

The Hopi brave carrying the white flag had also started to turn away from the Texians. At the sight of his companions beginning to advance, he saw a way of gaining a great honour.

It was a dangerous – some might even consider foolhardy – thing to do, but he had elected to arm himself with a lance and there were obligations in accepting such a distinction.[1] One was an utter disregard for personal safety in battle.

Reversing his mount's direction with a speed and precision which would not have shamed the finest polo player and pony, the brave dropped the head of his weapon forward. Without even trying to shake off the white shirt which had served as a flag, he gave his 'kill or die' cry and signalled his intentions with his heels. Instantly, the well trained horse sprang forward. There was no need for him to think of selecting a victim. He had already decided that only one was suitable and would bring the acclaim deserved by his deed.

The *gringo* with the face of *el Diablo*!

Aiming the lance's needle-sharp head at the centre of the chest of the tall, slim Texian, the brave guided the horse towards him.

Although Ole Devil was looking away, he heard the Hopi's yell and the sound of the horse approaching. Knowing something of the Indians' regard for the lance as a weapon, he guessed what was happening and that he might have been chosen as the victim. What was more, as he had not laid aside his pistols while conducting the parley, he had the means to defend himself.

Swinging his attention to the front and confirming his suspicions, Ole Devil was already lifting his right hand pistol. However, he was not the only member of his party who had appreciated the danger. Equally aware of the responsibilities which went with carrying a lance, although he could not be sure that the house-Indian Hopis – with whom he had had no prior contact – adhered to such precepts, Tom Wolf had been keeping the warrior under observation. At the first suggestion of trouble, the Tejas chief snapped his rifle upwards.

Even as Ole Devil was squeezing the Manton's trigger, he heard the crack of two rifle shots; but too late for him to prevent himself from firing. Hit between the eyes and in the chest, either of which wounds would have been sufficient to kill him, the brave was flung bodily backwards from his horse. The lance flew from his hand as he went down and, frightened by the weapons going off in front of it, his mount swerved aside. At the same moment that death took the Hopi, the bullet fired by

[1] Further details of the importance set by Indian warriors to carrying a war lance are given in: SIDEWINDER.

old Jube struck the back of Mendez-Castillo's skull. Killed instantly, the Mexican joined his companion in crashing to the ground and became their Regiment's first two casualties.

Although Ole Devil saw his party had scored first blood in the encounter, he knew it was small cause for congratulations. Nor would it have the slightest effect upon the inevitable ending.

Well over two hundred mounted attackers were pouring into the basin and rushing closer at an ever increasing rate as they urged their horses to gallop!

Nearly a hundred more assailants, seeing that there was no hope of drawing nearer undetected, gave vent to war yells and started to run forward!

Following his orders, Sergeant Smith moved back until he joined Sammy Cope, who was behind the tarpaulin-covered mound of ammunition. Taking out and cocking his pistol, the non-com knelt and placed its muzzle on the tip of the quick match cord. The destruction of the supplies was his duty, or would fall to Cope if he should be prevented from carrying it out for some reason.

Scanning the enemy's ranks as he tossed the empty pistol behind him and on to the mound, so that it would not be taken away after the battle, Ole Devil noticed how the older Mexicans and Hopi war leaders were allowing their more imprudent juniors and the younger braves to draw ahead. The same thing had happened at Santa Cristóbal Bay, so he was not surprised to find out who would be bearing the brunt of his men's fire.

Despite being little older than his subalterns, Villena was one of those who were showing caution. He had done so during the previous battle and it had saved his life. Trying to locate him among the swarming mass of riders, Ole Devil intended to prevent him from escaping a second time if an opportunity was presented.

Onwards thundered the attackers!

Already the defenders were opening fire upon the still closely packed horde!

By Ole Devil's side, Tommy Okasi drew and loosed a *yanagi-ha* arrow, extracing another from his quiver with deft speed as soon as it was on its way. Dropping the rifle with which he had justified Mendez-Castillo's fears of how the treacherous betrayal of the flag of truce would be replayed, Jube snatched up his second weapon and put it to equally good use. Others aimed, fired and exchanged their spent caplocks for the loaded reserve arms laid close at hand.

At each shot, a man or a horse went down; but the remainder continued to charge without hesitation or alarm over the losses.

Another hundred yards and the leading Hopis would be on the defenders!

Seventy-five!

Every Texian and Tejas Indian had used three of his weapons to good effect!

Then it happened!

Louder than the barking of the defenders' rifles, even making itself heard above the rumbling thunder from the horses' hooves, came an unexpected noise.

'Whoo – ooo – whoo!'

The eerie sound, magnified and echoing from the sheer walls of the gorge, caused all the Hopis in particular to stare in that direction and brought the dismounted braves to a halt. It was something beyond their comprehension. So was the sight that greeted their amazed gaze a moment later.

'Good old *Yellow Stone*!' Ole Devil breathed, without looking around. 'Let's hope those horses aren't like Di's mules!'

Coming from where it had been concealed up to then by the sides of the gorge was the thing which had caused the young Texian to be concerned over travelling along the banks of the Brazos River with the mule train. He had known that, having been brought in sections from the United States and assembled on arrival, a steamboat operated between the coast and the inland cities. However, Diamond-Hitch Brindley had assured him that her animals had had sufficient contact with the *Yellow Stone* and similar vessels which plied the Red River in Arkansas to have lost all fear of them.

The same did not apply to the Hopis – or their mounts!

In spite of being smaller than the great passenger and cargo carriers using the mighty Mississippi–Missouri Rivers system, the *Yellow Stone* was still an impressive sight as she emerged from the gorge. Smoke, flames and sparks – the latter created deliberately on her captain's orders to enhance the dramatic effect – belched from her tall stack and her wheels churned the water as they drove her along. A trio of four-pounder boat cannon had been fitted at her bows since the commencement of hostility and these were manned, ready for use.

Coming from Arizona, the Indians had never seen a boat larger than was needed for an oxen-powered or 'compass' type of ferry, or even one that was driven by a sail. Nor were they aware of such a device as a steam engine as a means of motive power. So the sight of the *Yellow Stone* bearing down on them was the cause of consternation and terror. None of them could imagine what the strange apparition might be.

Turning his vessel towards the western shore, with all the easy facility granted by the paddle wheels on each side, the captain tugged on the lanyard and the whistle emitted another of its steam-powered whoops. In echo to the sound, the three cannons bellowed and vomited forth their loads of canister.[2]

Great as the shock delivered to the Hopis by the *Yellow Stone*'s appearance might be, it had an even more adverse effect upon their horses. Before the tempest of balls from the cannon reached them, the animals were registering their alarm by rearing, plunging or swerving wildly in an attempt to get away from the terrible fire breathing monstrosity that was coming towards them.

Nor did the Hopis and Mexicans who had avoided being unseated try to regain control of their panic-stricken mounts and resume the attack. Instead, like the animals, the braves in particular had only one idea. To flee as swiftly as possible from the demoniac device which they believed had been summoned up by some magical power of the *gringo* with the face of *el Diablo*, the Devil.

In an instant, the charge that had threatened to overrun the Texians' positions had been reduced to chaos. With one exception, even the Mexicans – who knew what the *Yellow Stone* was – did nothing to avert the panic. Instead, they joined in the flight. Nor was the exception, Villena, able to prevent the mass departure.

Thrown from his horse as it took grave exception to the appearance of the steamboat, the 'colonel' had contrived to alight without injury. However, his pistol had flown from his grasp while he was falling. Leaping to his feet and snatching the *épée de combat* from its sheath, he tried to avert the rout. Not one of the men who were still mounted took the slightest notice of his yells. Instead, they scattered and fled in the direction from which they had come. If he had looked, he would have learned that the two Companies on the sloping ground were also in full flight.

---

[2] Canister: a number of small balls packed in a metallic cylinder for ease of loading, but which spread like the charge from a shotgun on being fired.

157

Finding themselves left on foot and with no means of flight gave the Hopis the courage of desperation. Screaming war cries that held a timbre of terror, they rushed at the men in the rifle pits with the intention of dying fighting.

Rage filled Villena as he realized that he had been abandoned by the majority of his Regiment. Glaring around furiously, he located the man who had brought about his downfall and saw his chance of taking revenge. As he looked, the young Texian – whose face appeared even more like that of the devil than ever – shot a charging brave. Doing so had emptied his pistol and he did not have another on his person.

Realizing what it meant, the 'colonel' spat out a delighted exclamation and dashed forward. If he had been in control of his emotions, he would never have attempted such a wild attack. In his present frame of mind, he thought only of impaling the man for whom he had developed an all consuming hatred on the *épée-de-combat*.

On discharging the shot from his second pistol, Ole Devil released it. His right hand flashed across to close around the concave ivory hilt of the bowie knife. Even as he was drawing it from its sheath, he became aware of another threat to his life. Face distorted with rage, Villena was almost upon him.

Seeming to act of its own volition, the bowie knife swung to the right. The great blade met the advancing *épée-de-combat* and swept it aside. There was a major difference between the two weapons. Where the sword was designed purely for thrusting with its point, the shape of the knife's blade gave it a far greater scope. The rounded back of the blade was excellent for parrying without endangering the cutting edge, but the latter or the equally sharp false edge could be used to slash and thrust.

Disengaging his weapon as soon as it had deflected Villena's blade away from him, Ole Devil performed a lightning fast backhand chop. The false edge made contact before the Mexican could think of retaliation or evasion, passing under his chin to lay open his throat. As the weapon came free, although his every instinct told him he had already delivered a mortal blow, the Texian could not resist striking again. Around lashed his hand, directing the cutting edge to just below Villena's right ear. Biting in until it met bone, the blade shoved its recipient aside. His weight dragged him free and he blundered on for a few involuntary steps until he collapsed face down across the mound of ammunition that had, in part, cost him his life.

Then it was over.

Lowering his blood-stained knife, Ole Devil looked around. Not a single living enemy remained in the basin. Apart from a couple of minor wounds, the defenders had come through the fighting unscathed. Giving a sigh of relief, he walked to meet the men who were coming off the *Yellow Stone* and wondered how they had managed to arrive so fortuitously.[3]

Di Brindley was galloping towards the opposite bank, waving her hat and yelling in delight. Returning her salutation, Ole Devil felt sure that the consignment of caplocks and ammunition were safe. With the help of her mule train, he could complete the delivery and give Major General Samuel Houston a powerful aid in the struggle to gain independence for Texas.

---

[3] Having met with Mannen Blaze's party while on a routine patrol, the captain of the *Yellow Stone* had agreed to go in search of the mule train. He had been contacted by the Tejas scout whom Ole Devil had sent to find him and, learning of the danger, had come prepared to deal with it. Guessing that the Hopis would never have seen a steamboat, he had added to its shock value by blowing the whistle and causing the flames, extra thick smoke and sparks to be given out.

J.T. EDSON OMNIBUS VOL.10

THE BIG GUN
UNDER THE STARS AND BARS
THE FASTEST GUN IN TEXAS

He was small and unassuming. The sort of man
you'd dismiss as just another cowhand. But Dusty
Fog was one of the brightest officers in the
Confederate Army. Promoted in the field, he
commanded the roughest, toughest, and most
ornery fighting company in the Texas Light
Cavalry.

Three Civil War stories starring Dusty Fog.

Also available from Corgi Books:
J.T. Edson Omnibuses Vols 1-9